THIS SCORCHED EARTH

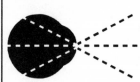

This Large Print Book carries the
Seal of Approval of N.A.V.H.

THIS SCORCHED EARTH

WILLIAM GEAR

THORNDIKE PRESS
A part of Gale, a Cengage Company

Farmington Hills, Mich • San Francisco • New York • Waterville, Maine
Meriden, Conn • Mason, Ohio • Chicago

LIBRARY OF CONGRESS CIP DATA ON FILE.
CATALOGUING IN PUBLICATION FOR THIS BOOK
IS AVAILABLE FROM THE LIBRARY OF CONGRESS.

ISBN-13: 978-1-4328-4604-6 (hardcover)

Published in 2018 by arrangement with Macmillan Publishing Group, LLC/Tor/Forge

Printed in the United States of America
1 2 3 4 5 6 7 22 21 20 19 18

To
KATHLEEN O'NEAL GEAR,
GAYDELL COLLIER,
and
JEANNE WILLIAMS,
who have always
believed in this story

ACKNOWLEDGMENTS

This novel finally came to fruition as a result of three remarkable women. The first was, of course, my charming and talented wife, Kathleen O'Neal Gear, a *New York Times* bestselling author in her own right. Kathleen read the first draft of *This Scorched Earth* in 1984. I had sold my archaeological consulting business to write full-time and Kathy was still working as an archaeologist for the U.S. Department of the Interior. As I labored on the novel, she was constantly being asked by her federal colleagues, "So, has your deadbeat husband sold a book yet?"

Kathy, fortunately, had faith.

The second great lady was Gaydell Collier — who was instrumental in catapulting me onto the writer's path in the first place. She had been reading my various attempts at fiction. I had sent her *This Scorched Earth.* Her response was: "You're making progress. Would you mind if I sent this to my friend Jeanne Williams? And are you going to the Western Writers of America meetings in Fort Worth this year? Jeanne will be there and might be persuaded to discuss the manuscript with you."

At the time we were unfamiliar with Jeanne Williams and her wonderful novels. We also hesitantly

7

explained that as unemployed writers we certainly couldn't *afford* to drive to Texas for a Western Writers' conference. Gaydell's response: "If you are serious about becoming published authors, you can't afford *not* to go."

We went. And true to Gaydell's word, Jeanne Williams took time from her busy schedule to go over the manuscript with me. Her editorial notes were precise, cutting, and perceptive. Everything a budding novelist needed to hear. I remain eternally grateful for her kindness and insight.

We sold our first novels at that WWA in Forth Worth, and with contracts in hand for other projects, we took a different turn with our writing. *This Scorched Earth* has always been there, an itch under the skin. Kathy has urged me, Gaydell goaded me until her death, and Jeanne's comments were still waiting to be addressed.

All these years later, I hope you find the story worth the wait.

1

April 12, 1861

Beginnings often hark back to a single, crystalline moment, as if it were a precursor for everything that followed. While mighty events unfold with what seems to be an inevitability, sometimes we are left to wonder at the implications of what seems a simple and inconsequential choice.

For Dr. Philip Hancock, that pivotal moment occurred in the back room of an upper-class New Orleans brothel.

For the previous three years, Philip Hancock had lived in a low-ceilinged, poorly lit attic in Boston where he had been attending medical school. In those narrow confines he'd frozen through the bitter winters, only to roast during the brief respite of summer. Nevertheless, he'd completed his studies, and though opportunities had abounded for a physician in bustling Boston, he'd longed for the semiwilderness of northwest Arkansas — the land of his boyhood.

To Doc's way of thinking, the fastest way home had been by sea on a merchant vessel loaded with textiles. Its next port: New Orleans. He'd only been able to afford a cheap berth, the bottommost hammock on a dark lower deck. Nevertheless, he'd completed the first leg of his journey and emerged in the sultry air of the New Orleans waterfront a free, and almost penniless, physician and surgeon.

As Doc had strolled down the wharves that morning, he had overheard a young boy — an apparent street urchin dressed in rags — calling to one of his friends, "Me? I can't play today. I gotta find me a doctor for Miss Meg!"

Doc had signaled the boy, asking, "And what service might your Miss Meg require?"

The black-haired urchin had stared suspiciously at Doc's surgical bag and cocked his head. Defiantly he had propped filth-encrusted hands on his skinny hips — a gesture no doubt mimicked from a much older man — in order to impart an air of importance.

"You can fix a man's leg?"

"I can fix as much as any physician can," Doc had replied. "Assuming your Miss Meg is financially solvent."

The boy's round and freckled face had puckered as if he were having trouble with the words "financially solvent."

Eyes still fixed on Doc's bag, he seemed to come to a decision. "Reckon you can make terms with Miss Meg. Foller me."

The way had led up cobblestoned streets where old French buildings rose to brood, gray-walled, with intricate wrought-iron balconies opening to cramped second-story rooms.

Miss Meg's occupied a neighborhood substantially higher in class than the waterfront where the urchin had been prowling.

Nevertheless, Doc had a moment of hesitation as the boy pointed him down a narrow alley, saying, "We gots ta go in the back."

"The back?"

The boy nodded with serene gravity. "The front door is for gentlemen." He emphasized "gentlemen" as if Doc might be just another bit of riffraff like himself.

Doc had suppressed a smile, following the urchin past piles of rotting horse manure that left a rainbowlike sheen across puddles of black water. Broken whiskey bottles had been kicked to the side, and the entwined reek of urine and excrement hung pungently in the air. In places, soot-stained white stucco had peeled like scabs from old wounds to expose the underlying brick.

The boy's discreet knock at a blue plank door had summoned an overweight black woman in her late forties. Dressed in a dark blue cotton smock fronted by a stroud apron stained with grease, she smelled of frying bacon.

"I brought Miss Meg a doctor!" the boy crowed.

"You all's a doctor?" the cook had demanded suspiciously as she stared Doc up and down. Her round face glistened with a sheen of perspiration. Before he could reply, she added, "Come on in. She be down the hall with Eli."

Only after passing through the kitchen and entering a velvet-walled hallway had Doc pegged the establishment as a bordello. A rather more sophisticated example of the trade than the shabby cribs a block back from the wharfs, but a house nonetheless.

Even as Doc had stopped short in hesitation, Miss Meg had come rustling down the wall-papered hallway. The woman was dressed in crimson taffeta layered with watered silk, her high-piled hair accenting a patrician forehead, angular

11

cheeks, and pointed jaw. She'd pinned Doc with a hard blue gaze that would have melted iron plate.

"Didn't expect anyone this quickly. This way!"

Not the sort of woman to deny.

And he did need the money.

Resigned, Doc followed Miss Meg to what appeared to be a cramped closet. Doc could have spit across the room's long axis. The stale air reeked of unwashed human, the stench of corrupt flesh, and old misery. And now he found himself face-to-face with his patient. A sweating man on the table blinked, swallowed hard. His black eyes darted this way and that but seemed unable to focus.

Eli appeared to be in his late forties, emaciated; his sunken narrow cheeks and knobby chin sported a four-day beard. In the amber light cast by the four oil lamps set on wall sconces, perspiration gleamed on the man's rounded forehead and around his glassy eyes. He wore only a smudged white shirt. Hairy bare legs protruded from beneath a gray blanket that draped his waist.

"Don't you touch dat leg! I ain't one of your girls what can be ordered around like a dog." He shifted to free his right arm long enough to shake a finger at Doc, the burning sincerity behind his eyes like a fire of the will.

Doc took in the whitewashed, rough-cut walls. A stained plank floor supported the raised table with its hanging leather straps. The stench of rot intensified in the sweltering air. In the lamplight the man's left leg — swollen, blackened, and stinking — extended beyond the table's edge.

Miss Meg, or Madam de Elaine, as she'd introduced herself, closed the door behind her to block the view from the small hallway. As news of

Doc's arrival spread, it had filled with women dressed as tarts who craned their necks to see into the confining room.

"What do you think, Doc?" Miss Meg's voice, softer now, was thick with the rasp of whiskey and cigar smoke.

Doc pushed a lock of dark blond hair off his brow and opened his surgical bag where it rested on the room's one rickety wooden chair. With the door closed, the air thickened with burned oil and the cloying smell of gangrene. He needed but one look at the grossly swollen foot to see sharp fragments of bone protruding from a black scab that leaked yellow pus.

"Cut dat leg and the world gonna go crazy," the man insisted as he began shaking his head in violent swings.

"Eli," she told him, "the only thing crazy in here is you."

For a woman closing on forty, Madam de Elaine might have passed as ten years younger had Doc not seen her in the light of day. Her makeup had been artfully applied; her thick black locks were curled, piled up, and held in place with diamond-studded tortoiseshell combs. She'd slipped a no-nonsense apron similar to the cook's over her crimson dress.

Given the stout leather straps and buckles dangling below the table, and the positioning of the four lamps, Doc realized Madam de Elaine was no stranger to ad hoc medical procedures in her back room.

This is not the reason I studied medicine.

He fought down his sudden distaste. This was the sort of place Paw would have frequented. Doc had spent most of his life struggling to outrun his

13

father's shadow. The flight had taken him all the way to Boston and the finest medical school in the land. Paw, of course, had paid for the schooling, but Philip had always wondered if it had been because of guilt, or as a final slap in the face. Whichever, the son need never emulate his dissipated and morally bankrupt sire.

I am a gentleman surgeon!

"Yes, tell yourself that," he murmured, pulling out his instruments.

"Tell yourself what?" Miss Meg asked. Her gaze narrowed. "You sure you're a physician? A mite young, aren't you?"

"You ain't touching dis leg," crazy Eli protested yet again. "Better you all let me die with dis leg. Take it off and nothing gonna be the same ever again. Madness. You all hear? Gonna be madness if'n you cut my leg."

"Madam de Elaine," Doc began, opening his bag, "I'm going to need you —"

"In this room? Given what we're about? Best call me Meg." She gestured toward the straps. "You want me to buckle him down?"

"Maybe after I've administered the anesthetic."

"Don't know that I want to pay for chloroform or ether."

Doc met her hard eyes. "I'm not cutting a man's leg off while he's awake." Then he added, "Meg."

She winced, nodded. "Very well."

"Don't do it! It be *your* fault!" Eli tried to struggle up from the table, reaching out with an imploring hand.

"Easy, Eli," Meg told him as she stepped over to the bed and laid a hand on his forehead. "No one's going to do anything you tell them not to."

Doc shot her a sidelong glance. The lie had

14

rolled so smoothly off her tongue. But then perhaps such facile prevarication came with her profession. He tried not to imagine all the things that had passed between those shapely rouged lips as he reached for his bottle and cloth.

Eli seemed to relax, dropped back on the table, his cracked and dry lips working. Anxious black eyes jerked back and forth, as though following fevered delusions.

"I seen it in my dreams, ma'am," Eli whispered. "Clear as you right now. All the world was right while I was dying. Flowers, they growed. Children was a-playing, doing chores. Young people, they's a-paying court, and young love was a-blooming." He swallowed hard, Adam's apple bobbing. "It come out of the darkness, a gleaming silver blade. Then . . . *swish.* And it done took my leg."

"What happened then, Eli?" Meg asked.

"The moment my leg dropped away, the blood started. World went crazy. Shooting, yelling, screaming, and dying. Wasn't just New Orleans, ma'am. No, it was the whole country. Men and boys, their arms and legs popping off their bodies like ticks off a hot plate. Not just no handful, neither, but by the thousands. Maybe tens of thousands, filling fields with legs and arms and heads popping right off their bodies. Crazy, I tell you. Plumb crazy."

He stared up at her face, panic-glazed eyes probing hers. "You gotta believe me, ma'am. You promise me you don't cut my leg."

She patted him on the bony shoulder. "Nothing's going to be your fault, Eli. Doc's here to take a look, that's all. He's going to make you well."

Eli sagged in apparent relief. "Thank you,

15

ma'am. Gotta tell you, I's plumb scared."

Doc dosed his cloth, stepped past Meg, and said, "Eli? I need you to smell this cloth. It will make you sleep."

"Don't want to smell no —"

"This is an order, Eli," Meg told him sharply. "You want to stay on here, you gotta get well. Now, pull your weight and smell the cloth."

Eli blinked, allowing Doc to place the cloth over his nose and mouth.

"Breathe deeply, Eli," Doc told him. "That's it. No, don't struggle. Just breathe."

Doc waited, finishing his count. Removing the rag, he checked Eli's breathing and heart.

"You're good at that, Dr. Hancock. And at so young an age? I wasn't certain when you knocked on my door."

He gave her a wistful smile. "I studied medicine and surgery for three years in Boston." He had observed and assisted on several amputations. This would be the first one he'd attempted on his own. He hoped Madam de Elaine remained blissfully ignorant of his tension.

"Your accent?" she mused. "Arkansas?"

"Very good. You have no idea how hard I have to work to keep the backwoods twang out of my voice." He rubbed his sweaty hands. Nerves. God, he hated the jitters. Eli's ravings about chaos hadn't helped.

Come on, Philip. Buck up. You know what to do.

"Arkansas to Boston to New Orleans? You travel, Doctor." She bent to retrieve the first of the heavy leather straps, and in moments had competently buckled Eli's passive body into the restraint.

"I think I inherited the wanderlust from my father. As much as he claimed to love the farm, he

16

loved being away from it even more."

"He was a surgeon as well?"

A smile thinned his lips. "If he's anything, he's a rogue and scoundrel. An irresponsible womanizing freebooter."

Doc squinted in the lamplight as he palpated Eli's gangrenous leg. "Do I want to know what you use this table and those straps for?"

"What does it look like?" Meg ripped the blanket from Eli's hips, leaving him naked from the waist down. Businesslike, she positioned his good right leg to the side and tightened it in a strap.

"I'd say you terminate the occasional pregnancy here."

"That and dose the girls for the clap when they need it. The straps keep the girls from moving at the wrong moment." She pinned him with her icy gaze. "I wouldn't like that to be talked about around town. If that's going to be a problem for you . . ."

Laying out his instruments, and hoping his hands wouldn't shake, Doc replied, "Impecunious young physicians, fresh off the boat, and new in town, should not consider themselves too high-and-mighty."

Her lips curled in a world-weary smile. "Then I guess we see eye to eye."

He removed the tourniquet from his bag and unwound the strap. "Not that Paw ever let us develop what he called airs."

She had bound Eli's left thigh to the table. "Sounds like an interesting man, this father of yours."

"Interesting covers a lot of territory." Doc tied on his apron. "I'm taking it at the knee."

17

"Do what you must."

"You don't have to watch this." Doc positioned his tourniquet, taking his time to screw it tight on Eli's skinny thigh.

"You're right. I don't." She crossed her arms beneath her full breasts and fixed her hard gaze on Eli's ruined foot and ankle.

Doc picked up his knife, reflexively wiping it on his apron. *Don't think. Just do it.*

Doc's blade traced a deep U in Eli's skin to create enough excess flap to cover the stump. He shot a sidelong glance at Meg, her blue eyes unflinching, face expressionless. Given other things she'd seen, perhaps an amputation wasn't among the worst.

How many girls have died on this table?

"Boston?" Meg mused. "What were they saying about secession up there?"

"Some are saying good riddance. Others are calling for troops to 'put down the rebellion.' Most, quite honestly, don't care if the country splits or not. Were it not for the abolitionists and Mr. Lincoln's rhetoric, my guess is that we'd be allowed to go peacefully. Still might as long as some lunatic doesn't start shooting at federal forces."

She spared him an inquisitive look. "And why did you choose Boston?"

"The best medical schools are there." Doc concentrated as he separated the thick web of ligaments around the knee. Synovial fluid drained like water as he punctured the joint. To his relief, the sepsis hadn't spread past the calf muscles. "After completing my studies I wanted to come home. The first ship bound for a Southern port was headed to New Orleans. Which brings me to

18

your back room and Eli's gangrenous leg."

"Eli lives under the stairs," she told him. "He's harmless, mostly. Just moon-touched crazy. Sees things that aren't there. Carries on conversations with invisible people. But you tell him to clean the floor? He pitches in and cleans and cleans. No letup until it's spotless. If I tell him to comb the carpets in the salon, or dust the shelves, it's done. And best of all, he's never pestering the girls for as much as a yank on his johnson."

"How did this happen?" Doc indicated the gangrenous lower leg.

"Moving a new cast-iron cookstove into the kitchen. Eli's not the strongest of men. He was on the downstairs end. Dropped it." She quickly added, "He wouldn't countenance the notion of having someone look at it. Didn't know how bad it really was till we cut his shoe off the next morning. Should have called for a physician then. But he insisted we leave him be. That it would heal."

"It might not have made any difference, as badly as his foot is crushed."

She raised an expressive eyebrow. "He kept insisting it was getting better, and I had more important things to do than keep track of his foot."

Doc's quick hands cut the last of the ligaments, and he caught the deadweight of the severed limb. He gently lowered it into a bucket placed conveniently beneath the table. One that had no doubt caught many an unwanted fetus.

A muffled bang, as if from a pistol shot, carried from the street. Then another and another. Meg stepped to the door, opened it a crack, and called, "Hattie? Go see what the commotion is about. If it's a fight, lock our front door."

"Yes'm."

19

The lower leg looked oddly forlorn where it canted in the bucket. "Well, there you go, Eli. The leg's gone, and the world is just the same as it was before."

Meg grunted. "I guess I can't very well order Eli to carry his own leg out, can I?"

"I'll see to it," Doc told her as he slipped silk suture over his tenaculum, the surgical hook. He used it to fish the arteries from the surrounding muscle. Sliding the surgical silk down, he carefully used it to ligate each of the major blood vessels.

She pursed her lips as if the notion were just sinking in. "How long until he can work again?"

"Maybe a month if there are no complications. The stump will have to heal. Keep him quiet and immobilized in a well-aired room to prevent the development of noxious effluvia. Expect fever for the next week or so. Dressings will need to be changed until the pus stops draining. It should be clear. You'll know from the smell if anything goes amiss. At the end of the month, you'll have to fit him with a prosthesis to —"

"A what?"

"A peg leg."

Her lips soured. "But he can still work?"

Doc pulled the flap taut and began to suture. "Physically he'll be a little slower. Expect him to be clumsy for the next six months. It takes a while to learn to balance and move with a prosthesis."

She turned her thoughtful gaze on him. "That was quickly done. I didn't know a leg could come off that fast."

"I grew up on a farm. Butchering pigs, deer, sheep, and cattle. Paw had me learning anatomy from a medical book, cutting up critters and

20

comparing their innards with human internal organs." He smiled, delighted with himself. She apparently had no idea how nervous he'd been. "There's not that much difference."

"You thinking of staying in New Orleans? Having just lost our old physician to the yellow fever, I'd be willing to offer you regular work here, checking the girls, dealing with our . . . special needs?"

Me? Service a bawdy house? Never again.

He finished his last knot. Bent down. Studied his suture. After wiping his hands on his apron, he slowly began unscrewing the tourniquet. A faint weeping of blood oozed along the incision's margins. This was the critical moment. Would the ligated arteries hold?

"Let me guess," Meg said tartly. "Your mother also taught you how to sew?"

"My father, actually. Harnesses, moccasins, and such. Life beyond the frontier taught him the skill, and he swore no son of his would ever be in a position where he couldn't 'repair his possibles' should the need arise."

Doc made quick work bandaging Eli's stump.

"Quite the man, this brigand father you so despise. Returning to my query. My girls are in need of a new physician. Young and handsome as you are —"

"I'm honored by your offer," he lied.

I'll see myself in hell before I lower myself to working in a brothel!

He'd never so much as set foot in a whorehouse before — and before God and the angels, he'd be damned if he'd ever do so again. That was Paw's realm, after all.

He began picking caked blood from his fingers,

21

still alert for the sudden rush should one of his ligatures fail. "Hopefully, I'm only going to be in New Orleans long enough to find a boat headed upriver. With the uncertainty of secession, I'd like to see my family again. It's been more than four years."

Then he added, "Assuming, that is, that Father's not home. Which, I must admit, is a high probability given his affinity for being anywhere else."

She smiled faintly, an amused look on her face. "But Arkansas?"

"Even worse, *western* Arkansas." Doc paused at her expression. "And it's true: as appalling as travel is in Arkansas, the politics are, indeed, even worse. Now, if someone could bring me a pan of water, I'd like to clean my instruments and hands."

"Of course." She opened the door, calling to someone out of sight. Then she turned back. "So that's it? Off to wild Arkansas to become a surgeon? They don't pay. Not even in Little Rock with its . . . what? Three thousand people? New Orleans, especially with the secession, *will* become the most powerful city in the Confederacy. Probably even become the capital as soon as this asinine notion of placing it in Montgomery over in Alabama wears off."

"I've no doubt that you're right. My dream, Madam de Elaine, is a small surgical practice. One where I can be close to the country. Hunt, fish, raise a family, and perhaps dabble in good-blooded horses."

He smiled at her as he checked Eli's pulse and breathing. "If I share anything with Paw, it's that I need a bit of wilderness. Paw settled in Arkansas, so he says, because it still has mountains and Indians, but with warmer winters and closer access to trade goods."

She vented a disbelieving sigh. "Well, what will it be then? Cash?" She narrowed her eye into a near wink. "Or could we interest you in a bit of trade? You, being a surgeon and all, should know your way around a female body. I'll have the girls —"

"Again, no disrespect, but cash would be preferred." He paused. "If I catch the spring-full rivers just right, I might make it all the way to Little Rock by boat."

"Very well." She nodded politely before stepping out. On her heels a young mulatto woman entered and set a pan of water on the rickety chair. Doc began washing the blood off his equipment and hands. He glanced at Eli, slumbering in drugged bliss.

What was it about the insane that they concocted such peculiarities of imagination?

Not my problem. I'm a surgeon. Destined to deal with medicine's higher and most noble calling.

Out in the hall, a young woman shouted, "It's war! In Charleston they're firing on Fort Sumter!"

Doc buckled up his surgical bag and reached down for the bucket with Eli's leg. He'd need a place to discard it, wishing the brothel had a garden. The outhouse would have to do.

"Hooraw!" another woman shouted in the hallway.

Bag in one hand, bucket in the other, Doc stepped out into the hallway.

"They're bombarding the Yankees!" one of the more buxom of the belles cried. She was a round-faced blonde, her cheeks rouged. "They're shouting it in the streets. The South Carolinians are going to war!"

23

"Get your rest while you can, girls," a thin black-haired young woman called drolly. "The loyal gentlemen of New Orleans will be primed for celebrating until long after dawn. And very free with their money, if I'm any judge."

"War in the distance," a redhead chortled, "profits in hand."

Doc glanced down at the bucket where the limp leg leaked blood and fluid.

2

May 6, 1861

Sounds of spring filled the forest: chirring insects; a mixed melody of birdsong; and occasional chattering from the squirrels as they leaped through the high branches. The fragrance of redbud and blooming dogwood permeated the Ozark highlands, enriched by the fresh smell of new leaves and early grass.

Billy Hancock flicked a thumb to dislodge the biting fly that had settled on his shooting hand and was fit to gorge itself. He glanced slyly at his companion; the big Cherokee lay unmoving on his right.

His large body dappled by the shadowing leaves, John Gritts cupped his hands, head slightly extended; the gobble that issued from his throat perfectly imitated the challenge call of a tom turkey.

Billy Hancock licked his lips and ran his fingers down the polished wooden stock on his rifle. Where he sat, his back to the hawthorn, his skin and clothing obscured by leaf shadows, he might have been invisible. The rifle, like all of his possessions, had been handed down. It had been Paw's to begin with — a .36-caliber cap-lock conversion. Despite care, the metal around the nipple had pitted over the years. The stock and forearm exhibited dents and dings, and the rifling had been shot out to the point that patches had to be thin and tight around the ball — and powder charges light — lest it blow right past the shallow grooves.

For fourteen-year-old Billy Hancock, the shot-out gun remained his most prized possession. His grip tightened on the rifle's wrist as a tom gobbled in response from behind the plum bushes across the small clearing.

John Gritts grinned at him, dark eyes flashing. Gritts was nearing forty, his long black hair gleaming and braided to hang down over his worn buckskin shirt. Thick muscle corded in the man's shoulders, and he shifted among the shadows like a cougar as he cupped his hands around his mouth and uttered his turkey call again.

Billy eased his knee up to prop his left arm where it supported the rifle. His right thumb eased the hammer back, his finger holding the trigger to keep the action from clicking. At full cock, he released the trigger and eased the hammer forward until it came to rest in the notch. An ant tickled his calf as it climbed past his moccasin top and started up under Billy's worn trousers. He ignored it.

Billy lowered his cheek to the rifle's comb as the first of the hens broke cover and stepped hesitantly out past the plum bush. With the slightest shift, Billy placed the silver front sight blade on the hen turkey's body.

Then another hen, and another, stepped out, their eyes gleaming and blinking as their heads jerked this way and that. One by one Billy sighted on them, finger barely caressing the trigger as he mentally shot them down. Someday someone was going to invent a rifle that would let a fella shoot and shoot. Not like Paw's slant-breech Sharps that had to be reloaded with a paper cartridge, but one after another, bang, bang, bang. When they did, a good hunter like Billy could really shine.

As it was, he lived for this moment. There they were: wily turkeys — and no more than a pebble's toss away. Unaware, completely at ease.

Exhilaration and power filled Billy's soul; euphoria spread a grin over his lips. His blood surged and ran hot with delight. Nothing, not even Maw's praise, filled him with excitement like this.

I got you!

Life and death . . . his to dispense. In that moment, he controlled the universe.

Gritts gobbled again. The hens stepped forward warily, heads bobbing. Then the tom emerged, searching for its potential rival. In full display, the tom drummed, speckled wing feathers dragging, tail spread into a full fan. April sunlight gleamed in the bird's feathers; the bright eyes twinkled.

The beat of Billy's heart settled as he studied the tom over the rifle's sights. He *loved* turkey hunting. The thrill of calling the birds in, of beating them at their own game, rushed in his very blood. The slightest movement, the wrong call, a glint of reflected light or the clink of metal, and the tom would bolt.

Gritts gobbled, and the tom froze, feathers puffing in irritation as it turned its stunning blue head. Sunlight flashed in the red wattle. Then the bird tilted its tail feathers in a dominant display, puffing and strutting.

27

Billy steadied his breathing as the big bird stepped warily through the spring grass. The feathers caught the sun just right, burning iridescent, shining copper, and almost purple.

No more than ten feet from Billy's hiding place, the bird hesitated. Billy put the last bit of pressure on the trigger, knowing where it would break.

The old squirrel rifle flashed fire and smoke, the loud bang silencing the birdsong and chirring insects. The hens exploded in flapping confusion.

Through the blue, sulfuric smoke, Billy watched the tom leap into the air, and then collapse to the ground. There it thrashed with a hollow popping of wings; the feet pumped, claws ripping at the grass.

"Nice shot," John Gritts told him. "I was wondering if you were going to let him walk down the barrel and stare you in the eye."

"Called him good, John," Billy told him. "Ain't nobody better in all the world. I swear, you're part turkey yourself."

"I'm Wolf Clan." He said it deadpan, the faintest of smiles on his broad lips.

"Yeah, and wolves eat turkeys, too."

"Only when they can catch 'em."

Crawling clear of the hawthorn, Billy stood in the April sunlight and walked over to the dying tom.

"Took out its spine at the base of the neck," Gritts noted as he picked up the heavy tom. The head and neck hung by the skin.

Billy slapped through his pants at the ant, now biting his thigh. He made a face and flipped his blond hair out of his eyes. "It was a choice. Lose the bullet, or take a chance on souring the meat with a body shot."

From the patch box he took a bit of cloth, plopped it into his mouth to wet it, and began swabbing his rifle barrel.

"Four shots, four birds. Your pap will buy you more lead." Gritts stared around the spring clearing, bounded on one side with redbud and with a stand of sassafras on the other. Behind it rose the billowed majesty of oak, hickory, and sycamore forest. Varying shades of green marked the different trees.

"Speaking of which," John said, "we better get these birds back to your maw. Warm as it is, you bring sour meat home, maybe I'm wrong and your paw won't buy you no more lead."

"Aw, hunting's good. Reckon another day out here wouldn't . . . Don't give me that disapproving look." Then Billy sighed. "I know. I promised Maw I'd be back."

"Promises is promises, boy." Gritts narrowed an eye, studying Billy's broad shoulders and strapping arms. "You think you can carry the four of them?"

"Nope," Billy lied with mock sincerity as he poured thirty grains of powder down the barrel. "But if you'd help, I'm betting Maw'd make sure you got a meal for your labor. Reckon we can throw a couple of these birds into the smokehouse for you. Paw will be home, too."

Billy squinted up at his friend, a devilish smile bending his lips. "And you'd best be a-gittin' it soon, 'cause with war talk, Paw ain't gonna be lounging around the farm for long."

Gritts seemed to be thinking hard as he attended to the bird. "Might be, too, that you're thinking that me being there is gonna keep your maw from going after you with a pitchfork for beating up

29

Matt Alsup."

Billy cut his patch and short-seated a ball before he rammed it home. "He needed a beating."

"What do you care if Alsup's sweet on Sarah? They got bottom, them Alsups. *Julichayasdi.* Tough men . . . if the Fleetwoods don't kill 'em all. That feud up north of the line could cook itself into a bigger war than secession. *Utana dinidah-nawi.* Big enemies."

"Them Alsups got Union leanings." Billy narrowed an eye as he capped his rifle and settled the hammer to half cock.

"So does your paw. You keep beating up Sarah's gentlemen callers, she's gonna be a old . . . What's that word white men use?"

"Old maid?"

"*Sgida.* That's it." Then he changed the subject. "When is your brother Butler going to be coming home?" Gritts threw the bird over his shoulder, holding it by the long legs. Together they skirted the plum bushes to a trail that led back into the shadows beneath the tall oaks and hickories. There, in a hollow between the roots, lay two toms and an incautious hen who'd stepped in front of Billy's rifle.

"Butler? Hell, he may already be there. He was due a week ago. But you know travel in Arkansas. Can't figger Butler. Never could. What kind of feller sits in a cabin reading about long-dead folks when he could be out huntin' squirrels and critters."

Gritts gave him a deadpan stare. "We have had this talk. He's the kind that feels things, dreams the spirit roads, and sees other worlds than this one. A different spirit power. He should have been born Cherokee. Your white men are going to break

30

something inside him before it's all done. You'll see."

Billy's squint tightened. "So, what do you think of Sarah?"

Gritts chuckled, throwing another of the turkeys over his shoulder to join the first. "Your sister is an unburned fire."

Billy heaved two toms over his right shoulder, and bent down to grasp his rifle. "An unburned fire?"

"You know of Selu?"

"The Cherokee corn maiden?" Billy resettled his load, watching a squirrel bound through the lower branches. Hitting a running squirrel in the trees was the toughest shot to make. Even tougher with his shot-out rifle, where, as distance increased, so did the amount of plain dumb luck required to hit anything.

A burning itch had started where his homespun trousers were belted at his waist. Hell, should have used more coal oil on his cuffs. Damn chiggers.

"Like beautiful Selu, she will stir the passions of men in her time."

Billy's heart leaped. "Ain't no one gonna be stirring nothing when it comes to my sister. Jus' 'cause you lost your . . ." He shook his head. "Ah hell, John. I didn't mean it."

Gritts's expression didn't change. "That was long ago."

"Never can trust them damn Northern people."

"Andrew Jackson was a Southerner. So were the men working with him. We call it the Trail of Tears now." He paused. "My sisters weren't the only ones who died."

"If I were you, I think I'd hate all white men."

"That means I'd hate you."

31

"Reckon so." Billy slipped Gritts a sidelong look. "You're my best friend. Maybe my only real friend."

"I've had things to teach you. The Creator made older men to teach younger men. A man without sisters has no one to teach. You know how it is among Cherokee. A man is responsible for teaching his sisters' sons to be men. Your father understands these things."

"Maw sure as hell don't." Billy shook his head. "Paw? He spent time out West. Still talks all the time about the Crow, about trappin', and that William Drummond Stewart. At least when Paw's home, that is."

"He should buy a house in Little Rock instead of renting that room. This convention on secession the governor called is going to take all summer."

"No it ain't. Not since that man Lincoln called for Arkansas to send troops to fight South Carolina and the secesh states. Even the Union men are mad about that. And that damn Lincoln, he shouldn't have sent that ship to reinforce Fort Sumter. That was a damn slap in the face to them Carolinians."

"So, you gonna go be a soldier?"

Billy grinned as he shook his head. "Paw told me about soldiering down in Mexico. As much as it didn't suit him, it'd suit me less. I ain't taking orders, marching to someone else's call." He paused. "And there ain't no hunting."

Gritts started down the winding trail, sniffing the flower-laden air on occasion, as if — like his Wolf Clan ancestors — he could scent the presence of prey and dangers. "Your mother likes to sound enraged, but like a nesting hawk, it is

32

mostly loud noise." He paused. "You confuse her. She is so proud, at the same time worried. You are her favorite."

"Favorite? Then why's she always yelling at me?"

"Because you are her favorite. The others, they are walking the path of their futures. Philip is already a trained healer, long gone. Butler now studies in the white man's school in Pennsylvania, and beautiful Sarah will choose any man she wishes."

"She damn well better choose smart, then, 'cause I'll whip any of these lazy bastards come sniffing around her. They only got one thing on their mind, John, and they ain't doing *that* with my sister."

"You can't stop Sarah from becoming a woman any more than you can stop the White River from flowing. Sometimes this preoccupation you have with her worries me. Guarding her honor is one thing, craving her, that becomes dangerous to the soul."

"I don't *crave* her! You've seen how men look at her. How that change comes to their eyes. And, damn it, you know they's figgering on what it would be like to peel her out of her dress. It just lights my fire. I see red and want to stomp every one of them for being sneaking bastards."

"Sarah is good to look at." John gave him a bland smile in return for Billy's hot glare. "All the curves are right . . . even if she's too pale with the wrong color hair for a man like me." He lifted a finger. "Even your maw worries that you take things too far."

"She's always yelling at me to let Sarah alone."

Gritts shot Billy a hard look. "You know your paw is taking her to Little Rock next fall. She's old enough to marry. She wants a rich and power-ful husband. One who will increase your paw's standing and power. Your paw and Sarah under-stand these things." He smiled tightly. "They could be Cherokee."

Billy ground his teeth, looking away. Maybe it wouldn't be so bad with Sarah married and living way off in Little Rock. To change the subject, he muttered, "Hell, John. I just want to have fun."

"Among my people, we have a word for your kind."

"Udiga udli," Billy replied. "Thrown Away Boy, the crazy brother." He'd been working hard to learn as much of the Cherokee language as he could, and John always helped him with the pronunciation. Said it might save his life one day.

"*Gehyahtahi.* The Wild One," Gritts corrected as they emerged from under the forest canopy and onto a high limestone cliff. Billy narrowed his eyes against the hard sunlight and stepped to the precipice. Patches of green moss clung to cracks in the eroded gray limestone. The sky beckoned, pale blue, with puffy white clouds in the distance over the rumpled ridges.

Perched on the lip, Billy looked out across the rounded tops of trees in the valley below. To the west lines of forested bluffs and ridges seemed to march away into the misty blue. The distant clouds beyond the horizon thickened in the southwest where they floated in from the Indian Nations, hinting of rain in the afternoon.

The fragrant air was heavy with the scent of blooming flowers and trees, the damp freshness of the soil, and the muggy warmth of the season. The different shades of green in the valley below marked elms, varieties of oaks and hickories, maples, and chestnuts. Redbuds, dogwoods, and vines of honeysuckle that added spots of color. He thought the forest greens to be achingly vivid in comparison to the stark blue of the sky. In the valley below, the White River ran high, its clear waters displaying the pale limestone bed that gave it its name. A thin line of white marked a logging road down in the bottom where it paralleled the river.

"This is an important place," John said, stopping beside him. With his left hand he pointed down to the base of the limestone cliff. "You see the trailhead where it comes through the rocks?"

"Yep." Billy used a sleeve of his grimy shirt to wipe the sweat from his forehead.

"I heard the story from a Caddo. He said that this place has seen many battles. That if a handful of warriors crouched up here they could hold the rimrock against hundreds of enemy warriors coming up from the bottom. You see the way the limestone overhangs the trail below? You can shoot right down on the enemy's head. They have no protection, and the trail is rocky and steep with drop-offs. Bad footing."

Billy shifted his load of turkeys and peered over the edge. Sure enough, every bend and twist of the trail below was visible as it zigzagged down to the trees a hundred feet below.

"All the times we been up and down here, how come you ain't never mentioned this a'fore?"

Gritts shrugged. *"Akto'uhisdi nula guhdi iyuwakdi."*

"Yep. Wisdom comes with time."

Gritts gave him a yellow-toothed grin. "Now you will never climb up or down this trail again without looking up and wondering who might be on top, ready to drop a rock on your head."

35

"And I thought the footing was scary enough on this son of a bitch."

Gritts glanced at the high sun. "If we hurry, we can just about be to your home by suppertime. Then you can face your mother and see what scary is really like." He gave Billy a deadpan look. "And don't forget to stop your cussing. She'll whack you for that."

"You just want a hot supper."

"And maybe to hear how your white man's war might change things. Cherokees keep slaves, too."

"Don't reckon much will change, John." Except Paw would be in the middle of the politics. And, as John had reminded him, he'd take Sarah off to Little Rock to "introduce" her to society. Which was just a fancy way to troll her like a lure to snag some rich and influential husband.

And then what am I going to do?

3

May 10, 1861

With his back propped in the chair, Butler Hancock idly rolled the bottom of his glass on the familiar scarred wood of the family table. His ass ached, as it had since he was a boy sitting on these selfsame chairs. They'd been locally made by a craftsman who'd learned the trade in New England and built a mill-powered lathe to turn spindles, legs, and bedposts. The chairs were every bit as uncomfortable as they were attractive.

His ass? Not his posterior?

He was home, all right. The cultured veneer he had worked so hard to learn and cultivate back in Philadelphia seemed to erode with every hour that passed, as if the very Arkansas air scuffed it away like grit ate the polish off a fine pair of shoes.

Philadelphia with its hustle and bustle had come as a shock after Little Rock. And Butler had paid a terrible price; he'd become the butt of jokes, scorned for his bucolic ways. To survive, he had dedicated himself to the task of learning the social graces, even inventing imaginary friends to practice with. But in the end, he'd survived because everything he read stuck in his head.

And, of course, the fact that he had grown up

wrestling, swinging an ax, and splitting rails didn't hurt anything, either. Wasn't a one of them he couldn't flatten in a knock-down brawl. It had only taken one to earn the complete respect of his fellow scholars.

And now I'm home. And it is as if nothing's changed.

Leaning his head back he found the soot-stained plank ceiling only a tad darker than it had been when he'd left two years past. Maw's pale hair, pinned back in a bun, might have acquired a whiter tint at the temples; but she still hurried back and forth in the kitchen with its counter, stove, and fireplace.

Paw Hancock's house had been the first frame structure built on the upper White after the sawmill opened. The original log cabin, ten by twelve, still stood out back. From those humble beginnings, Paw Hancock had built his curious estate.

Butler sucked on his pipe, enjoying the last of a mellow blend he'd brought with him from Memphis. Paw sat at the head of the table like a king, his own pipe working like the stack on a steam locomotive. His mane of white hair stood up from his high forehead like a wave that rolled over his skull and down to his collar. Now that he was nearing sixty, his once-red hair had surrendered to time. For the moment, Paw's angular face was clean shaven, the line of his jaw firm despite the missing teeth in his gums. Fierce blue eyes stared across the table at their guest, Isaac Murphy.

A redheaded Irishman, the normally affable Murphy wore a frock coat despite the late May weather, and his riding breeches were travel stained. He stared into the mug he cradled, attention absently focused on the light brown whiskey that remained mostly untouched.

How often could that be said of an Irishman? The thought brought an amused twist to Butler's lips.

Billy sat at the end of the table, fidgeting and pulling at his fingers. Burly for his age, Butler's younger brother acted as if a fire had been built beneath his seat. The boy's gaze kept straying first to John Gritts — the big Cherokee who sat to Billy's left — and then to the door behind him. Billy couldn't have been more eloquent were he Cicero addressing the Senate.

That's when Butler noticed the spider. A big one, brown and black, it came dropping down from the ceiling. Silk trailed out behind; the eight legs were held wide.

"Son of a bitch," Paw muttered, half rising, his hand lifted to swat the thing the moment it landed on the table.

"Wait!" Butler cried, laying his pipe to one side. He shot his hand out. The spider dropped into his palm, then skittered to the underside as Butler shoved his chair back and made for the door. The entire time he kept turning his hand so the spider couldn't drop off.

Hurrying outside, Butler let the spider drop at the edge of the porch. It hit the ground, then skittered into the dark safety under the planks. Billy's old dog Fly didn't even wake up where he was sleeping in the dust.

"Be just like you to get your hand bit, have it swell up, and fall off." Paw was giving him a scowl as Butler reseated himself.

"Spiders are good luck," Butler replied, glancing at John Gritts and winking. A smile spread on the big Cherokee's lips. Cherokees and spiders had a special relationship going back to the creation of the world. "And it's not like she was trying to hurt anything. Put yourself in the spider's position. Once she was in my hand, she just wanted to get away. Hard to fault a little soul for that."

"You've always worried me, boy," Paw muttered. "You'd go out of your way to save a rattlesnake when its fangs are stuck in your leg."

"I'm not as sensitive and delicate as you think. Believe it or not, scholars who read history and literature are a backstabbing and bloodthirsty bunch."

Paw sighed. "When I was young, a man I admired opened a whole new world to me. Taught me the value of education and scholarship. But Butler, when you spout Shakespeare, Plato, and Aquinas, it's like you are in their heads. I reckon that's a special gift." He pointed with his pipe. "Just don't lose track of this world."

Billy was making strangling noises.

John Gritts was still smiling.

Paw pointed with his pipe again. "Now, Isaac, finish your story. What happened at the secession convention?"

"I was the only one," Isaac stated dully. "The others, Bollinger, Campbell, Gunter, and the rest of the Unionists finally gave in. On the last vote, I was the only one who voted against secession. They cried, 'Traitor!' 'Get a rope!' 'Hang him!' Honestly, James, I thought some damn fool would walk up and shoot me on the spot."

Butler noted that Billy was finally paying attention. The mere idle mention of shooting something always brought Billy fully alert. John Gritts simply sat with his elbows on the table, fingers laced, and his thumbs touching. His head was down, as if in

40

prayer. But from long association with him, Butler knew the Cherokee was listening, thinking, keeping his own counsel.

"After Lincoln's blunder over Fort Sumter, from the moment he called for Arkansas to provide troops to put down the rebellion, the result was a foregone conclusion," Paw told him. "And it's just what our idiot governor down in Little Rock has been waiting for. Ever since seizing the federal arsenal, he's been on pins and needles to command an army."

"Oh, Governor Rector's already issuing orders. It's a swirling confusion, James. The convention is issuing its own orders. And there's a call to convene the legislature so yet more people can issue orders. There's a Confederate army being enlisted, an Arkansas state army being sworn in, and then there's the local militias. Three armies . . . and no one knows who's what!"

"What's the word on the abolitionist jayhawkers up in Kansas?" Butler asked.

"As of the moment I left Fayetteville" — Murphy gave him a clear-eyed look — "no one had heard anything. That firebrand Senator Jim Lane and his Kansas raiders, and that bastard Colonel Montgomery, could be marching on us at this very moment." He grunted. "Maybe we should wish he would. Settle this whole mess before it gets started."

"You don't want that kind of trouble," Paw said evenly. "And if Lane or Montgomery march their raiders anywhere, it will be into Missouri. If Missouri votes for secession, that's where the real fight will be. Arkansas is only famous for being an obstacle dropped smack in the way of anyone with ambition who's trying to get west to Texas."

41

"And our dysfunctional politics." Butler gestured with his pipe. "Even in Pennsylvania people have heard how corrupt Arkansas politics are."

"Careful about the politics, boy," Maw called from the kitchen. "Them's Paw's good friends, all them Johnsons and Conways and Boudinots and Danleys." She turned toward the table and raised her wooden spoon, aiming it like a scepter. "You can dress a jackass in silk breeches, but he's still a jackass."

At that moment Sarah stepped in from the springhouse, two pails of water hanging from a shoulder yoke. She shot Butler a flushed smile as she artfully maneuvered the buckets past the seated men. With locks of her pale blond hair loose, her cheeks flushed with exertion, and her blue eyes alight in her triangular face, to Butler she looked ethereal.

Isaac Murphy stopped in mid-thought, a look of wonderment on his face as he watched her pass behind the table.

After lowering her buckets, Sarah arched her back, resettling her gray cotton dress. The way her perfectly proportioned breasts rounded the fabric and how it clung to her full hips would have tantalized a dead man. She was going to be a sensation when Paw took her to Little Rock in the fall. Butler fought down a smile. His little sister apparently had no idea how her tall, ripening body affected Murphy.

Billy, however, had narrowed one eye to a slit, his jaw hardening as he fixed a lethal blue stare on the Irishman. Paw, having missed nothing, pulled on his pipe, eyes twinkling as he asked, "How soon are they figuring to fight this war?"

Murphy manfully forced himself back to the

42

subject at hand, glancing wistfully down at his whiskey. "If Arkansas were Virginia or the Carolinas, I'd say they'd have a sort of army by the fall. But Arkansas is Arkansas. Given our own divisions over slavery we'll be lucky if the northern counties aren't skirmishing with the southern by July fourth."

Paw chuckled. "I'm sure most of the slave owners in the counties south of the river are already enlisting men. The east, too. I'll bet my young friend Tom Hindman is already planning a regiment."

Murphy looked at Butler. "What about you, young man? Are you ready to charge off and fill your life with dash and glory? Or, as a Union man, will you go the other way?"

"Or be smart and avoid the whole blooming mess," Maw called from the kitchen. "There's no sense in my boys running off to get shot wholesale for someone else's lunacy."

Butler pushed back in the uncomfortable chair and rolled his whiskey glass as he quoted, " 'The battle where men were perishing shuddered. Now with the long man-tearing spears held in their hard hands, the men's eyes were blinded in the dazzle of bronze light, which shone from helmets, burnished armor, and polished shields. Men came on in confusion.' "

"What's that?" Isaac Murphy asked, forcing himself to keep from staring at Sarah, who pulled a fresh-baked loaf from the brick oven.

"Homer," Butler replied. "A section that stuck with me from the *Iliad*."

"They'll make you an officer," Murphy groused. "Nay, strike that. In Arkansas, they'll make you a general."

Butler waved it away. "Mr. Murphy, I'd be a book general, quoting Caesar, Xenophon, Thucydides, and von Clausewitz. Doesn't mean I'd be worth spit commanding troops."

Paw shifted. "Butler, no law says you've got to take sides. You could go west. Cowards don't head to the Shining Mountains."

Murphy snorted his dismay. "Butler can stay here. Fighting is going to be in the East. What's it to Washington or Richmond . . . or wherever the Confederate capital is today? A couple of battles will be fought to determine who's who. Then each side will have stood for their honor, and it'll all be over."

"If there's to be a war, I will bear arms for my state," Butler replied graciously. "What greater calling to manhood is there? Read your Homer, Scott, and Shakespeare. Or as is quoted in Thucydides, 'You do not see that peace is best secured by those who use their strength justly yet show their determination not to submit to wrong.' And in this case, should the Union attempt to force us back into the United States through force of arms the moral argument grants superiority to Arkansas."

Paw nodded. "I could give a damn about slavery, but a state's got as much right to leave a nation as a person has to emigrate." Then he fixed Butler with his hard gaze. "But war's not what you read in books, son. I was in Mexico."

Isaac Murphy opened his mouth, raised a finger . . . and stopped short.

Thinking better of what he was about to say, no doubt.

Butler pursed his lips. As much as Paw liked to remind folks that he'd been in Mexico during the

44

war, people still whispered behind his back that he'd been more interested in looting Mexican gold and silver. Indeed, Paw'd never enlisted, nor had he served in any known unit.

"A freebooter," it was suggested by men in the taverns — usually far into the night when they were deep in their cups. James Hancock had killed men who impugned his honor. Like so much about Paw, even his killings were veiled in controversy. Butler had been but a boy the first time he overheard a man claim that James Hancock had never killed a man in a fair fight.

That was the problem with Paw. No one knew him, least of all his own sons. Half the White River Valley considered James Hancock to be a scoundrel, and the other half thought of him as a solid man of the land, an entrepreneur, and a pillar of manifest destiny.

Was he the blackguard, backstabbing bastard that tough men dared not insinuate to his face, or the man who read *King Lear* by the fire at night, his long-stemmed pipe at hand?

Or is he both?

Why would such a self-serving cutpurse have encouraged his son Butler to pursue an education in letters? Paw claimed that the English adventurer Sir William Drummond Stewart had forever altered his appreciation for letters and a more cultured approach toward life.

James Hancock might be cold and calculating, but the man wouldn't brook disobedience or poor behavior. He insisted on the standards and comportment of a gentleman, and at the same time consorted in the company of illiterate backwoods farmers, Indians, Mexicans, and free blacks. Many of the more upstanding citizens of

Fayetteville — let alone the lordly planters in the Mississippi counties with whom Paw associated at the legislature — were appalled at the notion that he'd let a ragamuffin Cherokee like John Gritts share his table. Unfortunately, and to their immense discomfort, Paw's reputation as a duelist — and that he always seemed to have enough gold in pocket — made his company "acceptable." Not to mention his political influence with the illiterate voters in both Benton and Washington Counties.

Paw noticed Isaac's hesitation — read it with the same ease Butler had. "Isaac," he said, "I've been many things. One thing I am not is a traitor to my home. Arkansas has seceded. I'll place my fortune and honor with her." He raised a pale eyebrow. "And, my feelings about slavery be damned, that includes taking a commission in whatever military we cobble together."

In the kitchen, Maw's wooden spoon clattered as she and Sarah turned to stare their disbelief.

Butler straightened. "Then that decision steers my course, as well."

"Do I have to go, too?" Billy cried, having long ago exhausted his fidgeting. He shot a sidelong glance at John Gritts. The big Cherokee seemed to be enjoying some private amusement.

Paw pointed his pipe stem. "You will *not*! You are only fourteen. Philip's gone, God knows where. And by tarnal damnation, he'll probably fight for the North just to enrage me. That means someone's got to become the man of the house. Well, now's your chance. You've got three or four, why perhaps as much as six, months before this war squabble is over. That's your test, son. Take care of Maw and your sister. Keep the homestead and the fields productive. Do that, and you'll prove yourself a full man. Do yourself extra proud, and you'll merit a new rifle when it all comes to a conclusion."

Billy had swollen up like a strutting turkey. He shot Gritts a cunning smile and a wink, as if sealing some secret deal.

Butler chuckled under his breath, wondering what would drive his little brother to madness first. The lure of the forest and the hunt? His desire to whale the tar out of any young lad that looked sideways at Sarah? His desperate need to keep the home fires burning? Or his desire to escape Maw's incessant chastisement?

But when he looked in Maw's direction, it was to see her glacial stare fixed on Paw, a near desperation and disgust barely hidden behind her masklike expression.

I know, Maw. It's just another excuse for Paw to vanish on the trail of adventure. Thistledown on the wind. The only thing he's ever left you is alone.

4

July 29, 1861

The streets of Memphis — like all cities — gave that irritating offense to the nose. Something about horse urine and the particularly aromatic equine droppings imparted an acuity to the scent that seemed unusually prominent in the aftermath of the late-afternoon rain.

As Philip's heels drummed hollowly on the boardwalk, the thick and warm air seemed to burst with the sounds and smells of the city, augmented by the breeze-born odors off the great river where it roiled, swirled, and sucked on its way south.

Evening had fallen, the light having faded to a dark pewter in the partly cloudy sky. Lightning flashed in the black clouds now sulking their way toward the eastern horizon. The last of the evening birds were going quiet as the first bats wing-danced in the growing gloom.

To either side, redbrick buildings rose above Third Street in two or three stories, their wooden windows whitewashed and stark against the walls. Here and there the yellow glow of candlelight honeyed rooms behind wavy panes of poorly made glass.

Philip touched his hat and stepped onto the damp street as two matrons in taffeta and bonnets passed, their female slaves following demurely. His time in Boston — in addition to the western bias of his home country in northwest Arkansas — had left him uncomfortable with slavery. Yet here he was, smack in the middle of it, and fully aware that debate over its existence had driven the wedge of secession between North and South.

At Jefferson Street, he turned east, adjusted his hat, and proceeded to the address Dr. Morton had given him. A houseboy dressed in a satin jacket stood on the elevated porch of the frame structure. A lantern on a low table provided feeble illumination. As Doc climbed the steps, he could hear laughter from inside.

The boy drew himself up, his dark skin amber in the lantern light as he asked, "Can I be of service, sir?"

"Could you tell Dr. Morton that Philip Hancock has arrived?"

"Yassir," the boy told him. "If you will follow me, sir."

The boy led him up the steps to the porch, opened the great blue door, and ushered Doc into a lighted foyer. On the right a carpeted staircase ascended to the second floor. To either side doors opened to a living room on the right and parlor on the left. From this latter came the laughter and delicate clink of glassware.

An older black man, immaculately dressed, stepped forward as the boy said, "Dr. Hancock is arrived." Then the lad retreated outside.

"May I take your hat and coat, suh? And do you need a moment to attend to your toilet?"

Doc had doffed his hat upon entry, and shrugged

out of his coat before handing them to the servant. "No, I'm fine. Thank you."

"A moment, suh." The black man retreated with Doc's hat and coat, only to emerge from behind the stairs, bow, and lead Doc into the parlor, announcing, "Dr. Philip Hancock," to the assembled guests.

Doc took stock of the room. French windows gave a view of the street. A fireplace, grate closed, was built into the far wall; its mantel sported silver candlesticks and burning tapers. A Persian rug covered the polished hardwood floor, the room surrounded by chairs upon which several older ladies reposed. One rose at Doc's entry.

Dr. Benjamin Morton stood with another man before the door leading to the dining room, glasses of lemonade in their hands.

The woman who now approached offered her gloved hand as Doc bowed. He'd met Mrs. Morton at her husband's surgery twice before. In her early fifties, she had black hair barely touched by white and a kindly face dominated by spirited green eyes. She wore a sky-blue velveteen hoop dress with white lace.

She said, "Dr. Hancock, welcome. We are so delighted that you could come." Leading him forward she approached the white-haired man beside Dr. Morton, saying, "Reverend Nelson, I have the pleasure of presenting to you Dr. Philip Hancock, late of New Orleans and Boston."

"My pleasure, Reverend." Philip shook the man's hand.

"I have heard good things about you, young man." He indicated Morton. "Benjamin, here, says that you're a marvel in his surgery."

"He is very kind, sir, given my youth and inexperience."

"Oh, posh!" Ben Morton made an expansive gesture with his lemonade. "Theophilus, Philip can dissemble all that he likes. Since he started filling in, there are three at least that I can count who are alive because of his skill. Old dog that I am, he's teaching me new tricks."

The reverend raised a white eyebrow. "High praise indeed, Ben. So, if I come down with a goiter, you're telling me that my chances for survival are higher if I wait until *after* you've left your office?"

Ben made a face. "Much, I'm afraid."

"Dr. Morton is being much too kind," Philip replied, somewhat embarrassed.

"If you will excuse us, Reverend." Felicia led Philip to the woman in her sixties who remained seated, and said, "Mrs. Nelson, permit me to introduce Dr. Philip Hancock, late of New Orleans and Boston."

"My pleasure, ma'am," Philip replied as he took her gloved hand.

"Boston, Doctor? Surely you're not a Yankee." She gave him a forced smile, lips closed to hide missing teeth.

"No, ma'am. I'm from Arkansas originally. I was only in Boston to study."

"When Felicia finishes her gauntlet of introductions, do come and tell me about Boston. I've heard the most ghastly stories about the place."

"Of course."

A young man in his early twenties had appeared in the doorway behind Morton and the Reverend. A strapping redhead, a glass of lemonade in his hand, he cocked his head and studied Doc with blue-eyed curiosity.

51

Felicia led Doc to the young man saying, "Dr. Philip Hancock, may I present Nathanial Nelson, soon to be of the Fourth Tennessee Infantry."

Doc took the young man's hand. "Congratulations."

"Good to meet you, Dr. Hancock." A lopsided smile bent the young man's lips. "I'm trying to talk James into joining me."

"And not having much success," James Morton called from the doorway as he entered the salon. "Hello, sir." The young man with chestnut hair and green eyes stepped forward to firmly shake Doc's hand. Doc had met him several times at Morton's surgery. "Glad Father could talk you into coming."

"James, I declare! Don't know why you'd want to fool around with steamboats when you could march off to glory with me," Nathaniel interjected airily. "Doctor, surely you can dissuade my dear friend James from his obsession for piloting a steamboat. That's a trade rather below the calling of a true gentleman, whereas the military offers a young man of character ample opportunity to rise in the ranks."

"That's right," Reverend Nelson agreed as he made an expansive gesture with his half-full glass. "My old friend Leonidas Polk is in charge of Tennessee's defense now. Still an Episcopal bishop, he's made general in charge of Department No. Two."

"That's western Tennessee, Arkansas, Louisiana, and northern Mississippi and Alabama," Dr. Morton noted. "Quite an enterprise."

"I just want a chance to do my duty," Nathanial interjected. "After what happened at Manassas last week, the war will be over by the time I even get my uniform."

"And well it may," Mrs. Nelson noted to her son's dismay. "A smart young man, like James, here, dedicates himself to improving his lot. He's not just intent on piloting a steamboat, he wants to *own* one. And then another and so on. With the exclusion of the Yankee boats on our rivers, he's thinking of the endless opportunities to profit with the growth of our new nation. When has the army ever made a man rich?"

"You smile, Dr. Hancock?" Felicia Morton asked.

"I was just thinking how similar families are. Mrs. Nelson's words might have passed my own mother's lips. I've heard them often enough over the years."

"And do you have family in the military, Doctor?" Felicia asked.

"I am not sure, ma'am, having been out of touch with family and friends since leaving Boston. My suspicion, however, is that my father has not been able to deny the call to arms. Nor have I heard from my brother Butler. He was studying history and the classics at an academy in Pennsylvania."

"I take it they are loyal to Arkansas and the Confederacy?"

Doc shrugged. "I assume so."

Announced by a rustling of skirts, a young woman swept into the room.

Doc turned. The first thing he noticed were the most dazzling green eyes. Wearing a crinoline dress — cut low to expose smooth shoulders and a creamy chest — her auburn hair piled high, the young woman stopped short. Skirts swaying, she met Doc's gaze and smiled. Her face reddened as if in excitement and accented the fine lines of her cheeks and jaw. Thin waisted, her full bust barely disguised, she was nearly as tall as Doc. She took a breath and laced her hands before her.

"Excuse me," she said demurely. "I was detained in the kitchen."

Felicia Morton stepped forward, taking the young woman's hand. "The last of our guests has arrived, my dear. Dr. Hancock, please allow me to present my daughter, Miss Ann Marie Morton. Ann Marie, this is Dr. Philip Hancock, of whom your father has spoken so highly."

"My pleasure." Philip bowed, loath to break her gaze. Her green eyes seemed to sparkle in the candlelight.

"The pleasure is mine, Doctor." She gave him a perfect curtsy. "Father calls your abilities as a surgeon . . ." Her brow lined faintly, as though perplexed. "Brilliant? Isn't that the word you use, Father?"

"Your memory doesn't desert you, my dear," Morton told her dryly, a knowing smile on his lips.

Of course he'd known that Morton had a daughter. He just hadn't anticipated that she'd be a creature of such poise and beauty. Or with those dancing and sparkling eyes. Nor could he put name to the curious excitement that leaped within him when her eyes met his.

He inhaled, catching her faint scent of lilac.

Unsettled, he made himself retreat and take a place beside Reverend Nelson as Ann Marie crossed the room to sit beside Mrs. Nelson. Yes, she was beautiful, but some quality she possessed drew his gaze like a magnet.

Don't stare at her like an idiot, Philip.

James, having not missed Doc's reaction, and

unabashed in his amusement, asked, "Dr. Hancock, are you staying in Memphis for long?"

Ann Marie's green gaze fixed on his, accompanied by a ravishing smile. The whole world might have faded.

"Pardon me?" Doc gratefully took the opportunity to redirect his thoughts.

"Are you staying in Memphis for long?" James repeated with teasing emphasis.

"Oh . . . well, that remains to be seen." Doc struggled to focus on James. "My goal originally was to return to northwestern Arkansas and open my own surgery. I hadn't counted on the disruption to travel caused by either secession or the war. River travel has been considerably more expensive than I anticipated. I have the deepest gratitude to your father for allowing me to employ my skills in his surgery. As a result of his kindness I am able to keep body and soul together."

"You've been a godsend, Philip," Morton said as he studied his lemonade. "With all the goings-on, I've needed the extra help."

Aware as he was of Ann Marie's continued attention, Doc's skin seemed to tingle. His thoughts were tumbling. Desperate for any diversion, he asked, "Steamboats, James?"

"Yes, sir. They've always fascinated me. Most of the riverboats are owned by Northerners. No sooner did talk of war break out than north they went. Though how long they can remain tied up in St. Louis, Cairo, or Cincinnati remains to be seen."

"Plenty of work for them up north, I'd wager." Reverend Nelson tossed off the last of his lemonade. "Word is that Federal trade is booming up and down the Ohio and upper Mississippi."

"That's my opportunity," James stated with passion. "We're going to have to develop our own river commerce. Perhaps the right word dropped with Isaac Kirtland? All it would take is investment. We have the wood and skills to build our own boats. Plenty of labor. All we need to import in the beginning is the boilers, casements, and pistons."

Reverend Nelson laughed and laid a hand on James's shoulder. "I'll mention it to Isaac, as no doubt you will, but he's got enough trouble given the state of the banking industry. Bank notes, Federal dollars, Confederate currency coming in. For the moment everything is chaos."

Every time Doc glanced Ann Marie's way, her smile would warm as if in encouragement.

Dr. Morton added, "Things should settle down now that Mr. Lincoln's had his nose bloodied at Manassas Junction. We've established ourselves as a force to be reckoned with."

Doc took the glass of lemonade that Mrs. Morton handed him. "I hope you are right, Benjamin. My fears, however, are that this is far from over."

"How is that, Dr. Hancock?" the Reverend asked.

"I suspect we have a long and rocky road to hoe. The pit in the rooster's craw, as my father used to say, comes first from the abolitionists. Those people are maniacal in their cause. But with the surrender of Fort Sumter and the drubbing the Federals took at Manassas, Mr. Lincoln has not only his war, but a cause now sanctified in Union blood."

"Then we shall just have to beat them again and again," Ann Marie cried with spirit. She shared

56

another beguiling glance with Doc, adding, "It doesn't seem as if there is a Federal army that can stand against us."

The Reverend finished his lemonade. "I can tell you that my good friend General Polk has every confidence that he can repulse any Federal incursions into Tennessee. He is even now fortifying the river against Federal gunboats."

Felicia Morton placed a lace-gloved hand on her husband's arm, saying, "Enough talk of war, gentlemen. Elijia has prepared a marvelous roasted goose. If you will be so kind as to follow me into the dining room?"

To Doc's delight, Mrs. Morton seated him beside Ann Marie before the fish was served.

She began by asking, "I hear that you are lodging at the Gayoso House during your stay in Memphis. How do you find it?"

"Quite satisfactory. I've enjoyed Memphis. And working with your father has been both challenging and delightful."

His heart was beating too fast, he felt awkward. Bedazzled by her smile and those sparkling green eyes, he savored just being close to her. Again he caught the faint scent of her perfume as he poured her wine.

"I must confess," she told him conspiratorially, "when I heard you were from the wilds of Arkansas, and that you wanted to go back there, I wasn't sure what sort of man you'd be."

Doc chuckled. "Expected me to be picking my teeth with a Bowie knife? Wiping my mouth on my sleeve?"

"Well, your state does have something of a reputation."

"I was raised in the backwoods, Miss Morton,

so I can tell you it is well deserved."

"And after that you still wish to return to Arkansas?"

"I've seen remarkable changes to the upper White River Valley during my lifetime. With our mountains and streams, last I heard, we have thirty-eight mills and no shortage of tanyards. We're sawing milled lumber, building furniture, and processing, carding, and weaving more cotton into cloth than in the rest of the state. Most of our textiles are exported to Texas and Missouri."

"Then, how, Doctor, did you end up in Boston? Was your father a Northern man?"

"Actually his family came from eastern Tennessee. The mountains east of Knoxville. As a young man he ended up in St. Louis. Went west with Colonel Ashley. Trapped beaver. It was there that he met an Englishman, Sir William Drummond Stewart. Stewart encouraged him to read and better his position in society. In the early years we had the only bookshelf in either Benton or Washington Counties."

She arched a teasing eyebrow that he thought irresistible. "And did he insist that you be the perfect gentleman out there in the wilds with your backwoodsmen, Indians, and bookshelf?"

"That, Miss Morton, was suggested during my medical training. The nicer habits of a gentleman? That was a hard-won skill that I'm still struggling to master. Boston society, more than anywhere, decries the actions of the vulgar, but meeting their standards? Learning which fork to use? I fear that challenged me to an extent far beyond the intricacies of anatomy."

She laughed. "Father says you're a natural when it comes to medicine. We really appreciate the help you've been giving him."

"It was fortuitous. I suppose he's told you how we met?"

"Not really."

He realized that she had a dusting of freckles across her nose and cheeks.

"A large crate fell upon a workman unloading a wagon on First Street. I happened to be at hand, and while treating him as best I could, was told of your father's surgery two blocks away. I attended the poor fellow as he was carried to your father's . . . and, well, we both worked on him at the same time."

"That I did hear. Father said it was like you had been working side by side for years."

"Your father saved the man's arm while I worked on his leg. Afterward, we enjoyed a sherry, talked for no little time, and he asked if I might be persuaded to occasionally contribute my services to his practice."

As the various courses were served, Doc barely noticed the food. His entire world had funneled down to Ann Marie: her eyes, her enchanting laugh, and that smile that seemed to wring his very soul.

Too quickly the food was gone, the plates collected. Doc hated to stand, hold her chair, and leave her behind as he retired to the parlor with the men.

"Still thinking of heading back to Arkansas at your first opportunity, Dr. Hancock?" Reverend Nelson asked at the end of the evening. He indicated Ann Marie with a casual tilt of the head. She sat listening attentively to Mrs. Nelson, though she kept sneaking glances Doc's way. "Someone, I think, would miss your company should you leave."

"I am sure that Miss Morton has no shortage of gentleman callers, Reverend."

After he thanked Benjamin and Felicia for their hospitality, Ann Marie stepped forward, a gleam of delight in her eyes. "Do come again, Dr. Hancock. I can't think of when I have so enjoyed an evening. Mother and I would find your company most agreeable."

"Of course."

As he turned to leave, Dr. Morton had a suspiciously satisfied smile on his face.

So smitten was Doc by green eyes, a dusting of freckles, that musical laugh and auburn hair, that he got lost twice on his way back to his room.

5

August 10, 1861

Hoe in hand, Sarah chopped a gap in the ditch bank, watching water flood down the row of maturing green corn, intermixed as it was with spreading squash and the beans just starting their pods. Her bonnet shaded her eyes and face, and her bare feet gripped the grass-covered soil. She'd tied her pale blond hair into a ponytail that hung down her back.

Behind her, Billy used his spade to block yesterday's diversions and rechannel the ditch water downstream. The garden plot was only six acres, but with the war, food prices — along with everything else — were already soaring. The floodplain fields below the house were covered with twenty acres of wheat, ten of cotton, and five of tobacco.

In the three months since Paw and Butler had left to enlist, gold, silver, and even copper coins had nearly vanished from the country. State-issued Arkansas war bonds had begun to circulate in place of currency, but they were failing. Devalued to seventy cents on the dollar last she'd heard.

Barter — always the heart of the northwestern Arkansas economy — now resurged with a vengeance. Pratt's store, up on the Telegraph Wire Road, carried only locally produced goods. Down in Fayetteville — so the stories said — merchants' shelves were picked bare. Only last week General Ben McCulloch had marched his troops north into Missouri to "go whip the Federals."

Sarah and Billy had taken the springboard up to Elkhorn Tavern to watch them pass. And *that* was an army? That motley hoard? She'd seen a ragged mismatch of men bearing just about every sort of weapon from flintlock fowling pieces, to muskets, to engraved-and-inlaid hunting rifles. The poorest of them, barefoot and half naked, had only carried cane knives. They'd shuffled along, joking and jesting, as they choked Telegraph Wire Road. From the heights, she'd watched them funnel down into Cross Timber Hollow and on into Missouri.

All of her life Paw and Butler had told her stories of armies marching off to war. She'd been forced to read the histories. Armies were supposed to step high with their colorful banners, gleaming armor and steel, and dash and pomp. She'd expected something grand.

To say she'd been disappointed was an understatement.

More than anything, she wanted to get on with her life. Paw had taken her to Little Rock when she was fifteen, and she'd fallen in love with the bustling city. Given Paw's status in the legislature, she'd been introduced to some of Little Rock's most prominent ladies. Paw had taken her to one of the Conways' receptions. Awed by the peoples' manners, their fine clothes, servants, and the stunningly furnished brick houses they lived in, she felt that night had changed her life. She had marveled at the embroidered —

"Hey!" Billy's voice snapped her back to the present. "You dreaming again? You don't cut that bank right soon, it's gonna wash out the damn ditch!"

She shook herself, chopping with the hoe.

"Let me guess," Billy told her snidely. "Dreaming of Little Rock again."

Paw's house on the upper White might be among the most imposing in Benton County, but compared to what she'd seen in Little Rock, it was less than second rate. "What if I was? I gotta marry somebody. If I stay in Benton County, my choices will be farming, tanning, or tavern trade. Not only do you keep beating up any beau who sets foot here, but I ain't interested. Now, in Little Rock —"

"You still think Paw's gonna take you come November?"

"He promised." Her father made his seasonal journey to the capital every fall. Sure, Paw had his own motives for parading his beautiful blond daughter among Little Rock's rich and influential. He undoubtedly figured she'd give him an advantage while playing one beau off against another.

Sarah smiled warily. Two could play that game.

She knew exactly the sort of man she'd be interested in. Solid, smart, and ambitious. Little Rock, she'd been led to believe, was bursting with eligible young bachelors. And Paw would be her avenue into the finest parlors in the city.

"Promised, huh?" Billy muttered. "But there's no telling how the war's going to reshuffle the deck. Paw might still be fighting."

"War's gonna be over soon," she declared. But Billy had a point. Although in a way he hadn't intended. Young officers — men who previously had had limited opportunities — would rise to prominence. Everything hinged on finding the right man. Someone she could love and respect. Someone seeking the same advancement of his position. The town belles, however, might have the benefits of the inside track with their fine dresses and houses.

"Which means I just have to be smarter, stronger, and quicker," she whispered as she frowned down at the ditch.

Quick-eared like an owl, Billy said, "Yeah, I heard all this before. Gonna get your Little Rock gentleman with his big fancy house and slaves. Can't wait to see how you get around owning slaves. You know how Paw feels about it."

Sarah shrugged. Paw might rail against slavery. Butler might decry it as immoral. And, raised the way she'd been, the notion of it left her uneasy. But enough to scuttle the deal? Well, she'd have to attend to that problem if and when she encountered it.

And, by all that was holy, she'd have nice clothes.

Especially her dresses, many of which would be imported from Paris. Paw had bought her an imported dress the time he'd taken her to Little Rock. Real royal-blue silk from Paris. The lace had been from Belgium, and the collar and trim had been velvet. Though she'd outgrown it, she still had it up in her trunk. She'd figured she'd work on Paw to find her something before the fall trip.

Assuming Paw could get time from the war to take her like he'd promised. That it was now August, and no word —

"Damn all Friday!" Billy called. "You worthless

today, or what? We're trying to water the crops."

She cut another channel in the ditch bank. "You swear like that again, I'll have Maw whip you with a green willow switch, Billy Hancock."

Across the ditch, hazelnut trees gave way to the forested slope, thick with maple, oak, hickory, and gum. Farther along, the giant mulberry trees beyond the field marked the yard around the two-story Hancock house. Behind it, a grove of pines and sumac obscured the old cabin. In the flat above the river stood the corrals, barns, tobacco fields, and stables.

"Gotta do something to get your attention," Billy muttered. "You already wasted more of your life dreaming about living in a fancy house than you'll ever spend living in one. And what is so exciting about this theater that Mrs. Pennoyer is running in Little Rock? You went on about it all through breakfast. It's just people pretending to be other people."

"You'll *never* understand."

Billy's old yellow dog, Fly, lay in the shade beneath a tangle of honeysuckle and scratched as he dealt with a pesky flea. The yellow dog was a mongrel with light brown eyes. Sarah considered him more trouble than he was worth, but he kept the raccoons and deer from raiding the corn. Unfortunately crows and cutworms were a perplexing reality entirely beyond the old dog's comprehension.

Sarah checked her water and stepped off the distance to the next row. The midsummer sun burned down hot on her back, baking the faded blue of her worn and threadbare cotton dress.

But what if Paw *couldn't* take her this year? She'd be near to eighteen when he finally got around to it. A whole 'nuther year!

"What's the matter?" Billy asked as she half heartedly attacked the ditch bank with her hoe. "Yer not pinin' away for that Hank Adamson, are ya? *He* sure as spit ain't never going to own no fancy brick house in Little Rock. That's gospel, I tell you."

"Lot of good it would do me if'n I was. You bloodied his nose a'fore he left for General Pearce's state army."

"Some soldier he'll make," Billy muttered. "Three years older than me, and I didn't even dust up my britches whaling the tar outta his hide."

She slashed angrily at the soil, cutting a channel. "You've gotta stop it, Billy. He wasn't doing no harm."

"Oh? Why'd he want you to give him a token?" Billy propped his shovel, callused hands cupped over the handle top. He cocked his head so the August sun illuminated his battered straw hat and the insolent set of his shoulders. His half-squinted blue eyes studied her skeptically.

"Lots of soldiers carry tokens, something to remind them of home and people who care for them."

"You care *for him*?" Billy screwed his face up and spit. "He's not worth toad suck. Shifty, that's what Hank Adamson is. And lazy. And not only that, I figger all he was after was a kiss. Maybe more. Up at the tavern I heard how soldiers talk. If'n he was all so high and honorable, what was he doing, sneaking around trying to talk to you?"

"He was afraid you'd thrash him."

"Guess there's more sense in him than I thought."

66

"Billy, you . . . you *infuriate* me!" She hammered the hoe blade at the water, splashing it. "The only callers I get are the ones that Maw and Paw bring by. I'd like the chance to get to know some boy, that's all."

"Oh, like Shirley Winston? She's sixteen and married, sure nuff. 'Course Jackson Darrow, uh . . . 'got her with child,' ain't that what they say? And now what? Darrow, he done gone off to war. Probably gonna get his ass shot off and kilt. Then where's Shirley at? Widowed, with a baby, that's where. And what upstanding *gentleman* is gonna marry her and take her off to Little Rock to live in a big house?"

He shook his head, adding, "Paw left me in charge. Ain't no man gonna sweep my sister off her feet and leave me looking like a three-fingered fool."

Sarah fought down the burning rage. "Billy, ain't no man in these parts gonna sweep me off my feet." The last thing she wanted was to end up trapped in Benton County! But how was she going to learn how to enchant the right man without a little practice?

"I'm here to see to it, sis." He gave her a blue-eyed and deadly look. "And it's not just your honor. It's that new rifle Paw promised. Ain't nothing gonna get between me an' a new rifle."

She glared at him. "Why can't you run off to war like Danny Goodman?"

"And leave you at the mercy of all them rascals from up at Elkhorn Tavern, the tannery, and clear down to Van Winkle's mill?" He shook his head, grabbed up his shovel, and got back to work. "Paw left me in charge. It's my responsibility." He paused as he moved dirt. " 'Sides, ain't a man around that I ever seen was good enough for you."

Which, of course, was why she was so desperate to get to Little Rock. "Last thing I'd ever stomach is one of them rascals from up to the tavern. And sure enough not one of them whiskey-sotted fools. The man I marry? He's going to be an educated gentleman. Maybe like that lawyer John Mallory that Paw entertained last fall."

"Him? He's married!"

"Well, of course, you fool! I said a man 'like' him, not him. He had a way about him, graceful and strong. And I liked how he and Paw got on. You could see it. Paw respected him. And there ain't many men Paw really respects." She shot Billy a glance from beneath her bonnet. "Word is Mallory's shot two men in duels."

"You're just taken with that talk about his house. Three stories, all brick." Billy used the back of his shovel to slap the dirt flat where he banked the ditch. "And he's got slaves, which brings us right back around. That'd set a splinter in Paw's seat. He never cared much for the notion of folks having slaves."

"No matter what he thinks, he's off fighting to save the 'peculiar instittion,' " she shot back. "How's that for a Union man? Now he's a major in some Mississippi regiment."

Billy pulled off his hat and used his forearm to wipe the sweat from his brow. "Paw ain't so tied to a principle as to let it get in his way when it comes to a chance for travel, fun, and adventure." He shook his head, making a face. "You remember the look on Maw's face? She knew Paw was just waiting for an excuse, any chance to go 'chase the rainbow' as Maw'd say."

"Paw ain't done so bad chasing rainbows, Billy."

She stepped off to the next corn row and hacked a cut in the ditch bank. "But you know what people say about Paw when they're out of his hearing."

Billy scowled up at an eagle soaring above the forest in casual circles. "That if he couldn't steal it, it warn't worth working for? Yeah, I heard that. I was gonna thrash the last yahoo who said so, but John Gritts held me back."

"At least someone could. Wish he was still about."

Billy's face puckered. "Me, too. Figured he was smarter than joining up with McCulloch and going off expecting to whip the Federals. Ain't the same, going hunting without him."

Come back, John Gritts. And take my brother with you.

Billy's incessant preoccupation with her virtue was nigh onto smothering her. She wanted the damn war over. For life to get back to normal.

Otherwise she sure wasn't getting to Little Rock.

"So help me, God," she whispered under her breath, "I'd endure *anything* to get away from the White River and off to someplace with exciting prospects."

6

The mules shook their heads, rattling the harness and trace chains, flopping their ears as Billy's wagon climbed Telegraph Wire Road's tree-lined grade up from the tanyard. At the top, the mules snorted relief and changed from their determined pulling stride to an easier pace as the grade leveled out.

A quarter mile farther down the rutted trace, he pulled up at Elkhorn Tavern and set the brake. Elkhorn Tavern stood on the west side of the road. Erected on a timber frame, the whitewashed structure rose two stories above the ground with dressed-stone chimneys on the east and west sides. The small yard before the long porch was separated from the trampled and manure-spotted plaza by a post-and-rail fence. A cluster of rude sheds and square-notch log dwellings surrounded the place along with chickens and a couple of hog pens. Atop the tavern's gabled roof perched a bull elk skull with a sun-whitened rack of wide antlers.

A refuge for hardy souls traveling Telegraph Wire Road, Elkhorn Tavern rented rooms, dispensed locally distilled and brewed drink, and offered a hot and filling if not epicurean meal to those so inclined. For the scattered communities and sporadic farms around Pea Ridge, the nearby hollows, and the upper White River Valley, it provided a place to gather, conduct business, and most of all, socialize.

As Billy hopped down, it was to see a dozen or so soldiers in mismatched uniforms — or what he'd come to take for such. Mostly homespun or locally mill produced, the textiles had been dyed in hickory oils: what was called butternut. Some of the men wore battered hats, others were bareheaded, and all were fully bearded or sported goatees and mustaches.

They crowded the porch, tankards or tin cups in their hands. Belts supported the occasional large knife or pistol, and most wore blousy white or gray shirts in need of laundering. Footwear ranged from boots, to worn shoes, and not a few moccasins.

As a newcomer, Billy was the immediate center of their attention. Their hawkish gazes left him feeling oddly vulnerable and awkward.

"What have we here?" one asked. He might have been in his late twenties, with long brown hair pulled back in a way that accented his thin face and hatchet of a nose.

Someone raised his voice in reply: "What we have, gentlemen, is Billy Hancock, hunter extraordinaire, crack rifle shot, brawler, and woodsman outstanding."

One of the ragged soldiers pushed forward and trotted down the front steps in holey shoes. He stopped short and grinned as he tucked his thumbs into a brown leather belt from which hung a long-bladed Bowie knife.

"Danny Goodman?" Billy asked, a sudden feeling of relief adding a measure of reassurance to his words. He stepped forward, taking the older boy's hand in a firm shake.

Danny stepped back, looking Billy up and down. "Damn, boy. I swear you got another inch taller. And them shoulders is an inch wider."

"You cussing, now? Or did your paw lose his willow switch?"

Danny's grin thinned. "I reckon I don't see the world quite like I did afore I marched up North. But I tell you, it's good to see you, boy. How's your family? What's the news?"

Billy gestured at the wagon where the mules were happily lounging in their harnesses. "Just took a load of deer hides down to the tanyard in the holler. Old man Russell's going to give half to cover Paw's debts at the tavern. Ain't much in the way of money these days. Mostly it's just what they call scrip printed up by Governor Rector down to Little Rock."

That brought laughter from the men on the porch. "At least you got hides to trade," the lean one called. "We barely got spit."

"Heard the army was back. Heard some was making camp in Cross Hollow."

"We're mustered out," Danny told him, walking over to run a hand down the off mule's sweaty flank as he absently inspected the harness. "Soldiering ain't what they say it is, Billy. Hell, up to yesterday, we was gonna hang ol' Du Val. He's the paymaster. Or supposed to be. Till yesterday we hadn't seen a dollar. And they was gonna transfer us from the State Army to the Confederacy. Ship us off out of the state. For *three years,* if you can believe?"

"Like hell they was!" a skinny youth wearing

britches with the knees out cried.

"So . . . what's next?" Billy asked.

Danny shrugged. "Anything but the army, that's sure."

"Huzzaw, huzzaw!" called one of the men on the porch as he lifted his tin cup in a toast.

Billy shot his friend a sidelong look. "You all ain't sounding like the steely-eyed victors of that Oak Hill battle. Heard you made Wilson's Creek run red with Federal blood."

"Billy, I ain't never been so tired, so hot, so thirsty, so footsore, so cold, or so scared as I been in the last three months." Danny's fingers on the mule's side might have been like feathers, so lightly did they stroke. "What happened up on Wilson's Creek? That battle? You remember Jackson Darrow?"

"Married Shirley Winston."

"He was no farther from me than you is now. We's headed up that bloody hill right into the Federal guns. Solid shot from Federal artillery hit him square in the head." Danny's fingers rose from the mule to press into Billy's forehead just above his nose. "A jagged chunk of bone blasted out of Jackson's skull and cut my scalp. Spattered his blood and brains on my right side. Saw the air filled with a red haze as his body dropped to the ground. There wasn't nothing in his head, Billy. Just the empty bottom of his skull from his ears on down."

Billy had felt a crawling sensation at Danny's touch, as if his own skull had been in Federal gun sights.

Danny averted his face, as if away from the memory, his features twitching as if they itched. "Ain't nothing like the sound of war. The roar of

73

the guns . . . rifles and pistols firing. Men screaming and shouting, and blubbering, and praying.
Exploding shells. A thousand bullets whistle and
shriek in the air. And the smoke . . . the hell-stink
of smoke . . . and blood . . . and busted-open
guts."

The men on the porch had gone silent, listening, a couple of them nodding.

"What about John Gritts?" Billy asked.

Danny seemed to shake his stun away. "Hit in
the leg. Heard they took him to Springfield with
the rest of the wounded. 'Old Ben' " — as General
McCulloch's troops called him — "started us
home right smart, not wanting to leave us in Missouri."

The blond loudly insisted, "That Missouri
bunch under General Price? They's a thieving
bunch of weasels. Saw a bunch of them run from
the fighting."

"And don't fergit them that was robbing our
dead and wounded," the thin-faced man on the
porch declared hotly. "Taking the guns and
watches and personals off wounded Arkansans.
Right there in front of us."

"And they stole a bunch of our guns, too,"
another added. "Me, I ain't never fighting for no
Missouri bastard's freedom again."

Grunts of assent and the clicking of cups and
tankards emphasized their sentiment.

"How bad was John Gritts hit?" Billy endured a
sinking sensation.

"Hard, Billy. Minié ball took out a big chunk of
the bone just up from the knee."

"Think he's alive?"

"Don't know." Danny averted his eyes, going
back to running his fingers down the mule's short-

haired red hide.

"Anyone else you know of?"

Danny barely nodded. "You remember Hank Adamson?"

"Told him I'd whip his ass if'n he ever come sniffing around Sarah again."

"Well, he ain't gonna be sniffing around nobody no more. Case shot tore him clean in half. His innards was strung across the grass for twelve feet from his chest to what was left of his hips and legs."

Danny's words stuck down inside Billy like cobwebs on his soul. They haunted him as he climbed back on the wagon and took the familiar Huntsville Road back to the valley.

As he lay in his bed that night, listening to the crickets and the whippoorwill, he pressed lightly on his abdomen, wondering what that would be like to be blown apart and have his guts strewn along like bloody rope.

One thing's sure. They ain't never gonna make me into no soldier.

But then he really didn't need to worry. The war was over. Ben McCulloch had whipped the Federals at Wilson's Creek.

7

"If you would know and understand Cicero," Paw had recently said, "you must make the acquaintance of Thomas Hindman. As an orator, visionary, and patriot, Hindman is Cicero incarnate."

The words had stuck in Butler's head. He had been at loose ends, wondering about which regiment to join. Upon hearing that Congressman Hindman had arrived in Little Rock, Butler decided it was his sign from the gods that here was an opportunity to be seized.

"I don't always see eye to eye with the man, slave-owner as he is, but I did Hindman a great service one night," Paw had claimed. "The man owes me his life."

Butler had applied all of his calligraphic talents as he labored over the sheet of foolscap and carefully penned his letter of introduction to Arkansas's recently resigned congressman. He had written the letter while hunched over the cherrywood table in Mrs. Sorrenson's drawing room. For the moment, he was her only boarder, having been accepted based upon the widow's acquaintance with Paw.

Upon his arrival in Little Rock, Butler had

introduced himself to Mrs. Sorrenson. When he mentioned that he was James Hancock's son the woman's amber-eyed gaze had altered, a secret and knowing smile filling her full lips. Butler hadn't inquired further, but almost blushed when her oddly speculative appraisal dropped below his belt.

Now he waited in the Anthony House Hotel's lobby. The hotel, located as it was on the southwest corner of Markham and Scott Streets, was Little Rock's premier hostelry. Anyone of importance visiting the state capital stayed in the sprawling structure. More of the state's governance and commerce, it was said, took place in the hotel's lobby and bar than in the capitol itself.

As Butler glanced around at the fine furnishings, he wondered if he should just leave. The surroundings were a touch too opulent for his impecunious status as a budding scholar. And more to the point, according to the wall clock on the velvet-papered walls, the congressman was twenty-six minutes overdue.

Six long minutes ago, Butler had convinced himself to give Hindman but another five to appear. He paced back and forth before a leather-upholstered settee, glanced uncomfortably at the desk clerk, and took a deep breath. Things happened to important people. Last-minute interruptions. Important business.

He turned to leave, just reaching for the door as a voice called, "Mr. Hancock? Butler Hancock?"

Butler turned as a short man barely over five feet tall, spare of frame, and dapper in a fine broadcloth suit hurried into the lobby. He walked with a noticeable limp, and the built-up sole on one shoe indicated that an accident of some sort had left one leg shorter than the other. In his early thirties, Hindman had a neatly trimmed beard, a high forehead hinting at premature baldness, and wide-set blue-gray eyes. His shoes were polished to a fine shine, and his trousers pressed. Butler's familiar letter was in his hand.

"Congressman?"

Hindman offered his hand, a harried smile on his lips. "Colonel Thomas Hindman, at your service, Mr. Hancock. Forgive me, sir. My deepest apologies. It's the correspondence. I'm only in Little Rock for a couple of apparently frustrating days. I've been tasked by General Hardee to raise volunteers for the defense of Arkansas. And now, to my absolute irritation, Governor Rector — a man owing his election partly to my good graces — refuses me arms and rations as well as additional clothing for my troops."

"Why would he do that?"

"These regiments we've raised are to be *Confederate* units, not part of the State Army. It matters not to the good governor that one fights for all, and all for one. The reality that if we lose Virginia or Tennessee we lose our Confederacy seems totally beyond the poor man's comprehension." He smiled, a deadly twinkle in his eye. "Our good Governor Rector, keen-eyed myopic that he is, can only see as far as the wave-lapped western shores of the Mississippi River."

"I wish you the best of luck, sir. No doubt Vercingetorix was looking no farther than the Alps when he accepted command of the Gauls at Bibracte."

The smile was back, fiery this time, and Butler began to understand Hindman's political charisma. "Aptly put, Mr. Hancock. Let us pray that those in Richmond see farther. Now, how may I be of service? While your father and I have often been at odds politically, he did me a wonderful service one night. Despite our differences we have always maintained the most convivial of relationships. We share a certain compatibility as gentlemen. Is he well?"

"He is, and offers you his finest compliments. Last I heard he's somewhere in Mississippi serving as a major in a newly formed Mississippi regiment."

A slight frown lined Hindman's brow. "I find that odd for a Union man. Let alone an abolitionist. Surely I didn't misread James Hancock's sentiments. And why Mississippi when Arkansas regiments are desperate for solid men?"

Butler gave him a thin smile. "If you know my father, you are aware that a great many stories follow him around like mongrel dogs. And while colorful, they might bias the opinions of both his commanders and subordinates."

Hindman glanced at the wall clock, seemed to fidget, and asked, "And you, Mr. Hancock?"

"I wished to pay my father's respects, and on his advice ask if I could be of service."

"Can you make magic, snap your fingers, and cause a pile of correspondence to disappear?"

"Unfortunately, I cannot, but if you would be agreeable, I do have a most legible hand, and would be delighted to assist you with your correspondence if doing so would lighten your burden."

Hindman glanced thoughtfully down at Butler's letter of introduction. Hesitated, then reluctantly said, "I couldn't impose, sir."

"It would be no imposition. I've nothing else to

occupy myself while in Little Rock. I had thought to offer my services to one of the regiments . . ." He made a face. "I have to admit, however, that the recruiting agents I've encountered so far haven't exactly been . . ."

"Enticing?"

"Precisely. I was looking for a more salubrious company of men."

Hindman remained thoughtful, his capable gray-blue eyes taking Butler's measure. "Tell me, Mr. Hancock. Surely you didn't master such secretarial talents or nurture the taste for refinement in Benton County."

"I've just returned from university studies in Pennsylvania. I thought it prudent to change my situation given the Confederate revolution."

Hindman arched his back, almost adopting a photographic stance. "Given your experiences there, what do you see unfolding in the coming months? A quick and decisive war followed by a realization of our independence? Given the disasters suffered by the Black Republicans at Manassas and Wilson's Creek, that seems to be the passionate hope of most Southerners."

Butler shook his head, taking Hindman's measure in kind. This little man, with his sandy-colored hair and almost round and too youthful face, was being called the Lion of the South.

"Congressman, we may very well bloody the North's nose in the beginning. But people forget that the Yankees will have their own say in what happens next. Each time we humiliate them, bleed them, they'll just come back harder and with stiffening resolve."

A flintlike glint hardened in Hindman's eyes. "Perhaps, Mr. Hancock, we think alike. I may not have liked the Yankees I associated with in Congress. Many I not only detested but despised. I did learn, however, to never underestimate them." He paused. "Do you think they could whip us, Mr. Hancock?"

"Colonel, let us not forget the lessons of history. Northerners they may be, but they are still Americans. With all the resilience that implies. The only way we can lose this war is if we provide them with a reason to destroy us at all costs."

Hindman seemed to process Butler's words, then he said, "Here is how I see it: we must be audacious. Strike hard, recoil, and strike them again. We must defeat them quickly, sir, but only in defensive actions. By doing so, both England and France will understand that we are to be taken seriously, and that their advantage is best served by a rapid and resounding recognition of our rights as a nation."

Butler countered, "Recognition of our Confederacy balances with the economic benefits that we provide Europe on one side, and their philosophical objections to slavery on the other."

Hindman ran the toe of his polished shoe across the thick carpet, adding, "Without Southern cotton, European mills fall idle. Workers raise their voices in protest. The French have barely avoided revolution, and their workers are simmering. The English have their own multitudes in ferment. Southern raw materials provide gainful employment for their masses."

Hindman paused. "We have gambled that their need for our resources outweighs the quibbles of conscience."

"If we've wagered wrong, Colonel, we shall be in for a most interesting future, shan't we?"

"And what is your motivation, Mr. Hancock? Your father was a Union man opposed to slavery, though I am delighted to hear that he has become a patriot when it comes to the defense of his hearth, home, and the Constitution."

Butler raised his hands. "Colonel, in all honesty, like my father, I fear the rise of a tyrannical federal government. Nowhere in the Constitution does it say that once a state joins the Union, it cannot leave if that's the will of its people. Your fight is to keep your slaves, mine is to keep my freedom of association. Sharing that last makes us allies."

"Why come to me?"

"I am a classical scholar. My father said that if I wanted to understand Cicero, I should make your acquaintance. But now, I wonder if perhaps he was wrong."

"How's that?"

"I wonder if you aren't more a Caesar incarnate than Cicero."

Hindman fingered his beard, expression amused. "Mr. Hancock, if you are not indisposed this afternoon, perhaps I really could use your help with my correspondence."

8

When Doc arrived at the Morton house a little
after six on the night of December 2, a black
wreath had already been placed on the door. Puffing in the chill air, Doc climbed the steps and
hesitated. He glanced up at the overcast sky with
its low scudding clouds: a gray and depressing
day.

That morning, Doc had opened the surgery,
only mildly surprised that Benjamin hadn't beaten
him there. An hour later, having finished with his
first patient, and with another of Benjamin's waiting in the foyer, Doc had felt the first flickers of
worry.

The runner had arrived moments later with the
news: Dr. Morton was dead — passed away in his
sleep the night before.

Doc had responded by messenger that he would
see to the surgery and await Mrs. Morton's
instructions. All through the day, he'd tended to
his and Benjamin's patients. Everyone had been
stunned.

Late that afternoon he'd received a note asking
him to call at the Morton house after closing the
surgery.

Reluctantly, he knocked.

Moments later, Abel, the houseboy, answered, opening the door with the admonition, "Ev'nin, master. Mistress done tol' me to let you in and no other, suh."

"Thank you, Abel." Philip slipped his coat and hat off as Andrew, the household servant, arrived in the foyer. Taking the garments, he ushered Doc into the parlor.

Doc sighed, both expectant at, and dreading, the prospect of facing Ann Marie. But he hated the idea of imposing on the stricken Felicia. He walked to the hearth, extending his hands to where an oak and hickory fire burned low in the grate.

Moments later he heard the rustle of skirts and turned to find Felicia Morton and Ann Marie, both in black satin, their hair done demurely. The women had the puffy and red-eyed look of grief.

"Dr. Hancock," Felicia greeted him. "We hoped that you would come."

"I was as shocked as anyone," Doc told her as she extended a hand gloved in black lace. "You have my deepest sympathies. I will continue to fill in for Benjamin for as long as is necessary. If I can be of any additional service, I am at your disposal."

He struggled to focus on Felicia. While he grieved for both of them, his eyes and aching heart kept straying to Ann Marie's wounded expression. The past months had been filled with walks, conversation, and rising obsession. She filled his dreams, and every moment he could steal with her had been like a living miracle. Had he been asked before, Doc Hancock would have told the questioner that while a man might love a woman, he didn't, couldn't, worship her like a cherished idol. Fool that he'd been.

Benjamin and Felicia had both smiled knowingly, and each had given their approval to the courtship. But what now? Suddenly the plans, the notion of Benjamin walking his daughter down the aisle, seemed to have been from another world.

"She could do so much worse, Philip," Benjamin had let slip over cigars in the surgery one day after a particularly brutal procedure on a septic leg.

"I've never met a woman like her," Doc had confided with a smile. "Ann Marie has become my entire life. Somehow, Fayetteville doesn't seem to be the lure it once was."

"We haven't discussed it, but I know that you've considered buying into the surgery. If you and Ann Marie just happened to —"

"Whoa. You're a dear and valued friend, Benjamin. I know what you're about to say, and I appreciate it. I will not, however, take charity or a loan from my future father-in-law. Were I to make an offer on partial interest in the surgery, it will be after we've discussed what a reasonable down payment would be, and concluded fair market value."

"You dazzle her, you know. And Mrs. Morton dotes on you as well. But take your time, Philip. When you're ready, we'll talk."

That had been more than a month ago. And for all Philip had known, Benjamin Morton had been a model of health.

"What happened?" he asked as he looked into Felicia's shattered eyes.

In a brittle voice, she said, "I awakened this morning and thought everything was fine. He usually gets up when I do. Only later, when he hadn't come down, did I go back and check." Her gaze went vacant. "Philip, I would have called you, but he was already cold and stiff. It had to be early in the night when he . . ."

Ann Marie had stood stoically, her pleading eyes on Doc's. "I just can't believe it."

Then she stepped over, wrapping her arms around him, head against his shoulder as she wept.

"What do you need me to do?"

Felicia seemed to gird herself, as if for combat. "Philip, there are some things you should know. We consider you as family, as well as a gentleman. Therefore, I am taking you into my confidence. You know that Benjamin is . . . was a good friend to Colonel Rufus Neely."

Doc patted Ann Marie's firm shoulders, struggling between giving comfort to the woman he held while paying attention to Felicia. "Yes. He even supported the raising and outfitting of Neely's infantry regiment."

"It's now called the Fourth Tennessee Infantry," she said in agreement. "What you don't know is that Benjamin took out a loan to cover his share of the costs. Through Isaac Kirtland's bank."

Doc gave Felicia a reassuring smile. "Please do not worry yourself on that account. We've been doing well. It will mean additional hours, but I'm sure I can meet Benjamin's obligations as well as my own. It's not like Memphis is lacking surgery cases these days."

Ann Marie stepped back and seemed to have composed herself, her green eyes desperate as they met Doc's.

"I was aware that you would say that." Felicia took a deep breath and stared up at him through serious hazel eyes. "You, however, need to know that Isaac has been after my husband for years. He and Sam Tate own the rest of the block where the surgery is located, and they want desperately to construct a hotel on the property."

"But if we meet the terms on the note . . ."

"Philip, you are a jewel among men. I will not place Benjamin's obligations upon your shoulders. Unless, of course, you can pay off the note when Isaac comes knocking at the beginning of next week."

She read his consternation, adding, "No, of course you can't. But there are other surgeries, other buildings that you can rent."

"And what of you, ma'am?"

"Issac will make me an offer rather than take the chance that a certain young surgeon in my husband's employ might insist on finding a way to keep the property."

It made perfect sense. Suddenly a widow, Felicia had to be worried sick at the same time she was burdened with the loss of her beloved husband. Isaac Kirtland promised a semblance of financial security. At least until Ann Marie married or young James established himself professionally.

"Would you like for me to review Mr. Kirtland's offer? I would hope the man wouldn't take advantage."

Felicia almost managed a smile, her usual self trying to slip out past the grief. "Isaac may have his faults, Philip, but taking advantage of a friend's widow isn't one of them. Actually, it will be more than fair lest I be tempted to sell to another. Which means I shall be mercenary and hold your interest over his head should the terms not meet my expectations."

"You have my full support. Take the offer with my blessing, Mrs. Morton. I shall, indeed, find an alternate location to establish a surgery."

Ann Marie then asked, "Are you sure you will be all right?"

Doc gave her a reassuring wink. "I am in much better circumstances now than when I stepped off the boat onto the Memphis wharves."

"Philip, there is another option," Ann Marie said shyly.

No doubt aware of what was coming, Felicia said, "Philip, if you would excuse me, I'll take my leave now."

Philip inclined his head as Felicia stepped out in a rustle of black silk.

"Dear God, your poor mother."

"She's a formidable woman," Ann Marie said, eyes following as Felicia climbed the stairs. "I wonder if I'm really her daughter. I feel so lost."

Doc took her cold hands. "Will Isaac's offer be fair? Really?"

"I think so. He wants that building. And Father had so many friends in the city." She seemed to gird herself. "You know that James has enlisted in the Fourth Tennessee? Neely's regiment? They are in need of a regimental surgeon and are paying two hundred and fifty dollars a month. I know that Reverend Nelson and others are adding to that sum as an inducement. It's only a year, and you would come back with a substantial sum that would allow you to firmly establish yourself."

"We shouldn't be talking business," he told her. "Not today."

She smiled her gratitude, only to have it fade. "I

just can't believe he's gone. It *can't* be happening."

But it is, he thought to himself as Ann Marie's eyes turned glassy with grief. The feeling was as if some great opportunity were slipping away, as if the tragedy were greater than he could know.

The way she melted into his arms, her body conforming to his, sent a thrill through him.

"What if I lose my brother, too? That's why I was thinking of you being the regimental surgeon. You could be sure you'd bring him back to me."

9

December 10, 1861

At Fly's characteristic warning bark, Sarah lifted her head. Then ignored it. Instead of dominating some parlor in Little Rock where admirers could comment on her latest dress, she sat in the tobacco barn's cold and dim shelter and twisted leaves of tobacco into loops.

"Oh sure, Paw. Gone off to war, are you? And I'm stuck here making tobacco twists." She knew it was petty, but by Hob, a girl had the right to feel petty on occasion. She'd had to put her whole life on hold.

Not only had Paw failed to materialize with a new dress, but the war just kept dragging on. What had been keen heartbreak when she'd finally realized she was stuck at the farm for another year had dulled into a frustrated ache. It would be a whole year before Paw could take her to Little Rock. She'd be eighteen! Almost too old!

She plucked down another leaf, angrily twisting it into a string before bending it around in a loop. The seemingly endless task, however, provided its own rewards since a good twist of tobacco could be traded for a jar of honey, a sack of ground corn, a crock of molasses, salt, sugar, or any of the other sundries that were now in such short supply.

Come war, Yankees, hell or high water, the good news was that for the most part, northwestern Arkansas could pretty much supply its own needs. Even with as many men as had gone to war, and despite the shortages, corn, wheat, cotton, tobacco, barley, beef, and poultry were plentiful. The local mills were adept at turning raw materials into finished goods. But for luxuries like coffee and pepper — for which passable local substitutes could be had — or the occasional manufactured part for an engine or piece of machinery, Benton and Washington Counties could muddle on without the rest of the country.

Fly half howled his warning bark again, this time with more authority.

Sarah stepped out from the barn and shivered in the biting breeze as she stared down at the Huntsville Road where it ran along the river.

Seeing a wagon emerge from the riverside trees on that chilly and gray December day wasn't an unusual occurrence. Benton County's denizens had developed an interesting and constantly evolving economy based on the swapping of local resources and food stocks.

Sarah worked her tobacco-stained hands to ease the cramps in her fingers as the first wagon was followed by four more and a party of riders. Worse, the first of the wagons was making the turn onto the Hancock farm lane. Even more concerning, each was topped by two soldiers.

Wiping her hands on her wool skirt, she hurried across the yard to the house, stepped into the delightful warmth, and called, "Maw! Soldiers coming with wagons!"

Shoes thumping on the risers, her mother

91

descended the stairs, a look of concern on her face. She wore a gingham housedress with a white apron tied to her hips. "Coming here?"

"Riders and four wagons," Sarah told her, catching her mother's sudden worry. "What would they want here? We're a long way from Fayetteville."

Word was that Louis Hébert's brigade down around Fayetteville in Washington County had been provisioning itself from the surrounding countryside.

"Let's go see. Maybe they're lost." Then Maw hesitated. "Where's your brother?"

"Where do you think?" Sarah slapped an irritated hand to her side. "Said he was after a coon that got into the corn crib last night."

Some of the tension in Maw's face relaxed, and she whipped a shawl around her shoulders before stepping out onto the porch. Her breath swirled whitely around her head as the cool breeze ruffled her age-silvered hair.

Sarah followed her mother down into the yard, stopping as an officer — a sergeant she realized from the chevrons on his uniform coat — pulled up before the house. The wagons slowed, swinging out in the cramped yard, a couple of the teamsters cursing as the animals balked and got in each other's way.

"Good day, ma'am," the sergeant greeted, leaning forward on his saddle, reins in his hands. "Is this the Hancock farm?"

To Sarah's surprise, he was a handsome man, young, with a well-formed face, the most enchanting blue eyes, and curly chestnut hair. She wondered what it would be like to run her fingers through it. His wide lips looked practiced at smiling.

And then he glanced at her, his eyes widening slightly, the smile she expected finding its home.

"It is," Maw replied, pulling her shawl tight against the chill. "How can I help you, Officer?"

"Supplies, ma'am." He tore his glance from Sarah's. Turned. "Dewey, you, Haskell, and Branton may begin your inventory."

The men behind him dismounted, one heading for the corn crib, one to the barn, the other for the smokehouse.

"I don't understand," Maw cried, stepping forward. "You're here to take our food?"

The sergeant dismounted and unhooked a leather sack from his saddle. "It's a requisition, ma'am, for which you will be reimbursed fairly by the government."

"What if I say no?"

His eyes, friendly up to that moment, hardened slightly. "Your country requests your aid, ma'am." He glanced suggestively at Sarah, as if imploring her support. "My orders are to obtain whatever supplies are available. You may, of course, take any complaints to the commanding officer of the Army of the West should you find our reimbursement insufficient in return for goods surrendered."

He glanced again at Sarah, as if torn.

Maw, sharp as the hawk she was, caught it. The look she flashed at Sarah was filled with irritation. "Sergeant, how are we to be reimbursed?"

From his leather pack he removed a bundle of bills, and lifted them. "My clerks will provide you with an inventory of the grain and livestock requisitioned, each having a set value, for which I am authorized to reimburse you."

"Arkansas scrip?" Maw asked distastefully.

The sergeant's smile was back. "No, ma'am.

Good Confederate dollars, backed by the government."

"What if I want coins?" she asked, crossing her arms.

"You'll get bills, ma'am."

"And if I really do put my foot down and say no?"

Sarah felt her heart begin to beat as she read Maw's brewing anger.

The sergeant took a deep breath. "One way or another, ma'am, I *will* follow my orders." He paused. "Where are the men, ma'am?"

Maw drew herself to her full five feet and four inches. "My husband is a major in a Mississippi regiment. My son is a lieutenant with Hardee's division in Tennessee."

The growing glacial blue in the sergeant's eyes softened again, relieving Sarah's worry.

"That being the case, ma'am," he told her cheerfully, "we shall take only what we need. I was starting to worry that you might have been black Republicans, Union by predisposition, in which case, we'd have stripped the place bare."

To Sarah's horror, as she stood shivering and watching the sergeant's skilled foragers go about their work, it seemed as if her loyalty to the Confederacy might have been suspect.

After the heavily laden wagons finally pulled out, she and Maw walked in devastation past the corn crib, cleaned out down to the board floor, through the chicken coop where but three hens of the twenty-two remained, and then into the barn.

Were there any bright side, it was that she no longer had any tobacco to knot into twists.

As Maw shook her head, she slowly counted the Confederate bills. "Girl, it's a fair sum, but let's hope this actually spends."

"What if they had stripped the place bare?" Sarah asked.

"I don't know. But thank God your brother wasn't here."

"Dear God, Mother. What's he going to say?"

Maw's jaw had hardened. "If we can keep that boy from getting himself killed, it'll be a miracle. But you've got to help me, Sarah." She shook the Confederate bills suggestively. "No matter what this is really worth, we tell him we *sold* everything to the government."

"I understand."

But the cold was due to more than just the blustery December day. A crawling sensation of disaster began to eat at her.

10

February 8, 1862

Candles and oil lamps illuminated the spacious drawing room with a warm yellow glow that defied the dark rain falling in the frigid Kentucky night outside. Lieutenant Butler Hancock stood beside Brigadier General Thomas C. Hindman. The table before them was spread with maps, the corners held in place by silver candlestick holders.

The house occupied by Major General Hardee's staff was a grand two-story affair, generously offered by a Kentucky gentleman with strong Southern sympathies. The mansion, along with his plantation's grounds, now served as General Hardee's headquarters. Slaves provided most of the labor, hauling firewood and water to the bivouacked troops. But for the hideous winter storms, the regiments would have considered the plantation perfect winter quarters. Located on the Green River at Munfordville, Kentucky, the cantonment was eighteen miles north of Bowling Green, where General Albert Sidney Johnston had established his headquarters for the newly fashioned Army of Central Kentucky.

As Butler and Thomas Hindman pored over the maps, they awaited the arrival of General Johnston and some of his staff officers.

Hindman's Second Arkansas had already been bloodied in battle with Federal forces at Rowlett's Station on the Green River last December 17 after having reinforced Buckner. Now they waited, deployed, knowing the Federals under General Don Carlos Buell were building a great army just north of the trees and fields beyond their pickets.

"Libations," General William Hardee called as he stepped into the room; a bottle of brandy dangled by the neck from his left hand. Hardee was a Georgian in his late forties, a graduate of West Point, a Mexican War veteran, and career soldier. Prior to the war he had returned to West Point where he both taught and wrote about tactics. Butler had immediately obtained and avidly devoured Hardee's *Rifle and Light Infantry Tactics: For the Exercise and Manoeuvres of Troops When Acting as Light Infantry or Riflemen.*

The reading had been as ponderous as the work's title. While Butler understood in theory how troops were supposed to move, maneuver, and attack, he was delighted to remain at headquarters and allow others to implement the field orders he wrote out and distributed.

Back in Arkansas, General Hardee had taken command of the volunteer regiments assembling at Pocahontas in northeastern Arkansas. Hardee had trained them, drilled them, and cleverly solved serious problems with supply, arms, and munitions. The Arkansas troops had taken to calling him "Old Reliable," and the name stuck.

Atop the general's broad forehead his blond hair had already begun to shade into silver, and his eyebrows had thickened into tufts. A reddish beard shaded with white and a full mustache obscured his jawline, but didn't hide the smile that rode his lips as he stepped over to the glasses and poured.

"Our noble leader is late," Hindman noted, glancing up at the mantel clock as he took a glass from Hardee. Hindman rarely so much as took a sip, having once been active in the temperance movement, but he was politically savvy enough to know the value of maintaining the convivial atmosphere.

"The weather out there is miserable," Hardee replied. "And something always comes up. He may have gotten a late start from Bowling Green."

Butler could agree. Something did always come up. Somehow — since his meeting with Colonel Hindman that day in Little Rock — life reminded him of riding a rocket skyward. Every day had turned into a virtual blizzard of activity. Not only had Butler managed to prove himself able at correspondence, but Hindman admired his organizational abilities, and delighted in Butler's quotations of Caesar, Shakespeare, and Xenophon. As Hindman's staff officer, Butler rarely got a full night's sleep. He had come to understand that just doubling the size of a military command led to an exponential increase in the number of details, problems, and interruptions with which a commander had to deal.

The sound of voices, along with the hollow thump of boots on the mansion's wooden porch, presaged the commanding general's arrival, and moments later the door opened to admit General Johnston and several of his staff officers. They divested themselves of capes slick with rain, sodden hats, and overcoats to reveal darkly soaked uniforms where the water had crept in around collars and sleeves.

"It's a frog strangler out there," the general greeted them as he returned his officers' salutes and stepped into the parlor. He grinned. "The next requisition I send to Richmond, I'm asking for horses with gills and fins." He slapped rain-soaked white gloves against his pants. "Since they're not providing us with arms, munitions, or equipment as it is, their refusal won't come as a surprise."

That brought a laugh from the assembled officers. The joke that was circulating among Johnston's command staff was that Jefferson Davis and the Confederacy had given the good general everything he needed to succeed in the west, except for an army, arms and artillery, munitions, and supplies.

Albert Sidney Johnston dazzled Butler every time he was in the general's presence. The man looked like a human lion with a mane of white hair rising from a widow's peak, steely blue eyes, and — unlike so many of his subordinates — a clean-shaven jaw, though water beaded on his full white mustache.

General Hardee had poured another glass of brandy, handing it to the commanding general before seeing to his staff. As he did, he stated, "We were surprised by your courier, sir. This isn't a night fit for man or beast, let alone riding up to see us. I sincerely hope your motivation isn't a lack of good company in Bowling Green. If so, I'm afraid you'll be terribly disappointed as we're a poor substitute for gentlemen and scholars."

Hardee hesitated, glancing at Butler. "Well, all but Lieutenant Hancock, here, who is so much better read in the classics and doesn't mispronounce his Greek the way the rest of us do."

Butler flushed at the recognition, having stepped back into a corner in an attempt to stay out of his superiors' way.

General Johnston gave Butler a slight nod of recognition as he sipped his brandy, which added to Butler's fluster. Then the general added, "I regret, gentlemen, that as much as I admire your fine companionship, conviviality isn't on my mind."

He stepped over to the table, limping slightly, the chill having seeped into the old dueling wound General Felix Huston's pistol ball had inflicted when they had squabbled over control of the Texas army back in 1836.

"Surely the Federals aren't moving in this soup," Hindman scoffed. "Our pickets and scouts would have informed us. We've had a couple of Texans spying on Buell's camps. We'll have good warning if they try to march."

"I could only wish," Johnston said softly.

"Dear God, it's Fort Donelson, isn't it?" Hardee, more astute, read Johnston's expression.

Johnston rubbed a hand over his head, as if the red line where his hat had impressed his forehead itched. "Last night I received word that on the Tennessee River, Fort Henry has fallen. This same damnable storm has raised the Cumberland to the point the Federal gunboats are bombarding the works at Fort Donelson. It is reported that General Grant's troops have taken control of the land approaches. In short, gentlemen, it would take a miracle to keep Fort Donelson from capitulating given the strength arrayed against it."

He pointed to the map. "With Zollicoffer's

defeat outside of Knoxville last month, and the imminent loss of Fort Donelson, our first line of defense is in shambles. Strategically, gentlemen, our best choice is to abandon Kentucky and fall back to Nashville while we await the Federals' next move."

Hardee's back seemed to stiffen. "Surely there is some alternative, sir."

Johnston's lips thinned in despair. "We could move on Fort Henry, pull Grant's strength from Donelson, but if we did Buell would push aside any force we left behind to hold this line. He'd be sleeping in your bed and drinking your brandy before we were halfway to Fort Henry."

Hindman smiled sadly. "If we move on Fort Henry, Buell will hit us from behind, probably after he burns Nashville and circles around to crush us between his forces and Grant's."

Johnston took a deep breath, held it, and exhaled. "To my dismay, our best hope lies in falling back. We need to see what General Halleck does. If he sends Grant west, he can flank the Mississippi River defenses at Columbia. If he swings east, he can easily hit the Army of Central Kentucky from the rear, smashing it against the anvil of Buell's command."

"Are you thinking of holding the line at Nashville, sir?" Hardee asked, thoughtfully stroking his beard as he looked down at the map. "We'll need engineers, some way of creating fortifications. Situated as the city is in the loop of the Cumberland River, and with all the pikes approaching from the west, south, and east —"

"We have no way of stopping the Union gunboats," Johnston told him. "Yes, we can dig in, turn the city into a fortress against infantry, but to take out those gunboats? We need heavy artillery. Columbiads and Dahlgren shore batteries. If Fort Henry teaches us anything, it's that shooting at an ironclad with a field piece is like using your thumb to flick gravel at a snapping turtle's shell."

"Then what are you thinking, sir?" Hardee braced his arms on the table, brow lined, mouth pursed.

Johnston straightened. "I fought in Texas, gentlemen. Sometimes, to beat a superior force, you draw him in, retreat while his strength dissipates, and strike him hard on ground of your own choosing when he is at his weakest and most vulnerable."

"And you don't think Nashville is the place to draw that line?" Hindman asked.

"I don't have enough men or guns, General. We'll delay the Federals, fight a rear guard, bleed him on the way south, but it means abandoning Nashville. Finding a place of our choosing. Perhaps like Sam Houston did with Santa Anna at San Jacinto. A place where his army has the river at its back, and there is no place to go but to the devil."

Hardee turned, speculative eyes on Hindman, as he said, "Well, General, do you think you can effectively withdraw your division? We need to do it smartly, leave nothing behind."

"If there's a way, sir, we can do it." Hindman turned to Butler. "Lieutenant, I think I'm going to need your consummate skills in crafting the orders."

Butler replied, " 'It appears that Hektor has breached the sharp-staked ditch. Let us only hope that he doesn't drive us back among the ships.' "

"Lieutenant?" Hardee asked, confused.

"He refers to Homer's *Iliad*," Johnston replied thoughtfully. "Because if we're like the Greeks being forced back among our ships, we can only hope the British or French will turn out to be our Achilles."

"And if they are not?"

Hardee answered, "Then we are in for a long and deadly affair."

11

February 10, 1862

Billy pounded up the lane riding Clyde, their big buckskin-colored horse. From the saddle he glanced back to make sure the pack on old Swat was riding well despite his hurried pace. One of the first skills Paw had taught him was to throw a proper diamond hitch on a packhorse.

As if the weather would never turn, this cold February day, too, was dreary with the threat of rain. He had been down to Fayetteville in Washington County where Confederate money was traded at a higher value than here in the hinterlands. After all, Hébert's brigade was quartered there, and the soldiers insisted on their currency being honored.

The salt, sugar, powder, shot, caps, ax head, saw, and horseshoes were supplies not locally available in Benton County. Maw had thought that with the soldiers around, powder, shot, and caps might have been hard to come by. What Billy had found, however, was a thriving contraband trade, whereby military goods were flowing into the civilian market in exchange for luxuries in a soldier's life, particularly alcohol and tobacco.

More than that, he had gone for news. And

news, he'd discovered, was available by the bucketful. Especially given the excitement that had broken within an hour of a courier's announcement that General Price had abandoned Springfield, ninety miles north of the Arkansas line, and was fleeing ahead of a massive Federal force bent on the invasion of Arkansas.

While pleas had been coming rapid-fire from General Price for a couple of weeks, no one had taken the threat of a Union winter campaign seriously, chalking it up to Sterling Price's paranoia.

Now, as Billy clattered into the yard and jumped from the saddle, he ran to the door, flung it open, and called, "Maw? I got news! The Federals is coming!"

Then he turned back to the horses, walking both Clyde and Swat in circles to cool them down before he led them to the barn and unloaded the packhorse's load.

Maw, swinging her shawl around her shoulders, led Sarah at a hurried walk as she crossed the yard, demanding, "What on earth are you shouting about? Federals? What Federals?"

Billy glanced over his shoulder as he began to rub Clyde down. "It's all over Fayetteville, and I heard it on the road north, too. Some Yankee general by the name of Curtis has taken Springfield. Kicked old 'Pap' Price out of his winter quarters and is nipping at his hindmost. Price's Missouri Rebel army is running like scared hares down the Wire Road."

Sarah had stripped the pack saddle off Swat and was using straw to rub him down. "Are they coming here?"

Billy shrugged. "Depends on if McCulloch's troops can stop them, I guess. I didn't want no part of it, so I took the Cross Hollow trail from Mud Town and followed it over to Van Winkle's Mill. For all I know, Price's Missouri cowards may have reached the tavern by now." He shot Maw a knowing look. "And, with any luck, the Federals will chase their scrawny Missouri arses all the way to Fort Smith and out of our county."

Maw stood, head down, back arched, fingering her chin. "You're *sure* of this, Billy?"

"Yes'am. As sure as anyone else, anyway. Yankees ain't more than three or four days away at most according to the last reports. And I passed a heap of folks, soldiers and common folk, on the Wire Road before I turned off. All of them is fleeing ahead of the Yankees."

Maw took a deep breath, making a decision. "Then we'd better be ready. No telling which army we should fear the most. Rebels or Federals. You two, pack as much meal as you can, take the hens, the horses, and get them up Hancock Creek and into the forest. Maybe up to that trapper's cabin Paw used to use. Back in that cul-de-sac like it is, it's as good a hideout as any in these hills. Then, Billy, you stay there until Sarah comes with the all clear."

"Maw?" he protested, turning. "You want me to hide out?"

Maw stepped close, a wan smile on her lips. "Federals or Rebels, they're not going to bother women. Not even Missouri men are that low. But the food and livestock? They'll steal it all without a moment's notice."

She poked a finger into his breast. "And they'll take you, too, those Yankees will. And maybe, if there's a fight brewing, Ben McCulloch might forget you're only coming on fifteen, stick a rifle

106

in your arms, and march you out in the front lines to get shot."

Billy ground his jaws as he looked around at the familiar house, the pens, barn, corn crib, and fields. An odd tingling filled his chest.

"What is it, son?" Maw asked, eyes on his.

"Just don't seem right. This is home. It's just that a fella ought to feel safe at home." He waved a hand at the world at large. "It's out there that oughta be scary."

A twinkle appeared in Maw's eye. "And where, Billy Hancock, will you be safest? Sitting here waiting to be pressed into someone's army? Or out there in the woods? Just do your hunting with a bow and arrow, or a snare. Don't you go bringing no trouble down on yourself with a rifle shot."

She stepped back, adding, "You can come round after dark. Sarah and me, we'll leave the bucket on the porch when it's safe. If you sneak in and don't see that bucket? You skedaddle right back up the creek."

Billy rocked his jaw, nodded, and led Clyde into his stall before pitching out hay. Sarah had just about finished with Swat, unbuckling his bridle and lead rope. "We got time though, don't we? I mean, Billy don't have to go tonight?"

"Morning will be good," Maw agreed. "But just in case, we'll leave a pack by the back door. Should any soldiers show up, Sarah, you and I will occupy them while Billy sneaks out the back and through the pines. But by dawn tomorrow, I want the stock and what grain we've got left off this property and hidden."

Billy nodded. But it seemed that the world was turned on its head. It didn't seem right that the women were at less risk than he was.

12

Doc kept hearing the complaints from his fellow Southerners that Island No. 10, sitting as it did in the middle of the Mississippi River, was the coldest place on earth. He had arrived but three days past, accompanied by four other young men — boys, if the truth be known — dedicated to enlisting in Neely's Fourth Tennessee Infantry.

They had traveled north from Memphis after he had seen to the closing of Benjamin's surgery, and the dispersion of its assets for Mrs. Morton. And yes, Isaac Kirtland had made good on his offer. Felicia had been paid handsomely in newly printed Confederate dollars, all of which had been deposited in Isaac's bank.

The first thing Doc had done was to look up young James Morton to give him his mother's and sister's regards, love, and best wishes. Both the chestnut-haired Morton, and the strapping redheaded Nathanial Nelson served as privates in the Shelby Grays.

James had greeted Doc with a wild hug, his green eyes alight, and so reminiscent of Ann Marie's. Compared to so many, at least the young man looked healthy.

"I tell you," James insisted, rubbing the sleeves of his new gray uniform, "polar bears ought to live in Kentucky."

Doc was attending to his instruments, having just finished extracting a pistol ball from a private's arm after an accidental discharge. They'd given him a tent to serve as his surgery, along with two "assistant surgeons."

Doc raised an eyebrow as the oldest, Augustus Clyde, recently of Tyler, Texas, replied, "Naw, James, they'd freeze this far north. Even a polar bear'd have sense enough to head south . . . at least as far as Hernando."

The town to which he referred was in Mississippi just south of the Tennessee line.

Clyde was a thick-set and muscular man, just turned twenty-two. A mat of rich black hair crowned his head and contrasted with his almost brilliant blue eyes. His father was a Methodist minister back in Texas, and while Clyde had apprenticed with a surgeon in Tyler, he had no formal medical training. He did, however, have a quick mind, and rarely needed to be told twice.

James tucked his hands into his sleeves, puffing out breath as he watched the slushy rain fall from the gray sky. Beyond the surgery, the Fourth Tennessee camped in cramped quarters within the Island No. 10 fortifications. Lines of muddy tents sagged wetly, while before them, men clustered around sputtering fires that spewed redolent blue smoke into the air. When the wind changed, not only was the smoke so thick it would choke a man and leave his eyes weeping, but the smell of urine and feces from back in the trees would, as the troops unkindly said, "Gag a maggot."

Half of the regiment was down with diarrhea,

and, though Doc had mentioned it to Colonel Neely, a proper latrine had to be a priority. Sanitation was simply appalling.

As miserable as conditions were for the soldiers, Doc's heart went out to the battalions of slaves who labored building the defenses. Ragged, cold, and shivering, they dug out the dirt, piled it to create ramparts, and hauled timbers to build gun emplacements.

If they had any brightness in their lives, it was that as valuable "property" they were at least fed and provided shelter. As if, in the grand balance of things, that in any way tempered their endless labor and misery. But at least the effort was made on their behalf. Unlike each time a soldier died of dysentery or pneumonia, when a slave died, it was money out of the Confederacy's war budget to reimburse the distant owner.

Doc had never been comfortable with slavery, given his raising and time in Boston. *If the Confederacy is to fall,* he thought, *it will be through divine justice coming home to roost.*

"You have no idea what cold is." Doc turned his thoughts back to the conversation. "I lived in Boston for three years. My father used to tell me about winter out in the western mountains, how it got down to twenty and thirty below zero. He said the trees would pop as they froze. But something about Boston, the damp cold, the wind blowing across that half-frozen harbor . . . It slices through a man like a saber."

"Don't suppose I need to give that a try if it's worse than this," James said as he wrapped his arms tightly about his chest. In the cold, the freckles dusting the bridge of his nose stood out. "So, you're really going to be my brother-in-law?"

"Your sister, having taken leave of her good senses, has agreed. We will set the date as soon as my enlistment is up." Doc glanced at the young man. "Don't know where I'll find a best man."

James grinned, looking around. "Well, you sure won't find one among any of these lazy bastards, if I'm any judge of men."

Doc shot him a wink and buckled his surgical chest closed. He turned to the small tin stove he'd been provided with. The embers inside had just about burned out. He'd sent what little wood he had left with his other assistant, John Mays, a lanky nineteen-year-old blond lad from Tupelo, Mississippi. John had been instructed to keep the fire going in the pest tent next door. Each bed was full with the worst cases. Those who were still ambulatory had been sent back to their tents to either recover, or be carried back as they continued to decline.

"How'd you get here, Doc?" Clyde asked. "We been so busy, I been wondering."

"Hell," James cried, delighted to indulge in profanity now that he was not only a soldier, but far from his mother's strict censure. "He's in love, Augustus. With my sister. She's the one talked him into this madness. Thinks that after the war's over, he's going back to Memphis with a pocketful of money to set up his own surgery and marry her."

Doc took a deep breath, adding, "I'd be there now if James, here, hadn't enlisted. It's his sister's fault. She said her brother wasn't capable of taking care of himself, and if I didn't get him back to her in one piece, she'd marry a Yankee selling tinware before she'd marry me."

James grinned self-consciously and hugged

111

himself tighter against the cold. "I think she's about as smitten as you are, Doc. After Father's death . . . shucks, I don't know what we'd a done without you." He paused, gaze vacant. "It was like I just stopped. Sort of like I'd been cored out like an old apple."

Which was when James had given up on the dream of steamboats. At least for the moment.

Doc lifted an eyebrow in Clyde's direction. "I'm here because of freckles."

"Freckles?" Clyde shot him a sidelong glance. James was smiling, sharing the joke.

"She has the cutest freckles on the bridge of her nose and cheeks. So, assuming I can keep James from getting shot up, when my service is completed a year from now, I'm going back to Memphis, establishing my surgery, and I'm going to look at those freckles for the rest of my life."

And more, of course, but that wasn't any of their business.

That last night in Memphis, Ann Marie had given him a hint and promise of things to come. Betrothed though they might be, she'd somehow managed to remain a lady, and he'd forced himself to be a gentleman. Nevertheless, the desperation in her lips as they'd kissed, and the arching of her body against his, hinted of the magic their wedding night would conjure.

"Dear God, I love you so much," she'd whispered as her green eyes had fixed on his, pupils wide with desire and intimacy. Her lips had parted, breasts rising and falling with each panting breath she'd taken.

A year had suddenly become an unbearable eternity.

A deep boom carried through the storm, causing the men around the regimental fires to look up, shift, and stare off to the west.

Artillery. It wasn't an uncommon occurrence. Just beyond the tents, earthworks had turned the island into a fortress. If you laid a letter *S* on its side and turned it upside down, Island No. 10 was situated at the south end of the first bend with shore batteries on either side. Any approach down the river would have to run a gauntlet of cannonfire.

Doc had only had time for a glimpse, but he wondered how even the supposedly vaunted Federal ironclads could withstand bombardment from the mass of heavy artillery.

As the boom from the shore battery faded into the gray day, John Mays slopped his way out of the pest tent and shivered as he stepped under the surgery awning. "That's the last of the wood, Doc. I banked the stove down as far as it would go. Then I checked beds. Private Jenks is still hanging on, but it wouldn't surprise me if'n he's dead come morning."

Another boom carried on the sodden air.

"Hope their aim has improved." James shook his head. "It didn't do them a hell of a lot of good at Fort Donelson. Can you believe the whole garrison surrendered? Thought one Southerner was supposed to whip ten soft-bellied Yankees."

"Thinking like that will lose us this war," Doc told him as he shrugged into his winter coat. "Heard that Johnston is pulling our forces back all along the line. With Donelson and Fort Henry gone, the guns up at Columbus can't be protected from an army coming from the east."

"Wonder where General Johnston is going to make a stand?" James said. "I talked to Nathan

113

last night. The rumor is that Nashville is being abandoned without a fight. That all the supplies are being burned rather than let them fall into Federal hands."

"That's just a rumor," Mays muttered truculently. "Johnston will hold the line at Nashville. By Hob, it's the capital of Tennessee. He can't let that fall. What kind of message would that send to the rest of the state?"

As if in response, the lilting call of a bugle sounded assembly. Doc was barely familiar with the melody himself. Mays had to say, "That's your call, James. You'd better be in formation pronto, or you're going to find out what sergeants and punishment can really be like."

James grabbed up his wet slouch hat and charged off into the slushy rain.

Doc had just turned to make a bed check, when Lieutenant Francis came slopping out of the murk, saluted, and said, "Dr. Hancock? Colonel Neely's compliments, sir. You are ordered to pack up and be ready to move. General Johnston is relocating the regiment."

"Where to?" Doc asked. "My hospital is full of men who can't be moved."

The lieutenant hesitated, glanced uneasily at Mays and Clyde, and said, "Corinth, Mississippi, sir. We'll see about ambulances and wagons to transport the sick."

"You do that, and you'll kill some of these men."

"Then we'll have to leave them behind to catch as best they can, sir."

With that the lieutenant snapped off another salute, spun on his heel, and slogged off through the mud.

"Just leave them behind?" Doc wondered, stunned.

"Reckon it's the army, now, Doc," Clyde said softly, his eyes on the vanishing lieutenant.

"War's different, Doc," Mays agreed. "It's devil take the hindmost."

With a gnawing unease in his gut, Doc took a deep breath and headed for his hospital. It was the army, damn it. Of course they couldn't wait for the sick to heal before moving out.

13

February 22, 1862

The sleet, snow, and freezing rain during the tactical withdrawal from positions along the Green River toward Bowling Green, Kentucky, left Butler feeling colder than he'd ever been. And, miserable though it was for him, he suffered nothing in comparison to what the rank and file of the Second Arkansas endured as they muscled wagons and artillery down boglike, half-frozen roads.

Tasked with covering the Army of Central Kentucky's retreat, they had no sooner occupied positions around Bowling Green, than the companies were ordered to move out. Hindman's men set fire to the commissary and quartermaster stores and any supplies they couldn't carry. Next they put the torch to bridges, the railroad depot, and any structures the Federals might consider of military value.

Either some of Bowling Green's panicked citizens — already on the verge of hysteria — caught the fever, or arsonists with an agenda of their own began setting fires in the town.

On General Hindman's orders, his troops had spent the night battling the blaze in freezing temperatures, only to evacuate the town the next morning as Federal shells announced the arrival of Buell's forces.

"Lieutenant," Hindman had told Butler as he reached from his saddle and handed over a leather bag, "I need these dispatches delivered, with my compliments, to General Johnston in Nashville. You will await the general's response and rejoin us in Murfreesboro. We will be encamped there."

"Yes, sir," Butler had replied, glancing back at the plumes of black smoke rising from Bowling Green. The boom of Federal artillery carried on the cold morning air. Flakes of snow drifted down, indistinguishable from the falling ash that melted and ran in black streamers down his coat.

"Ride safely, Lieutenant," Hindman had told him grimly. "You shouldn't have too much trouble finding our new headquarters when you reach Murfreesboro. We'll be crowded around the biggest bonfire in the area, staying warm!"

"I would have thought you'd had enough of big fires last night, sir," Butler told him with a grin. "Go with God, General."

Then he had wheeled his sorrel mare and pounded off along the treacherous and frozen road toward Nashville some sixty-five miles to the southeast. The way was not hard to follow, given the abandoned equipment, scattered personal items, broken wagons, and dead horses along the way. And then there were the stragglers, looking miserable as they stumbled their way toward Nashville in ever greater numbers as Butler overtook them.

As a staff officer on horseback, he shivered, and his teeth chattered. The poor infantry slogged through the snow and half-frozen mud, thinly clad, many suffering from frostbite; each morning men were found dead and partially frozen in their blankets.

Along with them went the fleeing civilians, most improperly dressed, carrying their most cherished valuables. The most miserable of all, however, were the lines of slaves. In long lines they plodded, barefoot, in the half-frozen mud, worn blankets over their heads and shoulders. Shivering, starved, often roped together and huddling, they were the living reminder of the root of secession. Property — planters' wealth — being herded south out of reach of Yankee confiscation and the lure of freedom.

It brought a crawling sensation to Butler's gut, an unsettling reminder — like a slap in the face — that the glorious cause of secession meant the continued abuse of an entire class of human beings.

God forgive us for inflicting such misery.

While Butler might question the ethics of such humanity, behind the grimace on his cold lips and chattering teeth, he was more proud than he'd ever been in his life. The organization behind Hindman's clockwork retreat was his: a model of efficiency that even General Hardee praised.

Catching up with Hardee's brigade as it entered Nashville, Butler might have marched headlong into chaos. The streets of the panicked city were full of desperate people, many of them wheeling their personal property out in wagons, carriages, on wheelbarrows, packed on horseback, or even in valises held over their heads against the cruel freezing rain.

Governor Harris and the state government had already fled to Memphis, adding to the sense of despair.

Here and there, structures burned. Sparks and smoke shot into the sky. Furtive groups of skulkers looted stores and residences. Women shrieked and pleaded, some groveling before drunken men who carried off household furnishings.

On a street corner, a lunatic laughed maniacally, a whiskey bottle dangling from his hand, his face reflecting a crazy relief at the sight of troops.

The arrival of Hardee's half-frozen, sick, and dispirited men only added to the insanity of defeat. At the sight of them, even more people picked up and joined the columns of refugees that clogged the roads out of town. But most striking — the image Butler would carry away — was the terror in the children's eyes. Their pale faces tear-streaked, gaping mouths like black holes.

This was the stuff of nightmares, the literature of disaster come to life. Like Euripides would have penned in *Trojan Women.* The sack of Rome. The razing of Carthage. Napoleon at Moscow.

In a daze he rode through the streets, his pistol in his hand for protection. He kept asking himself: *Am I really seeing this!*

If there were any joy to be found in the city's misery, it was that after delivering his dispatches, and for the first time in a fortnight, Butler had enjoyed a full night's sleep in a warm bed. Had had his uniform cleaned, and paid to have a seamstress add gold piping to his sleeves to augment his promotion to first lieutenant.

In too short a time, General Johnston's replies were prepared.

Partially recuperated and refreshed, Butler rode south on the Murfreesboro Pike. He tried not to think of the cries and dismay expressed by the remaining terror-crazed citizens of Tennessee's

119

onetime capital on the Cumberland.

What was war, anyway? He wanted to cry for the poor people, broken, terrified, fleeing into the cold, rain, and mud, as the Yankee hordes swept down from the north. It was the children, the women, the frightened families, many of them without the comfort of men, that speared his heart with pain.

Nor did it let up.

Wagons clogged the road. Loaded as they were with the treasures of a lifetime, they still couldn't come close to evacuating the tens of tons of provisions left behind for Nathan Bedford Forrest's cavalry to burn or destroy before the pursuing Federals could seize them.

Had Butler not been there to see for himself as Confederate troops fought with lawless civilians, he would never have believed such madness could be occurring in an *American* city.

And then had come the final look over his shoulder as Hardee's small army marched south on the Murfreesboro Pike. Columns of smoke rose into the sullen sky as warehouses were set fire; steamboats, still under construction, were immolated in their docks; and military stores were put to the torch to deny their use to Buell's pursuing Federals.

This part of war, Butler hadn't imagined.

"Your thoughts, Lieutenant?" Colonel Daniel Govan asked. Govan had raised a company of Phillips County men from around Helena, and been promoted to regimental command in the wake of Hindman's promotion to brigadier general. In the reorganization and integration into the Army of Central Kentucky, the Second Arkansas had been placed in Liddel's Brigade, Third Division, Hardee's Corps.

"I was thinking I can't have seen the things I've seen. Was that really Nashville? I mean, that might have been Moscow on the eve of Napoleon's advance, or perhaps Rome as the barbarian vanguard approached. Not *our* Nashville."

He glanced at the line of chained slaves who rested at the side of the road. *If the price of secession is the abolition of slavery, let them go. Each and every last one.*

Colonel Govan now walked his gelding beside Butler's sorrel, their pace set by the infantry and overloaded wagons thronging the pike. The column seemed to proceed like some huge antediluvian serpent as it flowed unbroken over hill and field. Here and there exhausted civilians waited off the side of the road, huddled under blankets, cold, shivering, their meager possessions piled around them. When they met Butler's gaze, it was with hopeless and hollow eyes. They might have been wraiths instead of corporeal beings. Images whose reality faded the moment they were out of sight.

Interspersed among them were more lines of slaves — driven south by mounted overseers who rode with shotguns over their saddle bows. Human wealth, suffering from the cold and lack of food. Many marched shackled and chained, a sight that sent a spear of pain through Butler's soul.

Is this what I'm fighting for?

With each step, the horses splashed, hooves sucking as they pulled from the mud. The wet creak of leather, the snuffle of tired horses, and occasional shouts carried on the chill air. Butler was assailed by the curious scent of unwashed human mixed with wet wool, mud, manure, and horseflesh; it almost overwhelmed when the breeze changed quarter.

Colonel Govan's hat, like everything, was soaked from the drizzle, the brim dripping and partially obscuring his bearded face as he peered sidelong at Butler.

"It defies imagination. Americans acting like Vandals?" Butler wondered as he lifted his right hand and made a fist. As he squeezed, water dribbled out of his saturated glove. Then he shifted his reins.

"We saw it, Lieutenant. Sort of like some drunken nightmare." Govan glanced up at the bruised sky. "Except I haven't woke up from it yet."

Just past the stone walls lining the sunken road the country was gray and barren. Winter-bare trees lined the fallow tobacco and cornfields before surrendering to thick stands of forest that blocked the horizon. Occasional cabins and barns were set back from the road, all looking abandoned. Word was that the locals had removed themselves — and most of all their livestock — from any possible depredations by the passing army or the hoard of refugees.

"Seems a damn shame." Govan's shoulders slumped beneath his slicker. He claimed he hadn't been much of a horseman before enlisting, but Butler hadn't seen any proof of it. The man seemed one with his animal.

" 'Strategic withdrawal,' that's what General Johnston called it." Govan tilted his head and squinted out from under the brim. "I'd rather we stuck it out and fought."

"Never found much in my reading that implied any dash or élan to 'strategic withdrawal.' " Butler agreed. "Not even Caesar managed to turn the event into anything stirring. Homer, however, had it easier. Any reversal was always the fault of the gods. Their fated decree. Worked out nice. Leaders never had to take the blame for their mistakes."

"I don't think we can fall back on that old saw." Govan smiled thinly. "God's supposedly on our side."

"It was Napoleon's observation that 'God is on the side with the most cannon.' "

"Then we're whipped before we start," Govan said gloomily.

They rode a while in silence, the patter of rain on Butler's hat barely audible over the splashing and sucking of mud beneath the horse's feet. His sorrel mare — called Red during a moment of inspired revelation — shook her head; the fine spray rode back on the breeze to mist Butler's face.

"You heard that a Union army is heading for Fayetteville? Invading Arkansas?" Govan asked.

"Just that it was headed that way." Butler shook his head. "My family is there. On the upper White. Benton County."

"They'll be all right. My guess, if I know anything about war, which, I got to admit, Lieutenant, I'm starting to question, is that Earl Van Dorn will draw them south close to Fort Smith and crush them from strength."

Butler ground his teeth, catching himself as Red slipped on the poor footing. "Is that our strategy, Colonel? Like the Russians on the retreat to Moscow? Lead them deep into our territory, and then strike so that we send them reeling back in starvation?"

Govan shrugged, refusing to answer, his head

bowed just enough that the water streamed from his hat brim.

Butler glanced off to the west, trying to see past the tree-clad hills, on beyond the Tennessee River, beyond the Mississippi, the lower White, and the far distant Ozarks.

Are you all right, Maw? Is Sarah? And Billy? Surely, like here in Tennessee, the armies will just pass and leave you to your own devices.

But now when he looked at the huddled refugees beside the road, at the forlorn farms they passed, the dark and empty windows seemed to mock him.

14

March 7, 1862

On that frozen March morning Sarah had just filled two buckets at the springhouse. She stepped out, turned to latch the door, and heard it: the faint crackling and popping sound was barely audible on the cold, clear air. It might have been twigs snapping beneath a heavy boot. A lot of twigs. Under a lot of boots.

She sniffed the air, watched her frosted breath rise, and started for the house. A curl of blue smoke trailed off to the southeast from the chimney top, hinting of the warmth inside the tight plank-sided house.

The crackling was louder now.

Sarah was sure of it: the sound came from the direction of Elkhorn Tavern, no more than eight miles away as the crow flew. For the last three days, she and Maw had known that the Federals were up on Pea Ridge. Not only had they seen small parties of armed horsemen cantering down the Huntsville Road, but Elias Hatt, their neighbor downriver, had dropped by with the news the evening before.

She glanced up at the forested slope on the eastern side of the valley, hoping desperately that

Billy had enough sense to stay away. It would be just like him to let curiosity get the best of him.

Hollow booms — louder and deeper than the crackling — could now be heard. The sound didn't reverberate the way thunder did with that low rolling; instead the booms seemed to bounce off the land.

Sarah stopped on the porch, her heart leaping. Through some trick of the ear the crackle seemed louder now, only to fade.

She rushed in, sloshing water, turning toward the kitchen. "Maw! There's gunfire! I think the Yankees and Ben McCulloch are fighting!"

Maw wiped the grease from her hands, her face pinching as she followed Sarah to the door and out onto the chill-cold porch.

The distant crackling continued to rise and fall, sort of like devilish bacon frying.

"Where's your brother?"

"He took off just before dawn. I reckon . . . I *pray* that he's headed up to the trapper's cabin to look for deer." She swallowed hard, throat suddenly dry. "If that's a battle, surely he'd have more sense than to head over that way."

Maw narrowed her eyes; a series of louder bangs shivered the clear, cold morning. "God knows, girl, just this one time I hope he uses that head of his for something besides holding up his hat."

Maw cast a worried glance up the slope, only to stop and squint. "Wait. That's him." She extended her arm.

Sarah followed her mother's finger and detected movement among the trees. Something dark crossed the snow on the shadowed slope.

Moments later, Billy burst from the woods, coming at a run. Halfway across the yard, he called,

126

"You hear that?"

"It's a battle!" Sarah shouted back.

Billy, chest heaving, bobbed his way across the frozen ruts in the yard, his old rifle cradled in wool mittens. His face beneath his black slouch hat was red and flushed, eyes glittering with excitement. Puffing for breath, he led the way to the edge of the porch where they all looked to the northwest. There was more of it now, like a loud tearing of some brittle cloth.

For long minutes they stood, the three of them, heads cocked, listening.

Sarah's heart had begun to race. That was war up there. Men shooting and dying. She'd heard enough stories of Oak Hill, up on Wilson's Creek, where so many of their friends had been killed.

"Will it come here?" she asked, a sense of dread rising.

"Hope not," Billy mumbled. "But I bet the Fords, Cox, Fosters, and all them folks up by the tavern are having a lively old morning wishing they was somewhere else."

Maw turned. "It's still far off, but Sarah, you get the hens. Billy, take the horses, lead them way up the creek path. Reckon we can't do anything with the pigs but turn them loose and hope we can catch them again when this is all over."

"Why, Maw?" Sarah asked, suddenly perplexed. "The battle's up on Pea Ridge."

Maw fixed on Sarah, her blue eyes like cold marbles. "Maybe it will stay up there. Let's hope so. But what happens afterward, girl? That's what worries me."

She turned to Billy. "Son, you keep yourself and them horses out of sight. You so much as catch sight of soldiers, you take to the thickets."

"Yes, ma'am." Billy's eyes narrowed. "What about you and sis?"

"We'll be all right. They won't bother us. After that battle yonder is over, you wait a couple of days. You don't come back until after dark." Maw looked around. "There's that bucket. If it's a-sitting on the corner of the porch, you'll find the back door unlatched. And you pay attention here, Billy. If that bucket isn't sitting out, you stay away because it isn't safe, you hear?"

"Yes, ma'am." Billy sucked at his lips, gaze fixing on the house and yard.

To Sarah it seemed as if he were trying to memorize it, to keep it all in his mind.

"It's all right, Billy. They can fight all they want up there. Nobody's gonna bother us clear down here on the river."

As if to accent her words, something detonated in the distance. The sound echoed off down the valley like the clap of doomsday.

15

Spring, at least for the day, had come to northern Mississippi. As Doc stepped out from the Corinth post office, his heart was joyous. He had come hoping for just one, but had *three* letters from Ann Marie clutched in his hands!

He stepped out onto the street, hardly aware of Corinth, bathed as it was in bright sunlight. He could care less about the once-sleepy town's bustle as soldiers, wagons, men on horses, and columns of laborers and slaves marched down Jackson Street toward Main. Fronted by brick buildings, with occasional frame structures, Corinth had blossomed as the crossroads of the north-south Mobile and Ohio Railroad and east-west Memphis and Charleston line.

Here General Johnston was consolidating his widely dispersed Confederate forces, and not a single soldier didn't fully understand that two massive Federal armies were gathering just north of the Tennessee line. One under the irrepressible "Unconditional Surrender" Grant, and the other led by the supposed "Conqueror of Nashville," Don Carlos Buell.

For the most part, the mood of the troops was

glum. First Kentucky and then central Tennessee had been lost. At this rate the war would be over by Christmas, and the South reconquered.

"I didn't join the damn army to run like a whipped puppy," one Shelby County volunteer had told Doc as he stitched up a cut in the man's arm.

The sentiment was common — and just about everyone laid the blame squarely on General Albert Sidney Johnston's doorstep. Now the general was reportedly on his way, along with the Army of Central Kentucky — whatever that was — to personally take control of the gathering Confederate forces.

Assuming the man somehow managed to remain in charge.

Thousands of letters, not to mention several delegations of irate citizens, had arrived at President Jefferson Davis's desk asking that the transplanted Texan be relieved and replaced for incompetence.

As if any of that mattered.

Doc stopped short on the boardwalk, taking the moment to read, once again, the careful womanly script that addressed each envelope to Dr. Philip Hancock, Surgeon, Fourth Tennessee, Corinth, Mississippi.

Bursting with delight, he couldn't wait to hurry back to his tent, pour a glass of brandy, and based upon the dates, open them one by one. He would take his time, savor each and every word that Ann Marie had written.

He ducked around a party of jauntily dressed Texas cavalrymen, their high-heeled boots pounding on the boards and spurs jingling. He turned on Linden, hoping to catch a supply wagon back to his surgery and tent in the middle of the Fourth Tennessee encampment.

From the open door of a saloon, the twang of a guitar matched the light notes of a mandolin as the habitués inside sang "Lorena."

Doc hesitated in the doorway, head cocked, oddly stirred that he held letters from the woman he loved, and how melancholy the song's lyrics and tune made him for Memphis and Ann Marie's company.

He had taken no more than three steps before a voice called from behind. "Philip?"

He turned, startled to see his father, bright sunlight almost glowing in the man's high mane of white hair. James Hancock had aged since Doc had seen him last, the lines in his face deeper, the strong chin more chiseled. Those hard gray eyes, however, remained just as stony and unforgiving.

"I thought that was you." Paw lifted a pewter cup, as if in salute. "A regimental surgeon, I see. Which one?"

"The Fourth Tennessee." Doc's throat had gone tight, his back stiffening. "I see that you've become a major."

"Blyth's Mississippi. First Brigade. They're digging ditches and rifle pits. My duties pertain to supply. Notably, through the applied arts of poker. The quartermaster, who is an atrocious gambler, is more than willing to cover his losses by granting my most deserving company the first choice of commissary and supply."

The feel of Ann Marie's letters crumpling in his knotting fist caused him to breathe deeply. He forced a smile. "Nothing changes, does it?"

His father walked up, tilting his head back to the brilliant March sun. He squinted, weathered

131

cheeks taut. "Word is that General Van Dorn, commanding Ben McCulloch and Sterling Price, is fighting a Union army just south of the border in Arkansas. I thought I might hear more details. Especially given that one of the colonels in yonder" — he nodded toward the saloon — "has responsibility for the telegraph office."

Doc crossed his arms. "Last I heard Curtis and his Federal army were pursuing Price south toward Fort Smith."

"He was. The good general Curtis — if my sources can be trusted — was smart enough not to overrun his supply lines or to be caught by ambush. Word is that he doubled back from Fayetteville and dug in on the bluff overlooking Little Sugar Creek above Trott's store."

Doc's heart skipped. "What about Maw and the family?"

Paw shrugged, the crowsfeet around his eyes tightening. "They're still miles away. If Van Dorn wins, the Federals will flee to Springfield. If Curtis wins, he'll chase Van Dorn back to Fort Smith. Either way, no one is going to stay around and fight over Benton County."

Doc chewed his lip, nodding, but he wasn't sure. It was one thing to hear about battles in Kentucky and Tennessee. Another to think of battles in one's own front yard.

"Haven't heard from you for a while, Philip. I trust, given your position as regimental surgeon, that you completed your studies." He smiled thinly, took a drink, and added, "It would have been nice to have known. Perhaps shared in your achievement. Especially since it was my gold that bought you that education."

The twisting down inside added to Doc's

discomfort. "I wasn't aware that you cared."

"I don't. I only required that you be a man. Stand on your own two feet and make something of yourself. Your mother, however, would appreciate hearing from you." He arched a suggestive eyebrow. "Since I'm no longer in residence, you needn't be hesitant about reestablishing contact."

"I see."

James turned his attention to an artillery limber as it rolled by. "Butler is a lieutenant on General Hindman's staff." A pause. "He writes. Last I heard, you had nothing against your brother. He might like to know your whereabouts. Word is that Hardee's Third Corps is heading this way. You might look your brother up when he gets here."

"I will."

Philip had shifted, forgetting the letters. James using the sleight of scuffing his boot on the walk, looked down. Glanced sideways. "I see you have a female admirer. Three letters?"

Flushing, Doc knotted his muscles, stuffing the letters behind his back as if he were a child caught stealing hard rock candy. "An acquaintance. Nothing more."

A flicker of annoyed smile played at his father's lips and then died. "I can't put the past back the way it was before. As you've no doubt discovered by now, she wasn't worth your time."

"But she was worth yours? Married man that you were, and are?" Doc demanded hotly, the sour rage starting to burn in his gut.

"She would have been a millstone around your neck, son. She'd have tied you down, killed your dreams, and left you a broken man when she ran off with whatever feller made her a better offer."

"You don't know that!"

"Sure I do. Reckon she wouldn't have let me into her bed otherwise."

"Sometimes I wonder why Maw never slipped in with an ax in the middle of the night to put you out of our misery."

"She might have. It certainly wasn't beyond her, Philip. But she had something I never did." He shot Doc a knowing look. "Belief in family and kin."

Doc swallowed hard, struggling for words.

"Good day, sir." Paw touched his high forehead in a salute, turned, and walked back into the saloon where the celebratory strains of "The Bonnie Blue Flag" were belting forth in a harmony of tenors and a bass.

16

Blood. So much blood. The worst cases, the horribly wounded and dying, had been carried inside the house. Others, most no less critical, had been laid on the porch or lay bleeding in the yard.

The sights, smells, and sounds of torn, blood-soaked, and dying men overwhelmed Sarah's senses. Raised on a farm as she was, she was more than capable of cutting a shoat's throat, gutting and butchering it. She had long been accustomed to the feel of hot red blood on her skin, the sight of entrails as they spilled from an animal's body behind her knife.

When she killed, the act had always been quick, clean, and merciful. Suffering and filth of this magnitude — let alone that it was endured by human beings — had her sick in soul and body. Senses reeling.

The first units of the fleeing Confederate Army had appeared around noon the day before, announced only by the clanking of metal and the soft clatter of hooves on the cold ground.

She and Maw — having almost grown used to the distant sound of battle — had walked out, staring in awe at the first columns of weary horsemen, many swaying in the saddle from exhaustion, their horses plodding and stumbling. Some lame.

The wagons hadn't been far behind, turning off the Huntsville Road and climbing the lane to the Hancock farmyard. She and Maw had walked out, unsure of the meaning, only to stare in horror at the wounded men groaning, gasping, and crying in the wagon beds.

"Ma'am," a bleary-eyed teamster in the first wagon greeted, his hands blood-blackened as they held the ribbons. "We need your help. These wounded can't go no farther. We'll have a surgeon here soon to take over. But I gots to get back to the field hospital. We got more to evacuate."

"But I . . ." Maw had gaped, her eyes wide as she stared at the grisly, writhing men in the ambulance.

Three more were pulling up, the seats crowded with dirty men, their clothing bloodstained. The whites of their eyes were a stark contrast to their blackened faces, but something in their stare was hollow and lost.

They seemed to fix on Sarah alone — as though she were an apparition from a heavenly realm. The look unnerved her more than the sudden appearance of so many strangers with their cargoes of torn and dying men.

"Thank you, ma'am." He turned. "Let's get these boys out. Move now! Take the worst inside."

"But what's *happened?*" Maw had pleaded, stepping forward as the men on the wagon boxes climbed down and began pulling litters from where they'd been lashed to the sides.

"Army of the West is withdrawing," one of the other men told her. "Orders were for us to start moving the wounded down Huntsville Road. That's all I know."

Sarah stared at the column of men and horses now choking the narrow road. They might have been souls of the damned marching into hell. It was the way they walked, exhausted, desolate, loose-jointed and without hope as they shuffled, head down, shoulders slumped, guns dangling.

And then perdition unfolded before her as she hurried into the house ahead of the first of the casualties. Unable to think, she stepped aside as the teamsters laid the first poor man on the rug in the main room. To her horror, she realized his arm was missing; a blood-soaked bandage began weeping blood onto Paw's Persian carpet.

Just as quickly, another was borne in, and another, each being laid next to his fellow, like cordwood on the floor.

As each of the bleeding wretches was laid out, he gasped or cried out in pain. Some trembled, others had tears streaking their powder-blackened faces. A few, jaws clamped, bore the pain in stoic agony.

"But what do we do with them?" Sarah had cried plaintively.

"Someone will be along," another of the teamsters told her.

"When?"

"That's up to the officers, ma'am."

And then he was out the door with his companion and litter to get another one.

Sarah had watched the ambulances as they jostled and backed in a clumsy turn around the yard; then they headed down the lane to the mass of troops thronging southward on the road.

There they sat, shouting impotently that they

137

needed to get back. That more men needed rescuing. As if God himself could part that river of men, horses, and guns. Even as she watched, the walking wounded, some limping, others with blood-soaked arms or head wounds, began to be loaded into the ambulances by their comrades. When the teamster in charge protested, a musket was pointed at his breast by an angry lieutenant, and the loading of wounded soldiers proceeded.

"Sarah!" Maw called from the porch. "I need water!"

By the time she was back from the springhouse with her buckets, the ambulances were gone, swallowed by the shuffling and beaten horde as it surged south toward Van Winkle's mill.

The impossibility of it numbed her as she stepped between the prostrate men, her buckets sloshing. Twenty-some were in the yard and on the porch, another thirty or so in the house. Most were calling to her, weakly asking for a drink, some for a blanket, others delirious as they called out names, or seemed to be talking to the very air.

"What do we do?" Sarah almost wept as she stepped around a boy laid before the door. He looked no older than sixteen; black blood soaked a torn section of coat that had been tied around his middle, and he kept whispering, "Cain't move m'legs."

Maw shoved a cup into Sarah's hand as she took one of the buckets. "Get them a drink first."

Panic lurked just under Maw's hard veneer. "Then . . . then someone's going to come for them." Maw swallowed hard, bending down to scoop a cup of water from the bucket as she murmured, "Someone has to."

But they didn't.

Through that long afternoon, Sarah trudged back and forth from the springhouse. The worst of the lot kept crying out to her, and it nearly drove her to madness. They insisted that Sarah was their mother, or they called her the names of their sweethearts or sisters. They implored her to stop the pain, or in agony, they called out to God.

And he just didn't seem to hear.

When they died, she and Maw just let them lie on the floor, their eyes wide and empty, mouths ajar, faces sunken and waxy. She wasn't sure they could carry the bigger ones, had no idea where to put the dead.

Somehow she held her teetering thoughts together. As if she could shut off the suffering and horror.

More men kept arriving, some trudging up the road, guns hanging from their shoulders. Others appeared out of the woods, only to look about, peer into the barn or sheds, and then amble slowly down to the main body of men hobbling south on the road.

Early on she saw five men emerge from behind the house with the old black boar. She recognized the pig's hide, but it had already been gutted and quartered. As they walked with the animal's various pieces thrown over their shoulders they were chewing thankfully on strips of raw meat.

A melee almost developed as others caught sight of the prize, but a corporal who tipped his hat at her ordered the scavengers to pass the booty around. A long-barreled revolver gave authority to his rank. By the time the looters reached the Huntsville Road, all that remained were the boar's bones scattered along the lane. And by dark, they, too, were gone. No doubt for the marrow they contained.

Sarah turned her attention to that first man — the one with the missing arm. The blood wasn't obvious where it had soaked into the dark blue Persian carpet. When she bent down, the man kept staring fixedly at the ceiling. Numb, she wondered when. If he'd made a sound that she'd missed.

"Sarah? Help me please." Maw was bent over a blond, bearded fellow.

"He's dead," Sarah heard herself whimper. "They're all dying. Right on our floor!"

"Sarah!"

She caught herself, stood, managed to step around the slowly moving men who groaned and wheezed to where Maw crouched with sparkling and desperate eyes.

"No one's coming, Sarah. It's just you and me. It's a job to be done, that's all. Like shucking corn or hoeing weeds. Just pitch in and do it."

Sarah swallowed hard. "What do you need?"

Maw had pulled the blond man's shirt up, revealing small holes around his navel that leaked dark blood. The man's throat worked, and he said, "I can't feel nothing down there."

"Might be a blessing, son," Maw said as she unbuckled his belt. "Sarah, help me here."

"Maw! You're undoing his . . ." She couldn't finish.

Maw's eyes were blazing. "*Help me* ease these trousers off!"

Sarah ground her teeth as she took hold of the man's pants; the blood-saturated fabric was already ripped and torn. Maw's quick fingers undid the few remaining fly buttons, and he gasped as she pulled the flaps back. Blood squeezed between Sarah's fingers as Maw nod-

140

ded, and she eased her side of the pants down.

Her stomach rose in her throat. The smell of urine and sour bowel was bad enough. Clotted with blood, the man's penis hung by a shred of skin, a testicle dangled by its cord. A deep puncture above the pubis was partially plugged by a swollen knot of intestines.

"What do we do?" Sarah heard herself squeak as she labored for breath.

"How . . . bad?" the blond man asked.

Maw, her resolve crumbling, had settled back on her haunches, face gone pale. "Bad, son."

"Write my mother. Sally Adams. She's on Izard Street. In Pine Bluff. Tell her I love her." He swallowed again. "God . . . it's so . . . cold."

Sarah blinked, forced herself to look away from his mangled manhood and the coagulated blood and urine pooling in the grotesque wound.

"We'll get you a blanket, son." Maw stood, swaying on her feet. "Sarah, get the quilt off my bed."

Sarah stood, almost staggering as she stumbled back into Maw's bedroom and tugged the quilt off the bed. She stared in horror at the stains her blood-caked fingers left on the fabric, and then burst into tears.

17

March 11, 1862

Billy picked his way across the dark yard and
slipped in the back door. The main room was illuminated by lamplight, what Billy would have
considered a flagrant luxury given the cost and
scarcity of lamp oil. But when he stopped at the
end of the pantry and counted the number of men
lying on the floor, heard their soft whimpers and
ravings, he forgave the excess.

He'd never smelled such a stench. The odor of
blood, urine, and shit mingled with the unpleas-
ant sourness of unwashed men, all accented by
the sulfuric tang of burned gunpowder. That it
pervaded the air of Maw's house made it that
much more horrifying.

The floor seemed to move as the suffering men
drew breath, shifted, and squirmed. Some were
covered with blankets or coats, others just lay in
their rended clothes. A low fire burned in the
hearth.

Sarah perched in one of the ornate chairs at the
kitchen table, her head pillowed in her arms, apparently asleep.

"Who're you?" a voice whispered from beside
the front door.

Billy took the man's measure. Maybe a couple of years older, oily black hair, a haggard expression on his thin face. He wore a filthy gray coat, the knees out in his pants as he sat with his back propped against the wall beside the front door.

"I'm Billy Hancock. I live here. Who are you?"

"Private Josiah Armand. Third Louisiana, Hébert's Division." He gestured wearily. "I stayed to help Mrs. Hancock and Miss Sarah. Got to go in the mawnin' though. Reckon they'd think I's a deserter if'n I didn't show for muster. And 'sides, them damn Yankees is gonna be hot on our butts come sunup."

"Where's Maw?"

Armand gestured toward the bedroom. "Gone to ketch herseff a nap. Me, I ain't hardly slept in three days. Just been marchin', shiverin', and shootin'. Cain't figger why I can't sleep now." He smiled faintly. " 'Cept when I close my eyes, all I see is horrors like hell broke loose on earth."

Armand frowned slightly. "Where you been all day?"

"Up in the woods. Since your army took most of our food, I've been hunting, trapping." He smiled crookedly. "And avoiding being took into the army."

Armand nodded absently. "A couple 'o days ago, I'da called you a yellow-bellied coward, Billy Hancock. But after what I seen these last days, you be de smartest boy I know." Armand's eyes drooped. "Gonna catch some shuteye now. You keep watch."

Instantly, the man was asleep.

Billy wrinkled his nose at the smell, and picked his way among the bodies. Most, he discovered, had one of Paw's thick books under their heads for pillows — some blood-soaked and now ruined. Adding to his unease, the floor that Maw had kept so spotless was tacky with pooled blood, dried urine, and other gore.

"Sis?" he asked, pulling out a chair next to her. "Wake up."

"What?" She blinked, lifting her head. Her long blond hair was awry, clotted where she'd pulled it back with blood-sticky fingers. Red smudges, as though she had rouged her face, showed where she'd rubbed it with those same unwashed fingers. She stared at him through wounded and puffy eyes.

Billy glanced around. "Why'd Maw let them in?"

"You think we had a choice? Someone is supposed to come for them. Maybe tomorrow." She reached up with blood-blackened fingers and rubbed her eyes. "We've finally got a line of the dead laid out in the front yard. Nine of them at last count. If Private Armand hadn't stayed, Maw and I wouldn't have been able to carry the boys out. We just didn't want to have to drag them. Not in front of the others. It wouldn't have been seemly."

"How are you doing?"

"Billy . . . I've seen things. God in heaven help me, the worst is when they cry out and call on you to save them. I tell them that it will be all right. But it won't." She knotted her hands, forearms swelling. "It's lying, Billy. I wonder . . . will God forgive me? Or am I just as damned as these poor fellows?"

"God led them into this mess, so I reckon He could care less."

He looked out over the crowded floor where one of the men cried out, "Mary? Where have you

144

been?" and then his voice dropped back to a mumble, his eyes blinking as he stared vacantly at the ceiling.

"Damnation," Billy whispered. "Who's Mary?"

"His wife." Sarah shook her head. "He's gut shot. God help me, Billy, but I wish he'd die. Somewhere today I heard that being gut shot . . . it could take four or five days."

She seemed to suddenly come to her senses. "Why are you here? Soldiers could come anytime."

Billy shrugged. "Hell, sis, nobody cares. There's men all over. Half the country is crawling with Van Dorn's fleeing soldiers. I'll be gone come dawn." He narrowed an eye. "Ain't none of them been out of place, have they? They been treating you with respect?"

She gave him a disbelieving stare. "Are you insane? I'm surrounded by gut shots, bullet-broke arms and legs, head wounds, and blown-off limbs and you think any of these poor boys would be trying to sport me off to the woods?"

She dropped her head into her hands. "You amaze me sometimes."

He took a deep breath. "Never can tell about a man."

She peeked at him from between her stained fingers. "I did get two proposals for marriage today. One of them thought I was Amanda, and that I lived in Arkadelphia, the other insisted that I was Eudora over to Searcy."

"What did you tell them?"

"I told them yes, you fool. And then I watched them smile, and we talked about weddings, and relatives . . . and then I watched them *die*! God help me, I don't never want to spend another day like this. My soul can't take it."

145

"Come morning, let's you and me head up to the trapper's cabin. This is army business. Let the army take care of it."

Her look pronounced him a fool again. "Do you really want to leave this all to Maw?"

"No. Hell, I don't want neither of you to have to put up with this." He paused. "What is there to eat?"

"Nothing."

"I don't need much. Maybe a corn mush."

Her eyes darkened. "We cooked everything today. Threw the last we had, flour, meal, dried meat, sugar, into the big pot and boiled it. They stripped the cupboards. Blackstrap molasses, the sugar tin, raw flour, our dried fruits. It's all gone. They came at the smell. From clear down at the road. We fed the wounded first, and then the rest. They hadn't eaten in three days, most of them. *Three days!* What kind of army doesn't feed troops going to a hard fight for three days?"

He sighed. "Well, it's a long shot, but I'll check the hens for an egg when I take feed up the creek to them tomorrow morning."

"There is no chicken feed."

"There was a whole sack full of cracked corn when I left. Ain't no chickens down here to eat it."

She turned those somber eyes on his. "They *ate* it. One handful per man. Washed down by a cup of water from the springhouse. The hay is gone, too. Cavalry took it. What was left of the black boar didn't even make it down the lane. Don't know about the brood sow. If she wasn't well hid, she's headed south in a couple dozen stomachs."

Billy stared into his sister's wooden eyes. "How did this happen to us?"

On the floor, one of the men gave off a rattling gasp, trembled, and went stiff. His back arched, face twitching, and then he relaxed, jaw opening slackly, his wide eyes empty and fixed on the ceiling.

"Thank you, God," Sarah whispered as she closed her eyes. "I was supposed to write his mother. Some street in Pine Bluff. Can't remember the rest." She paused. "Shotgun blast nearly ripped off his cock and blew one of his nuts away."

"Sarah!" Billy hissed his shock and anger.

Her eyes had that flat emptiness, no change in her expression. "The things I've seen . . ." She chuckled hollowly, as if mocking herself. "I'm not the same girl I was, brother. But I'd give anything to be her again someday."

18

March 12, 1862

Doc made a face as he tried to organize his pharmacy on the flimsy wooden shelves. The shelves weren't anything to write home about, being only four high in a sort of boxlike contraption. He had placed them on a battered oak kitchen table. A fine and sturdy piece of craftsmanship that he'd "confiscated" from one of the messes in Company A. They in turn had no doubt "appropriated" it from one of the local households in Corinth. Most likely right out of some citizen's living room when the unwary occupant — trusting in human nature — had stepped out for a moment.

The original owners of the stout table were undoubtedly raising hell, trying to discover where their valued centerpiece had vanished to. Since they had most of General Beauregard's army to regard as likely culprits, their task was no doubt proving to be a daunting one.

Built like a slab, the table was heavy enough that Doc figured he could trust his medicine shelf to it, and had placed it against the hospital tent's back wall. Getting his varied-sized bottles organized, however, was another matter.

Taking an alphabetical approach, he was down to *Q* for quinine when a shout from beyond the tent's confines caused him to pause.

"Yo! Doc? You 'round?" a voice called.

Doc crossed his hospital tent and stepped out into the late evening. Against the backdrop of the Fourth Tennessee's tents, messes, and cook fires, a sergeant marched ahead of an obvious prisoner flanked by two privates.

Doc glanced up at the evening light where it filtered through clouds above the hilly country to the west. "What can I do for you, Sergeant?"

"Colonel's orders, Doc. He wants an evaluation of Private Shumaker, here. Wonders if he's fit for duty." The sergeant gave the cringing Shumaker a disgusted look.

As the small squad drew to a halt before the tent, Doc rolled up his sleeves and stepped close. The private stared back with a somewhat cowed but clear-eyed expression. Shumaker might have been eighteen, thin, medium height, with a narrow face and a razor-thin beak of a nose. Like so many, his unwashed black hair hung to his collar. He watched Doc with wary black eyes that reeked of worry.

Doc checked the man's pulse, poked and prodded, finding the usual slightly malnourished Confederate volunteer in his ragged but serviceable homespun uniform.

"Any complaints, soldier?"

"No, suh."

"Are your bowels fit? No runs, squirts, or pains?"

"No, suh."

"What about his head?" the sergeant asked. "Anything wrong with his head?"

Doc shot a wary glance at the sergeant. The two

149

guards had a strained expression — as if they were struggling to keep amusement firmly throttled in the presence of their irritated sergeant.

Doc turned his attention back to Shumaker. "What's this about, Private?"

"It's about the prisoner, suh."

"What prisoner?"

"The Yankee, suh."

"What Yankee?"

"The one the sergeant, here, caught just outside our lines day afore yestiddy."

Doc glanced at the sergeant, seeing the man's hot blue eyes narrow to an angry squint. His knuckles turned white where they gripped the stock on his Enfield musket, as if he wanted to wring the wood.

"Go on, Private," Doc coaxed, seeing nothing about the man's cognition or wits that seemed amiss.

"Well, Doc . . . er, suh, I's given the guard duty. You know, to hold the prisoner till he could be sent back East on a train. Right pleasant feller this Yank was. Said he's from Ioway. Some little town called —"

"Git ter the point, Willy!" the sergeant barked.

"Yes, suh." Shumaker flinched. Then he glanced at Doc. "Well, suh, I'd been a-watchin' him all day. Finally, he looks me right in the eye and says, 'Hey, Reb. You know y'all is gonna be whipped.' "

" 'How's that?' I says."

" 'Why, us Yankees, we's better so'jers than you Rebs. Better dressed, better fed, better led, and we sure is a heap better at so'jering.'

" 'How's that?' I asks." Shumaker fixed Doc with serious eyes. "I's gittin' a mite perturbed, ya see."

Doc crossed his arms and arched an inquisitive eyebrow.

"So next, the Yank says, 'Take that rifle yer a-holdin. Any Yank in the army knows the manual of arms better'n even the best Johnny y'all gots in yer army. Fer instance, y'all couldn't come close to matching me, move fer move, at rifle drill.' "

Shumaker's face puckered with a frown. "So I tells him, 'Count her out, Yank.' And he does. And I do the drill, calling, 'Load in the nines!' He calls one, and I pass my rifle left and drop the butt. As he calls out the numbers, I play like I'm reaching for my c'tridge box. Pull a round on the number, play like I rip it with my teeth, and act like I'm pouring the powder. I shucks out the ramrod, drops it down, pulls it out. And he's still a-counting. I fix the ramrod and bring the gun up right, cocking. Then I play like I'm reaching for a cap a'for I tap my thumb on the nipple like I's capping, and bring her up, ready to fire."

Doc noticed that the sergeant was almost vibrating with rage. The two privates on either side looked like they had something stuck in their throats.

Shumaker, warming to his story, added, "So the Yankee says, 'I kin beat that all holler. Hand me that rifle.' So I does. And I start the count, and he's right fast, dropping the butt, playing like he's reaching for a ca'tridge. Then he whips out the ramrod and drops it clear down the barrel where it goes *tink*."

Doc understood. It was regulation that guns were unloaded inside the Corinth works and around the tents.

"So he finishes the drill," Shumaker continued. "And but for dropping the ramrod down the barrel, he'da beat me."

"Then what happened, you damn idiot?" the sergeant demanded, his face blacker than a midsummer thunderstorm.

Shumaker shrugged nervously. "That Yank, he done tossed me the rifle and declares, 'See y'all in Richmond, Reb!' And he takes off running like lickety-split!"

Doc took a breath, seeing it all in his mind.

"I whipped my rifle t' my shoulder, took aim, and hollered, 'Stop, Yank! Or I'll shoot!' And over his shoulder, he shouts back, 'Give 'er hell, Reb! Ye ain't loaded!' So I takes out after, but he's passed the rest of the camps, and he's rabbit-gone inter the trees. And we search and cain't none of us find hide ner hair of him."

Doc nodded to himself. Glanced at the sergeant. "And what, exactly, does the colonel want me to determine here?"

"Well, Doc, my orders from the colonel, and I quote, were 'Before I decide if I'm gonna shoot him, or have him diggin' latrines for the next twenty years, take this moron to the regimental surgeon and see if he's got so much as a single brain in his head!' "

Doc smiled, fighting a chuckle. "Well, Sergeant, tell the colonel, with my compliments, that given Private Shumaker's apparent mental capacity, the Army of Mississippi might be best served if the private were given the opportunity to enlist in the *Federal* Army."

19

The wagon stopped short as it hit the half-rotted log. The horses strained in their traces as they leaned into their collars. Muscles bunched in their hindquarters, the trace chains taught.

"Gee!" Sarah yelled, using her long-handled whip to touch the black's offside flank. The horses leaned right, hooves shredding the leaf mat and twigs underfoot.

"Haw!" she cried and touched the brown's onside flank. This time the team staggered left, pulling the wagon's right front wheel over the decaying log where it lay almost buried in the leaf mat.

The wagon lurched up, dropped down, and rocked Sarah back and forth on the seat as she called, "Git up, there!" The horses gained enough momentum to bounce the back wheels over the log with a bump.

Sarah turned, keeping an eye on the corpses piled in the wagon bed as they bounced and flopped, but none shifted enough to be in danger of falling out — limp weight in their torn uniforms. Lifeless. Ruined. Decomposing, and leaking.

But for the stench, she could almost believe the

bloated corpses were anything but dead men.

Men didn't look like that. Or shouldn't. Not blackened, swollen, and gurgling, eyes dried out and sunken into skulls. Men had lips that covered their teeth, not these gaping rictus grins that exposed blood-blackened and filth-stained teeth.

And the stench. It never let a person forget. Even through the layers of cloth she'd wound around her mouth and nose, even though she tried to parse her breathing to little sniffs, it was enough to leave her on the perpetual verge of throwing up.

She turned her attention back to guiding her wagon through the tangle of gun-shattered forest, and back to the path where it wound through the thick confusion of oak, maple, and hickory timber. Through trial and error, a circuitous path had been hacked out of the thick woods, signs of ax work visible where saplings and vines had been cut. Piles of branches and deadfall had been dragged off to the side. But wagons could reach most of the battlefield now.

"By God, Miss Hancock," one of the privates behind her called, "that was a fine bit of driving!"

She looked back where the four Yankee privates stood among the trees, and waved. Then they were bending to lift the remains of a Confederate private. They'd carry his body to the dead pile and sling it on top. When all the Rebs in the area had been picked up, they'd be buried in a single trench close to where they'd fallen.

The Union dead got individual graves.

The horses knew the way now, following the trace as it wound around the tree trunks in Morgan's Wood like a drunken snake. Here and there she could see bullet scars in the bark. One old oak had taken a direct hit and been blown into splinters. Dark patches on the fall-pale leaves marked bloody spots were men had died.

This was ground that Hébert's Divison had fought over for most of a day before Davis's Federals had finally driven them from the dense tangle of forest. It was literally crawling with soldiers now, their job to search the brush and forest litter for bodies, weapons, and abandoned equipment.

She broke out onto the Leetown Road where Captain Stengel waited with his clerk. He was dressed in his blue overcoat, gloves on his hands, and a black felt hat pulled low over his ears. His breath fogged in the cold evening air. The sun was setting in the west across the field at Foster's farm.

"Got fifteen, Captain. All Federal."

As the clerk scribbled in his bound book, Captain Stengel called, "Thank you, Miss Hancock." Then he stepped close, waving at her to wait. His brown eyes were filled with concern. "Are you all right?" His German accent tainted the English.

"Fine, Captain." She fought a smile beneath her cloth mask. "Well . . . as fine as could be, given the kind of work this is."

"We appreciate, *ja.* None of the men have been untoward?"

"No, sir."

"You let me know, *ja?*" He shook his head. "You are no older than my daughter Ilsa. I cannot imagine her doing this."

"Just a job, Captain. A dollar a day."

His nose wrinkled as an eddy in the breeze carried the full stench to his nose. "And you get to keep your wagon, *ja.*"

155

That had been the deal when he had come in command of the small wagon train sent to finally evacuate the Rebel wounded and dead from the Hancock farm.

Sarah had been watching from the porch as the last of the wounded were being loaded. That was when one of the Yankee corporals had pointed to the Hancock's wagon, saying, "If we had the horses, there's another wagon for us, Captain."

Sarah had walked out, placing herself firmly before Captain Stengel. "That's ours. Maw's and mine. You wouldn't steal a woman's wagon, would you?"

Stengel had studied her appreciatively, aware that the corporal was watching her the way a young man did when in the company of a most attractive young woman. He had looked around, taking in the empty barn and outbuildings.

"Where are the horses?"

"Taken by the Rebels. Captain Stengel, come next fall, we can borrow horses, but that wagon is the only way we can take our crops to market."

"Miss Hancock," he had said gently, "I am in need of wagons, *ja*? I have men to collect all over the battlefield."

It had hit Sarah like a thrown stone. "I'll rent it to you. And better yet, you find me the horses, I'll drive it. Dollar a day."

"Sarah!" Maw had protested, but desisted at Sarah's lifted hand.

She'd thought the figure outrageous. A dollar? He could have hired all the wagons he wanted at two bits.

Something had warmed behind Captain Stengel's eyes. "*Ja,* you have a deal, Miss Hancock. Corporal Steinmetz, you will send for two horses."

156

To Sarah he'd asked, "You start today?"

"Yes, sir!" Sarah had cried, somewhat stunned by the rapidity of it. "I'll have the harness laid out by the time you get me a team."

"It will not be pleasant work, Miss Hancock."

She'd looked over to where four Yankee soldiers were loading the last of the Rebel corpses into a field ambulance. "Captain, after the last few days, I can handle anything."

Now, two days into the work, she wondered. Down deep inside it was as if some part of her soul had gone eternally numb and unfeeling. Given the things she'd seen, a distant part of her wondered if she'd ever believe in God again.

What she'd give to be home with Maw, sitting in the chair, watching the flames in the hearth and wishing she could forget. This time of night, Maw would have tea made. Maybe Billy would have dropped by with a squirrel or opossum.

"Is almost sunset, *ja?*" Stengel waved her forward. "You deliver these to burial detail, and to the camp you proceed. Tomorrow, we start again."

She nodded, slapping the reins, and tried to breathe through her nose as the breeze blew from behind. As she bounced down the road, she glanced back at her gruesome load. The ones on the bottom were just dead. Shot through the body or head mostly. Still human looking.

And then there were the others. The things of nightmares. Had she not seen it with her own eyes, she wouldn't have believed it. The boy couldn't have been more than fifteen, slight, thin faced. Some bursting shell had splintered a high branch over his head. He had tried to duck, only to have the falling branch drive through his back and pin him to the forest floor like a speared rabbit. She'd watched the amazed burial detail pull the wood back through the boy's body and gone queasy as his guts came with it.

God, he was younger looking than Billy.

It still sent a shiver down her back.

Oddly, the pieces, the severed arms, legs, and heads no longer gave her the willies. She averted her eyes, however, when they loaded the bayoneted ones with their gaping holes, or the ones who'd been hit in the guts by the occasional cannon shot.

She wasn't even sure who she was anymore.

Little Rock and the future she'd dreamed about might have been like a golden haze of memory.

After delivering her load to the burial detail, she drove her wagon to the camp set aside for the civilians who'd been drafted into the Union cause. Twilight was fading into the cold March night as she cared for the horses and led them to their picket.

The tent Captain Stengel had provided was pitched in a row just down from the fire where a couple of soldiers dispensed plates of stew. Even though she'd removed the cloth mask, the stench of death seemed to linger in her nostrils, as if it permeated her dress, skin, and hair.

"Here you go, miss," the burly private from Iowa told her as he handed her a tin bowl of the stew. He glanced around, lowered his voice. "Supposed to get cold tonight."

"I reckon," she agreed, reaching for a handful of squares of hardtack to soak in her stew. "It's still March."

His dark gaze fixed on her. "If you need a body to keep you warm in that bed of yours tonight, it'd be worth five dollars to me."

It took a couple of seconds for his meaning to

sink in. "What?"

He gestured around. "Well, some of these other gals doing the mending and all. They come down from Springfield. They been making a little extra on the side. Didn't know if'n you was interested, but pretty as you is? I'd raise that to ten dollars for the whole night."

Sarah's heart was pounding. "I am not a . . . a . . . One of *them* women!"

He ducked his head, looking appalled, and winced. "I'm most sorry, ma'am. So very, very sorry. I didn't . . ." He swallowed hard. "Oh, damn. Please forget I said anything."

But Sarah was already headed back to her tent, almost at a run, the hot soup slopping in her plate. *How dare he?*

In her tent, she pulled the flaps tight and tied them, sitting in the darkness on her blanket. *Ten dollars?*

Thoughts roiled in her mind. What kind of madness had she fallen into? Memories of the dead as they bounced in her wagon, the sights, smells, and horrors. And then to be taken for a common whore? They were giving her a dollar a day to endure this? But was even that outrageous sum worth the horror and now the humiliation?

She shook her head. "So, this is what the real world is like?" Who would have believed that a soldier would give his entire month's pay . . . for *that?*

More than anything, she just wanted it to be over so that Paw would come and get her, take her to Little Rock where she could begin the task of building the life she'd always dreamed of. A life far from battlefields and death, where she could marry a decent husband, bear his children, and forget the soldiers, the battlefield, and the kind of men who'd offer her ten dollars for the use of her body.

20

A gentle rain fell just beyond the flap of Doc's surgery. On the pole, his yellow hospital flag hung limp and dripping, each drop reminiscent of urine as the dye leached out of the fabric.

Doc had just lanced a boil on an Obion County volunteer's neck, and John Mays was collecting the rags he'd used to absorb the effluvium. These, his young surgical assistant now tossed into the small stove for disposal.

Doc turned to the wash pan and cleaned both his hands and the trocar before drying them neatly. Next he inserted the trocar into its pouch. He was bent over, replacing it in his surgical bag, when a smooth Mississippi drawl stopped him short.

"Aw do declare, that must indeed be the regimental surgeon, identifiable to all the world by his wide and prepossessing ass."

Doc turned to find a nattily dressed first lieutenant standing beneath the protection of his awning. The man's slouch hat hung low over a shadowed face and dripped water onto a slicker. A large black leather case hung from his right hand. The new arrival sported long sandy hair, a dark blond

161

mustache and goatee. Devilish blue eyes were sparkling on either side of a familiar nose.

"Butler?" Doc cried, straightening.

Butler set his case down and wrapped Doc in a bear hug. The Mississippi accent was gone when he said, "Good to see you, brother! My God, it's been what? Four years?"

Doc pushed him back. "Damn, boy! Let me look at you. Where's the goggle-eyed lad I left behind? You've grown into a man . . . and a damned solid one at that."

"I'd like to say you haven't changed," Butler told him with a smile. "But you're still uglier than a mud fence."

"God, but it's good to see you. John Mays, may I present my brother, Butler Hancock. John, here, is one of my surgical assistants. The other, Augustus Clyde, will be along directly."

"My pleasure, sir." Butler shook his hand. "However, from here on out I would stay away from poker games."

"Poker games?" Mays asked, taken by surprise.

"Why, Mr. Mays, the only explanation I can think of that would have brought you so low as to have to serve with my brother is that you were trying to bluff against four showing aces and lost your soul to the devil."

Mays grinned, lifting the pan with its wash water. "If you two will excuse me, I think I'll go see if I can find a game crooked enough to take my bottom deal, and see if I can't win my soul back."

"He's a good man," Doc said as he watched Mays leave. "When did you get in? I'd heard that General Johnston had arrived from Tennessee."

"Last night. Hardee's Corps is settling in outside

162

of the town. I've been up to my eyebrows in meet-ings at headquarters. They just can't get on without me. If they didn't have someone to hand orders to, which means me and a couple of oth-ers, the whole generals' staff would have no other occupation than the consumption of fine brandies, ports, and Madeira."

Butler cocked his head, water still dripping from his hat. "Paw said you were here. Seen him?"

"Unfortunately." Doc crossed his arms. "He inconvenienced himself enough to step out of a saloon and share his felicitations as I was walking down the street."

"What happened between the two of you? It was never spoken of."

Doc considered, the reality sinking in that his brother was no longer the dreamy-eyed, tow-headed boy who once had lain before the fire, a book propped in the flickering light.

"A woman. You remember Sally Spears?"

"Up at Elkhorn Tavern. Tall, raven-black hair, daring dark eyes, and a rather large female endow-ment that challenged restraint by the sturdiest of garments. Half the men in northern Arkansas were in love with her. I do remember that you spent considerable time up there."

"I thought I had the inside track." Doc hesitated, reading Butler's expression. "Until the night I found her entertaining another. In ways that I had hoped she would entertain me. After we were mar-ried."

Butler sucked in a breath. "Paw?"

Doc nodded, tensing his crossed arms. "Now, don't you go passing that around. Maw need never know."

Butler smiled sadly. "Philip, never suppose that

163

Maw isn't among the canniest of the fair sex to have ever drawn breath. Reckon she's fully aware of Paw's weaknesses. It's a wonder she didn't throw him out years ago."

"I wasn't sure I should tell you. Wouldn't have. But seeing you now . . . ?"

"I know Paw as well as you do, better probably. It's good you told me. Means I won't put the two of you in the same room by mistake." He pulled his hat off, hanging it on a wooden chair back and plucking up the black leather case. "But enough of that! I brought you something. Spoils purloined from behind Federal lines just prior to our precipitous retreat from Kentucky."

Setting the square case on Doc's surgical table, he began unbuckling the long straps that allowed it to be attached to a saddle or wagon. Opening the leather exterior, he produced a wooden mahogany box, its corners fitted with brass caps and lockset. The top had been emblazoned with an escutcheon marked "U.S.A. Hosp. Dept."

"You know what this is?"

Doc gasped, running his fingers down the waxed wood. "My God, it's a surgeon's operating case. And a cussed expensive one at that."

Doc flipped the latches open and exposed the fine instruments, each held in place by dark blue velvet dividers. Tourniquets, scalpels, amputating knives, catlins, the various saws, scissors, probes, and sounders, it was all there.

"I thought it would do a heap more good in your possession than it would among the Federals. Those bastards are rich enough they can buy more."

"Butler, I don't know what to say. My dear Lord, it's a Hernstein & Son set. Among the best in the world." He lifted out the straight forceps, marveling at the serrated surface inside of the curved beaks.

"Just keep our boys alive. That's all the thanks I need." Butler looked around and stepped over to the cupboard, peering at the bottles in their lines. "Some surgical hospital. Where's the medicine?"

"Which medicine precisely are you interested in?"

"I think the medicinal term is 'pop-skull,' or 'Who-hit-John.' On some occasions it hangs on to the moniker 'oh, be joyful.' "

Doc grinned, used his foot to lift the lid on a trunk, and tossed his brother a bottle of whiskey. "That came from a distiller outside of Memphis. I'd tell you it's most likely the finest sour mash you'd ever tasted, but I reckon that hanging out with the kind of generals you do, you'll only find it passable."

Butler pulled the cork, took a drink, and worked it with his tongue before swallowing. "I'd say it's every bit as good as what we sampled from Lynchburg." He found two of Doc's tin cups, pouring liberally. After handing one to Doc, he parked himself backward in the chair, arms braced on the back to steady the cup.

Doc seated himself on the trunk, clicking rims with his brother in toast. He studied Butler for a moment, wondering again at the intense young man across from him. "You've heard about the fight at Elkhorn Tavern?"

"That's one of the reasons I came to see you. I've read the report Van Dorn sent to General Johnston. After Curtis finished kicking the stuffings out of the Army of the West, Van Dorn extracted what was left of his army down the

Huntsville Road. Maw, Sarah, and Billy would have been right in the middle of the retreat. Abusing my position, I've shamelessly sent five separate letters, but who knows what condition the post is in. All I can tell you is that the battle itself was up on the ridge around Elkhorn Tavern and over around Foster's farm. The family should be all right."

Doc nodded. "What about you? What's it like serving with Tom Hindman of all people? Most folks say he's a pompous prig."

Butler raised an expressive eyebrow. "When it comes to a firebrand, the man's hotter than a burning corncob. He and I don't see eye to eye on every subject — especially slavery — but he's smart. Really smart. If this war could be won on passion, he'd be the one to win it. No one I've met has ever impressed me like he has."

"How on earth did you come to his attention?"

"Paw. Of course. I finally got the story out of Hindman. The man draws trouble like a lightning rod. After a rather fiery speech in the legislature, Hindman stepped out into the street. Five of Johnson's thugs jumped him. One grabbed Hindman from behind and pinned his arms so he couldn't draw his pistol while the others prepared to beat him to death with clubs. Paw appeared out of the darkness and laid about him with that sap he always carried.

"According to Hindman, Paw helped him to the nearest tavern where Hindman medicated Paw with brandy until all hours. Hindman drank soda water. They both decided that politics aside, they were, and I quote, 'the most convivial of kindred spirits.' At least when it came to a street brawl."

"You've come a long way. You talk like a gentleman instead of a Benton County Arkansan. But then I always expected you to be a professor of history or philosophy. A lecturer on the classics. How life has taken us by surprise."

Butler stared into his whiskey. "Surprised indeed. Fact is, I rather like being an officer. To my wondrous discovery, war is not only fun, but exhilarating. I organized our withdrawal from Bowling Green. I'm at the heart of the army, watching history being spun off the looms of great men."

Butler paused, his sensitive face thinning. "But some of the things I've seen? I get the night chills, brother. I see the faces of the suffering. They call out in my dreams. It is like . . . Dante's Hell, newly broken loose in America. And we may see worse to come."

"John Gritts used to say you heard the spirit voices."

"Enough of me. What of you? The last I heard you were in Boston, and pop, you're a regimental surgeon? Ain't that a twist to chaw on?"

"I'm betrothed."

"Do tell?"

"Her name is Ann Marie Morton, a physician's daughter in Memphis." Doc smiled. "Seems that I fell for the most wondrous laughter, beauty, and poise. I think, though, looking back, it was the freckles that God scattered across her nose that laid me low. You could do a lot worse for a sister-in-law, and I would consider it my greatest honor if you would stand up with me on the day I finally marry her."

He'd deal with Young James on that subject when it came around. Surely his friend would understand.

"Of course I will. Come hell or high creek water! When is the event?"

"Perhaps next spring. For the time being, I'm sort of looking after her brother, James. He's in A Company. The Shelby Grays. Meantime, I'm saving every penny, hoping to purchase a building where I can open a surgery in Memphis. I'm hoping that by then the war will be over, and we can all go back to our lives."

Butler's lips pursed in that old familiar way.

"What is it?"

"Nothing."

"I know that look. You used to get it when you were hiding something. Like the time you let those horses Paw bought in Fayetteville get away because you didn't latch the corral gate."

Butler glanced around as if for reassurance, and leaned forward. He indicated the surgical case, and, voice low, said, "I think you're going to be needing that soon. A Federal army is building at Pittsburg Landing on the Tennessee River about twenty-five miles north of here. Meanwhile our old friend Don Carlos Buell is marching his army to join Grant's. We're going to crush Grant *before* Buell can arrive. And that, brother, is information as privileged as what you told me about Sally Spears."

"And when is this happening?"

"We're moving within days. If all goes according to plan, Grant's army will be destroyed in the first week of April. Then we'll catch Buell on the other side of the river, and send him reeling back in defeat. By the end of May, we should be back in Nashville, reestablishing our northern line. And, best of all, the British and French, seeing the Union take yet another licking, will grant recognition and protection to the Confederacy."

"And you can come be my best man," Doc said with finality.

"As Paw'd say, here's to it, you ol' coon," Butler agreed, clicking his tin cup to Doc's in toast.

21

Insanity! It brewed and stormed, boiling around Butler's head. Lost in the instant, to Butler it seemed that the world had splintered. Blown apart. As if reality had vanished in this ear-shattering banging, screaming, and shrieking.

Time had been consumed in the whirlwind of hideous images, sounds, and smells. Rational thought no longer existed. Reality had funneled down to terror, thirst, confusion, and the frantic beating of his heart.

They were making another of the endless assaults on Union General Prentiss's retreating forces. It had started in the morning when they caught the sleepy Yankee camp by surprise. All day they'd been driving them northward toward Pittsburg Landing, launching one bloody assault after another on the wavering Yankee lines.

Until they'd reached this place: a sloping open field. Someone said it belonged to a farmer named Duncan. At its crest a little-used and sunken road crossed before a thick stand of vine-laced brown timber.

The Federals finally had managed to hold the line at the sunken road just across the bloody and torn field. At Hindman's side, Butler watched the Arkansas brigade — its ranks already thinned by the morning's fighting — charge with the shrieking scream of banshees. So far they'd broken every formation the Federals had thrown together to stop them.

"Come on, boys," Butler whispered as the gray and butternut formations surged out of the trees and into the body-dotted field. The Arkansas companies made no more than ten paces before the first rounds of canister and grape tore into them. Butler winced at the mayhem as bodies were torn and tossed. Gaps, like swaths, cut through the ranks.

And then a volley of musketry exploded from the sunken road. Whizzing death made a pattering sound as men were shot down.

They'd made it less than halfway across the open field before great clouds of blue-gray smoke spurted and puffed along the Federal line of fire, and a blizzard of lead savaged the ranks. Men dropped. Spun. Staggered. Shrieked in pain. As if of its own accord, the gray mass stopped, hesitated. All the while, the Yankee batteries blasted death and carnage as the Federal infantry shot at will, their position hidden by a wall of expanding smoke.

"By the Lord God!" Hindman cried as his troops staggered back, the once-tight formation breaking into confusion. "Arkansas! You shall not break!"

When Hindman spurred his horse forward, Butler followed, keeping Red to the general's rear.

Dear God, what are we doing? A cold wash of fear, like a winter wave, ran through Butler's soul.

Hindman's mount dashed out before the mill-

171

ing ranks of confused, frightened, and disorganized Arkansas regiments. In his dress uniform, little Tom Hindman lifted his sword on high, shouting, "Re-form your ranks! One more charge and they'll break! Arkansas! *Follow me!*"

Hindman kept swinging his sword, heedless of the balls that cut the air around him in rasping whirs.

Butler, terrified to the point of tears, Red plunging and prancing, shouted his encouragement. As the Arkansas regiments rallied at the sight of their commanding general, Hindman turned his horse to face the enemy.

What the hell are you doing, Tom? Charging them headlong? You won't make ten paces.

A wreath of thick gray smoke, like a miasmic fog, hung over the sunken road and hid the Federal soldiers. Lances of fire and the bang of the Union artillery in the trees added to the hellish scene.

Red shied as she stepped on the dead and screaming wounded that lay strewn across the bruised grass. The smell of gunpowder, blood, and brutalized guts mixed with the scent of crushed grass.

It happened in an instant. Butler would replay it again and again in his memory. Hindman laid spurs to his horse, the big black gathering itself, muscles bunching under the sleek and sweaty hide.

In a blink, the animal exploded. The horse's head and neck shot up. The muscular shoulders and ribs ballooned wide. The front legs burst out sideways like wings. The right rear hip and leg vanished in a jetting spray of blood, chunks of muscle, and fragments of splintered bone.

Hindman, still in his saddle, was smacked into

the air. At the height of his flight, he twisted like a rag doll before falling limp onto the blasted carnage of his mangled horse.

Butler didn't remember dismounting, only that in the next instant he was crouched beside the unconscious Hindman. The smell from the horse, gutted stem to stern by artillery round shot, was overpowering.

"Help me!" Butler cried, wondering if Hindman were alive or dead. Bullets were zipping past his head, the sound mixing with the shouts of panicked men and the screams of the wounded and dying.

And then Hindman blinked, sucked in a frantic breath, and moaned.

The air beside Butler's shoulder was torn away as a round shot ripped past. Standing, powered by panic, Butler jerked Hindman up and tossed him over his shoulder. Turning, he ran like he'd never run in all his life. At the rear of the receding gray wave, he pounded over the torn grass. His boots slipped in the blood, clawed for purchase as he leaped over the sprawled dead, and darted to one side or the other of the crawling wounded.

Dear God, save me. Please, just let me live!

The memory faded into a confused swirling of images. He was back among the shot-chewed trees. Weaving through disorganized formations of weary and dispirited Arkansas volunteers.

Then he was placing a groggy Tom Hindman on the ground, leaning him against a tree. Around them, the shattered formations were fleeing Duncan field. Butler stayed at his general's side until a stretcher could be brought from the medical service, and two privates loaded the dazed Hindman onto the stretcher.

As the stretcher bearers bore him to the rear, Hindman called, "Butler?"

"Yes, Tom?"

"Stay with the brigade! You are my eyes and ears!"

"But Tom, you've just —"

"Damn it, man! *Stay with the brigade!*"

Butler stopped short, a feeling of disbelief eating a hole in his chest.

As the general vanished behind the wall of trees, Butler looked around at the stunned and horrified men who had dropped to the ground beneath the trees.

Hindman's final order.

Stay with the brigade? And do what?

Overhead a shell burst, shrapnel cutting the air with a fluttering sound followed by twigs, branches, and spring-green leaves as they rained down from above.

22

2:30 P.M., April 6, 1862

Tom Hindman's horse had exploded in the morning. Since then, Butler had ridden Red back and forth through the chaos as the remains of the division fell back and replenished their ammunition. With Hindman and his replacement, General Wood, disabled, Alexander Stewart of the First Corps had taken command of the disorganized Arkansas brigades.

Butler had been told that Hindman had been evacuated, and even then was on his way back to Corinth.

It was two-thirty. The weary survivors of the re-formed Arkansas regiments again charged the Union position. Word was they were calling it the Hornet's Nest — for every time a Confederate formation attacked it, the result was the same: a buzzing, painful, and devastating response.

Instead of crossing the open Duncan field, now the Arkansans approached up the thickly wooded slope. Slipping among the trees, the gray-clad men wound past fallen heaps of dead and dying men. Gibson's Louisiana volunteers. They had tried and failed to break the Yankee line but an hour past.

As he rode in the rear, Butler's throat had gone dry. To either side, hidden behind the trees, the crackling hell of battle could be heard. And here, moving up among the boles, he was aware of the irregular tight whirring of bullets as they cut the air and smacked into wood and leaves.

Somewhere the woods were on fire, a fact known only by the sweeter smell of wood smoke and presence of ash that whipped and whirled through the relentless Confederate advance.

Butler clamped his eyes shut, hard and tight, left hand tightening on Red's reins as if to squeeze them like soft mud between his fingers. Beneath him, his horse trembled. Danced sideways around a bled-out corpse that lay facedown in last year's moldy leaves. And stilled at Butler's insistent tug.

He opened his eyes, and the vision remained the same: men dressed in gray and brown, staggering forward through the rough-barked trees and hanging vines. Ghosts, they intertwined and separated from the smoke and noise and stench of battle. Like hunters they proceeded in a half crouch, their rifles held low until, at an instant, they would straighten, shoulder, and fire. Each shot but a single snap in the popping, crashing cacophony of banshee sound and banging explosions. With each discharge came another puff of the vile and sulfurous blue-gray smoke that blew around like corrupt and hellish mist.

Afterward, the men slowed, ripped a cartridge from their box, bit off the paper tail. The sides of their mouths bore a darker streak left from the powder. Eyes half panicked and wide, they poured the charge into their still smoking rifles and shotguns. The clatter of the ramrods was drowned in the deafening roar as they seated the ball or shot. Fumbling a cap onto the nipple, or priming a pan, the man would start forward again in his half crouch, his eyes fixed on the drifting smoke ahead. He advanced with his face slightly averted, shoulder up, as though edging into a frightful storm.

As they went, they stepped around or over gray-and-butternut-clad bodies: the wreckage of Gibson's previous assault. Some dead, lying in puddles of darkening blood, others crawling in the grass, leaves, and twigs, heads up, mouths open in screams that were devoured by the clatter of musketry, the shouts of officers, and the calls of terrified men.

A Federal soldier stumbled out of the smoke-wreathed hell of splintered trees. Bareheaded, blood streaming from a long cut that had laid the right side of his head open above the ear. With both hands he struggled to hold his intestines inside his belly by using the torn fabric of his shirt as a sort of basket.

Colonel Shaver's First Brigade paid him no heed, as if he were nothing more than a vaporous apparition. A spectral phantom conjured of a nightmare.

As though stunned by that very realization, the Federal dropped to his knees in the trampled leaves. The impact defeated his groping hands. An instant later he toppled onto his face, only to vanish into the swirling smoke as the snorting and trembling sorrel carried Butler beyond sight of the wretch.

A shell burst above Butler's head, the shrapnel almost musical as it tore and twisted through the air and pattered like absurd hail onto the ground around him. Two men fell, hit by the hissing fragments. Branches clattered down where they'd been severed from their anchoring trunks.

A shriek ripped the air away beside Butler's left ear. The passing shot batted at his head, blowing his hair, mustache, and goatee sideways. His hearing popped painfully on that side.

Cannon.

Solid shot.

A finger's width from his ear.

Damn, that was close!

The image of Hindman's horse exploding replayed in his tortured brain. He should have been terrified.

Instead he was numb. His thoughts ex-corporeal.

Just ahead, calling encouragement, Lieutenant Colonel Dean of the Seventh Arkansas followed behind his line of men. The ground rose before dropping into a sunken track at the crest. There, behind a mat of brush, a large force of Federals had fortified themselves: Prentiss. He had stubbornly been holding up the entire Confederate advance on Pittsburg Landing.

Is this where it ends?

So far, word was that the morning had gone well. The wretched two-day march up clogged roads — though tedious, and infuriating with its delays, bogged wagons, and mismanaged movement — had been a success.

That morning Hardee's Third Corps had taken Prentiss's Sunday morning encampment by surprise. Hindman's brigades had routed Peabody's panicked troops and driven them in a desperate flight that had reminded Butler of flushing quail.

Then had come the disastrous assault at Duncan Field.

They'd restocked their ammunition from the plundered Union camp, and been ordered here, to these woods, to dislodge some general named Wallace and his stubborn Iowans.

"Stay with the brigade! You are my eyes and ears!"

Butler watched the approaching tree line across the sunken road; the smoke was brushed back as though by the breath of a providential God.

The first elements of his massed brigade, maintaining a solid line, were no more than fifty yards from the trees. The demarcation was clearly seen by the piles of dead left after Gibson's previous assault.

Oddly, the rattle of guns slowed, the battle gone quiet to the point that Butler heard the Yankee commander's order: a plaintive voice from the other side of the brush that cried, *"Have at 'em, boys! Fire!"*

Magically, a rank of dirty blue-clad forms — faces powder-blackened, their hair unkempt — popped up like manikins on strings. Their rifles clattered against each other, so closely were they packed. The silver of fixed bayonets gleamed in the afternoon light.

Then the entire line vanished in a wall of flickering orange fire and spewing smoke. The sound of it, like hell's own hail, hit with the impact of a hammer. And in it, the tortured air screamed with the whiz of the bullets. Red bunched, spooked, and seemed to hunker beneath a great dark weight.

Butler heard the volley as it tore through the Arkansas infantry, popping into flesh, pocking through rifle stocks and skulls, clacking as hot lead struck metal.

A great moan went up from the troops ahead of

him, and the ranks literally wavered and melted as men dropped, curled, pitched sideways, or threw up their arms, weapons flying.

"Onward! Forward, Arkansas!" Dean's bellowed order was picked up and relayed by the captains and lieutenants. "Onward, Arkansas!" the shout rose.

Guns popped, the ranks stepping over or around the piles of fallen, as though the formation were a great and ponderous snail-like creature. They were close now, the smoke rising enough that Butler could discern the Iowans, ramrods clattering as they reloaded. Capped their guns, and leveled them.

"Forward!" Dean screamed again, his sword held high as he followed his men. "Onward, Ark . . ."

The great wall of curling orange fire, sparks, and rolling smoke was accompanied by the crackling hammer of sound.

As another pattering impact tore the Arkansas regiments apart, Colonel Dean spun, his sword cutting a corkscrew pattern out of the smoky air. For the briefest instant, Dean's eyes met Butler's, and then he was down, sprawled on the trampled grass.

Red stopped short, trembling as if about to burst.

Butler glanced up from the colonel's limp body. Fixed on the falling soldiers — at the gaping holes in the ranks. He could see the indecision as men slowed, firing, glancing this way and that.

Filling his lungs, he was about to shout encouragement, take up Dean's cry.

Impossibly, the Iowans dropped, falling flat into their sunken road. It was so surreal that Butler hesitated, another of the lulls having gone quiet enough that his order would carry down the entire line.

The woods behind the Federal line erupted in cannonfire. The air screamed as canister and grape tore into the massed Arkansans. Concentrations of men burst into red haze. Entire ranks vanished into a flying melee of arms, heads, hands, broken rifles, flying cloth, and wide-splayed ribs. One severed leg flipped on high, twisted toward the afternoon sky; a shoe flew off the foot before the limb thudded down onto cowering soldiers.

The line stopped, stunned at the impossibility of what it had just endured.

Butler could feel it, as if the massed ranks of men were an organism — some primordial beast with a horrified conscience of its own.

Before the beast could react, the Iowans rose from the dirt and gore. Their guns swung level, heads bending to the stocks, squinting eyes on the sights. A wall of sound, fury, and flame again blasted into the Rebel line. The slapping of the bullets as they blew through cloth, skin, muscle, and bone was dazing in its effect.

Butler watched his soldiers falling out of ranks the way corn might be cut when a hundred workers slashed randomly through a field with cane knives.

"Fire!" one of the Seventh Arkansas sergeants bellowed, and from the decimated lines, a ragged and irregular staccato of musketry hammered at the Iowans. The men in blue knew their jobs. They'd dropped flat, the majority of the Confederate balls smacking harmlessly into the wall of ruined timber behind them.

"Forward!" Major Martin cried.

Butler saw him, perhaps thirty yards to the west as he tried to exhort his men to the attack.

Too much time had been lost. The advance had stalled.

An Iowan screamed, *"Down!"*

The Federals dropped like rocks.

The Federal gunners hidden back in the trees had reloaded. Again the howitzers and rifled cannon blasted their wrath into the stumbling Confederate ranks. Men vanished in another red haze of flying body parts, bits of them spattering in all directions to bounce off the leaf mat, to rain down on their cowering fellows, or to catch in gruesome patterns to hang from the splintered branches in shot-broken trees.

Butler gaped at one such display: a man's entrails strung like Christmas bunting in the jagged branches of a hickory.

As quickly the Iowans leaped up from behind the brush, their rifles leveled. Another popping and crackling wall of flame shot from their muskets, the balls ripping through the broken and dazed formations.

What remained of the Seventh Arkansas, groups and individuals, turned and ran. Some managed to hang on to their guns, others just threw them down, arms pumping as they fled the insane wreckage of human flesh that had been piled in mangled heaps. Hundreds of voices rose in screams, pitiful wailing, and pleas for help, as wounded soldiers crawled among the broken, bleeding pieces of dead human beings, and reached out to the backs of their fleeing comrades.

Behind them, a shout of victory rose from the Yankee lines, as men waved their hats, shook fists, and held up rifles.

Butler froze, disbelieving eyes on the bleeding piles of meat and splintered bone strewn over and around the dead and dying that still had human form.

Is this real? Or am I living a deluded nightmare?

The impossibility of the scene before him defied . . . *defied* comprehension. Let alone belief.

Someone pulled at his stirrup, breaking the trance. Butler glanced down, saw a panic-crazed man, saw him drag at Butler's pant leg. The man's mouth was working as though he were shouting, but nothing permeated the ringing scream in Butler's ears.

The man jerked again at his leg, as if trying to pull him from the saddle. The action spurred Red, who turned away. As she did, something slashed through the air where Butler's body had been but an instant before.

The spell, the horror, whatever it was, broke, and Butler heard the Federal balls ripping through the air around him.

The man now clasped his leg, screaming, his eyes crazy, and refused to let go. Then a minié ball blew the back of his head off; the man dropped as if his strings had been cut.

Butler jammed his spurs into Red's side, and let her carry him down the slope. He was faintly aware that at least two men were knocked flat in the horse's terrified flight. And then, ducking and weaving, he and Red were through the trees.

Butler heard whimpering, as if from a distance. The sobs were soft, like those of a child whose beloved dog had just died. The forest through which he rode shimmered, going silver in his vision.

23

April 8, 1862

Doc Hancock blinked the fatigue from his eyes. He steadied the capital saw in his grip, nodded at John Mays, and began his first cut.

At the feel of the saw on bone, the young man on the table cried out, "Oh God!"

Doc ignored it.

"No! Not my leg!" The young man's face, gleaming with sweat, had a look of absolute horror. He swallowed hard, the Adam's apple bobbing in his throat. The wide brown eyes had an almost angelic softness. He broke into whimpers, his other limbs bucking against the straps Augustus Clyde had adapted out of harness.

The saw ate its way through the lower femur, and the youth's shattered knee rolled loose under Doc's left hand.

Augustus flung the useless and bloody lower leg into the pile in the corner where it added its leaking gore to the pool in which the other amputated limbs lay. With the rongeur Doc dressed the rough edges of bone, pausing only to wipe the sweat from his brow.

Augustus had already wrapped the surgical suture silk around the hook-shaped tenaculum,

184

and Doc used it to pull the arteries free of the severed muscle. Dropping the ligating loop around the arterial end, Doc tied it off.

The boy on the table was quivering like a desperate rabbit as Doc worked his fingers to relieve the stiffness. His hands ached, his fingers cramped from fatigue. Outside the rattle of wagons and the shouts of men announced the arrival of another load of wounded.

Hurry. Got more to do.

How many more? Where was the end of it? He'd been working straight through since Sunday morning when the fighting started.

It dawned on him that the crackling and banging of battle had grown louder. That things were not going well for the Army of the Mississippi.

General Albert Sidney Johnston was dead. The story from Dr. Yandell — after he had finally been led to Johnston's body — was that the commanding general had bled to death. The irony was that all the while the general had had a field tourniquet in his pocket.

The boy on the table — for he was little more than that — had ceased crying, his expression pale with shock. Doc battled against the trembling in his fingers as he stitched the flap closed as best he could. The caked blood, thick on his fingers, made matters worse. He didn't have the "feel" he needed for elegant stitches.

Damn it, these things needed time to do right. Sloppy. So damned sloppy. But the suture held after Doc nodded, and John Mays carefully released the tourniquet.

"Next," Doc called, wondering when his voice had gone hoarse. Wasn't there anything to drink? Just a cup of water?

185

Mays and Clyde undid the straps and lifted the boy from the bloodstained table.

Two men bore another, hanging between them, as Mays and Clyde carried the boy out. Doc stared dully at the bloody oak tabletop. Once it had been the center of family life, graced with holiday feasts in a better day. His brain had that fiery feeling that came of fatigue, stress, and too many hours awake.

With care the two men eased their sagging burden onto the table. Doc's clot-thick fingers eased the blood-soaked wool jacket open. The seeping wound was just under the man's armpit. Doc put a hand over the man's gaping mouth, noticed the gray deep behind the expanded pupils, and then touched the right eye. No reaction.

"Too late," he said wearily. "Next!"

"No, suh," one of the ragged soldiers said. "You fix my brother."

Doc focused on the chestnut hair, the freckled skin, and the round chin. The family resemblance to the man on the table couldn't be missed. "I can't do anything for him."

The younger of the two reached down, slipping his hand under the flap of his holster, drawing out a revolver and leveling it with deadly intent.

"You *save* my brother! You're a doctor. Damn it, fix him!"

The older brother blinked, as if confused. He glanced at the trembling pistol, and then at Doc, worry and hope welling.

Doc raised his hands as Clyde and Mays stepped in and stopped short, staring in disbelief.

"I *promised* Mother!" the pistoleer cried. "We all did! We have to go home!" Tears now glistened, then streaked down his dirty powder-blackened face. The hazel eyes widened.

"Son, put the gun away." Doc reached out, pressing the long barrel down. "I can't bring back the dead. He was gone before you brought him in here. I'm sorry, son. Just plain damned sorry."

The younger brother's head tilted, the confusion back, his mouth working as if struggling for words. Not finding them.

The older brother, blinking and stunned, reached out and ran fingers along the dead man's cheek. "Put the gun away, Tad. Andy's dead. Got to go bury him now. Nothing more we can do."

"But we told Maw!"

"I know. Damn it all, *I know!*"

The pistol slowly wobbled back into its holster. Tad seemed to sway, his blood-smeared jacket hanging open to expose a filthy white shirt. He stared emptily at the tracked-through blood coating the floor. "But we promised . . ."

The older brother reached out, knotting his fingers in the dead man's jacket. Dragging the body through the tacky gore, he shouldered the burden. Then he turned, staggering under the load, and plodded for the door.

A moment later, the young one, still struggling with disbelief, turned, almost stumbling as he followed.

Clyde took a deep breath. "Damn, Doc. That's the bravest thing I've ever seen."

"What? Picking up a dead man?"

"No, pushing a pistol down with your bare hand."

"Pointing a pistol with empty cylinders? Sort of defeats the purpose. Next."

The angry sounds of battle were growing. A nearby shell burst startled them. A volley of

187

musketry sounded, louder than they'd heard that Monday.

"They better hold that line," Mays muttered.

"God help us if they can't," Doc agreed, wiping his forehead with a blood-slick hand. Using his sticky apron, he did the best he could to wipe the forceps clean. They had used the last of their water early that morning.

God, what I'd give for a drink.

The next young soldier, barely twenty, had sweat-damp and filthy blond hair along with the beginnings of a beard. His side was bare where he'd pulled the bloody cotton shirt up to expose the wound.

"Am I going to live, Doc?" he asked in a wheezing voice.

"I'll do what I can. Where you from?"

"Biloxi. By the sea."

"You peed?"

"It come out all blood." He swallowed hard. "Didn't know a man could hurt like this. Am I gonna live?"

Doc shifted him, eliciting a yelp of pain. Feeling around the man's back, he located the lump of bullet under the skin on the far side.

Doc eased him back down. "I can't do anything."

Impassioned blue eyes searched Doc's. "What?"

"The bullet went through your liver and smashed your kidney. If I take it out, most of your guts will come with it." Doc looked down at his trembling hands and picked anxiously at the clotted blood that coated them. "I'm sorry."

The young man's throat worked, obviously thirsty. "It's all right. There's others out there. Help them, Doc." He blinked his eyes, brow lined.

"Damn."

Doc reeled under the weight of impotence as the young Mississippian was carried out. He braced himself on the table, the room spinning slightly as he swayed and blinked to clear his vision. This was just thirst and fatigue, that's all.

He had *nothing* to give them. The last of the morphine, ether, and opiates had been exhausted before noon yesterday. The bandages had been used up by early Sunday afternoon. The small well, enough for a family, only recharged with a bucket of water every hour or so. Even his surgical silk, the one thing he'd had an abundance of, was down to a single spool. And what would he use when that was gone? Strip the thread from uniform coats?

Unbearable impotence gave way to a building rage. "What the *hell* were they thinking? Didn't the damn fools understand?" He raised his hands, imploring the plank roof overhead.

Reeling again, he wondered if the disorientation wasn't hunger. He hadn't eaten for two days. And damn, he really, really was thirsty. Somehow he hadn't been able to make himself drink from the occasional canteens that came through. Not when wounded and dying men needed it more than he did.

The gut-shot, brain-shot, and spinal injuries were beyond his help. When they looked up at him, pleading, no matter how he hardened his heart the desperation in their eyes was torture. They expected him to make them whole again.

How, in God's name?

He wanted to shut them out, to cover his ears and close his eyes, to sag against the wall and curl into a defensive ball. If he could just let the madness pass.

It didn't.

It wouldn't.

They continued to come: shattered, broken, maimed. So many with pieces gone, the missing parts of their bodies spattered somewhere out there in the mud and mire. Others torn, their flesh ripped by jagged pieces of flying metal. So many punctured with deformed lead that expanded and crushed bone, muscle, and artery.

He had become their last chance. Hope that they'd continue to draw breath, see their homes and families, hug their loved ones, fulfill even the simplest dream, or make love with a beautiful woman. All depended on Doc's skill, as though he could conjure magic from his blood-thick fingers.

They have to see that I'm a fraud. That I'm failing them, one after another.

Something hit the wall with a loud crack, startling him from his near stupor.

"Bullet," Mays muttered.

Doc cocked his head, surprised at the growing sound of the battle, amazed that he'd been able to completely ignore it. Artillery banged loudly. This was the close range of war: men shouting; the clatter of ramrods; gasping breath; the rattle of accoutrements; and the cocking of gun hammers.

"We might have to leave, Doc," Clyde said.

"Can't." Doc bent down to his work. The man he worked on was raving through a gargling exhalation of sound. Something large had hit his head side-on, blowing away most of his lower jaw. Doc had cut away the shreds of cheek that would die anyway, had ligated the spurting arteries, and removed the bloodshot remains of the tongue.

Is this right? Does he even want to live this way?

Doc hesitated, weaving on his feet, kept blinking as he stared at the facial wreckage. It would only take a slip with the scalpel. Drive it down under the mastoid and sever the carotid artery. He glanced guiltily at Augustus Clyde. The man had fixed horrified eyes on Doc's as if reading his thoughts.

Am I acting as an angel of mercy? Or am I some demon from hell, damning him to an endless humiliation and misery?

Clyde surprised him, however, when he asked, "Can't leave? But Doc, our lines are folding up like a lady's fan."

Doc swallowed hard, setting his scalpel aside, trying to fill his lungs with the smoky air and find enough resolve to finish his surgery.

"John, we've got that yellow hospital flag out front. I don't care how you do it, but make sure it's up on the roof where the Federals can see it." He bent back to scraping clotted blood from the man's mouth. "God knows, even that might not save us."

Doc barely noticed the officer's arrival in the doorway. A discharge of muskets just west of the house drowned out the man's words.

"What was that?" He was finishing — as much as he could — with the jaw-shot patient.

"I said, sir, that you are ordered to evacuate!"

"Major, we can't." Doc gestured at the door. "Most of those men can't be moved."

"Those are my orders from General Beauregard."

Doc stepped back from the table, yawned, rubbed his eyes, and watched as Clyde and Mays removed the hideously wounded man who still uttered his wavering vocalizations. The major's face

191

blanched, and he stepped back, a hand going to his stomach.

Doc could only stare dully as he tried to get his head around the problem. "If you have wagons, the superficial wounds and amputees can go." He glanced at Mays. "Who's next?"

"Did you hear me, sir? I *ordered* you to evacuate. You're a regimental surgeon. I could order you shot."

"Pistol's on your hip, Major." Even as he said it, Clyde and Mays were laying another bleeding man, a sergeant, on the table.

Doc wobbled his way back around the table to inspect the gunshot to the man's groin. The major remained, as if fixed, his hand resting on the butt of his still-holstered revolver.

Doc never saw him leave.

"He was going to shoot you," Clyde said woodenly, as if past caring. They were all tired enough that death would have been a relief.

Clyde worked his dry mouth as if to get up enough spit to swallow. "Some of the things you've done? Where did you learn to save things like that wounded jaw?"

"Nowhere." He snorted his surprise. "It just had to be done. Thank the Lord they had us work on all those cadavers back in Boston. Some people think medicine need only be taught out of a book, you know."

The sergeant on the table cried out, bucking, as Doc's probe located the bullet. Small. A pistol ball. God, he'd learned to tell by the feel. When had that happened?

Did he dare try and take it out? The bladder had been punctured, hence the urine. Or did he leave it in, located as it was, beside the prostate?

He bent over the wincing sergeant. "It's a pistol ball. I'm afraid I'll do more harm removing it. Sergeant, we're just going to bandage you, and give it some time to see if it heals."

"Am I still going to work?" he asked, plaintively. "I mean, you know, with a woman?"

"I think so."

The man's expression softened, becoming almost beatific as he smiled. "Thank you, God. And I meant everything I told you in that prayer."

Wagons and horses rattled their way into the yard, men calling orders. The evacuation.

And then they were gone, the musketry breaking with a fury. Two more bullets whacked into the log wall behind Doc.

"Don't tense your leg, damn it!" he snarled at the young Shelby Gray he worked on. The private nodded, lifted his sleeve to his mouth, and bit down on it to keep from screaming.

When Doc had removed the bullet, thankfully without rupturing the femoral artery, he tossed it toward the pile in the corner, surprised to see blue-coated Federal soldiers peering in the door.

Even as he did, two Yankees carried a third, a captain, through the doorway, declaring, "We've got a wounded man here!"

"Put him on the table." The leg was a mess of blood and broken bone just above the knee.

"Hope you don't hold a grudge, Reb," one of the Federals, a red-haired man with a powder-grimed face, said.

Doc blinked, almost weaving on his feet. "No grudges." He looked down. "Captain, you're going to lose that leg."

"Just do it, Reb," the captain managed through gritted teeth.

To the two privates, Doc said, "You two, find me some water, bandages, any medical supplies you can. And if you can find me another surgeon, get him here. I don't give a goddamn whose army he's in."

He was working on his fifth or sixth Federal casualty before another wounded Rebel was brought to the table.

"Doc?" the young man gasped as he was laid out on his back.

For a moment, Doc blinked, struggling through his fatigued mind, lost in anatomy and surgical concerns. When he finally found the dormant part of his brain, it still took a moment to place the strained, filthy face, the chestnut hair, and green eyes.

"James? James Morton?"

James blinked, his eyes pain glazed. His uniform was covered with dried blood. "I been laying out for two days now. God, I'm thirsty."

"We'll get you water."

"Am I gonna die?"

"Not if I can help it." *Promised your sister I'd look out for you.*

Doc blinked again, almost in tears as he fought to shed the cobwebs in his brain. He had just exposed the sucking chest wound. Then the world turned oddly gray and soft. He felt himself reel, collapse. It hurt when he hit the floor, bringing him awake.

Hands were lifting him, helping him to one of the chairs, and then he faded off, dropping into an exhausted slumber.

He wasn't aware that he'd failed Ann Marie, that fifteen minutes after he'd collapsed, a Federal surgeon, riding atop a wagon filled with supplies, had patched James's pneumothorax, and done it while the young man was peacefully under the chloroform's merciful spell.

24

May 5, 1862

Billy felt free as he and Sarah drove the wagon up the Pea Ridge grade toward Elkhorn Tavern. Spring had come. The day was warm, filled with the smell of dogwood, honeysuckle, and redbud. Wildflowers added both color and their delicate perfumes to the air.

The Federal army had finally packed up and marched back north along Telegraph Wire Road, headed, so the rumors said, for eastern Arkansas where General Van Dorn was supposedly raising hell.

Or invading Missouri.

Or both.

He, Maw, and Sarah had had their fill of Yankees and Confederates, and war, and battles. First had come the Confederates who had hauled off most everything. Then they'd been inundated with wounded and dying men. Then had come the Federals, who, fortunately, had finally evacuated the surviving Confederates from the farm and hauled off the dead for burial.

Sarah, of course, had saved the wagon — and made a dollar a day for nine days to boot, driving for the Yankees. But that she'd done so was still a burr under Billy's butt.

"Unfitting," Maw had insisted.

Sarah had stared back with a blue-eyed hardness Billy had never seen before. "Lots of things ain't the same anymore, Maw."

He was chewing on that, jaw clamped, when Sarah asked, "What's got you riled?"

"I'm the man. I should have driven the wagon for the Yankees. Maw was right. It ain't fittin' for a young woman to be hauling dead men. Let alone by herself out among all them strange men. There's no telling what they thought of you."

But he knew, all right. In their minds they'd been pulling her clothes off, fondling her high round breasts, and slipping between her muscular thighs. That's what men did when they saw a full-bodied woman like Sarah.

She eyed him warily. "Captain Stengel treated me with respect and courtesy. Some . . . well, shucks, a girl's got to figure out how to deal with them sometime." She raised her hands, let them fall. "All that matters is that they thought we were loyal Unionists. The ones like the Fosters, that they knew were Rebels, got cleaned out."

"So did we," Billy muttered.

The Federal occupation meant constant depredations. The Hancock farm was eternally crawling with blue-coated soldiers looking for eggs, silver, grain, cornmeal, or anything edible. Billy had been forced to relocate the remaining chickens, horses, and milk cow ever higher into the hills. Of course a fox got the hens first thing. The cow broke her rope and strayed off where it took Billy three days to track her down. By then, she'd stopped giving milk.

Sarah added, "Don't know what we'd have done

if you hadn't been out in the woods hunting."

Unlike so many who were thrown into destitution, Maw and Sarah had had full bellies. The constant supply of squirrels, rabbits, turkeys, and the occasional venison quarter beat starvation all hollow.

"Tough work having to live in the forest, setting snares and deadfalls. Barking the occasional squirrel. Had to do something to stay away from all them Federal soldiers and scavenging parties."

"You ask me, you were just getting away from the drudgery of scrubbing gore off of the floors, burning the bloody rugs and bedding, and having to tackle any of the less-than-manly cleaning up."

He gave her a triumphant smile.

She scowled, adding, "Never had to work so hard in all my life. Maw wouldn't tolerate so much as a stain."

"At least you didn't marry one of them damn Yankees." How would he deal with the knowledge that some strange Yankee was driving his pizzle into his only sister?

But to his immense relief Sarah — though inundated by soldiers — had resolutely ignored them.

"By all that's holy, why do you think I'd want to marry one of them Yankees? Have my husband traipse off to get shot and bleed to death in some strange woman's house?" She shook her head as if at the very ridiculousness of the notion. "Besides, these were all enlisted men and a couple of lieutenants. If this war's done anything, it's made me even more committed to marrying a man who wants the same things I do. Someone with prospects."

She stopped short, her smooth brow furrowing

as a mockingbird's song trilled in the branches overhead. "I tell you, Billy, I just want this war over. I got a belly full of it — more than I ever bargained for as it is. I'll be eighteen a'fore Paw can get me to Little Rock."

Despite the Confederate defeats, Billy hadn't heard talk of surrender yet. "You go right ahead and plan on snaring your mystery man. Me? I figure we got us a hard row to hoe yet, sis."

The seed corn he'd hidden had survived the snooping Federals. And what the Yankees had confiscated had been paid for in Yankee coin, whereas the Confederates had paid in paper money, or worse, "requisition" forms that needed to be taken to the nearest Confederate commander. That being the case, whichever side won, Maw had their kind of money to buy replacement supplies.

Assuming that freight wagons ever rolled up from Fort Smith or down from Springfield again.

Meantime, he and Sarah would plant as much acreage as they could. Come fall, prices would be sky-high since so many of the farms in both Benton and Washington Counties had been stripped of their grains.

The hired men were gone though, enlisted, which meant the cotton and tobacco crops would be severely curtailed. But who knew, maybe they'd be back in time to pitch in if the war was stopped.

The wagon bucked and banged over the rocks as they continued up the road toward Elkhorn Tavern. Old Fly, Billy's arthritic yellow dog, rode in the back, his aging bones cushioned by a folded blanket Billy had saved. Once it had been thick with its owner's blood. Left behind after the man had been evacuated, Billy had taken it down, staked it out in the White River, and left the current to leach it clean. Beside the old dog were the fruits of Billy's labor: fox, deer, rabbit, and squirrel skins, all dried and pressed.

In addition, Sarah had nine dollars in gold in her purse to buy whatever staples might be had at either Elkhorn Tavern or down to Pratt's store.

The horses seemed to enjoy the warm morning, their ears twitching at flies as they pulled their way up onto Pea Ridge and leveled out.

"Holy Jehoshaphat!" Billy exclaimed as they broke out of the trees.

The Clemons' farm was devastated. "What happened here?"

"All of the split-rail fencing was torn up by Federal soldiers for firewood. The outbuildings was torn down, too; the planks they used for coffins. The timbers went for other Union repairs on their wagons and gun carriages and such." Sarah pointed. "The trees? That's all damage from cannons shooting canister and grape."

Billy stared wide-eyed at the once familiar forest lands. In patches, the spring trees looked normal with new leaves on full branches, and then would come a swath of splintered and broken timber. What had once been thick branches ended in chopped-short and frayed chaos. Whole trunks had been shattered to resemble giant overchewed toothpicks. On other boles, sections of bark had been blown away. Gouges marked other trunks.

What had been fields were now trampled mud flats, and word was that all the stock had been snatched up by either Federal or Confederate troops during the battle. Where the Clemons family was going to find a draft animal to pull their plow was anybody's guess, but until they did, their once proud fields were going to remain weed patches.

Sarah pointed west beyond the tavern into the savaged trees. "You ought to see out beyond Little Mountain and down to Morgan's Woods. They paid me to haul dead men out of the woods and off of Oberson's fields." She made a face. "I didn't tell Maw. And don't you, neither. But the things I saw? Billy, they was the most horrible mutilated corpses. Don't you *never* go off to war to be marched out and shot like that."

"What do you mean?"

"I mean pieces of men, others with their guts blown out, mangled." She shrugged, gaze distant. "Wasn't nothing like the ones what died at the farm." Expression clearing, she added, "And now I've seen it, and I don't want to see it never again. When I find the right man, I'm leaving Arkansas. Going someplace fancy. Maybe New Orleans where they don't have no war. Or New York, or Philadelphia."

"Back to satin dresses, huh? Well, at least you can court this gentleman caller with your belly full. Assuming he ever comes." Billy smiled widely, his chest feeling as if it were about to burst with pride. The Hancocks, because of him, not only had their horses, but a future. Whenever Paw got back, he was going to have to fetch up with that new rifle.

Billy drove the wagon onto the Telegraph Wire Road, surprised to find that what had been a country lane was now a low and wide swale. The clearing around Elkhorn Tavern had to be four or five times the size it had been, the ground trampled and trails worn into the dirt where lines of tents had stood.

Sarah pulled her bonnet up to cover her gold-blond hair as they pulled into the rutted yard. Billy set the brake, jumping down to offer her his hand.

Pointedly, she ignored it, dropping lightly beside him in a puffing wave of gingham.

Old Ezra Taylor, long-stemmed pipe in hand, stepped out the door, calling, "Well, well, it's Billy Hancock and the lovely young Sarah. What can we do for you today?"

"Got hides to sell," Billy told him as he clumped up the steps. "That and we're looking for flour, cornmeal, candles, and lard."

Taylor cocked his head, peering first at Billy and then at Sarah, his dark brown eyes amused. "Well, first off, the tanyard's closed. Maybe forever. Had their belly full of the fighting and packed up and left. Flour? Cornmeal? Haw! Good luck."

He waved the pipe stem. "Oh, they's some. But it's hidden away in the woods by individual families and dipped into for special occasions. Now, candles? Yankees took every one. God His-self knows when we'll see more. Can't even make 'em. Sure, we can spin wicks, but where you gonna get the tallow? Every cotton-picking beef cow in the country's been eaten. There's nothing to render for the tallow. Same thing with the pigs. Or do you still have that old sow hid away?"

"Yankees got her the second day they was at our place," Sarah confided.

"Well, there you have it."

Billy wrinkled his nose. "What are you smoking?"

"Smells wretched, don't it?" Old man Taylor looked askance at his pipe. "Chokecherry bark and grape leaves. You can't find a twist of tobacco in this country to save your life. So I made this up. It ain't the same, but at least it feels like normal."

"Well, maybe we'll find something down to Pratt's store," Sarah said, voice soft to mask her disappointment.

"I'll save you the trip, Miss Hancock," Taylor told her. "There's nothing to be had. Shelves are empty but for some crockery. Same in Bentonville and Fayetteville." He paused for effect. "Come right down to it, bellies is going to grow a mite tight until crops come up."

"We don't need much," Sarah insisted, giving him her best beguiling smile. "Just a jar of flour. Maybe the same of cornmeal. Maw's birthday is coming up, and we wanted to make her a special celebration."

"Ah, you must have had good news then. I'd been worried."

"About what?" Billy crossed his arms.

"About the battle. Knowing your Paw, James, and Butler was involved, and given the number of the dead . . ."

"They're in Mississippi," Sarah insisted. "They were nowhere close to here, sir."

Taylor narrowed an eye. "It's the big battle at Shiloh Church that I'm talking about. Pittsburg Landing. That one."

Billy and Sarah glanced at each other, mystified.

Billy spoke first: "Where's Shiloh Church?"

"Tennessee, just north of Corinth, Mississippi. Albert Sidney Johnston marched forty thousand men up to beat the Federals. They fought for nearly three days. Near two thousand Secesh killed . . . another eight thousand wounded. A quarter of the Reb army . . . gone. Just like that."

He waved his pipe stem at the surroundings. "Makes what happened around here seem like child's play. Van Dorn only lost fifteen hundred dead and wounded. Not even a tenth of his army."

Sarah had gone white, swallowing hard. "We hadn't heard. God, I hope Paw and Butler are all right. And we have another brother there. Philip. He's a surgeon with the Fourth Tennessee."

"At least he'd have been out of the fight and safe."

She shook her head slowly, and Billy could see the pain and panic behind her eyes as she said, "I know what it's like, Mr. Taylor. Caring for them while they're crying and dying. Washing away the blood, seeing the life drain out of them. It's a horror if Paw or Butler was shot or butchered, but a nightmare if Philip had to watch them die."

"So." Billy shifted uneasily, wondering if Paw were even alive to bring him that new rifle. "Did the South surrender? Does this mean they're whipped and the war's over?"

"Just the opposite, young Billy." He pointed at the telegraph wire, recently fixed after the battle. "The Confederate congress passed a conscription bill a week or so back. They are going to fight it out to the bitter end."

"What's a conscription bill?" Billy cocked his head.

"Conscription," Sarah told him. "It means they can order you to be a soldier with a stroke of the pen."

"Anyone over eighteen," Taylor agreed. "Local governments, mayors, county men, the voting precincts. The government can impress you into the service."

"Then, since I'm fifteen, they can't touch me."

Taylor shrugged, but Sarah turned on him, eyes fiery blue. She jabbed a finger into his chest. "You listen to me, Billy Hancock. Don't let 'em catch you. I was with them soldiers, and I know it as God's truth. Some of them were fifteen, and they didn't look nothing like as old as you do. We got enough men in the fight with Paw, Butler, and Philip. We're doing our share."

Taylor pulled the pipe from his mouth, adding, "I'd listen to your sister, Billy. I've had just about everybody through here, Confederates, Yankees, state militia, Indian regiments, and God alone knows who's going to be next. This I can tell you, having heard them all: it's going to be a long war, and before it's over, they're going to be putting every man in the fight who can hold a rifle. Reckon they're going to want you, Billy. Strong as you are, tough as we all know you to be, they'll *make* you fight for one side or the other."

Sarah took a deep breath. "It'd break Maw's heart."

Billy scuffed the worn wood on the stair tread. "Guess they'd have to find me first, huh? Ain't nobody better than me when it comes to hiding in the woods."

When he met Sarah's eyes, he almost flinched. It hit him that he'd never seen Sarah so scared.

25

May 30, 1862

The last time that Butler had set foot in Little
Rock's imposing Anthony House Hotel it had
been as a supplicant to Thomas Carmichael Hindman. Now he strode imperiously into the lobby as
First Lieutenant Hancock, a member of Major
General Hindman's staff. The gold piping on his
sleeves and the polished buttons added to the
dashing effect.

Paw would have called him a strutting peacock
— a thought that brought a heartbroken smile to
Butler's lips. Paw — along with more than six
hundred others from Bragg's Second Corps —
was listed among the missing after the bloody
disaster at Shiloh.

As a tonic to his constant worry, Butler imagined
Paw's amused distaste for his current sartorial af-
fectations. Could see his father's face screw up as
the old man muttered, "You look like a damned
popinjay."

Yes, he would have loved that with all his heart.
It would mean old James was still alive instead of
blown to pieces or rotting in a brush thicket where
he had crawled away to die.

Stop it! Don't go there.

He already wondered if his sanity was eroding. And the thought that it might be scared him to death. God, he couldn't get the battle out of his mind or thoughts. The others didn't seem to share his terrors. Hindman, despite the explosion of his horse, remained a rock. The others — though they often stared into space, expressions pinched — never let on that they were anything but pillars of strength.

Ghosts. Too many damned ghosts.

He thought he heard a scream — a man dying in pain and fear — and started to turn, only to have the sound cut off, as if it had never been. Several times he'd heard things. Voices. Sounds that others, when he asked about them, had not heard.

Concentrate. You are here. In the hotel. An officer and a gentleman.

Butler straightened his gold-piped sleeves, aware of the glances he and his party received from the folks idling in the lobby.

With him were Hindman's aide-de-camp, Lieutenant Jerome P. Wilson, a planter from Mississippi's landed gentry. Following closely came Hindman's new commissary officer, Major John Palmer. Palmer had been the general's old law partner from Helena, Arkansas.

Butler and his companions had just checked into their rooms at the Anthony House that afternoon. General Hindman himself, along with his young wife Mollie and their three children, were renting a house in Little Rock.

Additionally, Hindman's adjutant and chief of staff, the one-time Little Rock attorney Major Robert Newton, had his own residence in the city; after Shiloh the man's family was more than delighted to have him at home.

The final member of Hindman's staff was Major Francis Shoup, who had been in charge of Hardee's artillery at Shiloh and had now been conscripted into Hindman's new command. A graduate of West Point, Shoup was an ordnance specialist and key to Hindman's plans.

Their task could be simply stated: save Arkansas from Union conquest. A curiously daunting prospect given the reality on the ground. After General Van Dorn's defeat at Pea Ridge he had stripped just about everything of military value from the state, including men, small arms, artillery, equipment, and supplies. Hindman — come hell or high water — had been sent to save the situation.

How? That was the question of the day. To Butler, it seemed that the only thing Tom Hindman had in his favor was an arrogant, vainglorious, and self-righteous belief in himself. If that was the single necessary criterion for success, the sawed-off little general had it in spades.

Butler had had little more than fifteen minutes to refresh himself in his room when a knock came at his door.

Lieutenant Wilson gave him a salute, saying, "The general sends his compliments, sir. He has just arrived for our meeting."

"Where?"

Wilson's smile enlarged. "The barroom, sir. Seven-thirty."

"I'll see you there." Butler closed the door. Leaned his head against it. Nearly two months had passed since he'd ridden from the disaster at the Hornet's Nest, followed the Corinth Road south in the darkness, and finally located Tom

Hindman's battered body in a hospital tent outside of town.

The notion that anyone could "barely survive the explosion of his horse" would have been ludicrous had Butler not witnessed it with his own eyes on Duncan Field. Let alone the other horrors that preyed on his mind after the battle.

Since then, he'd been unable to sleep. The macabre images of blood-misty gore, the eerie shrieks and screams, the impossibility of things he'd seen with his own eyes, kept reaching out of his deepest brain to claw their way into his dreams.

A soldier he'd seen dragging himself forward with his hands, his hips shattered, legs blown away, would look up as Butler rode past, but instead of the black-bearded man, it would be Paw's face, or Philip's. With a cry, Butler would jerk awake, heart hammering, skin gone clammy.

The dreams were one thing. When the images popped into his head during waking moments, they left him scared and sweating, panting for breath.

He'd given his report to Hindman outside Corinth, struggling to keep the tears from welling; but the general had lain there, his blue eyes distant. The only sign that he'd heard was the quivering at the corner of his mouth.

When Butler had finished, Tom Hindman had said, "It's all right, Lieutenant. If the cost of victory was our entire brigade, it was a price well paid."

That had been but hours before the first hints of disaster were carried down from the battlefield by broken and retreating soldiers. Despite that, in the following days the generals continued to hawk

209

the carnage at Shiloh as a triumph of Confederate arms.

"If we inflicted such a damaging defeat," one squint-eyed sergeant who sipped from a tin cup filled with whiskey had asked, "wouldn't the damned Federals be running for the Ohio instead of strengthening their forces up at Pittsburg Landing? And why are us graybacks digging trenches and building abatis around Corinth?"

Before that question could be answered, Hindman had been given overall command of the Trans-Mississippi District, consisting of Arkansas, Louisiana north of the Red River, Indian Territory, and all of Missouri.

They had traveled through Memphis — a city in panic and on the verge of being abandoned to the relentless advance of the Federal forces. There Hindman had requisitioned what few rifles, artillery rounds, and military supplies remained. In addition, he drew a million dollars in Confederate bills from the Memphis banks to cover his expected expenses in Arkansas.

I am home, Butler thought in relief as he walked into the hotel's bar — a brick establishment attached to the main building. He found the door guarded by two privates with Enfield muskets, and the interior cleared of patrons.

Major General Hindman, still on crutches, was perched over one of the billiard tables, arranging the balls on the felt. Major Newton, consulting a map in his hand, was watching the placement of the balls. Shoup, arms crossed, was staring at the arrangement with a frown.

Behind the bar, a single bartender was pouring what looked like sherry from a cut-crystal decanter.

At Butler's approach, Hindman cried, "Good to see you, Lieutenant. No need for a salute. This is an informal occasion."

As Butler looked down at the table he realized it was for pool, having six pockets. He'd heard the game was played with fifteen numbered balls, but this table had more than thirty, scrounged from other tables nearby. In addition, strings had been laid out in patterns that Butler recognized as representing Arkansas's rivers.

At that moment, Lieutenant Wilson entered — glanced around to make sure that everyone was accounted for — and crossed to the bar where he summarily dismissed the bartender.

As the man exited, Hindman raised his hands, balancing on his crutches. "What do you think? Lamplight, velvet wallpaper, an ample supply of sherry, wine, and good spirits, and complete privacy. What better place to figure our way out of one hell of a nasty mess?"

"And a mess it is," Newton said, squinting at his map and comparing it with the balls on the pool table.

Lieutenant Wilson brought a silver tray bearing glasses of sherry as Hindman gestured at the tabletop. "What do you see, gentlemen?"

"Arkansas," Butler noted. "With a lot of billiard balls in the northeast. And . . . Oh, I see. The striped ones are Federal positions, aren't they?"

"Very good, Lieutenant," Newton agreed. He pointed with a pool cue. "These few balls here at Helena, and here at Arkansas Point on the lower river, these at Little Rock, and this one at Fort Smith comprise the roughly fifteen hundred troops under our command."

He shifted his pointer to the huge collection of

211

balls in the north-central region around what Butler recognized as the Batesville area. "That's General Curtis and his estimated *fifteen thousand* men. Here, at Jacksonport, are General Fred Steel's five thousand Yankees. These balls here on the northeast along the Mississippi are the Federal gunboats advancing on Memphis." He looked from eye to eye. "Unless God grants us a miracle, Memphis can't last the month."

"What's the number eight ball down in the southwest?" Shoup asked, pointing.

"That," said Hindman dryly, "is my old bosom friend Governor Rector who abandoned Little Rock and fled to Hot Springs, taking the state government with him."

Shoup took a glass of sherry and sipped. "Is there *any* good news here?"

Hindman shifted on his crutches. "Our predecessor, Brigadier General Roane, declared martial law in Pulaski County on May seventeenth. I have inherited that order." He paused. "I am declaring martial law for the entire state."

Newton and Palmer, lawyers both, simultaneously said, "But that's . . ." They looked at each other, surprised.

"Illegal," Newton finished. "According to the Confederate constitution, only the president, in this case, Jefferson Davis, can declare martial law."

Hindman raised an eyebrow. "Nevertheless, Roane did it with General Beauregard's blessing and approval — in writing no less — and based on that precedent, I will extend it." He raised a finger. "Now, I'm not in a position to question my commanding general. Nor would I dare to. Do you get my point, gentlemen?"

Newton and Palmer were nodding. Butler

looked at Lieutenant Wilson, who simply shrugged.

"What about Rector?" Palmer asked. "He's a bit of a prig. He won't take well to this."

"He abdicated when he fled Little Rock." Hindman shifted on his crutches, gesturing at the table. "As far as I am concerned, I *am* the Arkansas government. And you, gentlemen, are my cabinet. We may have to take some distasteful actions if we are going to save this state from Federal occupation."

"And how do we do that?" Shoup asked, his thoughtful eyes on the collection of balls marking Federal superiority. "They could run right across to Helena and flank the Mississippi defenses. Or their advance units could be in Little Rock tomorrow night. We might as well spit at them as try and stop them with scarcely fifteen hundred men. We're not even sure that all of our troops have weapons, let alone training."

"And there's no supply. You saw what was left in Memphis," Palmer reminded. "Even when we were in Corinth, on the *other side* of the river, with the benefit of railroads, you know the pitiful state of supply for the Army of Mississippi. Only a lunatic would think the Confederacy is going to supply us on this side of the river." He looked mystified. "Tom, we're on our own."

Hindman's secretive smile widened. "Precisely. And I mean to rely on exactly that."

"How?" Newton asked, thoughtful gaze on the table.

"You have to become Caesar," Butler whispered, understanding. "Supporting and maintaining your own legions. Running your own economy. Building your own bridges across the Rhine, and taking them down again."

Hindman's eyes flashed with that old excitement, his smile thinning in satisfaction. "*Veni. Vidi. Vici.* I came. I saw. I conquered."

"Dear God," Newton whispered. "Do you know what you're saying?"

"Here's the reality." Hindman resettled on his crutches. "You're right. There will be no supplies from the Confederacy. No arms, caps, powder, or cannon. We have to make our own. I know for a fact that there's a rifling machine for making gun barrels in Little Rock."

"And only fifteen *hundred* ill-trained troops to fight with." Palmer looked unconvinced.

Hindman propped himself on his crutches and lifted a glass of sherry, studying it in the lamplight. Butler gaped. The man's commitment to temperance was well-known. "We've got the conscription act, and on my honor, I'm going to use it if I have to lasso, drag, and herd every last male of military age into the ranks."

"This isn't Virginia. Push too hard and our Arkansas frontiersmen *will* rebel. Try and force them and they'll take to the swamps and forests. Hell, Tom, Rector already told Jefferson Davis he was going to secede from the Confederacy if he didn't get his way."

"And become what?" Wilson cried. "The United *State* of Arkansas?"

Butler, half afraid, said, "We could have all the men we need."

"How?" Palmer demanded.

"Slave owners are filling our part of Arkansas with their slaves in hopes of keeping them out of Federal hands. If we conscripted them, offered them their freedom for fighting, we could —"

"Have you *lost your mind*?" Palmer gaped, expression incredulous. "*Arm* Negroes?"

Butler smiled his discomfort. "It would do two things. First we could fill our ranks, and second, it would send a powerful message to the —"

A cacophony of shouts overwhelmed him as all but Hindman crowded around.

"*Gentlemen!*" Hindman bellowed, restoring order. He glanced from face to face. "Lieutenant Hancock makes a valid — if impossible — point. He's a westerner who sees the issue differently. And yes, Negro regiments would swell our numbers and make a statement to the Yankees that even Negroes will fight for secession and slavery. But it won't happen. Not in the Confederacy *as we know it.*"

Palmer asked, "Are you serious?"

Hindman shrugged. "If it came down to slavery or secession? I choose secession. But we haven't been driven to that extreme yet." He paused. "We have the resources, caves with niter deposits, lead mines, foundries, and mills. Enough textile mills, though small, exist for some uniform production, and women can be enticed first to spin and then weave additional garments for the men. We don't much care what it looks like as long as men are warm.

"Francis" — Hindman turned to Shoup — "I am giving you free rein. Requisition bells, boilers, and brass, but build me a cannon foundry and an arsenal. Offer fair compensation from the funds we took from Memphis. If anyone stands in your way, arrest them."

"Some people won't take Confederate notes," Palmer reminded.

"They will. From this moment on, the use of

215

Federal currency or specie is illegal. Violators will be arrested for treason."

Palmer looked worried. "Tom, if you alienate the people, this whole thing could turn on us. We could have our own civil war within a civil war. General Curtis is already recruiting Arkansas regiments to fight for the Union."

Hindman's eyes narrowed. "John, if it takes a dictator to save a democracy, then I am indeed Arkansas's Caesar. But I guarantee you this: when it's all said and done, Arkansas will be free, or I will be dead for the trying."

26

Sixty-one men, including Doc, John Mays, and Augustus Clyde, had been captured when Doc Hancock's makeshift field hospital was overrun at Shiloh. The other fifty-eight were wounded so badly the fleeing Confederates hadn't been able to evacuate them before Brigadier General William Sherman's Federal troops arrived on the late afternoon of April 7.

Transported through the streets of Chicago, past the scornful eyes of gawking citizens, twenty-seven of his charges made it alive to the round-arched gate at Camp Douglas prison camp.

The rest had died on the long and abusive journey from Shiloh to St. Louis, and then in the cramped cattle cars that had brought them to Chicago and prison camp. For Doc the journey had been a living hell as he'd watched helplessly, doing what he could for his suffering patients.

As he watched them being processed, papers were compared by bored and careless officers, names checked off, one by one, on the lists.

"Where's Charles Masson?" one would call.

"Dead," Doc would answer. "He died in St. Louis."

And the name would be scratched off.

Next they were searched, their bodies patted down, pockets turned inside out. A physician's assistant asked if they were ill, looked in their eyes and mouths, and ushered them along.

After finally being passed through the gate, he, Mays, and Clyde found themselves in bedlam and chaos. And then the stench hit them. They were locked in a twenty-acre compound with nearly eight thousand other Confederate prisoners of war. The smell of excrement, urine, unwashed mankind, and rot was immediately overpowering. Hovering columns of flies filled the air like a Mosaic plague.

The swarms of mosquitoes, Doc would learn, arrived at dusk.

The lice would take a full day to make their presence known.

The camp was surrounded by a fence, armed sentries, and manned guard towers. The high observation platform outside the fence had been built by an entrepreneur who charged local Chicagoans ten cents to climb the steps where they could look over into the camp and see the thousands of prisoners.

Wooden barracks, twenty-four feet by ninety, and filled with stacked bunks, were elevated three feet above the muddy soil. Originally designed to discourage escape tunnels and hiding places, the elevation did serve the positive value of raising the rickety wooden floors above the flooding each time it rained, and allowed some air circulation during the hot summer months.

Matters would change in winter when men froze to death sleeping on the uninsulated plank floors while the Chicago winds blew snow beneath.

Windows on the south side let in light, and each barracks had a fireplace and tin stove.

"What do we do with our wounded?" Doc asked one of the guards, appalled that his amputees and immobile wounded had just been shifted off litters and left in the shade of the gate.

"Not my problem, Reb. You might get some of the canned mackerel in here to carry them to the hospital square."

"Canned mackerel?"

"With eight thousand of you bastards packed in here, and more coming, that's pretty much your situation, ain't it?"

"Yeah," one of the prisoners called. "We'll he'p y'all." He was a tall man, bearded, perhaps in his late twenties. "McNeish," he called. "You others, give us a hand here."

"We appreciate it," Doc told him.

"Lieutenant Ab Smith," he said, offering his hand. "Seventh Louisiana. This hyar nasty piece of work is Andy McNeish. Welcome to Camp Douglas." He gestured to the others standing around. "Come on, boys. Grab a man and help us git 'em over to the hospital square. Ain't like y'all was doing anything important anyway."

Within moments, the motley crowd had shuffled forward, grabbed up Doc's wounded, and carefully borne them into the heart of the camp.

Doc, last in line, tagged along behind James, who was carried on an impromptu blanket litter to join the rest in the hospital square with its infirmary and separate pesthouse: a barracks area for the isolation of the contagiously ill and dying. Doc followed James's stretcher bearers into the clapboard building, and winced. Instinctively, he placed a hand to his nose against the stench and flies.

Every bed was already taken. The worst of Doc's wounded were laid on the barracks floor. To Doc's horror, the only place the wood could be seen was where the passing of feet had worn away the coating of feces, blood, urine, and vomit. The plank-walled building was a hothouse; the fly-filled air hummed, and the walls crawled. Not with a simple army of the beasts, but a true swarming Mongolian horde of them that set the air humming as Ab Smith's volunteers beat a hasty retreat from the horrible place.

As James was removed from the litter and laid on the floor, Doc noticed a writhing white mass inhabited the damp pile of feces beneath the nearest bed. Maggots. Looking around, Doc realized, to his horror, they were everywhere.

"Doc?" Augustus Clyde asked, his hand over his mouth as he gazed at the suffering wretches in the beds. "God Almighty, is this place real?"

"I'm going to see who's in charge." He made a beeline for what looked like an orderly lingering on the steps outside. The man pointed Doc to the pesthouse, where another orderly gave him directions to the surgeon's office.

"What would you have me do?" a bleary-eyed surgeon named Phineas Higbee asked when Doc finally ran him to ground in a small office behind the main hospital barracks. The man's desk was piled with papers. Overweight as Higbee was, Doc wondered how he could stand food after the smell of his hospital. He wore a blue uniform with the prominent *MS* of the medical corps on his shoulder straps. A round face with jowls was partially hidden by a thick graying beard, in stark contrast

220

to his shining bald pate.

"We don't have the water," the surgeon said, leaning back in his chair. "It comes in wagons every day, and it's barely enough for the men's basic consumption, let alone the frivolity of washing."

"Good God, man! Even shovels would be an improvement. The floors could be scraped if nothing else!" Doc stood, fists clenched, his anger rising.

"Shovels?" Higbee chortled in amusement. "You want me to give prisoners of war shovels? And have Camp Douglas turned into a rabbit's warren of escape tunnels?"

Doc paused, willing his temper under control. "Can you at least find me the materials to get some of those poor wretches off the floor and out of the miasma? Even a tent outside would be —"

"You needn't worry, Dr. Hancock. In this heat, and at the rate diarrhea and complaint are disposing of the worst cases, your men shall have beds aplenty." Higbee smiled. "Probably within the next day or two."

Fury, hot and liquid, stirred at Doc's core. "We're talking about human beings, sir. Men. The worst besotted swineherd wouldn't allow his hogs to inhabit such filth. Are you a physician or a —"

"They are *Secesh,* Doctor!" Higbee shot to his feet, slamming his palm on the desk. "Rebels. As are you! Maybe you all should have thought about the consequences *before* you went to war with your government."

"That does not negate basic humanity!" Doc replied through gritted teeth.

Higbee bellowed, "I am doing the best that I can given the conditions! No one expected the war to go on this long, or that we'd take so many prisoners, so *don't* call me inhumane. How dare you, you insolent . . . stinking . . ."

"My apologies, sir." Doc tried to defuse the situation. "Is there any hope?"

Higbee was fuming, face red. "I've heard the government is working on an exchange system. We have more than eight thousand of you bastards stuffed into a camp made for six, and if your people keep losing battles, another couple of thousand could be packed in here like sardines in a tin by the end of the month."

"Then allow me to at least offer my services in the surgery. They confiscated my surgical case at Shiloh. I was trained in Boston, at —"

"You're a *damned* Rebel! A traitor! I will *not* be bullied about conditions. You wanted your war? Well, Secesh, you got it! Now, get the hell out of my office."

A sense of desperation slowly replaced Doc's rage. "Do you all hate us that much?"

"It's your war. And the nerve of you, coming in here to snap at me like some mongrel dog. I'll make you pay for that. Guard!"

The guard was there immediately, a dark-haired private with a flamboyant mustache that covered his mouth and flared out over his cheeks.

Higbee pointed. "Get him out of here."

Doc raised his hands in a gesture of surrender, hearing Higbee mutter, "Call me inhumane? I'll show him . . ."

As Doc stepped out into the yard, the mustachioed guard following warily, he said, "Well, at least he didn't order you to shoot me."

The man barely cracked a smile. "Oh, Surgeon Higbee? He's a heap more devious than that. If 'n you was shot, you'd be dead. He'll figger some way to string it out for you, Reb."

27

July 15, 1862

"I think I am the most hated man in Arkansas," Tom Hindman noted as he and Butler rode their horses into Little Rock at the head of a small detachment of Texas cavalry.

The day had been dismal for Butler, despite the unseasonably cool midsummer weather. Just enough of a shower had blown over to settle the dust and drop the temperature. The smell of the damp ground, the flowering corn, and the diaphanous wings of the insects against the sunlight would have delighted him once. But not today.

The purpose of their excursion, however, had been the trial and execution of nine conscripted Arkansas men for desertion. The accused had consisted of three Searcy brothers, a father and his two sons from Prairie County, and three best friends from Arkadelphia. All had been rounded up by Texas cavalry in June pursuant to Hindman's conscription order. Believing their rights had been trampled, they'd deserted with the intention of traveling to Helena, Arkansas, to join General Curtis and his Federal forces.

Not only did the notion of desertion sit poorly with Hindman, but General Curtis — after having been artfully dissuaded from attacking Little Rock — had marched cross-country to Helena. There, he'd moved into Tom Hindman's newly built, and very imposing, brick house. The opulent dwelling now served as Curtis's headquarters. That the Union general was sleeping in Hindman's bed, eating off his table, and sending military communiqués from Tom's parlor, had been like pouring coal oil in a cut.

"The most hated?" Butler asked absently. While his eyes might have been on the back of Red's head, he kept seeing the men and boys, their arms bound, bags over their heads. One of the Searcy brothers had collapsed at the last moment, breaking out into sobs. The youngest son from the Prairie County family had cried out, *"Dear God, Paw! I don't want to die!"*

The Texans had shot them to rags as the deserters' regiment watched with wide eyes.

Is this what war has become?

"Well, lookee there!" Hindman cried, breaking Butler's introspection.

Butler raised his gaze to the brick warehouse they were passing. In white paint had been scrawled the words HINDMAN! HAIL SEESUR! and THREE HEADED DEMON! The latter referred to Hindman as judge, jury, and executioner. Or, as the more politically savvy tended to think: executive, legislative, and judicial all rolled into one.

"Do you think he means 'Hail Caesar?' " Hindman wondered.

"He does," Butler said wearily. "It's being whispered about. The affluent and educated are divided. Most understand that it has taken harsh measures to accomplish what you have. A couple

225

of months ago, the city was in a panic and General Curtis was two days' march away. Now, because of what our spies have planted and the artful use of misdirection, Curtis thinks we've got thirty thousand men waiting for him in Pulaski County."

"We've got about fifteen thousand untrained, unequipped, barely fed conscripts," Hindman countered sourly.

"That's ten times what we had when we started." Butler waved his hand around. "You've saved Arkansas. With General Orders Number Seventeen you created the Independent Companies of Rangers to harass the Federal rear. You've opened the mines, started factories, and terrified poor Governor Rector into handing the State Guard over to your command. When you issued General Orders Number Eighteen at the end of June, you placed the entire state under martial law. *Your* martial law. Maybe the comparisons to Julius Caesar aren't that much out of line."

"What do you think, Butler? Since Shiloh, you haven't been yourself." Hindman walked his horse closer as they passed the first of Little Rock's famed gas streetlights atop its pole. They didn't work, of course, due to the lack of fuel.

Butler felt as burned out and dark inside as the light. "I don't know, Tom. I feel adrift, as if my mind is at sea. After Shiloh I *know* what's at stake. We *need* a Caesar . . . and Jefferson Davis is not that man."

Hindman glanced absently at the people they passed on the sidewalks, many pausing to watch the small cavalcade, some nodding, others bending heads close to whisper to their companions. None — Butler couldn't help but note — smiled, and many didn't offer so much as a curt nod of the head.

"That's the dilemma, isn't it?" Hindman admitted, his blue eyes hardening. "It takes tyranny to preserve freedom."

"What about when it's over? Assume we win this thing. Tomorrow, Lincoln and Davis declare peace and a cease to all hostilities. Do you just let loose of the reins?" He gestured around at the city. "Little Rock . . . Hell, all of Arkansas is a mess. If you just hold on to power, use the troops, you can order people back to work. Order prison details to rebuild the destroyed bridges and railroads. Supervise investment in new steamboats and rail lines."

Hindman's expression was lined in thought as they pulled up before the Anthony House. "It will all be different. New."

"And Tom, it's going to take an iron hand to deal with slavery. The Negroes are going to know how close they came to freedom. That's going to fester. Like it or not, if we win, you're going to have to put them on a path to freedom. That may well be the ultimate price of secession. You willing to pay it?"

Hindman's expression soured. "I don't know."

The doorman emerged, arms behind him as he awaited instructions.

"That's the perpetual trap, isn't it?" Hindman almost mumbled, still seeing things in his head.

"Call it the irony of revolution. Your policies have split the state. Even alienated some of your generals. Palmer predicted it correctly when he said a lot of folks would slip away into the swamps and forest to avoid conscription. Pro-Union sentiment has never been higher."

"At its roots, Butler, Arkansas is a Southern

state. It wouldn't be happy in the Union. You know that."

"Tom, my guess is that maybe one in ten people here have any idea of how much sacrifice, blood, and treasure it will take to win independence. I fear the explosion when they finally find out."

"I will pay any price. Even if I have to drag the people by their ears to get them into the fight. I know that many of the prominent ones have been complaining to Beauregard. Some have even traveled to Richmond to air their grievances to Jefferson Davis in person." He shrugged, looked back at the Texans sitting on their horses like centaurs. "Whatever it takes. I've crossed the Rubicon."

Butler lowered his voice to a whisper. "Negro regiments?"

"As an absolute, last means to stave off defeat, yes."

Butler swung down from his horse, handing the reins to the doorman. "I'm with you. But Tom, remember something else. The reason we had a republic in the first place was because George Washington didn't declare himself a king. And yes, Caesar was able to seize the reins of power in Rome . . . but it didn't work out well for him in the end."

Hindman chuckled softly. "Something I'll keep in mind, Butler. Now, may I wish you a pleasant —"

"General!" Robert Newton called as he burst from the door, a piece of paper in hand. "Good to see you back, sir. This came by courier today."

Newton handed the missive up. Hindman broke the seal and squinted in the dying summer light. His face had the look of stone when he lowered

228

the paper. Stared up at the evening sky where a couple of bats fluttered against the purpling heavens. Then he met Newton's curious gaze before raising an eyebrow.

"Perhaps, Butler, you're not the only one worried about my dictatorship. President Davis has just appointed Major General Theophilus Holmes as commander of the Trans-Mississippi. I am to offer him every courtesy."

"So . . . the complainers and traitors have won?" Newton asked.

"That, my friends, depends on Theophilus Holmes. Meanwhile, we have some time before he arrives. A couple of weeks, a month at most. Let's make the best of it, shall we?"

He knocked off a salute, turning his mare and trotting off toward his home where Mollie and the children were waiting.

"Never seen a man with such faith in himself," Newton muttered.

Butler nodded, clamping his eyes shut, seeing the nine deserters as muskets and shotgun blasts blew them apart. Exhausted and depressed, he swallowed hard, as if to choke off the horror.

Dear God, are they going to fill my dreams like the dying and maimed wretches from Shiloh?

"Oh, it will be all right, Hancock," Newton assured him, clapping him on the back. "Sometimes I think you care too much. Join me. I'll stand you for a whiskey in the bar."

"No, I'm tired, Robert. I'll see you in the morning."

He turned, heading for his room. As his boots trod the carpet, the execution of the nine deserters kept running over and over in his head. This would be another night of twisting and turning, of

229

nightmares filled with blood and terror.

Nine more helpless human beings. Add them to the growing tally of ghosts and demons.

"Dear God, Paw! I don't want to die!" The boy's scream — clear as a bell — was deafening in Butler's head.

"Not my responsibility," Butler whispered to himself.

But what happens when it finally is?

The voice seemed to whisper out of the very air. A sob caught in his throat.

28

October 1, 1862

The problem with a field of corn, beans, and squash was that it couldn't be moved. Sarah pondered that change of perspective. All of her life, she'd preferred farming because the field was right there, next to the house. You always knew exactly where to find it. Convenient and close at hand.

Unlike cattle, horses, or sheep that had to be followed around from one patch of grass to the next — or chickens or hogs that could wander off and get into trouble — plants just sat there, waiting to be watered and weeded, to have pests like hornworms picked off, and the raccoons kept at bay.

She had always thought planting safe and tidy.

War changed everything.

Fields, and their ripening crops, were impossible to hide. They sat naked and vulnerable to anyone passing on the road. And a lot of people had been passing since General Rains had ordered a Confederate cavalry regiment to be camped over at Cross Hollow, just south of Pea Ridge. Not only that, but new recruits were being brought in from Missouri and were being trained up at Elkhorn

Tavern. Those were a lot of mouths to be fed.

Fed what?

And by whom?

The first ears of corn were ripening, the squash full, and pods of beans at the edge of maturation. Sarah had no illusions about how her field would look to half-famished soldiers.

If only she could figure out how to keep her harvest from being "requisitioned" by desperate Confederates with empty commissary wagons.

Her few chickens, one cow, and two horses at least had been shinnied up into the mountains where Billy shuttled them back and forth out of sight. A skill at which her brother was becoming most adept.

The fields, ripening in the new October sun, were now lush from the efforts of her hard work — and Billy's, whenever he was around. It would be enough to keep her and Maw in high style through the winter, as well as provide enough of a surplus she could trade down in Fayetteville.

Assuming she could get her harvest safely past the soldiers and all the way to market. That meant driving a wagon full of food down the Telegraph Wire Road and right past the soldiers' noses. Even if she could get her crop to Fayetteville and the staples back, the army would know she had two horses hidden somewhere, and that the wagon — now propped up and "broken" — was actually sound and worth taking.

"I hate this damn war," she whispered, surprised that the profanity not only came with such ease, but that God didn't strike her down with a lightning bolt for blasphemy. But then, after what she'd seen in the aftermath of the fight up on Pea Ridge, maybe everything she'd ever been told about God was a lie.

Word was that General Curtis and his Federals had marched clear over to Helena on the far side of the state. In the Union Army's wake, General Hindman had taken cavalry up into Missouri, establishing a headquarters just across the border at Pineville. As a result, trickles of flour, molasses, salt, and sugar had been making their way up the line from Fort Smith and Van Buren, traded all the way across Texas. Clear from Mexico, of all places.

Sarah, more than anything, wanted a winter's supply — especially the flour, sugar, salt, and molasses. Little Rock and its magical future had faded like a winter mist.

She wiped her sweaty face, glancing out at the road where a lone horseman appeared from the trees, apparently on his way north from the ruins of Van Winkle's mill. The Federals had destroyed the mill just before they pulled out, thinking it to be a meeting place for Confederate bushwhackers. A lot of mills — unless they'd declared themselves Union — had been destroyed. Almost a third of them. And now the tannery was gone, too.

She glanced speculatively at her corn, then back at the rider who had stopped short where the Hancock farm lane turned off the Huntsville Road.

She murmured, "Just keep going, mister. We ain't got nothing here for you."

From his gray outfit and slouch hat, he was a Confederate officer. Following in his wake came the sound of more horses. Moments later a small band of cavalry appeared out of the trees, the distant clatter of their approach barely audible

233

over the White River's soft hush.

Sarah took a deep breath. It wasn't that unusual to see, but most Confederate cavalry used the Telegraph Road, heading up to raid Missouri.

Now the officer turned his horse, walking it up the farm lane in an almost leisurely way; he slouched in the saddle as he stared at the fallow field where the tobacco and cotton had once grown.

"Damn it!" Sarah dropped her hoe, running full tilt to the house, calling, "Maw! Riders coming! Reb cavalry!"

She dashed up onto the porch, hurrying to remove the warning bucket from the corner where Billy couldn't help but notice.

Not that he'd come stumbling into the house with a couple dozen strange horses tethered in the yard.

Sarah turned as Maw stepped out the door, wiping her hands in her apron. They were thick with acorn dough, made after leaching the nuts and then mashing them. What little flour and meal they had been able to find was now augmented by the natural produce of the forest: acorns, hickory nuts, walnuts, and hazelnuts. On racks out back wild plums were drying along with persimmon, mulberries, and chinquapins.

Again, that had been Billy's work, wild foods he'd learned from John Gritts.

The officer dallied until his small command caught up, then stepped up his approach. He seemed unusually interested in the buildings, glanced curiously at the wagon where it was propped on a timber, the splintered wheel weathering next to it.

He wouldn't see any sign of the horses, of

course. They stayed hidden up in the hills. And the real wheel — good and true — was stashed back in the wild rosebushes. The broken one had been picked up on the battlefield and was prominently displayed as a ruse that the wagon was immobile, and therefore not worth requisitioning.

Then the officer turned his eyes on Sarah and Maw. A slow smile spread beneath a ragged dark-blond beard. A glittering in the eyes where they squinted out from either side of a straight and patrician nose. Something about him . . .

Maw gasped. "Dear God!"

"Butler!" Sarah cried, dashing down off the porch.

He stepped down from the saddle, ground-reining his sorrell mare. Throwing his arms wide, he gathered her into a great hug, drawing her to his breast.

"Sarah! Sarah!" he cried. "By the sun, moon, and stars, I've missed you." He pushed her back, his gray eyes intense as he studied her. Reaching out, he pushed a couple of sun-bleached blond locks from her tanned forehead, saying, "I don't think any man alive has such a beautiful sister. Helen herself would slink from the halls of Troy at the mere mention of your name."

"You look thin," she told him. Then wrinkled her nose. "And you smell like —"

"Don't." He put fingers to her lips. "Such words should never cross a lady's lips."

Then he pushed her aside and grabbed Maw up in his bear hug, crying, "And how are you, most lovely of fine ladies?"

"I'm happy!" Maw was crying. "So happy to see you."

She held him at arm's length, looking him up

235

and down. "You've been traveling far?"

"From Fort Smith. I have a dispatch from General Hindman for General Rains. My men and I need to rest the horses and be off in the morning."

He turned, ordering, "Corporal. Bivouac the men in the field down by the river and see to my horse, please."

"Yes, Lieutenant," the corporal, a dust-covered and weary-looking young man with a Texas drawl, replied. Stepping his horse forward, he gave Sarah a dashing and devil-may-care grin, doffing his ill-shaped felt hat in the process and bowing deeply from the saddle.

She demurely responded with a slight curtsy, and lowered her eyes. Blessed be, he was a charmer with his wild honeyed locks, full-lipped smile, and dancing brown eyes.

Butler chuckled, whispering under his breath, "Don't even think it, sis. Corporal Baldy Taylor may draw women like stink draws flies, but the last thing on his mind is a fancy brick house in the city."

As the corporal led Butler's mare away, throwing appreciative glances over his shoulder the whole way, Sarah grabbed Butler's arm, saying, "Just as well. Billy'd beat the tar out of him for just looking."

Butler lifted an eyebrow. "If he's going to take on Baldy, he'd better wear his working clothes and pack a lunch."

"Working clothes is all we've got left," Maw said sourly. "And they're starting to get threadbare. But enough of this, how have you been, son? We got the one letter."

"Then you know about Paw?" he asked, as they

walked inside.

"Yes. You've heard nothing more?" Maw pulled a chair out for him.

"Not a word." Butler stood, hat in hand, as he eyed the chair. "My rear is sore enough, Mother. Let me get my land legs back. Got anything to drink?"

"Horsemint tea or spring water. What we call coffee is made from chicory root and dark-roasted corn. Can't get real coffee anymore."

Butler was staring around the house. A slow look of confusion supplanted his apparent delight at being home. "Water's fine. Where are the rugs? The divan? And half the books are missing."

"Burned after being blood-soaked," Sarah told him, walking over to slice acorn bread and dig out the tin of lard Billy had rendered from a black bear he'd killed. With the milk cow dry they had no butter. "We were used as a hospital after the big battle. Took weeks after the last of the wounded was carted off to get the blood out of the floor. Wasn't till later that Billy figured out we could have staked some of the rugs in the river and left them to clean in the current. By then it was too late."

"Didn't want 'em in here after that," Maw told Butler as she handed him a cup of water. "Just seeing the patterns again would remind me of them poor boys." Her sharp eyes fixed on Butler. "But you'd know better than we would after Shiloh."

Sarah saw the paling of Butler's face, saw his mouth quiver, the slight shake of his right hand. He dropped his gaze to the water, clasping the cup in both hands to steady it. Maw had missed his reaction, hustling back to her kitchen to open the dampers on the woodstove.

"What word of Philip?" Sarah asked quickly. "You just said he'd been taken."

Butler almost trembled as he grabbed the grease-slathered bread from her hand. Closing his eyes, he savored it as he chewed. "What kind of bread is this?"

"Made of acorns and cattail roots," Maw called, apparently satisfied with her stove. "Thank your little brother. If he wasn't half wild Indian, we'd starve."

Butler wolfed the rest of the bread and washed it down with water; then he noticed Sarah's still raised eyebrow, and said, "All I know is that Philip stayed with his wounded when Bragg's corps withdrew. As a regimental surgeon, he'll no doubt be paroled and exchanged sometime soon. He may already be free. Since he was taken, surgeons have been declared noncombatants."

Maw ladled a bowl of stew from the pot on the stove, found a spoon, and set it before Butler, who finally seated himself. "Is he still sore as a nose-twitched bear? Mad at your paw?"

Butler nodded as he spooned soup into his mouth, heedless of the drops that stuck to his mustache. "That hurt of his, it turns out, runs deep. Some wounds . . ." He paused, eyes lowered. "Well, enough said."

"What was it?" Sarah demanded. "Did you ever find out? Everything was fine one day, and the next, Philip stormed out and was gone."

Butler nodded, started to speak. Then he glanced furtively at Maw, jaws clamped tight.

"Oh, tell her," Maw said, turning tiredly away. "I knew all about it when it happened, so you're not sparing me any grief. Given what Sarah's been through, she's a grown woman now." Maw pointed her ladle at Sarah. "But don't you breathe a word to your little brother! Your word on that!"

"Yes, ma'am." Sarah turned back to Butler. "Why'd he leave?"

"He left because of a woman." Butler bit off the words.

A woman? But Paw wouldn't have cared who Philip wanted to court. It wasn't like they would have been after the same . . . She stiffened, uncertain gaze going to Maw, who'd turned her back, her attention on the stove.

Oh, Paw, how could you? But it figured. It was always the ones who loved him that he hurt the most.

"On the brighter side," Butler said with false cheer, "Philip is engaged to a socially prominent Memphis belle named Ann Marie Morton. A surgeon's daughter of good reputation. They are to be married next spring. Assuming Philip can escape the Yankees, and doesn't mind the turmoil of Memphis being a Union town."

"Is she a nice girl?" Maw asked.

"I can't tell you. The one time I was in Memphis, Tom Hindman had me running from dawn till half past midnight. Otherwise I would have called and paid my compliments. Philip, however, is besotted with love. Which, given his normally dour persuasion, is really something of a miracle in and of itself."

"Will he be all right?" Sarah asked. "I mean, what do Yankees do to prisoners? All we heard after Pea Ridge was that the Confederate prisoners were marched off to Saint Louis before finally being exchanged. They won't hurt him, will they?"

"Oh, I don't imagine it will be any fun for Philip,

but they won't go out of their way to hurt him. Like I said, he may already be free. The commission in charge worked out some complicated scheme of what rank can be traded for how many of a lesser rank, and so on and so forth. Problem is, that on a one-for-one trade, there's ten Reb prisoners for every Yank."

Sarah heard the strain in her mother's voice. "Before the battle, you did see your paw, didn't you?"

"Yes, ma'am." Butler spooned more of his soup. "He was . . . in his element. A raconteur in fine form, and his men loved him."

"What's your guess, son? Was he killed, or did he just cut and run?" Maw asked too casually.

Sarah felt her heart skip.

Butler considered, toying with his soup spoon. "Mother, I honestly don't know." His voice almost broke. "The things I saw . . ." He swallowed hard, the right hand shaking again. "Whole men just vanished . . . Blown into atoms of red mist. And the ground was so cut with ravines and woods and creeks."

"Paw wouldn't run," Sarah insisted hotly. "He killed men in duels who so much as suggested he was a coward."

Butler turned oddly glittering eyes on hers, his expression pinched and brittle. "Sister, I saw braver men than me run from that hell. I wish I'd . . . never . . ." His gaze went empty, the hand shaking again, a twitching at the corner of his mouth.

"Well, that's over with," Maw insisted as she pulled out a chair and dropped into it beside Butler. "We're so proud of you. My son, an officer. And on a general's staff."

Butler's vision seemed to clear. "And not a very popular general's staff at that. What do they say about us in Benton County? Despot? Tyrant Hindman?"

"Secesh is behind you to the Green River, as your paw would say. Union men would as soon hang Tom Hindman naked from a chinquapin tree and leave him to rot." Maw knotted her hands on the table before her. "That Order Seventeen? The one that lets any ten men declare themselves as a company of rangers? Don't you all know down in Little Rock that that sword cuts both ways?"

Butler nodded soberly. "It was that, or surrender the whole state to the Yankees. General Hindman bet that when push came to shove, most of the state would side with secession."

"Most," Maw agreed. "You'd be surprised at the number of men in Benton and Washington Counties who've slipped away in the night with their rifles to join the Union army. And then with General Curtis leaving? Tempers are starting to burn hot, son. For the moment, the county is in Rebel control, and those that suffered, like the mill owners, and the ones with sons and fathers killed by Yankees in the fighting? They've got a call for revenge on the Unionists. I've heard tell of two farms that were burned over by Bentonville. There's tales of men shot from ambush as they stepped out their front doors."

She leveled her finger at him. "Word is the Union families have started forming their own bands of rangers. There's talk of secret societies, of passwords, and meetings held in the darkest of night. Lots of folks is feeling betrayed by their neighbors, Butler. And if the army can't keep a lid on the pot, it's going to boil over."

"We're going to do our best to make sure the Federals stay gone," Butler said softly. "Under old Granny Holmes's orders, we've got nearly five thousand cavalry tying the Federals in knots up in Missouri. If we can get the country folk up there to rise for the Confederacy, the state will turn in our favor."

Sarah said, "Billy was talking to one of his friends up at the tavern. He said there was just as much Union recruitment in Missouri as there was Secesh recruitment in Arkansas. That in the end, the Federals just plain have more men."

"I suggested the recruitment of Negro regiments, offering freedom for service. To save Arkansas, Hindman would have done it. Though God alone knows what the reaction from Richmond would have been. But with Granny Holmes in charge, even that hope is gone."

"Heard the Federals recruited several Negro regiments of runaway slaves." Maw studied him thoughtfully. "How do they fight?"

"They fight as well as any other men. Which makes a lie of the old notion of Negro inferiority." Butler looked suddenly fatigued. "It boils down to a matter of will. In the end, we just have to want it more than the Federals do. Just like when we were ordered back here after Shiloh and Pea Ridge. Arkansas was defeated, and now she's back in the fight." He glanced around, as if noticing. "Where is Billy anyway?"

"Out in the woods," Maw told him. "Where none of the recruiters can find him."

"He doesn't have to hide. Not from our soldiers," Butler protested. "They can't take anyone under eighteen."

Sarah laughed, the sound of it bitter. "You've

242

been in headquarters too long. Big strapping boy like Billy? Your soldiers don't care. If Billy falls into their hands, one will look to the other and say, 'Why, I do declare, he looks like he's a solid eighteen to me.' And the other will say, 'Of course he's lying about being fifteen. He's eighteen sure. And besides, once we get him to camp, it's his word agin' ours.' "

Butler sucked his lips for a moment, an unfamiliar tension in the set of his brow. Sarah thought he looked pale, and his hair, sweat-darkened, hung in strands.

Butler asked, "He ever said so much as a word about enlisting?"

Sarah laughed. "Your brother? Last thing he wants to be is a soldier. Butler, he's the happiest he's been in his entire life! He's *hunting for a living,* and we're so thankful he is."

"Then you keep him out there, sis. You, too, Maw. I don't want him to see the things I have. You promise me."

The intensity of his words unnerved her. "Of course, Butler."

"Too many ghosts already," Butler whispered under his breath, then dropped his head into his hands, as if his soul had shriveled away inside him.

29

November 24, 1862

Did anyone ever get used to a place like Camp Douglas prison camp? Doc wondered as he exhaled frosty breath in the chill air. He plodded along, feet numb where the holes in his shoes sucked in cold with each step.

He had volunteered at the hospital and spent most of his days there. Regimental surgeon Higbee rarely stuck his nose into the place, and when he did, it was with an expression of absolute disgust.

As a result, however, Doc was subtly and occasionally successful in his attempts to influence the "medical" assistants in their ministrations to the wretched prisoners. None had had anything beyond the most rudimentary medical training. As a result, they listened when Doc made a suggestion.

For the most part, however, it had been an exercise in frustration. The lack of supplies, the intransigence of the authorities — and most of all, Higbee — to improve sanititation.

Maybe I'm just fooling myself.

He plodded his way through the crowds, glancing up at the wall: a plank fence that surrounded the prison barracks and "bull pen" where the Reb soldiers congregated and attempted to fight the incessant boredom.

Doc had to step carefully around a clot of soldiers clustered around a game of chuck-a-luck. Someone had carved a board onto which wagers could be placed. Shouts of delight or dismay went up as each roll of the three dice was made. With each round of play a fortune in tobacco and hardtack — the only wealth a prisoner in Camp Douglas could amass — hung in the balance. But it was the crafty board owner, with his dice, who was going to go back to his bunk a winner.

Young James — who didn't gamble — had a biscuit tin half full of hardtack "crackers" that he'd been carefully hoarding since the summer. His stash had made him a somewhat renowned personage among the other prisoners, and several schemes had been concocted to separate James from his crackers, but to no avail. They remained James's most prized possession.

Rounding the corner of his barracks, Doc was surprised to see James. The subject of his thoughts sat on the ground, hunched, arms crossed tight on his stomach, back against one of the posts supporting the elevated floor of the barracks. Doc needed no more than a glance: something was terribly wrong.

Hurrying forward, Doc crouched, asking, "James? You all right?"

"Nothing I won't get over." James gave him a queasy sidelong look.

"What's wrong? Stomach? You got the squirts? Cramps in your guts?"

"Naw, just feel like spewing my guts. Sick over something I ate. What it made me do."

Doc sighed, diarrhea was a constant scourge. "I know it's hard, but you've got to stick to fresh servings that have been boiled before they can turn foul."

"It ain't that, Doc," James told him with a weak grin. "Hell, neither of us has had a full belly since we got here. And all we get is slops. Reckon the Yankees enjoy keeping us ganted up and half starved. But Walker Coleman . . . You know, that big guy across the way? From down in Louisiana? It was his idea. He says, 'Reckon I'm hankering for meat, boys.' And he allows that down in the swamps he ate anything that ran, flew, swum, or slithered. And that included rat. 'Why, when you think about it, it's just meat, boys. 'Tain't no worse than opossum.' And he organizes a rat hunt."

"You went rat hunting?" Doc rubbed his chin dubiously.

James nodded, his young face morose. "It's just that when you think of it, what's a rat made of but meat? And how long's it been since any of us chewed on a piece of meat, Doc?

"So we go over to the cookhouse right at dusk last night and start hunting. You know, them damn rats have a whole city of tunnels over there. And we commences a-chasing, and stomping, and grabbing for rats every time one pokes out of his hole."

"Catch any?"

"Rats is harder t' catch than you'd think. Fast little bastards. But there's this big one. The fatted calf of all rats. He ducks into this hole, and he's gone and we got to get back to barracks for roll call. So this morning we go back with a couple of spoons, and it takes us half the day to dig this old rat out. And just as we get the hole big enough,

246

he comes shooting out.

" 'Grab 'im!' Walker yells, and I catch his tail just as he scoots down a different hole. He bunches up and sets his claws in the dirt, but I figure I got him. So I give a hard yank, and the skin just pulls off his tail, leaving bare meat and bone."

James made a face. "I'm just sitting there on my butt holding that empty skin, and it sends the shivers clear through me. It's about the most awful and horrible feeling."

"I can guess."

"So Walker gives a howl and we start digging, and sure enough, this time we get him."

James scrunched up his nose. "Doesn't take but two shakes of the lamb's tail and we're cooking spitted rat. And I got to tell you, Philip, it smells wonderful. Roasting meat. You know, it's like heaven. There's three of us, Walker, Hetch, and me, and when the rat's declared roasted, we burn our fingers picking the meat off. I put a piece on one of my crackers and take a bite, forgetting what it is I'm eating.

"I tell you, I envision it's beef. Fine veal. Some of Mama's pot roast. My eyes are closed, and I'm home in the dining room, hearing the clink of the fine china.

"And the next thing, Walker says, 'Reckon I never saw a feller look sicker than ol' James did when that rat tail come off in his fingers!' "

Doc watched James's expression turn green. "And that was it, Doc. It was like I couldn't get the feel of that loose skin off my hand, no matter how I rubbed it. Collywobbled my gut something fierce at just the memory."

"And?"

James tightened his hold on his stomach. "And I charged outside. I can't stand to have it in me. Tried to puke it up. I just keep remembering that tail pulling through my fingers and leaving that skin behind all loose and warm."

"Well, I guess you've got a right to look sick. I suppose rat's off the menu from here on out?"

James shot him a reproachful glance. "Hell, no. It's just *that* rat. 'Cause I pulled his tail off."

"Then what's bothering you?"

"You know I been saving those crackers for months now? Waiting for a special occasion to eat 'em? What really makes me sick is I run outside to poke my finger down my throat. And while I was fooling around, trying to puke up that damn rat, Walker and Hetch ate my precious biscuits. Along with what was left of my rat!"

30

December 8, 1862

The smell of roasting human flesh and burned hay pierced and clung to Butler's memory like cockleburs in his soul. For the rest of his life the mere sight of a hog would trigger his memory of the horror. The pigs were eating them! Ripping off strips of cooked human beings, snorting, chewing.

His mind seemed to reel, and he swayed in the saddle, as if the frigid night air were pressing down around him as he sat on Red. Alone in the darkness. In the middle of the battlefield.

Dear Lord God, how did I ever get here?

The plan had been audacious from the start, but something *had* to be done in northwest Arkansas.

Just not this.

Butler fought tears, as he tightened his grip on the reins. Why did every turn end in the sort of horror that left his soul on the verge of screaming, and tears streaking down his face?

The pigs are eating cooked human flesh!

The original plan of taking the war north to Missouri had collapsed as two Federal armies drove Confederate forces back south into Arkansas. Union General James G. Blunt had parked five thousand Federal troops in the vicinity of Fayetteville and Cane Hill to spend the winter.

This "army made of Pin Indians, free Negroes, Southern tories, Kansas jayhawkers, and hired Dutch cutthroats," as Tom Hindman called it in his railing diatribe, would ruin Arkansas and the Confederate cause were it not routed. And what better time than in early winter when the Federal forces were scattered across four states, in winter bivouac, and could be destroyed a piece at a time?

The winter march north from Fort Smith had been miserable. A thousand had to be left behind for want of shoes, blankets, training, or even adequate clothing. Of those ordered north, Butler had watched half-clothed — often barefoot — men marching on partially frozen roads. Despite all the rations Hindman's command could gather in advance of the campaign, for all intents and purposes, the men received half of a maintenance ration — let alone full bellies for a march. Of the nine thousand men, hundreds marched carrying weapons no more lethal than kitchen knives. The hope was that they could pick up arms from the fallen on the battlefield. Only one day's supply of ammunition was available for those who were armed.

But Arkansas had changed since Van Dorn marched north to surprise Curtis at Pea Ridge earlier that year. The state's loyalties were split; Union passion was driven by Hindman's Draconian measures. Spies and scouts were everywhere. Up in Fayetteville, Blunt knew the moment that Hindman started his First Corps north into the Boston Mountains.

What should have been an overwhelming attack

on Blunt's five thousand Yankees at Cane Hill turned out to be a daylong brawl of a battle when Francis Herron's reinforcing two divisions hit Hindman head-on at Prairie Grove Church just south of Fayetteville.

By dusk the two armies had fought to a draw.

Tom Hindman and his desperate, half-naked army had exhausted its limited ammunition. As the Federals dug in for the night, hundreds of wounded and dying lay in the bloody, burning, and shell-torn fields between the armies.

Butler had just delivered a message from General Marmaduke to Hindman at his headquarters in the Prairie Grove Church. He had waited while Francis Shoup finished his report on the few artillery rounds remaining among his batteries. Silence lay on the small gathering, broken only by the sporadic fire from the lines.

"Lieutenant Hancock, I need you to carry the flag of truce to the Yankees," Hindman had told him. "Ask for a cease-fire in order that we may retrieve our dead and wounded." Hindman's cold blue glare had burned into Butler. "Then get back here, Lieutenant, because we're out of ammunition, and we don't have rations enough to get the men back to Van Buren as it is. I need you to figure out a plan to disengage this army tonight. How can we withdraw without them damn Yankees having a clue?"

As he rode Red back across the battlefield, his white flag sagging on his shoulder, he saw the hogs in the deepening evening light. In the beginning, he couldn't figure what had drawn them to the burned and still-smoking haystacks. If they should have been at anything, they should have been worrying the tumbled corpses that were strewn across

251

the battlefield.

The haystacks — set afire during the fighting — were nothing more than heaps of white-gray ash, oddly mounded with irregular-looking lumps.

Avoiding a pile of mixed Union and Confederate dead, Butler had ridden closer — pulled Red up and stared. In the dying winter twilight, he had seen the nearest hog biting at something round. The frigid air had carried the oddly sweet smell of cooked meat, like barbecue mixed with bitter smoke.

The hog gave a vigorous yank and pulled what looked like cooked tissue free from the round . . .

"Dear God!" Butler gasped. The pale bones of a stripped human skull gleamed in the half-light as the hog's jaws snapped and chewed before going back for another bite. Yes, that swell of charred material was the chest, the legs and arms having been stirred from the powdery ash. Nor was that the only roasted corpse. To Butler's horror, he could see three or four more just in this pool of ash alone.

No more than a stone's throw to the east, more hogs were rooting in the ashes where another of the haystacks had burned.

Squealing and fighting, the hogs savaged long strips of human meat from men's legs. With tusks they sliced bellies open and gulped down long strands of roasted intestines.

Could this be real? Was he really seeing this? His breath twisted whitely about his face in the cold December air.

How? Why?

A chill deeper than the winter air leached into his soul as he glanced down at the Confederate dead in their skimpy summer-weight clothing.

Beside them, the dead Yankees wore thick coats made of wool. Frost was already settling on the grass.

The cold. That was it. They'd been wounded, crawled into the haystacks in search of warmth. Then they'd bled out or stiffened. Sparks, maybe from bursting artillery, maybe from rifles fired from the protection of the haystacks, had set the dry grass on fire.

"Dear God in heaven. The wounded . . . they burned alive in the haystacks!" Butler heard a keening sound, unaware it was his own horrified cry escaping the strangling knot in his throat.

Got to get back. Got to get the army away.

He was shaking, tears streaking his face, as he backed Red from the horrid porcine feast.

He almost lost his seat as Red shied, spooked at the half-frozen corpses she stepped on.

Butler laid spurs to her flanks.

The hogs would turn to the rest of the dead, but not until they'd finished the cooked meat.

How much can a man stand? he wondered, his thoughts spinning and sick. *When does his soul finally break to leave him weeping and weak in defeat?*

31

December 28, 1862

"I missed Butler's visit in October," Billy groused as he rode through the cold Arkansas night. "But then, not much is working out the way it's supposed to in the whole damned war."

"You're telling me?" Danny Goodman said through a grunt. He rode half a horse length behind Billy on the right, his wary eyes on the darkened woods to either side of the narrow road. It had to be nigh onto midnight.

"Butler left Maw and Sarah with the impression that the Confederate army was going to carry the war up north to Missouri. Said that General Hindman's forces would sweep in through the Yankee back door, turning the state into a staunch Rebel ally."

Danny's gray horse stumbled over a rock, Danny shifting to help the animal recover. "Yeah, well, Billy Hancock, the way that worked out was that two Union armies chased both Cooper's and Shelby's cavalry out of southwestern Missouri the way hounds chase coons out of a henhouse."

Billy nodded. "One of them Yank armies, Schofield's, marched right past the farm on their way to Huntsville. They didn't even pause long enough

254

to try to steal food. Chased them poor Rebs around Benton and Washington Counties like cats after packrats. In the end they finally managed to corner and whip a bunch over by Fort Wayne."

Hindman's Confederates had responded, marching, starved and barefoot, up from Fort Smith to that bloody fight in the snow at Prairie Grove. Through audacious skill, Hindman had managed to extricate his entire army in the middle of the night and withdraw to Fort Smith. But this time the Federals were right behind him, chasing him all the way to the Arkansas River.

Run, Brother Butler. Run!

Billy gave the whole thing his devoted consideration as he and Danny Goodman rode through the winter night, the hooves of their horses clopping on the frozen road. Around them, the trees rose like twisted black apparitions, winter-bare branches stark against the half-moon-lit and starry sky. Patches of snow — almost shining in the darkness where they lay back in the timber and along the north slopes — added to the illumination.

The buffalo coat Billy wore had been Paw's, and it had come as something of a surprise that it fit him so well. Despite the cold and snow the thing was so warm he rode with it hanging open to keep from sweating.

Danny's rather bony gray panted as it climbed the incline to the top of the ridge as they topped out of Cross Hollow with its abandoned military camps.

Billy had taken them by way of Lightning Oak Trail in order to avoid the main road as they cut west from the ruins of Van Winkle's mill. Now, after breaking out on Telegraph Wire Road, he could look back, surprised to see that the farms

255

that had once filled the bottom were gone.

"What happened to all the houses?" Billy asked.

"Abandoned, and then torn apart by the armies for firewood and coffins." Danny blew into his hands to warm them. He was huddled in a coat made from an old blanket. "I really appreciate you doing this."

Danny had tracked him down in the hills above the Hancock farm the night before, arriving at the trapper's cabin with a sack of poorly ground cornmeal and a small bottle of whiskey. A blanket had been rolled over the cantle of his saddle.

Danny interrupted his thoughts, saying, "Sam Darrow never got over it when his boy, Jackson, was killed up to Wilson's Creek. Formed himself one of them ranger companies. Said he was gonna ride down and visit the Shockup and Altee farms." He looked around at the brooding woods again. "God, I hope I'm wrong about this."

Billy, too, kept his gaze roaming. "Both Shockup and Altee came out as Union when Curtis was here. With a Federal army down to Fort Smith, and Yank troops going back and forth, a man'd have to have the bark on for sure to cause any trouble for Union folks."

"According to what I heard, that is Darrow's whole plan," Goodman said, his breath fogging in the cold moonlight. "Said he wanted to make a point to the Yankees. Said he wanted to teach 'em a thing or two. That they might march through this country, but they wasn't never going to hold it. As for me, I want to see what comes of it." He paused. "Glad you came with me."

"Why me?"

"Because I don't want to be seen. And there ain't no one can get us away if'n either Darrow's bushwhackers or the Federals spot us."

"Why do you care?"

Danny Goodman shrugged, worked his jaw. "If Darrow does this, harasses them farms, it's gonna change this country. Not 'cause old man Altee or Ben Shockup did the Darrows dirt. It's 'cause they ain't got no other sin than that they's Union."

"What of it? I ain't neither Yank or Secesh."

"Your paw and brother are Rebs, old friend. That makes you and yours Rebs. I fought for Ben McCulloch at Wilson's Creek and Oak Hill. That makes me a Reb."

"You quit. You're hiding from the conscription just like I am."

He'd taken Danny along the back ways, reveling in his proficiency at "Injuning around in the dark" and moving quietly. He just wished Danny Goodman had a better horse.

The way Billy remembered it, if he kept to the Wire Road just this side of Mud Town, in a mile or so he'd hit the lane that led to the Altee farm. It sat back a quarter mile or so from the road. Of course, if they approached that way, they'd be in the wide open where the lane ran along the fields.

But if they turned off sooner, made their way through the woods . . .

"This way." Billy reined his horse off into the forest. The snow patches and half moon allowed him to pick his way, the faint shadows giving him direction as they wound through the trees, ducking vines.

The first awareness he had of getting close came from the faint yellow glow that seemed to dance and flicker through the trees. Even as he picked it out, burning wood popped, the sound muted by the forest.

"Something's on fire," Danny whispered.

"Something big," Billy agreed, kneeing his horse around a thick black oak and onto what looked like a trail. Must have been something the Altees used for it widened into a path and led them straight to the gap between what had been the chicken coop and the tobacco barn. Both were now collapsed into burning wreckage.

As they pulled up at the edge of the trees, the scene before them was sobering. The Altee place had been built of logs, steeple-notched, and had had a shake-shingle roof and plank floors. The charred walls still stood, the roof having fallen in to feed the inferno that still shot flames toward the moon-paled night.

A woman's choked sob penetrated the fire's roar. Billy edged Swat around the fires, until he could see. The big mulberry tree in the Altee front yard was bathed in flickering yellow light. Two macabre figures hung by the neck from one of the mulberry's thick branches.

At the feet of one, a woman lay partially collapsed on the frozen dirt. She was propped up by one hand. Elsie Altee looked like a rag doll thrown down too hard on the ground. Her hair was in wild disarray, clothes scorched. Beside her, both of the girls, Eudora and Nattie, ages nine and five, crouched weeping, their heads down, hands clasped.

Something popped in the burning house, making the women and girls jump.

Billy rode closer, staring in disbelief. He'd never seen a man hung. Old man Altee, as Josiah was called, had been stripped bare, his flesh torn and filthy, as if he'd been dragged. Now he swayed with the evening breeze that blew smoke off to the southeast. Five feet down the limb, Nathaniel Altee, Josiah's son, age twelve, swung slightly out of synch with his father's corpse. Nathaniel was still dressed, but his gray cotton pants were dark down the legs where his bladder had emptied.

Both corpses hung with the heads bent awkwardly, eyes bugged out, tongues swollen and protruding from their slack jaws.

"Dear God . . . Dear God . . . Dear God . . ." Elsie kept blubbering through the sobs. As if catching the horses' movement, she blinked hard, eyes going wide, and placed a hand to her mouth. Billy had never seen such terror in another human's eyes.

"No! No! No!" She began scrambling back, reaching out, grabbing the girls to her. As each of the children caught sight of Billy and Danny, they began to shriek hysterically.

"Whoa!" Danny cried as he pulled up and stepped out of the saddle. "Easy! Mrs. Altee, we're friends. We're not here to hurt you!"

Seeing no break in her terror, Danny dropped to his knees, arms out. "See? We're here to help."

Billy watched in horrid fascination as Elsie Altee collapsed into a quivering pile, the girls clawing their way free of her suddenly limp arms.

Billy took another look at the corpses, stirred again by the breeze to sway and slowly twist back and forth. Then he turned his attention back to the incinerated remains of the house. "Sam Darrow did this?"

At his words, Elsie began to come to, lifting her head. The woman's eyes were puffy and slitted, her face swollen. "He was our friend! *We helped him build his barn!* Sent him stew when Esther was sick with the typhoid! He . . . He . . ." Her throat

259

worked, expression wild, then she reached up and clawed at her eyes.

"Here now," Danny soothed, pulling her hands down. The two girls were wide-eyed as tears rolled down their thin cheeks.

Then the wind changed, blowing hot smoke their way.

Billy bent his head, eyes slitted, covering his nose. Something inside the house burned with a sulfurous sting.

Damn! Hell's done busted loose on earth.

Old Man Altee had kin, three brothers and some cousins, down the other side of Mud Town. Elsie came from the McPhee clan over in Conway County. She was one of the patriarch's daughters. And if Sam Darrow and his rangers had hit Ben Shockup's place the way he had Altee's?

"By God, Danny, you were right. There's gonna be the devil to pay. This country's about to bust wide open."

But what did that mean for him, Maw, and Sarah?

Danny looked up. "Billy? What are we going to do?"

Billy stepped down from his horse. He wasn't sure how Darrow's bushwhackers had tied the ropes like they did, but he'd have to figure a way to get them down. Baffled by the intricate knot, he reached for his pocketknife.

"We got to care for the men, Danny. When I cut the rope, this isn't going to be pretty. Make sure the women look the other way. Then we've got to get Mrs. Altee and the girls down to kin just on the other side of Mud Town. And we got to do it before dawn."

"Why before dawn?"

" 'Cause you was right. We don't want to be seen by neither side, or we get tarred by the same brush. And me, I don't want my family looking like they're taking sides."

32

February 6, 1863

Doc shuffled and stamped as he climbed the rickety steps to the barracks. If anyone but the guards were to see — let alone care — he looked like a bundle of walking rags. He wondered when he'd grown used to lice. Somehow the perpetual burning and itching, the red welts, and constant infestation had just become "the way it is."

The wind tore his breath away, sending it cold and white to blow along the shoddy clapboard barracks wall. It had been whitewashed originally, but the thin coat of paint had faded and peeled, allowing the boards to warp. Here and there in the widest of the cracks, bits of cloth, mud chinking, and even whittled strips of bone had been used to partially seal the gaps.

Were there any good to come from the miserable cold, it was the ice-and-track-stippled, hard-frozen mud. It made footing treacherous, but stemmed the transmission of disease. Of course, when it melted, it would become a cesslike sea of excrement, thawing urine, and clinging filth.

Doc unlatched the door and hurried in, slamming it closed behind him and securing it against the wind. It should have felt warmer inside. The little tin stove was burning, its pile of sticks already dwindled to less than ten pieces.

A wood ration would be granted again tomorrow, but the small bundle of waste wood — mostly garnered from Chicago's trash — was barely enough to keep the stove alive for eight hours. Just enough fuel was provided to cook a meal in the "kitchen area" fireplace. Once the gruel was boiled, they'd stuff a dead man's frayed and pest-infested garments up into the flue to stop the exodus of what little warm air remained.

Their barracks — packed with humanity as it was — should have been appreciatively warmer than outside, but to Doc's numb face, it didn't feel like it.

As he passed down the central aisle among the bunks, curious eyes lifted and the coughing started. Anything, even Doc's passage, was of remarkable interest to the prisoners. The coughing, of course, provided the background symphony in Camp Douglas.

Near the stove he found a chess game in process. No less than ten men crowded around to watch as Baker and Halloway moved their hand-carved pieces. The board with its squares had been engraved into the floor using a piece of broken glass as a chisel.

Sylvester Moulton sat hunched beneath one of the windows reading aloud from the tattered remains of a Chicago newspaper. As Doc passed, he hid a smile. Moulton was nearing the paper's end, reading ads for employment, a piano for sale, and the incredible claims for various patent medicines. His audience sat enrapt.

Doc took a seat on the lower bunk where James Morton lay propped, his thin body wrapped in a series of blankets. He had arranged them so that the holes in one were covered by intact portions of another.

"What news?" James asked, his deep-sunk green eyes meeting Doc's.

"We're down to seven," Doc told him. "Levi Harvath died this morning. I accompanied his body when it was carried to the deadhouse. Then I went to the chief surgeon's office and made sure the paperwork was filled out. Like so many, it was typhoid."

"The paperwork? Do they do anything with that? Or does it just go into a drawer somewhere in the War Department? How many times have we heard that anyone back home was ever informed? Twice? Three times?"

"The post is unreliable. You know I don't put much stock in rumors, but I've heard on good authority that someone is fighting a war somewhere or other."

James fished inside his blankets, extracting a stained and worn envelope. "Mother manages to write."

"Wish your sister would. Four letters I've sent. If I could get the money, I'd write her every day."

The camp provost allowed a prisoner one page. It would be carefully read before being placed in the post, and it cost a relative fortune without any guarantee that it would be delivered behind the lines. To Memphis, in Union control as it was, the letters should have gone through fine.

So why hasn't Ann Marie written?

James broke into a coughing fit. At least it didn't leave him in agony anymore. His convalescence had taken much too long, and truth be told, had James been asked to walk all the way across the compound, he'd have collapsed at the halfway point.

Seven of us left.

Of those captured with Doc at Shiloh, only John Mays and Augustus Clyde had been paroled and exchanged. Paperwork had come through that they were surgeon's assistants, and noncombatants. Doc had stood by the main gate, watched as they were searched, and then led out to begin the march to the railroad station. That had finally happened in September.

"I think it's my fault," Doc said, looking down at his dirt-encrusted hands.

"That Ann Marie hasn't written? What did you tell her in that last letter?"

"No. I mean I think it's my fault that we haven't all been paroled."

"How?" James asked.

"When I talked to the provost, he protested that he had no paperwork for the release of any Dr. Philip Hancock. That surely it was a paperwork error, and eventually it would be straightened out."

The man had smiled as he'd said it.

"Can't blame yourself for a paperwork error."

"James, it was after I made that first big fuss. When I bearded Higbee about conditions. That's when the records for our group of Shiloh prisoners disappeared. The miracle is that Clyde and Mays made it out."

When Doc had asked, an arrogant, fresh-faced lieutenant had told him: "I'm sorry, sir. While we have records of your interment here, we have no records of when or where you were originally processed. Therefore, we cannot give you preference for parole and exchange."

It's my fault! These men are dying because of me.
He'd gone after Higbee. Raised too much hell. Complained to the Sanitary Commission.

"I know that look," James told him. "You're punishing yourself again."

"Since that first time I've tried to make amends, James. Kept my silence. Hoped that the occasional hint, the dropped suggestion, might get our Shiloh prisoners finally placed onto the list."

And then there was James. And his promise to Ann Marie.

Who never wrote.

Only seven of them left.

Camp Douglas was better at killing Confederates than the entire Federal army. In any given month, roughly ten percent of the camp's prisoners died from pneumonia, typhoid, diarrhea, influenza, the periodic outbreak of measles or mumps, catarrh, and, God forbid, the occasional smallpox case.

Since no one else cared — except for the occasional inspector from the Sanitary Commission — Doc had taken it on himself to look after the pesthouse where the worst of the cases were taken.

She should have at least received one of those letters.

"I see that look," James said softly. He waved the missive from Felicia again. "There have just been two of Mother's letters that have been delivered. And in this last one from October Mother states that she'd written at least four before this. We don't know how many get lost."

"I know." He closed his eyes, imagining Ann Marie's face, the freckles on her nose. How her eyes . . . Dear God, they were green, weren't they? And her hair. Chestnut, yes? Auburn?

A sense of panic sent a shiver through his nerves.

266

The freckles. Hold on to the freckles. They were a constant.

"Are you all right, Doc?"

He took a deep breath of the cold air, wondering when he'd stopped smelling the stench. "It's the damnedest thing, James. For an instant . . . I couldn't remember what Ann Marie looked like."

"Philip, for the love of God, take yourself down from this impossible meat hook you've hung yourself on. You've done everything you could to save each and every one of us. You're using up so much of yourself for the rest of us that there is nothing left for you."

But it is my fault.

"Besides," James told him with a smile. "I know Ann Marie. She's my sister. Writing just isn't one of her talents. Drawing, singing, sewing, and planning entertainments? That's her."

"At least your mother said she was all right." Doc looked down at his hands, the nails black, grime seemingly ground into the lines. Would they ever be clean again? "It's just that it's a year, James. My time is up. I am supposed to be back in Memphis, my accumulated pay in hand. With her. That was the dream."

He placed his head in his hands, whispering, "I shouldn't be struggling to remember her. She should be laughing for me in life, and not just in a fading memory. I've failed her."

He felt James's hand on his shoulder. "No you haven't. You enlisted with Neely's Fourth Tennessee promising her that you'd take care of me, remember? I'm still alive, Doc. You've kept your word to Ann Marie."

Then why aren't we back in Memphis, James?

33

March 17, 1863

Butler climbed the steps to Major General Hindman's residence in Little Rock — the house the general had rented for Mollie, himself, and the children. A private, in a much-too-clean uniform, saluted from port arms, and said, "The general asked that you proceed inside, Lieutenant. He is in the parlor."

Butler nodded, entered, and immediately wished he'd attended to his boots — muddy and scuffed as they were. Nor had his uniform been cleaned in days, and he knew he smelled like horse, mud, and sweat.

To minimize the damage, he tried to mince his way across the hall so as not to leave tracks or soil the carpet. Glancing sideways into the main room he saw it was filled with trunks and valises: evidence of the general's immediate departure. Then Butler caught the barest glimpse of Mollie Hindman in a rustling green crinoline dress as she hurried past a far door.

At the entrance to the parlor, Butler stopped and cleared his throat. Hindman sat at his desk, his uniform immaculate. He was in the act of dipping his pen into the ink bottle before he continued writing on a piece of foolscap.

"Come in, Lieutenant. And don't mind your boots."

"Sir?"

"Tiptoeing across the floor?" Hindman, not even bothering to straighten, pointed the end of his pen at the mirror set off to one side. It gave the general a perfect view of anyone entering the parlor. "Had that installed back after we declared martial law. I figured that the guards would keep me from getting shot through the window, but I wanted to have an edge if someone were to sneak in from behind."

That was when Butler noted the Colt on the desk beside Hindman's right hand. Tom Hindman, after all, might be the most hated man in Arkansas, but he had never acted the fool.

Relaxing, Butler strode into the parlor, taking in the fine furniture, the polished mantel over the fireplace, and the gleaming piano with its silver candlestick holder. Beyond the general's teakwood desk, the street was visible through beveled-glass panes in the French window.

"They've won," Hindman said as he signed the missive he'd been working on. "It was inevitable, I suppose. Turns out that it proves impossible to save a people who, quite simply, do not want to be saved. Think of how much worse it would have been if I'd agreed to your Negro regiments."

Butler shifted uncomfortably. "Sir, if it hadn't been for the condition of our troops at the Prairie Grove fight . . . Half-starved, barefoot soldiers, with a day's supply of ammunition, can't be expected to best —"

"Don't blame the troops, Lieutenant. It was a long shot. We knew the odds when we marched

north." Hindman turned in his chair, his thoughtful blue eyes focusing on Butler's. "Unfortunately,
long shots are all that we have. The Federals have
more resources, including men, commissary,
arms, artillery, and . . . well, everything else. The
only thing we have more of is audacity and will.
Robert E. Lee can fight a defensive war in Virginia.
That strategy in the west is nothing more than a
hurtling disaster coming our way."

"Which is why you've stressed the cavalry?"

"If nothing else, that may be my greatest contribution."

Hindman stood and walked over to the map that
remained open on the parlor table and pointed.
"Where have we ever prevailed in a defensive position, Butler? Fort Hindman down at Arkansas
Post? They marched thirty thousand Federals and
sent a slew of gunboats against it. Our fight at
Prairie Grove? We didn't have the commissary or
ammunition to have exploited an advantage even
if we had gained one. But large bodies of cavalry?
Ah, yes. They have the mobility, the speed, and
the tactical ability to turn the Yankees' advantage
of men, resources, and area into a liability. Five
thousand cavalry can attack Independence, Missouri, one day, and two weeks later, raid Saint
Louis itself. And in the meantime, they can rip up
railroads, burn bridges, tear down telegraph wire,
and burn out pro-Union settlements, sending
those people into flight. By the time the Federals
can muster enough force to repel the threat, our
cavalry is already back in Arkansas."

Hindman gestured with his pen. "It will change
the entire nature of the war in the west. And
perhaps, just perhaps, it will jade the people to
the point they rise and give the Federal Congress

an ultimatum: stop the war!"

This isn't war against armies that he's talking about. It's war against people.

Butler realized his right hand was trembling and stuffed it into his coat. God, it just kept getting worse.

"But that is for another to deal with," Hindman said as he turned away, a seething behind his eyes. "I have never shied from a political fight, Butler. You warned me that pursuing my policies would prod the hornet's nest."

At mention of the hornet's nest, the scene from Shiloh flashed in Butler's mind: men being blown apart, others screaming agony, the whistle of the minié balls. So intense and real was it that he jerked, ducking.

"Lieutenant? Are you all right?"

Butler blinked, suddenly back in Hindman's parlor. "Sorry, sir. Perhaps I am fatigued." He smiled, and to change the subject said, "This isn't your fault. Governor Rector hates you. As does Henry Foote. That journalist James Butler and his ilk would allow Arkansas to suffocate in its own blood before they'd admit you were right. General Pike did everything he could to cut your throat. Were you an ordinary man, Tom, the entire Arkansas congressional delegation in Richmond wouldn't have marched up to the Confederate white house and demanded that Jefferson Davis replace you."

That brought a humorless smile to Hindman's lips. "Yes, I suppose that one's qualities can indeed be judged by the number and caliber of his enemies. But enough of that. The reason I called you here is to give you this."

Hindman took an envelope from the desk, hand-

271

ing it to Butler. "Those are your orders. I am having you transferred out of Arkansas."

"I'm not going with you to Vicksburg? To work on the Board of Inquiry? I thought we were supposed to investigate culpability in the surrender of New Orleans to the Federals?"

"Butler, you have become my friend . . . and in many ways, my conscience. For that I am eternally grateful. What you are not, is a political animal. You don't have the necessary killer instinct for the sport. In the coming months I shall be pilloried in the press, and perhaps even indicted over my actions here. I would spare you the trauma and trial, let alone have your career further tarnished by my association."

"Tom, I may not have —"

"Therefore," Hindman interrupted, "I am sending you back to General Hardee. You impressed him in the past, and I've written to him about the immense help you have been to me in the governing of Arkansas. I emphasized how your genius for organization allowed our successful retreat from Prairie Grove. You are to report to his headquarters at the Army of Tennessee in Chattanooga where you will accept a field command and promotion to the rank of captain."

Butler stared woodenly at the envelope. He was going to the front lines? He would be in command of a company, leading men into the cannons and massed musketry?

The tremor in his hand worsened, and he flexed the muscles in his arm to stop it. The sensation of panic tightened the insides of his chest; he took a deep breath, forcing it away.

In a dry voice, he said, "Thank you, sir. I don't think that I'm the right —"

"It's done, Butler." Hindman's eyes had hardened into a stone-cold blue. "Don't let me down."

34

July 17, 1863

The first Sarah knew of the riders was when old Fly lifted his nose and began to sniff the breeze. His ancient eyes had been going white, and the dog could barely see. Nothing was wrong with the fur on his back, however. It now rose into a bristling mane.

Sarah straightened from where she was hoeing weeds from among the bean plants. Fly growled, struggled to his arthritic feet, then he *bowwww-wooowed* his warning bark.

Sarah carefully looked around. The hot air was filled with the clicking sounds of insects, backed by the White River's soft murmur. Heat waves rose over the fallow cotton and tobacco fields down by the river, now gone back to weeds and grass. The Huntsville Road beyond the lane looked like a white scar in the green.

The breeze, however, came from the east, down from the forested slope that rose behind the house. And it was in that direction that Fly continued to sniff and growl. Again he let out his half-howling bark.

"What is it, Fly?" She set her hoe down, leaning close to the dog. A stick snapped up in the forest, barely audible over the hum of insects.

She could feel it, some wrongness.

She was halfway to the house when she caught the first hint of movement back in the trees. Then another, and another.

A horse and rider slipped between a gap in the green forest wall.

"Maw! Riders coming!"

Sarah slowed as the first of the riders emerged from the trees: a young bearded man in a buckskin jacket, his stringy black hair hanging down past his collar. The thin face, pointed nose, and hunger-hollowed cheeks reminded her of a living skull. Nor did the scrawny beard do much to offset the youth's hard brown eyes. He held a carbine at the ready on the saddle.

From the right, the hazelnut, rosebushes, and honeysuckle crackled as another man forced a big black horse through the tangle. Older, perhaps in his late twenties, he cradled a shotgun, his thickly bearded features hidden by a low-brimmed hat. What she could see of his face was round, the mouth small and pursed. His eyes, like blue ice, fixed on Sarah with a predatory intensity so powerful she started as if physically violated.

He seemed to read her sudden fear, his mocking leer adding to her discomfort.

A line of horses emerged from the creek trail behind the house, and yet another horseman appeared from the river trail to the west.

Nine in all, they rode into the yard, taking positions around the house. All of them hard-looking men, wearing filthy gray, butternut, and homespun. Most of them had blue Yankee uniform coats tied atop the blankets on their saddle cantles.

"Good day, ma'am," one of the older men,

maybe thirty, said, touching a finger to his worn hat brim as he gave a slight nod of the head. "This hyar might be the Hancock farm?"

Sarah's heart had started to pound, that sick sensation of fear tightening her muscles. "Who might be asking?"

It was the black-bearded, blue-eyed rider who spoke: "They call me Colonel Dewley. Dewley's Home Guard, at your service ma'am." When he grinned, it was to expose broken teeth behind his small pursed lips. His wide nose and plump cheeks gave his face a full look. But his eyes, already so cold, were changing as he looked her up and down. A predatory tension sharpened his gaze, his lips beginning to twitch as he fixed on the way her shirt clung to her sweat-damp breasts.

Sarah stepped back reflexively, and crossed her arms over her chest.

"It's the Hancock farm," Maw called from the porch. "What's your business here, Colonel?"

Dewley's smile, like some deadly insolent thing, widened. For a long moment, he let his gaze linger on Sarah, then turned his attention to Maw. He fixed on the double-barrel shotgun she rested butt-down on the floorboards.

The second he did, the spell seemed to break, and Sarah fled to the porch, stumbling, almost shaking as she rushed, childlike, behind her mother's protection. Her joints had gone weak, as if her legs didn't want to hold her.

In the yard, Fly continued with his drawling bark, tail wagging slowly as if trying to decipher the good or evil of the invaders.

"Ma'am," Dewley said with the flick of a finger to his brim. "We're just passing through. I think they call it canvassing. A sort of campaign. Where might your sympathies lie in the current troubles?"

Sarah glanced again at the Union-blue coats behind the saddles, and then at the weapons Dewley's men carried. An assortment of shotguns, and a sprinkle of different, apparently new, breechloading carbines. Rumor told of bushwhackers who wore stolen Yankee uniforms to ride into Union territory before murdering all around them.

"We're Secesh," Sarah called proudly. "Paw was killed at Shiloh under Bragg. My brother's a captain in Hardee's Corps."

A look of disappointment crossed Dewley's face. "That is good to hear, Miss Hancock. Good indeed. We were almost deceived by the apparent prosperity of your farm. So many loyal Southerners have not fared so well, having paid for their dedication to our cause. Suffering Yankee aggression and persecution, they are left destitute. All this in the wake of Captain Darrow's foul ambush and murder by traitorous, jayhawking Altee and Shockup Unionists."

"I don't recognize you, Colonel," Maw said warily. "And I know most folks hereabouts."

"We hail from over to Marion County, ma'am. It has been our honor to cleanse our home country of traitors and defeatist cowards. We have been asked by friends and patriots to extend our patrols here. In the wake of that inept despot Hindman's defeat at Prairie Grove, we have been told that a vile taint of Unionism has been springing up here in the northwest. We cannot allow that to happen." He smiled again, showing his broken teeth.

"Thank you for your concern, Colonel." Maw stepped to the edge of the porch, pointing. "At the end of the lane, take a right on the road. Six miles up, atop Pea Ridge, you'll come to Elkhorn Tavern and the Telegraph Wire Road. Watch out for Federal cavalry and patrols. If you're looking for the latest information, the tavern is the place to find it. Be careful, Colonel."

Dewley's lips were twitching again as once more he turned his attention to Sarah, a quickening in his ice-cold eyes. His hands clenched and unclenched, fingers working over the reins, as if he were grasping and caressing something in his mind.

The rest of the men, too, were staring at Sarah as if they'd never seen a woman before. The thin-faced young man had started to smile, licking his lips, a curious glittering in his eyes.

"We've had a long ride, ma'am," Colonel Dewley said casually. "Might there be a drink to be had? Forage for our horses?"

"River's yonder," she told him. "You see them trees down to the south? Five miles beyond, on the Huntsville Road, is the ruins of Van Winkle's mill. It's all gone to grass, flat for good camping, and sweet water. You can see clearly for a mile in every direction. That's the junction between the Huntsville Road and the cut-across through Cross Hollow. If a Yankee cavalry patrol were to appear, you'd have time to withdraw. There's the three roads and another six trails that take off up into the hills and up War Eagle Creek."

"I take your meaning, Mrs. Hancock." He kept his hungry eyes on Sarah. "With my deepest respect, ma'am," he added, but Sarah wasn't sure if he meant Maw or her, or if it were being said in mockery.

With a flip of the reins, Colonel Dewley spurred his big black horse and led the way out of the yard. One by one, the men withdrew to follow, each one taking a last look about as if memorizing the yard, the buildings, and house. But most of all, they kept looking at Sarah, each with a promise behind his eyes that she didn't want to think about.

Heart still pounding, Sarah gasped in relief as the last of them rode down the lane. "I've never been that frightened by a man in my life."

Maw picked up the shotgun, her eyes hard as she watched the bushwhackers wade their horses into the White River to drink. They were talking among themselves now, all of them looking back, some laughing.

"Sarah, I want you to go in the house and stay out of sight for a couple of days."

Just the tone in Maw's voice kept the shiver alive along Sarah's backbone.

"Do you think they'll be back?"

"Hope not." Maw drew a deep breath and blew it out as if exhaling an unreasonable tension. "I've never hoped for any man's death before, but it would suit me just fine if they ride up to the tavern and smack into a company of Federal cavalry."

For the rest of the day, Sarah had the jitters. And that night, even though she propped chairs against the doors in addition to throwing the bolts, Dewley's blue eyes burned through her dreams and left her trembling, alone, and scared.

35

September 3, 1863

The last of the light was fading over Lookout Mountain where it rose like a dark leviathan to the west. The mountain's northernmost point dropped off to mark the Tennessee River Valley west of Chattanooga. To the north, past the lines of worn tents, the rooftops of the city were barely visible in the shadows.

The smell of wood smoke hung low in the warm summer air, accented by frying bacon, roasting corn dogers, and what passed for coffee among General Bragg's ragtag Army of the Tennessee.

Butler's Company A served in a regiment composed of the combined Second and Fifteenth Arkansas, of Liddel's brigade, in Hill's Corps. His old friend Colonel Daniel Govan was in charge. The second and fifteenth had been combined like so many of the original Arkansas units. After two and a half years of war and endless losses from disease and fighting, the ranks had been worn so thin that combining them was the only way to keep them operational.

Where they were camped south of Chattanooga, Butler's Company A was but one in the long rows of hodgepodge tents and shelters. Men gathered around their evening fires, playing cards, mending, talking softly. The firelight played on their bearded faces, sparkling in their eyes.

"My men," Butler whispered to himself as he strolled slowly down the line.

Until Butler had walked into General Hardee's headquarters, he'd hoped he could convince the general that he was best suited for a staff position, carrying orders, organizing movement, commissary, and supply. The timing of his arrival could not have been worse. Butler had arrived just as Hardee was being transferred to the Department of Mississippi; General Daniel Hill was taking command of Hardee's old corps.

Hardee, however, had given Butler a paternal smile, and said, "I know for a fact that in the old Arkansas regiment there is a company that needs a captain. The boys there know you and will be delighted to have you at the helm."

Why hadn't he protested?

The words seemed to pop out of the still evening air: *You fool! You were too much of a coward to say no.*

He looked around him, seeing no one close. Sometimes, like tonight, the voices would speak out of thin air. He heard them so clearly.

He made a face, worried. It still surprised him when others didn't react, showed no sign at all that they'd heard.

"What's wrong with me?"

"Cap'n?" Sergeant Amos Kershaw asked from the nearest fire, apparently having overheard. The big Cajun with his blocky face, midnight hair, and black eyes had enlisted in Helena, Arkansas, back in '61 when Tom Hindman first called for volunteers. He'd risen through the ranks to sergeant, and the men loved him.

Dan Govan had told Butler, "If I could give you one piece of advice? Pay attention to whatever Sergeant Kershaw says or suggests. The man knows his business."

Butler pulled his pipe from his pocket as he stepped over to Kershaw's fire. Squatting in the circle of men, he used his thumb to pack tobacco into the bowl, and Corporal Willy Pettigrew to his left reached for a burning stick to light it.

Butler puffed, then exhaled, aware that the men were watching him curiously. "I was just talking to myself. Happens sometimes."

"Reckon we all do." Kershaw smiled wistfully in agreement. " 'Specially around dis outfit. Ain't nobody worth talkin' to but yerseff, Cap'n. The rest of these here scoundrels cain't hardly string a sentence t'gether."

"Well, Sergeant, stringing a sentence doesn't make a man a good soldier." Butler noticed that blond-headed Jimmy Peterson, across the fire, seemed to be antsy, looking every direction except toward Butler, and his right hand was held behind him.

"Private?" Butler asked. "Something wrong with your hand?"

"No, suh." Peterson swallowed hard, the others in the circle suddenly looking uneasy.

"Produce that hand, Private, and whatever's in it."

Peterson went pale, winced, and eased a tin cup from behind his back. "Just my drink, Captain."

Butler nodded in sudden understanding. "Orders are that no alcohol is to be consumed in camp. Penalties for violation are a bit draconian."

"Draconian?" Kershaw wondered, all the while looking sorrowfully at Peterson. Panic filled the private's blue eyes.

"Severe, Sergeant," Butler said, aware that the men had all frozen, expecting something terrible. "Flogging is prescribed in extreme cases."

Peterson's eyes closed, and he swallowed hard.

None of the men would meet Butler's eyes.

"Now me," Butler resumed casually, "I'm a stickler for regulations, and I've served with Tom Hindman for all these years, and you all know his feelings on spirits."

"Cap'n, it's just a cup," Kershaw said reasonably. "And I reckon we's all sharing it a'fore ya'll walked up."

"Actually, it's my cup," Johnny Baker admitted and ran a hand through his long brown hair. "Anybody gonna be punished, it otta be me."

So, they'd all take the blame for each other? Touched, Butler reached out a hand. "Private Peterson, pass me that cup if you please, and for God's sake don't spill any of it."

The cup was carefully passed from hand to hand around the circle. Butler grasped it by the handle, lifted it to his nose, and sniffed. Rotgut for sure. He sipped and made a face as the stuff burned on his tongue. "Dear Lord God, that's terrible!"

Butler passed it to Kershaw. "Try that, Sergeant. Take a good taste."

Kershaw did so warily. "Reckon I've had better, Cap'n."

"Sergeant, anything that tastes that vile can't be drinking whiskey. No, indeed. That has to be medicinal spirits."

Kershaw was giving him a speculative, sidelong glance, the cup handle grasped in his thick fingers.

Butler waved a hand at him. "Well, pass it on, Sergeant. Each and every one of you men, take a taste."

Kershaw passed it to Corporal Pettigrew, who sipped, and passed it along to Private Phil Vail, who passed it to Baker, and on around the circle until it came back to Butler, who forced himself to drain the last couple of drops from the cup.

The soldiers were watching him with no little confusion and uncertainty.

Butler took a pull on his pipe to dull the taste of what had been pure corn liquor, then said, "My brother is a surgeon, therefore I have some understanding of the uses for medicinal spirits. Private Baker, I assume there's more where that came from?"

"Some." Baker winced. "Yes, suh."

"My standing orders with regard to your medicinal supply are no more than one sip per man per night as a precaution against the ague." He winked at Baker. "Am I understood?"

"Yes, sir!" Baker snapped off a salute. The rest of the men were grinning.

"Pass the word, Sergeant, that according to orders, there will be no drinking in this company. *Medicinal* spirits are another matter." He looked around at the expectant faces, and pointed with his pipe stem. "But if I catch anyone drunk, that privilege goes away. We understood?"

"Reckon the company appreciates that, Cap'n." Kershaw grinned and gave him a respectful nod.

Butler shifted and stared at the fire. "Colonel Govan has it from headquarters that most of the Federal army is on this side of the Tennessee and moving in from the west." He pointed at where Lookout Mountain lay like a black lump along

284

the western horizon. "They're just over yonder. Bragg is probably going to withdraw us into Georgia to make a stand."

"That ain't gonna sit well with the Tennessee boys. They ain't gonna want to leave the state," Corporal Pettigrew noted.

Baker whispered under his breath, just loudly enough that Butler could hear: "Bully for General Bragg. He's just hell on a retreat."

"The city of Chattanooga can't be defended. It's in the bottom of a bowl. Our only hope to whip them is to withdraw."

"So we drop back and hit 'em on ground of our own choosing," Kershaw said as he fingered his beard and stared at the fire.

"That's the plan."

"When we moving, Cap'n?"

"Govan says tomorrow. My take is that he's pretty good at reading General Bragg."

"I just want it over," Frank Thompson said. "I ain't been back to Helena in two years. That's home. And now, with the Yankees there, I can't go back even if I get furlough."

"Yeah," Phil Vail muttered. "Most of eastern Arkansas is filled with Yankees."

"All but the far southwest corner," Butler agreed. "But if we finally can deliver one crushing blow to the Federals here, maybe they'll withdraw some of their forces from Arkansas."

"Do you think so, sir?" Corporal Pettigrew asked. "Last I heard they was dug in all along the Arkansas River from Fort Smith to the Mississippi."

Butler pulled contemplatively on his pipe, eyes on the fire.

"I just want to go home," Johnny Baker said

wistfully. "It's three years since I seen my wife, Missey. My boy, Jasper, is five now. My daughter, Lillie, is coming four."

"At least you seen yor kids," Billy Templeton told him. "I got to spend lessen a month with Serena after we's married. My boy William? He's most three now hisseff, and I ain't never so much as laid eyes on him."

Phil Vail looked around with green eyes. "Eighteen of us enlisted together at Barley Station. Not that it's much, out in the swamp like it is. 'Cept for me, ain't a man from there still alive." He shook his head. "Pap, Marcus, and the rest? Who'd a thought it would be me that made it?"

"They ain't a-gonna get you, Vail." Kershaw's smile created a deep dimple in his cheek. "All them fights you been in and you ain't so much as got a scratch, *sans dommage*."

"What about you, Sergeant?" Butler asked. "How'd you end up in an Arkansas regiment?"

Kershaw's dark eyes sparkled. "How's a man ever get hisself in trouble? *La femme fatale.* A woman, *oui*? She owns one of the establishments on de riverfront. A place you, Cap'n, as a gentleman, would not go. My wish was always to take her back to Bayou Teche, but I am not sure she would be happy."

Phil Vail grinned to expose crooked teeth and declared, "I got three women waiting for me. There's mother and my two sisters." He wrapped his arms around his knees where they poked out of the worn holes in his trousers. "I'd like to go back to Arkadelphia and find me a wife. I promised God that if he'd get me through this, I'd be the best husband and father ever. I'd never cuss, and I'd be in church every Sabbath." He paused.

286

"Not so much to ask, is it?"

"Reckon not," Jimmy Peterson told him as he pulled at his ear. "Sometimes I just cain't figger God's doin' in all this. Most of the boys we lost up to now was good men. Lot of 'em better than me by a long shot. And they's some black sinners that I'd figger God would'a taken right off, or at least mangled and maimed fer being dastardly. And they've come through without so much as a close nick. And if anything, they's worse scoundrels now than when the war started."

"And don't fergit the Yankees," Matthew Johnson said. "They catch as much grief as we do come a hard fight. So it ain't like God's playing sides."

"Yep," Kershaw agreed. "They just catch it with a stomach full of food, wrapped in a thick blanket, with good shoes an' wool socks on their feet, and wearing a warm uniform what don't got holes in the elbows, knees. Or seat of the britches."

Corporal Pettigrew's expression soured. "So, you're saying God's a Yankee supply officer?"

"Lordy," Jimmy Peterson whispered. "Makes sense, because the only reason we could be as short as we always are on clothing, food, ammunition, and guns is if Lucifer himself is in charge of our rations and supply."

"You ever think of what this army could do if we had half of what the Yankees get?" Frank Thompson wondered. "Hell, we'd be camping on Abe Lincoln's White House lawn!"

"Reckon if'n they'd a give us the shoes, we coulda marched circles around the damn Yank army and took Washington from behind," Vail groused.

Butler thought back to Prairie Grove. They'd

had to leave a thousand men behind for lack of shoes. Had to leave the battlefield to the Federals because Hindman's scarecrow Rebel soldiers didn't have the powder to fight a second day, or even a meal to see them on the start of the long retreat.

Thinking of those men, he stared at the firelit faces around him. All they wanted was a chance to get home. Was that such a bother to God? Was it worth the right for rich men to keep slaves? Or even Lincoln's supposed sanctity of federal Union?

One by one he studied them, cataloging their eyes, faces, the set of their mouths, the mannerisms. Each a vibrant life full of dreams and hopes. Some of the bravest men alive, most were little more than boys annealed by fires into a different kind of metal. If the preachers were right, and this was God's work, where was the justice that denied a man from seeing his son, wife, or mother and sisters?

It's up to you to keep them alive, the voice whispered beside his ear. *Your responsibility to get them home.*

36

September 7, 1863

Dear James:

We received your letter of July 28, and understand that its brevity is dictated by the rules of your captors. You are constantly in our prayers, and we pray earnestly that this ghastly war will be over and you can come home to the family that loves you. We are all well here.

You would be surprised to learn that Memphis has been thriving under Federal rule. And with the fall of Vicksburg, river traffic has once again begun to boom. Your dreams of a steamboat of your own are better now than ever before. With the river open we have been receiving plenty of flour, sugar, and coffee and the prices have fallen. Good thing we kept our northern currency since Confederate paper is worth nothing here anymore.

Mollie Henderson stopped by for a marvelous visit this morning, having been relieved to discover her husband, Peter, is alive and well and back in the ranks after having been listed as missing in the fighting over at Murfreesboro.

Colonel Mason tells us that we can send packages to you at Camp Douglas through the regular post and we shall do so. As I mentioned in my last letter, the good Colonel will be making enquiries about the possibility of getting you paroled. He also noted that if you would be willing to swear a loyalty oath to the United States he might be able to get you back to Memphis. I think you two would hit it off splendidly, and he is such a good match for your sister.

Do consider the parole. From the looks of things the war will be over by next summer, and the question of secession will have been decided one way or another. It was bad enough that you missed your sister's wedding. Should providence permit, we would love to have you home in the event you might become an uncle.

All of our love,
Mother.

"I don't understand." Doc dropped limply to the ground where James sat in the sunlight. For the moment even the itching and burning of lice and flea bites was forgotten.

James reached out, carefully taking the letter from Doc's nerveless fingers. James leaned his head back, eyes closed in the bright sunlight. The letter hung between his fingers to waffle in the cool breeze blowing in from Lake Michigan.

"All them times you wrote her? Maybe she never got them letters. Maybe she thought you forgot her."

Doc reached a hand to his chest as if he could soothe the odd emptiness inside. All he felt was bones, the fragile skin beneath his threadbare shirt, and the hollow where his shrunken gut receded under the rib cage. But then they were all walking skeletons, especially if they'd been in the camp for any length of time.

In his memory, Ann Marie smiled at him with love, eyes dancing with promise.

"She married a colonel. Whose colonel? Reb? Yank?"

"Reckon Yank," James said softly. "No Reb colonel would be wanting me to give a loyalty oath to the Union."

Doc blinked his eyes. An eerie keening wanted to rise up through his lungs and trachea.

She's married?

"Doc, don't," James told him. "I know how much you loved her."

"Loved?" His voice broke. *"Loved?"*

He staggered to his feet, aware of the hundreds of bored men crowding the yard around them.

James was standing, hands on Doc's shoulders. "Why the hell didn't you leave, Doc? You could have made a stink, demanded that they release you on parole as a noncombatant! *You could have gone home!"*

Doc shrugged off the restraining grip. He staggered forward, vision silvered.

From long familiarity, he knew the slope of the deadline. All he had to do was march up that angled soil. So many others had taken the route before him.

"Doc!" James screamed in his ear. "Damn you! Stop it!"

Doc angrily flung James's restraining hand from his shoulder. In the process, he blinked enough of the tears away to see the slope. Four paces, three, two, just another . . .

Hard hands grabbed him from behind. He was jerked backward, his foot lifted high for the next and fatal step. With a grunt, he hit the ground, smelling the reek of piss. Confederate prisoners made a point of urinating on the deadline. One of the few acts of defiance that they could actually get away with.

Three bodies landed on top of his, knocking the wind from his lungs.

"What the hell are you doing, Doc?" Andy McNeish's face shoved close, his ragged gray kepi at an angle on his blond head.

"He just learned his fiancée married another," James said.

"Thought that was your sister!"

James sounded miserable. "Just . . . leave it be, okay?"

"Goddamn," one of the other men holding Doc declared. "If Doc, of all people, can give up like this? Ain't none of us safe."

Doc felt his shoulders shaking, and reached out desperately, pleadingly, for the Yankee guard up on the walk.

The man was watching him, rifle raised, waiting for him to set foot on the deadline. A slight smile lay on the guard's lips, his aiming eye bright with anticipation over the rifle's sights, the other squinted closed.

"Just let me go," Doc pleaded.

"You ain't thinkin' right, Doc," McNeish growled into his ear. "You kept too many of us alive to let you squander yourself like this."

They jerked him to his feet, keeping their hold. A ragamuffin crowd had formed, delighted for this break in the ceaseless boredom. Now they waited, watching to see what would happen next.

As James, McNeish, and Ab Smith dragged Doc back toward the barracks, the guard up on the walk sighed and lowered his rifle. At Camp Douglas there was always another chance to kill a prisoner. He need only wait.

37

September 19, 1863

Bully for General Bragg. He's hell unleashed when it comes to a retreat. That was the joke in the Army of Tennessee.

And right now, we could use a little retreat, Butler thought.

The day's fighting had been a bloody seesawing through the thick Georgia forest southwest of Chattanooga. Men shot, ducked behind trees to reload, and popped out to shoot again. A mayhem of bullets hissed through wreaths of smoke, the smacking of lead into hardwood. Falling branches and leaves — ripped from on high by shot and shell — came raining down from the thick canopy above. Masses of men had struggled to maintain their formations as they clambered over fallen logs, around tree trunks, through brush, and a nightmare of vines. It had been primitive and bloody.

Butler's decimated Company A tried to sleep where they'd stopped at nightfall. Whipped, demoralized, and shamed, they now suffered as the temperature dropped to freezing.

No fires allowed.

Just wolf down cold rations — assuming you

had any. The smart ones had grabbed Yankee haversacks and packs from the dead as they passed. Confederate commissary sure as spit and fire couldn't be trusted for a meal.

To Butler's relief, Kershaw had seen to the posting of pickets. They hid out there in the darkness, not more than fifty yards from where Butler stood looking out at the cold forest.

He could hear the pleas of the desperately wounded men lying just out there beyond the pickets. They all could. Between the lines. Gut shot, legs broken or shot off, hit in the head or spine shot, they called piteously for water, rescue, or their mothers or wives. The only answer to their pleas had been the Yankee axes as the Federals a couple of hundred yards farther to the west built breastworks.

Butler lifted shaking hands to his head, trying to block the sound. Like ice picks, they seemed to pierce his skin, muscle, and bones.

"Stop it," he whispered. "In the name of God, please make them quiet."

Tears streaked down his face, his stomach tickling with the urge to throw up.

"Played hell today, didn't we, Cap'n?" Kershaw asked as he stepped up beside Butler.

"It's so different," Butler whispered hoarsely as he struggled to hide his trembling in the Cajun's presence. "I'm used to being on the staff, to knowing what's happening around the battle. Here, I just have such a small piece of it. Orders coming down, just my little piece, the men around me."

Dear God, he felt lost.

Just hold it together.

That's all he had to do. Cobble his courage into some semblance of a backbone.

The men are depending on you.

"Reckon, Cap'n, we done had us better days. Had 'em right smart this maw'nin when we started driving the Yankees north past Brotherton Road and Winfrey field."

Butler closed his eyes, the cries of his dying and wounded from that morning mixed with those out in the darkness. "It all came apart this afternoon, though, didn't it?"

Govan's Arkansans had been routed by an enfilading vise of blue-coated troops. They'd fled through the forest in a disorganized frenzy.

"Got the boys back together," Kershaw told him, his dark form shivering in the frosty night. "Reckon they'll be more'n ready to make up for it tomorrow."

Butler thought back to that precipitous retreat. When had he ever felt as desperate? Had it not been for Red following the retreat, he'd have died there on the field, tears streaking down his face. It was as if he'd lost himself. His brain and body had shut off. He couldn't shake the image of his men falling, shot down, as they ran from the hideous blue line.

"This is Shiloh all over again." Both of Butler's hands were shaking. He thought he saw lights glimmering out in the forest. But when he blinked, they were gone. "We pushed them back all morning long, chasing them through the forest. Only to have them throw us back in the afternoon."

"Tomorrow, we whip 'em," Kershaw told him firmly. "The difference dis time? We got Longstreet's Corps. *À vue de nez.* It gonna do foah us what Buell did foah Grant at Shiloh. You see."

Butler looked out into the forest darkness, smelling smoke and blood on the night breeze. "Bloody as today was, tomorrow's going to be worse, Sergeant."

There, again, he saw the lights. "Do you see them, Sergeant? Right out there in the night?"

"See what, Cap'n?" Kershaw was squinting, following Butler's pointing finger.

"Like little twinkles. Sort of like stars. They're just . . ." He blinked again, and felt foolish. "Now they're just . . . gone."

"Didn't see nothing out der, Cap'n."

"Maybe it was just the souls of the dead," Butler whispered under his breath.

"You all right, Cap'n? Maybe you'all otta get some shut-eye. Been a long hard day, suh."

"Maybe I should."

Butler hunkered down, back to a tree, his gaze on the dark battlefield with its cold smell of blood, smoke, and death. Tomorrow they would once again march into the enemy's guns.

How many of his men would die?

And you can't save them, the voice seemed to hiss from the darkness around his head.

"You don't hear that, do you?" Butler asked.

"Hear what, Cap'n?"

"Echoes of hell in the darkness."

"Speaking of hell, Cap'n, what happened to that preacher? Dat one who give dat blood-and-guts sermon on de march up here? I hear'd most of it. Damning Yankee Puritans fo' witch-burning bastards, and how God gonna chase der souls through fire and brimstone? Last I hear, he say if'n he but have a gun, he ride into the fight with us, *non?* Dat we be de chosen of God. Dat any man who fall, he gonna be eating supper in heaven at de Lord's right hand."

Butler's trembling lips bent in a smile. "Yep. I

heard all that, Sergeant. The ol' reverend was with us right up to the moment a Federal shell exploded in the tree above him. As the fragments whistled past his ear, he turned a vacuous shade of pale. Then a couple of balls whistled past his ear, and he reined that horse around and lit for the rear. Word among the ranks was that the good reverend had taken on a sudden case of the stomach flu and wished to excuse himself from supper from here on out."

Kershaw chuckled, then sobered, listening to the ominous sounds coming from the darkness.

God, I wish I could excuse myself, too.

All Butler had to do was bind himself together. Just one more day. He could do that, couldn't he?

38

September 20, 1863

Butler leaned, panting, against the rough bark of a hickory tree, thankful for the thick copse of woods that hid him and what was left of his tattered and exhausted Arkansas volunteers.

He rubbed the sleeve of his dirty uniform across his mouth and wished for a drink of water. Any water. Even the bloody, fouled, and muddy stuff rolling down Chickamauga Creek. It lay just a half mile over east, screened by woods, and behind the sounds of battle.

Terrified, he stared up at the thick and sinuous branches overheard. The fall-dark leaves stirred in the breeze — the sound of their rustling drowned by the hammering crackle of musketry, the banging of artillery, and sharp cracks of exploding shells.

The sound was more of a tearing thunder, a ripping staccato, as if the world's very fabric were being sundered. Rising and falling, the demonic crackle was accented by irregular bangs, many of them deafening.

Even here, so far into the timber, gray wisps of smoke, like phantom wraiths, brought the acrid smell of burned powder to his nostrils.

Butler's reeling brain kept replaying the things he'd witnessed: men's bodies jerked comically as they exploded. Gore-spattered and maimed limbs were sent wheeling through the air as if ripped and flung from torsos. Decapitated heads just seemed to pop up as the bodies disintegrated beneath them. Entrails burst from ruptured flesh and clothing, or were strewn in the grass where cruel shells had tossed limp and broken fragments of men.

He couldn't stop his hands from trembling.

Butler blinked hard, as if by clearing his sight, he could also clear the horrors playing so vividly in his mind. Chickamauga's scenes mixed. Flowed together. And parted. Haunting memories.

Or were they from Shiloh?

Or perhaps from frozen Prairie Grove?

Impossible to tell after the eternity of the last two days.

Among the haunting visions, Private Newsome — so young and vivacious — with midnight hair, soft brown eyes, and a round, freckled face — kept grinning widely as he looked over his shoulder at Butler. Captured in the instant that a minié ball hit him in the back of the head. The soft lead had mushroomed and blown Newsome's brains out through the center of his face.

Or it might be Harper Angrue, the fast-talking wheelwright's son from Chicot County, Arkansas, who was thin faced with slick brown hair. Yankee canister had torn the lad's belly open, slinging ropes of his intestines this way and that like macabre, whipping strings of sausage to slap onto the cringing men closest to him.

My men. My soldiers.

Who said that?

Where did the words come from?

He kept hearing obscene voices as they formed out of the nearby racket of battle. Like devil's talk, they hissed through the trees, riding upon the acrid smoke. Could be heard as syllables in the rising and falling chatter of musketry. If he concentrated, picked out the cadence, the voices had an almost female tone.

Had to be the names of the dead.

Mocking him. Mocking his incompetence at command.

Chickamauga.

Even the sound of it boded of no good.

"What do we do, Cap'n?" Sergeant Amos Kershaw asked, his dark Cajun face blocky and grim under his sweat-stained kepi. Starbursts in the powder grime around his eyes betrayed how he'd been squinting.

Butler raised his hands from the bark, pressing hard against his ears, trying to shut out the guns, the screams of the wounded and dying out there just beyond the trees. Shut out the voices that hung just below his hearing.

Think! If I could just think?

His men were cowering among the trees. Panting and scared. Looking to him for salvation after the mauling they'd taken as they charged around the Federal right in a supposed flanking movement — and marched right into massed Federal guns.

We fell apart, fled the only direction we could: west, into the trees behind the Yankee lines.

In the melee, Butler's company — his lieutenants shot dead — lost track of the rest as they skedaddled through the smoky maze of dense hardwoods, clambering through thickets, dodging among dangling vines. They'd crawled over tangles of deadfall, clawed through brush, and plunged through low-hanging smoke and mist to this small clearing. If it could be called such.

South! the voices seemed to say despite his plugged ears.

"South?" he questioned, wondering if the words in his teetering and exhausted mind had been whispered past the devil's lips.

"Why south, suh?" Kershaw asked. "We's a'hind the Yankee lines." His crowsfeet deepened as he considered, and nodded his head as if in understanding. "I see, suh. *C'est bon.*"

See what? Butler was still struggling, too many voices whispering in his head, the words confusing to him, woven as they were into the cackle of gunfire.

Kershaw was putting it together. "Most of the battle is just over east. The rest off to the west a mile or so. Reckon y'all thinks there be a hole a'tween, right, suh?"

Was that what he thought? He nodded faintly, cocking his head in an attempt to hear the voices as they called to him from the hot air with its reek of sulfurous smoke.

"Got to be careful, though," Kershaw said, nodding. "On yor feet, boys. The cap'n done figgered us a way out. Corporal Pettigrew, you follow on along behind. Make sure nobody lags."

"Yes, sir," Willy Pettigrew told him, cradling the Yankee Springfield he'd carried since picking it up on the battlefield at Shiloh. "C'mon, y'all." He waved the tired men to their feet.

Butler took a quick count. Twenty-seven. He had only twenty-seven left. He'd seen nearly a hundred die in the last day and a half.

Dear God, tell me the rest are with the brigade.

"We all capped and loaded?" Kershaw asked. "Check yor guns, boys. We stumble unexpected-like on Yankees, I want volley fire. Only my number ones shoot. Number twos, y'all wait till the ones step back to reload. Only then aim, take yor time, and shoot."

All along the line the men nodded, faces hard, jaws clamped. Some wore kepis, others had shapeless felt hats atop their heads. Their coats were threadbare. Some carried Yankee knapsacks picked up here and there. Others kept their meager possessions in cloth sacks hanging from their belts or rolled in their blankets. The various rifles might have been battered and hard used, but what was left of Company A kept them well cared for. Cartridge boxes on their belts were unsnapped and ready. Their caps within reach.

"Cap'n?" Kershaw asked.

Butler's heart trembled in his chest. What if he were wrong?

"Move out," he whispered as he made a fist of his right hand to keep it from shaking.

"Phil, y'all take the lead," Kershaw ordered. "Ten paces ahead, and aim us a'tween the fighting. We don't want to stumble into no pile of Yankees here."

"Just 'cause I'm half Injun?" Vail, a tall boy with cinnamon hair, gave him a grin.

"You be all Injun for me today, boy," the burly Cajun told him.

"Yes, suh!" Vail clipped off a salute, his smile exposing white teeth in a soot-encrusted face.

Twice during that long and twisting passage through the woods, Vail raised his arm. Both times Kershaw copied the move, and when Vail slashed

303

his arm down, the whole command dropped to the forest floor, merging with the sticks and old leaves.

Each time, a panicked group of Yankees went crashing past. So fixed were they on escape, they never so much as glanced sideways in their flight.

Sticking to the west side of a small creek, they crossed two beaten roads and had proceeded maybe a mile before Vail raised his arm, ducked down, and went still, his head cocked.

Butler's small command could have been a Cherokee raiding party the way it hunched down in the brush or melted behind trees. With a hand signal to wait, Vail slithered off into the thickening honeysuckle and currants.

A nasty battle was taking place less than a mile to the west. Great crashes of musketry kept firing in volleys that rolled over the sporadic background of shooting. And through it all, the popping bark of the howitzers and the sharper bang of the rifled cannon spoke of massed artillery.

This sounded worse than the Hornet's Nest at Shiloh.

Just give us a hole to creep through. That's all I ask, dear Lord.

If he could just save these remaining men, it would be enough. He could resign his commission, find another way to serve. Perhaps in the commissary or supply. Anything to relieve himself of the knowledge that he'd failed so many of these boys who trusted him to . . .

Vail barely shifted the brush as he stepped out and grinned. "We're saved! Just ahead. They's Humphrey's brigade of Longstreet's Corps."

Turning he led the way, parting the stiff branches like Moses through the Red Sea and out onto a road packed with Mississippi volunteers. There wasn't any mistake given the actual matching uniforms, the better-fed look, and modern Enfield rifles on their shoulders.

"Who're y'all?" one lieutenant called.

"Company A, Second and Fifteenth Arkansas," Kershaw answered proudly, though the words were drowned by a swelling thunder from the battle just behind the trees.

Looking that way, Butler could see the thick pall of battle smoke that wreathed a treed ridge and blew slowly off to the northeast.

"Arkansas?" a voice called, and Butler turned to see a horseman, his uniform splotched with mud and smoke. "Butler? Is that you?"

"Jerome?" Butler gaped at Hindman's aide-de-camp. For the first time that day, he felt his heart go light in his chest. God had indeed delivered him. "What are you doing here?"

"Looking for a lost company." Wilson propped a gloved hand on his hip as his horse, a white-footed sorrel, sidestepped. "Thought Govan was on the right?"

"We were. Once," Butler told him with a grin. A great weight lifted from his soul. His men were safe. He'd done it.

"The general will be delighted to see you. That all of your men?"

"I hope there's more up north."

Jerome Wilson looked at Butler's little command, calling out, "How about it, boys? Will you make one last fight for Tom Hindman and Arkansas?"

"Hoorawww!" his boys shouted. "Show us where, Lieutenant Wilson!" They were raising their rifles, showing off for the Mississippi troops.

"By God, we'll drive them sons of bitches off that hill now!" Wilson crowed. "Follow me."

"But I need . . . Wait!" Butler's words died as his men, of their own volition, headed off after Wilson and wound their way through the Mississippi volunteers.

Should he protest?

Voices laughed in the air around him as he followed, feeling confused, as if his thoughts were as tangled as the forest they'd just crossed.

Across Kelly Road, they threaded their way through hickory, gum, oak, and maple forest, until they encountered massed gray infantry milling among the trees.

Butler glanced uneasily at the tens of wounded — soaked in their own blood — who were laid out in a line broken only by the trunks of trees. A regimental surgeon, pompously dressed in a full, and blood-saturated, uniform was pointing out cases for his assistants to haul off in captured Yankee field litters.

"Grab up what cartridges you can," Wilson called at a captured Yankee wagon.

Inside the wagon a sergeant — an older man with a gray beard and filthy uniform — handed down boxes of cartridges, calling, "Twenty rounds to a man!"

Butler's men surged forward, reaching out with grimy and blackened hands. The cartridges came in bundles of ten, each rolled in paper with an extra twist that held twelve caps. His men were grinning, each man stuffing the largess into his mostly empty cartridge box.

Butler watched with an eerie distraction, as if he were a spectator inside his own body. The disembodied voices were all chattering at once, adding to his confusion. Panic shot electricity through his breast, as if, when each of his soldiers laid his hands on the ammunition, the man's face turned into a skull, his arm going skeletal.

Was that real? Did he really see that?

"I don't want to do this," he said, words partially drowned by a crescendo of firing up on the smoke-wreathed ridge.

Kershaw, standing beside him, gave him an off-balance smile that displayed his crooked teeth. "Word is the Yankees is breaking all up and down de line. We win dis, we destroy Rosecrans's army. Do dat and the Federals is gonna have to rethink dis whole thing. Might win us de war, suh. *C'est bon!*"

"I don't want a disaster, Kershaw. I've lost too many as it is."

Kershaw hesitated, looking hard into Butler's eyes, seeming to read his soul. "Cap'n, yor in c'mand, *mais oui?*"

Go! Run! the voices whispered.

He was taking a breath to order just that, when Tom Hindman himself appeared through the trees. A bloody bandage swathed the neck of the "Lion of the South," his glass-blue eyes agleam with pain and the thrill of battle.

"Butler? Who'd have guessed. Whose men are these?"

"Why . . . mine, Tom. Company A, Second and Fifteenth Arkansas."

"Hello, General!" Willy Pettigrew called out with a wave. "We's come to drive them damn Yankees off yonder hill fer ye!"

"Then, by all means, get to it, gentlemen," Hindman cried. "Front and center! Double quick! The last charge is forming as we speak. Today, my fellow Arkansans, we win the war!"

The hearty cry that rose from his men sent a shiver of fear through Butler's breast, but he could do nothing except follow along behind as his decimated company trotted forward, guns at the ready. Passing through the confusion of the rear were more wounded being carried back. Butler saw soldiers, sitting, gazes empty, shoulders fallen, seemingly in a daze.

On Hindman's order a captain put them in line between two of Anderson's Mississippi companies.

Shells screamed in from the Federal guns on the heights and exploded with loud pops overhead. Fragments of metal tore several of the Mississippians apart in the ranks off to Butler's right.

"Forward at the quick step!" The order came down the line, and Butler, his heart pounding, his throat frozen, stood mutely.

"Cap'n?" Kershaw demanded, awaiting his order.

Unable to stop himself, Butler said, "Forward."

Drowned by the swelling cheer, Kershaw waited until he could be heard to bellow, "Arkansas! Forward at the quick step!"

Like some slothful monster the ponderous gray line started, a surging thousand men, pouring around the trees while branches, leaves, and fragments of hot metal came falling from the savaged skies.

As they approached the edge of the trees, musket balls began to whiz past, cracked into the tree trunks. A few thudded into men; others hit damp soil with a *phutt.*

Then they were out, pouring across the Vittetoe Road. The real storm broke with an explosion of musketry from the crest of the ridge before them.

The zipping and meaty impact of the minié balls staggered the entire line. Men fell. Others ducked or flinched. But onward they went, crouching down as if against a hard sleeting rain.

"Forward!" Kershaw's bellow carried over the screaming men. "At 'em, boys! *Arkansas!*"

With an ululating scream, Butler's men charged up the slope, past the splintered and fallen trees, scrambling over branches, stepping on and over mounds of dead and dying men who'd tried and failed at previous assaults.

Another blast of musketry flashed up on the crest — chained sparks of lightning amid the billowing of smoke. Butler saw Simon, Deveroux, McCreedy, and Smith fall.

Panting, he raced after his men as they ran full-bore up the slope. Into the Yankee guns.

Twenty-three left.

The devil's voice keened in his ear, as though the beast rode upon his shoulder.

The slope here was torn — leaf mat, shattered wood, bruised leaves all making footing treacherous. Butler slipped on a dead man's bloody intestines. Fell flat, just as a Federal howitzer unleashed a charge of grape that tore a swath in the air above his back.

As he thrashed his way to his feet, he felt the wet sprinkles, and instinctively glanced up at the late afternoon sky. Found it clear beyond the haze of smoke. Realized the light patter was blood and little bits of tissue blown out of his men by the grapeshot.

They lay before him, broken and bloody, some still, others writhing and kicking as they died. He stared. Barnabas O'Toole's entire jaw was missing.

"Cap'n!" Kershaw was pulling on his arm, the man's voice, disembodied, seeming to echo in Butler's head. The Cajun pointed up the slope. "They's breaking! We got 'em on the run!"

Butler scrambled up the slope and over the bleeding bodies of his men. Vail, Pettigrew, Baker, Templeton, and some of the others were just ahead of him. The crest was so close.

On either side, the Mississippians were screaming, shooting, some stumbling or falling as they were shot down.

Thick clouds of stinking smoke darkened the sky, the smell of burned powder, blood, damp soil, and bruised vegetation choked his nostrils.

An eerie howl broke Butler's lips as he charged past the first dead Yankee soldier, and then there were others, blue-coated, blood-soaked, some in piles. He leaped across a rudimentary breastwork, locking eyes with a wounded Federal private who crouched down, eyes wide with terror, his gun across his lap.

Fragments of hot metal sliced the air past his head as Butler charged into the Union rear. Saw the blue line ahead of him stop in its flight. Even as he watched, the line re-formed. A Yankee captain, sword out, ordered his men to stand.

The Yankees leveled their rifles.

"No!" Butler screamed.

Perhaps twenty feet separated them as the volley flashed fire from the muzzles. Smoke jetted out along the line. Bullets smacked into flesh and bone. Butler's soldiers stumbled and fell.

As Butler staggered, tried to see who remained, the Yankees shouted and charged.

This is the last.

A keening sounded in Butler's ears; his pistol,

like an extension of his hand, steadied as he raised it. Time seemed to slow into an inexorable eternity.

Kershaw paused beside him, ramming another load into his rifle. Pettigrew's gun was up, flashing fire and smoke as it rolled the man's shoulder back in recoil. Parsons was still running forward as a Yankee rose from the earth like a perverted lotus and thrust with a bayonet. Its point lanced upward through Parsons's chest. The Yankee planted the butt of his rifle and Parsons's momentum carried him up and over in a full arc that ripped the rifle from the Yankee's grip and planted Parsons face-first in the trampled grass.

A clubbed rifle caught Matthew Johnson across the face, knocking his head back, flinging him off his feet.

"Fall back!" Butler screamed as he cocked and triggered his Colt, snapping shots at the Federal line. *"Fall back!"*

Kershaw capped his rifle, drew it to his shoulder, and discharged it into a Yankee private's face just as the black-haired man took aim at Butler's chest.

At the same time Kershaw shot, he jerked, rose up on his toes, and staggered sideways. The Cajun's piercing black eyes fixed on Butler's. A question hung behind them, as though he were asking for an explanation. His knees buckled and blood spurted from his mouth; Kershaw was trying to say something as he smacked onto the ground.

Dead! You've killed them all!

Throwing down his pistol, Butler dropped to his knees and clapped his hands to his ears, shouting, "Quiet! Damn you all, *quiet!*"

He blinked, aware that the Yankees had stopped,

311

staring, eyes wide. At their feet lay the torn and mangled bodies of Butler's men, all intermingled with the corpses of their foes.

"I couldn't save them," he pleaded to the Yankees. "I would have. Tried."

You killed them!

"Shut up! Stop it! Don't talk to me anymore! It's *not* my fault!"

The world had turned into crystal, brittle and clear, each detail so perfectly rendered. He could see the sweat trickling down beneath the Yankees' kepis, streaking their smoke-stained faces. See their damp mustaches and each individual hair in their beards. The separate threads of their uniforms. The intricate hide patterns on their leather belts. The polish on their buckles and the smudges on their elbows, sleeves, and jackets.

Movement broke the spell.

"Cap'n?" Peterson was crawling, trailing blood across the grass, a heavy rasping audible with each breath he drew. He reached out to Butler with a smoke-blackened and bloody hand.

One of the Yankees followed Butler's gaze, pulled out a pistol, and shot Peterson in the back of the head. The young man from St. Francis County jerked and went limp.

Still on his knees, Butler reached out and pulled Jimmy Peterson into his lap, heedless of the blood that leaked out the hole in the back of the man's head.

"You can go home now, Jimmy. You and your brother. You, too, Kershaw. Baker? Pettigrew? You can all go." He choked on a sob. "All of you, go home."

Then he looked up at the stunned Yankees who surrounded him, rifles half raised, bayonets sleek and silver. "Go home. *All of you just goddamned go home!*"

They stared, as if in awe.

"Are you stupid? We can't keep them alive! What's the point?" Butler swallowed against a lump in his throat and screamed, *"I told you stupid bastards to go home!"*

A Yankee major stepped forward, a Colt .44 Army in his right hand, his left out in a calming gesture. "It's all right, Captain. My boys have to stay here. But we're going to have to get you off the line. Can you come with me?"

"I didn't save my men," Butler said weakly, Peterson's head heavy, the blood sticky on his fingers.

"We'll tend to them, Captain. But we've got to get you out of here."

"I have to save my men." Butler dropped his head into his hands, weeping and empty. *"I have to save my men!"*

39

October 1, 1863

Doc studied Private Nelson's foot as he massaged the swollen member. He stood in the hospital as the Federal private lay belly-down on the operating table. The sound of coughing could be heard from the beds just outside the door. Typhus was loose again. A slanting yellow shaft of sunlight illuminated motes of dust floating in the still air.

With each ministration Doc drained a foul-smelling pus from the trocar puncture he'd made in the sole of Private Nelson's foot. Again he took a two-handed hold and squeezed.

"Jesus! Son of Mary!" Private Thomas Nelson screamed through gritted teeth. "Damn and hell, that hurts!"

"You ask me, Tom," surgeon's assistant Percy Anthony said from the side, "you're a heap better off with Doc squeezing that corruption out of your foot than having Dr. Sullivan cut it off."

"Hope you're right, Percy." Nelson squirmed on the table, twisting his head around to gaze suspiciously at Doc. Sweat beaded on the young man's face, his blue uniform looking incongruous on the table where Doc had examined so many Confederate prisoners dressed in rags.

Nelson swallowed hard. "You making it hurt worse just 'cause I'm a Yankee?"

Doc smiled his amusement. "Sorry, Private, but it would hurt just as bad if you had a Rebel foot as it does with a Federal one."

He glanced at Anthony, who watched from the side. The physician's assistant had paid attention to every move Doc had made, followed by the occasional question. The young assistant had arrived as green as a pine tree. Hadn't known a suture from a probe. Doc thought that with a little training, Anthony had the makings of a first-class physician.

"Glad I sent for you," Anthony told him. "Sullivan's off to see his family in Springfield. He'll be back in a few days. Said he'd take off Tom's foot when he got back."

"It was just a *nail*!" Nelson cried. "That's all. Nothing to lose a foot over."

"No guarantees," Doc said softly. "But so far all I'm seeing is infection. Not necrosis. Erysipelas isn't gangrene, though it can lead to it. See, Percy? How this is red and swollen, but not dark and lined? And the odor of the effluvium, while bad, isn't tainted by the smell of decomposition?"

Percy leaned forward and sniffed, his nose quivering. "That's why I sent for you, Doc." He glanced around warily. "But remember, not a word of this. I could get in real trouble. But I didn't think Tom's foot was bad enough to amputate."

"Jesus help me, no," Tom Nelson agreed.

Doc left the foot alone and let Anthony wipe up the effluvium. He was encouraged by the clear pus now draining from the wound. "Where you from, Tom?"

315

"Moline, Doc. A town over west on the river. Pap has a hardware store. Mama was so delighted that I was sent here to guard Rebs. Figured I'd be safe from getting shot or killed." He made a face. "And then I step on a nail. A single, solitary nail, and they're talking about taking my foot! What kind of life would that be? Huh?"

Nelson turned, eyes pleading as he lowered his voice in mimicry, " 'Where'd you lose your foot, son? Antietam? Gettysburg?' And all I can answer back is, 'Walking across the infirmary yard at Camp Douglas!' I'd be a laughingstock."

Anthony crossed his arms. "I'd tell 'em Chickamauga with Thomas, saving the Union center."

"I *can't* lie, Percy." Nelson dropped his head back on his arm. "Man's gotta have some sense of honor. Ain't that right, Doc?"

"I suppose. Though this damn war makes me wonder sometimes if whatever you want to call honor isn't being used as a weapon by the political bosses to turn us all into animals."

"You mean Jeff Davis?" Anthony asked.

"Him and Abe Lincoln. And the congresses in Washington and Richmond. And the generals on both sides. Let's not leave them out."

"*Both* sides?" Nelson asked.

Doc hitched his butt onto the table to take the weight off. "Back when the war started, I read the papers from North and South. All the fiery editorials. Each side was going to save the Constitution, defeat tyranny, and ensure freedom and democracy. One side wanted to stop Yankee despotism, and the other wanted to stamp out secessionist despotism. How could the North and South each be fighting for their freedom and the ultimate salvation of democracy and in defense of the *same* constitution?" He shrugged. "I guess I found that little philosophical problem worthy of Socrates himself."

"What about slavery?" Nelson asked. "That's at the root of all this, isn't it? You Rebs want to keep slaves."

"The high and mighty do." Doc sighed. "Those politicians we were talking about? The rich ones? They've jiggered this whole thing. Most people in the South don't want to run out and get shot just so that the landed gentry and slave traders can keep Negroes in bondage. They'd rather be left alone to raise their crops, see their children grow, and enjoy their lives."

"My mama didn't want me getting shot in the process of freeing no niggers, neither," Nelson asserted. "Everything's different in the war now that Lincoln announced that emancipation."

"Should have been a way to keep from fighting a war over it," Anthony said softly, his eyes distant. "What about you, Doc? You for slavery, or against it?"

"Against. Prior to the war, a growing number of Southerners were of that opinion. That's changed some since the fighting started. Hardened what was once reasonable discourse. Death and destruction make people kind of crazy."

"So, what would you have done different?" Anthony asked.

"Let the South go. The market for Confederate cotton is in Europe and New England where slavery is despised and revolution and human rights is in the air. I'd bet that in less than a decade the cry for free-labor cotton would be so persuasive the slave owners would be figuring a way to pay Negroes rather than own them. And it would be a

317

hell of a lot cheaper than fighting this damn war, and lot more humane for the Negroes making the transition."

"You're not so bad a feller for a Rebel, Doc," Private Nelson told him. "Don't know how I'm gonna explain that I owe my foot to a dirty louse-infested prisoner."

"Louse-infested!" Doc protested. "I stand before you as a fine Arkansas physician and surgeon. One that not even the most impetuous louse would dare to infest."

"Then what's that crawling across your left sleeve, Doc?" Anthony asked.

Doc glanced down, spotting the little beast as it scurried toward a hole in his sleeve.

"There you are!" Doc cried, pinching the vermin between thumb and forefinger. "Trying to escape, weren't you?"

"Not even the most impetuous louse?" Nelson asked slyly.

"Why, he's not mine," Doc replied seriously. "I just borrowed him from my friend James. I use him in my introductory lessons with each batch of Fresh Fish that come in. I want them to be able to recognize a real Yankee louse when they see one."

"What in hell are you talking about, Doc?" Anthony asked.

"Well, Percy, in order to understand Rebels, you need to realize that we're an egalitarian lot. New prisoners coming in want to share in all the things us canned mackerel — you know, the old-timers — take for granted."

Doc lifted the louse that was wiggling between his thumb and forefinger and studied it. "Wouldn't want them to feel left out or deprived, so I make

318

sure they know just what to look for as they take off in search of their own personal herd of Yankee lice."

"Yankee lice?" Nelson asked. "They different than Rebel lice?"

"Most assuredly, Private. Yankee lice are more industrious. They like to chew on a fella all night long whereas Rebel lice knock off at midnight and don't go back to work until dawn."

And saying that, Doc stuck the vile little creature in his pocket and turned to Nelson. "Now that that's settled, let's see if we can't get some more pus out of this foot of yours."

40

October 29, 1863

Something was wrong. As Billy rode down the
Spring Canyon trail he felt it even before he
caught the faint scent of something sour. He knew
that smell: the tang of severed and spilled guts.
Billy stopped and shifted his old .36 caliber
muzzleloader from his shoulder.

He had taken no more than ten paces down the
trail before he stopped short. Tracks in the loamy
soil. Maybe six hours old. Two men on horses had
descended the steep slope, winding through the
trees before taking the trail down the narrow valley.

Billy's heart skipped. *Two riders? Here?*

Surely they wouldn't have come cross-country
along the White River breaks. Anyone with a lick
of sense would follow the Huntsville Road. Or, if
they were desperate to avoid notice, would have
taken any of the ridge trails that wound up to
higher, flatter country. The only reason riders
would cut across the ridges was if they were
circling to come in behind . . .

"Damn and hell."

Swiftly, silently, he hurried down the trail, his
eyes taking in the brushy spots, the shadowed

overhangs beneath the weathered gray limestone, any place a person could hide and watch the trail.

The horses' hooves had chipped little crescents from the damp ground. The back hooves printed more than three quarters of the front. These weren't made by skulkers, but men in a hurry to cover ground. Men who had pushed their mounts at a fast walk.

Billy could just see the springhouse at the mouth of the canyon. The door was open. Something he, Sarah, and Maw never did in the constant effort to keep pests out. Slowing, he slipped into the trees, familiar with every stealthy approach to the house.

He eased into the thick rosebushes, saw the wagon wheel. But out in the yard, the wagon itself was gone. The old broken wheel still lay in the dirt beside the tire tracks where the iron rims had cut the soil. Whoever had taken the wagon had brought their own wheel, which meant they had been here before, had planned their raid.

In the center of the yard lay Fly, his belly torn open, entrails trailed behind him as if he'd crawled to his death.

A slow-burning rage began to glow in Billy's gut. Any bastard who'd do that to Fly . . .

A man lay facedown in front of the porch, his arms out, legs spread. Blood had dried black on his flour-sack shirt, his boots were missing. But who was he? Who'd shot him? And why?

And more worrisome, where were Maw and Sarah?

On the front porch, the warning bucket was missing.

He tried to think it through as fear began to eat inside him. They'd been raided. Pro-Union jayhawkers would have burned the place after looting it. Maw would have told partisan Rebel guerillas that she had sons in the Confederate army, and while they might have conscripted the wagon with its load of vegetables, they wouldn't have had to shoot one of their own men in the yard. Nor would they have killed Fly.

Billy shifted, easing back, circling before slipping up behind the newly harvested corn rows until he could see the front of the house. The door was open, sheets, clothing, a couple of Maw's chests lying open and spilled on the ground before the steps.

The anger and panic burned hotter.

From here he could see where the wagon had been drawn up before the porch, and how it had followed the horses out of the yard and down the lane.

Billy faded back into the brush, made his way along the wooded slope to the rear of the house. As he eased out of the trees, he cut the trapper's cabin trail, seeing where a man in boots had led Old Clyde and Swat toward the yard. They'd been hidden a quarter mile up the canyon. So, they'd known to look for the horses, too.

A quick dash took him to the pines behind the house, and from there he wiggled his way under the boughs until he could see the back door. Open. He could see clear through the hallway, and out the gaping front door.

He watched for long minutes. Nothing moved.

A rasping moan came from inside.

Billy tightened his grip on the rifle, worked his jaw to sharpen his hearing. He could feel the stillness, the aloneness, in a way he'd never felt while at home.

He sprinted for the back wall, stuck his ear against it and listened. But for the hammering of his heart he could hear nothing.

On moccasin feet he slipped in the door, rifle at the ready. All the cabinets were open, the clothes, normally on the pegs, were jumbled on the floor. He glanced into Maw's room to see everything in disarray, even the mattress slit open and shredded. What kind of lunatic would ruin an old woman's mattress?

Maw lay curled on her side in the front room. A smeared streak of blood marked where she'd crawled in from the porch.

"Maw!" Billy cried, rushing to her side.

He winced at the dark blood matting her blouse. High. Had to be a liver and stomach shot. "Who shot you?"

"Colonel Dewley." She swallowed hard, the action pumping blood out through the wound to rewet the front of her dress. "Took her."

"Sarah?"

"They *took* her!" Maw said through gritted teeth. "Leaped on him. Clawed at him."

"What happened then?"

She blinked, eyes flicking back and forth as if her vision were blurred. "Went at him . . . he shot me."

Stunned disbelief left him reeling. "Where did he take her?"

"Don't know."

Maw's body tensed, the rasping in her throat louder now.

"They's a dead man out there, Maw. Who is he?"

"One of Dewley's. Tried to stop it. Said he'd be damned to be part of molesting a white woman. Dewley shot him down. Asked if anyone else objected."

"Think, Maw. Where would they have taken her?"

"Get her back, son. Keep her safe. Your responsibility to . . . see . . ."

Maw tensed, eyes opening wide to flutter in her head. They slowed. Fixed. Her breath made a bubbling sound in her throat, her body going limp.

"Maw?"

Billy laid his finger on her neck, feeling no pulse. He swallowed a knot of grief and forced himself to touch her still, blue eye. She didn't blink.

Billy gathered her into his lap, hugging her frail body to his, feeling her blood as it soaked into his worn trousers.

By the time he'd cried himself out, sunlight slanted through the west window. Lifting her, he wondered at how light she was and carried her outside. He left her wrapped in a blanket on the porch. He and Sarah would bury her after they got back. The same for the gallant man who'd objected.

Billy stopped long enough to pat Fly on the head, another rush of tears silvering his vision. He and Fly had grown up together. Hunted side by side, played in the forest, gotten in trouble. For most of Billy's life, Fly had been a best friend. Forever forgiving, a companion without complaint and unstintingly faithful. Right up to the end when the half-blind dog had obviously given his life fighting for his family.

Propping his rifle over his shoulder, Billy started down the lane at a trot. He still had a couple of hours of light left, and there just weren't that many places Dewley could have gotten off to. Not with a wagon filled with corn and squash . . . and an obviously captive white girl.

The rage was a smoldering heat in his belly when he determined they'd turned south on the Huntsville Road. Seeing the country in his head, he had a hunch where they would go. Down by the ruins of Van Winkle's mill. Someplace accessible for the wagon, but off the road. Out of sight of Yankee patrols, but close enough they could take the wagon into Fayetteville to sell the produce. It was a gamble, but that's where Billy would go. To do it smart, he'd have to take the mountain trail.

The thought of their dirty hands on her soft skin, of them throwing her down and exposing her. Of an unwashed man grinning as he drove himself into her . . .

Billy threw his head back, throat swelling in rage as he screamed his pain up at the evening sky.

41

October 30, 1863

The midday sun shone behind a haze of high, thin clouds. They looked like finely drawn feathers stretched across the blue. Billy Hancock, weary, almost stumbling from fatigue and hunger, worked his way down the old deer trail that descended a steep and thickly wooded slope. The trail wound around outcrops of weather-grayed limestone, the footing rocky and loose.

It had been a couple of years since Billy had taken the mountain trail, and then he and John Gritts had been on horseback. He hadn't realized how long the thirteen-mile loop would take on foot, let alone at night, where — to his self-disgust and frustration — he'd gotten lost in the dark and had to backtrack.

He worked his way through colorful autumn forest as he descended the ridge trail, easing down slopes that were barely covered by the newly fallen leaves.

What if I'm wrong? What if I took too long?

The very thought of it left him sick to his stomach. If he were too late . . . No, trust to God and Cherokee spirit power, he *would* find her. She *had* to be all right!

Men didn't treat a girl that way. Even the worst of the guerrillas maintained a code of honor when it came to women. He had to believe that.

Desperation built until he wanted to explode.

Struggling to keep his feet light, he stepped from stone to stone as he made his way down a water gap that led to a sheer drop-off in the limestone rimrock.

He'd been here before. From the rim he could look down into the War Eagle Valley, and more specifically into the cove where Angus McConahough had had his little farm and distillery, with its corn, barley, and wheat fields.

If the raiders were Colonel Dewley's, they'd been in the country long enough to know this place. It was close enough to the main road that they would have arrived here at dusk the night before, and the road in and out was passable by a wagon.

Billy dropped to his belly and slithered out on the limestone outcrop where it overlooked the rounded hollow.

In McConahough's little pasture, eight horses were grazing. The cabin, however, was a charred shell with weeds growing up through the fallen-in roof. McConahough, a known Union sympathizer, had burned his house, loaded up his still, and followed in Curtis's tracks when the victor of Pea Ridge took his army away.

A campfire sent a single wreath of blue smoke up from before a stand of pines. It was just back of the willow-filled creek bottom and the spring that had once provided water for McConahough's famed whiskey. Four men were seated around the fire, looking relaxed. A man dressed in brown with a shapeless felt hat and a rifle in his hands walked past an opening in the trees on his way to check the horses.

But there was no wagon.

Is this the right place?

He heard distant male laughter, the clink of metal.

One way to find out.

Billy eased back, stood, and made his way to the steep trail. Most of the way it wound down through square limestone boulders tumbled from the rimrock above. Scrubby oaks, chinquapin, and gnarly-looking maples, all densely wound with honeysuckle, grape, and bindweed, were losing their orange, red, and yellow leaves.

He took his time, fighting against his desperate urge to hurry.

"Done teached you better than that," John Gritts's voice echoed in his head.

He tried not to think of Maw's blood where it stained his pants, of her dying in his arms. Or Sarah, and what she might be enduring. The thought of men sucking on her breasts, crawling between her legs brought a hellish bile to the base of his throat.

At the sudden whiff of tobacco, Billy froze short of a great, square, moss-covered boulder broken off from above.

Sniffed.

Caught it again.

Close.

He lifted his rifle. The sound of a shot would spoil everything. But where was the guard?

The trail led down around the wagon-sized rock. Again the tobacco's aroma filled a curl of breeze.

Billy eased forward and stopped short when a booted foot scuffed dirt and was followed by a man clearing his throat. Then came the sound of the dottle being knocked out of a pipe.

Billy peeked around the boulder's edge.

The man was standing. In the act of slipping his pipe into a pocket. He was big, maybe six feet. An old jacket hung on his shoulders, elbows out of the sleeves. But the color blended into that of the weathered stone. A fine slant-breech Model 1855 Sharps dangled from his left hand as he stepped forward to a drop-off and scanned the small cove.

Billy's mouth had gone dry. He didn't dare shoot. Could he take him? Did he even dare try?

Debts have to be paid.

On silent moccasins he crept forward, collected himself. With all the strength in his work-toughened body, he grabbed the old muzzle loader by the barrel and swung.

As he did, the man turned. Billy had a momentary glimpse of his face: lean, almost like a living skull, with shocked wide brown eyes and a scraggly beard that was darker than his dirty blond locks.

The stock caught the blond man full in the face. The power of the blow popped the hat up off his head. A muffled crack could be heard over the snap of bone as the maple stock split.

The man fell back into a currant bush, but Billy was on him. Gripping the barrel like an iron bar he swung the lock down into the man's face, gratified with the meaty thunk. Again and again he swung. Each impact sent a tremor through the man's body, causing his arms and legs to jerk.

Panting, every muscle in his body on fire, Billy stopped, gasped, and wiped his sleeve across his face.

What if this ain't the bunch? What if he was just a

329

guard for a family or something?

The moment of horror filled him, sent a shiver through his bones. He turned, staring anxiously down into the cove. Saw no movement, heard no shouts of warning. Heard only the rattle of the dying man's lungs.

God!

I killed a man.

Beat him to death.

Billy swallowed hard, realized he was shaking, and sat down. "What if he wasn't one of Dewley's?"

Too late. The milk's done been spilt.

"Got to find Sarah."

He stared at his broken rifle, the stock cracked off at the wrist, the hammer broken off the lock, the nipple and metal streaked with gore.

Still shaking, he got up, searched the man's pockets, finding a roll of Confederate bills, a couple of gold coins, the pipe and tobacco, a pocketknife, and a beautiful gold watch.

From the dead man's belt, Billy took the cartridge box, opening it to find fourteen paper cartridges for the Sharps. A quick check showed half a roll of caps in the rifle's Maynard primer.

The dead man had a Colt .44 Dragoon stuffed in his left waistband. Billy pulled it out and found five cylinders loaded and capped, hammer resting on an empty. The right grip on the revolver was charred, as if it had been in a fire. Finally, in the back of the dead man's belt hung a long-bladed Bowie fighting knife in a hard leather scabbard.

What if he's not one of Sarah's abductors?

He started to shake again.

"Better get your tail down to that camp and see," he told himself.

He wanted to scream, to run home to Maw, and let her hug him. Make him safe. She'd know what to do. Tell him if it were all right or not.

He glanced down, seeing her blood, now gone black on his fingers. It clung in his cuticles and under his fingernails. Tears came welling again. He thought of the still form he'd left wrapped in the blanket on the porch. She'd be stone-cold by now, stiff with the rigor.

Taking the dead man's belt, he strapped on the Bowie, stuck the Dragoon down into the waistband, and picked up the Sharps.

Got to go Injun now.

The fatigue and stumbling weariness was gone. Muscles charged, he crept down the trail, keeping low as he sneaked from one patch of cover to the next. At the bottom, he eased left behind the stand of willows and heard the loud laughter, the clinking of tin pans. He was close enough now to hear their talk.

"Dewley ought to be back any time now. Then what?"

"Think we ought to be shut of Benton County, that's what I think. Hancocks has friends hereabouts. They's gonna be talk."

"I tell you, should'a buried that old woman. Women disappear. No one knows but what they just up and left the country. Leaving a woman shot like that? In her own yard? And the daughter missing? I tell you, that be a calling card fer trouble down the line."

Billy's blood ran cold.

He knew the instant he changed. Felt it. Like a spigot being turned on. One instant he'd been scared, confused, and grieving. The next, he was filled with clarity. His senses — honed by years of

331

hunting — now focused. He might have become a cougar: silent, deadly, his only purpose distilled down to the essence.

Weeds had grown thick around McConahough's corral, which allowed Billy to slither close to their fire. With the horse guard returned, five men were now seated around it; pans were steaming on the stones.

"Damn," one said, grinning. "They may hang us, but boys, I ain't sure but what fucking that gal ain't worth it."

"Yep," said another, "and Tucker's still at it. The little shit gets his first ride on a damn fine-looking girl . . . and as many times as he can stiffen his wick in her. Me, I got my first cunt from a old black whore what was uglier than sin on Sunday . . . and loose as a mare's ass to boot! And worst of all, I paid two whole dollars for that!"

The others laughed.

Billy's heart slowed, the trembling gone from his hands.

The redheaded man on the end, however, looked worriedly over to where packs had been piled. "I'm telling you, boys, we shouldn't have brought this one with us. Should have taken our turns at the place, cut her throat, and burned her and the old woman with the house."

"Dewley never seen one this purty a'fore," a dirty-faced, short man told him. "I ain't never neither. Hair like snowy blond sunlight, eh? A goddess. That's what Dewley called her. And them tits, why, they ain't the biggest I ever got my hands around, but they sure fill a man's hands." He paused. "Reckon when Tucker's finished, I'm taking me another turn."

Later, Billy would realize that was when the

devil took him over. In the mindless clarity, he walked forward, pulling the Dragoon from his belt.

The redhead. He's the dangerous one.

"Hey," a brown-haired man in a straw hat said, pointing at Billy.

The others turned, two of them reaching for pistols.

"Ya'll got the Hancock girl? Say she's a good fuck?" Billy was laughing, feeling the craziness of the moment. "Bet she is."

Billy cocked the big Dragoon and shot the redhead through the center of his chest. Cocking and triggering, he shot the dirty-faced man, and then the blond. A black-eyed bearded man shot wildly with his pistol. Billy calmly laid the Dragoon's front sight to cover the shooter's nose and triggered. The man vanished in the billow of smoke.

The last man, sallow-faced, brown eyes wide, had leaped to his feet, tugging on his pistol. The Remington revolver's hammer had caught in his shirt, fouling his attempt to free it. Finally, he tore it loose.

Billy shot him in the lights. Sallow-face staggered. The Remington wavered. His mouth worked — rage in his eyes as he worked the hammer back.

Billy cocked the Dragoon, smiled. The hammer clicked on an empty cylinder.

The sallow-faced man smiled his victory, taking his time, letting Billy see his death coming.

Even as the Remington discharged, Billy dropped the Colt. Threw himself right, and down as he shifted the Sharps.

The sallow-faced man blinked, seemingly fixed on the expanding puff of black powder smoke, then glanced down in time to see the Sharps's black muzzle as Billy shot him in the chest.

Like an undercut tree, the sallow-faced man tilted, leaned, and toppled backward.

Like all good hunters, Billy took stock of his kills. The redheaded man was stone dead, as was the face-shot bearded man. The two others might have been mortally wounded, but Billy took no chances. Used the Bowie to cut their throats, left them choking and blowing blood in red misty sprays.

Sarah. Where's Sarah?

Behind the packs and saddles a young boy had risen, his arms spread. Face pale with horror, his eyes were wide with disbelief. Pants wadded down around his ankles, his penis jutted hard, proud, and glistened wetly above the damp brown thatch of pubic hair. His shirt hung open exposing a thin white belly and protruding navel.

Billy started forward, the Bowie dripping blood from its tip.

The boy turned to run, tripped on his pants, and fell flat, trying desperately to jerk them up. "No, no, no," he kept pleading as he tried again to leap to his feet, still tangled.

Billy launched himself, his body slamming down on the boy, driving the air from his lungs. His face inches from the boy's, he stuck the Bowie in low, watched the youth's eyes widen at the sting burning its way deep inside his guts.

"Was my sister good?" he gritted through clenched teeth, his powerful arm sliding the sharp knife up through muscle, intestine, and liver.

The boy's limbs quivered, his head jerking this way and that. Terror-wide brown eyes fixed on Billy's.

334

Billy rose to his feet, leaving the boy's guts to spill out the long slit in his side.

"God! Dear God!" the boy cried, reaching down with frantically trembling hands to clutch at his bloody intestines.

Billy sucked a deep breath. A crazy joy began to dance through his chest. A feeling of ecstasy like nothing he'd ever experienced. His entire body might have become electric. Never had he felt so alive, so powerful and joyful.

And then he stopped short, blinked.

For a second the sight didn't make sense, didn't register.

Sarah lay on her back, spread-eagled. Short lengths of chain ran from the shackles on her wrists and ankles to stakes driven into the ground. The torn remains of her dress and camisole lay in shreds beneath her. Her long pale blond hair had been spread out over the grass as if arranged. A cloth gag had been stuffed in her mouth.

As he met her desperate, half-crazed stare, Billy's breath stopped in his throat. His heart was banging like a wild thing. Knees buckling, he sank slowly to the ground.

This wasn't the heavenly dream. Wasn't the purity that had been his sister.

Distantly — as though he were gone from his body — he stared at her. Each bruise on her white skin, the bite marks around her nipples, the bloody fluids on the inside of her thighs and around her swollen . . . Around . . .

She saw, read his shock, and jerked her head away, as if to hide herself.

Billy struggled for breath. Felt himself float. How long? An eternity?

Sarah's pleas, shouted against the gag, her jerking sobs, finally broke through the screaming in his mind.

He crawled forward on all fours, fingers fumbling as he pulled the pins from the shackles — watched her curl into a ball as she was freed. He untied the knotted rag from around her head. Pulled the wad of cloth from her mouth.

"Billy?" Her voice sounded small. Wounded.

He pulled her into his arms. She wept, huge racking sobs that shook her like a broken bird.

"Sorry," he whispered in her ear. "I'm so . . . so sorry. My fault. I . . ."

Sarah hoarsely said, "Got to go. Dewley's coming with the rest of them. They's twenty-one in all. So that's fifteen that went to Fayetteville to sell the wagon and what they took."

"Can you ride? I mean, after what they done to your . . ."

"I think so."

He helped her to her feet, aware of every inch of her naked body. "Got to get you something to wear."

"Tucker's pants, for one," she said unsteadily, her eyes drifting, half mad in her head. "He's my size."

"Who's Tucker?"

Her head sort of wobbled as she jerked it toward the dying boy. The kid was breathing fast, kept swallowing hard. His glittering gaze kept fixing on Billy's when he wasn't trying to stuff his spilling guts back inside him. Whimpers sounded half-choked in his throat.

Out by the road, Billy heard someone distantly calling, "Hurry up! They's shooting back to the camp!"

"Who's that?"

"Road guard," she said through a sob as she tried, clumsily, to jerk Tucker's pants from his limp legs. "Dewley's coming."

"Can't take horses if they're on the road." He jerked the boy's pants free and handed them to her. Picking up his knife, he stared down at the gutted boy. "Tucker, you say?"

The boy glanced his way with pain-glazed eyes.

Billy bent, grabbed Tucker by the privates and pulled.

"Billy! No!" Sarah screamed as Billy neatly severed the boy's penis and testicles.

"Guess your first was your last, huh?" He threw the boy's parts full into his face.

Sarah stood, frozen and gaping, her face twitching. Glazed blue madness danced behind her eyes.

Walking to the packs, Billy found blankets, a red wool shirt that he tossed her, and then hurried to pick up the Sharps rifle. He ripped the pistol flask and bullet pouch from Sallow-face and took his Remington, leaving the Dragoon. Danny Goodman had a .36-caliber Remington that Billy had always admired. Now he had his own Model 1858, and a .44 at that.

He hesitated, looking at the men he'd killed. The ones who had raped Sarah.

Billy used the Bowie on each of them, leaving their castrated parts in their gaping mouths as John Gritts had told him the Cherokee once did.

"Come on!"

Sarah — shaking like a leaf in a hurricane — stumbled toward him, the pants tight around the swell of her hips. One sleeve of the red shirt kept evading her searching arm.

"What about shoes?" she asked.

"Where are yours?"

337

"I was barefoot when they come."

"You been barefoot before." He led the way back through the corral, behind the willows, and to the trail. "Can you climb?"

Shouts and horses were heard from the mouth of the cove. She literally sprang up the trail.

Billy followed, watching her bare feet as they dug into the damp soil. He was breathing hard by the time they passed the dead guard.

Maybe it's only fifteen behind us?

Working his way through the cut up to the rim, he realized that Sarah was limping, her legs shaking with the effort.

No way they were going to make any kind of time.

"Sis, wait."

He led the way to the limestone rim that overlooked the cove. Standing at the edge, he studied the camp, saw the horses, heard the shouts as men stomped back and forth.

A pistol shot rang out.

Someone must have taken pity on Tucker.

Billy dropped the block on the Sharps, slipped in a cartridge and raised the lever, neatly shearing open the back of the paper to expose the powder. Billy figured the distance at four hundred yards. Then he guesstimated the drop as he raised the Lawrence-patent sight for three hundred yards. Cocking the gun, he drew a bead on the big, black-bearded man stomping around, kicking the dead men around the fire.

The Sharps boomed, smoke billowing, and Billy raised his head. Through the blue haze, he wasn't exactly sure of where the bullet hit, but the big man leaped as if he were scalded.

Cupping his mouth with both hands, Billy

shouted, "You see what I did to them! I'll get each one of you! You bastards are dead men!"

"Billy," Sarah cried, "don't!"

"Come on, sis," he growled as he pushed past her. "We got a ways to go before nightfall."

She stepped in behind him. "They'll be coming for you."

"I'm planning on it."

42

November 3, 1863

Sarah looked up at the trees, most of the leaves gone now. Around them, the slopes were just catching the first light. Sparkling frost lay on the fall-brown grass. Her breath hung white in the cold air. She shivered in the blanket Billy had made her take.

She beat herself in the head again, self-induced pain bringing her back to the now. Tears, so hot and wet, silvered her eyes, dripping down one by one.

"Stop it!" Billy's unforgiving hand caught her wrists, heedless of the scabs, or how it hurt.

But everything hurt. Her abused breasts. Where they'd bitten her neck. Stones had cut her tender feet, now gone numb from the cold. Her vagina burned and ached. Everything down there was raw and sore when she walked. Blood and fluid still soaked the pad she'd made for herself from dried moss.

"You're hurting me," she whispered dully, shooting him a hard sidelong glance where he gripped her wrists.

"You're hurting yourself, beatin' on your head that way."

340

They'd spent the night under a limestone outcrop — the place long used for such things given the charcoal, the bits of broken Indian pottery, stone chips, and broken glass. The morning fire smoldered. Billy had carefully buried the bones from the turkey they'd had for supper and breakfast.

"Why go to the trouble?" she'd asked.

"So they think we're starved and weak," he had told her.

Finally turning her wrists loose, he said, "We gotta be going."

"You don't know Dewley. What you did to them men? Cutting them that way? He ain't never going to stop."

Who is this brother of mine? Castrating those bodies, that wasn't the Billy she'd always known.

"Good." Billy checked the cartridge box where it hung on his belt.

"Good?" She started to tremble again. "Billy, he's mad-dog crazy! Something's twisted in his mind. Broken like. He's got the devil in his eyes, and there ain't no beating the devil!"

Billy's lips trembled as he looked out at the oaks, maples, and elms that filled the little valley. "He ain't the only one with the devil in him. We laid us a good trail yesterday. That tracker of his?"

"Silas?"

"If he's good, he'll be a couple of hours behind us."

A dull terror settled in her gut. "You're *letting* them follow us?"

He gave a slight nod, his lips pressed hard, jaws bulging.

"Billy, I just want to go home. Get away. I want away." Tears beaded. "I just want to be safe! To go

341

somewhere and *die!*"

His expression hardened, eyes stony. "Debts gotta be paid, sis."

She laid a hand on his shoulder, feeling the packed muscle under his shirt. "Billy, you don't understand. You got lucky back at McConahough's Cove. You caught 'em by surprise."

"Me and Satan." He looped his rolled blanket around his shoulders and reached a hand down to pull her up. She could see the hardness behind his eyes, the fact that something was tearing him up on the inside. Maybe it was that they still hadn't seen to Maw's body? He said he'd left it on the porch in a blanket.

She winced as she got painfully to her feet, looped her own blanket around her shoulders, and picked her tender way out onto the frosted grass. Her injured bare feet burned with the cold.

To her surprise, Billy stopped long enough to pick up a piece of white ash he'd been whittling on, and leaned on it like a crutch.

"What are you doing?"

"Making it look like I'm hurt."

"But you ain't!"

"They don't know that."

He led her on an easy trail that dropped down into the White River bottom, past an old logging camp, and along a partially overgrown haul road to the base of a cliff. Their progress, given Billy's crutch, had proven uncomfortably slow.

"We got to go faster!" she called from ahead as he lagged.

"Stop a minute," he said, glancing at the boggy ground.

She walked back, mud squishing between her toes, irritated that Billy was looking approvingly at the tracks she was leaving in the damp soil.

"We got to *hurry*!" she pleaded. "God, Billy, it's bad enough with what I see . . . relive . . . every time I close my eyes!" She thrust an arm out. "They're just back there! They're coming!"

"Uh-huh." One by one, he removed paper cartridges from the black cartridge box and carefully rolled them into his blanket. Leaving three in the box, he gestured her forward as he stumped along on his crutch, saying, "Take the trail to the right at the foot of the slope."

"Up that cliff?"

"That's right."

She just happened to look back as they rounded the brush, seeing Billy drop the cartridge box with its precious three rounds.

"What are you doing?"

"Laying trail, sis."

"They'll think that's your ammunition."

"Reckon they will."

Fifteen minutes later, sweating, her feet bleeding and raw from the abrasive limestone, she wondered when, if ever, they'd reach the top. In places she had to pull herself up, scrambling on all fours, only to find the trail edging along a limestone shelf above a sheer drop. Looking over the edge she saw jagged boulders at the bottom. By crickets, that was nothing to fall on.

Billy was stumbling, making a racket, dislodging small stones, as if he were on his last legs. She looked back, froze, that terrible cold wash numbing her to the core.

"Billy?"

He looked back, stopped short, seeing Dewley's riders as they emerged from the haul road and stopped at the boggy stretch. There Silas stepped

343

down from his horse and bent over their tracks.

Billy grinned for the first time that day. " 'Bout time."

Sarah scrambled for the next switchback, trying to forget the pain in her feet.

"Hold up," Billy called as he lay down over a boulder, propped the Sharps, and adjusted the rear sight. The muzzle shot flame and smoke as the report carried out over the valley.

Sarah shaded her eyes. To her surprise, Dewley's big black horse, called Locomotive, rose up, shook its head, and staggered sideways. Colonel Dewley barely kept his seat. Immediately, men scattered into the trees. Dewley stepped out of the saddle, checking his horse's neck. Turning, he glared up at the steep trail.

Sarah said, "He sets store by that horse."

One of the men was pointing at where Sarah in her red wool shirt and Billy stood exposed on the trail.

"Guess that got their attention," Billy noted. "They got spyglasses?"

"Of course!"

He then made a show of reaching for his belt where the cartridge box should be. Fumbling, jerking his head around as if looking for it, he slapped his pockets, and lifted the Sharps, staring at it wistfully.

"They're shooting!" Sarah cried as blue puffs were followed by the popping sound of guns. Moments later, bullets slapped the rocks and soil around them.

Billy pulled up his pistol, banging away. He shot three times, then bellowed, "Go away! Leave us alone!"

"You killed my men! Mutilated them, you son

of a bitch!" Dewley shouted across the distance. "You shot my horse! You run, you little pissant!"

Billy fired another shot from the Remington before turning and saying, "I want you to scream 'Billy, you stupid fool!' as loud and angry as you can, then turn and see how fast you can scramble up to the top."

"Billy, *you stupid fool!*" With the patter and snap of bullets wanging off rocks and the distant pop of the guns, her torn feet were forgotten as she scrambled for footing.

For the last twenty or thirty feet the trail clung to the face of the rock before entering a narrow defile that was little more than a crack in the limestone cap rock. The cleft gave her the willies.

A bullet spattered her with rock fragments and hot lead.

Panting, she made the crest, followed moments later by Billy, struggling along on his crutch.

As soon as he was hidden from sight, he tossed the crutch aside, dropping to his knees as he laid out his blanket, unrolled it, and loaded the first cartridge. Then he turned to the Remington, loading all six.

"What are we doing here?"

Billy looked up at her, eyes crystalline and cold. "John Gritts showed me this place afore he went off to war. It's old, this trail here. And we're not the first ones to use it."

He pointed. "I need you to start collecting them rocks. The head-sized ones. Here, take the crutch in case you need to lever any out of the ground. Pile them up on that point beside the trail."

"You sure they're coming? It'd be suicide."

"They think I'm hurt. By now they found the cartridge box and think I lost it. Without ammunition, hurt, and you screaming at me, they're thinking they got the scare on us. That we'll break like rabbits."

"What if they circle around? Ketch us from behind? They're bushwhackers, Billy!"

"If you're right about Dewley and his mad pride, I killed and cut his men, took a woman out from under him, and just wounded his horse. Reckon he ought t' be right fit to chew nails about now."

As she turned to collect rocks, Billy crawled up behind a currant bush and stared over the edge. "Here they come. Maybe five minutes, sis. When I shoot, you start tossing rocks down onto the trail."

She willed herself to forget the agony in her feet; the cold rocks cut and bruised her fingers. Some she could barely lift. She piled them just back from the edge, wondering at the dull acceptance in her numb heart.

If we lose here, I'm throwing myself off the edge before they can lay hands on me again.

Billy's shot surprised her.

She peeked over, saw Silas, the tracker, fall backward and bowl Dewley over on a particularly steep section just ten feet below the cleft. She picked up a head-sized chunk of limestone, aimed, and slung it out into the cleft. It hit the trail literally at Dewley's feet, took his legs out from under him, bounced off a boulder and struck O'Shaunessee full in the chest where the man followed close behind. He screamed as he toppled off the ledge.

Billy's rifle barked again as a man clambered out of the mass of falling, screaming men. The fellow arched his back, then sagged limply across the stone before tumbling out of sight.

Sarah reached for another of her rocks, surprised that it lifted so easily. Stepping to the edge, she lofted it and sent it crashing down into the screaming melee.

Guns were banging, bullets whirring off the cap rock and ripping harmlessly into the midday sky. Billy shot again. Someone screamed, others cursed.

Sarah returned with another rock, smaller, and picked her target before she tossed it out. Again it bounced off the slope before thudding into the men clinging to the trail below the cleft. She had a glimpse of the man they called Tennessee as he slipped and dropped over the precipice. She caught sight of him as he smacked onto an outcrop farther down the slope, and plunged headfirst onto the rocks.

Billy shot again, and someone shouted, *"Fall back!"*

"Get back here, *you bastards*!" The voice was Dewley's.

Sarah carried her rock to the edge. Men were leaping, jumping, falling, in their mad descent. At the report of Billy's rifle, a thickset blond man pitched face-first down the trail, knocking two of his companions off their feet to disappear over the drop. Someone was screaming from where he'd fallen onto the rocks.

At the bottom, seven of the survivors ran full-out to where a man held the horses. Each vaulted into his saddle, looking back as if to see who was following.

Billy's Sharps cracked. A second later one of the riders cried out and clapped a hand to his thigh, his horse shying. With an oath, one of the others wheeled his animal, and leaning into the lunge

347

laid spurs to it. The others, after a moment's hesitation, bellowed their defeat as they charged off in pursuit. The rest of the horses broke free of the handler and followed at a gallop across the track-stippled bottom.

One by one, three men hobbled down the trail, each fleeing as fast as he could in the wake of the horse handler who was pelting off behind the vanished horses.

Sarah threw her last rock, watching it land squarely on Dewley's leg where he was crawling back down the trail. Dewley screamed. Then the rock clattered down the slope, dislodging more stones as it did.

Sarah stood at the crest, the wind blowing through her hair, fluttering her red wool shirt, waffling her pants.

Dewley cried out in pain. "Help me! Damn it, boys, come help me! My leg's busted."

Billy stepped up beside Sarah and offered her the big Bowie. "You want Dewley?"

She looked at the blade and sniffed, a burning at the base of her throat. "I don't know how."

"Just like butchering a pig, sis." He paused. "Nothing much different to it that I can see."

She took the Bowie. "Reckon, little brother, there's a heap of difference."

She didn't feel the pain in her feet as she started down the trail. But then, who could feel anything when all of her dreams had been murdered?

43

November 5, 1863

Billy tossed the shovel aside and climbed up out of the grave. Head back, he looked up at the leaden sky, the clouds dark, bruised, and torn as they worried their way toward the southeast. A bitter wind alternately gusted and harried its way through the trees, and called forth a rasping howl from among the branches. Streamers of leaves, ripped away by the gale, scattered and whirled, as though fleeing desperately before the approach of some terrifying beast.

They had chosen the flat out back and next to the old cabin. At the end of the line where they had buried pets, he and Sarah had taken turns digging Fly's grave first, and after having placed the dog's few remains and covered them, now dealt with Maw's.

The wind moaned through the pines, flipping the brim of Billy's hat. Sarah stood, arms crossed against the cold, her rag of a dress — the only one left after Dewley's looting — was pressed against her legs. Wind kept whipping her long blond locks.

A dull emptiness lay behind his sister's face — a glittering despair — as though hell had reached out from some dark place and clawed away everything that was she.

"Reckon that's deep enough," Billy said through a tight throat. His heart could have been a cold stone in his breast. He looked over at the tattered blanket that wrapped Maw. Clothing, let alone blankets, being so rare in the country, this was the only one Dewley had left behind. It had lined Fly's bed. Had served as Maw's shroud. Now it was her coffin.

The wind whisked the blanket's flap from Maw's face, teasing her loose white hair.

Her eyes were empty sockets lined with torn tissue, the eyes having been pecked away by the magpies. The flesh on her left cheek was ripped where some critter had worried her. At the sight, a cry died in his throat, a spear of pain lanced his heart.

He was living a nightmare.

Sarah, as though aroused from her lethargy, bent. Her fingers shook as she tugged the old red blanket back over the ruins of Maw's face.

"Let's . . ." Billy blinked at the tears. "Let's get her in the ground, sis."

He tried not to think of how they'd found Maw when they'd arrived at dusk last night. How she'd been dragged from the porch where he'd so thoughtlessly left her. How her gut had been torn open and her insides savaged by some hog gone wild. He tried not to remember the mewling sounds that had risen from his throat, or the horror glittering behind Sarah's half-mad eyes as they'd lifted Maw's remains back into the blanket.

Or the smell, God forbid.

If only I had been here that day . . .

Sarah met his gaze, nodded, and together they lifted and carried Maw to the side of the grave.

350

They swung her out and tried to lower her into the depths. Even as they did, the old blanket tore with a rip, and Maw's scavenged corpse fell to land with a thump in the bottom.

"No!" Billy cried out, his stomach flipping. "Oh, God, Maw! I'm sorry! So . . . sorry!"

"It's all right, Billy," Sarah said woodenly.

Before he could move, she'd crawled down into the narrow grave and set herself to the task of straightening Maw's flopped body. But he'd never forget the way Maw seemed to stare up at him out of those empty sockets, as if her ghost were glaring in disgust. It was in the set of her half-open mouth, the dried lips pulled back from the brown, peglike teeth.

"God in hell," he whispered, falling back, his legs no longer able to hold him. A banshee scream sounded inside his head. Something burst apart in his chest. Dropping his head into his hands, he wept.

44

February 7, 1864

On his twenty-third birthday James Morton looked up from his bunk with glassy eyes. When he coughed his entire body convulsed — the sound of it racking and deep. His flesh had sunk into his bones, leaving his face cadaverous. The eyes appeared slightly bugged and bloodshot. A sort of living skull beneath thin waxy skin.

"It's bad, ain't it, Doc?" Just that short statement brought on another fit of coughing that left blood and bits of tissue on James's lips.

Doc exhaled, watching his breath rise in a feathery mist where it was illuminated by the shaft of light slanting through the barracks window. He wondered if life were nothing more tenuous and fleeting. Appearing warm and animated, only to dissipate into nothingness within moments.

For more than a month now, he and James had watched the shaft of sunlight shift from the solstice maximum in December. Some wit had marked the farthest the sun had shone into the barracks on the solstice noon by scratching a bunk post. Now at midday, it only reached to a spot lower on the floor.

The slow crawling of light might have encapsulated all of existence.

Around him men huddled in blankets and old campaign jackets, many coughing, others muttering among themselves. All of them were scratching, pinching at their hair and beards in an attempt to catch a louse and crush it between their finger and thumbnails.

Outside, the wind off frozen Lake Michigan was agonizingly bitter. In the Camp Douglas barracks — as snug and windproof as a rusted-out colander in a blizzard — the temperature was just ordinary bitter.

Doc stared helplessly up at the ceiling tresses where thin strips of daylight could be seen between the shrunken planks in the roof. "I don't suppose a lie would do any good, James. You've seen too much of tuberculosis."

James nodded and wiped his lips with a bloody rag. "You taught me too much medicine." He averted his eyes. "I guess that steamboat just gets farther and farther away, don't it?"

"I wouldn't give up. Not yet. Your sister's husband said that the paperwork should be coming through any day now. Sometimes, getting a sick man out of an environment like this, back into his home, can work wonders."

"I think I'm going to become a Catholic."

Doc craned his neck, squinting. "Where did *that* come from?"

James waved his bloody rag to take in the rest of the barracks and the ragged, half-starved, vermin-infested prisoners. "Them Catholics, they're the only ones that recognize saints, don't they?"

"You Baptists are depressing. What about the Episcopalians?"

James chuckled, which precipitated another fit

353

of coughing. When he finished, he whispered, "Dear God, each time it feels like I'm ripping the insides of my throat and lungs out." A tear squeezed past his eye. "But I meant what I said, Doc. All of us in here, we think you're a saint. We know what you've done for us. Your volunteering in the hospital? How many of them green Yankee surgeons have you trained? That man Jenkins hadn't even held a scalpel before he was sent here. You're the one what taught him how to amputate a limb. You're the one as got that General Meigs to order a sewer system put in last summer."

"No I didn't. They wouldn't even let me talk to him." That had been Henry Bellows of the Unitarian Church of New York. Bellows had candidly told the whole world that the only way to clean Camp Douglas was to burn it to the ground. Right down to the last stick of wood.

Doc looked down at his hands, still so thin and grime-encrusted. Word had finally filtered through the guards that because of Doc's complaining, starting with Higbee, all of his letters to Ann Marie had been confiscated by the provost and burned. It was said that the provost had feared Doc was using some code to expose abuses within the prison that would be used as Confederate propaganda.

No wonder Ann Marie had thought him uninterested.

Could men really be that petty?

James wheezed. "Most of the men in here think you did. That's the trouble with being a saint."

"Why don't you rest now?"

"Because I got a funny feeling, Doc." He coughed, shivered, and sucked for a breath that just didn't seem to come. Doc could hear the rattling in the man's lungs from where he sat.

"What feeling is that?"

"That I ought to say what I need to say."

"Nothing need be said."

"My sister . . ." He looked away, wincing with shame.

"She thought I'd forgotten her, James."

"I should have wrote her on my own. Told her how much you loved her."

"It wasn't your place. We could only send a single page. That was the provost's order. The god-damned provost . . . Well, it needn't matter. Can't change the past."

"She always was flighty." James closed his eyes, his skin so pale and delicate it looked like it might tear at the faintest touch. "I wish that . . . Well, I wish you really were my brother."

"I am, James. We've shared more than brothers." He thought back to Butler and Billy, wondering where they were. If they'd ever all be home together again.

James swallowed hard, coughed. "Afterward," he whispered, "just send Mother a letter. Don't go . . . Don't go telling them in person. You've suffered too much already at Ann Marie's hands."

"She didn't know." Doc reached out, laid his hand on James's and tightened it. "You just get a good night's sleep, and you can tell them yourself when your papers come through."

James broke into a fit of coughing, then spit blood into his rag. "Why'd you get into medicine?"

"Because my dog died when I was a lad. Called him Sandy. Went everywhere with me. Loved to play fetch with a stick. One day he chewed one up. Did that all the time, but this time he swallowed a sliver."

Doc glanced off to the side so James wouldn't see the hurt. "Took him a week to die, and it was agony the whole time. Paw and I cut him open to see what went wrong. And there was that sliver, poking through his stomach wall and into the intestines."

"They'll have a place for you in heaven, Doc. Saint Hancock . . . got a ring to it."

Sure. And where is God in all this horror, sickness, and death?

"Don't grieve for me, Doc. You gotta promise."

Doc sat with James until he dropped into an uneasy slumber.

After a time he rose, walked over to the window, and stared out at the slanting winter sun. Crystals of ice glinted in the air like tiny diamonds. Light gleamed on the snow-covered roofs, cast shadows in the track-dimpled and hard-frozen mud in the yard.

A group of shivering men, hugging their sleeves to their breasts for warmth, were harassing a scarecrow of a madman. Bending down, teasing him, asking him questions. The lunatic looked pathetic — a considerable achievement when compared to the rest of the vermin-ridden ragamuffins in Camp Douglas.

"A real saint would go out there and put a stop to that." He sighed unhappily and walked back to the bed. James was . . .

Doc's heart dropped.

When had he gotten so good at recognizing death? James should have had days. Weeks. Maybe, if his parole papers had come through, even months before consumption took him.

Or perhaps it was a complication from the old chest wound from Shiloh. Or maybe James had

356

just finally given up.

Doc stared woodenly at the empty green eyes, the chestnut hair . . . the dusting of freckles on the pale bridge of the young man's nose.

He should grieve, feel the aching loss. But inside lay only a dark emptiness. Like that of a worn-out boiler abandoned in the desert, which, when rapped with the knuckles, echoed hollowly of rust.

"Thomas? Corporal Willy? Do you want to give me a hand here? James needs to go to the deadhouse, and here's another bunk we can free up for whoever's next in line."

The men went suddenly quiet, turning owlish eyes on Doc.

"You sure, Doc?" Corporal Willy asked. "He was just talking to you not fifteen . . ."

At Doc's look, Corporal Willy looked away. "All right. Come on. All of you. Burial detail. Form up!"

"What for? It's colder 'an hell and a bat's ass out there! Five men died in here in the last week. Didn't do no burial detail for none of them," one of the Fresh Fish protested — a newcomer from Chickamauga.

Brady Duncan leaned down, practically nose to nose with the Fresh Fish, his eyes thin. "Because James is Doc's friend. Now get your chapped ass off that floor and form up, or they'll find you under the barracks in the morning, froze solid in the mud with a broke neck. You get my point?"

They carried James across the frozen yard on a blanket stretcher supported by planks. The guards watched from the high fence, stamping, blowing into their hands as the wicked wind off the lake blew their breath away in frosty streamers.

The guard outside the deadhouse looked worried at first, raising his rifle, uneasy gaze flicking this way and that.

"Private Nelson," Doc told him, stepping forward. "James Morton passed. We're just showing our respect. Come to lay him out for burial."

To his surprise, Nelson saluted. "I see, sir. Uh, Doc. My sympathies." He stepped aside, allowed them to carry James into the dark interior. The stack of frozen corpses, piled like macabre lengths of firewood, looked ghastly. A work detail would dig a trench for them as soon as the ground thawed.

With great care, James was placed high atop the pile in a position where he wouldn't be covered by other dead: the only respect they could show him.

Doc climbed down, now used to the unyielding, frozen corpses. Not even their expressions, the half-lidded and frost-filled eyes, or the partially gaping mouths bothered him.

"Attenshun!" Corporal Willy cried. Feet, some only clad in socks, shuffled.

"Salute!"

Arms flashed.

"Troooop . . . dismissed!"

One by one they filed out. Doc, the last, turned in the doorway to whisper, "Go with God, my friend. Hope they got steamboats in heaven."

Then Doc stepped out into the bitter cold.

The others had gone, waddling off across the uneven frozen ground, already chilled to the core in their threadbare uniforms.

Nelson glanced inside to make sure no one had stayed behind in an attempt to escape, and then closed the door. "Again, so sorry, Doc."

"How's the foot doing?"

"Healed up fine, Doc. Can't believe that surgeon wanted to cut it off. I'da been a cripple but for you."

"Dr. Sullivan just hadn't seen an abscess like that before. Erysipelas presents differently than gangrene. Just don't step on rusty nails anymore."

"No, sir."

Doc gave him a nod and began the slow walk toward the barracks. It hadn't hit him yet. But it would. James had been like an anchor, a reason to live. He'd promised Ann Marie and Felicia that he'd take care of the boy.

Oh, God. When this finally sinks in, it's going to break my heart.

He'd made it halfway when the lunatic cried out hoarsely, "Private Baker, back in the ranks. I'm your captain, and you'll not tarry. This is hostile territory, and we've got to stay close."

The cold had become so intense that even the lunatic's tormenters — delighted to have any distraction from the boredom — had retreated to the relative protection of their barracks.

Doc shivered, actually happy to suffer in the frigid wind. It proved he could still feel something — even if it were misery. He marched past the lunatic.

Can't save the whole world. Couldn't even save James.

"Vail, I know you're not an Indian, but you will be today. Can't let the Yanks know you're scouting their flanks."

Doc stopped short, shivering. He closed his eyes, asking God what more could possibly lie in store for him today.

Left alone, the lunatic would be dead by morning. Curled into a stiffly frozen ball, he'd make a mess of the stack in the deadhouse. Maybe even cause Nelson to reshuffle the corpses.

Doc turned back, walking over. "Hey, you! Come on. Get up."

The man didn't so much as look up, but whispered, "You're not real." He shivered hard, asking, "Corporal Pettigrew, do you see him?"

Doc reached down, gripped the man by his torn coat, and lifted. The scarecrow barely tottered to his feet, swaying, leaning against Doc. Jesus, he stank of urine and shit.

"Walk with me . . . uh, Captain."

"I'll need to send Private Templeton to report."

"You do that. I'm sure the private is an exemplary soldier."

The lunatic sounded hoarse, as if he'd been yelling and had strained his voice. He barely kept one foot ahead of the other, shivering uncontrollably, like a rack of bones in a buckboard.

Doc barely made it to the hospital yard, just feet from the hospital door, before the ragamuffin collapsed in a limp heap, his face in the snow.

"I see." Doc shivered and hugged himself. "Maybe Private Templeton didn't manage to report."

Doc stepped inside, made his way down between the rows of beds filled with the dying. Typhoid was epidemic again. He found Surgeon's Assistant Percy Anthony boiling water. Probably because that was a good excuse to stand by the single stove.

"Percy, could you give me a hand? I've got a sick call outside."

Anthony looked up, glanced longingly at the stove, and said, "Sure, Doc."

Outside the lunatic was muttering into the snow, still facedown.

"Oh, him."

"Been here before?"

"He's the worst case of fatigue we've ever seen, Doc. Can't do a thing with him."

"At least let me get him inside. Leaving him out here? It's a death sentence."

Percy Anthony crossed his arms, eyes fixed meaningfully on Doc's. "Sometimes, Doc, leaving someone out is the kindest thing you can do. You've told me that yourself. More than a couple of times over the last six months that I been here. So, let me ask you the question you asked me just last week: do you really want to prolong this man's suffering?"

Doc pursed his lips, a memory of James's ever so fragile skin, his green eyes softly imploring.

"I guess you're right. What's another . . ."

In a rasping whisper the lunatic said, "I think it's Philip, Sergeant. At least, it sounds like his voice."

Doc whirled, staring down at the filthy, snow-encrusted form. "You know me?"

The man laughed into the snow, his fingers opening and closing, water melting on his dirt-encrusted skin.

"Let's get him in," Doc said. "Do me this one favor, will you?"

Together — well, mostly it was Percy Anthony — they lifted the bone rack and muscled him through the door, down the aisle, and propped him in the cabinet corner closest to the stove.

"Got something I can clean his face with?" From the looks of it, the lunatic had been kicked or punched. One side of his face was swollen; dried blood had clotted in his once amber beard. One eye was puffed shut.

Anthony handed him a damp cloth and watched over Doc's shoulder as he sponged the grime from the lunatic's sunken features.

Even as he did, Doc swallowed hard, his hand beginning to shake. "Butler?" he whispered in disbelief.

"Yes, yes," the lunatic cried, "but it doesn't matter anymore." His voice changed, as if explaining something to someone. "Of course he does. He's my older brother. He and Paw don't get along. Hear he's a fine surgeon, however. Any of you need sick call? You go straight to Philip."

"Who are you talking to?" Doc demanded, grasping Butler by his snow-caked jacket.

"He talks to people all the time," Anthony said as he straightened. "They shipped him in with the Chickamauga prisoners. Said his whole command was wiped out, and he went raving insane."

Butler cocked his head. "Chickamauga. Now that was a fight, wasn't it, Sergeant? Company A wouldn't have charged that hill for anyone but Tom Hindman." He paused. "You think?" Another pause. "Maybe. I'll ask."

"Ask what?" Doc demanded.

Butler's open eye seemed to clear, and he looked straight at Doc. "The men want to know if there's any food. It's been weeks without rations. We know commissary is bad, but they'd give anything for even some hardtack."

"The men?" Doc felt his insides go runny. "What men?"

Butler pointed a bony finger at the space next to the stove with its boiling pot. "There's Corporal Pettigrew." The finger moved. "And sitting on that closest bunk, that's Phil Vail. Jimmy Peterson, he's the private looking over your friend's shoulder."

Philip and Anthony followed Butler's finger as it pointed here and there. Anthony actually shivered and backed away.

"We don't see anyone," Doc told him gently, unsure what to make of it.

"You don't?" Butler seemed genuinely distraught. "Most people don't. We're used to that. But you, Philip, you're my brother."

"Butler, there's no one there."

"They're not phantoms. They are my men. I'm taking them home. My responsibility. I promised them." Butler tried to smile, only to have it flicker and vanish. "I think it was Caesar, perhaps Napoleon, who said an army marches on its stomach. Can we see about rations?"

"Doc?" Percy Anthony asked. "You really know him?"

Doc felt the world reel, as if the ether that the scientists talked about had just spun around him. "He's my brother," Doc said hoarsely. "Butler Hancock."

And his mind is broken. Something I can't fix any more than I could cure James of his consumption.

45

Sarah tended the pit fire before the trapper's cabin. The day was blustery, rain having fallen earlier. The log structure, not ten by ten feet, sat back under the trees. The branches, so stark against the bruised gray clouds, were budded, about to flower. The first blades of spring grass had come up on the hillsides and in the flat before the cabin.

She tossed another broken branch — collected from forest litter an hour's walk up the small canyon — onto the fire. They'd scrounged most of the easily available wood from the little valley, and between the bucksaw and ax had cut up most of the smaller dead stuff.

She'd become adept at pit roasting, having dug a hip-deep hole, dropped in stones, and built a snapping fire. When a thick bed of coals had covered the glowing rocks, she'd shoveled in four inches of dirt, laid a venison quarter wrapped in burlap atop the steaming dirt, and shoveled another four inches atop the meat. Finally, she had built a fire on top, sandwiching the meat between layers of fire to slow-roast through the day.

Beyond that their diet consisted of leached acorns, cattail roots, and processed countie root, sassafrass tea, occasional corn or wheat that Billy procured. When he did manage such a treat, Sarah pounded the kernels with a homemade wooden pestle to make coarse flour. And finally, just about anything that walked, crawled, flew, or scampered in the forest was fodder for the stew pot.

Such bounty — after a full winter of scavenging and hunting — had become scarce enough that her belly had shrunk. Hard muscles contoured her thin arms and legs. She hated being hungry all the time, but knew that with spring greenup, a passel of new foods would grow.

Could that old life before the war have ever been possible? Had it all been a dream, or did those days of full bellies, roasting breads, bacon, pork, chicken, and hot buttered corn bread really exist? Were her memories of family, a warm hearth, sugar, molasses, and salt and pepper real? Had Butler once reclined in the rocker, his eyes alight as he read aloud from Xenophon or Shakespeare? Had Paw presided at the head of the table, pulling on his pipe, a smile on his bearded lips? Were Maw's looks of idle amusement as she kneaded bread dough but a figment of imagination?

Had Sarah once dreamed of a prominent husband, a fancy house in Little Rock, and gas streetlights? Were the velvet and silk dresses she had once imagined but flights of a spoiled little girl's fancy?

God, I was a fool.

Life consisted of before the rape, and after.

Sarah took a deep breath, stretching her ribs; she pressed a hand into the hollow of her abdomen. She had lived on the precipice of terror after the rape. Dewley's burning blue eyes still pierced her dreams — and sometimes her waking moments as well. She'd hear the ripping of her clothes, feel his body on hers. Her insides would curl at the memory of his penis probing inside her.

At odd times, just popping into her head, she would relive the moment when different men had thrown themselves onto her. She would hear the distinctive sounds each man made as he cooed endearments.

Endearments, for God's sake!

Then her skin would crawl at the memory of how differently each had reacted as he shot his seed into her. How odd that her damaged soul insisted on remembering their individual peculiarities. And then there had been Tucker, the virgin who had come the moment he'd entered, and then lay atop her crying.

The images, the sensations, possessed her with such clarity. How could that be? The actual event was months past. If God were truly merciful, shouldn't they be fading?

She laid her hands against the sides of her head, pressing, as if she could pop the memories from her skull. In the following weeks she had had the horrible certainty that they'd impregnated her. Night after night she'd lain awake, a hand pressed above her womb as if she could expel their seed.

Desperately she'd counted the days to her next flux, the fear rising as day after day her loins remained passive and the certainty, fear, and disgust grew.

Until the morning she'd been savagely chopping wood; a terrible cramp had doubled her over. She had sat down in the snow, grabbed her belly, and felt the hot wet rush between her thighs.

Unable to even stand, she had lain there until a final cramp — like something tearing inside — triggered a gasp from her heaving lungs. She felt when it finally passed. Weak and shivering, she'd pulled off her bloody pants and stared at the little blob of tissue — a thing that reminded her of a naked and bloody mouse.

Sobbing, trembling, she'd stumbled down to the trickle of a stream and washed herself in the cold water. Then she'd scrubbed out Tucker's pants with sand and wrung them out. Shivering in the cold, breath puffing, she pulled them on and staggered back to the trapper's cabin where she'd lain in bed for three days, much to Billy's chagrin.

She'd never told him. She never would.

But for a month afterward, she had savaged herself. Hated herself for ever having been born.

"What's the matter with you?" Billy had asked over a steaming cup of chicory root. "Get over it. Or are you just doing this to keep reminding me?"

"Reminding you?" she'd cried in disbelief, then, bursting into tears, she'd run out into the night to stumble up the slippery, snow-covered slope until she could stare up at the winter-white moon and pray to God to kill her.

But He hadn't.

She still lived. Hungry. Desperate. And loathing herself.

Not that Billy, with his dreams, was any better. She'd never seen her brother scared. But when the dream came upon him in the middle of the night, he'd cry. Whispering, "No, Maw! Please don't! I'm sorry! Don't hurt me!"

Once she'd shaken him awake, asking, "Billy, what is it?"

And before he could come to his senses, he'd hoarsely admitted, "Maw. She's climbing out of the grave. Her eyes are like fire, and she's pointing at me."

And then he'd taken to shaking as if his soul were frozen.

The crack of a hoof on rock carried up the canyon.

Sarah froze, head turning as she listened. Rider coming. Then she scrambled for the cabin door, reached inside, and wrapped her fingers around the revolver's polished grip. Tossing a brown blanket — stained green with grass — over her shoulders, she hurried to the currant thicket and crouched down behind the stems. Covered so, she was as near to invisible as a whippoorwill on the forest floor.

One hand on the grip, the other around the cold cylinder, she cradled the Colt she'd taken from Dewley's body. The gun that he'd shot Maw with. Capped, and all six loaded, she need only cock, aim, and fire.

Dewley. Her jaw clamped, the eerie memory of his demon-blue eyes stared out from inside her. Billy had been right. She had slaughtered enough pigs in her time. Killing a man wasn't that much different.

That she'd done so should have given her peace. Instead she wondered if she hadn't just released his dastardly soul — freed it from his body to possess a previously unknown corner of her own.

Along with everything else in her shattered world, her relationship with Billy was just as wounded. They barely talked — each locked sullenly in his or her head. The looks he gave her were bitter, filled with guilt. As if, by whatever fool reasoning, he considered her abduction and rape to be his fault.

As if it all went back to Paw saying, "You take care of your mother and sister."

Worst of all, however, were the nightmares that brought Billy screaming upright in his blanket. Several times, she'd seen him reflexively grab his privates. Seen the shame in his eyes the next morning when he wouldn't even so much as look at her.

She'd heard that men sometimes ejaculated in the night. Did he blame himself for that, too? As if his dream emission condemned him to the likes of Dewley and his rapists?

"And how, Sarah, do you go about discussing *that* with your brother?"

Her entire world was in shambles, and she could see no way out.

A hint of movement down the creek trail.

Her heart began to hammer.

A horse and rider appeared; another followed down in the trees.

Should have run!

Too late now. She'd have to let them get . . .

"Sis? We're coming in!"

She puffed out a relieved breath as Billy's voice carried on the cold air. But who had he brought? And why here? This was to be their secret. Their refuge.

Inviolate.

She stood — pistol still at the ready — as Danny Goodman led the way, his bone-rack of a blood-bay horse looking exhausted and sweaty. Danny — a worn butternut cape about his shoulders, a misshapen felt hat on his head — wore high boots in need of polish; a Burnside carbine rested in a saddle scabbard made from old boot tops. A ground cloth and lumpy blanket were tied to his cantle.

"Miss Sarah," Danny greeted, touching a gloved finger to the brim of his hat. Then he wearily stepped out of the saddle, bracing himself on the horse as if unwilling to trust his legs.

Billy, on a gray — another walking pile of bones — swung easily off, patting the horse. Both animals had immediately and greedily started cropping the spring grass in the small clearing.

"Billy?" Her anger was rising. "Why'd you bring Danny here?"

He gave her his hot gaze — the one that said, "I'm the man, and I'm responsible!" That look always incensed her.

Aloud, almost apologetically, he said, "Danny's in trouble. He needed a place to hole up."

"That's not *our* problem!"

"Miss Sarah," Danny said with a smile, eyes averted. "I understand. Just give me a moment, and I'll be on my way."

"No you won't," Billy declared adamantly, ground-reining the horse — not that the gray beast looked like it had the energy, or the inclination, to leave with fresh grass on the ground.

Billy stepped up, jaw set, a finger pointing her way. "We don't turn away friends in need, and Danny's *my* friend. It ain't Christian, and it ain't our way. Paw taught us better than that."

Danny's fatigued eyes fixed on the 1860 Army Colt she held. "Miss Sarah, you all want to shoot me, go right ahead. Given the way I feel right now, being dead might be a tolerable improvement."

She lowered the pistol.

"Billy, you promised . . ." She couldn't finish,

walking around the currants, stepping wide around the horses, and leaning in the door to slip the revolver back into its holster.

Then she turned, rubbing the backs of her arms as she asked, "Where'd you get the horse?"

"It's Danny's spare. Ride one, switch to the other when the first is tuckered." He reached up and unbuckled the bridle and bit, the horse barely letting him as it cropped for grass.

"You on the run, Danny Goodman?"

He grinned in her direction, his eyes on the ground at her feet. "Been up to Missouri and into Kansas some. Living the life of the partisan ranger." He tapped at his waist. "I got enough gold sewed into my belt to buy me a nice place when this is all over and done."

"You go sit, Danny my boy," Billy told him. "I'll see to the horses. Give 'em a chance to roll." As he started on the blood bay's cinch, he said, "Sarah, you reckon that haunch of deer meat is done?"

" 'Nuther hour," she told him, a feeling of futility sucking at her insides as she watched Danny settle himself on her stump before the fire and extend his hands. He was dirty, his eyes baggy, and he stank so powerfully of horse sweat, old burned powder, and long-caked body odor that her stomach surged, causing her to step back, her hand to her mouth.

"Good to sit so," Danny said to no one in particular, his eyes on the fire.

"Well, after you catch your wind, you go down yonder to the creek and wash up," she told him, unable to stop from making a disgusted face. "Though, God knows, it'll probably kill the fish and crawdads when you do."

He reacted with a slight smile. "Reckon I am a mite ripe."

He still hadn't really looked at her since he'd arrived. Maybe he was afraid Billy'd thrash him? As if Billy needed to worry. To put it mildly, she wasn't particularly keen on *any* kind of male attention these days.

She busied herself making sassafras tea, warming some of the cattail-root bread, and watched as Billy laid Danny's saddle forward against the cabin wall.

"This is quite the hideout you got," Danny called. "Unlash that blanket, Billy. Reckon they's a bottle in it."

Billy did, unrolling the dirt-smudged wool enough to retrieve a brown glass bottle three-fourths filled with liquid. This he handed to Danny, who used his teeth to pull the cork. Then he took a swig before handing it over to Billy, and asked, "How come you all are up here instead of down to the big house?"

"On account of the fact that we didn't kill all of Dewley's men. Reckon the ones still alive are biding their time, checking on the place periodically. I would." Billy took a drink, made a face, and wiped his lips with his sleeve. "Besides, there's too many riders these days. Right on the road like the house is? There ain't no way for just me to defend it. And the way bands of cavalry run up and down the Huntsville Road? Like as not I'd be swept up as a conscript by one side or the other, or shot as an enemy, or a deserter, or just for the fun of it."

He handed the bottle back and added, "An' I got to take care of Sarah. I let her down once. Ain't gonna happen again."

Danny didn't even so much as look up, didn't

bother to ask how Billy might have let her down.

It hit Sarah like a thrown rock: *He knows. Knows who Dewley was, why the riders would periodically check on the house. He knows what they did to me!*

Every muscle in her body went rigid; her stomach knotted harder than an Irish prizefighter's fist. First the fear. Then cold anger settled deep in her bones.

Billy told!

She could imagine how it had been. Billy, his face grim, saying, "Now you be damned careful of Sarah. Given what they done to her, don't you so much as smile at her, or wink, or nothing that might make her remember, you understand?"

Humiliation and shame brought tears to her eyes.

Struggling for breath, she looked away at the somber trees, their branches now heavy with budding flowers, leaves ready to burst. The faint trickle of water in the little creek, the grinding of horses' teeth, and the crackle of the fire were the only sounds.

She closed her eyes, and the sensation of futility left her swaying on her feet. Billy had told. Danny would tell . . . who knew? And they would tell. And within months, the whole county — what was left of it — would know.

The story would go from lip to lip: renegade bushwhackers — worse than jayhawkers — had killed Maw Hancock, abducted and violated young Sarah. Then plucky young Billy killed the worst of them, getting her back.

Billy Hancock, the brave and resolute hero. Men would buy him drinks; women would smile and nod their heads out of respect.

For Sarah, however, there would only be the

shame and ruin. She'd be the woman to be pitied and kept at arm's length. A forever peripheral person, sullied and fouled through no fault of her own — but eternally tainted nonetheless. When men gazed at her, they would be seeing her as Dewley's men did: naked and many times used.

For women she would be the ever-present reminder of "a fate worse than death." A horrifying living example that even the ironclad walls of chivalry provided no absolute protection. They would want to distance themselves, as though Sarah might be a lodestone that could draw similar disaster to their doorstep. A woman so abandoned by God — perhaps for good reason — as to be living proof that nightmares could become real.

She already understood that no decent man would want her. What gentleman would want to take her into his sacred marriage bed, knowing that as she disrobed before him, he was seeing what others had already ogled in lust? That as he laid her on the sheets what he might have considered a temple had been used by so many as sewer?

She felt faint, head swimming.

How could my own brother do *this to me?*

Numb to the soul, she leaned against the rough log wall, barely hearing as Billy said, "Critters had been at Maw, but we dug a grave for what remained. Took what little was left in the house, and hightailed it up here."

"Whole county is empty," Danny noted. "I been gone since last July so it come as a shock to come home. The farms is all abandoned, and half of 'em burned. Fields growed up with weeds. The roads is like trenches. Bridges all burned. But the worst part is the mills, all ruint. Some's blowed up, others burned to the ground. Ditches washed out. Stores like Trott's is all abandoned. What's Benton County come to, Billy?"

"Just a highway for armies going up or down the Wire Road, and for guerrillas to hide out between bushwhacking each other. We'd a never hung on if'n I weren't a hunter."

"So . . . what are you thinking? Just hide out up here until the war's over?"

"Think it'll ever be over?"

Danny laughed, took a swig from the bottle. "Reckon so. The way people is killing each other, sooner or later, won't be no farms nowhere. No mills to grind flour. No tanyards to make leather. No powder mills, lead mines, nor textile mills to make clothing. And then, finally, the last Yankee will kill the last Rebel with a rock, and he'll win. Standing alone in some field."

"Him and me," Billy said, taking the bottle and tilting it to his lips. After he'd swallowed, he added, "That's when I'll come down from the hills and start farming again."

"Where are you gonna get the seed corn?" Danny took the bottle and gestured with the neck as if to emphasize the point. "Without roads and railroads and steamboats, ain't none coming from back East."

"Might have to go to Mexico!" Billy laughed in a hysterical way Sarah had never heard. "Hey! Sis! Come dig up this hyar venison, and let's eat us some."

Trembling with rage, she pushed off the wall, saying, "Dig it yourself, you son of a bitch." Then she stalked off into the growing gloom.

As she did, she heard Billy say, "What the hell's got into her?"

Long after dark, she slipped back, shivering, and found the pit dug up, but still radiating heat. The brown-glass whiskey bottle lay on its side, empty. The door hung open a crack, and she slipped in, hardly surprised to find Billy passed out facedown on his blanket, still fully clothed with his boots on.

Danny lay wrapped in his blanket on the dirt floor, snoring like a bucksaw cutting hardwood.

She stepped around him, pulled her blanket from the bed, and tugged her gingham dress — the only one she'd saved from the house — down from its peg. Easing back out, she unhooked the holstered Colt from its peg by the door and, careful not to bang the powder flask, looped the pistol belt over her shoulder.

The blanket she folded; then she grabbed up the still warm remains of the venison haunch. The two men hadn't left more than a pound or two of meat clinging to the bones, but it would take her a ways. Once the last of the meat was chewed off, she could break the long bones for their marrow.

The gray horse fought the bridle and bit, but she managed. Then she turned, leading the gelding down the trail. The farm was little more than a mile away down the trapper's cabin draw. Once she reached it, she'd turn south on the Huntsville Road toward the ruins of Van Winkle's mill.

She'd leave the road at one of the creek crossings, walk the horse upstream through the water, then take one of the forest trails to the Wire Road. From there she'd head south to . . .

Well, it didn't matter.

If she was going to be a pariah, she would be one someplace where tongues wouldn't wag, and the gossips wouldn't delight in chewing her up like a slab of fresh meat. Where people wouldn't look at her through eyes eloquent with revulsion and pity.

Damn you, Billy. I trusted you!

46

May 2, 1864

"*Peut-être.* You gonna carry yo'self over to the mess an' see what commissary dey got?" Sergeant Kershaw asked. "Bin getting used t' them vittles."

Butler lay in his bunk, his wasted body still recuperating. Hard to believe that he'd actually *gained* weight on the gruel and weevil-ridden flour the prison provided.

"It ain't like I used to get at home where Missy makes that roast ham, biscuits, and hominy! Bet you never had hominy with red pepper in it." Pettigrew folded his arms, elbows sticking out through the ragged holes in his sleeves. He shot a challenging glance at the rest of the men who crowded around the barracks bunks. They were illuminated by slanting light that came through the window with its broken panes.

"You and that wife of yourn," Phil Vail said with a shake of his head. He sat on Brewster's bunk, whittling on a piece of wood with a pocketknife.

"Oh, stop," Butler chided them as he sat up on his bunk. "It's a prison camp."

"Cap'n," Jimmy Peterson reminded, "you was the one said y'all was gonna take us home." He stood back in the shadows, looking uncertainly at the other men.

"Told the Yankees," Butler replied sullenly. "Ordered them to go home, too."

"And since when, Cap'n," Kershaw's deep Cajun voice asked, "do dem Yankees ever do anythin' you tells 'em?"

"Sergeant, Yankees are beyond my ability to fathom."

"What ch'all mean? Fathom? What's dat?"

"It means to understand."

"Butler!" Doc's sharp voice brought him up, and Butler blinked. His men were grinning where they lounged around, not even making room as Doc walked up, his face concerned.

"Hello, Philip. We were just discussing the obstinate intransigence of the North and why —"

"You were raving," Doc insisted wearily, seating himself across from Butler on Brewster's bunk. Next to him, Vail gave him a sidelong look before peeling another sliver from his whittling.

"Not raving. That implies an emotional quality, a rising of the voice that —"

"All right. Not raving." Doc studied him from under lowered brows. "The men are back, aren't they?"

Butler pursed his lips, staring down at the floor, rocking slowly back and forth as he did so. Rocking helped. It soothed him when he knew Philip was going to lecture him. The men were always present, but Philip didn't want to hear that. When Butler concentrated, he could converse silently with his soldiers. But it took so much effort. And they didn't always understand.

Doc sighed, slapping his torn pants. The man was mostly skin and bones, and while he kept a cheery expression on his face, and a light tone in

379

his voice, Butler had caught glimpses of Doc when he didn't think Butler was looking. At those times his brother's face was a mask of worry and pain.

Doc raised his hands, as if in surrender. "You've been doing so much better. What's caused you to —"

"Sergeant Kershaw says it's the food."

Doc's expression pained for the briefest instant, then he pasted the placid mask back on his face. "The last time we tried to talk about this —"

"You became unreasonably angry," Butler reminded.

"I just . . ." Doc swallowed hard, as if struggling to keep his voice calm. "I want to understand."

"The men are *my* responsibility," Butler told him reasonably. "My command. I have to take them home."

"To each of their homes?"

The question was confusing, requiring too much effort to sort through. "No, Doc." He'd come to calling Philip "Doc" like so many of the prisoners did. "Just have to get them home."

"Home? That can mean a lot of things. Our home? On White River? I don't understand."

"I'm not sure I do either, but the sergeant will tell me when it's time."

"The one you call Kershaw?"

"He don' know me fer frog spit, Cap'n," Kershaw said. "*Bonhomme,* he t'ink I's just a ghost or spirit!"

"Aren't you?"

" 'Course not, Cap'n."

"Then why don't you show yourself like the rest of the men? You just talk into my ear like a —"

"*Butler!*" Doc barked. "I need you to concentrate. Pay attention."

380

"That's all I do, Doc. Do you think it's easy to be a captain? The entire company is counting on me. I have to keep them alive."

Doc's face was pained again. "You say that with such simple faith it wounds me. Don't you know . . . *know* that your men died at Chickamauga? You've told me that they were all shot down in the attack against the Union breastworks."

Butler said nothing, nodding slightly. When Doc kept looking insistently at him, Butler finally told him, "We've gone over this before."

"If you know they're dead, how can you still see them?"

"You're going to tell me I'm crazy again." Butler smiled in weary amusement. "So, all right, I'm crazy. You want to talk crazy? General Hardee put me in charge of the company! Made me, of all people, responsible for all these men. And they call me a lunatic?"

Kershaw was laughing, the others smiling in amusement. Butler gave them a conspiratorial wink.

Doc grimaced, his thin face working. "I'm trying to get you to admit that your men, the ones you think you see, aren't real."

Pettigrew threw his hands up. "Here we go again. I'll say fer sure, yer brother's like a bulldog when he sink his teeth into something."

Butler gestured for Philip to desist. "So I'm seeing ghosts. Philip, they're here. Just as real to me as you are. I can't make them go away any more than I seem to be able to make you go away. Go ahead, say it. I'm crazy."

Philip looked panicked. "I didn't mean . . ."

Frowning, Butler tried to find the words. "It's a

381

most peculiar thing. I don't *feel* crazy, just . . . well, a little confused by the way people act around me."

"It's what we call the fatigue. It's in your mind, Butler."

"Philip, you don't see them clustered around all the time."

"We's a cluster!" Johnny Baker crowed, breaking Butler's concentration.

Butler's lips twitched. Baker never took things seriously.

Doc sighed, blinked his eyes wearily.

"Doc," Butler said softly, "you think you've got to take care of me. You don't understand, do you? Me and the men, we're going to take care of you."

Doc gave him a dull stare. "I can hardly wait."

"Sarcasm ill suits you, big brother." Butler scratched where a louse kept biting his side. "Did you have a reason for disrupting the men and me, or just the indefatigable urge to harangue me back to whatever version of sanity currently preoccupies you?"

Doc coughed hard into his hand, and when he got his breath, said, "I finally got my appointment with Colonel Sweet today. He said he'd have his staff start on the paperwork. Given your improvement from the raving scarecrow I found in the yard, to merely delusional, I think I can take you home."

"By damn, boys!" Willy Pettigrew cried. "Ole Doc's gonna see us outta hyar!"

"Wait!" Butler called as the men cheered. "Doc, how are you going to do this?"

"I took what they've started to call the yellow dog oath — the oath of allegiance to the United States." Doc laughed, coughed again. That deep-

382

lung kind of cough. "As if I ever had any loyalty to the Confederacy. Given your, um, condition, you'll be released into my custody. For some reason, the good colonel doesn't seem to think you'll be a threat to the continued survival of the Union."

"Dat show what he know 'bout us," Kershaw said darkly. "We could still whip us a full regiment of blue bellies."

"As you proved so well at Chickamauga, Sergeant," Butler reminded.

Kershaw only growled in response. From where they crowded around the bunks, the rest of the men were looking uncertainly at Butler.

"Philip?" Butler asked. "What about your own men, the ones who depend on you here?"

Doc gave him a hollow look. "I'm tired, Butler. I save so few. I'm just . . . sick. Sick of death and suffering, and . . ." He coughed into his hand. "I've lost everything. Except perhaps you. I want to go home. I want to see Maw, Billy, and Sarah."

His eyes went dreamy. "I want to go down and sit on that flat rock and look at the sunlight on the river. I want to enjoy a cup of coffee on the porch and talk to Maw about the weather and the tobacco crop. Beyond that, I want . . ." He blinked away a tear. "I want to forget."

"The men and I," Butler told him, "we'll get you there, Philip. You'll see."

"Oh, that makes me feel so much better." Philip broke into maniacal laughter until the coughing grew so severe he gagged and almost threw up.

47

May 5, 1864

A fire continued to burn — white ash smoking — in the center of the small camp. Packs and blankets lay around the periphery of the clearing. Horses, tethered back in the brush, watched with pricked ears.

Odd how the simplest things, like building a fire, didn't seem to mean anything to a man. The men in this camp hadn't had the foggiest notion they were building the last fire they'd ever see.

Billy stood over the wounded man, staring down at him over the Remington's sights. The fellow lay on his back, air wheezing in and out through the hole blown out of his chest. With each breath the wound frothed with bubbly lung blood that soaked into the man's blue wool shirt, exposed where the stained and patched buckskin coat hung open.

The dying man looked up with shocked, disbelieving gray eyes. Speckles of frothy blood stained his dark blond beard. His nose was razor-thin, a pearling of lung-blood on his lips.

He lay where he'd fallen on his bedding, stunned by Billy's shot.

Two more bodies lay to either side, one facedown, legs akimbo, the other looking like he'd just fallen asleep on his side, but for the pool of dark crimson leaking out of the hole in his head.

Three down. One got away.

Danny was bent over the facedown man: George Fletcher as Billy had heard him called. He'd been one of Dewley's riders. One of the men who'd haunted the Hancock Farm looking for Billy and Sarah. Now Danny was rifling Fletcher's pockets and possessions. Most of Dewley's men carried gold, fancy watches, rings and jewelry, and other plunder they'd made off with from raiding.

The second man, the one who looked asleep, had been called Francis Scopol, a burly black-haired man in his thirties. He'd been the man wounded in the thigh by Billy's last shot the day after he rescued Sarah. The last of Dewley's riders to be brought to justice.

Maybe Maw's hideous ghost would no longer rise up from the grave, clods of dirt falling from the old red blanket. Maybe the glowing hellfire in her empty eye sockets would dim. Hopefully she wouldn't turn her rotted face toward him and reach out and unleash damnation from the tip of her skeletal finger.

Hopefully the terrible demon image of Sarah wouldn't slip into his nightmares anymore. She had first haunted his dreams the night he'd freed Sarah after the rape. That night her naked, abused apparition had hovered over him. To his horror and shame she had reached down and grabbed him. As her fingers wrapped around his cock he'd pumped seed into his trousers.

What kind of head-sick son of a bitch had dreams like that about his sister anyway?

God, he hated to sleep. Never knew if he'd rest,

or if Maw would come to condemn his soul, or Sarah would corrupt his body with the most forbidden kind of sin.

"Who're you?" Billy asked the lung-shot man.

"George Crawford," the man whispered through the blood. "Why'd you shoot me?"

Billy tilted his head at where Danny was pulling the pockets inside out on Scopol's pants. "You were riding with Dewley's men. They kilt my maw, raped my sister. Makes us at war."

"Raped . . . ? You . . . swear?" Crawford's wounded voice was barely audible.

"Swear," Billy agreed.

"Didn't . . . know that. Thought they'd join Paw's rangers."

"Debts gotta be paid."

Crawford coughed weakly, blood spurting from the hole in his chest. He spit blood to clear his mouth and said, "My brother? Tobe? He . . . get away?"

"Yep. But if he wasn't part of Dewley's rangers, well, I don't got no fight with him."

"Reckon you do," Crawford said, his eyes starting to flutter in his head. "You jist kilt me. He'll be coming. Along with the rest."

"Crawford?" Danny asked, stepping over. "From down to Van Buren County? Relation to Amos?"

"My . . . grandpap . . . Amos." Crawford's gaze drifted off, his mouth working weakly.

"Shit and hellfire!" Danny cursed, stamping off to the side. He straightened, looking off in the direction Tobe had fled. "Reckon it's too late to catch him?"

"I heard of the Van Buren County Crawfords." Billy looked down at where George was fading, his chest pumping weakly as his lungs filled with blood. "What in tarnal hell was any of the Crawfords doing riding with Dewley's lot? Crawfords is Yankee guerrillas. Dewley's lot was Rebel."

"Maybe they's looking to change sides." Danny licked his lips, looking nervously down the trail where Tobe had fled. He clicked the short stack of coins together that he'd culled from the dead men's pockets. At the picket, the horses snuffled and whickered as they looked off in the direction Tobe had taken.

"And what will the Crawfords do when good old Tobe reports?"

"Come looking for us," Danny said. "That Crawford bunch, they's thick with Jeff Williams and his Yankee jayhawkers. They got them a regular war going with Allen Witt and his guerrillas over to Quitman. And somehow, Billy boy, we just got ourselves stuck right in the middle of it."

Billy looked down at the dying man. "Reckon I'm sorry I kilt you. Just bad luck. You was camping with the wrong men."

Even as he said, it, Crawford's chest expanded one last time, the sucking wound under his right breast gurgling and going still.

"Billy? What are we gonna do?"

Billy turned his attention to the Boston Mountains where they rose to the south. They were smack in the middle of Franklin County, in unfamiliar territory. Billy glanced up at the sun, just nearing midday. "Reckon we'll head home. Them are three good horses on that picket yonder. With our mounts, we can switch off. By this time tomorrow, we can be at the trapper's cabin."

"They'll figure it out, Billy. You don't know them Crawfords. They'll hear that you was hunting anybody what rode with Dewley. You done made a point of it to too many people since Sarah left. Reckon they'll comb the whole length and width of the Upper White until they flush us out like lice."

"Might want to be shut of this country for a while."

"What if Sarah comes back?"

Billy shook his head, thinking of how craftily she'd outfoxed even his abilities as a tracker. In the beginning, he just couldn't believe she'd leave him so, but once it had soaked in, he'd come to understand that it was his fault. That he'd betrayed her trust. Hurt her to the bone.

And she ain't never gonna forgive me.

Just the thought of it made him sick to his stomach.

"She won't. Not after this long. I ain't told you, but I been having dreams. Maw comes back from the dead, shaking that finger of hers, telling me I done let her down. Got Sarah raped, and then I made her leave."

"You *didn't* make her leave. She done it on her own. Took my damned horse in the process."

"Nope. I made her run. Did it the moment I told you how she'd been violated." He shoved the dead Crawford with his toe. "Maw knows. That's why she's come back from the dead. She's damning me to hell for failing her. My fault. I done it all wrong."

Danny bent down and started the task of going through Crawford's pockets, saying, "Reckon they'll kill us just as fast for looting the body as for making him dust in the first place."

Billy holstered his Remington and started going through the blankets and packs, setting aside anything they could use. It wasn't a bad start:

three more horses and a couple of sides of bacon, cornmeal, some pans, and money. He and Danny were well armed, had enough powder and shot, and the whole countryside was at war with itself. Travel by night, hole up by day, the biggest problem was staying clear of Union jayhawkers and Rebel guerrillas.

And after they packed up their belongings at the trapper's cabin? Where then?

Missouri was out of the question. That truly was jumping from the frying pan right into the fire. Kansas was Yankee country. But just west was the Indian Nations. He could probably get through the Cherokee country, knowing enough of the language. Granted, Chief John Ross's Union Cherokee were killing Stand Watie's Confederate Cherokee — and vice versa — just as fast as Arkansans were killing each other. But beyond that, if the stories were true, Texas wasn't at war with itself.

"Crawfords can't kill us if they can't find us, Danny." He picked up his Sharps and propped it on his shoulder. "What the hell is left for us in Arkansas anyway? Your family's gone south, fled to Louisiana. Mine's dead. Aren't but a handful of farms left in Benton County. Elkhorn Tavern's burned. We can't farm 'cause anything we raise, whichever bunch of bushwhackers, Reb cavalry, or Yank army would confiscate it all anyway."

"And we'd be conscripted by whoever finds us first. Yank or Reb. We'd be tossed smack into the ranks to march, starve, and sleep shivering in the mud before being shot in battle."

"We got close to three hundred dollars in gold from Dewley's bunch." Billy grinned. "Reckon we could live pretty damn well on that in Texas."

389

Danny was staring at him as Billy hunched down and pulled his powder flask from his belt. Half cocking the Remington's hammer, he rotated the empty cylinder and poured a measure of powder into the first empty chamber. Fishing a ball from his pouch, he seated it, turned the cylinder, and used the loading lever to press the ball home. He repeated the process on the two remaining empty chambers, sealed the loads with grease, and finally pinched caps onto the nipples before setting the hammer on the revolver's safety notch.

Danny had been watching pensively. "You ain't leaving the hammer on an empty? You gonna trust the safety notch?"

Billy worked his jaws as he looked around at the spring-green hills. "The way I figure it, Danny, I got a whole lot better chance of being shot by somebody else than I got of shooting myself if'n I snagged the hammer. Reckon it's up in the air as to whether I'll need that sixth shot before we even get out of this damn county."

Strapping their plunder onto one of the horses, Billy wondered, *Where the hell are you, sis?*

For an instant, he had a vision. Like he'd heard tell of among religious folk. He thought he saw her, tall, naked, her golden hair streaming out behind her as if blowing in the wind. She lifted her arms in his direction. Blood was leaking down the insides of her long legs, and her high full breasts were bruised, bitten, and bleeding. Her pink nipples stood hard and erect. The dark shadow of her navel contrasted with the milky flat of her abdomen, and droplets of semen glittered on her golden pubic hair.

Her eyes pinned his, and flashed — angry, damning, and unforgiving.

The dream demon. This time in the light of day. And just as quickly, it was gone.

Gasping, he struggled for breath. His heart was pounding.

"C'mon, Danny. Sooner we get ourselves to Texas, the happier I'm gonna be."

48

May 8, 1864

In the days since he and Butler had walked out beneath the arched entry to Camp Douglas, Doc found himself in dire straits. Dressed in tatters, not a penny to their names, he and Butler were starved and sick. As he and his brother walked slowly south from Chicago along the Springfield Road, northwest Arkansas might have been on the other side of the world.

A spring rain pattered on their bare heads, running down their faces. Their clothes were soaked, cold, and clinging. Mud squished between Butler's toes. It clung to Doc's old brogans and worked up through the holes in the soles.

Not since the days after Shiloh had Doc been this hungry, wanting nothing more than to chew on something, anything, just for the taste if not the sustenance.

A sense of complete despair filled him. Were it not for Butler, he would have loved nothing more than to fall prostrate in the mud and weep.

He glanced at his brother. Butler's eyes were flickering, lips moving as he "talked to his men." He did it so rationally, as if — as he claimed — he could see them as clearly as the real world around him.

What had happened to the young man who read Plato, recounted tales of the kings of England, quoted Voltaire, Hume, and Rousseau, and told of Julius Caesar and his conquests? What terrible thing had broken such a fine intellect and sent it scurrying into delusion?

Doc had carefully felt Butler's skull, seeking any sign of injury or wound. Nor did Butler remember being hit in the head at any time. The madness had just come upon him, according to the way Butler told it.

Doc winced. As if his own hightailing for the deadline that day he'd read that Ann Marie had married precluded him of any such charge of insanity.

He coughed, spitting the production into the wet grass at the side of the road.

"Kershaw tells me the men are in need of rations," Butler said off handedly as he looked around at the cultivated fields on either side of the road. Lines of newly leafed beans, the first shoots of corn, and lettuce sprouted in lines behind the rail fences.

"Well, Butler, you tell the good sergeant for me that I just don't have an answer for him. If I hadn't 'swallowed the yellow dog' and been paroled, we'd still be getting something at the mess in Camp Douglas."

He barely had the strength to gesture. "After dark we might be able to sneak past one of these fences and pick some of the lettuce without getting shot. On the other hand, our tracks would give us away come morning."

"Kershaw says that the men could probably

mount a raid," Butler agreed in a tone of voice that indicated it might be a military option.

"Kershaw and the men," Doc whispered under his breath. "Mount a raid." He shook his head, water dripping from his cold nose. "All of Illinois should tremble."

Somehow he plodded on, each foot he managed to place ahead of the other being a small victory. Time after time, he and Butler would move aside as a wagon, carriage, or coach would pass. So, too, did riders. And more than once, pedestrians who gave them furtive looks, and who kept hands tucked into coat pockets where the smooth grip of a pistol or revolver no doubt reassured them.

To each, Butler would smile and call a greeting, as if he were meeting a longtime acquaintance. And the travelers' lack of a reply seemed not to bother him in the slightest.

Not for the first time did Doc wonder if, of the two of them, Butler's insanity wasn't the better bargain.

They stopped that night under a bridge. It was moderately dry, though water dripped between the planks. At their feet the rain-swollen creek would wake them should the waters rise up past the banks.

"I could sure snuggle up to Colonel Armstrong's donkey tonight," Butler said absently.

Doc wasn't sure if he were talking to him or to his delusions. "Whose donkey?"

Butler's eyes went rubbery, his expression shifting from pinched to slack. "It's the gospel truth. I swear it."

"Swear what?" Doc asked in irritation. "Sometimes, Butler, so help me . . ." But there was no use. A deep and yawning pit seemed to open before him, as if he could fall into the swirling water below his feet and let it carry him down into an eternal darkness.

"Fella by the name of Chillon, so the story goes, walked all the way from California to join up with the Third Louisiana Infantry. Hébert's regiment. Fought at Pea Ridge. Anyhow, Chillon had served in the French army and considered himself indispensible." Butler paused. "Yes, Sergeant. That's the man."

The pause was so long, Doc figured Butler had lost the thread of the story, and just as he was about to stretch out on the timbers, Butler added, "Chillon walked all that way from California, but he'd packed his possessions on the donkey. Being winter, every night he and the donkey slept all huddled up together for warmth."

"Are you making this up?"

"Oh no. It's told all over Arkansas. Chillon, of course, marched off to Pea Ridge and was killed in the fighting. It was winter, if you'll recall. And on the retreat, Hébert had been captured, and Colonel Frank Armstrong had taken over.

"Now, Armstrong looked a lot like Chillon. Older, bearded, wore the same style uniform, but he was a stuffy, self-aggrandized sort. So arrogant his men hated him." A pause. "Yes, Corporal. Very much like General Bragg."

"Butler, does this have a point?"

"It's snowing, cold, and men are sleeping near naked in the snow, and of course, Chillon's donkey can't find his master anywhere. Armstrong, like everyone, was exhausted, and pitched out on the ground without so much as a tarp.

"Which is where his first lieutenant found him the next morning, sort of spooned around

395

Chillon's donkey. Right plastered around him, and supposedly smiling blissfully in his sleep. Word is his trousers were at full attention, if you follow."

"God help Armstrong. Men have erections in their sleep. Doesn't mean anything," Doc said with a weary smile.

"From that moment onward," Butler stated gravely, "it was taken as proof that old Colonel Armstrong couldn't tell the difference between a whore's rear and a jackass."

Sometime around midnight, Doc was aware that the rain had stopped. He listened to Butler's deep breathing where he lay on a square bridge timber.

Sleep, brother. And I pray you have more peace in your dreams than in waking . . .

Sometime later the clatter of iron-shod horses and wheels brought Doc out of a sound sleep.

He blinked, surprised to see it was late morning, the sun high.

Beside him, Butler sat on the timber, his bare feet dangling down to trail in the water as it swirled past. As he did, he munched on a piece of apple pie, and a white cotton cloth bag stuffed half full rested on the timber beside him.

Doc's nose caught the sweet smell of the pie, his mouth watering as he pushed himself up.

"Food? Butler? Where did you get the pie?" Doc couldn't take his eyes off the prize as Butler took another bite, crumbs sticking in his mustache and beard.

"Raiding Yankees isn't half bad, Doc," Butler mumbled through a full mouth. "You were sleeping so soundly, Sergeant Kershaw said it would be a shame to wake you."

"You *stole* that!" Doc stiffened, expecting to

hear shouts and the hue and cry of pursuit.

"Seized as spoils," Butler replied after swallowing. "Sort of like John Hunt Morgan did so well in Ohio. But the men couldn't find a telegraph to send any messages proclaiming the fact to the Yankee authorities."

"A telegraph?" Doc blinked, trying to clear the cobwebs from his sleep-slow brain.

Butler frowned. "Major road like this? You'd think they'd have strung a telegraph along it. Of course, we'd have to have a telegraph operator. None of the men know how to operate one. Although Billy Templeton has a cousin who ran a telegraph station in Mississippi."

Doc rubbed his face, his stomach flipping in contortions at the smell of the pie. "You got any more of that?"

"Of course! I saved you half. And there's smoked ham and bread in the bag. Phil Vail reminded me that war being an uncertain thing, I should start with the pie first. Corporal Pettigrew argued for starting with the ham, but the exegesis of command is to make hard decisions."

"The . . . *what* of command?"

The look Butler gave him was curiously full of pity. "You are starting to sound as unlettered as the men. But then, I'm sure you employ medical terms that would be similarly beyond my ability to ken." Butler reached around, offering a slice. "Pie?"

Greedily, Doc devoured it, almost crushing the sticky sweetness into his mouth. Dear God! Cinnamon and sugar, tart apple, and a perfect crust! He closed his eyes, savoring.

How long had it been since he'd enjoyed those tastes? At least since Memphis. He swallowed the last of it, placing a hand on his stomach as it cramped slightly.

"Don't eat too much, Butler," Doc warned. "It will make you sick."

"We have time," Butler replied easily. "Sergeant Kershaw cautions us to hole up and refresh, at least for the day. It will allow Yankee cavalry to disperse before we take up the march again."

Doc took a breath, his impulse being to challenge Butler's delusion. *No, let it pass.*

"You really loved her, didn't you?"

Doc flinched. "Who?"

"Ann Marie. You were talking to her in your sleep. Asking over and over, 'How could you?' "

"I'll never take an interest in a woman again, Butler. Every time I do, they end up with another man. First it was Sally Spears. I found Paw in her bed. Ann Marie, she was as different from Sally as day and night. She was a lady, Butler. So refined, mannered, and poised. Where Sally was wild, dangerous, and spirited, Ann Marie was the essence of feminine purity. A belle in the truest terms." Doc licked his fingers. "And now she's someone else's. Just the same as Sally."

Butler yawned as another wagon rattled and banged over the bridge. "I've never spent time in the company of a woman. Sergeant Kershaw, Corporal Pettigrew, Parsons, and Johnson, they're married. Billy Templeton, he's a sort of rascal and frequents soiled doves. They tell me about what it's like to be with a woman." Butler's expression tensed. "Wouldn't it be wonderful to have a pipe? I could go for a smoke now."

"I think it's because we both went off to get schooling," Doc told him. "Farm people marry young. The work requires it. Farming is family business. And I think there's an earthy attraction for young people. The life is all about fertility and making life." He paused. "I wonder if Sarah's married?"

Butler smiled wistfully. "I wouldn't doubt it. Unless Billy's whipped them all. She was the most beautiful girl when I left. Pale blond hair, glowing blue eyes, and Doc, she's grown into a full woman. Not classical in figure like Aphrodite, but more of a Nordic goddess's beauty. Think Freya come to earth."

Doc smiled at that, feeling his stomach settling in. A horse could be heard approaching fast. It hammered over the bridge and cantered away.

"There goes your cavalry."

"Sergeant Kershaw says there will be more." Butler pulled an earthen-ware jug around. "And I brought this. It's hard cider."

Doc took a sip of the cider, its taste awakening long-dormant parts of his mouth. "Well, who am I to argue with Sergeant Kershaw?"

And as weak as he and Butler were, a day of rest, eating slowly, might just make the difference.

He glanced over at his mad brother, seeing the man's eyes flickering, his lips moving, the odd twitching of his hands.

Wouldn't it be nice if you really did have a company of soldiers to keep you safe?

49

July 8, 1864

Mrs. Pennington's redbrick house in Little Rock was a two-story affair with sandstone lintels over the white-trimmed French windows. A full porch faced Eighth Street just west of Broadway. Mrs. Pennington was a widow, her husband John having died of pneumonia a couple of years before the war.

John had made his fortune as a wholesale importer of goods by steamboat, and had owned a warehouse off First Street where he'd stored his wares before dispersing them to the various merchants about the city and state.

After his death, the sale of that property had provided Mrs. Pennington with enough of a financial stake that she could live comfortably, if not in the opulence she had enjoyed before the war, let alone before her husband's death.

That she fed Sarah and allowed her to live in the old slave's room in the basement, under the stairs, in return for the labor Sarah provided, was compensation enough. Mostly Sarah's duties consisted of running errands, cooking, cleaning, laundry, and occasional mending. In addition, the old woman had delighted to discover that Sarah could not only do sums, but actually manage money and accounts.

In the beginning, the columns of numbers had been intimidating. Especially after the farm's simplicity. But Sarah was getting a handle on them, and had already determined that the butcher was taking her employer for ten dollars a month by adding a one to his monthly bill.

"Where are you from?" Julia Pennington had asked when Sarah arrived at her door, the *Gazette* ad in hand. She had introduced herself as Sarah Rogers, come to apply for the position of housekeeper.

"Baxter County, ma'am," Sarah had lied. "My James was killed at Shiloh and jayhawkers burned the farm. Nothing left up north for me. What kin ain't dead up and left to get away from the bushwhackers."

"Don't suppose you'd have a reference?"

"Not among the living," Sarah had replied, looking into the woman's calculating brown eyes.

"You seem well dressed for a refugee."

"Sold my gray horse, ma'am. I got twenty dollars for him, and five went for the dress. Don't know when I'll find work so the rest goes to keep me fed in the meantime."

"That everything you own?" Mrs. Pennington had pointed at the bundled blanket rolled over Sarah's shoulder.

"Yes, ma'am."

For long moments, Julia Pennington had peered at Sarah as if she could scry into her very soul. Then she said, "Five dollars a month, room, and board. Since the Yankees arrived, the slaves have all left. You can have Percy's old room under the stairs. It's not much, and hardly fit for a white

401

woman, but I suppose it's better than the streets."

Sarah might have taken on the role of slave as well as having moved into the household quarters. Pennington expected her to be up at five, have a fire in the cookstove and both hot tea and breakfast prepared by the time Mrs. Pennington awakened at seven. At night, Sarah was expected to be the last one in bed after seeing to the dishes, making sure the doors were locked, and ensuring the lamps were extinguished.

For the first month all Sarah had done was clean the big and beautiful house. Nor was the irony lost upon her. This was the house of her dreams with its ornate woodwork, grand parlor, tiled fireplaces, fine staircase, and tall ceilings.

Had she really promised God she'd endure anything to live in a house like this?

The nightmares still came upon her, and she'd awaken in the middle of the night, her fist tight on the pistol grip, her body trembling as Dewley's frigid blue eyes burned into hers. But the odd moments in the middle of the day — when out of thin air she'd be back in that clearing, shuddering as men laid hands on her skin — had been fewer and farther between.

She had been doing so well. But that afternoon Maxwell Johnson, one of Julia Pennington's cousins from New Orleans, had arrived. He was in his early thirties, well dressed in pressed brown suit with ribbon-lined lapels, and had a cravat at his throat. Thick curly brown hair seemed to sweep up from his high forehead like a wave. His eyes, however, were hard, dark, and impenetrable.

As Sarah served the dessert cake, she was aware of how he watched her. Just knowing that she was the center of his attention brought on a shiver that made her almost drop Mrs. Pennington's fine china plate.

"Sarah? Goodness gracious, what makes you so clumsy tonight?"

"Nothing. I'm sorry, ma'am," she replied as she beat a fast retreat from the lamp-lit dining room and into the safety of the kitchen. There she took a deep breath, hand to her heart, feeling it pound beneath her apron.

"It's all right, Sarah. You're in Little Rock. You're safe." She looked around, reassured by the familiar kitchen with its big cookstove, the counters, and the dishes soaking in soapy water.

When she managed to still her breathing, she leaned her ear against the door, hearing Julia Pennington. ". . . no doubt some hardscrabble farm up north. Lost her husband at Shiloh. There are so many like her."

"Is she honest?"

"Nothing she's done would indicate otherwise. Oh, I tested her, believe me. I left some jewelry, fake things, where she'd find them. Not only did she not take them, but she brought them to me with a reminder that I best not leave such things lying about. Can you believe it? Her work is exemplary. Better than Percy on her finest day. And unlike having a slave, I can ask her to leave at any time."

"She has a man?" Maxwell's voice rose suggestively.

"Not the slightest interest, and I've entertained some of our city's leading lights . . . even Yankees. She never so much as looks them in the eyes let alone flirts." A pause. "You ask me? She's better off with that husband of hers dead. I'm sure he used to beat her."

"Why would you think?"

"I've seen her, Maxwell. At times something will set her off. She just freezes and shakes. Terrified and paralyzed. Then it will pass."

Sarah bit her lip and closed her eyes. Damn! Was she that transparent?

"But something about her doesn't ring true," Julia Pennington continued, lowering her voice. "She's educated. Knows the classics, reads well above her station, and writes in a most legible hand. She does sums well enough to be a book-keeper. Then just as you would think she were a lady, some word will slip out like she was raised in a backwoods frontier cabin."

"A most attractive young woman," Maxwell added. "Very well formed. Were she properly groomed, dressed, and had her hair —"

"You're married."

Maxwell laughed. "Vanessa could care less. You know as well as I do that I married her for financial reasons. Besides, she's happy to dedicate herself to the children. That's all she wanted out of the marriage anyway. Well, and the status, of course."

"And I suppose you, as a healthy young man, have your amusements?" The tone in Julia's voice was curiously cold. "I know you and Percy had an arrangement. And because it was mutual, I never said anything."

"Men will be men, cousin."

There was a silence, then Mrs. Pennington said, "I suppose I should have grown used to it. John never threw it in my face. Was always dignified." Another pause. "My advice here is that you leave that girl alone. Don't even suggest it."

"Of course, Julia. I wouldn't think of imposing

on your kind hospitality."

Sarah had turned hard as a board, every muscle knotted. "Thank you, Julia," she whispered under her breath. Then she staggered over to the washbasin and attacked the supper dishes with such violence she broke one of the bone-china plates.

"Sarah?"

She jumped at the sound of Pennington's voice, wheeling to face the woman. Pennington leaned in the kitchen door, her face oddly pensive, as she read Sarah's near panic.

"Ma'am?"

"You may clear the dining room. Maxwell and I are retiring to the parlor. I shan't need you for anything else tonight. I'll see to closing up. After you are finished you are free to retire."

"Yes, ma'am." A flush of relief ran through Sarah's breast as Mrs. Pennington closed the door behind her.

Thank God! She wouldn't have to see Maxwell again. All she had to do was set his breakfast on the table in the morning, and he'd be gone by midday.

Peeking into the dining room, she satisfied herself that it was vacant before retrieving the plates. She removed the soiled tablecloth — Maxwell had spilled gravy — and adjusted the chairs. Then she blew out the lamps, finished in the kitchen, and made her way down the stairs to her cramped bedroom.

She lifted the latch on the door, slipped out of her clothes, and crawled under the blanket before blowing out her candle.

Mrs. Pennington thought she'd been beaten by her husband? That that accounted for her sudden panics?

If you only knew.

She curled her knees up to her chest in the small bed, her hands knotted into fists.

"Please, God. Don't let me have nightmares just because Maxwell was asking about me."

Forcing herself to be calm, she struggled to make her mind blank, but in the end, she reached under her blanket, and pulled the long Colt revolver from its holster.

Her fingers on the wood grips and cool steel, she felt herself begin to relax.

She came awake, unsure of when she'd finally dropped off to sleep. Fragments of dreams clung to her like gossamer strands, images fleeting and fading.

Something creaked in the room.

Her heart leaped. "Who's there?"

"Sarah?" a man's voice asked softly in the darkness. "Don't be afraid. It's Maxwell, Mrs. Pennington's cousin. I just —"

"Get out."

"I just want to talk. You're a most attractive girl, and well, I can do things for you."

A vise seemed to tighten on her throat. Sudden terror strained her voice into a whimper. "Get away from me."

"Julia tells me that you've lost everything. I can help. You were a married woman so there are no secrets when it comes to men. What if I were to tell you that by tomorrow morning you could earn yourself a ten-dollar gold piece?"

Sarah fought for breath, her arms beginning to shake. Images of Dewley flashed behind her eyes. "No. Don't do this."

"Sarah." His voice was so smooth in the darkness. "You're such a beautiful woman, you shouldn't be locked away in prudish old Julia's house like a common house slave."

"Get away from me." Her voice came out as a squeak.

"Would it help if I sweetened the pot? Think of what you could do with fifteen dollars, Sarah. Yankee gold. Not paper."

"I'll scream."

"Shhh. No need." He shifted in the darkness. "It's your eyes, Sarah. That pale hair of yours. All I'm asking is a simple joining in the night, nothing you haven't done before. And if I don't make you feel things you've never felt before, I'll toss in another five dollars."

Blue eyes flashed in her memory, her body recoiling as she felt a heavy weight settle on the bed. Dewley was grinning down at her, stinking breath blowing past his broken teeth.

She felt a hand laid on her hip, a voice saying, "Just let me give you a hint of the pleasure I can stir from your beautiful body."

"No! God, please! No!"

"I won't hurt you." The voice wasn't Dewley's, but the eyes were, the weight of the body. The terror beating through her veins. She opened her mouth to scream, but no sound came from her spasming lungs.

"There," the voice soothed.

She remembered Dewley whispering softly into her ear as he lowered himself onto her. *There, there. Easy. Yes!*

She fought a sob, fear electric and charging her muscles. Her fingers curled into fists, her right hand tightening around cool wood and metal.

Dear God. Dear God, no!

"Sarah?" The hand settled on her, pulled the

407

blanket back.

Dewley loomed over her in the darkness.

"Sarah? I'm going to touch you now."

"Get away from me, Dewley!" she screamed as she scrambled back in the bedding, lifting the heavy Colt. She felt for the hammer, heard the clicking as she thumbed it back.

"I'll kill you, you son of a bitch!"

The revolver blasted fire into the blackness, the flash illuminated her room. As the concussion deafened her, she caught a glimpse of Maxwell Johnson's frightened face. His eyes were wide, his mouth open in an O, hands out as if to stop her.

And then the room went black and silent.

For a moment she sat in shock, gasping for breath. The sulfuric smell of burned powder clogged her nose. Her ears were ringing.

"Dear God!" she whispered.

"You silly cunt!" Maxwell whined. "You could have killed me!"

Through her ringing ears, she heard him scramble to his feet, knock over her little table, and fling the door open with a crash. She saw his figure silhouetted against the slight light of the basement, and then his feet pounded on the stairs.

Shivering and sobbing, she lowered the heavy pistol. God, if only she could stop her skin from crawling, banish the blue gleam of Dewley's eyes where they stared at her from the back of her mind.

50

December 31, 1864

"They have soup at Madame Sabrina's," Butler reminded his brother. "Kershaw says the men are getting a mite weary of short rations." Butler hunched on the foot of his bed where it was stuffed back under the sloping roof.

Doc continued to ignore him as he lifted the newspaper to the feeble light coming through the small glass window in the dormer. Their tiny upstairs room was cramped and cold. Doc's breath rose in the chill.

Doc announced, "Listen to this. It's a telegraph sent from General Sherman in Georgia to Lincoln. 'I beg to present you, as a Christmas present, the city of Savannah, with one hundred and fifty heavy guns and plenty of ammunition, and also about twenty-five thousand bales of cotton.' "

Butler huddled deeper in his coat. Just behind his ear, Kershaw muttered, "The Confederacy is dun foah. That damn Texan Gen'ral Hood has what's left of the Army of Tennessee skeedadling south. Atlanta and Savannah gone. Marse Robert's got that bulldog Grant's teeth locked in his throat at Petersburg."

"Reckon we all otta jist head on home," Corporal Pettigrew offered where he sat on the foot of Doc's bed. The rest of the men were crowded around in the small room, some looking over Doc's shoulder as he read the St. Louis paper in the fading light.

To his brother, Butler said, "That cook, Hallie Louise, makes a most amazing stew. And it is New Year's Eve. There will probably be special victuals prepared for a night as auspicious as this."

Doc shot him a sidelong glance, his lips pursed. "No doubt," he replied, and then went back to squinting at the paper.

"Why do you answer me sometimes and not others?" Butler demanded, slapping his hands to his knees.

"I've decided that when you mention the men, I will no longer respond. That by doing so I'm contributing to your mental illness. Abetting, if not downright rewarding it, as the case may be."

"Reckon that man's forever agin' us," Phil Vail groused where he sat cross-legged on the floor and fingered a Bowie knife.

Butler almost responded, then grinned to himself, gesturing for Vail to desist. Time to take a more erudite approach. "Philip, on this cold night, would it not behoove us to journey down to Madame Sabrina's and determine if she needs our assistance?"

"No." Philip glared at him over the top of the paper. "There is a loaf of bread and some salt pork in the paper wrapper by the windowsill. That will assuage your hunger."

"Might as well be back in Camp Douglas," Kershaw muttered behind Butler's ear.

"Something more filling and tasteful might —"

"We're saving money, Butler. Train fare to

Kansas City or Rolla, let alone the cost of getting from there to Springfield, is substantial." Doc rubbed his face. "We might be able to find someone willing to let us ride on their wagon, but more likely, we'll have to walk that last one hundred and fifty miles."

"We walked from Chicago to St. Louis."

Doc smiled, as if warily amused. "You ask me, it was a miracle we weren't strung up as thieves."

"Who he calling thieves?" Pettigrew asked, scowling. "Them's Yankees we raided."

Doc pointed to the worn medical bag by the door. "And I still owe five dollars for the instruments. It was a miracle that I found a used set, let alone that old man Gower would allow me to pay them off on time." Glaring over the paper, Doc met Butler's eyes. "Unless you just happen to have another Hernstein surgical case hidden away among all those imaginary men of yours."

"Philip, you have no reason to turn trite and sarcastic."

Doc's smile flickered and died. "I'm sorry. You're right." He lowered the paper. "We just have to build ourselves up from the bottom, Butler. A physician is judged by his appearance as well as his skill. Once upon a time I swore I'd never again sell my services to a brothel, but in the five months we've been in St. Louis, I've made enough to put a roof — such as it is — over our heads. We've warm clothes and full stomachs. My reputation is such that I can charge more, and the referrals have created a steady business for me."

"And I get to do odd jobs like painting and cleaning. That helps."

"Whorehouses seem to have an affinity for the mentally deranged that more elevated establish-

411

ments do not. Odd that they are so forgiving, but I didn't devote myself to medicine to spend the rest of my life treating women for hysteria, dosing for syphilis and the clap, and terminating the occasional pregnancy." Doc pointed a finger. "Come spring, I intend to have enough money to leave this all behind and make our way home."

"Once past Springfield," Butler reminded, "there's not that many fat Yankee farms to raid. And that General Curtis has ordered all the counties in western Missouri to be evacuated. Might be slim pickings until we get to White River."

"Heard they's still fighting down to Arkansas," Kershaw agreed. " 'Specially in yor country in de nor'west."

"Bushwhackers and guerrillas," Butler agreed. "I wonder what Tom would say if he could see how the independent rangers turned into such an outlaw bunch of —"

"Butler!" Doc snapped, irritation straining his face.

Butler evaded his gaze, knowing full well how Philip hated it when he started talking to his men. But then Philip had been out of sorts since they'd arrived in St. Louis. Butler and the men had "raided" them some clothes from a line over in Illinois, but Philip still wasn't presentable as a surgeon, let alone a Rebel one. He'd only taken to working the bawdy houses since the girls didn't care who he was or where he came from. And they paid in coin.

"And they lets you do odd jobs in return for a plate of vittles," Phil Vail crowed as he studied his knife.

"That's right," Butler agreed. "I could sure do with a plate of Madame Sabrin—" He let the rest drop as Doc gave him a sidelong squint.

Keen-eared, Butler heard it first. Hurried steps on the stairway. Doc turned his head just before the rapid knock came.

"Yes?"

"Dr. Hancock? Madame Sabrina sent me. We got a problem. She said to bring you no matter what."

"What happened?" Doc demanded, rising and walking over to open the door.

Sally Hamilton, no more than sixteen, shivered in a long wool coat. Her thin face — almost unrecognizable washed of its makeup — looked worried. Her hazel eyes widened as she said, "One of the johnnies got a little out of control. Started beating on Chloe. Tanner heard the ruckus and busted a chair across his face. Chloe and the johnny, they's both in need of stitches."

Doc shook his head wearily, then reached for his coat.

"Looks like we gonna get a *fine* New Year's Eve supper after all," Kershaw murmured in Butler's ear.

"Ya'll reckon they gots black-eyed peas and ham?" Jimmy Peterson wondered.

"While Philip stitches, I'll be most happy to clean up the blood and dispose of the wrecked furniture. That surely will be worth a bowl or two of whatever feast Hallie Louise has prepared."

"I don't know how you do it," Doc muttered as he picked up his hat and bag. "If I didn't know you were cursed, I'd say you were blessed."

Clapping his hat onto his head, Doc followed Sally Hamilton down the stairs. Butler slammed the door behind him, grinning ear to ear as he followed them down the rickety stairs to the alley.

413

51

Billy Hancock rode his tired and stumbling gelding through the thicket along the creekside trail. A good felt hat was clamped tight to his head, his long locks hanging down over the collar of his coat. The Sharps rested across his saddle, easy at hand, and high cavalry boots rose to above his knees. Compliments of a Yankee trooper who no longer had need of them.

All in all, with his linsey shirt and tan pants, Billy thought he cut quite the figure.

Evening was coming, and the birds sounded as full of spring as the flowers that blossomed in the newly sprouted grass. In the south, lightning flickered in tall, bruised clouds.

"Who comes?" a voice called from the scrub oak to the right.

"Billy Hancock. As if you, Bub Dix, didn't have eyes in yer head to recognize me."

Billy followed the trail into the small camp where nine stained-and-moldy tents and a couple of lean-tos surrounded a clearing. The camp was home to about twenty men, former Confederate soldiers. Most were deserters, hiding out to avoid conscription at best — trial and execution for desertion at worst. In Billy's mind, the only crime they'd committed was being smart enough to want out of the whole damn mess back East.

"What news?" Charlie Deveroux asked as he stood. His Enfield rifle hung from one hand, a tin coffee cup in the other. Charlie was closing in on forty. A thin man with weary brown eyes and a thick black beard, he walked with a slight limp from a wound received at Vicksburg. He was sort of the leader, if any man could be called that.

"Not much. I slipped into a tavern outside Fort Worth a couple of nights ago. Talk is that the militia is going to leave Waco and make a sweep north looking for conscripts." Billy smiled. "Word is they ain't gonna be looking any too hard even if they get their lazy asses out of camp."

"What's changed?"

"The war, Charlie."

Here and there men appeared out of tents and the brush down by the creek. Any arrival of news was greeted with curiosity.

"Is it over?"

"Not yet. Reckon it'll be soon, though. South Carolina is wrecked and Sherman is marching into North Carolina. Won't be another month and he'll be coming in ahind Gen'ral Lee. Ain't nothing but guerrilla bands fighting the Yankees. Little pockets of Rebs like in Texas, southwest Arkansas, and northwest Louisiana. Heard that Florida's mostly untouched, but who'd want it?"

Charlie scratched his beard, black eyes thoughtful. "Where's Danny?"

"Looking to a young lady at a place called Eulalia's in Fort Worth." Billy walked his horse to cool him out after shucking the saddle. "Told him I'd ride up and give you boys the word that it won't be long and we'll all be free."

"You starting to sound like a Yankee?" Amos Kern asked facetiously. He was a lanky and tall man in his thirties who longed constantly for his wife in Shreveport.

Satisfied that his worn-out gelding had been seen to, Billy tied him to the picket rope before walking over and seating himself by the fire.

Charlie was watching him with those hard black eyes, a curious reservation in his face.

"What?" Billy demanded.

"You going back to Arkansas after it's over?"

Billy chewed his lip, frowned. "Maw's dead. Reckon Paw is too, since no one heard a word of him after Shiloh. If Sarah's back at the farm, she sure as hell don't want to see me. Had one brother in prison camp up to Camp Douglas. And Butler? If he survived Chickamauga, there was the Atlanta battles, then Franklin and Nashville. He was an officer, so *if* he survived, Yankees'll most likely throw his bones into a prison camp after the surrender. Maybe hang him. No telling what's gonna happen to all them Rebels."

"So . . . what're you gonna do?"

Billy could feel this leading up to something. "You got a suggestion?"

"You been pinch-mouthed about it, but I heard you killed a renegade Confederate lieutenant in a card game up in the Nations."

"He was a bottom dealer. Danny caught him cheatin'."

"Heard he got off the first shot and missed. That cool as a springhouse, you shot him through the heart. That he'd killed five men in pistol fights, and a heap more riding with Bloody Bill Anderson. That he was known as a mighty mean man."

416

Billy narrowed his eyes. "He's a cheat. Don't matter how tough a man is said to be, a bullet to the heart'll make him dust."

"And there's the Dewley bunch over to Arkansas." Charlie lifted a calming hand. "Yes, I been asking about you. I'da been a fool not to. Something about you is like a coiled snake, Billy Hancock. Cold and deadly."

"You got a point to all this?"

Charlie glanced around, making sure the others had drifted off. From his boot top, he pulled a whiskey flask and offered it to Billy. "Not a point. A proposition."

"Then make it." Billy took a swig of the whiskey.

"War's ending, and the Rebs are losing. There's scores to be settled, and bad blood to be dealt with. That means there's money to be made." Charlie's dark eyes seemed to sharpen. "Assuming, that is, that a man isn't any too squeamish about killing."

Billy took another sip of the whiskey, waiting.

Charlie added, "You know about the Dutchies down 'round Fredericksburg? Large community. Most had Union loyalty. Lot of Texas Rebels had it out for them. You heard about the 'Butcher of Fredericksburg,' the People's Court?"

"Yep. Local justice looking for traitors and deserters. If'n they'da caught Danny and me, and we'd Injuned away from the conscription, they'da been the ones in Texas to judge and hang us by our scrawny necks."

"A friend of mine is a Dutchy. His sons were hung by a People's Court. All four of them. For treason. Funny thing is, the judge of that People's Court now claims title to my friend's land and holdings. All of it."

"Sounds like this judge is a lying and thievin' bastard, but he ain't *my* bastard to worry about. So why would I care?"

"What if I told you two hundred dollars in gold could be yours if that judge was found dead some morning."

Billy took another swig of the whiskey. "That's a lot of money."

"My friend is willing to pay for justice. His youngest boy was just thirteen. Only reason my friend didn't swing with them is because his wife's sister over in Burnet took sick the afternoon before the riders arrived. So he wasn't home."

Two hundred dollars? Billy rocked his jaw back and forth. Just to kill a thief? Of course, the judge would be an important man, somebody with local connections to county or state. But the time to get him would be now, before the Yankees marched in and declared martial law. And as soon as they did, there'd be confusion everywhere.

"Where do I have to go?"

"Lampasas."

"Why don't your friend do it hisself?"

"And swing for the murder of the man who hung his boys? No, he's got to be somewhere else. Austin. San Antonio. Someplace where he can prove he didn't do it."

Billy felt the devil warm the area around his heart. It would be hunting, just like he'd done with Dewley's bastards. And it was still justice, doing right by bringing down the evildoers.

"How do I get paid?"

"If you're right, and the war's about over, I'd meet you at Eulalia's first of April." Charlie took the whiskey flask and drank from it. Swallowing he added, "And the money *will* be there, Billy

418

Hancock. Not only do you got my word, but you're the last person on earth I want to spend my life running from, you spooky bastard."

Billy grinned at that, clasping his arms around the knees of his high-topped boots. "Better tell your friend to spend the rest of the month in San Antonio. Tell Danny I'll meet him at Eulalia's that same night."

He liked Eulalia's. There was a whore there who never made fun of him if his pizzle stayed limp. That seemed to happen more often these days, especially if he'd had one of the nightmares recently.

52

The man's name was Anson Hartlee. True to Billy's instincts, Hartlee was everything Billy had figured he'd be. Hartlee was active in the Texas Democratic Party — one of the most prominent men in both Lampasas and Burnet Counties, with connections in Austin. He was the director of two local banks, and one of the biggest landholders in the county. During the war, his empire had grown to include quite a bit of land confiscated from the Germans down around Fredericksburg.

Hartlee's ranch lay five miles south of Lampasas on the Burnet Road and consisted of a two-story stone house, large barn, cotton, corn, and tobacco fields, and several outbuildings.

For three days, Billy applied his skills as he scouted around the Hartlee ranch, learning the lay of the land. Watching the comings and goings. The five hunting dogs might have been a problem, but Billy began sneaking close from downwind and leaving treats for the dogs. These he'd carry under his armpit to ensure they were doused with his scent, and he'd urinate close by to ensure the dogs were accustomed to his presence.

By the fourth day, the dogs didn't react when he

approached the house from upwind.

Hartlee lived alone, his wife having died of the typhoid three years earlier. Of his three sons, one had died at Shiloh, another at Chancellorsville, and the third was reportedly convalescing in Chimborazo hospital in Richmond after losing his left leg.

The banker had four Negro slaves who worked the fields and retired at sunset. A fifth, a male house servant, prepared the meals and saw to the domestic duties.

Each morning Hartlee had ridden off on his big black horse at just before seven. Each evening he returned home a little after six. When he did, he rode the black into the barn, stripped the saddle and bridle, curried the animal, watered it, and locked it into a stall for the night. Only then did he walk to the slave quarters for a report on the day's activities. That done, he retired to the house and a supper laid on the dining room table.

The only difference on the night of March 22 was that Billy stood in the shadows behind the saddle racks where they stuck out from the wall.

What would Maw say?

Billy cocked his head, unsure. Hartlee had abused his authority to hang four of Billy's un-named employer's sons. A fate that, in another time, could have been Billy's own. Over the years, more than one envious rival of Paw's had desired the farm. And say that Paw hadn't sided with Arkansas. Say he'd remained loyal to the Union. Any of the bushwhackers like Dewley would have shot, burned, or hung Philip, Butler, and Billy in a hot second if it had meant getting the farm.

There but for the grace of God.

Come to think of it, what he was doing now

wasn't any damn different than what he'd done to get Sarah back. Slipping around underneath it all was justice. Plain and simple.

That, and the incestuous Sarah demon who still lurked just beneath his dreams. What wouldn't he do to murder that apparitional bitch?

His heart was beating faster, the warm anticipation running through him. By Hob and thunder, he never felt as alive as he did when he was hunting a man. That surge of joy rising in his chest was every bit as intoxicating as a good bottle of whiskey. Every nerve seemed to sing, every vein and artery pumped, his senses sharp as a razor and his soul humming with anticipation.

The sound of a horse's hooves carried, the dogs running out to bark a greeting as they had done each night that Billy watched the place from his vantage back in the trees.

"Whoa, now, Midnight." Hartlee's thick Texas accent carried on the warm evening air. "That's a good boy. Bait of oats fer y'all tonight."

Hartlee led the big black horse through the barn door, missing the black gelding's nostrils as they flared at the unfamiliar scent of a strange human.

Billy smiled.

I got you!

He waited, his entire body electric. No need to rush. Like John Gritts had always said, he liked them right up close. The ultimate triumph of the perfect hunter.

Hartlee finished rubbing the horse down, poured water from a bucket, and scooped grain out of a sack and into the stall's manger.

He backed out, cooing to the horse, taking one final look at the magnificent sixteen-hand gelding.

As Hartlee hesitated, Billy stepped out, his

422

Cherokee moccasins silent on the straw-covered dirt. As Billy lifted the ax, Anson Hartlee had no more warning than the tom turkey that long-ago day when Billy had last hunted with John Gritts.

53

April 10, 1865

News had come by telegraph. Robert E. Lee had surrendered the Army of Northern Virginia the day before. The final vertebra in the spine of Confederate resistance had been broken.

A line of flashing yellow-orange light leaped outward in the darkness. Not even a second later Sarah heard the crashing boom of the cannons. The sound reverberated across the Arkansas River Valley. A cheer went up from the crowd that had gathered on the Belle Point heights before Fort Smith.

While the crowd shouted their enthusiasm and seemed to wash back and forth before the fort's stone walls, Sarah wasn't sure what she should be feeling. The war had ruined their lives. Paw declared dead, no word from Butler or Doc, Maw shot, Sarah running from life itself, the farm abandoned, and who knew where Billy was. She should have felt relief, but the future loomed before her like a descending and ugly black cloud.

Men were singing "The Battle Hymn of the Republic." Women sobbed and cried. Little girls hugged their mothers' skirts and chattered back and forth. The little boys whooped and cavorted as they ran back and forth through the maze of adult legs.

Another flash of light and fire shot forth even as the evening breeze carried the acrid stench of burned powder across the crowd. The clapping thunder of the celebratory guns echoed across the valley. Hats were being waved. Two men danced with each other, arms interlaced as they kicked and shuffled. Sarah heard liquid as a bottle was passed back and forth. The sound of a fiddle came from somewhere.

These were Union folk — or so they said — farmers and refugees for the most part who had come to live and till fields beneath the protective umbrella and within the military boundary protected by the fort. Similar military sanctuaries had been set up around Van Buren on the other side of the river, and up in Washington and Benton Counties. Literally armed agricultural compounds protected by Federal cavalry. Islands of survival in the ruined sea that had once been northwest Arkansas. The rest was a wild no-man's-land of forest and abandoned farms. The domain of the jayhawker and bushwhacker as they raided and murdered each other among burned mills and along overgrown roads.

The Confederacy was dying before her eyes. Its memory would pass like an autumn leaf, grown brittle and cast loose, tossed on the currents of passion to settle softly, brown and desiccated. The only certainty remaining was decomposition.

Looking back, what had it all been for?

The gnawing in her belly distracted her from any deeper philosophical explorations. Her only food that day had been a biscuit for breakfast.

Compensation for washing a Yankee captain's coat.

The cannons in Fort Smith flashed and boomed once more. People cheered as the reverberations rose to the cloud-dark night sky.

She placed a hand to her breast. The war was over.

Butler, Philip, and Billy — if any of them were still alive — would be safe now. They could go home, pick up the plow, and reclaim the farm from the weeds, assuming no one had burned the house.

"But what of me?" she wondered, knowing full well that she'd never go back. The looming black cloud that was her future seemed to hang even lower over her head.

Two men, obviously drunk, staggered toward her. One jabbed the other with his elbow, indicating Sarah. They both grinned foolishly, doffed their hats, and cried in unison, "Best of the evening, ma'am!" Then broke into giggles.

"Y'all need an escort?" the taller asked as he replaced his hat.

"Thank you, but my husband wouldn't understand." She craned her neck, looking past them. "He should be back any moment."

"Y'all have a nice night," the short one said with a sigh. Then dragged his associate away into the crowd.

Sarah exhaled her tension. She felt the Colt revolver's cool grip under her fingers and wondered when she'd reached into the heavy canvas sack that hung from her shoulder.

The ugly lump of steel, brass, and wood — capped and loaded — remained her one true and dependable ally in life.

A smile came to her chapped lips as she remembered Maxwell Johnson's panic-white face as he dabbed at the furrow her bullet had cut through the web of his neck. The young dandy would think twice before he entered a woman's room in the middle of the night. Of course, it had cost Sarah her job.

When everything a woman owned fit into a blanket roll, packing didn't take long.

She and Maxwell had both been lucky. Hearing the hammer click as she cocked the big revolver, he'd thrown himself to the side. Doing so had not only saved his life, but probably hers as well. A woman of Mrs. Pennington's influence easily could have sent Sarah to the gallows. A sobering fact the enraged woman had made a point of: "It would be your word against mine, you little harlot."

"Well, madam," Sarah whispered to the April night, "you can bet I'm going to be a whole lot more careful in the future."

She'd taken the first ride she could find out of Little Rock — a wagon headed for Fort Smith. Arriving, she'd joined the throng of refugees, and hung on, advertising her services to the soldiers as a washerwoman: three shirts and a pair of pants for a slice of bread. Include underwear and an overcoat, and throw in a can of beans.

Dealing with the soldiers had been hard at first. She kept her eyes downcast when she talked to them, and remained coldly polite. Her mouth would go dry, and the knot would tighten in her throat. She wore a baggy, oversized sack of a dress to hide her body and kept her long blond hair pinned up under a sun-faded bonnet. She had adopted a slightly stooped walk to keep her hips

427

from swaying. Her sole expense was for soap, the river providing ample free water.

Nevertheless, most days she went to bed with something in her stomach. Today had been different; the news of the surrender had distracted the troops. Hopefully in the morning there would be a rush for her services. Maybe in advance of a parade or display of some sort.

The last cannonade of the two-hundred-round salute boomed into the night, and a bugle accompanied the troops as they sang "Union Forever" before the lone horn blew their dismissal.

Sarah pulled her worn blanket about her shoulders, feeling the slight chill of the night. People were beginning to disperse. Someone in the crowd struck up "Yankee Doodle" and the song went from lip to lip as Sarah followed the mass of the crowd toward the encampment. She dared not linger, or travel out of sight of others.

She hadn't taken four steps before a man matched her pace, his baritone voice saying, "Quite a show. Glad it's finally over."

"Yes." She felt the rising anxiety. "Good night."

"Mind if I walk with you?"

"No. Please. My husband should be here somewhere close." She looked around anxiously as if searching for her man.

"Whoa, now, Sarah. There's no husband waiting in that chicken coop you sleep in. Unless, of course, he's a rooster." He paused. "And the last of that hardy breed of fowl was eaten three years ago."

"Please, sir. Leave . . . me . . . alone."

"Ah, of course. My apologies. A gentleman shouldn't intrude upon a lady's company without a proper introduction. My mother would wilt should she ever discover that I've become such a low brute." He gracefully removed his hat, sweeping into a slight bow, and in a Southern accent, stated: "Bret Anderson at yoah service, ma'am."

Bret Anderson? Ah yes. He was one of the gamblers who hung around the peripheries of the fort. He was known to prey upon unwary and cocky soldiers, especially around payday. Though on those occasions he was in direct competition with the brothels and whiskey dealers down by the river.

She had seen him a time or two around the fort, having stood out because of his finely tailored clothing, vest, and old-style frock coat. His patent boots were always polished. She figured him for being in his thirties, with a well-trimmed black mustache and hair cut just above his collar.

"It's late, Mr. Anderson. I really must be going."

"I would be obliged to walk you partway. My camp is on the way."

"Thank you, but no."

As if he hadn't heard, he kept pace, adding, "What a wonderful day. This vile war is all but over. The dying and senseless destruction is finally coming to an end. I don't know about you, but I think the country is just worn out and exhausted."

The familiar anxiety had tightened like a band around her chest. She suddenly felt dizzy, swayed, and caught herself, fighting for balance.

"Are you all right?" Bret asked.

"Light-headed. I'll be fine."

"Good thing I'm with you." He was studying her in the darkness. "Not much washing today, was there? I mean with the news and all."

"No."

"Bet you haven't eaten today."

"I had a fine meal," she lied.

"Snuck that in while you were standing at the fort gate all day? Caging a wash job takes diligence given the number of women anxious for the task. Maybe you slipped away sometime when I wasn't looking?"

"I'm fine."

"I'd say you were strong, proud, independent, and resolute, but not exactly fine. They talk about you, you know. You're a mystery woman to them. You and that big pistol you keep in your bag there."

"They know about . . ."

"Of course, and they know that you are no doubt proficient with it given the way you keep it oiled and don't let the caps corrode. Some even watch over you when you don't know it."

She felt herself on the verge of fainting again. Dear God, did they suspect? *Time to leave . . . put this place behind me.*

"So, tell me, Sarah, how long has it been since you've had a fresh-roasted duck?"

Maybe it was her light-headedness, but she spoke before she could think it through. "Almost . . . forever."

His white teeth flashed in the dark. "I happen to have a duck roasting at this very moment. I shot it this morning down on the river. Nice young bird. Fat. I imagine the meat is cleaving from the bone, steamed in its own juices."

Sarah swallowed, her mouth watering unexpectedly.

Bastard that he was, he saw and chuckled. "Come and join me. I would consider it an honor. And while we eat, you may lay your big gun at hand lest I act anything but the gentleman. And afterward I shall see you to your chicken coop and bid you a most glorious evening."

"Why?" she asked suspiciously.

"Because the war is over. It is a night to celebrate. One I will remember for the rest of my life, and I would like to remember having shared it in the company of a remarkable lady."

She stopped short. "Lady? Mister, you don't know anything about me."

He cocked his head, that lazy smile just visible in the darkness. "I know that you call yourself Sarah Rogers. From your accent you were raised in western Arkansas. You wash clothes in exchange for food and live in the last standing chicken coop in western Arkansas. The others long since having been torn down for firewood."

She shook her head, clutching the blanket tightly to her chest. "I don't —"

"Just two people sharing a meal, Sarah. Sharing a duck on a night they will remember forever. After today, everything is going to be different. I eat alone most nights. I'd like this one to be filled with amiable discourse."

She felt that light-headed hunger again. Her stomach growled at the thought of greasy, succulent duck. And she did have her pistol.

"I would be delighted to share your duck, Mr. Anderson."

"Splendid!" He almost chortled, leading the way.

His camp consisted of a Sibley tent and awning beneath which stood a table and collection of rickety chairs where he conducted his card games. The fire in the center was a round eye of glowing coals. A light carriage, painted black, stood to the side, and she could see a harness hung on a rack at the back of the awning. By Fort Smith standards, Bret Anderson was a very rich man.

"Now, feast your eyes on this!" he proclaimed as he used an iron tong to fish a clay-wrapped object from the depths of the coals. The outside glowed a dark red as he rolled it from the fire. Then he tossed a couple of pieces of driftwood onto the coals where they leaped into flame.

Bret carried two chairs from his card table and set them across from each other on either side of the fire. "Please do me the honor of being seated." He gestured, holding the chair as she seated herself. Fingers of worry kneaded her gut.

Then Bret proceeded to hurry about his camp, producing mismatched plates, forks, and knives, and finally, a bottle from which he worried a cork. At the pop, he grinned in the firelight, pouring something that fizzed into two tin cups.

One he proffered to Sarah, then, with a flourish, clinked the rim of her cup, saying, "To better days ahead, may the Confederacy rest in peace."

Then he seated himself across from her, a smile on his lips, firelight playing in his dark eyes. He had a firm and straight nose, finely shaped cheeks, and his smile was just visible behind his mustache.

Sarah sipped the bubbly contents of her cup. "What is this?"

"Champagne. The real thing. From France. One of Fred Steele's colonels, having lost everything else, thought that with three aces showing, he could recoup the entire evening with this prized bottle of his. A possibility my heart flush completely precluded." He paused. "Do sip slowly. Unused to it as you are, half starved, and on an empty stomach, you shouldn't overindulge."

"What about the duck?"

"We need to let it cool until I can crack it open." He leaned forward in his chair, hands cupping his tin cup. "The big question is what are the Yankees going to do now? How are they going to treat the Southern states? Arrest all the Rebel generals and politicians? Try and execute them for treason? Demand reparations? And the Reb armies are filled with fanatical men who have dedicated their lives to the cause. Do the Yankees expect them to just lay down their arms and go back to farming like nothing has happened? And what about the millions of freed slaves? Where do they go? Who employs them? Feeds them? Sarah, it's all a mess."

She studied him, feeling an odd warmth in her stomach from the champagne. "Mr. Anderson, there's nothing but hatred and heartbreak out there. Maybe too much to ever heal. Some wounds run too deep. Nothing will ever be whole again."

He studied her thoughtfully. "I do pray that you're wrong, but I have learned the hard way not to put too much hope or faith in humanity's good side. Word is that the Union lost nearly three hundred thousand men. That's a lot of empty chairs, as the song goes. All them families, they're going to want to punish someone."

"Then where does it end?"

"I expect the Union to do its worst. So me, I think I'm going west. Think I'll cast my future and fortune to a new land instead of seeking to rebuild it among the wreckage of the old." He paused. "What about you?"

"I'd love nothing more than a full-time laundry job at the fort. But them's all taken by soldiers' wives."

His lips twitched. "You're a puzzle, Miss Rogers. One minute you talk like a woman with a finishing-school education sitting in her parlor, the next you sound like a frontier Arkansan. It's as if you can shift skins."

"Paw made me read. Made me learn my numbers, too. Said I might need them to keep a big fancy house," she admitted, taking another sip of the delightful champagne. She'd always heard of it, but the few times Paw had had a bottle, he'd reserved it for influential guests. Champagne, she decided, was something she could enjoy more of. "He insisted that I learn to talk like a lady. Said I'd need such skills one day. But growing up in Benton County, and the last four years? It was all hardscrabble."

She blinked, wondering what possessed her to speak so freely — as if the worry and fear had suddenly faded. She peered uncertainly across the fire, expecting to see some crafty glint in Bret Anderson's eyes. Instead he was staring thoughtfully into the fire, as if in profound consideration.

"Anyway," she said defensively. "Where are you from? You seem to sound Southern one minute, and Yankee the next."

"Boston," he said softly. "My father has a house on the Commons. He's a banker." He pointed at her bag. "His money went to Colonel Colt, among others, to build the New England weapons factories. As well as he was doing before the war, I can't imagine what he's worth now."

"My brother went to Boston. Became a surgeon." She paused. "Last I heard he was in Camp Douglas prison camp. But that's been three years now."

"Your parents?"

"Killed in the war. My brothers are gone, maybe dead. I'm all that's left."

"Look at us! Grown maudlin. I'll bet that duck's cooled." He stood, rolling the clay-coated ball around into better light. "This is the tricky part. I've got to split the clay just right and part it so it pulls the feathers free and doesn't drop dirt onto the meat."

"Are you really that good, Mr. Anderson?"

"Hope so." He grinned up at her. "Let me get you another glass of champagne, and I'll give it a try."

54

April 11, 1865

It took two tries. Sarah finally blinked her eyes open, the lids gritty and dry. Nothing made sense. She was staring at canvas illuminated by bright sunlight. Her body was comfortably supported by a cot, a warm and soft blanket tucked around her.

She sat up, suddenly afraid as she stared around. The tent was spacious with a rug on the dirt floor, a metal-bound trunk to one side, a fine saddle in one corner, and a fine double-barreled shotgun rested in a scabbard to the left. An enameled pan, filled with water, had been placed on a folding table at the head of the bed. Beside it rested a small leather bag. Her Colt revolver lay beside the wadded pillow upon which she'd been sleeping.

She remained fully clothed, her worn shoes placed neatly on the rug beside the cot.

Outside she could hear birdsong and faint voices along with the clanking of metal. Somewhere a child broke out in laughter and the sharp rhythm of someone chopping wood carried on the morning.

"Oh, dear God," she whispered, reaching up to rub her face. Memories came back in bits and pieces. The firing of the fort's cannons in the night. Bret Anderson enticing her to his camp. The champagne, the remarkable duck he had stuffed with sage, cornmeal, and real pepper before baking it to perfection.

"And I ate the whole thing!" she reminded herself. "He barely had any." She'd cracked the duck's bones with her teeth to suck out the last of the marrow.

The same with the champagne. She remembered, somewhere in the small hours of the night, how he'd dribbled the last of the *second* bottle into her cup.

And then . . .

She shook her aching head, aware of her pressing and irritated bladder. God, how could her mouth be this dry, her thirst so great, at the same time she was so full of pee?

"What happened then, Sarah?" she asked herself.

Vaguely she remembered him steadying her as she walked around the fire.

God forbid, was that right? He'd actually touched her? And she hadn't frozen, hadn't begun to tremble and quake?

She looked down at the pistol, cold, blue, and deadly.

"I'm putting your revolver right here, Sarah. Right where it will be handy if you need it."

Bret's words. So reassuring. Damn! He'd really said that?

She combed her hair back with her fingers, realizing what a mess it must be. Her bonnet was folded and had been placed atop her canvas sack. Rising, she smoothed the blanket, replaced the pistol in its holster inside the sack, and checked her pitiful few belongings. Nothing seemed to have been rifled.

"Sarah?" Bret's voice from outside brought her bolt upright, heart hammering. "There's a chamber pot beneath the bed. If you need it, there's also a mirror on the tent pole. I don't have a brush, but you'll find a comb in my kit on the table."

"I . . . I . . ." The words didn't come.

"No rush," he called. "There's water to wash if you'd like. Breakfast will be ready whenever you are."

Breakfast?

For a moment she labored for breath, disbelief vying with instinctive panic. Damn! Her head hurt too much to think. What the hell was he doing? What did he want?

Just . . . run! She looped her sack over her shoulder, and reached for her blanket.

Her gaze fixed on the washbowl. And then went to the mirror. She hesitated. Damnation! She was making a mistake. One she'd regret. Nevertheless she unslung her bag, walked over and washed her face.

She considered the leather bag. Did she dare?

With trembling fingers she opened it, found a man's shaving kit and the comb. For whatever reason, she tiptoed to the mirror and began to work at the tangles in her hair. Before she could finish, she succumbed to her insistent bladder and used the chamber pot, holding it so he couldn't hear. Then she returned to the challenge of her hair.

"What's the matter with you?" she asked under her breath. "You need to be away from here. Away from him. He's just another goddamned man."

Finally she collected her things, and stepped

438

out, her heart pounding. Muscles charged, she fought the impulse to run.

"Might as well attack the day on a full stomach. Got bacon frying. Have a seat." Bret crouched at the fire and tended a pan that sizzled on the hearthstones. "The corn bread, poor as it is, is my own recipe. Can you believe they can powder both milk and eggs? What's the world coming to next? Powdered beef?"

She glanced over. Two of his mismatched tin plates had been set at the card table, in the shade. The silverware was placed as if for a formal affair.

Run!

She sniffed the bacon. Her legs might have had a mind of their own. Confused, she seated herself in the far chair.

Bret straightened and brought the enameled coffeepot with him, aromatic steam rising from its spout. He didn't even glance at her as he poured hot black coffee into her cup.

Blessed heaven! Real coffee! She carefully picked up the hot cup, inhaling the fragrance. "Where did you get this?"

"A corporal in commissary fancied himself a master of five-card stud. Those coffee beans were supposedly destined for General Bussey. A gift from General Halleck. Special, you see. All the way from Africa."

He had a twinkle in his eyes, as if inordinately proud of himself. Wind tousled a loose wave of his brown hair. He had a high forehead. A secret humor seemed to hide behind his lips.

Within moments, he had filled her plate with hot corn bread and bacon and seated himself. As he unfolded the rag that was supposed to serve as a napkin, he asked, "I hope that you slept well."

"I shouldn't have taken your bed."

He shrugged, pointing to a rolled blanket before the door. "It was a pleasant evening to be outside. I just lay there and watched the stars after the clouds cleared. Mostly I just relived the evening." He paused, meeting her eyes. "Thank you. Not only was yesterday a milestone, but that was the most enjoyable evening I've spent in years. I shall treasure it."

Sarah paused, a forkful of bacon halfway to her lips. "What do you want from me, Mr. Anderson?"

He cocked his head in that surprised, birdlike manner of his, and said, "I'd like to offer you a job."

"I don't understand."

"I keep irregular hours. I have been the victim of petty theft in the past, this camp being what it is. But with the end of the war, our population is going to be considerably more fluid. I'd like the security of knowing my possessions will be here when I return. I'm also a vain man. I want to come back to my camp in the middle of the night and find a fire and warm meal waiting for me. Keep my clothes clean and pressed, see to the care of Jefferson, my horse, and keep my camp and equipment in order." He pointed with his fork. "And that is *all* that I am asking of you."

"Why me?"

"Because through the good graces of champagne and roast duck, you lowered your defenses last night and I got to see the woman who disguises herself within that cotton sack of a dress. The fact that I need someone to take care of my things discomforts me somewhat. While necessity might require that I hire someone, my requirement is that that person be someone whose company, intellect, and competence I respect and enjoy."

"Where will I sleep?"

"You shall have your own tent and cot. Not only do you have my word that you will not be molested, you also have your revolver."

He said it with such sincerity, a hardness in his eyes.

"I don't know if I could —"

"Fifteen dollars a month to start with. If, by freeing me to concentrate on what I do best, I find my income rising, you shall profit thereby."

She sat stunned.

"Take it, Sarah. If nothing else it will get you out of old lady McGurdy's chicken house. Though how she's saved it from being firewood this long is a miracle, I'd imagine that with the war over, she's going to want to put chickens in it again."

"People will think I'm your bed thing."

He nodded frankly, a slight irritation behind his soft brown eyes. "Would it make any real difference in your life? Where you are now an object of pity, you would become one of occasional scorn. You already keep your distance from people, aloof and apart. When approached by a man, you'd no longer have to hide behind that feeble fiction of" — he mimicked her voice — " 'excuse me, I'm looking for my husband.' If maintaining that reputation of a chaste and frightened woman is important to you, by all means decline my offer. Although what you lose on one hand might gain you some peace and security on the other. Making you unavailable, you might say."

She ate in silence, relishing every single bite. Food. Money. And a semblance of safety.

She looked him hard in the eyes. "My last employment was in Little Rock. I was the housekeeper for one of the city's most important women. Her nephew tried to crawl into my bed one night. He ducked at the last instant. Which is why he walked away with only a bleeding neck. Mr. Anderson, I will kill any man who tries to crawl into my bed at night." She paused. "Even if he's my employer."

His pensive stare didn't waver. Reaching into his pocket, he laid a twenty-dollar gold piece on the table between them, and said, "If those are your only terms, I think we have a deal."

55

June 6, 1865

Doc coughed as he looked out at the once familiar Arkansas forests and ridges. He reached up with one hand and pulled his dripping hat down over his ears. Wet weather always brought the cough on. He just couldn't shake the damn thing. It continued to live deep in his chest like a constant tickle.

Butler was driving the rickety spring wagon and doing a good job with the mule. If the rain had served no other purpose, it had swollen the wood and firmed up the wobbly spokes in the wheels and tightened the iron tires on rims he and Butler had been shimming with whittled wedges.

Doc had somehow managed to shut his ears to the incessant chattering as Butler talked to the men. Butler kept pointing things out, saying, "This here's the Cross Timbers. Last I rode through here was with a detachment of cavalry in service to Tom Hindman." Or, "Oh, look! There's the ruins of the tanyard. We used to deliver hides there. Now it's all gone to disrepair and weeds. Not even a building left."

As they began to climb the grade onto Pea Ridge, Doc glanced around at the savaged countryside, wet and dripping from the warm rain. Clouds hung low over the wreckage of what had once been forest. Broken and splintered trees had regrown some branches, but not enough to hide the shattered trunks and limbs. Here and there shot and shell had gouged out chunks of bark that would never be healed, or a bole had been shot clear through, the tree growing around gray splinters that protruded from the holes.

"Dear God," Doc whispered. "Look at this."

"Hell of a fight, indeed. What do you think, Sergeant? As bad as the Hornet's Nest or Chickamauga?" Butler's lips worked. "Corporal, I most surely agree. You can almost smell the burnt powder and spilt blood." A pause. "No, no, Philip spent most of Shiloh cutting pieces off of people."

"This is worse than I imagined," Doc said as they topped out on the ridge. Moments later, Butler pulled the mule up, letting him cool and twitch his ears as they looked at the thick weeds filling the expanse where once Elkhorn Tavern had stood. Only the remains of the tavern's blackened chimneys and the lone telegraph line stuck up from the field of weeds. To the west, battered forest extended toward the rounded knob of Little Mountain.

A few blackened fire rings had been left by passing campers at the Huntsville Road junction, but other than that the tavern had gone back to wilderness.

Butler said, "Last time I was here you could see clear back to the graves. After the battle Sarah hauled Federal dead for the Yankee army. Made a dollar a day doing it."

"You never told me that," Doc replied.

"Of course I did." Then Butler looked confused.

444

"Or was that Johnny Baker I was talking to?" He listened for a moment, nodded seriously and said, "Yes, I recall now. Funny how family members can have that effect on you. I was just —"

"Butler!" Doc snapped, fought off a cough, and added, "Can we go home now? I'd prefer to *see* Sarah with my own eyes rather than listen to you discuss her with your phantoms."

Butler slapped the reins, turning the mule onto the Huntsville Road. "You're being short, Philip."

Doc glared at him, then took a deep breath and relented. "I'm sorry." He gestured around, disturbed by the empty field where the Clemons farm had been. Weeds were already giving way to encroaching forest. "I just didn't expect so much . . . I mean, in my mind I thought . . ."

"That home was still home?" Butler suggested, his eyes oddly unfocused as he stared at the rutted and rocky road, as though seeing it in his imagination.

Doc grabbed the wagon seat, bracing his feet on the dashboard as the mule started down the rocky descent. The swale, washed and eroded, was more like a gully than the road he remembered having been here.

His skills as a physician had indeed brought them through the winter, carried them to Rolla, and allowed him to purchase the old spring wagon and mule, both having lately been acquired from a military auction. Beyond a dutch oven and a sack of flour, they had only the clothes on their backs, his surgical kit, and some surplus blankets to their names.

Maybe he was as crazy as Butler. In his fantasies the farm had remained inviolate, as though immune to the war. Untouched and pristine, it

445

awaited him, ready to fold him into its embrace and heal the wounds in his soul.

Home is not going to be what I remember.

Doc knotted his fists, a quiver of worry mixing with the anticipation.

He told himself, "The buildings will be shabby. Some probably missing. Sarah is twenty now. Billy's a man. Maw will have aged."

Butler was studying him sidelong. "And you get after me for talking to myself?"

"You've seen the rest of the country we've ridden through from Springfield south. It's a desolate wasteland. One farm after another abandoned and burned." Doc worked his lips and looked at his brother. "Now that we're this close, I'm actually scared."

Butler nodded, tilted his head as if listening, then twitched his lips, biting off a comment. After a moment, he looked at Doc, that curious satisfaction behind his blue eyes that indicated that he'd managed to avoid talking to his men instead of answering his brother.

Butler said, "Last time I was here, Billy was spending his time out in the woods hunting. He was keeping food on the table when most of the folks hereabouts were starving. Neither Maw nor Sarah were anybody's fools. Unlike some . . . like the Clemonses who loudly announced their Rebel sympathies, they catered to whichever side was in control at the moment."

"That hope has kept me going, Butler." He glanced around at the familiar countryside. "I've just got the jitters, that's all."

He coughed into his hand, water droplets flying from his hat with each racking of his lungs. They had met a steady stream of people on the road south from Springfield. Most had been men, most of them disbanded soldiers. While the raggedly dressed Rebels and blue-clad Federals had mostly been tolerant of each other, if not patently curious, the families and some of the tight-lipped, heavily armed bands had not. The hatred among the latter had been as hot as a coke-fired oven.

The war might be over, but the wounds remained open and oozing.

To Doc's eyes the destruction in western Missouri — let alone the little he'd seen since entering Arkansas — defied belief. What the hell had happened here?

"Dear God, please. Let Maw and Sarah and Billy be all right," Doc prayed softly as Butler eased them through a rough section of the road.

"Lot of cavalry passed this way, Sergeant," Butler was explaining, apparently to one of his men. "Cavalry was the key to keeping the war going in this country. Not like the big armies you were used to in Tennessee."

Doc studied his brother from the corner of his eye. The Kershaw character seemed to show up when Butler was worried or under pressure. Sometimes when Doc asked, Butler would tell him Kershaw wasn't there. And, to add to the peculiarity, Butler had patiently explained that Kershaw was "invisible." A fascinating twist and glimpse into Butler's broken mind. He had invisible men among his already invisible men?

"I imagine your farm is pretty rundown, too, Private." Butler seemed to concentrate on something, and added, "I suppose so. But you'll feel better when you meet Maw, Sarah, and Billy." He paused. "Yes, it will have been a long time since we've eaten food like she can cook."

Doc lowered his head, bracing himself as the wagon slipped and slid over weathered limestone. Rain trickled down the back of his neck.

How do I explain to Maw that her son is a madman? What do I tell her?

She would expect him, as a medical man, to know what to do about it. How did he tell her he hadn't a clue?

And what was he going to do if — now that the fighting was over — Paw wasn't dead, but was sitting at home, fat and sassy, with another bag of gold? It would be just like the old reprobate.

Bear that cross when it's dropped on your shoulder.

He would be civil to the man. No matter what. It wouldn't be worth getting into a bitter, yelling fight. He was a physician and would act like one. Nor could he afford to upset Butler. God alone knew what further damage an acrimonious shouting match with Paw might do to his poor brother's already teetering mind.

Doc swallowed hard, so shaken he barely recognized the old lightning-scarred tree. When he was sixteen he'd spent the night under it, having sneaked away to the tavern. It had been the first time he'd drank whiskey. A lot of it. And the lightning tree was as far as he'd made it before vomiting his guts out, and passing out beneath the scarred branches.

"I hear you," Butler almost snapped. "You'll remain in ranks. You're soldiers not border ruffians."

What was that about? It was a tone he rarely heard Butler use with his men. Doc bit his lip, the anxiety rising as they finally dropped down into the White River floodplain. Butler had insisted from the very beginning that it was his responsibility to get his men home. So, was there a chance that as soon as Butler walked into the house, he'd slip back into being himself?

"Butler?" he asked cautiously.

At the tone in his voice, Butler gave him that wary look. "Yes, Philip?"

"When we get to the farm, are you going to let the rest of the men muster out? Let them continue on to their homes on their own?"

Butler's expression pinched, his eyes adopted that vacant look that he got when all of his men were talking at once.

"Butler?" Doc asked after several minutes. The man's face had gone completely blank. "Did you hear me?"

Finally Butler's eyes cleared. "Sergeant Kershaw says we all have to stay together for the time being. No telling what Yankee intentions are. And someone might get lost. Remember Chickamauga?"

"Damn it! It's not Chickamauga. The war's over!"

"I am an officer," Butler insisted. "Responsibility is the burden of command. It's up to me to keep the men alive. My men are safe now, and by God, I'll keep them that way."

"They *are* safe!" Doc almost shouted. "Just past these trees, we are home! Safe! And I . . ." He'd strained his throat, breaking into a fit of coughing that doubled him over. For moments he couldn't breathe, his throat pain-racked, stars of light dancing before his darkening vision. Finally spent, he gasped for air.

"You worry me, Philip." Butler shook his head.

"Yes," Doc said through a rasping breath. "Sometimes I worry myself, too."

449

And then they broke out of the trees. Doc and Butler turned in unison to see the farm.

"Dear God," Doc whispered. "There's barely anything left. The tobacco barn's gone, the barn and sheds are missing. The fields are gone back to wild."

"Smoke in the chimney," Butler noted. "They're home, Philip. They made it."

"Thank God!" Philip sagged on the seat, the wash of relief unmanning him. "Odd how a man's priorities can change. If I never have to set foot off of the place again, I'll be a happy man. Somehow, after everything I've been through, I can spend the rest of my life growing corn, cotton, and tobacco, and be forever grateful."

As they turned off onto the lane, Doc glanced down at the river. That big limestone rock was still there. Tonight, after greetings and supper were over, he was going to retreat there. Atop that rock, he was going to stare at the river, and begin the process of healing his tortured soul.

Butler pulled the mule to a stop and set the brake as they entered the yard. Philip hardly noticed his brother's pursed lips, the narrowing of his eyes.

Doc stepped down, dropped to his knees on the rain-damp dirt, bent and kissed it. Then he clawed up some of the soil, squeezing it tight in his fists, savoring the feel of familiar earth. His earth. He felt a tear break loose and streak down his face.

"Sergeant Kershaw says we're not home."

Doc turned, staring up at Butler, who sat stone upright. Then he stood, looking at the house, its sides weathered and gray and in need of paint. Glass was missing in the windows, oilcloth having been hung over what panes remained. Three saddles were front-laid on the porch, a dented bucket by the door. Paw's old rocker, missing a couple of slats in the back, sat to one side.

"Maw! Sarah! Billy!" Doc cried. "We're home!"

No one appeared at the door. "Maw! It's Philip and Butler!"

He started for the porch.

"Hold it right there, mister!" a sharp voice called from off to the right.

Doc turned. A man had risen from behind the rosebushes, a double-barrel shotgun at the ready. He approached carefully, dark eyes gleaming from beneath his wet hat. His jaws were working, making his black beard twitch.

"Got 'em covered from this side, Dube!" another voice called, and Doc turned, seeing two young men with carbines as they emerged from around the far side of the house.

"Whoa!" Doc said easily. "I'm Philip Hancock. This is my brother Butler. James Hancock was our father. Is Maw around? Or Billy or Sarah? This is the Hancock farm. Our home."

"Might have been." The man with the shotgun smiled. "Once. We been here nigh on two years now. Heard it was a Rebel farm. Reckon if'n yer Rebels, you'll be the last ones we drive out of Benton County."

"Two years?" Doc whispered.

"Federals cleared this country of Rebels after Prairie Grove. Ain't none o' yer kind here no more. Now, why don't you be smart, Johnny Rebs, and turn that wagon around. If'n ye don't, you'll end up good Rebels. You can tell yer a good Rebel 'cause you'll be buried next t' them two graves out back."

Doc swallowed hard. "There's *two* graves out back?"

"Ain't no names on 'em."

"You don't understand! This is our home! Where is our mother? My brother Billy and sister Sarah? Have you at least heard of them? Do you know where they are?"

As he spoke a young woman stepped out on the porch, her belly distended in pregnancy. She cocked her head, studying Doc and Butler. "Who's this, Dube?"

"Says they used to live here."

She stared distastefully at Doc. "I heard tell that the girl was carried off by jayhawkers. That boy, Billy? Word is Crawfords, from down to Van Buren County, was hunting him. Heard he killed one of old Amos's boys. Either they got him, or he done left the country a couple of years back."

"What happened here?" Doc asked, throwing his arms wide.

"Reckon y'all went to war with the Union and ye lost. Now, spoils of war, mister. This hyar land is ours. We found it. Took it. And ain't no two broke-down Johnny Rebs coming to take it away from us. So, this hyar's my last words. You git your arse back up on that wagon seat, and if'n I ever sees your stinkin' face around here again, I'll kill ye!"

"Dube?" one of the younger men asked as he raised his carbine. "We shoot 'em, we could sure use that spring wagon. Looks a mite used, but it's better'n what we got."

"War's over, Grady. We cain't jist shoot 'em down." Dube grinned evilly behind his beard. "Unless, of course, these two Rebs want to open the ball again."

452

"Sergeant," Butler called out, "form up the men!"

Dube's eyes widened as he brought the shotgun to his cheek, taking a sight on Butler.

"Whoa!" Doc shouted, throwing his arms up. "We're leaving! Don't shoot! For God's sake, he's crazy. Sees things that aren't there. Just . . . *please* let me get him out of here!"

"Well, go on. And don't ye never come back, neither."

Doc was shaking as he climbed up on the seat, reaching for the reins where they lay in Butler's hands. Even as Doc clawed them away, Butler shouted, "Advance by the right oblique. At the quick step. Forward!"

Doc slapped the reins across the mule's back, wheeling the animal around the yard, and started him down the lane toward the river road. He only looked back once to see the invaders, lined up, weapons at the ready. Three dark men and a pregnant woman. Standing between him and the last of his memories and hopes.

56

July 4, 1865

"I tell ye, it whar them damned high-an'-mighty politicians in Richmond what done the Confeder'cy in. We'da won the war if'n it hadn't been fer that Jeff'son Davis and that collection o' skunks he kep' around hisseff back East."

The speaker was a gray-headed old man with a wedge of a face, and deep lines around his oversized hooked nose. The few teeth in his mouth were tobacco-brown incisors that matched the color of his faded brown eyes. White wisps of beard clung to his cheeks. He held a chipped ceramic cup above his head as he pontificated.

The duffer stood atop a chair in the middle of McMannaman's Saloon; the place was a dusty and drab clapboard structure along a similarly dusty and drab trail on the bank of the Trinity River just outside of Fort Worth.

Billy waited in the darkness outside. Through the open door he studied the saloon's lamplit interior. The Confederate leanings were apparent given the battle flag hung behind the plank bar where McMannaman held sway. The central table was the codger's domain along with his collection of elderly companions: fiery gray and white-headed elders in faded flannel and canvas coveralls. A huge Texas flag covered the north wall, its bottom stained from the high-water line the last time the Trinity had flooded.

Two tables of young men, barely more than boys, sat in the back right. They wore the attire of stock herders, what the locals had taken to calling cowboys, as more and more of the border ruffians and "bush soldiers" had taken to rounding up strayed and unclaimed beef, herding them north into the Nations, and selling them to the army.

The table nearest the door was empty, but a lone man sat at the back table next to the open door that led out to the outhouse. Though he wore his hat pulled low, Billy knew Charlie Deveroux when he saw him. The bulk in the man's shoulders just couldn't be disguised. At Charlie's elbow was a second mug, the chair pulled back as if just vacated.

Taking one last look around, Billy satisfied himself that the fifteen horses tied around didn't seem interested in anything but switching their tails and shifting from standing hipshot on the left to hipshot on the right.

An owl hooted out in the brush along the river, and a bat fluttered past his ear.

"Hell, did ye ever see Texas invaded? We beat them bastards back time after time!" the old man crowed.

"You want to know where to cast blame?" a round-bellied elder at the table asked. "It's them damn Easterners. Shoulda let Texans fight the whole thing. What in tarnal hell does a Virginian know about war? Not like Texas boys what fit the Commanch' and Mexicans all their lives."

"Eastern bastards," the standing patriarch

455

agreed. "They drained poor ol' blood-sucked Texas for all we had. Took our boys first, then they took our wagons and stock. Then they took our food, and then that damn Jeff Davis kilt our cotton trade! He'da broke us but for Governor Murrah."

"Hoooraw fer Murrah!" the elders bellowed as Billy slipped in the door, kept a sidelong glance on the others, and made his way to Charlie's table.

The standing elder added, "Texas shoulda seceded from the Confederacy, too. We stood fine on our own two feet, and by God's hairy balls, we don't need nobody else!"

"It was them generals, I tell ye," old round face bellowed before slugging down a drink from a tin cup. "I heard tell of how Bragg lost battle after battle, never following up. His whole staff hated him. Warn't no different no matter whar ye was. Hindman and Holmes in Arkansas. Bragg in Tennessee. They all had their heads stuck so far up their asses they farted when they sneezed."

A bottle stood front and center on Charlie's table as Billy took hold of the empty chair and shifted it so he could sit with his back to the wall.

"Everything go all right?" Charlie asked.

"Reckon so." Billy shot him a measuring glance from under the brim of his hat. "Reckon tomorrow morning someone's gonna find your Nate Holloway behind some rain barrels in the alley behind Second Street. He never made a peep."

Charlie studied him thoughtfully. "How'd you do it?"

Billy tapped the pommel of his Bowie. "Slipped up behind him and ran nine inches of steel through his kidney, liver, heart, and lungs. Man

456

can't scream when that flap of muscle in the chest is cut."

Charlie glanced down at Billy's side. "Don't see no blood."

"I spent my whole life gutting hogs, Charlie. Man's no different, and sometimes a heap easier."

"Can't pay you until I got proof he's dead."

Billy nodded. "Fair enough."

Charlie shook his head, reached into his pocket, and slipped a small cloth sack across the table. Billy retrieved it, felt the familiar outline of coins beneath the fabric, and dropped it into his vest pocket. "Thought you needed proof."

"You read like a book. When you come off a kill you got a glow. It's in your eyes, the set of your mouth. You got an inner light like you was about to explode. You ain't never as full of yourself as you are right now."

"So you got something else for me?"

"Reckon he does," a voice called from the back door.

Billy's hand dropped instinctively to his Remington. Then he smiled as Danny Goodman stepped in from the darkness. "Ain't seen you since who flung the chunk."

"Heard you been keeping to the thick brush, Billy." Danny offered his hand, a silly grin on his wet lips.

"I don't spend much time around Lampasas these days. Not that anybody down there would know me, but they'd sure as hell know Locomotive."

"Locomotive?" Danny asked as he slipped into the empty chair and poured from the bottle into the mug. "Wasn't that Dewley's horse?"

"*Was.* Turns out I kilt that animal with a neck

457

shot, so I figure I own it. 'Sides, I sort of liked the name. Fits a big black horse, don't you think? I got tired of riding these broke-down old nags and took me a solid mount from a man what suddenly had no use for a big black gelding." Billy grinned. "Besides, I set the damn barn on fire on the way out so the damn horse might just as well go with me as burn to cinders."

"Still a stone-cold killer?" Danny asked.

"That bother you?"

"Nope." Danny pursed his lips, staring down into the whiskey. "Given where we been and what we seen, reckon that's about all we know anymore."

"I'll tell ye why we lost," the scarecrow at the elders' table finally cried in his reedy voice. "It was the damn deserters. Bush soldiers. Cowards that ran an' hid. Weak-livered bastards what couldn't stand the gaff. Piss fer blood. That's what they had."

Danny turned, snapping, "And you got shit between your ears that's leaking outta your damn mouth, you dried-up old cunt!"

The room was instantly silent.

"Danny?" Charlie warned.

Billy's grin began to widen, his heart ticking up as he tightened his grip on his revolver.

The elders were staring in disbelief, the tall one, his drink still elevated, had a startled look, as if he'd been slapped.

"You talking to me?" the reedy scarecrow asked, clambering uncertainly to his feet. "I fought Mexicans and Comanche for the Republic, you little wet-eared pup! In my day I coulda whipped a dozen of you and your kind. An' dun it with one hand tied ahin't my back. I otta —"

Danny swiveled in his chair, his revolver casually in his hand. "Don't got to get physical, old man. Somebody give this old goat a pistol. We'll do it like a duel. Count to three and shoot. Age won't make no difference, just plain old guts and steady nerves."

"Enough!" McMannaman roared from behind the bar. "Ain't gonna be no shooting in my place."

The double-barreled shotgun that had magically appeared on the bar planks clicked as McMannaman eared back the hammers. "Now, this being Texas, and you both being Southern gentlemen who shot off yer mouths, you'll each say yer sorry to the other, fergit it, and go on with yer drinking. If you can't, you'll both haul yer sorry damn carcasses out of my place and never set foot in here again. Right, laddies?"

Danny stared woodenly at the old man.

"Do it," Charlie murmured.

Danny stood, reholstering his Remington, and offered his hand. "Mister, I killed my share of Yankees in Missouri and Kansas. Seven of 'em. And a couple men that needed killing in Arkansas. Maybe some was cowards. Not me."

The old man worked his receded jaws, white bristles standing out from his shrunken cheeks and chin. "Reckon ye did, boy. Reckon ye got grit." And the old man offered his hand.

Billy felt the building thrill begin to ebb. He let his hand shift from the butt of his pistol. In the other corner, the cowboys were looking uneasily at each other, talking low as they discussed the near fight.

"Need a cup here," Charlie called to McMannaman.

The latter tossed it, Charlie grabbing it out of

459

the air with one hand. He reached for the bottle and poured Billy a full cup of whiskey. Billy, continuing to grin, took a swallow and recognized alcohol seasoned with tobacco juice and hot peppers for color and taste.

Charlie said, "Now that we got that settled, tell Billy where you been."

"Down to Brownsville," Danny said. "Heard that a fella could make a good fortune in the contraband trade. Ended up in Bagdad after Rip Ford drove the Yankees out. Met a fella there that really taught me how to play poker. Made me a small fortune. Nigh onto a hundred bucks. Greenbacks, not Confederate."

Danny's expression changed, thinning. "Then I run into a fella who *really* knew poker. He proceeded to teach me a thing or two about cards, like how he spotted my bottom deal. Then he taught me about hideout guns. Like the one he had up his wrist when I went to pull my belt gun."

"Guess you crawfished your way out of it?" Billy sipped his whiskey again, enjoying the warmth building in his belly.

Danny shrugged. "Won't make that mistake again."

"What?" Charlie asked. "The bottom deal or the hideout gun?"

"Both." Then the grin faded. "So, reckon I'm headed back to Arkansas. Got nothing else to do."

"Want a job?" Billy asked.

"What kind?" Danny lifted his whiskey, taking a swig.

"The kind that pays you twenty-five dollars a month. And if you prove yourself, and I don't have to shoot you, it goes up."

"Doing what?" Danny asked. "Waking you up

460

from them damn nightmares you get?"

Billy narrowed his eyes, thankful Danny didn't know the extent of them. Of how Sarah rose naked, something foul growing in her womb, her long blond hair blowing around her body. Or how his cock popped its load when the demon grasped it.

"First off, Danny Goodman, you keep your damned mouth shut. About anything having to do with me. Second, you care for the stock, sometimes hold the horses. Cook along the trail, see to keeping the outfit in top-notch shape, and sometimes you ride in and get information for me. Like a sort of scout." He paused. "Might be times when there's hard riding. Maybe some shooting."

Charlie was watching Billy through veiled eyes. To forestall him, Billy raised his palm, attention still fixed on Danny. "It would be just like it was when we run Dewley's bunch down."

"Twenty-five a month?" Danny frowned, trying to figure the catch. "And just keep the camp?"

"I mean it, Danny. I know you. If you got a fault, it's like tonight with that old duffer. You get likkered up, start wagging your tongue and bragging? I swear to God, and on Maw's bones, I'll kill you dead on the spot."

"Thirty a month," Danny said, obviously shaken by the intensity of Billy's cold blue stare. "And I promise I'll be worth every penny of it." He grinned, as if to defuse the tension, and added, "Hell, ain't nothing in Arkansas I need to see again anyway."

Billy then turned to Charlie. "So, what's the job?"

Charlie glanced uneasily at Danny. "Yankee captain and a bunch of Negro cavalry. Word is he's never alone. Five hundred to the man who drops him."

"I'll take it."

"Killing him is gonna be like throwing coal oil on a fire. They'll be looking long and hard fer the killer."

"Why, Charlie, they might even find me. God help the hindmost."

"You worry me at times, Billy Hancock. It's like you got a death wish."

"Yep. Maybe." He thought about the Sarah demon. " 'Cept the Devil's already claimed me for his own. Longer I string it out on earth, the longer I keep that son of a bitch waiting."

57

July 6, 1865

Lightning flashed white and hot in the inky storm. The crashing bangs that followed left Butler shaken as he crouched on the spring wagon seat. God had become the Lord of Battle: blasts of light, sound, and battering gusts of wind betrayed His fury as He tore the storm-filled sky asunder.

From Butler's mind came spinning images of Shiloh, of Prairie Grove and Chickamauga. In the afterimages of lightning, visions and faces flickered and faded. The gutted Yankee captain at Shiloh, Amos Kershaw at Chickamauga. Hogs fed on half-burned corpses at Prairie Grove.

Terrified, and on the point of weeping, Butler huddled as another blast of wind tried to rip his hat away and tumble him from his seat. Then the rain beat down in a savage fury. Balls of hail mixed with the pounding rain, while unrelenting wind ripped his blanket loose from his shoulders.

"For the love of God!" Butler cried, his voice lost in the earth-shattering crack of thunder as lightning splintered a cottonwood tree in the creek bottom not two hundred yards from the road.

He *hated* Kansas.

The panicked mule kicked and bucked in his

harness, adding a squealing bray of fear to the tempest's howl.

Squinting, wincing, as hail balls the size of walnuts beat on his head and shoulders, Butler fought to control the frightened mule. White lightning showed that they were still on the Fort Scott Road, though the rutted depression was filling with water and floating hail.

Not an hour before, Butler had been sweating, worried sick. Doc had been raving in the heat as he fell deeper into delirium. Now Butler's breath glowed white and frosty each time the lightning flashed.

The hail came harder and faster. Butler hunched in misery, one arm over his head, the other clamping the reins. In dull anguish he endured. Cold water leached through his blanket and clothes, running icy into his pants and down around his testicles.

"Oh, God, oh, God," he kept whispering, half prayer, half whimper.

The transition to hard rain was warmer, almost a relief.

Butler opened his eyes. The mule had stopped, defeated, head down and hunched. Around them the world had turned weirdly luminous — an almost dazzling white in the flashes of lightning. Thunder now echoed and boomed rather than blasted.

Butler slapped the reins, yelling, "Giddup there, Jake!"

For long seconds the mule resisted, then finally started forward, sloshing through a floating sea of hail. As the lightning flashed again, Butler could see that they were still in the road, the hail there flowing as the water slowly drained.

"Doc?" Butler called, shivering against the cold. "You all right?"

No answer.

Butler turned, staring at the damp mass where Doc had curled into a ball under his hail-covered blanket. Rain was inexorably washing hailstones from the bed, leaving it black and shining in the lightning flashes.

"We'll get there, Doc. You'll see."

No answer came from the blanketed form.

"Son of a bloody bitch," Butler muttered, turning forward.

Had to be close to midnight. The storm was rolling off to the northwest, lightning now more intermittent, the darkness deeper, blacker.

"Think he's gonna make it?" Kershaw asked unexpectedly.

"Where've you been?" Violent shivers ran through Butler's shoulders. "Could have used some help in the storm."

"Gone scoutin', Cap'n. Fort's just ahead. *C'est bon.*"

"Thank God." Butler wiped at the water leaking through his hat and down the sides of his face. "Doc's worse. The cough's bad enough. He's been fevered and raving all day. Talking about Ann Marie, and James, and letters being burned. And the farm being lost."

"Y'all think he about t' give up?"

"I don't know, Sergeant." Butler gritted his teeth against a spasm of shivering.

At the same time, Doc broke into violent coughing, causing Butler to look back, unable to see anything in the inky blackness.

"I hate Kansas," Kershaw muttered from behind Butler's ear. "And going into some damn Yankee

465

fort? Dat be foolishness if'n you ask me."

"They have a doctor."

"Dey gots more'n that, Cap'n. Fort Scott's a supply depot. Reckon dey all got the kind of supply we gonna need for to cross the Plains."

Lightning flashed again in the distance, and this time Butler could see buildings in the momentary flicker. Within a matter of yards they passed out of the pale, glowing hail zone, the air warming by ten degrees or more.

The tired mule plodded forward, each step accompanied by the sucking of mud around its hooves.

On the outskirts of Fort Scott the ramshackle buildings and tents they passed were dark; most had animals tied or staked close by. Dogs barked. These were mostly the saloons, cribs, and gambling dens that popped up around any military post — no matter whose army.

The military road turned into the town's main street. After what Butler and the men had seen in Arkansas, the dark houses, stores, liveries, and carriage houses spoke of a prosperity they hadn't seen since leaving Saint Louis.

"Looks to be a lot of people," Kershaw muttered.

Doc broke into a coughing fit in the wagon box, the tearing sound of it wrenching.

"There will be a physician at the fort. He'll know what to do."

"You better hope them damn Yankees'll take a sick Reb, Cap'n," Pettigrew called from where he walked beside the wagon.

Butler had no more than entered the parade ground when a voice up ahead called, "Halt. Who goes there?"

Butler pulled the tired mule to a stop. "I'm Captain Butler Hancock. I've got a sick man in need of the physician."

Dark forms appeared out of the night. "How bad is he, Captain?"

"Bad. Fevered, raving, coughing. That rain and hail didn't help."

"Silas, escort the captain to the hospital."

"Yes, suh." The accented voice sounded distinctly like a Negro's. Butler smiled. Funny how the world had changed.

One of the forms took the mule's bit and started forward. A break in the clouds provided just enough starlight that Butler could see the buildings in the darkness around him. Only here and there did he see a window backlit by the glow of an oil lamp. Fort Scott had played a pivotal role in the border war, a bustling supply depot that kept the Yankee juggernaut in constant motion against the ragged, half-starved Rebels.

"Dis be the den of the enemy, Cap'n," Kershaw whispered softly. "Reckon the men better be right careful."

"Sergeant, you have no idea."

The man leading the mule called back, "I'm just a private, suh." A pause. "But, suh, I's gonna make sergeant someday. All I gots t' do is be better than the next man. Last two years, I done taught myseff to read. I know the Army Manual by heart. Gonna reenlist until I make sergeant and retire with a pension."

"Where were you from?"

"Arkansas, suh. I's a slave till Gen'ral Curtis come. Got a chance to make something of myseff, and I swear, I gonna do it. We heah, suh."

The colored soldier let loose of the bridle and

hurried past the stone pillars supporting the second-story porch. The building was massive, with two rising chimneys.

"Got a sick man. Need a litter out heah," Silas called at the door.

Butler groaned, shivered, and stepped down, his blanket drizzling water. His stiff legs almost failed him.

The black private stopped, no doubt mistaking Butler's rain-slouched hat and dark blanket for a Federal uniform, and snapped off a salute. "Cap'n."

Butler pulled himself straight and returned his best salute, saying, "Carry on, Private. Dismissed."

He grinned to himself as he watched the man's form disappear into the darkness. Then in poetic cadence, said, "What manner of fools can men be . . . that they resort to sword, blood, and mayhem to keep other men from being free."

"Excuse me, Captain?" asked one of the orderlies who had emerged from the hospital with a litter.

"Thinking of the idiotic reasons human beings have for killing each other." Butler gestured toward the back of the wagon. "My brother's sick. An irony since he's the regimental surgeon for Neely's regiment. That's the Fourth, you know. Bad cough, fever, hot and cold spells, delirium. His name is Philip."

"With respect, Captain, just who are you?" the second of the men asked as the two of them shifted the shivering Philip to the litter.

"Captain Butler Hancock. Late of Company A, the Second Arkansas."

"Ah, the colored regiment. No wonder the private saluted you."

468

"He know what the hell he talking about?" Kershaw asked from behind Butler's ear.

"One of General Thomas's first Federal colored regiments. Ironically recruited at Helena, Arkansas, in 1863, long after you'd gone to the Army of Tennessee."

"Sir?" one of the orderlies asked as they started Doc up the stairs.

Butler studied the man thoughtfully. "Did you know that the success of the U.S. Second Arkansas colored Regiment even made Tom Hindman change his tune? Last I heard, just before Chickamauga, he was proposing Negro soldiers for Confederate regiments. Can't imagine how General Bragg and his flint-nosed cronies would have reacted to that."

"Probably why they lost the war, sir," the orderly returned.

"Yankee scum belly!" Phil Vail wailed as he appeared around the corner of the hospital. "Oughta whip his arse until it's red and raw!"

"Cap'n?" Pettigrew asked as he leaned against the spring wagon. "You better set that popinjay straight on a few things or we're gonna go through him like a stallion through corn stalks."

"Time we taught these smug Yankees a lesson or two." Peterson added his own ire.

"Gentlemen, we can discuss the outcome of the war later," Butler replied. "First let's get Doc taken care of. Then we can deal with the tactical realities."

"Of course, Captain," the first of the litter bearers said as they bore Doc's frail body into the dimly lit hospital. "With respect, sir, since he is a civilian, we may have to relocate your brother to a private physician's care."

469

"Doc never mustered out," Butler responded. "He should still be on the regimental rolls."

"Tactical realities?" the second wondered as he vanished into the hospital.

Behind Butler's ear, Kershaw growled, "Can't wait to chop these cocksure Yankees down to size. You got a plan, Cap'n?"

Butler smiled in anticipation. "Of course. Fort Scott served as a supply depot, and gentlemen, we're going on a raid."

58

July 8, 1865

Doc coughed himself awake, blinked at the world through rheumy eyes, and rubbed them with a weak hand. Nothing made sense. Phantasms seemed oddly interlinked in his memory: Ann Marie; shattered and bleeding limbs coming loose in his hands; freezing and starving men staring at him from sunken eyes; as if all the worst of his memories were patched together and merging into each other.

The taste in his mouth was nothing short of vile. He swallowed dryly, coughed again, and barely managed to sit up, only to trigger that racking and painful cough.

He was in a bed. For a moment he wondered if he were in a prison camp. No. Too clean and dry. A hospital, no doubt about it. Only four beds in the long line were occupied, most of them broken bones and injuries from what he could see. The building was frame, and it was delightfully warm. Bright sunlight shone beyond the shadowed windows. A powder magazine and flagpole shone in what was obviously a parade ground. Beyond were officers' quarters and barracks.

"Dr. Hancock?" a voice asked.

"Yes?" Doc's voice sounded like gravel rubbed on oak.

An orderly in an apron came striding down between the rows of beds. He was a young man, maybe early twenties, bearded, with curious light brown eyes. "How are you feeling?"

"Thirsty. Hungry. Where am I?"

"Fort Scott, sir. Captain Hancock brought you in. We've been treating your chest with mustard packs and a spoonful of syrup of squills four times a day."

That explained the taste in his mouth.

"How long have I been here?"

"Two days." The orderly offered his hand. "Bryan Miles, sir. The post surgeon was called away to see to a broken leg. He'll be delighted to learn that you've come back to us. For a time we thought you were a goner."

"Two days?" Doc wondered, feeling dizzy. He leaned back, resting his head on the pillow. "Could I get a glass of water, please?"

"Of course." Miles hurried away.

Doc pinched his brow, trying to remember. Last he could recall, he'd been in the wagon. One minute he was burning up, the next his bones were shivering with a cold so intense he might have been back in Camp Douglas. Each jolt of the wagon had been like a sledgehammer beating his body.

And then the phantasms had come. Eerie and unreal, dream and memory melting together. Ann Marie, Sally Spears, Paw and Maw, images from Boston, and Shiloh, and prison camp. The bearded man staring at him over the shotgun as he drove Butler from the Hancock farm.

"Why the hell didn't I just let myself die?"

472

"Dr. Hancock? Here's your water, sir."

Doc struggled to sit up, broke into coughing, and was helped by Miles. Gratefully he sucked down drafts of the warm water until the glass was empty. Then a second.

"Miles, my stomach is like an empty hole. Is there anything to eat?"

"Got some stew back on the stove. It's not much, but —"

"It will be wondrous," Doc said wearily.

"And as soon as you've eaten, I should give you a dose of quinine sulfate with a strong opiate in addition to your syrup of squills. What you need more than anything now is to rest and rebuild your strength."

"Lovely." Doc fought another round of coughing.

"And after that, a good dosing of spirits of turpentine."

"What for?"

Miles shrugged, failing to meet Doc's eyes. "Don't know where you've been, but somewhere along the way you've picked up a solid infestation of intestinal worms. I hope you weren't sharing mess with the colored troops?"

Doc cocked his head. "Colored troops?"

"In the Second Arkansas." Miles waved it away. "In the meantime, we have a clerical issue. We can't find Neely's regiment in the records."

"I don't understand."

"Probably just an error in records. Happens a lot, sir. We're just about on the edge of the world out here, but it is correct that you were never mustered out of your unit?"

"Um . . . no. They would have me listed as missing." Dear Lord, they thought he was a Federal medical officer who was still on the rolls? How had that happened? He was too tired to think about it.

Doc sighed, feeling exhausted as he closed his eyes. *Second Arkansas? Colored troops? What colored troops?*

"Forget it for the moment, sir. Concentrate on getting well."

"Forget? Hell, Miles, I can't even remember how I got here."

59

July 9, 1865

The night was warm and balmy, the breeze from the west filled with the scent of grass and the slightly astringent tang of horse manure. Not that a man could get away from it anywhere on the Fort Scott grounds. Private Golding Baird was most of the way around his patrol, his Springfield rifle musket over his shoulder. His feet, pinched in the brogans, already hurt and he had until sunrise before he'd be relieved.

Though he couldn't see his watch, he suspected that longed-for moment was still four or five hours away.

As he marched around the big wooden warehouse he gripped his rifle, squinting into the darkness. Yep. Here came the Rebs!

Dancing forward, he jabbed his rifle at the darkness, whispering, "Take that! And that, you dirty Reb!"

In Golding's imagination he mowed a swath through tight formations of gray-clad enemies.

He'd just turned eighteen, having been allowed, finally, to enlist last winter. He'd been desperately afraid that the war would be over before he could kill him a Reb. Mother and Uncle Frank had seen him off at the station in Atchison in February. So far, he'd only shot his rifle ten times. At a wooden target. When they were teaching how to load it. He'd actually hit the target — some fifty yards away — twice. That had been in the beginning. Before he knew what the blast of fire and smoke was like, or how the damn gun hurt his shoulder. At the end he pinched his eyes shut, pointed the malevolent thing, and winced at the bruise it was purpling on his skinny shoulder.

Far better to employ the bayonet. And in the darkness of night, out here on guard duty, no one could see him. Here he was in the front lines at Antietam, or Gettysburg, or Chickamauga, or even just whipping Sterling Price at Westport.

Which was as close as he'd get to actual fighting now that the war was over. Not only were the Rebels whipped, but even Fort Scott was going to be shut down by the end of September. Most of the other soldiers had been mustered out. Those who remained were guarding the last of the dwindling military supplies, caring for stock animals and wagons, and closing down the buildings. With a few exceptions even the gamblers, whiskey traders, and whores had already pulled stakes for Kansas City or points east.

Golding cocked his head, hearing coyotes out in the grass.

"It's the Rebel yell!" he rasped, lifting his rifle, shooting straight and true into Stonewall Jackson's advancing ranks of butternut infantry. In his mind, his ball blew through three of the Rebs who'd made the mistake of standing in line.

"Hah!" he mouthed as he charged forward, his bloody bayonet pinning and tossing Rebs this way and that.

476

He'd just reached the corner of the warehouse. Hearing voices, Golding stopped short, his heart pounding. Dear God! There was someone there! At the front entrance.

He swallowed hard, the rifle suddenly clammy in his hands. He was about to holler a warning when he stopped short, hearing, "If you want a passel of trouble, Corporal, I'm the one who can give it to you!"

The voice sounded sharp and commanding. Not the sort of furtive tone used by thieves.

"I'm a captain, soldier, and you'll snap to it, or I'll have that chevron from your sleeve! You're going to wake up tomorrow and look forward to the whole rest of your military career digging latrines!"

Golding swallowed hard and crept to the corner of the warehouse. The captain sounded really mad.

"Sergeant Kershaw, do you understand the nature of our assignment? Why it is important that we comport ourselves as gentlemen and soldiers? A sentry is supposed to be alert, not parading around like a buffoon!"

Golding felt a little sick to his stomach and snapped to attention, shouldering his rifle.

"We don't have time to stand around so that I can dress him down properly. Not and stay on schedule."

Thank God. Golding felt a cold sweat breaking out. He needed an excuse, something. He'd seen something. Yes, that was it. Moving out in the night. Maybe Indians or skulking Rebs.

Then why hadn't he called out the alarm?

Ah yes. Because it had turned out to be coyotes. But he was making sure. That's why he was late.

Squaring his shoulders, he prepared to step around the corner. Hestitated. The captain was going to dress him down?

He saw me killing Rebs.

Golding's gut fell.

Somehow he couldn't make himself round that corner and march forward into the captain's wrath.

"I don't want to spend the rest of my enlistment digging latrines." He felt like crying.

He was still standing there, rifle shouldered, when a spring wagon, loaded full, was pulled past. In the darkness, he could just make out the figure on the seat, tall, a slouch hat pulled low, what looked like an officer's cloak about his shoulders.

Golding froze, saluted, and stood at attention.

He waited, eyes following the wagon.

Only then did he exhale the breath he held. Where was the rest of the command?

Timidly, he peered around the corner, seeing nothing but the dark ground before the warehouse entrance.

"Must be pretty damn good soldiers," Golding muttered. "They vanished without a trace."

60

"Philip?" Butler's voice pierced the fragmentary dreams.

Doc opened his eyes, aware that he was in the wagon, his body propped uncomfortably. With every jolt, something sharp jabbed into his back. The sky overhead was a pale blue dotted with white puffs of cloud. He could hear birdsong over the creaking and muffled rumble of the wagon and trace chains.

He tried to sit up. The cough seemed to tear its way through his throat. He cupped his hand, enduring the fit, only to gasp for air when it was all over.

"Philip?" Butler asked again.

"Yes?" he said through a groan.

"I'm tired. I think we should camp now."

Doc lifted his head and stared around. The country was gently rolling grassland; here and there in the distance a small farm could be seen. The drainage to the south was filled with cottonwoods, elm, and ash. The tall grass around them undulated like waves as the southwestern breeze ran across it.

"Where are we?"

"We're in Kansas." Butler turned. "You took a turn for the worse again."

"Last thing I remember is being in a hospital." He made a face. "Or was that delirium?"

"You were in a hospital."

"Where?"

"Fort Scott."

"The Union military fort? What on earth possessed you to go there?"

"You were sick. Doing what you always accuse me of: raving."

"And they just treated me?"

"Of course. I'm a captain in the Second Arkansas."

"You *were* a captain in the *Confederate* Second Arkansas."

"The men and I have noticed that Yankees confuse easily. Poor fellows."

"What if they'd caught you impersonating a Federal officer? Butler, they might have shot you."

"The men were keeping watch."

"Oh, dear God." Doc closed his eyes, wondering just how close they had come to disaster.

It took him a moment to muster the courage to ask, "Where are we now? I mean, where are we going?"

"We are on the Fort Scott cutoff to the Santa Fe Trail. We are headed to Colorado."

"What? Why?"

"We discussed this. You agreed."

"Agreed to what?"

"Traveling to Colorado. About the gold there. And getting a new start. The altitude and dry air will be good for your cough. At Fort Scott they weren't sure if it was tuberculosis or not. And I remember Paw talking about how the damp air in

Missouri killed John Colter. Remember him? The mountain man? You mumbled something about nothing left in the east, so why not?"

"And why don't I remember?"

"I'm not sure you react well to opiates, Philip. When we left Fort Scott it was the middle of the night. They had filled you full of opium and a lot of other medicines. Jimmy Peterson reported to me that the hospital staff was growing suspicious about you being a regimental surgeon."

"Peterson? He's one of your phantoms, isn't he?"

"I had detailed Private Peterson to keep an eye on you while we were behind enemy lines. After completing the raid, I decided it was prudent to extract you from the Yankees. It was all the men and I could do to get you to stand up. It took all of us to carry you out to the wagon."

"And where was the surgeon and his staff during all this?"

"Corporal Pettigrew was distracting them. The corporal was on his best behavior. Earlier, his expertise in picking the quartermaster storehouse lock was less than exemplary. Could have got us caught by the Yankees."

"Why don't I remember any of this?"

"Because you were very collywobbled from the medicines. Most of the time you were talking to James Morton and Anne Marie, sometimes to Maw, and occasionally to me. But when I answered, you didn't seem to hear me." Butler glanced over the seat in reproach. "As dark and grim as your conversations are with people who aren't here, the men and I wonder if your mind isn't becoming unhinged."

"*My* mind?"

"We're not sure that what happened at the farm hasn't delivered you into an irreversible state of melancholy."

Doc looked around at the packed wagon, taking stock of barrels, kegs, a tent, folded wool blankets, sacks labeled as wheat and cornmeal, canvas-wrapped bacon, cookware, and various crates and boxes. A new Spencer rifle and several of the long cylindrical cartridge tubes lay just behind the seat. Additionally he could see an ax and shovel handle. He had no idea what the stacks of tins contained.

Peering into the sack beside him, Doc found it to be full of new shoes. Must have been at least fifty pairs.

"Butler? Where did we get all this stuff? It's all marked as U.S. property."

Butler vented an exasperated sigh. "While you were in the hospital, the men and I raided the Fort Scott quartermaster stores. With the exception of Corporal Pettigrew's fumbling of the padlock, the entire raid was flawlessly executed. Private Vail successfully scouted the location, determining the patterns and movements of the nightly guard. Privates Templeton and Thompson were placed as pickets, and Sergeant Kershaw and I supervised the recovery and packing of both commissary and supply."

Doc wilted, realizing the edge of a wooden crate was the culprit eating into his back. "You *stole* all this from under the Yankees' very noses?"

"We have a long crossing of the plains ahead of us. It is the responsibility of the commanding officer to see to the supply of his troops. When others — even Tom Hindman — were in charge, there were too many shortages. It cost us the fight at Prairie Grove, you know."

"Why do we have a sack of shoes?"

"I won't see the men march to Colorado on bare feet. You heard Paw. The plains are filled with cactus."

"Lord God, spare me." Doc rubbed his face. "We have shoes for invisible men." He glanced back over the wagon's tailgate at the tracks they left in the soft soil of the road. "And a squad of Yankee cavalry is going to appear at any second to arrest us and haul us back to Fort Scott for trial and execution."

"Oh no," Butler called cheerily back from the wagon seat. "Corporal Pettigrew is watching the rear. He'll give us ample warning if we need it."

"Right." Doc lasted out another coughing fit, and stared at the shoes, wondering how Butler's *men* were going to put them on.

61

August 28, 1865

As the summer commenced, Sarah was a casual observer as troops continued to muster out of the Federal army at Fort Smith. Confederate generals and irregulars continued to hand in their arms and apply for parole. More and more units were disbanded, beginning with the Arkansas militias, then the First Arkansas Infantry, followed by the Eighteenth Iowa, the Second Kansas Battery, then the Fortieth Iowa. They came in a steady stream through Fort Smith.

She kept Bret Anderson's camp, and he continued to play poker the entire time — forever careful to win just enough from the soldiers but still maintain a reputation for a fair game. Not that his winnings weren't more than satisfactory. The mustering troops were flush.

Who would have thought that a tidy living could be made playing poker, of all things? She'd always considered gamblers to be shifty, slovenly, and most of all, perpetually penniless.

By the middle of July, Anderson took over a spacious dugout with an actual window and two bedrooms. The previous owners, farmers from northern Franklin County, had determined that it was probably safe enough to return to their land, rebuild their burned house, and commence with the hope of rebuilding their lives.

Though Bret offered her the larger of the rooms, Sarah categorically refused, moving her bed into the smaller room in the back rear. There, outfitted with most of the necessities of a home, she continued to cook his meals, wash his clothes, care for Jefferson, his big black horse, and do the dishes.

Not once in the passing weeks had Bret treated her as anything but a valued employee, though more and more, he seemed to spend his leisure hours sitting at the handcrafted wooden table, a cup of coffee in hand, just talking with her. He said it soothed him.

For her part, Sarah had begun to relax, though on more than one occasion, she had been awakened from terrifying dreams when Bret had called from her door, "Sarah, wake up. You're safe. It's just a nightmare."

"Bret?"

"Yes. It's me. Go back to sleep now. I'm right outside, and I'll shoot the first booger that walks through the door."

For the most part, she'd sighed, and drifted back to sleep.

In the security of the house, Sarah began to let her hair down again. With her wages she had purchased two nice cotton dresses — both of which actually fit her — one blue the other red. She bathed each day, as if by doing so, she could distance herself from the event. As if being scrubbed were a repudiation of what Dewley and his men had done to her.

She was in the yard that afternoon, sleeves rolled

485

up, hair tied behind her head as she scrubbed a pair of Bret's pants in the washtub, suds beading on her forearms.

She glanced up as the horseman appeared out of the brush down by the creek. Close-shaven, he had short-cropped blond hair that was confined by a campaign hat. From his insignia, he was a provost marshal, and the blue double-breasted officer's coat hung open revealing no less than two pistols holstered butt-first in his belt. A well-varnished carbine stock protruded from the saddle scabbard.

"Ma'am," he greeted, touching a finger to his hat.

Sarah stared up into hard blue eyes, the kind with no give to them.

"Officer," she answered warily, every instinct warning her to back care fully away to where her pistol hung just inside the door.

"I'm looking for Major Bretford Jerome Anderson, Tenth Massachusetts Light Battery. Is this his residence?"

"The Mr. Anderson who lives here has not, to my knowledge, ever served in the military. Nor is he in residence at the moment, having gone to Little Rock on business. My suggestion, sir, is to return here tomorrow evening. Say about five? My employer should have returned by that time."

"Your employer?" His thin lips twitched. "Has such an honest ring to it, don't you think?"

Sarah stiffened, her heart beginning to pound. "Yes. I take care of Mr. Anderson's household. And *only* his household." Forcing herself to move slowly, she backed to the door. The pistol hung just inside. If he dismounted, followed her, she would let him back her through the door. As soon as he stepped inside, she'd shoot him through the chest.

But he just sat on his oversized black horse, his cold eyes taking her measure. He seemed to be weighing his choices, then said, "Now, if I were to await Anderson here, what sort of entertainment do you think we could devise to occupy ourselves, *housekeeper?*"

"I said, good day, sir." Sarah crossed her arms, the proximity to the pistol filling her with courage.

"You're a liar, ma'am. Reckon I'll be back just as soon as I deal with the belly-crawling bastard you're sharing the blankets with."

He was a very competent horseman. She didn't see the cue he gave, the horse just seemed to wheel on its own, breaking into a trot as it headed off across the flat toward the fort.

Sarah sucked in a deep breath, trying to calm her humming nerves. "Bret, what the hell did you do?"

She pursed her lips. He'd never mentioned being a soldier. Let alone being a major. But then, there was a lot about him she didn't know. She damned well knew what provost marshals did: they arrested people.

"So, think, Sarah."

She had no idea where Bret's game was, and even if she did, he often moved it. Did she dare go warn him? Or would that provost marshal just be waiting out of sight and follow her?

What was the smart thing to do?

Making a decision, she quickly and efficiently began packing Bret's belongings into his trunk. As she did, the ultimate irony struck her that she was so intimately familiar with a man's wardrobe.

She'd always anticipated being so, but with a husband, not a footloose gambler.

She left the house long enough to fetch the two mares Bret had bought at auction, and tied them off behind the dugout. The cookware and loose items she folded into blankets, remembering how Paw had once showed Billy when he was boy. Done up so, they could be tied on a horse with a diamond hitch.

"Blessed be, Sarah, can you remember how that went?"

Having nothing better to do as the sun inched slowly across the sky, she practiced until she got it right. Then it was just a matter of waiting as her imagination conjured one horrible thing after another. The provost marshal's blue eyes faded into Dewley's, sending a shiver up her spine.

Sarah strapped the .44 Colt around her hips, taking a moment to check the caps and loads. The hammer clicked crisply as she ensured the cylinder rotated freely.

She saw Jefferson as the black horse appeared on the fort trail. Bret rode hunched in the saddle, as if the weight of the world depressed his normally broad shoulders.

She ran to meet him, stopped short at the pale strain in his face, his eyes glazed, lips clamped in a pained line.

"Bret! A provost was here. My God, what's wrong?"

He swayed in the saddle, as if balance had deserted him. She'd seen him come home drunk before, but this was different.

"Bret?"

"Sarah? I'm shot." He grimaced. "I don't think it's bad, but by damn it sure hurts."

Shot! Images of dying men, bleeding on the farmhouse floor, came flooding from her memory. Her heart skipped in sudden fear.

"Hang on to the saddle," she told him, taking Jefferson by the bridle and leading him back to the house. There she tied him off and stepped over. "Easy now, kick loose of the stirrup. That's right. Now, help me. I'll take your weight."

"No time. Gotta . . . gotta pack my war bag. Can't stay. Have to leave everything behind as it is. They'll be after me right quick."

"I already packed everything, Bret. First, I gotta see to that wound."

Somehow she got him off the horse, into the house, and lowered him to the bed. Pulling back his coat she winced at the sight of the blood. She might have been back at the farm after Pea Ridge. Reaching out she grabbed his bloody shirt and ripped it open. Grinding her teeth together kept her from gasping at the sight. Broken fragments of rib stuck out from the bleeding mess, but she couldn't hear the sucking sounds she'd heard among the chest-shot men after Pea Ridge.

Dear God, Bret. Don't die on me! Not like that.

"Didn't figger ol' Winston Parmelee was that good with a gun."

"Who?" She reached down under her skirt, slipping her petticoat off her hips. As Bret gasped on the bed she began ripping it into long strips. She stepped outside long enough to drop them in the hot water she'd left steaming on the fire.

"That provost." His eyes went rubbery in his head. "Damn. Hurts."

"Gonna hurt worse right quick, but it's got to be done, Bret." She seated herself beside him with a rag and began picking at the bone fragments.

"Yaaa! Shit!" he screamed. "What are you do-ing?"

"Picking the bone out of the wound. You leave it in there, it's gonna rot." She bent over him, star-ing down into his eyes. "Bret, I'm sorry, but it's the only chance you've got."

He blinked. "Get me a piece of wood. Something to bite on."

She stepped out, found a stick he'd been whit-tling on. With it, she fished out her boiled pet-ticoat strips.

As soon as one cooled, she used it to dampen the wound. As Bret clamped the stick in his teeth, she began cleaning and picking the broken frag-ments loose.

Screams and whimpers came out muffled against the stick and Bret's sucking cheeks. Sweat beaded on his face, his body tensing and bucking. When she was satisfied, she managed to wrap the strips of petticoat around him, used the stick for a handle, and wound the bandages tight.

"Better?" she asked.

"Dear God in heaven," he said, sucking shallow breaths. "Wish he'da just killed me."

"You can't ride," she told him. "Not with those splintered ribs." She pulled his pistol from the holster, finding two cylinders empty. Pausing only long enough to load them, she left the gun in his hand.

"Parmelee walks through that door, shoot first. I'll be back."

"What . . . ?"

Sarah hurried around the back of the house and pulled the picket on the horses. Fifteen minutes later she was at Hervy Johnson's, catching the old man by the fire as he enjoyed his evening cup of coffee.

"Hervy? How much you want for that spring wagon and harness?"

"Why, I couldn't let that go fer lessn' twenty dollars, Miss Sarah."

"It's a *light* wagon. You'll take five. In gold."

"Ten."

"Five. In gold."

"Why'd I sell it for five?"

" 'Cause only a blind idiot would give you ten. Lessen it was Confederate funds."

"Seven."

"Five. In gold."

"Sold."

God smiled. The two horses had been broken to harness sometime in the past, though they were a bit fractious getting back to the dugout. Loading the belongings was easy. Getting Bret on his feet and to the spring wagon? That was a labor of Hercules.

She barely looked back as she slapped the ribbons, and the wagon lurched forward into the evening. Jefferson snuffled where he was tied on behind. She took the road down to the ferry, having just crossed the main road. Looking back, she saw the dark horses, maybe fifteen, that took the turn toward Bret's. In the darkness they barely gave her a second glance. Then were lost in the gloom as they cantered toward the dugout.

"Guess we just made it," she told herself. "Now, Bret, when we get to the ferry, you don't say a word. You hear me?"

"I do," he gasped from where he lay curled in the back.

By midnight she had passed through Van Buren,

following the road north into the Boston Mountains.

"Where are you going, Sarah?" she asked herself as she blinked and let the horses walk. Enough moonlight glowed in the night sky to ensure she was staying to the road.

They would expect Bret to flee east along the river toward Little Rock. It was in her bones to head into home country. Assuming they made it to Fayetteville, she knew all the back roads and trails. It would take more than a provost to ferret her out of the Upper White backcountry.

She allowed herself a humorless chuckle. Her last five dollars might have gone for the wagon, but before — having been hungry for too long — she'd stocked up on cornmeal, wheat, oats, and baking soda. Bret's Henry rifle along with fifty cartridges was behind the seat next to his shotgun, and she had her pistol on her hip.

"So now, Bret, darling," she told the sleeping man behind her, "all I need is to keep you from dying on me."

But that, she realized, might be a dream beyond hope.

62

September 2, 1865

Five hundred dollars!

The thought of it filled Billy's brain like a fever as he lay in the dappled shade beneath the mesquite. The occasional fly buzzed around his head, apparently desperate for his sweat or enticed by the way he smelled after a week in the brasada. Not an hour earlier he'd watched a scorpion — worried by the way he'd shifted on the hot white limestone rock — skitter away.

A family of wrens had passed by not fifteen minutes ago, hardly paying him any heed at all as they hopped about in the cedars surrounding him.

Across the canyon, heat shimmered on the white rock and dark green foliage of live oak, redolent cedars, mesquite, and currants. From his perch, Billy could see down to the trail below where it skirted a dry and rock-filled streambed. In the distance he could see Packsaddle Mountain. Every two weeks, the captain and his patrol of mounted Negro cavalry made this loop. At Llano, they would spend the night before riding down to Fredericksburg, then back to Austin.

Billy hadn't a clue why anyone would want to kill the captain — let alone pay five hundred dollars for it. Nor did he particularly care. The man was a Yankee, a pawn on the conqueror's game board.

He shooed a fly. Maybe, if he made a good kill, the dreams would stop. He had awakened Danny last night after the nightmare image of Sarah, naked, her breasts bruised and bitten, had risen over his supine body. As her hair billowed and twisted around her, she'd looked down at him with icy blue eyes and her lips, looking rotted, had twisted around fanglike teeth.

She had bent down then, her hands fastening on his pizzle.

Billy's pumping loins had brought him awake screaming.

God in heaven, he hated that dream.

Miracle was, Danny hadn't shot him dead when he jerked upright in the blankets.

The crack of a hoof on rock, followed a moment later by the metallic clink of buckles, gave Billy his warning. A shod hoof clicked on stone. A man laughed. The sound funneled up the canyon.

Soon now.

Billy's heart began to slow, the feeling of euphoria rising. He shifted the Sharps where it lay propped on his pack and snuggled behind the stock. With the gun up, he peered through the sights to the place where the trail climbed up through the limestone rim. One hundred and twenty paces. He could see the cracked rock he'd practiced on yesterday. The elevation and windage were perfect.

"What you gonna do wit dat gal, Samuel? She gonna wan' you t' marry her. Den you'se gonna get transferred someplace else," one of the colored troops called out.

"I's gwine t' marry her," another called back. "An' if'n I's be transferred, I's gwine t' give her money t' come. Dat's what. Don' gotta let massa break no marriages no mo'. Even if massa's de army. Ain't dat right, Cap'n?"

"Reckon so, Samuel," a white voice, Northern accent, called back. "Though God alone knows how you can keep a woman on army wages."

The first of them passed below Billy's perch. The point riders, three black men in blue uniforms, kepis strapped tightly under their chins. They and their mounts looked tired and sweaty.

Then came the captain, crossed sabers glinting gold on the front of his campaign hat. He rode as if one with his mount, a big blood bay. Though he scanned the rim as he passed, it was with a trained soldier's casualness, not that of a man expecting trouble.

The rest of the column followed in twos, the black soldiers in various postures, their carbines muzzle-down in the thimbles attached to their stirrup straps. The carbines yanked and swayed, tugging on the broad shoulder straps, as their horses labored up the grade.

Billy began to breathe as he settled the front sight on the notch. Inhale, hold, exhale; he followed the mantra Paw had taught him so long ago.

The point riders climbed through the narrow defile one by one, and then came the captain.

Billy let him ride into the sight picture, applied the slightest pressure to the trigger, and felt the Sharps punch back into his shoulder. Even as the report boomed in the narrow canyon, he heard the meaty smack of his minié ball into flesh.

Through the spinning cloud of blue smoke he

saw the captain sag forward, then tumble sideways off his mount. The blood bay panicked, trying to shy sideways in the narrow gap, then bucked and kicked as it fought free.

Billy had already snapped the lever down, dropping the block. He shoved another greased cartridge into the smoking chamber and flicked the lever closed, shearing the paper to expose the powder. Plucking up the cap he'd set to the side, he pressed it over the nipple and resettled the rifle over his pack.

Below him was chaos, men shouting, horses milling, the clatter of confusion.

Two of the colored troops had dismounted and rushed to the captain. A sergeant was bellowing orders, pointing this way and that.

Billy waited.

As the two soldiers attended to the captain and raised him into a sitting position, Billy took up the slack on the trigger. One of the men was supporting the captain's head.

Now!

The Sharps boomed again and spewed another wreath of smoke into the air.

Billy didn't see the captain's head explode as the lead bullet hit it — but the mess was apparent: the two stunned soldiers were spattered with blood, brains, and bone.

Then Billy was wiggling backward, bullets whacking off the limestone below his hiding place.

Getting to his feet, he ran. From long practice, he dropped the block, fishing another cartridge from his shirt pocket and slipping it into the chamber. Keeping low, he zigzagged through the brush — cat's claw and mesquite thorns tearing at his clothing. He leaped from one limestone boulder to another, sprinted across an open expanse of stone, and slipped and slid his way down through a crack into a side canyon on the other side of the ridge.

Wasn't no horse in the world going to follow him across or down that.

"How'd it go?" Danny asked as Billy burst into the small clearing. Danny was already mounted on his own horse, holding the reins for Locomotive.

"One through the lights, the second through his head. Now we gotta make tracks, Danny. Them might be freed black boys back there, but that ain't to say they ain't got one hell of a mad on, right now. And they might have some coon who can track us. Let's go."

He leaped into the saddle, jamming the Sharps into its scabbard as Locomotive sidestepped. Grabbing the reins, Billy gigged Locomotive into motion, leading the way down the narrow trail.

"What's the plan?" Danny called from behind.

"Reckon we can make it to Magdelena's roadhouse by midnight." He grinned. "When we do, we're celebrating. Reckon we'll dip our wicks in a couple of whores and drink us a bottle of whiskey. Then it's the back trails north to pick up our pay."

"You paying?"

"Yep."

"I want Rosalia."

"Fine with me, I'll settle for Helga."

"That flat-chested skinny red-haired Dutch gal?"

"Yep."

"Why her?"

" 'Cause she lets me make believe."

"Make believe? What kind of talk is that?"

"None of your damn business." Fact was, she'd

let him close his eyes, lay back, and imagine whoever he wanted while she rode him. And even if she suspected that he imagined a tall blond woman with blue eyes, and if he lost himself in the moment and called her "Sarah" she didn't care.

63

September 10, 1865

Bret clung to life. For four days fever sought to burn him up. Then he began to mend.

At the end of each day's travel, Sarah stopped, cared for the horses, built a fire, started supper, and stepped to the back of the wagon where she peeled off Bret's pus-filled and blood-speckled bandages. Allowing the festering wound to air, she'd boil the old bandages while wrapping the previous day's around Bret's slowly healing chest.

The night of the tenth, just north of Fort Scott, Kansas, Bret actually sat up. He positioned himself with his legs dangling from the back of the wagon and watched her as she went about her evening chores.

"You saved my life, Sarah."

"You're not out of the thick timber yet, Bret." She shot him a measuring look from the stew pot. She'd traded with a farmer that day: a tin of salt for a chicken.

Bret nodded faintly, glancing around the copse of trees where they'd camped by a small creek. Cottonwood and ash leaves rattled softly in the wind. From the fire rings and grazed areas they were far from the first to use it.

"I'm going to live," he told her. "I'm going to do it for you."

She avoided his eyes. "Why'd you desert?"

"How'd you know that?"

"Parmelee told me before he went off to shoot you."

He took a breath, as if testing his ribs, and strangled a gasp. For a moment he was silent, then said, "I guess the war wasn't making much sense to me." A pause. "Battle after battle, my battery was in the thick of it. All I saw was the mass murder of men. Chancellorsville. That's when I quit. The Rebs tried to take our battery. I had my boys wait until they were right at the cannon muzzles . . . and blew them away with canister. Then we fell to rifles and pistols. Drove them back."

Bret used his thumbnail to pick at the wood tailgate. "I shot this boy. Little guy looked half starved. Dressed in rags. Maybe he was sixteen. Maybe. After the Rebs fell back, this boy kept crawling toward me. He was choking on his blood, crying, 'Help me, please, mister.' "

Bret glanced up at the night sky. "Can you believe that? He was looking me in the eyes. Knew it was me who'd shot him. But there he was, crawling toward me, reaching out with that shaking bloody hand. Wanted me to save him. Comfort him." He paused. "And then later I walked out among the dead. You don't know what canister, shot point-blank, does to people. Something inside me just couldn't stand it anymore."

"Paw made me read history. I don't guess there's ever been a war like this one. I heard a half-million men died."

"I walked away after the battle, Sarah. I've

always had a talent with cards. I can remember what's played, know how to calculate the chance that an unplayed card will turn up. I just thought, like Thoreau, that my steps would take me west until I ran out of war."

"I guess it worked until Parmelee caught up with you."

His eyes were vacant. "Never will figure how he followed me all that way."

"He scared me." She straightened from the fire, a wooden spoon in her hand. "Glad you shot straighter than he did. That look he gave me when he left? He meant it when he said he'd see me again."

Bret nodded, expression perplexed, as though struggling with something. "But for you, they'd have run me down. We both know that. I'd have hung for killing him." He spread his hands, looking at them as if in wonder. "I'd be dead but for you."

"Reckon I didn't want to lose my thirty dollars." She gave him a conspiratorial wink.

Bret's dark brown eyes filled with intensity. "I think . . . Well, you and I have gone beyond a boss and the hired help." He seemed to pick his words.

"Maybe."

"I need you to understand something. Just hear me out before you say anything. I have come to love you with all of my heart. My life is yours, Sarah. It's yours in any way you want to have it. I will remain as your friend. I would be your husband if you would have me. Or I will be thankful to act as just a casual acquaintance. But having said what I have, I will never impose myself on you."

She stood, heart beginning to pound. Not that

his words surprised her, but she had anticipated a sense of panic were he ever to say it. Instead, she seemed paralyzed, standing stupidly, the wooden spoon in her hand.

"Sarah?"

"I'm . . . just a little confused, that's all."

He smiled wistfully. "Part of loving someone, *really* loving them, is accepting them entirely on their terms. I meant what I said. I shall be honored to simply remain your friend. I just . . ." He made a face. "I *had* to tell you. Even at risk of driving you away. I couldn't have forgiven myself if I'd never said it."

She took a deep breath, then blew it out, saying, "Dear me." She laughed at the irony. "You don't want to love me, Bret. It's a bad idea. Find some woman who can dream and love and laugh. I'm nothing more than a walking ruin."

"You're a pillar of steel, Sarah. And each day I marvel at your strength and resilience. Your courage inspires me."

"You're an idiot, Bret Anderson." She turned away, the hollow sensation of loss in her belly.

"I know what happened to you. You cry out in your nightmares. And it's the same nightmare over and over. If I prove nothing else to you, it will be that I am not like those men. That eventually, you won't have to run anymore."

She stared down at the fire, swallowing hard. The demons down inside her tried to claw their way out.

"I killed the leader," she heard herself say, as if from a great distance. "Used Billy's Bowie knife."

She felt herself sway.

In her mind she relived those moments, perched on the steep trail. Dewley was staring at her in horror, his leg broken. He kept trying to reach the Colt where it had fallen among the rocks. His fingers kept slipping off the end of the barrel. The memory of Dewley's screams, the blood jetting from his severed arteries. It had spattered on her skin, warm and viscous.

"It was like Billy said. Not much different than butchering a hog." She paused, gaze gone distant. "I was crazy, Bret. Like some mindless banshee. Possessed of the devil." She hesitated, still feeling remote and separate from the world. "Maybe I still am."

"My nightmares are of the war," he told her. "That boy. Or seeing ranks of men blown to red bits in front of my guns. We all have our devils. It's what we do with them that matters."

She shrugged, bent down and stirred the chicken where it boiled with carrots she'd found outside of Fort Scott.

"I think we should go to Colorado," Bret told her, his voice dropping into its familiar and easygoing cadence. "Someplace new for both of us. A place where no one will be looking for me, either as a deserter or for killing that scoundrel Parmelee. In addition, we can set ourselves up in a better residence. People don't ask as many questions in places like mining camps. And Sarah, there are fortunes to be made."

"Colorado is a long way from here, Bret. And winter's coming."

"In Fort Scott I overheard that there's a new stage line running across the plains from Atchison, Kansas. That's a week or so north of us. I'll be fit enough to sit up by then. And it will be fast."

"What about the wagon?"

503

"Sell it. Like you said, it's September. It would take us months to make the crossing on our own. We'd freeze out there in some blizzard. The stage will have us in Denver in weeks. And Jefferson can follow behind the coach on a lead."

Colorado? Did she want to go to Colorado?

"Aren't stagecoaches expensive?"

"The fare is one hundred and seventy-five a person."

"Dear Lord God, where are we going to find three hundred and fifty —"

"Here." He reached over to pat his trunk. "In the lining, lower right side. We shall travel in style."

"You are a man of surprises tonight, Bretford Jerome Anderson." The more she thought about it, the more intriguing the idea was. Colorado was such a long way from Benton County, Arkansas, and the ruins of her old life. For the first time since the start of the war, a flicker of hope began to burn inside her. It would be new. A place where some horrible memory didn't lurk around the corner. Where no former acquaintance might meet her on the street and cry, *"Why, aren't you Sarah Hancock? James's raped daughter?"*

She studied Bret thoughtfully, her gaze locked with his dark and anxious eyes. Was the fool really in love with her? Could a man really and truly love her, knowing what he did about her?

He's never so much as hinted that I sleep with him.

And she knew he was interested, had seen the longing in his eyes. Had seen the quickening in him when she wore her red form-fitting dress and stood tall before him.

Oddly, just thinking of it kindled a flicker of warmth inside her.

"As to Colorado? I say we do it, Bret."

"You're sure? Just like that?"

"Paw always talked about the Shining Mountains. I never figured I'd see them. They were just kind of a dream, something for adventurous men."

Bret gave her a sparkling smile. "We'll do it up right, Sarah. I promise. You shall never want for anything. Once we climb into that stage, we'll leave the devil behind us and never look back."

"You're a fool, Bret. You almost make me believe you."

64

September 15, 1865

The camp was situated a half mile north of the Santa Fe Trail. It lay in the protection of a grassy draw that emptied into the Arkansas River floodplain. Doc and Butler were three days west of Fort Zarah on the Great Bend of the Arkansas, headed for Fort Larned. Word was that a caravan of freight wagons was about to leave under military escort and make its passage across the western trail.

Peace might have been declared in the east, but chaos reigned in the west where every Plains Indian tribe had taken the opportunity to declare war on the overland trails. In the south it was the Comanche, Kiowa, and Kiowa Apache. Move a little north and it was the Cheyenne, Arapaho, and Sioux.

As the depredations had increased, atrocity led to greater atrocity. Colorado Volunteers under a Colonel John Chivington had surprised a Cheyenne and Arapaho winter camp in November of 1864 and murdered men, women, and children. They had paraded through the streets of Denver exhibiting bits of female genitals they'd cut from the dead bodies.

Given the reactions of travelers Doc and Butler had met, the fighting on the Plains had degenerated into a war of mutual extermination.

They came on Doc by surprise. Though exactly who surprised whom might be up for grabs. Indians on ponies traveled with much greater stealth than Yankee cavalry. The first Doc knew of their presence was the whispering of tall grass under the unshod hooves of the small party of Cheyenne riders.

He looked up as they appeared from around a bend in the grassy drainage. The mule on its picket let out one of its screeching brays. Doc slowly stood from where he'd piled kindling inside a ring of stone left by previous travelers.

The Indians made not a sound, the first four split, two to the left and two to the right, as they circled him and the wagon. A fifth, leading a horse pulling a travois, stopped short.

One by one, Doc inspected them, seeing young men, perhaps in their twenties and early thirties. Thick black hair was greased, hanging long down their backs. Buffalo-hide shields were hung over their shoulders, along with bows and quivers. Their only clothing consisted of breechcloths and tall moccasins — though most had beaded and feathered arm and ankle bands. Their skin had been burned dark, the color of an old penny. All but the one to Doc's right who looked seasoned-oak brown. In addition he had wavy brown-tinted hair and the kind of straight nose that hinted of a white father.

They had fixed their unforgiving black eyes on his, no change of expressions on their faces. Each held a carbine at the ready, or propped on his leg. If the stories were true, no mercy was being given on either side.

"Hello," Doc greeted, glancing back to where the fifth rider had pulled up. The horse pulling the travois had stopped and was cropping the grass, the long poles extended over the horse's withers in an X.

"I'm Dr. Philip Hancock. I'm just passing through and mean you no harm."

One of the Cheyenne said something in what sounded to Doc's ignorant ear like chittering, and half-swallowed vowels.

The others laughed.

The tall young one kneed his horse forward and reached out with a quirt to slap Doc across the shoulders, then he yipped in triumph.

"What the hell!" Doc cried. "I said I was no harm to you!"

"Just the same, white man," the oak-brown one said as he rode his horse forward, "you are in wrong place, wrong time." Then he rattled off a quick smattering of Cheyenne to the others. They all laughed again — the sort of amused laugh an executioner gave to the condemned just before he cut off his head.

"Attenshun!" Butler's voice rang out from the top of the draw. He stood skylined above the drainage, calling out orders. "Company, form up. Sergeant Kershaw, order your men to cap their weapons. Private Johnson, advance at the oblique and prepare to engage. Corporal Pettigrew, by the right flank. Prepare to fire from the enfilade. Forward!" Butler raised his hand, signaling as if it held a sword.

The Cheyenne were wheeling their horses, staring at him as if in disbelief. The oak-skinned warrior called out, pointing this way and that, as if

508

looking for Butler's soldiers and telling his companions where to anticipate attack. Each had his carbine raised, cocked, ready to fire.

"No!" Doc cried. "They're not real!" He ran in front of the oak-skinned warrior, raising his hands and shouting, "They are *ghosts*! Do you understand?" God, what was that word Paw used to tell at the dinner table when he was going on about Indians in the west? *"Heyoka!"* But he wasn't sure that was the right word. "Do you understand? He's crazy. Not right in the head."

The Cheyenne on their sidestepping horses were staring over the sights, two of them fixed on Butler. They looked anything but relaxed as Butler continued to call out orders, gesturing this way and that.

"You know *heyoka*?" the oak-skinned warrior asked.

"Crazy, yes. Uh . . . possessed of the spirits. He calls orders to dead soldiers. They live in his head. My brother doesn't mean any harm. The soldiers he commands are . . . I mean, they're ghosts! God, what are the words? *Wakan?* Is that right? Don't hurt him!"

The oak-skinned warrior called a soft order. The Cheyenne, wary and nervous, circled their horses, black eyes flicking this way and that.

"I am a doctor. What you call a medicine man. I'm trying to heal my brother."

Oak Skin called to the apparent leader, the sharp-faced, slightly older man leading the travois. Seven eagle feathers — each cut in a different fashion — hung from his thick tangle of hair.

Butler, meanwhile, called, "Hold your positions! At the ready!"

The leader spoke to the oak-skinned warrior.

The latter replied and stared down from his horse at Doc. "You are *heseeotse*?" He pointed at Butler. "He is *Ma'hta'sooma Notakhe*?"

"I don't know your words."

"You doctor. Him spirit warrior."

"Yes. That's as good a description as any."

Oak Skin stared speculatively at the wagon, then called to the leader and pointed back at the travois. The leader said something in reply.

"You tell *Ma'hta'sooma Notakhe* to call off his spirits and come down. Tell him to call back his spirits. Then you doctor our warrior, yes?"

"Yes," Doc agreed. He cupped hands to his mouth and called, "Butler? Tell the men to stand down. The Cheyenne don't want to fight them. It's all right here."

Butler stared uncertainly. "Are you sure? Philip, the stories we've heard from everyone we've passed on the trail are that Indians are at war after that Sand Creek massacre in Colorado."

"You know Sand Creek?" Oak Skin asked, his expression harder if anything.

"We heard it was bad," Doc said.

There didn't seem to be any give in the man's hard eyes.

"If it makes any difference, we, too, fought the Yankee cavalry."

"One white man is pretty much like another." Oak Skin slipped off his horse, poking Doc in the chest. "Now, *heseeotse ve'ho'e,* heal our warrior." He pointed to the travois being brought forward.

Doc walked ahead of Oak Skin. A wounded man lay in the webbing between the travois poles, his chest tightly bound. Even through the blood-soaked bandages, Doc could see that it was probably a bullet wound.

"How long?" he asked.

"Two days."

"Butler. Get down here. I need your help."

Oak Skin said softly, "Warrior dies. You die."

"Bring him," Doc said as he turned and started for the wagon. "I have a surgical kit in the wagon. Tell them not to shoot me."

Oak Skin issued some kind of directive in Cheyenne.

Butler was slowly descending the slope, the canvas sack full of dried chips he'd been collecting, dragging along behind.

"Doesn't matter, Sergeant," Butler was saying. "We have a white flag. Just like when I went out between the lines at Prairie Grove. Looks like we're tending the wounded."

Just as Butler drew even with the still-mounted lead warrior, he turned, pointing, and crying, "Corporal Pettigrew! Reholster your pistol. We have a flag of truce."

The Cheyenne warrior, expression anxious, backed up his horse, as if frantic to put distance between himself and Butler. Doc noticed that the warrior did everything he could to keep from looking at Butler, but seemed to keep him at the edge of his vision.

Meanwhile Butler turned to his right, saying, "Sergeant Kershaw, you will maintain order among the men." He listened, nodding, "Of course, Sergeant."

Oak Skin called something, the other warriors backing out of Butler's way, expressions wary, avoiding his eyes and keeping their distance. Some were fingering the medicine bundles hanging from their throats and softly singing.

"What do you need, Philip?" Butler asked as he

511

dropped his bag of chips.

"That medical case you stole from Fort Scott. The one that almost wore a hole in my back."

"Coming." Butler climbed up on the bed, hesitating long enough to order, "Sergeant Kershaw, you will maintain the watch."

As Butler dragged the surgical case out, he added, "But you are not to attack unless you observe hostile intentions."

Oak Skin kept speaking in Cheyenne, apparently translating what Butler was saying. The rest of the warriors kept shifting, flinching each time the breeze stirred the grass or a bird flew past.

Butler smiled at the Cheyenne warrior, who immediately averted his eyes. Then Butler told him in a commanding voice, "You and your warriors are outnumbered, surrounded, and tactically disadvantaged. Do not make me order an attack."

Doc damned well knew he and Butler were about to die. He bent over the delirious warrior and began unwinding the bandage. "Butler? I need water to soak this free."

"Do you need to move him?" Butler asked.

"Never operated on a travois before. First time for everything."

He forgot the angry and ominous-looking warriors as he removed the bandage and studied the young warrior's wound. The bullet had entered just below the ribs on the right side. With a damp cloth Doc sponged the dried blood away. Entrance wounds were always hard to judge, but it looked like a smaller caliber.

He sniffed, encouraged by the lack of sour smell that would have indicated a punctured gut. Nor was the abdomen hard and swollen as was normal after either a punctured bowel or excessive internal bleeding.

Doc raised his eyes to where Oak Skin had dismounted and now stood on the opposite side of the travois, his rifle in his hands. "Has he made water? Pissed? Was it black? Bloody?"

"His water is good."

"Do you have a name?" Doc asked as he dripped ether onto a rag. He carefully shifted, holding the rag below the man's nose. Taking up the wounded warrior's wrist he could feel the pulse.

"Vehoc." Oak Skin replied in Cheyenne, then he added, "It means Little White Man. My father called me Billy Hawkins. I do not like that name."

"Vehoc," Doc repeated as he sponged away new blood, noting it contained small bits of necrotic liver. "Who is the man I'm working on?"

"In white tongue, he is Red Legs." Vehoc pointed to the leader, now watching from his horse. "He is *Honi'a'haka,* the Little Wolf. His wife and children were at Sand Creek. Only when the last white man is dead will he rest."

Doc shot Little Wolf a quick glance. "Does he know about your father? I mean about him being white and all?"

Vehoc smiled grimly. "I am *Tsi'tsi'ta,* Cheyenne." He pointed to puckered scars on his chest. "I have given my soul to my people."

Doc turned away to cough, then picked up his scalpel, saying, "I'm going to open the wound a little so that I can remove the clotted blood and dead tissue. I have to do this carefully, so please have someone hold the horse. The animal must not move while I am inside, do you understand?"

Vehoc barked orders. Another of the warriors dismounted, taking up the horse's lead rope and speaking soothingly to it. He looked in every direction except toward Butler, who was talking to Private Vail about the way the Cheyenne were dressed.

Doc began to carefully clean the clotted and dead tissue from below the diaphragm. With the slant of the sun, he wished for better light.

"Your brother is a powerful man. Our word for him is *hohnokha,*" Vehoc said cautiously. "You must be honored to travel with him."

"Sometimes it's scary."

Vehoc grunted in what Doc took to be Cheyenne understanding. "Then you are a very wise man. I would not have the courage, even if he were my brother." He paused. "These spirits he sees, are they good or bad?"

"A little of both, I suspect."

"Are they in his head . . . how do you say, because they want to be?"

Doc sighed. "Maybe you'd better ask him."

Vehoc pursed his lips, hesitated, and said, "Do you think I'm a fool? What if he takes control of my spirit, as well? Does he say what these spirits of the dead want?"

"He is taking them home," Doc replied. "And heaven help me, half the time I even think I see them myself these days."

"A'hee! He carries the souls of the dead to the white man's land of the dead? Their *Seana?*"

At mention of the word, the Cheyenne muttered uneasily among themselves.

Vehoc said something to Little Wolf, who whispered under his breath. The other riders backed their horses away, making more room between them and the wagon where Butler perched. The fingering of medicine bundles was more fervent, their efforts to avoid Butler's atten-

514

tion even more apparent.

"When I was little," Vehoc said, "a black robe came to our camp to talk about Jesus. We had an old *hohnokha* who called the rains and thunder. The black robe raised his book, called our *hohnokha* a devil, and shouted at him. That night lightning struck the black robe's camp and killed him dead. Only fools laugh at *Ma'heono.*"

"What's that?"

"The four sacred Powers. The spirit beings." He gestured in a wide loop that didn't include Butler. "They are all around. All that lives. Buffalo, grass, birds, the deer and antelope. The mice and grasshoppers. The flowing of the river. You white men know so little, yet here you are, filling our land."

Doc used his probe, located the bullet where it had stopped between the liver and diaphragm. With his straight forceps he reached into the wound and grasped the bullet, easing it out.

"Looks like a .36 caliber. From the scraped rifling, it was a revolver shot." He extended the bullet and dropped it into Oak Skin's hand. "You can give it to Red Legs as a remembrance."

Doc sponged up some of the blood, tied off a bleeder, and carefully began to suture the wound closed. "Make Red Legs drink all the water he can hold. Tell that to Little Wolf there. I don't want Red Legs walking or riding, so when he has to piss, tell him to just let it go. Do you understand?"

Little Wolf asked something. Vehoc translated, "Is he going to live?"

Doc tied his last knot, fixing his gaze on Oak Skin's. "I think so. The only thing I can't help is if the wound infects. Indian medicine or white,

515

that's up to the wounded man to beat. He has damage to his liver, but it will heal if you don't let him move for a moon or so. But if he gets bumped hard, or falls, it could break the wound open, and he'll bleed to death. Do you understand?"

Vehoc made a sign with his hands, saying, "Reckon so."

Doc smiled thinly, aware that the evening light was fading. "Can you find him a Cheyenne medicine man? A healer? Someone who can bathe him in smoke, feed him herbs. Maybe hold a sweat?"

"Maybe so."

"It would help his healing." Doc tapped the side of his head. "Up here. In the soul. You need to do this as quickly as you can."

Vehoc stood, turned to Little Wolf, and spoke hurriedly.

"Haahe," Little Wolf said. Then he asked something else as he made a fist-knocking hand sign that meant to kill.

Fear gripped Doc's spine with icy hands.

Vehoc made a sign that Doc thought meant no, and added something else. Then he made a slight gesture of the head toward Butler, as if indicating him without indicating him, and said something about the *hohnohka.*

Vehoc turned to Doc, a grim smile on his lips. "We are *Hotame'taneo.* Dog Soldiers. Unlike whites we are men of honor who will not harm a *hohnohka.* Tell your holy man that we offer prayers in honor of his journey to carry his dead to the white man's *Seana.* Because you serve him, we give him your life."

With that he backed carefully away, turned, and leaped onto his horse. The warrior holding the lead rope handed it to Little Wolf. The leader glared his hatred at Doc, but studiously ignored Butler as he led the travois forward.

Within minutes the last of them disappeared into the growing gloom of evening.

Doc sank onto his surgeon's chest, his heart hammering like a sledge on an anvil.

"At ease, gentlemen," Butler called to his men. "Surrounded and outnumbered as they were, they wouldn't have dared to try anything. Not against Company A. We had them boxed the entire time."

65

October 5, 1865

Sarah stood in the cold wind, arms crossed, and stared westward at the road. Little more than a rut in the overgrazed grass, it vanished into the growing darkness. Only a hint of light lay behind the low clouds to mark where the sun had set on the southwestern horizon.

She tried to ignore the sound of shovels grating in the hard ground, the rasping curses of the soldiers, or to think of the remains of the two men who would soon be laid under the High Plains sod.

Just at dusk their convoy of two stages and a detachment of cavalry had pulled into Willow Spring station to find the horses missing, and not a soul in sight. The two herders — the ones the soldiers were now burying — had been spread-eagled on the ground in front of the dugout. Dugout? Little more than a hole in the ground actually. Both men had been naked, each with his severed penis and testicles protruding from his bloody, open mouth. The tongues — cut out to make room for the genitals — had been stuffed into slits cut into their crotches, as though obscene vaginas were giving birth. The men's scalped

518

skulls had been split to expose the brains. As a final indignity, the Indians had piled poles ripped from the corral over their stomachs and set them on fire.

This is a damned and terrible country. Why the hell did we ever come here?

Worse. Seeing those mutilated and tortured men opened a door she'd wanted forever closed. It was as if she could hear the hinges creaking as she peered through a slit and saw Dewley's body lying there on that narrow ledge. She was rising, the knife in her hand dripping crimson, Dewley's severed genitals limp, warm, and squishy in her bloody hand.

God, Sarah, don't.

Even the bitter wind was savage as it gusted at her, bringing smells of grass, old manure, and the threat of frost.

The journey west had proven a great deal more arduous than Sarah had anticipated. The youthful enthusiasm with which she and Bret had left Atchison, Kansas, had rapidly dwindled. First had come the rude realization that riding inside a Concord coach was akin to being the target of a sparring pugilist. Suspended only on thick leather straps, she'd been jostled, bounced, banged, and slammed around the inside. On occasion the jolt was severe enough to send her airborne to land in her fellow travelers' laps if she were lucky, or to smack into the window frames were she not.

She hadn't been this battered and sore since she'd escaped from Dewley's camp.

The trip had rapidly devolved into a contest of physical endurance. The food had been reasonable — if not outstanding — in the home stations on the eastern leg. But after Junction City, it had declined to rancid bacon boiled in a pot of beans with the occasional venison or buffalo steak.

Sarah had marked their progress by the station names: Ellsworth, Buffalo Creek, Fossil Creek, Downer, Henshaw's Springs, and finally Camp Pond Creek. Here their Concord coach had been held up for a day to await the coach traveling a day behind them. For the two days prior, the eastbound coaches had failed to arrive. A sure sign of trouble.

Their driver, a bandy-legged man named Mapleton, had stared warily about, then scratched his bearded chin. "Won't bother me a bit to hole up here until Rep Barker's coach ketches up. And having them twenty so' jers along? That gives us nigh on forty guns. Jest hope y'all can shoot."

The arrival at Willow Spring had proven everyone's worst fears.

"What do you think?" Bret asked, stepping up beside her to stare out at the darkening grasslands.

"Wondering if we were fools, Bret." She rubbed her hands on the back of her arms. "You've heard the same stories I have from the eastbound coaches. And if you have any doubts just step over yonder and look what's left of those two boys they're burying."

"All of life's a gamble," he told her softly. "But if you're that scared, we can turn back."

She took a deep breath, fought a shiver from the chill. "I can shoot straighter than most men. Like Mapleton says, we've got forty guns." She chuckled nervously. "Funny what life comes down to sometimes, isn't it?"

She could feel the danger out there in the dark, smell it on the biting west wind. And what if the damned Sioux did manage to surround the coach, disable it? There'd be one hell of a fight. She'd save her last shot for herself. What did she have to live for anyway?

The band of gold on her ring finger still felt odd. Back in Atchison she had asked, "What are people going to think, Bret? A man and a woman traveling together? I say we act like we're married."

He had studied her through those liquid brown eyes. "It would make things easier. I have a ring, something I won someplace. No idea if it will fit."

She fingered the gold band as she considered the darkening Kansas night. All of her childhood dreams of marriage to a prominent gentleman and a grand house? Her fine dresses? The servants? The elegant parties she had intended to host? Well, here she was in the middle of dark and bloody Kansas, faking marriage to a rootless gambler.

God had to be laughing until His guts ached.

The wind flipped her hair back and pressed her skirt against her long legs. "I'd swear, Bret, I can almost feel them out there. I grew up with Indians. Cherokee, Choctaw, and some Chickasaw. But, seeing those men . . ."

Images flashed behind her eyes, cold fear clutching at her. As if in an instant she was back on the cliff, bending down as Dewley screamed.

She shivered, only to be reassured when Bret pulled her against him. "It was . . . I was . . ." She swallowed hard. "That's what Billy did. What I did when I cut Dewley apart. I didn't burn them alive. But I was back. Seeing it all again." She looked at him, adding, "I'm no damn different than a savage Indian, Bret."

"I've been wondering if this was the right decision. It sounded so easy. Eight days and we'd be in Denver. Able to start over. I didn't know we'd be walking right into a war."

"This is worse than Yankees and Rebels. The Sioux and Cheyenne want us dead, and we want them dead. Ain't gonna be no surrender. Won't be like the Cherokee, dispossessed by that lying cheat Andrew Jackson. This is blood and pain and death to the last."

"Cooler heads may well prevail in the end. Not all —"

"You and your Yankee Boston mind don't understand, Bret." She paused, guts gone hollow. "But I do. I lived it."

Another gust of wind rocked her; Bret stood so as to shield her with the flap of his coat. "We'll be all right now, Mrs. Anderson."

"I just have a premonition, Bret. That's all."

"Claiming future sight now, Mrs. Anderson?"

She glanced up at him, imagining more than seeing his smile in the darkness. "You're enjoying that, aren't you?"

He paused for a moment. "I know it's a sham, Sarah. But if you could ever feel comfortable with me, trust me enough, I would make it real."

She stepped away from him, turning to study him in the darkness. "Bret, I'm not sure I could ever . . ."

"I don't need your body, my dear. Men and women have made marriages without carnal relations. They have loved each other dearly for the enjoyment they took in simply sharing each other's company."

For a moment she couldn't breathe, then forced herself to fill her lungs. The mere act of doing so seemed to break the spell. "Bret, you need to find some fine and decent woman, one who can fulfill a man's needs. Give you children, build a home. You don't want a ruin like me."

He laughed softly, shivering as the cold wind ate into him. "A decent woman? We're both ruins in our own ways. I'm a disgraced gambler, a deserter, and murderer. Just where, my dear, do you see some decent and upright young virgin swooning into my arms? Let alone setting up hearth and home, and later explaining to the cherubic fruit of my loins, 'Oh, be good, little ones! Papa is due any moment with his take from the saloons!' "

"Bret, you're impossible."

"No, my love. We both are."

"What of your . . . needs?" She cocked her head, staring up at him. "I spent my days watching Paw slip away, always on the prowl. Since he shared a bed with Maw, it wasn't as if he had no outlet. For you, on the other hand, it would be a necessity."

"You sound sharp when you say it."

"I shouldn't." She shrugged. "What a hypocritical wretch I am. I'm spoiled goods. But were we married, I wouldn't want you between some stranger's legs. What's the old story about the dog in the manger?"

He lifted her chin with a finger, staring down at her in the darkness. "Do you trust me?"

"Up to a point. Sometimes you don't have the good sense a —"

He bent down and kissed her. His lips weren't on hers for more than two seconds, conforming, loving, and then he straightened.

"By God," he whispered as he walked back toward the coach. "I've wanted to do that for months."

She stood, fingering her lips, unsure if she were staggered by the wind, or the aftereffects.

66

December 1, 1865

Charlie Deveroux stood resplendent in his black broadcloth suit. Yellow lamplight filled his parlor, casting its soft light on his guests — and upon his resplendent Martha where she stood in her white muslin wedding dress. Occupying the place of honor beside the fireplace, she held a crystal glass of champagne in her delicate and white-gloved hand. Outside the window the night was black, the pattering of rain barely audible over the happy conversation filling the parlor.

The neck of the champagne bottle clinked as Hank Abrams poured another measure of fizzing champagne into Charlie's glass.

Phil Seymore, the Austin mayor's right-hand man, leaned close, a satisfied smile on his lips. "Mr. Deveroux, I'm afraid I shall have to make my apologies and take my leave. It was a most becoming wedding. And, while the mayor was unable to attend, again, I assure you that he sends you and Mrs. Deveroux his fondest regards and best wishes for your happiness."

Charlie inclined his head graciously. "I just hope that I have been of service, sir."

Seymore's smile was a fleeting thing. "Texas will

change under Reconstruction. Hamilton and Throckmorton are going to ease it back into the Union. But until then it falls upon those among us with insight to quell the violence and restore the peace. You have made the right choice. The information you've provided has allowed us to run down most of the worst of the lot."

"What about Billy Hancock?"

With a tilt of the head, Seymore indicated that Charlie should follow him out into the foyer. There he turned, sipped his champagne, and said, "You were right. His scout, Danny Goodman, showed up at that whorehouse outside San Marco two nights ago. Everywhere Billy Hancock goes, he sends Goodman in first. I thought I'd hear today that they'd either captured or killed him."

"That would have been the perfect wedding present." Charlie thoughtfully smoothed his mustache. "I want that five-thousand-dollar reward for fingering Captain Loomis's killer."

Seymore watched him through narrowed eyes. "How'd you know he'd be headed for Magdelena's?"

"He's developed a thing for Mexican whores." Charlie grinned. "Besides, I was supposed to meet him there. He expected me to pay him two hundred dollars for killing Antonio Guzman over in Bandera."

"Why?"

"Why what, sir?"

"What do you hope to gain from betraying all of your old comrades in arms?" Seymore crossed his arms, gaze intent.

"Look around, friend. I have a house, a wife, and new associates." He fought a smile. "There is a new political structure in Texas. The Yankees are

526

here to stay. You all are going to need a man like me. One who can attend to the less savory parts of running a government."

"And Billy Hancock?"

"Phil, I got to tell you, Billy Hancock scares the shit out of me. Men kill for lots of reasons: passion, lust, greed, revenge. Billy? He lives for the hunt. Killing fills his heart with a tingling fever. The way he tells it, the devil comes alive inside him." He paused. "That's why I told you to send ten men to ambush him."

"I sent five."

Charlie stiffened, his heart skipping. "Jesus jumping Jehoshaphat! You may have killed us all."

"Dear Lord, Charlie. He's just a single malicious young man. The five I sent are good. Ex-Rangers. All salt, sand, and tanned leather. They've taken down Comanche raiders, Mexican bandits, and some of the nastiest men this state's ever seen. If they can't take one young —"

"Billy says he's possessed by the devil himself."

"If he's not already tied crosswise over a horse with bullet holes through his heart and head, the devil better start looking for someone else to possess, because Billy Hancock's going to be swinging from the gallows within the week."

"How soon are you going to know if your men got him?"

"Might be someone waiting at the governor's office now." He glanced toward the front door. "Assuming the storm hasn't washed out the bridges between here and San Marco."

"You send me word, Phil. I don't care if it's the middle of the night."

Phil gave him an incredulous look as lightning flashed outside the window and, a second later, the bang shook the house. "Tonight? It's your wedding night, man. I'll send someone in the morning, late. You have other things to enjoy."

Clapping Charlie on the shoulder, Phil Seymore retrieved his coat and hat from the rack in the hall. Donning them, he graced Charlie with a farewell grin, then opened the door and stepped out into the storm.

"You better be goddamned right about this, Phil."

Charlie hesitated in the parlor doorway. Martha gave him a beaming smile where she stood talking to Clarissa Foxland, wife of a prominent Austin attorney. The other guests were enjoying the drink and conversation.

Another smashing of thunder startled the room, and left people laughing self-consciously.

Martha's first husband had been a blockade runner — a man intimately familiar with the coves and bars in the Laguna Madre and along the Texas Gulf Coast. She had been widowed two years ago when her husband had finally run afoul of a Federal steam packet and gone down with his ship.

After a whirlwind courtship, Charlie provided her with companionship and the promise of a man in her life. One who was politically ambitious and willing to work with the powers rising in Texas. He in turn derived a measure of respectability from her name and standing, not to mention her not inconsiderable wealth. And one thing Phil was indeed correct about, the new Mrs. Martha Deveroux was still a woman in her physical prime. Charlie had explored the delights of her full body several times since their engagement. Martha, after two years of enforced celibacy, was a woman of considerable appetite. And from the looks she kept casting his way, she was just waiting for the last guest to leave before sating her hunger.

Again thunder shook the house, and the frame rattled from a particularly vicious gust.

Five hardened Texas Rangers. He's either dead or captive. And even if they missed him, he couldn't know I turned him in.

Still, it wouldn't hurt to lock the back door and check the windows.

He gave Martha a reassuring wink and walked down the hall. The kitchen was dimly illuminated by a single lamp. A big pot stood steaming on the stove should anyone want coffee or tea, and a tray of pastries rested on the counter. No less than five were missing, and Charlie wondered which of the guests had sneaked back to pilfer them when he wasn't looking.

The dining room was dark, and in the dim light, the rear door behind the stairway where deliveries were made was firmly closed. Charlie reached down, flipping the lock, and glanced out at the small backyard and alley. At that moment a white flash of lightning cast the almond tree in the backyard in a stark light, its shadow falling across the toolshed and carriage house out back.

Nothing and no one there.

He reached down and checked the door, the knob feeling cold and wet.

As he turned, lightning flashed again, and Charlie had the briefest glimpse. A second flash confirmed it. The floor was wet.

He turned, running his thumb along the door as rain beat against it.

"Nope," a soft voice called from the dark shadows under the stairs. "Door don't leak.

Reckon that come off'n my slicker, Charlie."

He froze, breath choked in his lungs. It took him several tries to rasp out, "Billy? That you?"

A shadow moved under the stairs, a form emerging from the darkness. "Looks like a right fine wedding, Charlie. And this, why, it's a daisy of a place. Beats hell outta the bush where we first met. Now, how you reckon you come to all this good fortune?"

"Don't you go jumping to any conclusions." Charlie's heart had started to beat again. "Now, listen. I got another job for you. Best one yet. You know Anabelle's? You go there. I'll see you tomorrow at around noon. But for the moment, I gotta get back to my —"

"Reckon your friend Phil . . . wasn't that his name? Reckon he's wrong about them five he sent to San Marco."

"I don't know what you mean."

"Charlie, I'll be dad-swamped if'n those boys was tough old ex-Rangers. Hell, Danny hisself kilt two." Billy paused, head tilting, and Charlie heard the patter of water draining from the brim of Billy's hat. " 'Course, that last ol' boy. He might turn out tough in the end. And tough he'll be if he lives after being shot in the guts like he was."

"Billy, I . . ."

Lightning flashed through the rain-streaked window, illuminating Billy's pale face, sparkling with water drops that beaded on his cheeks and nose. The eyes were a weird pale blue.

Just in that white flash, Charlie saw the wet Remington where it stuck out of Billy's slicker.

"Billy, don't do this. There's money to be made. I just need time to . . ."

Between the lightning's white glare and the

yellow-red muzzle flash the back room was almost day-bright. The pistol's bang barely preceded the deafening crack of thunder.

The feeling was as if someone had punched Charlie hard in the solar plexus. He bent over, struggling for breath. Backed into the wall. Breath still wouldn't come.

"Aren't you one cool scoundrel, Charlie? Figgered to collect the reward fer that Yankee captain? Why, you made money all the way around on that deal. Took your share of the payoff, then figured to snag the reward, too."

"They know you," Charlie finally managed to gasp. "They'll get you now."

"Reckon not," Billy whispered as Charlie slid down the wainscoting. Billy leaned down, water dripping.

Charlie blinked in the dim light, hearing loud laughter from the parlor. God, wouldn't someone come? Hadn't they heard the shot?

Lightning flashed through the back-door window again. Gleamed off the long Bowie held low in Billy's hand.

The sting drove into Charlie's belly, then rose, fiery hot to his mule-kicked gut. A low squeal passed his lips, driven by his sudden fear. Then came the warm rush of urine between his legs. After wiping the blade on Charlie's pants, Billy stood.

Charlie heard the lock click, felt the door open, and close. For a long moment he sprawled there, warm fluids and guts spilling over his hands.

And then the world faded into a soft gray and vanished.

67

December 15, 1865

The sign proclaimed the place to be the REBELL SALUNE; the proprietor's spelling turned out to be every bit as atrocious as the vile alcohol he sold by the tin cup. Word was that it was little better than Indian whiskey: ten gallons of pure grain alcohol to which five twists of tobacco, a dram of gunpowder, two cups of molasses, and five rattlesnake heads had been added.

The establishment, were it to be called such, consisted of a weather-grayed canvas extended out, ramada fashion, from a rocked-up cavern overhang just below the Llano River bluffs, and about a half mile upstream from the town of the same name.

The bar — behind which One-Legged Shiloh Pete stood to dispense his heavenly spirits — was no more elaborate than a wagon tailgate laid atop two fifty-gallon barrels. Propped up on a stone shelf behind was the notorious ten-gallon keg of whiskey, cups of which were dispensed from the tap at its bottom.

Billy Hancock sat at one of the two rickety tables, his foot up on one of the three mismatched chairs that furnished seating for any weary customers who happened to pass by. Billy's butt was in the second chair, and Danny Goodman slouched in the third. Atop the battered table between them a deck of cards had been abandoned for lack of interest.

A meadowlark trilled out in the winter-bare mesquite along the river.

"You hear that?" Danny asked. "Wrong time of year for that ol' bird."

"Maybe it's the weather. Must be nigh on sixty degrees." Billy rocked the tin cup back and forth on its bottom. "If I know shit about anything, tonight the wind's gonna pick up, and by morning a blue norther's gonna be blowing down on us."

"Could be." Danny leaned forward, lips pursed.

"Spit it out. You're about to bust with whatever's been eating you since Austin."

Danny studied him thoughtfully and began. "Right now Texas is wide open. Lots of folks hate other folks over things done during the war. I'm not arguing that. But here's the thing: Charlie sold us out."

"You think I don't remember that?" Billy stared at his dusty boot where it was propped on the chair. "I never had such a bitter taste in my mouth as that. I can't say as I never felt better killing a man, but slipping a blade into old Charlie was right up there."

For whatever reason, the Sarah demon hadn't been haunting his dreams since. What was it about spilling a man's guts that would make a demon nightmare keep her distance?

"And we're still paying for it," Danny growled. "How we gonna do business?" He ticked off on

533

his fingers. "To start with, now they got a name for you and know what you look like. Next, they's a price on yer head. Five thousand dollars. In this country, that's all the money in the world. Third, we can't trust nobody. We's just lucky that that little whore down to Magdelena's liked you. If'n you hadn't overpaid her by ten dollars, she might not have gone outta her way to warn us. We'd a been dead men."

"Feller gets a right powerful kick out of ambushing the ambushers, don't he?" Billy grinned at the memory.

Danny continued to tick off on his fingers. "Fourth is that Charlie was the front man. He was the one that found the clients and set up the work. Did the business, if you will. He had the connections. We're just two bush soldiers out in the brasada."

"Then we have to make the connections ourselves."

"That's the part where we get killed." Danny leaned forward, expression earnest.

"How's that?"

"Me? If'n I was one of Throckmorton's boys? I'd place me an ad in the paper. Maybe just whisper it around in the saloons. 'Need Billy Hancock to do some killing. No questions asked. Five hundred dollars.' And then what? We just ride up to the Travis County courthouse a-singing out, 'We're your men! Whar's the Dick as needs to be shot?' "

"You're saying they'd bait us in."

"Damn right." Danny nodded soberly. "They want you for that Yankee captain. Want you enough they found Charlie and brought him in to heel on their leash. Then we kilt the five men they

534

sent to take us. Then you spilt Charlie's guts all over the hallway in his own house, in Austin, on his wedding day, with the mayor's right-hand man as good as in attendance. You think they ain't got a burn up their assholes over that?"

Billy grinned. "Right pert bit of work if'n you ask me."

"Maybe too good." Danny leaned back and sipped his whiskey. As he swallowed he made a face and screwed his eyes closed. "God in heaven, that's awful."

"Puts a fire in a man's gut, all right." Billy shook his head. "But that's about all, I reckon." He paused. "So what are you thinking, Danny? Go back to Arkansas?"

Danny reached into his coat pocket and pulled out a scrap of newspaper. "Read that."

"I ain't that good at reading." Nevertheless he picked it up, pronouncing the words as he made them out. "New ditch will free millions in gold at Last Chance Gulch, Montana." He licked his lips, frowning at the names. "Chessman and Cowan should be able to increase profits tenfold from rich aggregate. According to Mr. Chessman, over one million dollars should pour from the earth."

He looked up, puzzled. "What's Montana have to do with anything? How does a ditch make gold? What's aggregate? Who's Chessman?"

Danny thumped the table. "That don't matter. What does is mining. That's the business we need."

The meadowlark trilled in the brush again.

Billy gestured around, as if to include most of Texas. "And where is all this mining at?"

"New Mexico, Colorado, Nevada, Montana. Places where you ain't twisted every politician's pecker. Whoa, now." He held up a hand. "Next yer gonna tell me you don't know shit about no mining. My answer is that you don't need to. You're just my assistant. The man I send out to do mine scouting. Locate claims and all. Anyone asks why you ain't around I say you're headed to the Sangre de Cristo Mountains to look at a claim. Meantime you ride to Montana to shoot a man in Bozeman."

"What are you planning on doing? Hanging out a shingle with big block letters saying KILLER FOR HIRE?"

"That's the tricky part where I come in."

"Go ahead, Danny. You got my interest like a bee on a flower."

"I been learning a lot doing these scouting jobs. There's always trouble brewing somewhere. Sometimes it's in the papers, but other times it's just gossiped about in the bars and brothels. John is feuding with Dick. It's gonna come to blood. And that's when I step in and drop a word in the right ear. I offer to solve the problem, fast, simple, and without complications."

The meadowlark broke out in melodious song again.

"What is wrong with that bird?" Billy wondered.

"Maybe it's a sign. Just what we need. A new name. From here on out you're the Meadowlark. And we advertise that. But Billy, once we do, you cain't never tell no one. Not no whore you're poking your johnson into, nor no loudmouth you're drinking whiskey with. Cain't never be no tie a'twixt the two."

Billy's sober appraisal had Danny to the point of squirming. "That means I pretty much gotta trust you with my life. Like Charlie, you could

536

make a lot of money turning me in."

Danny swallowed hard, a glitter of fear behind his eyes. He jerked a nod, almost too fast. "Well, Billy, here's the thing: when I was a kid, I was in Fayetteville one day when a fella comes through with this snake in a glass box. Cost a nickel to see the snake. It was a pretty thing. Called it a cobra. In return for the nickel the man would reach in the box with a stick and make it rear up and spread its neck wide. Heard he got down to Van Buren and the snake bit him and killed him."

"I ain't following you, Danny Goodman."

"Billy, you're my snake. You'll make me a passel of money, but I know you'll kill me quicker than spit if I make the smallest mistake."

68

December 24, 1865

Since their arrival in Colorado life had been hectic. Bret had checked them into the Broadwell House on Sixteenth and Larimer. He had insisted Sarah take the bed, while he unrolled his bedroll on the floor. It was, as he reminded her, a vast improvement over the cold ground. And while Sarah amused herself during the day, Bret's nights were spent in pursuit of the tables.

Everything changed on Christmas Eve when Bret arrived back at the room early, sometime just after nine. A bottle of fine champagne dangled in one hand, and a folded piece of paper was clutched in the other. Sarah had been reading, the lamp turned low to save fuel. With a total of three books in her possession, she was on her third reading of Homer's *Odyssey.*

"Victory, my love," he said seriously. "Prepare to pack. We're off to Central City."

"Bret?" she asked, sitting up in bed, her hair in tangles. As she pulled it back out of her eyes, he turned up the lamp, cranking the wick. He kicked his bedding out of the way where she'd unrolled it on the floor, ready for his late-night return.

He plopped himself down beside her on the hard

frame and worked the champagne cork loose with a pop. He emptied her tin cup of water into the washstand, and poured her cup full.

"We own a gold claim," he told her proudly, handing her the deed. "It's up just above Central City, almost to Nevadaville, and consists of a discovery shaft, a cabin, a creek, and a tailings pile. But more to the point, it's a ten-minute walk from some of the richest poker tables in the territory."

He clinked the neck of the champagne bottle to her cup and they both took a drink.

She studied him over the rim, the champagne's fizzy sweetness tickling her tongue. "Central City? Up in the mountains? I have to tell you, I'm already about to go mad with boredom. Bret, I've got to have something to do. Are you sure that a snowed-in cabin up in —"

"You now have a house all your own, my dear." His eyes were dark and twinkling. "Though I've no idea what sort of shape it might be in. The man who just bet three sixes against my full house lamented not only its passing, but the six hundred and forty dollars he tried to recoup by wagering the value of the claim."

"My own house?" She felt herself warm on the inside. "Don't you mean *your* own house?"

His brow furrowed. "Odd, isn't it, but I've come to think of my life as before Sarah, and after Sarah." He paused, as if searching for words. "I've been giving our future a lot of thought. Central City should only be a stepping stone. I'll play conservatively, small pots, and each night I'll bring you a percentage. You're to be the banker. I want you to sock it away. When we reach twenty thousand, I say we leave. Pull stakes, and take a stage to San Francisco. Buy a nice house. Maybe I'll read the law, or invest in property. Something more stable and profitable. I have the skills and education."

She felt her heart skip. "Are you sure?"

"I would like to see you in a nice house, Sarah. One built of brick, with a proper parlor where we could spend our evenings sipping sherry, talking by the fire, and I could just watch you smile."

Dear God, he was serious, his expression taking on that solemn look.

"Bret, I . . ." She averted her eyes, watching the slowly flickering flame in the lamp. Her blood seemed to quicken, and she could feel the rapid beat of her heart. "Honestly, Bret, you leave me speechless sometimes."

She surrendered her hand when he took it and lifted it to his lips. "You are my reason for being, Sarah. I love you with all my heart, and I will do anything I have to just for the joy of sharing your company."

She drank down the champagne, her insides seeming to flutter. Over and over, she kept thinking, *I'm not worth it.*

She blinked, stared into his eyes, alternately frightened and excited. "Bret, I've . . . Oh God, I'm the luckiest woman on earth."

At that his lips broke into a beaming smile. "We'll do it, then! Twenty grand. And then we'll go to San Francisco." He poured her tin full again, looking bedazzled by his own machinations.

Dear God, do I want to do this? Can I?

The demons flickered, leering, whispering, making her soul shrivel. She forced the memory of groping hands away, stilled the violent ghosts. Sought to ignore the stench of sour breath, the cooing words accompanying her violation.

She slipped her legs past him, and stood. Setting her cup to the side, she pulled him to his feet and looked squarely into his eyes. All she saw was dancing anticipation of the future and a sense of shared excitement.

The pounding inside left her fingers trembling as she undid his coat, pulled his cravat loose.

"Sarah?" he asked softly, as though suddenly unmanned.

"Hush, Bret. I need to do this. I *have* to do this."

"By this, do you mean . . . I don't want you to think I . . ."

She placed her lips against his, letting them linger, slowly teaching herself how to kiss a man. Feeling her way.

As she slipped his shirt from his shoulders, she felt him shiver with anticipation. Backing up, she locked her eyes with his, willing herself to live in the moment. This moment. One where Dewley and McConahough's farm didn't exist.

His hands cupped her shoulders as she undid his trouser buttons. Next she tackled his long underwear, sliding it off his shoulders and letting it fall down the length of his muscular body. She traced her finger along the slick pink of his bullet scar.

She sounded uncommonly calm when she said, "You'll have to recline so that I can get these boots off."

As though a man in a dream, he sank to the bed, and one by one she removed his boots and shucked off his clothes. She knew his body, the muscles, the scar, the thick dark hair on his chest. She had managed to clean him when he was

541

fevered and delirious. But he'd been helpless, unaware.

The sight of his erection should have left her shuddering, but this was Bret. His arousal was different — from another existence than Dewley's and that of his demonic minions.

This is Bret, she reminded herself as she unbuttoned her nightshirt, shrugged, and let it slip down. Every muscle in her body went tense, electric, her stomach aquiver. The cold air brought gooseflesh to her skin and tightened her nipples.

Naked.

Vulnerable.

For a moment she panicked, fingers of terror eating at her. Flashes of memory behind her eyes.

Bret whispered, "God Almighty, you are the most beautiful woman on earth."

And she came back to herself. To this night. To the reality in Bret's eyes, brimming as they were with worship and love.

She lowered herself to the bed beside him, heart beating furiously. Her throat dry. Fear pulsed, and her breath seemed to catch in her throat.

Do it, Sarah. There's only one way to vanquish the demons. Swallowing hard, she battled to keep from trembling as she reached down and grasped his hard penis, watching him tense.

If she could be on top this first time, hold Bret's eyes, it would be different. "I need to go slowly. Do this my way."

"Tonight is yours, Sarah. Anything you decide to give me is a gift."

And then, as if to finally murder the last of Dewley's memory, she took a breath, let herself drown in Bret's eyes, and lowered herself onto him.

69

"For the love of mud, Butler." Doc turned his head away and coughed, then dabbed at Butler's face. "How many times have I told you to stay out of the street?"

"Yankees took us by surprise."

Butler winced as Doc cleaned the cut on his cheek. Bruises were darkening on his jaw, and his ear was swollen. After prodding Butler's ribs, he suspected that while not broken, they were most likely bruised from the kicking he had endured while down.

Doc coughed again.

With the cold weather, it was back, and getting worse. He shook his head, breath puffing in the chill only to vanish as it encountered the warmer air around their little tin heat stove. Doc blinked wearily as he huddled in his coat. On the snowy street beyond — if the path through the garbage could be called that — someone drove a wagon across the frozen, snow-covered ruts. The thing banged and rattled, trace chains clinking.

"Butler, you and the men can't just wander off." Doc reached down and opened the stove, tossing the blood-smeared bandage inside to incinerate on the glowing coals. "Half the men in Denver are drunk, and the other half are on the way to getting there. I can't take you with me everywhere I'm asked to go."

"Corporal Pettigrew wants to know why not? We've come all the way to Denver. We can help. Like when we doctored that Cheyenne warrior out on the trail. The men and I have watched you. You'd be surprised how much medicine we've learned."

Butler's blue eyes — the right one surely going to swell shut by morning — wavered in his head, as though confused by the voices he was hearing inside.

"When I'm asked to attend to someone sick, it distresses them to have you hovering in the background, carrying on conversations with the men about my patient's condition."

Doc slapped his knees, wishing they had more wood for the stove. "But if I leave you, you wander off like you did this morning. At best you end up the laughingstock of drunks, or worse, like just happened, some bummer takes a board and beats you."

"Private Peterson thinks you need to have cards made. Like the ones used to introduce gentlemen." Butler blinked, nodded, and said, "Yes, yes, I'll tell him." He looked at Doc. "You know Phil Vail, our scout? He has made the point that an ad in the *Rocky Mountain News* — and even an introduction to that man Byers — would have a most salubrious effect as you go about building a practice."

"Vail thinks this?" Doc asked dryly.

"It's like he says, people just don't know what a splendid physician you are."

Doc thrust his hands out to the dying stove, as if to absorb the last of its warmth. "Butler, I'm working out of a tent. I show up looking like a ragamuffin. People don't trust a physician who looks like a bummer. And finally there is you. In Saint Louis, you didn't seem as delusional. Yes, you cadged a little work in the brothels, but I want more here. I want to build a quality surgery. To take on challenging cases. Better our —"

"Taking that bullet out of Arne Stovensen's belly was pretty challenging. And he's still alive."

"Damn it, Butler, you can drag in all the penniless drunks and broken miners you want. Arne Stovensen? He had twenty-five cents to his name. That drunk you had me patch up last night? I set his broken arm, used up my last sling, and what? He's gone. With my sling. And not a penny to show for it. You and I *can't* survive giving away free medicine to the indigent and broke."

Butler blinked vacantly, his lips twitching.

"Then, this morning, I think there's a chance I can make a couple of dollars delivering a baby, and halfway through, I hear screams in the street, only to find you getting the lights beat out of you by two howling drunks! A physician's trade is dependent referrals and reputation. I'm known as 'that man with the crazy brother . . . the one who wears rags and has drunks for clients.' "

Doc dropped his head into his hands. Weary and desolate.

"Maybe in Golden City," Butler said softly. "Kershaw says that good things are being said about it. It might become the capital someday. And then there is Central City and Idaho Springs up Clear Creek."

"And what will be different there?" Doc asked,

his stomach gnawing at his ribs. They'd had less than a cup of oatmeal each that morning. What remained in the tin might make them each another cup for supper that night.

"Mines are dangerous places to work," Butler said solicitously. "Lots of injuries. I'm sure that physicians are always in short supply."

Doc endured a coughing fit, then whispered, "I had that one golden year in Memphis. You should have seen it, Butler. A real surgery, and a partner. I had a nice room. Fine clothes. What a difference it made knowing that I had a future. I felt young, bright, and alive."

"Phil Vail says that —"

"I *don't* give a damn!" Doc snapped. "Just shut up! I can't deal with your insanity now."

Futility. That was him. Cored out and empty.

Butler blinked, huddled defensively. His swelling lips moved soundlessly as he avoided Doc's eyes. His hands were twitching spasmodically, eyes darting this way and that, as if fixing on his imaginary men where they crowded around the cold and cramped tent.

The immensity of it overwhelmed. Came crashing down on Doc's shoulders. Fact was, he wasn't going to have his surgery. His life was going to be spent caring for his crazy brother. Keeping him from being the brunt of jokes in the streets, and subject to beatings by bullies and ruffians.

He had had his happiness. His one moment of respectability. During those brief days in Memphis, life had bloomed, each day a wondrous new possibility. He'd seen the totality of his fluorescence as a surgeon, teaching and being taught; that was medicine as he had only dreamed it could be. A mutual collaboration of like-minded colleagues, creating miracles with their scalpels and sutures.

Ann Marie had filled his heart with hope and promise. Every last ounce of his love and being. Hers. Without reserve. She would have been the cornerstone of his entire life, her smile and freckles, the children they would have produced, and the home they would have built.

"Sergeant, not now," Butler whispered, breaking Doc's reverie.

He should have been wept out. Empty. But he fought tears. Wondered how, in this cold, miserable, and disgusting excuse for a city, they could manage to replenish.

"I swear to God, Butler," Doc whispered, "you are a living Greek tragedy. Something straight out of one of those plays you used to read. Sophocles. That's who. We're brothers that the gods, for whatever peevish reason, have sworn to destroy. Probably for some thievery or seduction Paw committed. Something so offensive the gods had to wreak their vengeance on you and me."

"Philip, I just need to get the men home."

"They *were* home, you lunatic fool! Why didn't you dump your madness right there in the farmyard? Leave it to infest those shotgun-toting hicks? Why didn't you stay to befuddle them with your invisible men as payback for taking our home?"

He drove his fingers into the sides of his face, adding, "I didn't *ask* for this! I didn't *want* it. I wanted away! Away from Paw and the pain he caused. Away from the memories. I didn't want anything to do with family, and *now you're a damn millstone around my neck*!"

There, he'd said it. The thing he'd buried down deep inside his heart. And he'd uttered it with all

547

the vitriol and anger that swelled and pooled like a pestilence within him.

Silence.

Doc's anger crested, broke, and drained. In its wake lay only a sense of despicable guilt and desolation. That was followed by self-disgust. Damn it, it wasn't as if the bullies in the street were the only ones to mistreat his mad brother. And ultimately, Butler *was* his brother.

"I'm sorry. I didn't mean to hurt you."

"Oh, you didn't hurt me none, but you should have seen how the men took it. You might as well have bucked and gagged them."

"The men?" Laughter took Doc by surprise. "I *hurt* the men? Your damned and infernal ghosts? Bruised their incorporeal sensitivities?"

I'd do more than wound their egos. I'd flay them, scourge them, drive them from your soul, brother.

But how did he attack phantoms when they hid inside his brother's skull? The only alternative was to chop them out with an ax. But what ignorant and medieval kind of a solution was that?

Not to say that doing so wouldn't have made him feel better . . . but it didn't exactly bode well for Butler's recovery.

When had he begun to embrace such a sick sense of humor?

Or I could end the pain.

He'd come so close that day in Camp Douglas before James and the rest hauled him back. But here, in Denver, on the dismal outskirts of the city, there was no steely-eyed guard with a ready rifle. No deadline. Here, he'd have to do it himself.

He glanced down at the varnished wood of his surgical case. The one Butler had stolen during his "raid" at Fort Scott. All it would take was a scalpel. A small incision to open an artery. In cold like this, he'd hardly feel it, could bathe himself in the rising steam as his hot life pumped out onto the frozen tent floor. Dying from exsanguination wasn't such a bad way to go. He had watched the process so many times. Seen the slowing, the fading of the senses as the eyes stilled. Breath went shallow, and the muscles relaxed.

A graying that faded to darkness.

Eternity.

Peace.

"Doc?"

"Leave me to my fantasy, Butler."

"Doc? There's a man here."

Doc lifted his head, took a deep breath in the cold air, and fought the need to cough. The damned stove was going cold. Even that small joy was failing him. He had no more wood to toss in for fuel. The frozen horse apples filling the streets were too full of ice to burn.

The man outside was well dressed — a black broadcloth suit visible beneath the buffalo coat that hung open in front. A high beaver-felt hat — banded with a wide brown ribbon — topped his head. Long black hair, washed, hung over his collar. A fine black mustache flared in defiance of his thin face and arrogant black eyes.

"It is said that you are a doctor," he began in a well-modulated voice. Then his eyes flicked dismissively Butler's way. "Word is that you are remarkably skilled, but inconvenienced by having to care for your brother."

"People know a lot about me." Though why that should surprise him, he had no idea. Butler made enough public scenes they should have been the talk of the town.

"Word does pass, sir." The man looked around the shabby tent, at the rickety beds Doc had cobbled together on either side of the tin stove. This was everything. Doc had sold the wagon and mule back in November to pay for food.

"How can I help you?" Doc asked, forcing himself to rise and offer his hand. "I'm Dr. Philip Hancock. I was trained in Boston, worked as a prominent surgeon in Memphis until the war. Plied my trade at Shiloh, though it was more akin to butchery, given the conditions."

"Macy Hare. I've got a job for you, if you're a good enough surgeon."

"What is it?"

"Woman with female troubles. Bleeding from the cunt."

Doc stopped short, a dull acceptance making him draw a breath. "A man doesn't say a woman's 'bleeding from the cunt' if she's his wife or sister. I assume we are talking about a line girl?"

Another penniless bit of human wreckage who couldn't pay him enough to buy an evening meal?

"She's a burlesque dancer. Works for Big Ed Chase." Hare crossed his arms. "You've heard of him?"

"Runs the Cricket Club. Combination gambling hell, saloon, and variety theater. That, and I hear he has financial interests in several other gambling and recreational businesses. I guess he's what they call a kingpin."

"The woman we're concerned with, she's a dancer at the Cricket who suddenly found herself in a motherly situation. That good enough for you? Or do I need to go find another doc?"

"I'll come. Do what I can. I'll need to take my brother. If this morning's any indication, I can't leave him alone."

"The men and I will be fine, Philip." Butler grinned. A gesture meant to reassure, which only served to open his split lip. "We can go scouting for firewood. Maybe see if we can find Yankees to raid."

"Bring him. We can find someone to keep an eye on him, I suspect," Macy Hare said coolly.

"You can carry my case, Butler."

Doc stepped out into the cold day. Sunlight glittered on the thin crusting of snow. Ice floated in the Platte. The distant Rockies rose in white splendor against the sky. Doc and Butler's camp lay in the no-man's-land beside the river's rocky shores, just below the confluence with Cherry Creek. Ground abandoned as too dangerous after the '64 flood. Several other tents were pitched close by, the occupants similarly pressed in circumstances.

Hare led the way, winding through piles of empty and rusting tin cans, bottles, and accumulations of trash. Down at the water, a pack of dogs worried the frozen corpse of a dead mule. The occasional tang of offal, urine, and feces tickled the nose.

Word was that the spring runoff would finally "cleanse" the entire river bottom.

To Hare, Doc said, "My brother suffers from the fatigue. Not all casualties of the recent war were caused by bullets or flying metal."

"Yep," Hare said without concern as they climbed the bank and took the Cherry Creek trail. "He's kind of the talk o' the town. And looks like he's keeping you down on your luck, Doctor. As to my problem? It seems that, like today, Doc Flannagan can't always be found. And when he is, he's generally engaged in finding the bottom of a whiskey bottle. A talent at which he excels."

"Even sober I wouldn't trust him to lance a pimple with a —" Doc stopped himself short. "Excuse me. I have no right to vent my feelings about another physician."

Macy Hare bit off a smile, almost slipping on a patch of ice. The wind played with the silky hair on his fine buffalo coat. The thing looked remarkably warm.

Macy said, "Big Ed says Flannagan does more damage than good. And somehow the drinks he credits against his account are perpetually more than he's paid."

Doc looked back where Butler was following along, shivering, holding Doc's surgical case as if it were a holy relic. "We all have our burdens to bear, Mr. Hare."

The dapper man shot him a sidelong inspection. "You look about at the end of your line, sir."

"The war didn't leave me with much. But, to be honest, I didn't expect that getting a new start would prove so difficult."

"If I might ask, what were your sympathies in the recent unpleasantness?"

"Staying alive . . . and keeping as many of my fellows in that state as I could. A goal at which I often did not succeed."

"Big Ed served with the Colorado Volunteers. Under Colonel Chivington. He was proud to punish the red heathens hiding under the American flag at Sand Creek. Does that cause you any inconvenience of conscience, Doctor?"

"Mr. Hare, once upon a time I had the luxury of moral outrage and an amount of rectitude. Since then life has managed to stamp, slap, and beat me free of any such silly preoccupations. My purpose, these days, is to ply my craft to the best of my ability, to allay suffering, and establish a practice that allows me and my brother to live in comfort."

"We might have a solution for your current circumstances." Hare paused. "Assuming you have the requisite skills that some of the hoosieroons claim you have."

"And what solution might that be?" Doc coughed into his sleeve. What could the drunks and vagabonds be saying about him?

"Don't be so suspicious, Dr. Hancock. First, let's see if you can help Lottie."

"Ah, she has a name now."

Hare shot him a cold look as they turned onto Blake Street. The line of prominent two- and three-story brick buildings were the center of Denver's night life. A line of wagons, teams waiting head down, filled the center of the street. Despite the closed doors, the sound of a piano could be heard from the Arcadia.

Butler, who had remained remarkably quiet, made mumbling sounds as they stepped through the Cricket Club's doors and into a blessed warmth. Hare led the way through the restaurant and gaming room to the back, climbed the stairs, and into the back hallway.

At one of the doors a third of the way down the dark hall, Hare slowed, knocked, and called, "Lottie? It's Mace. I've brought a doctor."

"Mace?" The voice sounded weak as Hare opened the door.

Doc took his surgical box, inclining his head toward Butler, as he said, "If you could keep my brother out of trouble?"

"Sure, Doc." Macy Hare asked Butler, "Do you play monte?"

"Don't even think it," Doc told him. "Neither Butler nor his imaginary soldiers have a penny to their names. Nor will I cover their debts."

"Maybe we'll play for matchsticks."

"Hell, we've less than a dozen of those left." Doc closed the door behind him, and blinked in the dim interior. A coal oil lamp, its chimney black, barely cast a gleam in the room. Doc turned up the wick.

Lottie lay on a narrow, metal-frame bed against the wall; a thick sweater protected her from the chill. She stared at Doc through leaden eyes as he laid his case on the mirrored dresser.

"I'm Doc Hancock, Lottie. I'm told you're bleeding."

"Doc Flannagan said I'd be fine. That I'd be back to dancing for Mace in a week. But it just won't stop bleeding, Doc. And it sure stays sore down there."

Doc glanced down at the chamber pot next to the bed. Even in the poor light he could see it was full of bloody rags.

"Well, Lottie, let me clean your lamp, then I'll see if I can find the trouble."

His preliminary inspection sent a shiver down his spine. He'd seen the like in a female corpse once while in medical school in Boston. He glanced at his surgical kit. But for forceps and sutures, instruments for women weren't included.

"I'll be right back."

He hurried out into the hall, then down the stairs to the dingy kitchen, calling, "I need a gravy spoon. It's an emergency."

The cook, a toothless, gray-haired man wearing

554

a dirty apron, his cheeks covered with stubble, picked up a serving spoon from the counter. "All we gots is this."

Doc looked at it, grimaced, and wiped it off with a grease-impregnated rag. As he burst out the door, the cook called, "You bring that back when you're done!"

"Don't think you're going to want it when I'm through with it," Doc muttered, heading to the bar, stepping behind, and grabbing a whiskey bottle.

"Hey!" The bartender started his way. "You can't be back here."

Doc pointed at Macy Hare, who'd risen from his chair opposite Butler. "I'm working for Macy. I'll bring back what I don't use."

Then he was off, dashing for the stairs, splashing the dirty spoon with whiskey and wiping it on his pants. Stepping into Lottie's room, he bent down before her.

"Doc?" she whispered.

"Lottie. I'm going to have to anesthetize you. And then we're going to do our best to save your life."

After he'd placed the cloth to her nose and mouth, monitored her weakening struggles, he positioned her legs, and stared thoughtfully at the spoon. The story about Dr. Simms — the Alabama madman — had been apocryphal. That he'd used a bent gravy spoon prior to inventing his speculum.

"Philip," he told himself, "if you can do this, you're going to prove yourself one hell of a surgeon."

Then he crouched between her legs and began bending the spoon backward around its handle.

It might have been an hour later when he closed her door, arching his back against the cramp. He made his way down the hall, his case in hand, and descended the steps.

Butler still sat at the corner table, his concentration on the cards as Macy Hare dealt and shifted them around with fluid dexterity.

"How is she, Doc?" Hare asked, his eyes still on the cards.

"I think she'll make it, Mr. Hare. If — and I do say if — she doesn't come down with an infection." Doc pulled up a chair, lowering his voice. "Flannagan did the abortion?"

"He did."

"A man can murder a woman through incompetence just as thoroughly as if he put a revolver to her head and pulled the trigger." Doc leveled a finger. "You value these girls?"

"Of course."

"Then don't let that fraud close to them again. Now, I knocked her out with ether, cleaned her uterus, and put some stitches in the rip that butcher tore in her vagina. She's coming to, so you, Mace, have to get her a hot meal. I'd say stew thick with meat and vegetables if you can find any. She needs to drink water by the glass, or tea, but not coffee. No spirits. Keep her quiet for a week or so, and only then start with light exercise. Do it right and she'll be dancing by the end of the month. Do you understand all of that, and why I'm asking it of you?"

Mace's expression had pinched, his dark eyes curiously surprised. "I'd reckon so."

"Good. Then I'll give you the final order: she's not to have sexual relations until I declare her fit. None. She was torn up, and she needs time to heal. Do you understand?"

"You ask that a lot, Doctor."

"Mr. Hare, Lottie's life is still hanging in the balance. It's a coin toss if she's gonna make it. The only reason she's still got a chance is because she's a dancer and strong as a horse. Someone needs to sit with her. Maybe one of the other girls. If there's a change, you fetch me, pronto. Even if it's the middle of the night."

Hare seemed to consider, his dark eyes probing Doc's. "Why don't you stay with her yourself? I didn't notice the dying and consumptive tearing down your tent for services."

"I didn't want to wear out my welcome, but I'm happy to stay." Doc leveled a finger. "But if Flannagan shows up, you keep that son of a bitch out of my sight. I'm not feeling especially collegial after what he did to that girl."

Hare turned, raising his voice. "Joseph?"

"Yes, Mr. Hare?" a young man who was laying in bottles behind the bar answered, his expression expectant.

"You know where Doc Hancock's tent is down on the river? Take Isa and a cart and pack up his camp. When you get it here, fold the canvas and pile it out back. Put the bedding in Josiah's old room."

"What are you doing?" Doc asked.

"You keep that girl alive, and the boss will have more than enough work for you, Dr. Hancock." He pulled a cigar from his pocket, scratched one of the matches on the table, and lit it. Speaking around it, he said, "I think your ship just came in."

"What about my brother?"

"He says he can do chores, sweep, clean and

such. As long as he don't rile the chuckleheads, he can stay. At least until we see if you're worth a lot."

"A lot of what?"

Hare blinked behind the smoke. As the blue cloud rose, he said, "A town lot, Doctor. A place to build your office and surgery. That's what you want, isn't it?"

"And you would back me?"

"Big Ed always backs winners, Doc. Just keep Butler, here, away from our tables. Him and all these imaginary men he talks to."

"It's mostly Sergeant Kershaw," Butler murmured as he watched Hare manipulate the cards.

"Who's Kershaw?" Hare asked.

"He's the one no one ever sees," Doc replied.

"As compared to . . . ?"

"Oh, hell, Mr. Hare, he's even got me doing it now."

Of the fifty or so matchsticks on the table, all but five were piled before Butler.

70

March 1, 1866

The little adobe house stood at the side of a draw where it emptied from the western slope of the Sandia Mountains. A small ditch ran from the rocky creekbed to a reservoir that in turn could be diverted to a ceramic cistern buried in the rocky soil.

A low New Mexican sunset burned in the western sky as Billy led the way on Locomotive. Danny Goodman followed, continually turning as he did to stare at their back trail where it led down the ridge to the alluvial flats, and thence to the distant swath of cottonwoods along the bosque where the Rio Grande flowed.

To the south-southwest in the far distance, the naked eye could just make out the blocky outline of Albuquerque and the faint smudge of its evening fires. To the west the mountains had turned from violet to purple, the clouds taking on shades of gold, yellow, orange, and blood-red.

Billy pulled up, cocked his head as he studied the little adobe. The door was painted a bright blue, the window frames white where they were set back in the brown-plastered adobe. The faint glow of a lamp was already visible through the panes.

Out back, in a rickety corral, stood two very fine blood-bay horses, one of which was saddled. They watched Billy's approach with pricked pin ears and nickered a greeting to Locomotive.

"So this is the place?" Billy asked as Danny eased up beside him.

"Yep. This is where Nichols said the payoff was to be. You kilt Jessup, just as the contract said. Reckon all we gotta do is pick up the money and light a shuck for town."

He'd like that. Just last night the Sarah demon had paid him a visit and left him shaken and shamed by her nocturnal preoccupation with his manhood.

Maybe it was a warning. He wondered if Sarah wasn't dead. Be like her to have ended as a suicide. The reason the dreams were getting worse was because her ghost was coming to humiliate him. Some punishment from Hell for having allowed her to be taken by Dewley.

Or some cockeyed warning from the devil to take care. Be just like that tricky son of a bitch to send Sarah to yank on his cock as a way to let him know death was around the corner.

"Why don't I like this?" Billy asked, reaching down for his Sharps.

"Got yer back up, huh?" In reply Danny eased his Remington from its holster.

At that moment the door opened, a man in a black linen suit with old-style frock coat, and a dark derby set crooked on his head, stepped out. With his right hand he raised field glasses to his eyes, carefully studying them, and then turning his attention to their backtrail.

Only after lowering the glasses did he reach into his pocket for a cigar. Striking a Lucifer, he lit the stogie, puffed, and studied them across the hundred yards separating them.

His voice carried on the still air: "Why don't you all ride in? Keep your hands on your weapons if you'd like. While you might be tempted to shoot me and take what you're owed, it would preclude further, and potentially more lucrative, opportunities."

"He saying what I think he is?" Danny asked.

"Yep." Billy urged Locomotive forward, crossing the intervening distance before shoving the Sharps back into its scabbard. He did, however, keep the horse between him and the man as he dismounted and tied off the reins on the porch support.

The man with the cigar stepped forward, offering his hand. "George Nichols. You must be the one calling himself the Meadowlark."

"Reckon so. And it don't need go no further than that."

"On that we are agreed." He glanced at Danny. "Actually, Mr. Goodman, my expectations are exceeded. I've been appraised by my agents in the sheriff's office that they haven't a clue as to the reason behind Barney Jessup's unfortunate demise. Remarkable as it may seem, they are even considering an act of suicide as the most likely explanation of Barney's exuvitated existence."

"Says the sheriff leans toward the idea that Jessup killed hisself," Billy translated.

The man who called himself Nichols fastened his thoughtful night-brown eyes on Billy's. "That was your idea?"

"Killin's easy, Mr. Nichols. It's just hunting men, after all. But if'n they's kilt crude, sooner or

561

later, someone's gonna come a-hunting you. Leave 'em a different way to think? Maybe accident? Maybe a fire? Or like here, suicide? Then it ain't vendetta."

"And where'd you learn that?"

Billy chewed his lip, squinted up at Nichols, and said, "Some of the men what kilt my maw and raped my sister. Said they'd have been smarter to have left Maw and Sis burned in the house. If'n I'd a come home and found both dead and burned in the house like a couple of them coyotes suggested, I wouldn't have hunted them bastards down and kilt every one of 'em. Smart killers cover their tracks."

Nichols seemed to come to a decision. "Come on inside. We need to pursue this conversation over a bottle of whiskey and a plate of Maria Luisa's chili and beans. Hope you like peppers."

With a sidelong glance at Danny, Billy led the way, stopping at the door. Hand on his pistol he took in the little room with its kiva fireplace, single table, bed, and *trastero.*

He took a seat, back to the wall, as Nichols dished out steaming red chili from a pot perched near the fire. Only when he'd dished for them all, did he sit.

"Now, here's the thing," he began, filling his spoon. "The job was remarkably handled." He tested the chili by sipping loudly. Chewing, he waggled the spoon at Danny. "The approach, however, is not your forte, Mr. Goodman."

"My what?"

"Your strong point," Billy muttered. "You want to make a point here, Mr. Nichols?"

"Danny Goodman can no more sell himself as a front man for mining investments than I can pass myself off as a tinware drummer." The spoon waggled again. "The approach was so clumsy I figured the two of you would be caught, strung up, and hung for murder before Jessup's body was cold."

"Why are we having this palaver?" Danny demanded hotly.

Billy reached out, grabbing Danny's arm as he stood to leave. Tightening a viselike grip, he dragged Danny back down to his seat. "I suspect we're having it 'cause Mr. Nichols, here, is right."

"But I —"

"Shut your hole, Danny." He turned to Nichols. "Go on."

Nichols fixed on Goodman. "Do not take this as offensive. Your idea was correct, your thinking sound. A professional front is indeed necessary as a means of deflecting suspicion. Your vulnerability is that despite your intentions, your proclivities present you as what you are: an Arkansas hick with no formal training in mining or geology."

Danny roared, "Now, just a damn —"

Billy put all of his strength into his grip, seeing Danny wince.

"We had us a front man," Billy said softly. "Turns out he took the money, then he gave the law all the particulars on us so's he could fetch the reward, too. We didn't take well to the betrayal."

Nichols's lips quirked as he shoveled another spoonful of chili into his mouth. He seemed to savor the taste, then added, "Gamblers have a proper term for your late and lamented front man's game. They call it penny ante." He reached into his coat pocket, removed an envelope, and laid it before Billy.

563

Gesturing for Danny not to move, Billy pulled it over, opened it, and quickly counted, only to hand the envelope to Danny and say, "We took the job for fifty. There's a thousand dollars in there."

"Tell me a cardinal don't shit," Danny said in awe after he'd counted.

Nichols calmly continued eating his chili. "If I ever start offering you fifty-dollar jobs, it's because you're no longer working like the kind of professionals the Jessup job seemed to indicate. While I am not at liberty to impart particulars, I would like to employ your services again in the near future. As long as the work continues to be performed satisfactorily, we shall continue to maintain our relationship."

"Sounds good to us," Billy agreed. "But I reckon we need some things made clear."

"Indeed we do, Mr. Meadowlark." Nichols wiped his lips with a handkerchief. "Here are the ground rules: you never refer to yourself as the Meadowlark on a job, but leave a feather behind. You work for no one but me. No freelancing for penny-ante killings to make pocket change. You go where I send you, take your time, and kill the target in the most nonconfrontational manner. And, unlike tonight's crude transmission of cash, future financial remuneration will be through bank deposits in accounts under your name."

"Then how do we know who the johnny is?" Danny asked.

"Ads in the classified under the heading 'Meadowlark' will be placed in several major newspapers at the first of each month. It will contain an address where a letter addressed to Danny Goodman can be picked up. The person with whom I leave the letter will demand a

564

password. Danny will tell him or her 'impetuous.' Upon hearing the correct response, he will then be given the particulars on whomever the next target is."

"And how do we communicate with you?" Billy asked.

"Through a classified Meadowlark ad giving the particulars of a place and time whereby I can be reached by telegraph."

"Mr. Nichols, you're asking a lot of us. 'Specially restricting our jobs to your business alone. You sure you got enough employment to keep us busy?"

"Count on it." Nichols stirred his chili. "In fact, after you finish your meals, assuming you don't scald your tonsils, there's a man in Colorado City, Colorado, who needs to meet with an accident. If that could be attended to before the end of next month, I would be most delighted to add five hundred dollars to the thousand I will deposit in your names in the Kountze Brothers Bank in Denver City. Payable upon completion of the job."

Billy grinned, gave Danny a nod, and picked up his spoon. "Why don't you give us the details, Mr. Nichols? Colorado City ain't but a week or so north of here. Reckon Danny and me can figger something out to take care of your problem."

The chili was indeed hot. At the first spoonful, Billy expected his scalp was going to melt and slide off his skull. He figured this was how the food in hell burned a sinner's mouth.

Looking at George Nichols, who continued to eat the stuff without breaking a sweat, Billy wondered if, indeed, he hadn't just sold his soul to the devil incarnate.

71

Spring was coming slowly to the high Colorado Rockies. Glancing out the window, Sarah could see gray clouds; streamers of blowing snow trailed off the peaks to the north and west, and wreaths of white fell in hazy fingers across the valleys. Occasional flakes descended irregularly just beyond the porch.

Central City, just down the slope, was an ugly place. A collection of claptrap plank or log structures, shebangs, shanties, hovels, and tents packed wall to wall. Most of the privies hung out over the creek in back. The surrounding mountains had been logged of every stick of wood, leaving the slopes bare and eroded. Intermingled among the stumps were shacks, privies, prospect holes, waste and tailings piles, and the crisscrossing scars of roads.

Her yard — such as it was — had melted out last week for the first time, surprising her when a small flower bed emerged from the packed white coating of old snow.

Ezra Cummings — the man who'd lost the claim to Bret, along with six hundred dollars — had been a man of contrasts. She had practically had

566

to shovel the two-room cabin out when Bret first brought her here. Beneath piles of empty tin cans and bottles, wooden crates, empty kegs of blasting powder, and a mouse-chewed rug, she had discovered a plank floor. Glass-pane windows looked out on the mountains. An expensive cookstove with built-in water heater stood against the back wall, and a high brass bed with a cotton-ticking mattress dominated the bedroom.

And now she'd discovered an honest-to-God flower bed.

Sarah bent to open the oven and remove the rolls with a hot pad. They'd risen to perfection and smelled divine. Bret would be so pleased as he dipped them into the juices leaking from the elk roast. It now simmered in the Dutch oven atop the stove.

She left the rolls to cool and stepped over to the small desk beside the window. Looking out, she was pleased to see the stack of firewood Johnny Doolan had delivered. It would last them another two months at least. Longer if the weather warmed.

Then she studied her accounts book. She'd taken seriously Bret's promise to make her the banker. Paw had ensured that she learned sums and numbers by the time she was ten. And she had studied, figuring she would need it to run her fancy household when she married and moved to Little Rock.

That brought a wry smile to her lips. So here she was, mistress to a fancy gambler, living in a tight but small two-room cabin. Some four thousand and fifteen dollars were secreted in the tin box behind the foundation stone. Not bad for four months of labor on Bret's part.

Since he'd won the cabin and claim in Denver, he'd changed his tactics.

"You've got to keep the game balanced," Bret had told her one night after they'd exhausted each other's bodies. "I never clean a mark out. I just take a percentage and let him walk away with something. Never leave them feeling like they been cheated or humiliated. That's the true art of it. That way, they'll always come back. And better yet, they'll tell all their friends that you run a square game."

"I heard you buy everybody a drink."

"I always keep a bottle on the table. Half empty. That way they think I've got a head start on 'em and might be whiskey-headed already. If they sit down, and they're flush, I'll pour them a drink. Maybe two or three over the next hour."

"But you don't drink?"

"Only enough to look like I'm keeping up, and my cup's mostly full of water." He had shifted beside her, fingers playing through her hair. "Here's the trick: if you can take a big chunk of a chucklehead's money, and have him stagger away feeling happy, you'll come out ahead every time."

"So, are you the best gambler in Central City?"

"There's others as good at reading the cards and remembering what's been played, and what the odds are that a given card's in the other fella's hand. But when they play, it's with a sort of fever. They've got to be the best. Got to win." He shrugged. "For me it's a business."

She smiled at the memory. Hard to believe that she'd found happiness with a footloose, disgraced deserter. Nevertheless he had placed her at the center of his world, and in doing so had established himself as the center of hers. In his bed she had driven Dewley and his demons ever deeper into the hazy distance, and come to cherish not only Bret's body and sex, but a marvelous appetite and delight in her own.

"You are a miracle worker, Bret Anderson," she told herself, placing a hand on her abdomen just at the thought.

The clatter of wheels and a horse clopping on frozen ground caused her to look up as a phaeton pulled into the yard. The woman in the seat was hidden in a bearhide coat. A woolen bonnet was tight on her head, and a buffalo robe lay over her lap. All were dusted with snow. She set the brake and stepped down, pausing only long enough to deliver a sweet to the horse before she tied it to the hitch.

Sarah opened the door and greeted her. "You must be Aggie. Bret said you wished to call today. I'm sorry, but he didn't give your full name."

"Aggie's fine, Mrs. Anderson." The woman stamped off her shoes, puffing a cold breath into the gray day. In the yard occasional flakes of snow still drifted down.

"Do come in, and don't mind your shoes. It's just snow."

"Oh, my, Mrs. Anderson, it's cold out there." She slipped out of the bear coat as she entered. Then she removed her bonnet, careful to shake the snow off at the door. Both coat and bonnet she deposited on the floor before stepping over to the stove and extending her hands.

She looked to be in her late twenties, with curly red hair, and a delicately formed, heart-shaped face. Her complexion was pale, her skin creamy, and her petite mouth bore faint traces of rouge. She closed her green eyes and sighed in relief, as though in worship of the stove. She shifted, and her bright red day dress rustled.

And such a dress! Sarah admired the high-necked collar and ruffles. Below the jacket bodice, a trained overskirt fell in folds from her bustle.

Sarah conscientiously fingered her light blue wool skirt and realized she must look drab in comparison.

What a fool I am. She'd practically swooned when Bret presented it to her, it being the finest dress she'd owned since Paw took her to Little Rock.

Aggie turned, lifting a knowing eyebrow. "I been around women long enough to know what you're thinking. Stop it, Mrs. Anderson. A dress doesn't make a woman. Why, me? I'd kill to have your looks. Bret calls you his angel. Not sure I wouldn't kill to have a man worship me that way, either."

Flustered, Sarah asked, "Could I get you a cup of tea? Perhaps a hot roll?" She pointed to the water steaming on the stove next to the Dutch oven "The coffee's cold, but I could boil up some fresh."

"Tea's fine. Long as it's hot."

Sarah took down the tin from the cupboard and shook leaves into the cup before she poured hot water over it and handed it to Aggie. "Have a seat. I take it this isn't a social call."

Aggie chuckled in wry amusement. "Got two things on my mind, Mrs. Anderson. First, thank you for agreeing to see me. It ain't always considered proper. And even then, it would be back-door admittance only."

"We don't have a back door." Sarah shrugged. "And I've been down pretty far myself. A lot of the women I worked beside doing laundry kept their children fed by entertaining men on the side."

Aggie studied her through thoughtful green eyes as she held the tea before her. "In this world a woman either marries, lives on starvation wages when, and if, the men allow, or she sells her sex. Ain't hardly ever a way around it." She sipped at the tea, level green eyes on Sarah. "Me, I come to talk business."

"And what would that be?"

"Two things. One, I'd like your permission to let Mr. Anderson move his game to my parlor house one night a week." She lifted a lace-gloved hand. "And no, he's never set foot in my place. I would give you my word that neither I, nor any of my girls, will so much as bat an eye at him, let alone offer any other temptation. I'll make sure the professor enforces that when I'm not around."

"Professor?" Sarah couldn't help but think of Butler and his books.

"It's what we call the man who plays the piano, oversees the action, and ensures that our guests keep the rules and behave themselves." Aggie spread her hands wide. "I just want Bret's game on Saturday nights, ma'am. I'm guessing his take would more than compensate for my cut given the kind of money most of my clients toss around. And when he closes the table, I give you my word I'm sending him right home to you."

Sarah considered. "How much do you think his game is worth?"

"I reckon a thousand a night," she said without batting an eye. "And that's after my percentage."

Sarah frowned down into her tea. "Forgive me, but I don't understand. I thought men were there to . . ." She struggled for words.

571

"Oh, they're right keen to dip their sticks," Aggie told her with an amused smile. "But a parlor house is different than a dollar-a-whirl brothel. What I provide is a refuge where a certain class of men can congregate, listen to chamber music, drink the finest spirits imported from the east and Europe, read a volume from my library, discuss business over a perfectly cooked meal, and bed a beautiful woman who isn't going to milk their pricks and shout 'Next!' In return, I receive ample compensation."

"But why do you need Bret?"

"Mrs. Anderson, Pat O'Reilly, you heard of him? The mine owner? He started a weekly game at one of my tables. It breaks my heart to watch that wealth switch back and forth, and I'm not getting a cut."

"And what's the second thing?"

"Bret tells me you can keep figures."

"I can add columns and tally. But not like a real banker or such."

"I put my money in a ceramic pot." Aggie took a drink of tea, before adding, "I can't do sums. Don't have the head for it. I can count it, and sometimes there's more, and other times there's less." She glanced up, green eyes sincere. "I come up the hard way. Spent the last ten years learning to read, how to talk, trying to be smarter than the rest."

"I'm flattered, but it might be that one of the men at the bank could do a better —"

"Could be I want a woman," Aggie said firmly. "Maybe one as could *teach me* once she herself gets the way of it. No man from the bank would do that. I'd pay you what you think it was worth."

"You think I can do this?"

572

"Bret does. He thinks you can do anything. Says you're the strongest, toughest, smartest, and most courageous woman alive."

"Does he?" She paused, somewhat taken aback by his faith in her. "I don't know. I've never thought about it. How much money are we talking about?"

"A couple of thousand a night."

"Dear God!"

Aggie smiled humorlessly. "If I was doing so well, that ceramic pot would be busting out money all over. You start by paying for cognac, champagne, and wine all the way from France, whiskey from Ireland and Scotland, bourbon from Kentucky, Cuban rum and cigars, tinned oysters and Russian caviar, and it's all hauled across Indian-infested plains on a jerk line. That ain't cheap, ma'am. Not to mention fresh meat from the market hunters, real vegetables from down on the Arkansas River, and soda water from Saratoga, not to mention the laundry, the fabrics, the medical, and regular old expenses like firewood and coal oil, and money just seems to disappear."

Sarah stood, her mind in a fog. She walked over and stared down at her list of figures where it lay open on the desk.

Could I do this?

Hope filled Aggie's voice. "I could have Mick, the professor, bring the money up here for you to count every Monday."

"It doesn't work that way." Sarah turned, leaned back against the desk, and crossed her arms. "And carrying that much money around, especially on a schedule, would be asking for a robbery. There's more to it. You have to know how much money is coming in and from what. Is it from the girls, the

573

drink, or the food? How much is going out, and to which accounts? When I worked for a woman in Little Rock, I had to have a list of what I spent and what I charged at each store. Old Mrs. Pennington didn't teach me much, but she knew where every penny was going."

Aggie frowned. "Wagon shows up with supplies, I just pay 'em."

"It's a wonder you're not broke." Sarah slapped her hands to her sides. "What if I came down with Bret on Saturdays? He could run his game; I could sit in the back somewhere and make my sums. You'll need a ledger book. And you will be required to write down each expense. All of them. Right down to a nickel for a bar of soap from a street vendor. I had to for Mrs. Pennington."

"Come to my place? Mrs. Anderson, it's impossible. I run a parlor house, and you're a respectable lady. It wouldn't do to be seen within a stone's throw of my door."

Sarah chuckled, thinking of what Maw would say.

But this was a job. *I'd pay you what you would think it was worth!*

Something inside her came clear, as if a blindfold had fallen away, when she said, "I'm not a lady. I'm not even Bret's wife. The ring, and the lie, was to allow Bret and me to travel and room together without complications. I am *Miss* Sarah Rogers. An unmarried woman sharing a gambler's bed and keeping his house. Respectable? It's a front."

"You could lose even the illusion by setting foot in my place."

"I want to learn how to run a business. You want to learn how to sum accounts. As a gambler's

574

woman, I don't get invited to the women's sewing socials as it is. And, well, to be honest, Bret and I aren't long for Central City in the end. Where we're going, no one will know."

"Might be a high price just to learn a business," Aggie countered. "You'll be tarred, just as if you were in the trade and Bret were your pimp. And you might find yourself receiving unwanted male attention if they see you there."

Sarah fingered her ring. "They'll think I'm Bret's wife. I really want to learn this."

Aggie narrowed an eye. "I think Bret's right about you. About that courage and all."

72

June 28, 1866

The nightmare had been haunting Billy's sleep all during the long week before the job. It had bedeviled him as he waited in a camp hidden in the breaks up from the Mimbres River. Danny, meanwhile, had scouted the next target. All things considered, the job had been easy: eliminate a placer miner who was working a claim on a mostly dry tributary of the Mimbres. Up a canyon on the western slope of the Black Range.

Billy simply shot him in the back from ambush one morning as the man walked down to work his claim. He and Danny packed the body onto the man's mule — and dropped his corpse into a sheer-walled canyon as they made their way over Emory Pass. By the time anyone found his body, *if* anyone ever found his body, it would consist of sun-bleached, coyote-chewed bones. And damn few of them.

But the nightmare hadn't gone away.

Two days later, they were spending the night at a small roadhouse — what the New Mexicans called a cantina — in a four-adobe community known as San Marcial. Once it had been rife with trade from Fort Craig. The small settlement stood across the Rio Grande from the Valverde battle-field where General Sibley's Texans had whipped the Federals in 1862. With the end of the war, trade had fallen off significantly.

The cantina consisted of a small restaurant and bar with four tables. Turned out that they served beans, peppers, and some sort of stew with tortillas. The bar in the back — run by a dark-skinned, Spanish-speaking man with a thick black mustache and goatee — dispensed whiskey and something traded up from El Paso called mescal. River water was used to dilute it.

Two dark-haired young women, maybe in their teens, both thin, with deep-set eyes and the look of sisters, provided services of the horizontal kind in addition to dishing out food and carrying drinks from the bar to the tables.

As the evening deepened, Billy wasn't sure that he'd really been drinking whiskey. Coal oil might have left the same burning aftertaste as the house's fine blend. But feeling flush, his stomach full, and with the satisfaction of another job well done, he offered the mustachioed barkeep a twenty-dollar gold piece, pointing at both of the girls, and then at himself and Danny.

"Por toda la noche. ¿Comprende?"

The man had glanced back and forth between them, nodded, and barked some order in rapid-fire Spanish that Billy couldn't understand.

"All night?" Danny asked him as the older of the girls reached for a lamp, took him by the hand, and led him out the back to one of the *jacales.*

"Use her good," Billy answered, "and don't let her milk you dry on the first ride."

The girl he followed had long black hair that hung down below her waist. When she looked at

577

him, her eyes seemed large — almost like a deer's — in her thin face. Small breasts, the size of oranges, were set low on her chest; the baggy white cotton blouse exposed her brown shoulders and chest. Leading Billy to the second *jacal,* she demurely closed the door behind him and placed the lamp on a bedside table.

"You got a name?" he asked as she turned to him.

"Margarita," she replied as she laid herself on the bed and pulled her red frilly skirt up past her waist.

"Por toda la noche," Billy reminded, reaching down and pulling her back onto her feet. "Now, here's the thing," he told her reasonably as he reached down and unbuttoned her skirt, letting it fall to the floor. "I been having nightmares. I see my sister rise up, all bare, and bitten. Then she reaches down and grabs my pizzle. And there's a demon growing in her womb. It's cause the devil has a choke hold on my soul. You understand any of what I'm saying?"

She stared at him with those large and dark eyes. *"Toda la noche. Sí."*

"She's blond, my sister. You're dark. Now, I know a fella shouldn't oughta be having sin-filled dreams about his sister. If'n I wasn't already damned and possessed by the devil, he'd blast me to hell just for the dreams. So tonight, I'm gonna get it out of my system. Cure myself. *¿Comprende?"*

"No, Señor Billy."

He didn't understand the rest of what she said, the Spanish words coming much too fast.

He eased the white cotton blouse from her shoulders, letting it fall onto the dirt floor. She stood uncertainly before him, her hands at her sides, fingers working as if kneading tortilla dough.

Billy kicked off his boots, unbuckled his belt, and dropped his drawers. After skinning out of his shirt, he remembered to remove his hat. Some idle thought reminded him that given the dirt floor, he'd be smart to check his outfit for scorpions before he put them on again in the morning.

The bed was barely big enough for two, the mattress feeling like nothing more than straw sewed into ticking. She seemed to be waiting patiently for instructions.

"You come. That's right. Climb up here."

He positioned her in the lamplight. Tried to imagine Sarah's blond hair turning black. Her pale skin browning, her teats shrinking down into the size of Margarita's small round breasts.

It didn't work.

Reaching up, he took her hands and pulled her down on top of him. Trying to imagine she was Sarah.

Only when he closed his eyes — let his imagination run free — did the feel of her hair on his skin, her body against his, begin to match the dream.

He could feel his cock hardening against her, and she settled firmly onto him; her breasts, becoming Sarah's breasts, flattened against his chest.

Her hand slipped down, grabbing him and tightening.

He gasped at the strength in her grip.

"Yes," he said through a groan.

She shifted, rose, and settled onto him.

"Sarah?" he whispered, the dream image so vivid

in his brain.

Then he opened his eyes, and saw only a skinny, brown, black-haired girl, her gaze dull and unfocused as she rocked her hips back and forth.

"You're supposed to kill her," Billy told her. "Damn it, girl. You gotta *be* her. Don't you see? I'm killing a devil's dream. I'm trying to save my soul. A man who dreams of his sister in a carnal way? He's damned!"

Misunderstanding his words, she rocked back and forth with more vigor, thrusting her chest out, small breasts bouncing.

"Goddamn it!" Billy reached up, grabbed her by the neck and closed his eyes.

And in that instant, she was Sarah. Her panicked blue eyes were looking into his. Locks of her golden hair were falling around his shoulders as he thrust up, driving himself into her.

Sarah was bucking, struggling to break free as he tightened his grip.

"You're a demon," he hissed. "You're *not* my sister. She wouldn't do this to me. She'd never tempt me this way. But it ends tonight, you Satan-spawned bitch."

He thrust up into her again as she clawed to break free, the blue eyes beginning to burn red. And then Sarah laughed in his face, loud peals of it, mocking him, belittling his rage. Something hot kindled in his belly — a spear of devil-fire inside him that rose into his penis and mixed with the smoldering demon that radiated from Sarah's evil womb.

His loins exploded. He gasped, sucking great breaths of air. He wasn't prepared for the intensity — as if great throbbing waves burst from his cock, shot up his spine and down his legs.

He seemed to hang in midair, all of his body electric.

Slowly he came to. Sagged flat. A weight was pressing limply down onto his still tingling body.

"Damn," he said between sucking breaths.

Had he done it? Had he killed the demon?

He blinked at the mass of black hair tickling his face. Not blond. Not the Sarah demon. Margarita. The little Mexican whore. She'd done it. Helped free him from the nightmare demon.

He chuckled, saying, "By damn, girl. I'll give you a twenty-dollar gold piece extra. Maybe two, given how good that was. I never popped my cork like that before."

She remained limp as he relaxed his hands from around her throat.

"Come on, girl. Let me catch my wind, and we'll see if we can't ride that bronco again."

He reached down and slapped her skinny round ass.

"What the hell?"

When he shoved her to the side, she flopped loosely against the wall, arms akimbo, one of her legs like deadweight across his thigh.

"Hey, Margarita! Wake up!"

Through the tangle of her black hair, he could see her eyes, half-lidded and dull, gleaming in the lamplight. The girl's tongue protruded between her lips, giving her a foolish expression. On her bare throat he could see the bruises, her skin broken where his nails had cut deep.

"Hey!" He jerked her up, propped her flopping head, and slapped her hard across the face. "Wake up, damn it!"

He slapped her harder.

The eyes remained half-lidded, pupils wide. No

581

change of expression.

He let her go, watched her sag onto the rumpled bedding.

"Dear God in heaven," he whispered as he swung his feet to the dirt floor. "What the hell did she do to me?"

He studied the dead girl, her limbs still tangled, her small breasts flaccid, the round curve of her hip dropping to such a thin waist.

Shit. I killed her.

But what to do? Danny was next door, dipping his pizzle in the sister. The mustachioed pimp would be around in the morning, looking for his whore.

I could just walk in, kill every living soul in the place.

And that would have half the law in the territory riled enough to come looking.

Cursing himself under his breath, Billy dressed, checked his Remington, and slipped to the door. Dark as the night was, he had an idea.

Back at the bed, he fought with Margarita's limp arms and legs as he slipped the skirt back up over her hips and buttoned it. Then he pulled the blouse around her shoulders and got her arms through the sleeves.

The next couple of hours were some of the longest waiting he'd ever endured.

Finally, long after midnight, he led his horse around, tossed the dead girl over Locomotive's withers, and stopped at Danny's *jacal* just long enough to knock.

"Who's there?" Danny asked groggily.

"Me an' Margarita. We're headed for Santa Fe. Says she's never been to the city and wants to see the fandango. I'll meet you there in a couple of weeks. Look for me at La Fonda on the square."

"Are you outta yor mind?"

"I'm taking a couple of weeks by myself with a woman, Danny. Never done that afore. Hell, stay and screw this one for a while if you like. She's cheap. Don't you rile me by following along and trying to track me down. See you in two weeks."

Then he was in the saddle, spurring Locomotive north along the Rio Grande trail. Come morning he could turn up into the Magdalena Mountains and find an arroyo to leave the dead girl in, or stuff stones into her dress and blouse and sink her in the river.

"What the hell possessed you, Billy?" he kept asking himself.

Had to be the devil, just dragging him down deeper and deeper.

73

September 4, 1866

Butler crouched behind Doc, elevating the lamp so that it shone onto the woman's privates. He'd been amazed at the variety of shapes that the female vulva came in, and had blushed once when Corporal Pettigrew wanted to discuss it. The cramped room was also illuminated by a single, small window that looked out over the trash-filled alley.

"I need the Sims' speculum, please," Doc told him.

Butler reached to the open medical case and retrieved the device, one that Philip had just managed to obtain — at great expense — from back East. Just working the duck-billed device had filled his brother with delight.

"Gina, I'm sorry, this is going to be uncomfortable."

"Christ, Doc, it ain't the first uncomfortable thing ever shoved in down there," she told him.

Butler watched the woman tense as Philip slowly inserted the speculum. As Doc had said the first time he laid eyes on the device, it beat the living hell out of his old bent-up serving spoon.

"Could you raise the light a little higher,

Butler?" Doc asked as he spread the woman's privates and began his examination. Butler extended the lamp over Doc's shoulder.

"Don't burn my ear," Doc countered.

"Y'all'd think he didn't trust the cap'n's steady hand," Pettigrew muttered.

"I'm paying attention," Butler told the men who crowded around the room's confines.

The woman, who called herself Gina, reclined on her back, legs spread wide, her hands gripping the wooden headboard over her head. She might have been in her early twenties, but exhaustion and weary acceptance lay behind her light brown eyes. Her cinnamon-colored hair had been tightly curled, and she wore a white cotton pullover, now wadded up above her hips.

After peering inside her, Doc said, "I don't see any sign of disease. No discharge or odor. But you say you feel a fullness down here?"

"Like a slight ache, Doc," Gina told him. "Sort of like something's built up. Kind of a pressure."

"Been working a lot?"

"Eight johnnies last night. Five or six during the day. I been pulling more'n my share."

"New, aren't you?"

"Come in last week. Phillipa has been selling me as strange. Reckon at this rate, I'll pay her back what it cost to bring me here in another week. Or would have if she hadn't lost the place. No telling about the new owner."

"Tell me if you feel any pain or tenderness."

Butler watched Doc press his fingers here and there into her abdomen above her pubis.

"What's he a-doin'?" Billy Templeton wondered, bending over the bed and squinting.

"Checking for lumps or other trouble. Get back,

585

Private. Don't make a pest of yourself. The rest of you men, don't be obnoxious."

"He really is crazy like they say, ain't he?" Gina remarked. She shifted her head, uncertain brown eyes fixing on Butler.

"It's called the fatigue. Happened a lot to soldiers in the war. Butler's case is severe," Doc explained as he straightened and reached for his bag. "Have you been feeling nervous, out of sorts? Jittery?"

"Ain't been sleeping, Doc. Seems like I can't 'thout I take a swig of laudanum."

"I'd say it's the hysteria. Probably brought on by the stress of relocating and working in a new place. How long has it been since you've had a release?"

"What's a release? I pee and shit fine."

"That delightful tingling down in your privates after good sex. What we call a paroxysm."

"Been a while, Doc. You're the first as has ever asked."

"Why's he worried about that?" Jimmy Peterson wondered where he hovered near the door.

Butler explained. "That spasm of the female organs releases the pressures inside a woman. Supposed to be most pleasant."

Gina shot him a wary glance. "Who's he talking to?"

"People he imagines in his head." Doc settled on the bed beside her. "You've never been treated for hysteria?"

"No, sir."

"But you've heard about it. Probably from the other girls."

She nodded.

Doc told her, "When I was in medical school I

586

read a report by a doctor named George Taylor who claimed that one out of four women suffers from hysteria at some point or another." Reaching between her legs he began to massage her. "It used to be called the 'Widow's disease,' and was thought to be the result of sexual relations being cut off."

Gina laughed. "As many johnnys as I've drained the last couple of days, that ain't me."

"But like a widow you haven't released the tension that builds up in the female loins, either." Doc paused. "And don't ask me how it works, Gina. There's a lot about medicine we just don't know yet."

"Corporal, step back, please. Don't crowd, the room's already small enough." Butler glared at Pettigrew.

Gina swiveled her head, staring uneasily around the room.

"Don't worry about Butler," Doc told her. "He's harmless. And his imaginary soldiers are even more harmless than he is."

She chuckled, closing her legs and almost trapping Doc's hand.

"Just lie back and relax," Doc told her. "Clear your mind and think of something pleasant."

"You sure I shouldn't be charging your brother, Doc? Generally someone's paying when a man watches me get my cunny rubbed."

"Might not be a bad idea," Doc told her with a grin. "Given all the men he says he's got locked inside that head of his, you'd make a fortune."

"Ah, now!" Corporal Pettigrew groaned and shook his head.

"It's all right, Miss Gina," Butler said, waving the men back. "We're like surgical assistants. We're all learning to be medical men now that the war's over."

"Butler," Doc told him, "you could help by packing up my case and remaining silent while Gina concentrates on healing herself."

Butler placed a finger to his lips to silence the men, and slipped around Frank Thompson to replace Doc's instruments.

Tightening the case straps, he crouched on the floor and considered everything they still had to do. This was the last of the girls in Phillipa's parlor house. Doc had had to douse one with mercury when he'd discovered a discharge and prescribed a vinegar douche for another with pernicious odor.

"We all getting practiced at woman's medicine," Kershaw said behind his ear.

"All the better for you to take care of your wife when you get home, Sergeant," he whispered, hoping Kershaw could hear.

On the bed, Gina finally gasped and tensed, her hips rising as Doc's stimulation brought on the paroxysm. When she'd relaxed, Doc stood.

"Feeling better?" he asked as he turned to wash his hands in the small porcelain basin.

"Been a while," she told him.

"The sensation of pressure should be gone." Doc gave her a reassuring smile as Gina pulled her gown down. "If it isn't, send word and I'll come back. If it's bad, and I'm not around, you can conjure your own relief. Or have one of the girls do it for you."

"You mean . . ." She blinked. "Ain't that sinful? Agin' the Bible or something?"

"Not if it's for medical needs," Doc told her. "If it was sinful, God wouldn't have designed a woman's system the way He did when He made

Eve from Adam's rib."

Doc met Butler's eyes and led the way out into the hallway with its sconce lamps, thick Persian rug, and varnished-pine wainscoting.

"The men are still fascinated," Butler told him. "We've learned so much. A man never gives much thought to how different women are from men."

"Are they, Butler? How many times have we heard the story that a young man who bottles up his semen and does not find relief will go crazy?"

"You think that's what happened to me?" Butler blinked. "Are you making fun of the fact that I've never lain with a woman, Philip?"

Doc stopped short at the head of the stairs. "I wasn't aware that you'd never . . . And no, I'm not making fun of you."

"*C'est merde!* Reckon he gonna be thinking on dat something fierce now, Cap'n," Kershaw whispered behind his ear. "Doc dun got a twist in his tail when it come to driving us outta yor head."

Carrying Doc's case, Butler followed his brother down the creaking stairs and into the foyer. Bill Phillips, the "professor" who played the piano and saw to keeping order for Phillipa, beckoned him into the parlor.

Phillipa, a buxom woman in her late thirties, sat behind the parlor table, her cash box before her. She studied Doc and Butler with pale blue eyes that seemed to have lost their fire. She wore a taffeta dress that matched her eyes and accented her curled blond locks.

"Any problems, Doc?"

Butler watched his brother seat himself across from the woman. Doc just had a fluid way about him, an ease of movement, as though he were a man for whom the world had no more surprises.

589

Doc said, "Keep an eye on Amy. I dosed her for the clap. And I treated the new girl, Gina, for hysteria. I suspect that's all she needed, but if she complains about pressure in the next few days, I might need to relieve her again."

Phillipa nodded, lowering her head so that her double chins appeared. "Not my concern anymore. Not after tomorrow. I'm on the street."

"The girls said something about it. What happened?"

She gave him a humorless and wide-lipped grin that exposed the missing premolars in her jaws. "A woman like me shouldn't gamble. That's how I met Big Ed in the first place. He staked me to build this place. Fanciest house in Denver when it went up. Paid him off two years later. And what happens? I'm in the free and clear for less'n a year, and I wager it on a sure thing. A goddamned horse race. Oh, it was a sure thing, all right. Clear up to the moment my horse, two lengths ahead, snaps his right foreleg in two. Tossed the rider down the track for fifty yards."

"If we're talking about the same race," Doc told her, "I set the rider's broken bones."

Phillipa waved around at her fancy parlor with its cut-glass lamps, marble fireplace, and elegant piano. "Difficult come, but sure easy go. Maybe I can start over again. Get another stake from Big Ed."

"And if you can't?" Butler asked offhandedly.

Phillipa fixed him with her faded blue eyes. "Well, crazy man, there's always the whore's slow demise. For as long as the fine clothes last, I can set up in a crib. But at my age, it's gonna have to be dark if I'm going to lure the johnnies in. And after that runs its course, there's always the street.

Walking up on a drunk and riding his johnson in the alley for two bits a go."

"And after that?" Doc asked quietly.

"Maybe I'll land on your porch and beg for a full bottle of laudanum to take down to the river and chug to the dregs. But, enough of that. What do I owe you, Doc?"

"Same as always. Two dollars a girl and five for Amy's dosing."

Butler watched Phillipa count out twenty dollars, hesitate, and add another five.

"Call that last a gratuity, Doc. You were always decent with me and the girls." She glanced at Butler. "Even your crazy brother minded his manners when cunt was flashed in his face."

Doc pushed the five back. "You have more need of that, given the circumstances."

She studied Doc, nodded, and slipped the five into her bosom.

Doc stood, saying, "Phillipa, stay in touch. You have skills. If I hear of anyone needing a manager . . ."

"You're a good man, Doc Hancock." She winked. "You looking for a randy, older wife who could still squeeze your johnson hard enough to . . . Ah, I see. I didn't think you were. But it's nice to get a declining smile instead of a look of outright revulsion."

Doc led Butler to the door, saying, "It's a hard life they're facing, isn't it?"

" 'Oh, soft Eros and Cyprian lady, devise some surge of beauty, I pray.

" 'To smooth between our nipples, and oh, Aphrodite slip beautifully between our brave thighs!" Butler quoted.

"What dat be?" Kershaw asked behind his ear.

"Aristophanes at his cynical best in *Lysistrata.*"

Doc stopped at the door, giving him a look askance. Then he glanced back at Phillipa, still sitting at the table, and called, "This new owner? Who is it?"

"Some Yankee. Tough-looking bastard. Said his name was Win Parmelee."

74

October 5, 1866

That night in Aggie's parlor house, Sarah bent over the ledger book. Its columns of numbers had been carefully entered by her steady hand. Beside her — already stained by the grease on the kitchen table — were her work sheets. On them she first made her columns, writing down from each of the receipts what the expenses were. Only after she had totaled them three times did she laboriously copy them into the ledger book with the sums at the bottom.

She straightened her back, winced at the cramp in her muscles, and paused long enough to sip from her lukewarm coffee cup. Her butt was sore from the uncomfortable wooden chair. The kitchen — always too warm — had brought a sheen of perspiration to her underarms and neck.

Aggie had a cramped but efficient kitchen, with a cast-iron cookstove sporting a warming shelf and water heater. A wooden counter for preparing meats and vegetables stood waist-high along one wall. An icebox, the table at which she labored, and a wall full of shelves that brimmed with pots, pans, cups, and plates completed its furnishings. Just off the back door was a pantry stuffed full of tinned foods. Fresh meat hung in the closed-in porch out back.

Through the kitchen door she could hear the professor's voice rising and falling over the hired violinist and cellist playing music. Central City, with its cosmopolitan and diverse population, produced men with lots of unexpected talents — including remarkable musicians.

Raised as Sarah was in backcountry Arkansas, she'd heard of Mozart but never thought she'd actually hear his music played. The same with Brahms and Beethoven, Handel and Bach. In the months she'd worked at Aggie's, she'd come to appreciate how much life she had missed on the Upper White. As she did, bits and pieces had begun to form in her head. Things she anticipated she would do when she and Bret made their stake and moved to San Francisco. Opera. Symphony. Plays. Books she had never read. So many opportunities awaited her.

But dang! In the meantime she was finding out just how much it cost to run a bordello on the Colorado mining frontier. Central City was so far from anyplace. The most expensive items were the European spirits and specialty foods. She had been stunned just to discover that people ate fish eggs, and was completely floored the first time Aggie showed her one of the little fifty-dollar caviar tins imported from Russia.

In a town where hard-rock miners worked for less than a dollar a day, and twenty-five cents would buy a person a solid meal and a room, fifty dollars for a small can of fish eggs was almost more than she could get her head around.

Then came all the other expenses.

The first few weeks, Sarah had been appalled.

Aggie's ceramic jar had had five dollars that first night. Two the following week. On the third, Aggie had brought the jar down with one hundred and twenty dollars in it.

"I had to pay for a wagonload of supplies," Aggie had explained. "That's all them paper receipts I stacked there. To pay it off, Pat O'Reilly loaned me five hundred dollars."

Her pencil in hand, Sarah had stared, dumbfounded, at the woman. "Aggie, you borrowed five hundred dollars?"

"Well, it ain't the first time." Aggie had given her the look a dog might when caught lifting its leg on a chair.

"How much do you owe Pat O'Reilly?"

"All told?" She'd looked away. "Reckon it's close to six thousand or so. You'd have to ask him." Then she'd dropped down to take Sarah's hand. "That's why you gotta help me, Sarah. We gotta figure out how to make this pay."

And over the months, Sarah had done so. Cutting some expenses, keeping track of orders and deliveries, double-checking the invoices for fraud. The work was dry, for the most part boring, but with it had come triumphs. Aggie's was making a steady profit. Aggie had managed to pay Pat O'Reilly nearly a thousand dollars on her loan, and Sarah had another thousand saved away in a second ceramic jar for an emergency.

She finished her final total as Aggie hurried into the kitchen, her hand pressed to her belly. She wore a green satin dress with velvet trim, cut low on the shoulders to show the cleave between her breasts. Her expression seemed strained as she hurried through and out the back.

Sarah finished her figures, took another drink of

595

her coffee. She was thinking of refilling it, when Aggie stepped back in, her blanched face pinched.

"Are you all right?" Sarah asked.

"Food poisoning. I think." Aggie pressed her hand to her abdomen. "God, please tell me the girls aren't going to come down with . . ." She clapped a hand to her mouth, turned, and charged back out the door.

Sarah stood, poured more coffee, and gave her figures one last look. Aggie's had made a solid seven hundred and fifty dollars and seventy-two cents profit that week. She sat down to do a final count on the money in the ceramic jar when Aggie staggered back in, her dress spotted with vomit.

"Sarah? I'm sick. I hate to ask it, but there's no one else. Could you attend to the gentlemen at the card table? Mick can see to the girls and john-nies. But the men at the game . . ." Her throat worked, and she whirled, fleeing once again into the night in search of the privy.

Sarah took a deep breath, replaced the money, and closed the ledger. Standing, she brushed her skirt, a blue-and-white gingham, and smoothed her blouse. While her apparel was fit for a day dress, compared to Aggie's verdant splendor she looked like a miller moth in a butterfly's shadow. Nor was her hair done; it hung down her back in a simple ponytail.

Nevertheless, a faint smile bent her lips. She'd been desperately curious about Bret's game. Had never set foot beyond the kitchen during business hours. Generally, after the accounting was done, she'd compose herself in the kitchen chair, put her feet up on a keg or coal oil tin, and try to sleep until Bret came to get her. Usually sometime around dawn.

Very well! Sarah had had ample opportunity to watch Mrs. Pennington act the perfect hostess in Little Rock, surely she could do just as well. Sarah left the kitchen, paused long enough to glance in the hallway mirror to ensure she at least looked presentable, and stepped through the door into the small side parlor Aggie had dedicated to the game.

A thick blue cloud of cigar smoke hung low in the light of the oil lamps and stung her nose. She'd expected this, given the way Bret's hair and clothing smelled when he took her home.

Stuffed animal heads hung from two of the walls. A large painting of a much-too-fleshy nude dominated the wall across from her. The artist had apparently never seen how a woman's breasts looked when she reclined on a sofa; the nude's defied both gravity and anatomy.

A serving cart stood in the rear corner, bottles of cognac, whiskey, rum, sherry, and Madeira, ready to pour. Sparkling crystal glasses were stacked to either side, along with a box of two-dollar cigars from which four were missing.

The table was felt-covered and had five chairs, of which three were occupied. Cards, stacks of greenbacks and coins, glasses with various levels of tan-colored liquor, and brass ashtrays marked each player's position.

At her entry the men looked up, Bret's eyes going wide.

The man to his right she recognized as the infamous Pat O'Reilly — a big bluff Irishman with ruddy features, blazing hair tinged with silver at the temples, and a pug nose. He wore a fine charcoal-gray broadcloth suit; diamond cuff links glinted in the light. His hazel eyes fixed first on her face, then he looked her up and down with open admiration, a red eyebrow rising.

The fellow on Bret's left was dapper, mid-thirties, impeccably dressed in a black wool suit with a frock-cut jacket and a frilly cravat at his throat. He had a strong jaw, thick black hair, and dangerous midnight-dark eyes. He stopped short, a card half extended, a hawkish interest glittering behind his stygian gaze.

O'Reilly spoke first, quoting, " 'Oh, wonder! How many goodly creatures are there here. How beauteous womankind is. O brave new world. That has such people in it.' "

Sarah couldn't help herself. " ' 'Tis new to thee.' " She smiled. "But you make a poor Miranda."

The black-haired man, as if not to be outdone, stated, " 'Is she the goddess that hath served us and brought us together?' "

"The goddess, aye," O'Reilly agreed, his voice slightly awed. "And tell me, lassie, where has the lovely Miss Aggie been keeping ye that we've not the joy of yer previous acquaintance?"

Bret spoke firmly. "In the *kitchen*, gentlemen. Doing the accounts. May I present my wife, *Mrs.* Sarah Anderson. And I do stress the missus for a reason. Her employment here is strictly of the nonsporting sort."

Both O'Reilly and the dark-and-dangerous one immediately stood, O'Reilly beating his fellow to take her hand and bow. "My distinct pleasure, Mrs. Anderson. Patrick O'Reilly at your service, ma'am."

"The pleasure, I assure you, is mine, Mr. O'Reilly. I've heard a great deal about you from

Aggie and my husband."

"Alas, madam, I do hope they didn't speak the truth about me, or I'm desolate."

"They speak quite highly, sir."

"George Nichols, ma'am," the dark and handsome one said as he took her hand and kissed it. "Also at your service, though at the moment that service seems to be limited to losing hand after hand to your husband."

"My pleasure to meet you, Mr. Nichols." She took her hand back, oddly uneasy at his continued predatory inspection. Some primal instinct made her wish for her pistol, so long relegated to a place under the bed.

"Sarah?" Bret asked. "Is there a problem?"

"I'm so sorry to interrupt. Aggie has taken ill." She clasped her hands before her. "She has asked me to see to your needs. Can I get you anything?"

Nichols reseated himself, glancing at his fellows. "I might find a plate of oysters suddenly to my liking."

"George, you really are a cadger," O'Reilly said as he seated himself. Looking up at Sarah, he added, "Indeed, Mrs. Anderson, do bring George a plate of oysters. Low as he is, he no doubt needs all the help he can get."

"Coffee?" Bret suggested, the quirking of his lips she recognized as embarrassment.

"Yes, gentlemen."

Retreating to the hallway where the music was louder, she closed the door and frowned, then made her way to the kitchen.

Aggie was back, leaning against the door frame, her bodice unbuttoned, looking hot as she panted, eyes closed. "How are they?"

"Oddly literate. I was greeted with a quote from

599

Shakespeare's *Tempest*. O'Reilly —"

" 'O brave new world'?"

"That's it."

"He says that any time a new girl comes into the place. I hope Bret didn't shoot him."

"Bret was fine. Only asked for a cup of coffee. But after calling me a goddess, Mr. Nichols asked for a plate of oysters. Some interplay I didn't understand." She stepped past Aggie and into the pantry to reach down a tin.

"Bret didn't shoot him?"

"No. Why are you stuck on this?"

"Pat no doubt had a witty comeback?"

"Something about George needing all the help he can get. That's when Bret seemed embarrassed."

Aggie took a deep breath, seeming to be on the verge of agony. "You must have made quite the impression. Oysters? One of the reasons we sell them here? Men think that by eating them, they'll put a little more oak in their peckers."

"Oh, dear God."

Aggie smiled, fought her stomach, and added, "Don't worry, girl. Take George his oysters. If he's thinking along those lines, my guess is before morning, he's going to spend some time with Theresa. I'll have Mick raise her rate another five dollars tonight."

"Why Theresa?"

"Of the two blondes here, she's the one who looks the most like you."

Sarah had a queasy feeling in the pit of her stomach as she cut open the can and spilled the oysters into a china bowl. "How on earth am I going to set these on the table next to Mr. Nichols? I'll be burning red from embarrassment."

Aggie gulped air, hand still to her stomach. "Oh, you'll do fine. Just set them down, and give Bret a big old saucy wink as you do. And if you want to rub it in, tuck your blouse a little tighter into your skirt so that magnificent bust of yours stretches the fabric as you do."

"Aggie!"

"Think of it as strategy. A way to help Bret and our take. Tall and blond, built the way you are? You *are* a goddess. That slight sheen of perspiration and smelling the way you do? Neither O'Reilly nor Nichols is going to have his mind on the cards."

75

December 25, 1866

Billy cried out, sweating, fear running like water in his veins. His body seemed to burn as he backed away, terrified, from the hellish apparition.

"Hey, wake up!"

Billy jerked his eyes open to darkness. Instinctively reached for his pistol. Only to have an iron-like grip fasten on his wrist. Where the hell was he?

He struggled, his assailant pressing down on top of him. He threw himself sideways; they rolled off the bed and slammed to the floor. Panic gave him strength, the banshee presence holding him only adding to his terror.

"Billy! Damn it, it's Danny! Wake up!"

Danny? He stopped struggling, panting in cold air.

"That's it," Danny's voice soothed. "Now, I'm gonna let loose of you. Don't you go grabbing for no gun now, you hear?"

"Danny?" He blinked in the darkness, the floor hard and cold beneath him.

"Yes, *Danny,* you fool."

Billy felt the grip loosen, the weight lifting. He lay panting as Danny's dark form stood and backed away.

"Where the hell are we?"

"Planter's House Hotel. Denver City. You remember?"

Billy felt the fear drain away, sweat cooling in the cold. The terrible images from his nightmare slowly faded, his heart beginning to slow.

"Son of a bitch," he whispered, and sat up.

Danny walked over to the door. Opened it a crack and looked out. "Well, at least there ain't no crowd out here wondering what happened."

Billy pulled himself up to the bed. "What did happen?"

"You was howling. Like the devil hisself had hold o' you. Screaming, 'Maw, I didn't kill her.' And 'Sarah, go back to hell! Leave me alone!' And a whole lotta 'I'm sorry. I'm so sorry!' Like to waked the dead."

Billy rubbed his wet face. "I did?"

The image of Maw was still so clear. She'd risen from the grave, clods of dirt dropping away from her thin bones and gray flesh. Her torn-out eye sockets red and burning, her half-rotted finger pointed at him. Her death-bloated face had been filled with hate.

"This ain't the first time," Danny told him softly. "Mostly, it comes when we're out on the trail. Before a job. I just let you howl until it's all wore out."

"Why do you do that?"

" 'Cause I'm afraid if'n I wakes you up, you'll shoot my ass afore you figger out which world yer in."

Danny settled onto his bed. "Usually you're some better after a killing. Wasn't nothing different about the one you did tonight, was there?"

"Naw, I just walked up behind him and stuck the Bowie up under his ribs. He never had a clue until that blade sliced his insides apart. Wasn't enough left in one piece to let him pull a breath, let alone give off a scream." Billy grinned. "Merry Christmas. Reckon that's all the gift he's ever gonna get."

Danny was silent for a while, head bowed in the darkness.

Softly, he asked, "What happened to Margarita? Seriously? Warn't like you not to talk about her. That clip-jawed 'She run off with a gambler' don't cut no water with me." He paused. "Just answer me this: she didn't make it to Sante Fe at all, did she?"

He didn't know why he said it. Maybe it was the presence of Maw's ghost, ranting and raving mad from the afterlife. "No."

Danny took a deep breath. "Any way anybody gonna recognize her body?"

"No."

Danny exhaled. "Well, at least there's that."

Billy rubbed his face. "I think Sarah's dead, 'cause her spirit done become a demon. Like happens sometimes among the Cherokee. It's 'cause of me letting her get taken. Then all them men used her hard. You should have seen her eyes that day when she went down and cut up Dewley. All crazy and haunted."

"Did Margarita do something to you?"

Billy shook his head. "There's times . . . like with that little Margarita girl, that I got the devil in me. But Sarah's demon? She's plumb evil. Comes in the night, Danny. She's naked, all bit up and bruised, and her hair's blowing around. Her eyes is insane and hellish. I can't run. Can't

604

get up. She stands over me and reaches down. Grabs me by the cock . . . and all hell breaks loose."

"Jesus." Danny gestured his helplessness. "It ain't yer fault, Billy! You saw. You was there when old man Darrow started the raiding. Yankee or Reb. Wasn't no one safe. And it wouldn't have made no difference if'n you'd been there when Dewley rode in. They'd a shot you down without a chance. Yer Maw'd still be dead. And not only would Sarah have been taken and raped and kilt, but you'd be dead, too."

"I was responsible."

"That's no more than horse shit in the street. You saved your sister, and at least your maw got a decent burial. And you're still alive. She'd a wanted that."

"Not as a devil-filled killer."

"So, stop! We'll walk away. We got enough money. Hell, let's go back to Arkansas. Buy a farm. Make whiskey. Hunt for a living. Who cares?"

"Can't quit," Billy said quietly as he continued to rub his shaking hands over his hot face.

"Why not, fer God's sake? So what if the Meadowlark just up and disappears? George Nichols can do his own killin'."

"I gotta pay."

"You already paid enough, Billy."

He shook his head. "That's what Maw rises up from the grave to tell me. That I let the devil into my heart, and I'm his. It's just a matter of time, Danny. I'm damned. He can collect me whenever he wants, and God's gonna look the other way. Then it's just Sarah's demon and me, fighting it out for all eternity."

"Billy, if you'd just let me —"

"I *fuck* my sister in my dreams! I'm a *sick* son of a bitch, Danny." He laughed in open defiance of the desolation inside him. "And one of these days, I gotta burn in hell fer it."

76

December 27, 1866

"Who is he?" Doc asked as he stepped out of his surgery and into the front office where Big Ed Chase waited before the heat stove. Doc was still drying his hands after washing them. There had been a lot of blood as the frozen corpse thawed.

Doc's front office was ten by twenty, the room finished in cut pine, spruce, and fir — depending upon what had been hauled down from the mountains on any given day. The room still had the smell of fresh-cut lumber. Two windows looked out onto snowy Fifteenth Street. Pocked by horse and human tracks, lined from wheeled traffic, the street sported frozen piles of horse manure and a couple of empty bottles abandoned just out past Doc's boardwalk.

Big Ed Chase turned, fixing Doc with his hard blue eyes. The man was six foot four, with pale blond hair. The broad jaw, wide and firm mouth, and prominent nose gave his face a powerful look — one that complemented his position in Denver society. Chase wore a buffalo coat, now thrown back on his shoulders to expose his fine black wool sack suit and the boiled white shirt beneath.

Not only was Chase on the city council, he and

his partners controlled the city's entertainment business. When it came to the better gambling dens, parlor houses, theaters, dance halls, hurdy-gurdy, and burlesque, Big Ed had an interest, as he did in much of Denver City's prime real estate.

In the beginning, Big Ed had made a name for himself running fair games, and overseeing it all from a high stool in the middle of the tables. He always kept a loaded shotgun laid across his lap. So intimidating was he, that he had never had to use the scattergun to enforce his warnings. He backed people he thought were winners, investing in such diverse enterprises as Phillipa's parlor house, and Doc's surgery.

Big Ed said, "The man you just looked at back there was called Nelson Dunn. If it wasn't for these damn dog packs running loose all over the city, we might not have found him for months. The mongrels had dragged him out from under a pile of tin cans down by the river. One of the marshals recognized him and sent word to me. I had Macy bring him to you. What can you tell me about how he died?"

"Well" — Doc propped his butt on the corner of his desk, arms crossed — "he wasn't out for long. Cold as it is, he wasn't froze all the way through. It's a guess, and only a guess, but I'd say he was stabbed Christmas night. Whoever did it came up from behind, stuck a long, sharp knife in just under the floating ribs, and very efficiently cut through the diaphragm, lower lobes of both lungs, and the bottom of the heart."

"But what does that tell us, Doc? About the killer, I mean?"

Doc spread his hands wide. "Well, sir, I can tell you it wasn't a street fight, brawl, or misunderstanding that led to violence. It wasn't robbery. Mr. Dunn was wearing a money belt. Something any thief would have found. The killer was strong, silent, and right-handed. No way you could consider this as a random street crime. The assassin knew who his target was and wanted him dead."

"An assassin."

Doc shrugged. "Whoever killed Mr. Dunn did a damn competent job of it. He was either practiced, or damn lucky."

"It wasn't luck." Ed Chase took a deep breath and walked back over to the stove where he extended his large hands to the heat.

"Then you might have a better understanding than I do."

Chase's wide lips bent in a humorless smile. "Your brother back there?"

"We've rented a small house. I found a copy of *Uncle Tom's Cabin* and gave it to him for Christmas. When I left, he was reading it aloud to his imaginary men. Given they were all Confederates, it's been a lively old time."

The smile widened on Chase's lips. "You're a good man, Doc. You don't talk, so I'll tell you that Nelson Dunn was my agent in a land deal. The hope was to encourage a group of investors back East to build a smelter. The gold is still up there in the mountains, but it's locked up by something called sulfides. I don't understand the chemistry, but the mercury pans won't pick it up. The gold goes right out with the tailings."

Chase frowned down at the stove. "Building a smelter here, we could process the ore. Not just from the mines up around Central City, but the whole Front Range. That gold would flow through

Denver, making people rich from the top down to the workers. All of whom in turn need a fair game, entertainment, and refreshment."

Chase smiled tightly. "Which, along with the value of the land I was offering through Mr. Dunn, would continue to make me a tidy profit."

"So you think one of your rivals removed Mr. Dunn from making the play?"

"It appears so. Currently those investors are up in Black Hawk, looking at potential land. Nelson was supposed to carry the offer to them today. But one of the Black Hawk or Central City interests appears to have gotten to him first."

"What about Mr. Dunn's body?"

"Put him on ice, Doctor. I'll cover his burial out at Jack O'Neill's ranch when the ground thaws." Jack O'Neill's ranch. What they called the local cemetery.

Chase started for the door, and then turned back. "Doctor, I hear you've become quite the hero to the demimonde. But I understand that you don't seem to avail yourself of their charms as your predecessors did. Nor do I hear of you investigating the eligible young ladies on the respectable side of our city, few as they may be."

Doc lifted a skeptical eyebrow. "Sir, I am full-time caretaker for my brother. Until I find a cure for his ailment, I suspect my chances of paying court are rather limited." Doc wadded the washcloth into a ball. "It's hard to impress my fine prospects upon a young lady when I have an entire company of Arkansas infantry in attendance whenever Butler is around."

Chase narrowed his eyes. "I also hear that when you attend our most soiled of doves, you don't seem to betray the distaste that others in your profession do."

"Mr. Chase." Doc pushed off from his desk, walking over to look up at the man. "My first professional surgery was in a brothel, and at the time, I swore I'd never stoop that low again. Along came a war, and prison camp, the loss of everything. Butler dropped into my life. I had to live for him. After all that, I gave up worrying about morality, and virtue, and sin, and damnation. Because as low as these women might fall, I've been lower."

Chase considered him, the cold blue eyes thoughtful. Then he shrugged his buffalo coat onto his shoulders saying, "I would appreciate it if you'd keep our conversation about Nelson private."

"Of course, sir."

Chase stepped to the door, reached in his pocket and tossed Doc a twenty-dollar gold piece. "For looking after Nelson."

"Oh, Ed? One last thing." Doc reached into his pocket. "I found this on the body. Stuck in the wound actually."

Big Ed took it. "A feather?"

"I'm no expert, but I think it's from a meadowlark. And there are no meadowlarks around this time of year."

Almost beyond hearing, Big Ed whispered, "George Nichols." And then he was gone.

77

March 15, 1867

Sarah sat at her kitchen table, a flannel robe wrapped about her. She leaned with her elbows on the wood, watching the sky beyond her ice-rimmed window. A cup of coffee was cupped in her hands. Below her, Central City was dusted in white, as were the naked mountain slopes rising to all sides. Snow covered a lot of ugliness. It was the only time Central City and its sprawling, claptrap neighbor camps were in any way, manner, or form, pretty.

Only the distant peaks, so frosted and still-timbered, provided a sense of beauty. As if a beacon that heaven existed, but that to find it, a person was required to travel as far from Central City and its mine-scarred slopes as the eye and imagination would take them.

Sarah inhaled the aroma of her coffee as the woodstove popped and crackled behind her — the little explosions from the burning juniper powerful enough to puff tiny wreaths of smoke past the stove lids.

She'd been saving the few lengths of juniper that came mixed among the pine, spruce, and fir. It added a special aroma to the house.

Also, this day had been special. She and Bret had arrived home early from Aggie's. Bret's game was now two nights a week. Aggie had bought the lot next to her parlor house, and was expanding. She had hired two new girls brought in from Chicago by a cadet, or procurer, named Philo Waltee. In spite of the fact that many of the locals were worried about the reduced production from the mines, Aggie's continued to draw an ever larger and more prosperous clientele.

The gold was there, but in lode deposits, locked in sulfates, and impossible to separate from the ore. Miners, owners, and merchants alike waited, word having passed that a smelter was coming to Black Hawk. That a man named Hill had a process that offered the hope of as much as eighty to ninety percent gold recovery from the recalcitrant ore.

Those thoughts, however, barely nagged at her as she watched the intermittent clouds rolling off the high peaks.

By all accounts, she and Bret would be gone before the smelter was built. Together they had invested most of their stake — nearly six thousand dollars — to allow Aggie to buy the lot, raze the rickety laundry, and begin construction on an addition that would house a larger gaming room downstairs and additional girls on the second floor.

Construction was scheduled to be finished by the end of May. Sarah estimated that come September her twenty percent share of the additional income would have repaid her investment, and would put her and Bret above their ten-thousand-dollar goal.

By Christmas, she figured, they would be in San

Francisco and living like the lordly rich.

Funny how the world worked. All those childhood visions of fine houses, status, an influential husband in high society, raising children, and ordering servants about had been centered on her man's success alone. Not once had she anticipated happiness or love, or even considered them goals to be striven for, let alone achieved.

Bret opened the door, bursting in, and pressing it firmly closed. "Bloody hell, it's cold out there!" he blurted as he slipped his thick buffalo coat off and hung it on the hook by the door.

She laughed at the sight of him, shivering, as he clumped over to the stove and extended his hands to the heat. "Well, you fool, it has to be below zero. What kind of an idiot trots off to the outhouse in cold like this dressed only in long handles, a buffalo coat, and boots?"

He grinned at her, relishing the heat. Then he poured himself a cup of coffee, kicked the chair out, and seated himself opposite her.

His dark eyes were alight as he studied her through the steam rising from his enameled cup. That faint smile curled his lips. A couple of flakes of snow melted, gleaming like dew in his rich brown hair. Her stomach warmed at the animation in his eyes, the almost worship that seemed to radiate from his very soul.

"What are you thinking?" he asked.

"About happiness. I never thought I'd have it. And I thought love was some sort of mutual admiration and respect. A species of fond duty. Had you asked me, the notion of a lover as a best friend, a confidant and partner, would have entirely eluded me."

"We do rather suit each other, don't we? And

614

this morning was . . . ethereal." The little dimples were forming in his cheeks.

"Proud of yourself?" she asked.

His grin burst into a satisfied smile. "What do you think? A couple of times I thought my body was going to burst. Nor did I know you could move like that."

Even the thought of their long morning beneath the blankets brought a tingle to her loins. Dear God, was she insatiable?

She said, "We just seem to get better and better with each other. If I didn't keep the inventory, I'd think you'd been into Aggie's oysters. Where *do* you get the stamina?"

"You have the nerve to sit there with your hair spilling over your shoulders like flowing gold and piercing my soul with those sparkling blue eyes, your long, lithe body stretched out like the goddess you are, and ask me a question like that? I need only look at you, let alone run my hand over your skin, and somehow my cock can raise itself from the dead."

"Isn't it peculiar, Bret? As women we're raised with the notion that the connubial act is an unfortunate but necessary duty." She inclined her head. "The very idea that it is enjoyable, let alone that such sensations . . . Well, let's just say I feel like I've been catapulted out of a dark and benighted pit into a brilliant revelation." She paused. "Is this some secret married people keep among themselves?"

"No. For most it's considered a mere necessity to produce children. They've turned it into a moral battlefield filled with flying shot and shell. One that has to be negotiated so very carefully."

"And it's not like this for the line girls, either, is it?"

"To them it is a job. Get him on, get him in, trip his trigger, get him off, and entice the next one. Business. Pure and simple."

"So, how did we get so lucky?"

He gave her his tantalizing wink. "We are pariahs, you and I. And being so, we are set free to explore beyond the bounds of what our choke-throated, respectable brethren back in civilization consider prudent and godly."

He reached out, taking her hand and giving it a gentle squeeze. "I made the oath to love you with all of myself. Without reservation of body or soul, and in return, I would take any crumb you offered. First you gave me your companionship, and then your trust, and finally your body and soul. You gave me my life, a direction, and a way to discover who I am as a man. And being a pariah, I can love you down to the last drop of my blood." He squeezed her hand again. "If I could, I'd put you inside me and melt your soul into mine."

Her throat tightened; her heart skipped.

"Bret? I've never told you that I loved you."

"Nor would I ask you to."

She returned the squeeze of his hand. "I think, my dear, that we've saved each other. I spend most of my hours dreaming of you, seeing your smile, hearing what you'd say in response to my thoughts or notions. I try to keep that sparkle in your eyes down in a safe place inside my soul. I dream of your body, of holding you close, and locking you inside while we make love. If that isn't loving you with everything I've got, what is?"

He swallowed hard, his smile trembling, an upheaval behind his glistening eyes. His voice

616

almost broke as he said, "You have no idea what that means to me."

"Never leave me, Bret Anderson."

"Not even with my dying breath. We're going to live, Sarah. Do all those things you've been dreaming about. We're going to spend each day experiencing everything life has to offer. Never the trite or mediocre."

She raised an eyebrow. "And if a child should come along?"

He locked his eyes with hers. "I'm surprised one hasn't, given our healthy and athletic relationship. I will follow your wishes."

"Meaning?" She felt her curiosity rising, having wondered what his desires were.

"Sarah, I can live with you as we are. Just you and me, adventuring and savoring life to the fullest. Were we to have a child, I will dedicate myself to loving it and raising it as a shared and cherished creation of our love. And, by God above, I swear I will be a better father than that cold fish who raised me."

"I may not be able to have children, Bret. I've never told you. Never told anyone. After the rape . . . I knew I was pregnant. Hated it. Wanted it out. Did things. And one day, something tore inside me. Out it came."

She paused, watching his eyes. "I don't know what it did to my insides."

His smile comforted, his hand gentle on hers. "Whatever comes, I will welcome it with delight and anticipation. I just want you."

She smiled. "What about marriage?"

"Of course. If you'd like. Would it make a difference?"

"I have no idea." She shrugged. "I won't love

you more for having stood up in a church. As far as I am concerned, Bret, you're my husband. Right here. In the eyes of God, I declare it. In sickness and in health, until death do we part."

"And I you," he replied, his voice gone husky again.

She reveled in the glistening depths of his soft brown eyes, seeing right down to his emotional soul. Dear God, so this is what it really meant to be loved? How on earth had she ever managed to find this one man? This mate for her soul and dreams?

"Come on, Bret. I just declared our honeymoon." She pulled him to his feet, leading him back to the bed. "Hope you ate enough oysters, because now that we're officially man and wife, I want to see just how far beyond 'conjugal duties' two pariahs can go."

78

April 22, 1867

The knock in the middle of the night sounded oddly timid.

"Coming," Doc called as he slipped his feet into his worn slippers and made his way from the cramped bedroom in the back of the small frame house.

The night was as black as pitch, and he could hear water dripping from the eaves as he hurried across the front room.

At the door, he fumbled for the matches, struck one alight, and lifted the chimney as he lit the wick. Holding the light, he unbolted the door and opened it.

Three wet and bedraggled women, scantily dressed in white cotton chemises, huddled together under the protection of his small porch. Two were holding up the third, and now he could see the rain-washed pink of blood.

"Come in," he urged, throwing the door wide. As they did, he raised the lamp, peering out into the gently falling spring rain. The lamp's feeble light failed to pierce the cold stygian darkness.

Closing the door behind him, he followed the girls, who had veered into the small parlor and eased the bleeding girl onto Butler's chaise longue where he "read to his men."

"Sorry, Doc. Didn't know where else to go." The first of them turned to him, pulling back her wet and dark hair with thin white fingers. She stared at him with worried eyes made large where kohl had run and streaked her cheeks. Water beaded on her face, her thin cotton chemise clinging. Her nipples stood out on her breasts, the wet fabric outlining her belly and the concavity of her navel.

"What's happened?" Doc asked, bending down with his light. The second of the girls was holding the wounded one's hand, whispering, "Gina? We got you to Doc Hancock. It's gonna be all right."

"Excuse me." He bent down, holding the light as he raised Gina's chin, seeing the bruises, her left eye almost swollen closed. As he lifted, he felt bone rasp in her mandible. Broken jaw. "What happened? Who did this?"

"Parmelee. That mother-fucking bastard!" The first almost spat the words.

"Amy!" the second cried in shock. "You'll get us th'owed out! Then what?"

"No one's being thrown out for profanity," Doc told them, pressing fingers to Gina's neck and finding a strong pulse. "Let's get back to the beating. I assume that's what this Parmelee did?"

Amy crossed her arms, apparently unconcerned about how it displayed her breasts. "It ain't been the same since Phillipa left. Parmelee is a whore's nightmare. Don't know how, but he done found the roughest johnnies in Colorado. Advertises that we'll do exotic. Like he can find every headsick fuck in the country . . . and ain't no limit. Then Gina today, she had Collette and me giving her

620

the relief. You know, like you said we should when we get the hysteria?"

Collette, the second, interrupted. "Well, we was on Gina's bed, giving her the relief. She says it helps with two to do it, and Parmelee just busts in. He takes one look and bellows, 'By damn, I ain't even off to Central to kill that deserting son of a bitch, and you're giving it to each other for free.' And he just tore into us."

Doc watched Gina gasp as he felt along her ribs, finding a hardening bruise. "He kicked her? That how he broke her ribs?"

"Yes, sir. After he'd throw'd her on the floor," Amy added. "Collette and me, we just got hit and smacked a couple of times. But he was plumb gleeful going after Gina. She done give him lip a couple of times. Ain't the first time he beat her, neither. Said she bit his cock one time when he had her playing his flute."

"Why'd you bring her to me?"

" 'Cause you're a good man, Doc." Amy stared down at him with desperate eyes. "We gotta get her help. Parmelee, he don't got no doc. He just doses us once a month for the clap hisself. Says why should he pay a sawbones for what he can do for free."

Doc took a deep breath. "Oh, hell."

"Doc?" Butler asked, appearing in the parlor doorway. He was rubbing his eyes, wearing his long handles, partially exposed since the fly was unbuttoned. He glanced around at the girls, saying, "It's all right, Johnny. Report to the sergeant that the rest of the men should stay in bivouac."

"He thinks he's a johnny?" Collette wondered.

"He's referring to Johnny Baker, one of his phantom men," Doc told her. "This is crazy

621

Butler, my brother." He turned. "Butler, go get my case. We've got work to do."

As Butler vanished into the hallway, Doc asked, "What about Parmelee? Surely he knows you're missing."

Amy, arms still crossed, shrugged. "He lit out for Central City. The professor's running the house. We took Gina off the line, of course. Then when the last of the johnnies left, Elvina and Circe grabbed the professor by the cock and dragged him off to Circe's room. They figgered they could keep him the rest of the night with a twosome so's we could get Gina looked at."

"You gotta fix her," Collette insisted, "so's we can get her back a'fore the professor's back on watch."

Doc raised Gina's eyelids. Even in the lamplight he could see the two different sizes of pupils. "She's not going back," Doc said sadly. "He kicked her in the head, too, didn't he?"

"Doc," Amy pleaded. "Come morning, if the professor don't find her in bed, we're all gonna pay. He'll know he's been had."

Doc sat back, looking up at the terrified women. "She may not come out of this as it is. She's got a broken jaw and an injured brain. When I press on her abdomen, it's hard, which means she's bleeding on the inside."

Butler appeared, wedging himself into the small room and setting Doc's case on the floor. He bent to open it.

Doc said, "I'm going to treat her pain with opiates, and I can bind her ribs. Once she's out I'll see if there's anything I can do about her jaw. But if this girl's got any chance to live, you're not taking her back there."

Collette's thin face whitened, her wet hair leaking water onto her shoulders. "What are we gonna do? The professor's gonna know someone had to help Gina get away. And he's damn sure gonna know it was me and Amy."

Doc carefully rearranged Gina's wet hair then reached for his bottle of chloroform. "How about all three of you get out of there? If you want to relocate, I can find you safer houses either here or in Colorado Springs, Cheyenne, or Colorado City."

He had not only discreetly been treating Margaret Jane Chase, Big Ed's wife, but also the kingpin's mistress from the theater at the Cricket. Ed owed him a favor or two.

Amy's expression pinched, her eyes hardening. "And what's in it for you, Doc? You get a piece of our action from here on out? A man don't do for the likes of us w'thout he's gonna get his pockets lined or get his johnson slick for free from now on."

Doc smiled wearily, watching Butler's lips quiver as he whispered to his men in secret. "Nothing's in it for me. I can get you moved into houses under Big Ed's protection, or at least up to Cheyenne with enough for stage fare to End-of-the-Tracks or Salt Lake. Meanwhile I need one of you to slip back and get those other two out without the professor knowing. And once you're relocated, you'll never, ever, mention this again to another soul." He looked back and forth. "We clear?"

Amy looked warily at Collette. "If Circe and Elvina had any damned sense, they'd have doped him to the gills to keep him from thinking."

Collette, however, remained fixed on Doc. "So,

we just supposed to think you a saint? That it?"

"Actually, Collette, I don't know what I did to offend God, unless it was pride. But I made my deal. If, by my actions, I can convince God to restore my brother's sanity, I'll do whatever it takes." He paused. "And then there's the pragmatic. Parmelee left for Central City? To deal with some gambler?"

Amy shrugged. "Reckon he'll be gone a couple of days."

Doc turned to Butler. "It's a little after three. I need you to be at Macy's by six. Tell him I need a favor. A place for four, and hopefully five, girls under Big Ed's protection."

But even as he spoke, Gina twitched, her breath rattling in her throat as she spasmed and died.

79

May 4, 1867

Billy glanced up and down Eureka Street. He had just located a livery for Locomotive, paid the exorbitant rate for stabling, and was told, "This is Central City, boy. Got to haul in hay! It sure don't grow on these cussed mountains, young man." The gangly owner had stuck his thumbs in his hip pockets in emphasis.

Billy walked along the busy avenue, his boots thumping on the boardwalk. Around him, the denuded hills had begun to green, spring coming as late as it did to the high country. But, scarred as they were by diggings, roads, and colorful waste and tailings, they reminded him oddly of a battlefield and its fortifications.

So this was Central City? The "richest square mile on earth" sure as hell didn't look like much. Just a ragtag collection of frame and log buildings jumbled together in the valley bottoms. Unlike any town Billy had been in before; from the moment he'd ridden over Dory Hill and down the road to Gregory Toll Gate, the conglomeration of buildings had reminded him of a town on a string — crowded as the communities were along the bottoms of the gulches.

While mining had taken a downturn after the war, the big news was that a new smelter was going in down in Black Hawk. The one being built by Nathaniel Hill's Boston and Colorado Smelting Company. All Billy had heard was that it would unlock a fortune in gold from high-testing ore.

Stepping from the boardwalk, he started up the hill toward High Street. He got his bearings and made his way to the rather imposing frame house, whitewashed, with red trim around the windows. It had been set on a foundation of native rock, and smoke rose from a redbrick chimney.

Billy clumped his way up the steps, spurs jingling, cast a look up and down the street, then knocked at the ornately carved door.

Moments later a well-dressed woman answered, asking, "Yes, may I help you?" Her shrewd eyes took in Billy's travel-worn clothing, his muddy boots, and soot-stained coat.

"I'm looking for George Nichols. Heard he was boarding here."

"If you would be so kind as to give me your name, I will see if Mr. Nichols is scheduled to receive you."

Billy laughed, slapping his side. "Reckon he ain't scheduled to receive shit, ma'am. Why don't you run back and tell him that Billy Hancock would like a word. Tell him I want to talk about a little bird. That I'm an old friend from just outside Albuquerque." He flicked his fingers. "Now, go on. Shoo."

As he talked, her dark eyes had frosted, expression turning glacial. She closed the door in his face with a bang, and he heard her steps hurrying into the rear.

Billy grinned, worked his tongue around his dry lips, and looked up and down the street. No one was giving him a second glance.

He heard the woman's hammering steps approaching, and the door was opened. Her expression was, if anything, more prim. "I have relayed your information to Mr. Nichols. He asked me to convey his intent to meet with you at the Colorado Nugget at two P.M. You will find the establishment on Main, just past Gregory Street. Good day."

And the door closed again, the bolt clicking home.

Billy narrowed an eye at the door. Considered busting the damn thing down, and decided against it. Maybe George had his own concerns.

Billy skipped his way down the wooden steps to the rocky and rutted street, and proceeded — stopping to ask directions once — to the Colorado Nugget.

The place was a saloon, built wall to wall on a narrow half lot between a laundry on one side and a harness shop on the other. Entering, he found a long bar made of rough-cut lumber running the length of the place.

Bottles lined narrow shelves behind the bar, and a man in a stained white shirt wearing an apron stood ready to dispense drinks. As Billy entered, the barkeep was talking to two miners, their pants tucked into muddy boots.

All three looked up, taking Billy's measure as he walked down the narrow aisle, his shoulder rubbing the wall. Must have been a common practice because the wood looked polished.

"What time is it?" Billy asked.

"Little after one, mister. Make yourself at home.

627

What can I get you?"

"Supposed to meet a man here at two. You got a good rye?"

"Such as it is." The barkeep turned back to a bottle. "Can't hardly get the good stuff. The damn Injuns got the trails shut down to the point only large caravans with army escort make it through. That's what we get for turning that damn Chivington and his murderers loose."

Both the miners grunted, taking in Billy's garb.

"Some folks still call him a hero," Billy noted, tossing a silver dollar onto the bar.

The bartender offered him a tin cup filled with brown liquid. "Up to the Masonic lodge, it used to be called Chivington Lodge Number One. They got so disgusted they sent back the charter. Now they're Central Lodge Number Six. You see, here's the thing: you kill a man's wife, cut her privates out of her body and stretch her cunny into a hatband? Kill his little boy and little girl and scalp 'em? Don't matter that he's a red savage, he's gonna fight and kill every white man he sees till he's dead and gone to the spirit world to find his loved ones."

"Like poking a wasp nest with a stick," one of the miners said, his accent thick with Cornwall.

"I'll leave that for you gentlemen to decide." His eyes having adjusted, Billy could see a table in the back and made his way.

The rye — or whatever it was — warmed his belly, reminding him he ought to think about eating. His last meal had been beans and sowbelly at a roadhouse in Golden Gulch that morning.

The time passed slowly, Billy sitting in the back, nursing his drink, his coat thrown wide. He'd eased the thong off the Remington's hammer, just in case George had either caught a whiff of why Billy'd come, or even had a change of heart about their relationship.

It must have been a little before two when the back door opened and George Nichols slipped in wearing a slouch hat and an oiled canvas slicker. To look at him, he might not have been anything but a local miner. Unless one noticed his polished boots.

"How do, George?" Billy asked, his right hand easing the Remington out beneath the table.

"Mr. Hancock," George said, tipping the brim of his hat with a lazy finger. He walked to the bar, calling, "Whiskey, Mooney."

Mooney poured and asked, "You know a Win Parmelee, Mr. Nichols?"

"Not to my knowledge. Should I?"

"He's asking around about that gambler friend of yours as runs the games up at Aggie's. Just an impression, mind you, but you might want to keep an eye on Parmelee. To my reckoning, he's trouble."

"I'll have some of my people ask around, Mooney. Thanks."

"We'll give you your privacy, Mr. Nichols." Mooney told the others, "You boys, let's go down here by the front door so's we don't bother Mr. Nichols."

Cup in hand, George walked back, pulled out the opposite chair, and seated himself. He sipped at the drink, made a face, and said softly, "So, what brings you here, Billy?"

Billy eased the pistol back into its holster, then reached for his coat pocket. He slipped a piece of paper across the table. "Ripped that out of the *Rocky Mountain News.* As you might imagine, having just traveled down from South Pass City, Danny and I were somewhat out of sorts to read this."

Nichols pulled the torn sheaf of newsprint his way, glanced at it, and nodded, not even bothering to read it.

Barely above a whisper, Billy told him, "Headline says, 'South Pass City Speculator Murdered.' Then it goes on to say that Harold Jones was gunned down outside Atlantic City by an unknown party. Local sources suspect the paid assassin known as the 'Meadowlark.' "

"It does indeed say that."

"Why'd you tell them about me, George?"

Nichols made sure the barkeep and his clients were out of hearing. Voice low, he asked, "You left the feather, didn't you?"

"Sure. But someone had to give them the name."

"Billy, there's times that a threat has no value unless it has a name. A dangerous name. Time's come for the Meadowlark to gain a little notoriety. Sometimes, just leveling the threat is as powerful as the killing itself."

Billy felt his heart slow, the deadly hollow emptying his gut. His fingers danced lightly on the Remington's grip. "You start advertising my killings, they're gonna start putting the facts together. Lookin' to see who's profited by the killin' . . . and it's gonna lead right to you. The Meadowlark's a tool, just like a single jack, and you're the one a-swinging it."

"Way ahead of you, Billy." George leaned back, tilting his head so he could peer out from beneath the low brim. "Got Meadowlark stories planted in California, Nevada, and Arizona. Places you've never been. Unsolved murders of prominent folks

630

whose holdings I never had anything to do with. So, who's behind the Meadowlark? Some interest from the Comstock? Or Sacramento? You lay false trails to cover your tracks, just like I do mine."

"Wish you'd talked to me first."

"I would have loved to, had I known where you might have been on any given day or even in which territory." Nichols chuckled. "If anything, speculation about the Meadowlark will work to your advantage. Facile minds will soon attribute any unsolved murder to his name."

"What's facile?"

"Easy and simple. Even the garroting of a drunk in an alley in Cheyenne or Salt Lake will be blamed on the mysterious Meadowlark. People will latch onto it like wildfire; it will bring notoriety to their otherwise squalid little communities."

Billy took a deep breath and another sip of the whiskey. The thing about having money was that a person got used to good stuff. This was real piss in a cup.

"Other than discovering that nice new feather in your cap, if I may make a pun," Nichols asked, "how are you and Danny doing?"

"Got no complaints. It's been like you said, George. We get back to Denver, or wire a transfer, and the money's always been there. Sometimes it don't make no sense why we're killin' someone, but we assume you got yer reasons."

"Oh, yes." George leaned forward. "You or Danny ever decide you want to quit? Want to go back to being plain old Billy Hancock? I've got a separate account set aside for you. Enough you can buy a nice farm in Arkansas, New Mexico, or California. Hell, go back East if you want and be

631

a high roller."

"Why would you do that?"

George studied him thoughtfully. "You're not a stupid man, Billy. Neither am I. I'd be willing to bet you were ready to shoot me when I walked in here, which is why you didn't stand up and offer to shake hands. No, you had your pistol hid out under the table in case it was a double-cross."

"Maybe."

"So we're sort of like the scorpion and the tarantula dancing around each other. Both deadly. And how do we keep from killing each other? The best way is to be honest and fair. Do you know how much faith I put in the virtue of loyalty?"

"Haven't a clue."

"Loyalty for loyalty's sake isn't worth spit in the street." Nichols raised a cautionary finger. "But financial interest? That's where the daisies flourish. Each time you've removed an obstacle, I've made a pile of money. So, if you ever decide you want out? You'll get a piece. The longer you play, the bigger the pile."

"You expect me to believe you're doing this out of the better angels in your nature?"

"Hell, no. It keeps you from selling me out to one of my rivals, say, Ralston, Sharon, or Rockefeller. I have removed the financial incentive."

"Got an answer for everything, don't you?"

Nichols leaned back, arm extended to his whiskey. "Billy, when this is all said and done, I want to be the most powerful man in the Rocky Mountains. You take care of me, and I'll take care of you."

"What about Danny?"

"Do with him what you will. He's your associate. Your responsibility. You're the smart one with

632

vision. That is . . . as long as you don't let your personal demons destroy you."

"What demons?"

"Heard a girl disappeared down in New Mexico." Nichols smiled, adding lightly, "Heard she run off with a gambler?"

"Danny tell you that?"

Nichols shook his head slowly. "I'm not the one to go meddling in your business, but don't ever think I'm not keeping track of my interests."

At the words, the Devil's fingers stroked coolly down Billy's back.

80

May 6, 1867

Patrick O'Reilly clattered into Sarah and Bret's yard and reined his team to a stop.

Wiping her hands on a cloth, Sarah watched him through the window. She smoothed her dark chintz housedress and batted at the full cut of her bishop sleeves where flour clung to them. Why did she always turn into a mess when she was baking?

Her hair was tied back in a ponytail and unfit to be seen, but Pat was climbing down from his phaeton. She dared not leave him standing outside while she took the time to fix it.

Sarah opened the door and stepped out onto her porch. The midday sun glimmered on distant, snow-capped Mount Black Hawk. She shielded her eyes, calling, "Hello, Mr. O'Reilly. How are you today?" Her breath hung before her only to vanish in an instant in the cool air.

"Quite well, Mrs. Anderson." He pulled himself up, as if at attention. As he doffed his homburg hat, his ruddy Irish face bent with a smile. He wore a black wool sack coat over a thick brown-and-black checked vest. A high collar stuck up almost to his ears, and his trousers were wrinkled. Looking at him, it was hard to believe he was one of the city's most prominent men.

"I'd invite you in, but Bret is still asleep."

"No need, dear lady." Reaching into a coat pocket, he removed an envelope. "The game down to the hotel saloon ran a wee bit late last night. I had the most damnable luck, and Bret, saint that he is, covered my debts. I told him I'd repay him by noon, but — foul wretch that I be — you'll notice tis nearly two-thirty."

"Mr. O'Reilly, I sincerely doubt Bret would care. Not only does he refer to you as a gentleman, but he considers you a friend."

O'Reilly handed the envelope over, sighing as he did so. "I think he be the only mon in this dad-blasted excuse fer a city that I admire and envy, lassie." He gave her a twinkling wink. "And tis all because he has you."

"You're too kind."

O'Reilly's expression sobered. "Oh, not at all. You saved Aggie. I was on the verge o' calling her loan. I loike the lassie, but I wasn't throwing good money after bad. 'Twas her property and building I was after. And I told her right out."

"She just needed to figure it out, Mr. O'Reilly. No one trains women how to run a business."

"Nor yourself, either, I'd wager." He was watching her through wary Irish eyes. "And I'm well aware that you are the root o' her salvation. My dear old father, may he rest in peace, told me once that nothing on earth was more dangerous than a competent woman with a clever and cunning moind. But then, I've always appreciated and been drawn to danger."

He gave her a slight bow.

"I'll convey your warning to Bret."

"Aye, an' I've already told him till the poor

mon's ears are blue." O'Reilly waved it away. "But since we're sharing hearts and souls, I'll tell you this: a smart one he is. Perhaps the best hand at cards I've ever known. He plays us loike fiddles, ye know? Knows his odds as if he can see through the cards. Lets us win just enough that we don't know we're being skinned."

"Mr. O'Reilly? If you know, why do you play?"

"Why, to beat 'im, o' course! The mon is master! Loike one 'o them swordsmen in France, I know he's better, eh? But playing 'im, I sharpen me own skills."

She laughed. "I still do not understand men."

"Nor I women. Makes us even, lassie."

"Could I get you a cup of tea? Perhaps water?"

"No. I'm just going to admire the view for a moment more, and then I've got to get to the moine. The superintendents have need o' a decision before they dig me more gold."

"Not much of a view from here. Most of the high peaks are blocked by the clouds today."

"Wasn't the mountains I was lookin' at," he said easily.

"You are a tease." She caught movement down on the slope road where it wound past miners' shacks, sheds, and prospect holes. She squinted, knowing that familiar phaeton. "Speaking of which, isn't that Aggie now?"

O'Reilly turned, shaded his eyes, and added, "Aye, 'tis. Yor day fer foine comp'ny, I'd say."

"She seems to be in a hurry."

Moments later, Aggie drove her carriage into the yard, pulling up short of O'Reilly's. She fought the brake, spoke calmingly to her half-winded horse, and pulled up her full-cut poplin skirt to step down and hurry across the rocky yard.

"Aggie?" O'Reilly called. "What brings ye in such a rush? Were ye a-pining fer my comp'ny, I'd a stopped by at the house and saved ye a trip."

"Pat? Well, in a way I'm glad to see you." She let her hooped skirt drop. A velvet cap was tied at the high collar, and her coat was open to expose her corseted bodice. Then she turned worried hazel-green eyes on Sarah.

"What's wrong?" Sarah asked.

Aggie's expression was pinched. "You ever heard of a man called Win Parmelee?"

Sarah took a deep breath, her heart skipping a beat. "He was a Yankee provost marshal. Bret killed him down at Fort Smith just after the war."

"Tall man?" Aggie asked. "Blond, hard blue eyes, muscular? Likes to dress well? Maybe about thirty-five or so? Something almost snakelike about him?"

"Very like that. But like I said, Bret shot him at Fort Smith."

"Shot him . . . or killed him?" O'Reilly asked cautiously.

"Why, killed, of . . ." Or had he? All Bret had said was that he'd shot him. Dear God, could it be? "It was a shooting on an army post. It's not as if we stayed around to view the body. Bret was wounded. Badly. I put him in a wagon and we pulled stakes."

"I've heard of a Win Parmelee" — O'Reilly fingered his chin — "who runs a parlor house in Denver. A known killer. A man said to serve a clientele dedicated to the more brutal of Aphrodite's arts. A specialist, is what I think he calls himself."

"Wait." Sarah lifted her hands. "Aggie, why are you telling me this?"

637

"Because he's here, Sarah. In Central. He was at my house. Took Theresa upstairs for a trick. She said he was a rough ride, and while he was pumping, he was demanding information on Bret. Any time she hesitated, he hurt her just a little more."

"It could still be someone different," O'Reilly noted.

Aggie crossed her arms. "I might think so, Pat, but when he asked me about the Saturday game, he wanted to know if the Anderson who gambled still traveled with a tall blond servant woman. Said she was 'a damn beauty' that he kept for fucking."

Sarah stiffened; a cold wind blew through her soul. "Said he was coming back for me after he killed Bret," she heard herself say as if from a distance. Parmelee's rapacious look had stuck with her, as clear as it had been that day in Fort Smith.

"D' ye need anything from me, Mrs. Anderson?" O'Reilly asked. "A place to stay? Protection?"

"Thank you, Mr. O'Reilly. You are indeed a good friend. But, no. Thanks to Aggie, we have fair warning. I'm going to wake Bret and pack a few things. I think we'll take the pass over to Virginia Canyon and down to Idaho Springs."

"What about the snow up there?" Aggie asked.

"I heard that it's melted enough that two jerk-line teams brought wagons over the top yesterday. If they made it, we should surely be able to get across on two horses."

She turned to O'Reilly. "Sir, if you wouldn't mind, could you drop word at the stable and have Jefferson and my mare saddled and brought up? We would also need to rent a packhorse for a week or so."

"Of course, Mrs. Anderson." O'Reilly clamped

his homburg onto his red hair. "I'll be right aboot that. And as soon as I check with the moine, I'll be back to see t' anything else ye moight be need'n."

"By then, Mr. O'Reilly, we should be long gone," Sarah told him, forcing a smile.

As O'Reilly left, Aggie followed her inside. "How will you know if Parmelee's gone?"

"Pass the word, Aggie. Spread it around town. We're gone to the Comstock. We are shut of Colorado, and shortages, and sulfated ore, and headed west to Virginia City where there is real money to be made. You can mention that at the next game. George Nichols will surely ask, as will the others. Then, in a week, we'll send word. If he's gone, we'll come back and collect our things. We'll have time to plan by then."

She hurried into the back room, stopping beside the big brass bed. She'd never understood what could have possessed someone to haul it across the Plains in the first place, but she was sure going to miss it. She glanced around. Her chest. The mirror. A handmade wardrobe. Precious things that made her a rich woman by Colorado standards.

"Bret? Dear? You have to get up." She reached down, shaking his arm.

Bret jerked, sat up, his hair standing on end. "What's wrong?"

"We have to go. Now. Win Parmelee isn't dead. He's here. In Central. And he's looking for you. He traced you to Aggie's. Now, get up while I pack a few things."

"Parmelee? I shot him!"

"Well, my love, apparently you didn't kill him any more than he killed you. Now, hurry. I've made plans, and Pat O'Reilly's sent for the horses. Aggie's in the front room."

Bret rubbed his face, stood, and stretched. She admired his whip-strong body, the matted hair on his chest, his broad shoulders. How many times had she run her hands down his sides, along those lean hips and down his muscular thighs?

"Bret?"

"Yes, yes, I know. Let me think. I should have —"

"Bret, I just need you to know how much I love you." And she stepped into his arms, hugging his warm body to hers. "We're going over the pass to Idaho Springs. We'll wait until he's gone, and come back for our things. I've told Aggie to spread the word that we've gone to the Comstock."

"Got this all planned out, have you?" He grinned, chuckling in amusement as he broke away and reached for his trousers. "I'm tired of running. Wouldn't it just be better if I found him first and made sure of it this time?"

"It would not," she told him crossly. "Not that I don't want him dead, but I don't want the complications. There will be an inquiry. The marshals will have questions. Most likely a trial. And what? Sure, it was self-defense. Parmelee came to kill you. But it would come out that you were a deserter. One way or the other, Bret, our days in Central are over."

He studied her thoughtfully as he pulled on his warm wool shirt and buttoned it. "As always, you are right. Very well. You said you sent for the horses? Did you think of a packhorse, as well, to carry some things? And across the pass? It's going to be colder than Arctic hell up there."

"I did. We might want to camp at snow line

640

tonight and wait until morning to cross. We'll see when we get up there."

"I really do love you," he told her with a smile as he pulled on his boots. "First I've got to use the jakes out back, and then I'll help you pack."

She followed him out into the main room where Aggie had poured herself a cup of coffee and stood with her rear propped on the kitchen table.

"Morning, Aggie," Bret called. "I guess we owe you."

"Sorry for the bad news, Bret. I figgered you needed to know soonest."

"You're an angel." Bret turned to Sarah. "I'll be right back and give you a hand with the packing." But he paused. Bent to her, and kissed her. Then, with a wink, he patted her on the cheek.

"I do envy the two of you," Aggie said with a sigh. "And I am really going to miss you. When you get back, we're going to have to figure out how to handle interest in the house."

"We've got plenty of time," Sarah told her as Bret opened the door.

In that instant she didn't recognize the figure standing in the doorway. Backlit, he was just a silhouette. Tall, in a sack coat, his right hand extended. Light gleamed on the revolver's long barrel.

Bret had stopped short, one hand still on the door, the other at his side.

"Found you, you cod-sucking bastard." Parmelee's flat voice echoed out of the past.

Sarah had barely gasped a breath when the pistol was shoved into Bret's chest and fired. Bret's body blocked most of it, but Sarah saw the sparks and smoke as the cap split under the hammer.

Bret jerked.

Parmelee cocked the revolver. Triggered it again, the crack deafening.

And again.

As Bret collapsed backward, Parmelee shot him yet again.

Bret's body hit the floor like a limp sack. Sarah felt the impact through the boards. The back of Bret's head made a hollow thump. His shirt, right over the breastbone, was blackened and fingers of fire flickered from the cloth.

Sarah stood frozen, heart beating in her chest. Then she threw herself down, reaching for him.

Bret's eyes, brown and limpid, were wide with shock as they met hers. His mouth worked, tongue pink behind his irregular teeth.

She saw it. The fading of light. The widening of his pupils. The muscles in his face went slack; Bret's eyes fixed on emptiness and eternity.

"Bret? Oh, God. Bret?"

Stunned disbelief seemed to paralyze her.

As though from a great distance, she heard a pistol cock, a voice say, "Stay right where you are, you treacherous bitch."

Sarah, blinked, ran her fingers down Bret's still warm face, twined her fingers in his beard.

"You killed him, you son of a bitch! Shot him down like a dog!" Aggie's voice. Angry. Panicked.

Sarah glanced up, saw Parmelee, his deadly revolver on Aggie where she stood in horrified disbelief.

Sarah made herself stand on wobbling legs, turned to face Parmelee. She started forward, was going to claw his eyes out.

His pistol moved like a blur. Pain and lightning flashed behind her eyes, the impact of the gun against her temple heard through bone and blood.

Dazed, head ringing, she staggered.

In her swimming vision, she barely registered the fist that rose under her jaw. A thousand stars exploded through her head, and . . .

81

May 6, 1867

Like someone was driving a pick into her head.

Pain.

It speared through Sarah's brain. Through her whole being. Through her very soul.

Her skull was broken. She could feel the jagged pieces of it rubbing against each other. Tortured nerves speared agony through her.

A body couldn't survive pain like this.

She blinked, tried to clear her swimming vision.

When she would have felt her head, sought to discover the extent of the damage, she couldn't move her arms.

Blinking through the pain, she tried to focus. She seemed to be lying on her chest. Somewhere soft. The bed. Her bed. Her hands were bound to the big brass headboard. She could see the knotted ropes.

Couldn't . . . understand them.

For long moments, she just sucked in breaths, as if they'd soothe the pain.

Somewhere she heard whimpering, and wondered if it was her own.

Her arms ached. That reality came filtering through the pain in her head.

Something terrible.

Yes.

She tried to cling to the memory, but it slipped away.

Got to get loose.

She heard herself whine as she tried to rise. Through the jab of pain, she felt her foot slip, and flopped. She was half off the bed, her weight pulling her arms.

Slowly, she managed to get her feet under her.

Legs trembling, she lifted.

Shifted.

Raising her head, she looked around. Her mirror was broken. The bedroom door was swung wide. She could see late afternoon sunlight slanting into the kitchen as if the front door were open.

The whimpering came again.

From her angle, Sarah could see someone's arm on the tabletop, the wrist tied to the rear table leg.

It made no sense.

Who'd tie someone over a tabletop?

She swallowed, her mouth and tongue dried and sticking.

Think!

Her dress was wadded around her feet, the rounded moons of her bare buttocks goosefleshed from the cold. In agonizing slowness, she crawled onto the bed, felt the cool air blow around her breasts.

She looked down; her breasts hung and hurt. She'd seen bruises like that before.

In that instant, she lived it again. Hands were grasping her, cupping her breasts and squeezing, bringing a torn scream from between her gritted lips. With it came the jolting as she was taken from behind. Each thrust deep and brutal, as if to drive up through her center and into her heart.

And then it was gone. A mere memory. But from when?

Crawling forward, she used her teeth. Her head still radiated a splitting pain, as if an ax were driven into her skull; some animal instinct kept her chewing on the ropes until she worried the knot loose, and pulled her hand free. The skin on her wrists was pulled raw and bloody.

Her fingers thick, she undid the second knot, pulled her hand free, and slowly eased herself from the bed.

As she stood, the ruins of her dress slid down to pool around her feet.

Dizzy.

Damn! The room seemed to sway and dip. She braced a hand on the wall to steady herself.

Stepping out of the mound of cloth, she reached down, feeling the crusty dried smear of semen on her pubic hair and thighs.

Again the memory flashed of those violent thrusts, the banging against her buttocks, the gripping hands. She remembered his cry, how he'd tensed and jerked his penis this way and that.

But Bret wouldn't . . .

A fog seemed to float through her blinding headache.

"Not Bret," she whispered. And something in her soul sickened and curled.

She staggered to the door and stopped. Fought to understand what she was seeing.

Bret lay on his back, one of his feet out the door. He stared unblinking up at the ceiling. Cold as she was, he had to be chilled. Why didn't he close the damn door?

The whimper came again.

Sarah squinted against the pain. A woman was sprawled facedown over the table, her arms tied by the wrists to the table's back legs. Her dress was wadded around her feet. Hanging as she was, her knees were up off the floor. Red hair? Aggie?

What was she doing tied to the table?

Bret wouldn't . . .

Sarah staggered sideways as the room spun. Braced herself on the doorjamb. Her stomach tickled with the urge to throw up.

God, if she could just remember . . .

But the pain, it just kept spearing through her head, drowning every thought that tried to form. Her vision kept swimming.

And then she bent double, throwing up as her stomach squirmed and spasmed. Her balance fled. She sagged down in the doorway, gasping, the world spinning . . .

Hands lifted her, and through her swimming confusion, she heard someone say, "Get her onto the bed."

"Bret?" she whispered.

" 'Tis Pat," the voice told her in a familiar brogue. "Pat O'Reilly, Mrs. Anderson. Who did this?"

"Did this?" She stumbled over the words. Damn! Her head hurt.

"Was it Parmelee?"

Sarah blinked, opened her eyes to a stabbing of pain. Memory flooded back. "Win Parmelee. Shot Bret. Killed him when he opened the door. Never had a chance."

"That piece of shit doesn't know it yet, but he is dead," a cold voice said from the bedroom doorway.

Sarah made herself focus in the dim twilight. Someone had a lamp going in the front room. In profile she could see the man. "George Nichols?"

"Aye," O'Reilly told her. "Here, let me help raise you up and get a blanket around yer shoulders, Mrs. Anderson."

"How's Aggie?"

"We got her cut loose. Did Parmelee do that? Cut her face like that?"

The memory came back, the screams, the banging of the table against the cabin wall. Sarah had been tied, fighting the ropes, but she'd heard it all.

"Said she'd betrayed him. That he knew she was a lying cunt. Followed her here. Said he'd set her place afire. That it was burning to the ground. That she might have given him Bret, but he couldn't let treason or desertion pass."

She swallowed hard, fighting tears. "I couldn't see what he was doing. But I . . . I could hear."

"Well, he burned it all right. Mick and the girls barely got out alive. It's ashes, lassie."

She settled onto the bed as O'Reilly wrapped a blanket around her. It was coming back, tumbling into her memory like some eruption from hell.

Bret is dead.

She rose up again and staggered to her feet, shaking off O'Reilly's restraining hands. "No, Pat. I've got to see my husband."

"But Mrs. Anderson!"

"Let her go, Pat," Nichols said, stepping back from the door. "She has to see with her own eyes."

A bearded man was dabbing at Aggie's face with a wet cloth, cleaning blood from a series of slashes. Aggie cried and shook at each touch. What had been beautiful was now a hideous mask of blood and gaping slices.

Sarah swallowed hard, wondering why Parmelee hadn't done the same to her. The enormity of it didn't seem real. She would wake from this nightmare. The world would be the same. It *had* to be the same.

Sarah walked over, heedless of the stunned men staring in the doorway, and bent over Bret's body. Reaching out from the blanket, she ran her hand along his cold cheeks. When she tried to pull his eyelids down over his gray, staring eyes, they remained half-lidded, and in a way, more terrible.

His pants were damp from where his bladder had let loose. His lips, dry, were already receding to expose his teeth.

As she ran a hand over his chest where the muzzle blast had set the cloth on fire, it disintegrated and blew away in the breeze coming in the door. With her fingertips, she felt the bullet holes, dried and bloody.

Then, closing her eyes, she wept.

82

May 7, 1867

Hip propped on the desk in his surgery, Doc sipped at a cup of coffee and reflected on how peculiar his practice had become. "Mrs. B" as they referred to her, had come in the back way. She was one of Denver's most prominent and respected women. Active in numerous causes including the Women's Union Aid Society, she was the wife of an influential newspaperman in Denver politics and society. Nor was she the only well-placed and respectable patient he had; to his amusement, they *all* arrived through the back door rather than be seen entering the front.

Behind the privacy screen, Mrs. B now divested herself of her petticoats and stockings, laying them carefully upon the screen.

Thus prepared, but still wearing her dress, she stepped out, gave him a nervous smile, and settled herself onto his examination bench.

"Before we attend to the problem," Doc told her, "I'm going to give you an examination. To do so, I need you to relax. First, I'm going to look into your mouth and ears. Have you had any trouble with your teeth?"

"No."

"I'm going to use a tube to listen to your heart. Have you had any pain there?"

"No."

"Now, this isn't meant to embarrass you, but have you noticed anything unusual when you empty your bowels?"

"Doctor?"

"Mrs. B, any pain, any odd colors, or odors, especially blood, can indicate a problem. And if you ever *do* notice anything irregular, you come see me or Dr. Elsner immediately."

"I see. No. None."

Doc proceeded, finally attending to her actual complaint by relieving her pelvic congestion.

As she was dressing, she asked, "You are a puzzle, Dr. Hancock. No other physician has ever asked me so many questions, or poked or prodded so. They say you are the best, is that really necessary?"

Doc smiled at her over the screen, having retreated to his now cold coffee. "Mrs. B, I was trained in a forward-thinking institution that treated medicine as a science. Bodies are systems. If I can detect some malady early, I might be able to treat it before it gets bad. We're going to see remarkable changes in medicine in the next few years. Even out here, cut off from the world, I've heard about miraculous surgeries taking place back East as a result of things we learned during the war."

"Indeed?"

Doc studied her over the rim of his coffee cup. "For example, Mrs. B, have you ever thought of treating your congestion yourself?"

"You mean, touching myself?" Her eyes widened. "Down there? But to . . . I mean, a proper lady . . ."

"Yes, yes, you've been told all of your life that women who relieve themselves will become sexually obsessed and crazed creatures who slip out into the night in search of the first man to cross their paths. The kindest word I can use in reply is hogwash. Several of my most respected patients who were suffering severely have begun to treat themselves. I've monitored them closely, and they all report that if anything, they find their lives significantly less stressful and their home life more settled."

"Then why has no one mentioned this?"

Doc told her dryly, "Why should the men in my profession publicize self-relief when they're making two to five dollars with each office call?"

She studied him thoughtfully as she dressed. "I almost believe you, Dr. Hancock."

He walked to his cabinet, took down a bottle of sugar pills, and handed them to her as she stepped out from behind the screen. "Should you decide to try it yourself, recline under your covers and think about your husband, about how much he loves you, and massage yourself as I have. If, afterward, you have any discomforting thoughts about strange men, you take one of those pills and come see me immediately."

Mrs. B studied the pills. "You're sure this will work?"

"I want to see you in a month. Let's see if this new therapy works. And, I want you to bring the pills back to me unopened if you don't need them."

"Return the pills?"

"I'm betting I get my bottle back, and I'll refund you the cost of the medicine."

She continued to study him through skeptical eyes. "You really are such a puzzle, Dr. Hancock." She opened her purse. "How much do I owe you?"

"Five dollars, Mrs. B. Two for the visit and treatment, three for the pills."

"They are expensive pills."

"Potent and effective medicine — unlike the flavored alcohol and sweetened opiates sold by the street vendors. But I'm betting that next month, you'll bring them back unopened for a full refund."

"You've always had these returned?"

"All but once. And in that case the young woman's problem wasn't hysteria brought on by congestion. Quite the opposite. She just has . . . well, appetites."

"Good day, Dr. Hancock."

"My best, ma'am. And please give your husband my regards. I appreciated his last editorial on cleaning up the city." Doc watched her slip out the back door.

Yes, indeed, what a twist on the profession. Had he built his surgery in Memphis, he would no doubt have refused to treat the demimonde and the destitute. But on the odd chance that he had, he would have built a back-alley passage to obscure their arrival and departure from public view.

Here, in Denver, the city's prominent and socially upright slipped in the back while the riffraff entered and left brazenly through the front door.

"You are indeed a puzzle." Doc toasted himself and drained the last of his coffee.

He unlocked the door and stepped out into the office where Butler stood in a cluster of men. They

653

crowded solicitously around someone seated on his waiting-room bench.

"Butler? What's wrong?" he asked as he poured another cup of coffee from the pot on the tin stove. The men turned, Butler moving out of the way. A woman sagged on the bench, her face swathed in bloody bandages.

A burly fellow, a miner from his thick wool clothing, straightened. "We was tolt t' bring her here, Doc." The man had his hat in his hands, wringing it as if it were a wet washcloth. "Been on the road all night, we have, sir. We was told that her kind might not be well received at the new hospital, but that she'd be treated here."

Doc pursed his lips. "Who's financially responsible?"

"Sir?" The miner tilted his head as if he didn't understand.

"Who is paying?"

"Oh, why, that be Mr. O'Reilly."

"O'Reilly?"

"Up to Central City, sir."

"Ah, *that* O'Reilly." Curiouser and curiouser? So, was she his mistress?

"Bring her in."

Doc led the way as they steadied the wounded woman, and she slowly walked into the surgery. As Butler saw to seating her, Doc stopped the miner, asking in a low voice, "What happened?"

"Ah, an' 'twas bad, sir. A murder . . . an' two women raped. An' this one" — he crossed himself — "the fiend slashed her face fer good measure."

"In one of the houses?"

"Nay, 'twas in a man's home. Kilt he was. An' his wife and this one raped."

"O'Reilly did this?"

654

"Oh, God *no,* sir! The fam'ly, they's friends o' Mr. O'Reilly's. He's the one as found 'em, he did."

"I see." Doc stepped forward. "All right, all of you, outside, please. Let me see to my work."

"Sergeant Kershaw," Butler's voice rang out. "I need an escort detail. Baker, Mathews, and Vail, see to removing these men."

The miners stared incredulously at Butler.

Ahead of Doc's shooing hands, they retreated as he urged them toward the door. Turning to the woman, he told Butler, "Lock the door behind them if you would."

As Butler did, Doc studied the bloody cloth bandages. They looked like they'd been made from strips of torn dress poplin. "I'm Doc Hancock, ma'am. Do you have a name?"

"Aggie," she whispered weakly. "God, Doc, just let me die."

"You are going to feel my hands on your body, Aggie. I'm going to press to see if you are hurt anywhere else." He noticed the raw wounds on her wrists. "Were you tied up?"

"Yes." She swallowed hard. "He took me from behind."

"Well . . . we'll check down there, too. But does anything else hurt? I'm going to press along your ribs, around your breasts —"

"Don't! They're so sore. All bruised black. He tried to pull them off my body as he was shooting his cum."

Her language left no doubt about her profession. From the quality of her ruined and blood-stained dress, she came from one of the finer houses. "What about the other woman?"

"He didn't cut Mrs. Anderson. Not like me. He just hit her, knocked her out, and tied her up. She kept coming to and passing out as he dog-fucked her. Reckon it saved her from . . . from this. Mrs. Anderson just plain collapsed there at the end, and slap her as he might, he couldn't get her to come to."

Doc turned to his water. "I'm going to soak these bandages off, Aggie. Once I know what I'm dealing with, I'm going to give you chloroform before I start fixing things."

"Sure you shouldn't just let me die, Doc? What he done to my face? I'm going to be a monster. I been beautiful all my life. Don't think I can live with the way people will look at me, watching their faces screw up with . . . Ain't the word 'revulsion'?"

"Aggie, why don't you let me see what I can do?"

"He's the best," Butler chimed in. "Why, the men and I have seen him work miracles! Indians, whores, and Yankees, he's fixed them all."

Butler's expression pinched. "Why, no, Corporal, I don't think Doc could have saved Lieutenant Fisher, his brains were blown clear out of his skull."

"Butler, I don't think Aggie needs to hear —"

"Doc couldn't have done a thing about those poor souls who burned at Prairie Grove. It was bad enough that the hogs were eating the cooked corpses. Good thing there weren't hogs at Chickamauga."

Something in Doc snapped. He whirled, finger pointing. "Butler, I want *you* and your goddamned *delusions* out of my office! Stop being a damned nuisance! I have a woman's life to save here, and I can't do it with a lunatic discussing dead Confederates with other dead Confederates behind my damned back!"

"But Doc —"

"Out! Just . . . just go away! Leave me to my work."

Butler's jaw dropped, his blue eyes wide and pained. Then he straightened, knocked off a perfect salute, and wheeled on his heel.

Doc watched him march stiff-backed to the door, unbolt it, and close it behind him.

"Doc?" Aggie whispered. "Was that . . . ? I mean . . ."

Guilt rose as his anger drained. "Butler's my crazy brother. I didn't mean that. I'll apologize to him tonight, beg his forgiveness. I should be a better man than I am. I get so frustrated sometimes. With myself probably. For all of my gifts when it comes to medicine, I can't cure the one person who means more to me than the world."

"Sometimes, Doc," she said softly, "all the best of our dreams end in ruins."

Her words haunted him.

All the best of our dreams . . .

She could have written his life.

After peeling off her bandages and cataloging the damage, he walked out into the office and waiting room. Butler, however, was gone.

Damn it, he'd really hurt him.

Stepping out onto the street, Doc sent a runner for Dr. John Elsner — the only other colleague Doc considered worth a damn. In association with Sister Eliza from the Episcopal church, Elsner had formed the new hospital. The one the miners hadn't seen fit to deliver Aggie to.

With Elsner assisting, Doc devoted himself to Aggie's face. Damn it, she had been a beautiful young woman. Working while she was under anesthetic, he carefully stitched her lacerations back together. Hour after hour, his back aching, he worked with a fine suture and silk as Dr. Elsner helped him position skin and tissue.

Doc finally blinked, arching the kinks out of his back. "What do you think?"

"I think I have seen the finest facial surgery in the world, Doctor." Elsner worked his hands to relieve the cramp. "Should we bring her out of it?"

"I've kept you too long. Go home. I'll see to her recovery."

"It was a pleasure, sir. An honor."

"Let me know how much I owe you for your time and skill."

"No charge, Philip, if you promise to come to my rescue when I need it."

Elsner closed the door behind him.

Doc studied the woman, her expression slack, mouth open. She would never be as she'd been, but if the inevitable infection didn't complicate things, her appearance wouldn't conjure that revulsion she feared.

He checked the lamps. Normally Butler's job. Still half full of oil. Damn it, what had possessed him?

"Shouldn't have shot off my mouth." Again, he checked Aggie. She hadn't lied about the damage to her breasts, but the skin wasn't broken. Also to his relief, she wasn't bleeding from the vagina. For good measure, while she was out, he gave her a vinegar douche, known to prevent pregnancy, and dried her.

He was sitting in his chair, sipping the last of the cold coffee he'd poured so long ago when she came to.

"Don't reach for your face," Doc told her.

She stopped, hand half raised. Her hazel-green eyes fixed on his, the panicked question lurking there.

"You won't be the beauty that you were, Aggie. But you won't be a monster, either."

Doc handed her his examination mirror. She studied herself, fighting tears.

"Aggie, from here on out, it will just get better and better. Once the stitches are gone, and the redness fades . . . well, just trust me."

She looked around. "What time is it?"

Doc checked his watch. "A little after ten."

"I'm starved. And I have to piss."

"We can attend to the piss. I'll have to steady you and hold the pot."

"I'm not having some man . . ."

"Some physician who has been in and out of your body all day. My apologies, but you have no secrets left."

She smiled. Regretted it immediately.

"Nope. Keep that hand down," Doc ordered. "If you can't trust a physician, who can you trust?"

"After what's happened to me? Should I trust any man?"

"I wouldn't blame you if you didn't."

Nevertheless, she let him help her. Maybe it was the first step on a long road.

"Do you have a place to stay?"

"No. Not that I'd want to be seen in public anyway."

Doc yawned, blinked, and stretched. He couldn't just turn her out on the street. Nor did he want to leave her at the surgery while he went home to fix things with Butler. Nor was Aggie the sort of woman who worried about her reputation. "I have

659

a spare bed at home. I'd really like you close where Butler and I can ensure you don't fool with those sutures. I promise we will be gentlemen."

"Doc, I lost my place in decent society when I turned seventeen. And given what's been done to me, I doubt I'm going to tempt you to any assault upon my virtue. What about food?"

He smiled, liking her spirit. "On the way there's an all-night kitchen where I can procure two tins of soup."

"Soup?"

"Chewing isn't something you'd enjoy tonight. And believe me, as the anesthetic wears off, you're going to start taking me at my word."

"I can already feel it. It's like a tight prickling all over my face."

"I don't want you walking, so let me call a carriage. And after I get you home, you can help me apologize to Butler."

But when Doc finally arrived at his little house the windows were dark. Dismissing the carriage, he led Aggie inside.

The problem was, there was no Butler to apologize to.

And worse, Butler's clothing, bedding, and war bag were gone as well as the cash and the Spencer rifle.

83

The horse Butler had bought was named Apple, a buckskin gelding, supposedly a seven-year-old. Apple was a tall and rangy fourteen-and-a-half hands, with good brown hooves. He seemed to have good wind, and a sound gait, but the horse was just lazy. The packhorse following behind on a lead was Shandy, a ten-year-old dapple-gray mare of thirteen hands. Butler and the men had haggled with the man at the livery, for both animals. And in the end, Butler had dickered a fair price — mostly. Which brought a smile to his lips, because by the end, the man would have agreed to anything to get Butler and the men out of his livery.

Leaning over the pommel of his saddle, Butler studied the irregular buttes with their sandstone caps; spring-green grasses waved in the wind. The remarkable blue sky overhead gave way to clouds that packed over the mountains to the south and west.

Before him spread the Laramie Basin, a high and shallow bowl bounded by the low, timbered slopes of the Black Mountains on the east, the Laramie Range to the south, and irregular rounded hills to the distant north.

"Been hard riding," Kershaw noted from behind Butler's right ear. "Reckon y'all been pushin' yerseff, Cap'n. Same fer the hoss. He's a stout one, but, suh, y'all might want t' ease up a mite."

"Long march ahead, Sergeant," Butler told him, aware of the men dropping onto the ground around him. Good soldiers never stood when they could sit or lie down. They were looking winded and footsore. Butler was proud of them. Even with as many of them as were barefoot and threadbare, they'd tackled the Cherokee Trail north of Denver with enthusiasm. They'd forded streams, crossed the Cache la Poudre River, climbed up over the Virginia Dale divide, and marched over sagebrush and cactus without complaint.

"Cap'n?" Corporal Pettigrew called from where he propped his skinny arse on a sandstone outcrop. "Y'all reckon maybe we shouldn't outta just up and lef' yer brother thata way? Doc took care of us right fine. Leasta ways, that's how the men and me feels."

"You heard him, Corporal. He wanted us out." Butler lifted his hat and rubbed his forehead where the band had eaten into his skin. He'd had to clamp it down tight against the constant and worrying west wind.

My God, this was lonesome country.

"Reckon he mighta jist been a bit teched, suh?" Kershaw told him. "Times is, yor brother takes on too much. Man's only got shoulders so wide, suh."

Butler nodded, thinking back to the expression on Doc's face. Fury and frustration had been battling with each other. The cutting tone in Philip's voice still stung like a lash.

"Sergeant, I think it's time we struck out on our

own." He let his eyes trace the layers of low ridge and swale ahead. Wildflowers the likes of which he'd never seen dotted the grass in yellows, whites, purples, blues, and reds. The west wind plucked at his coat and teased the buckskin's mane.

"Suh?" Kershaw asked uneasily.

"War's over, Sergeant. And you all saw. Doc's got his practice. Just like he always wanted. He's got a house. Even standing in the community."

Butler read their expressions one by one. Jimmy Peterson, his blond locks tossing in the wind, looked pensive. Johnny Baker's long brown hair hung over the collar of his worn and stained uniform coat. He fiddled with his hands, as if having nothing to do. Willy Pettigrew, the shirker — unable to meet Butler's eyes — glanced away at the distant horizon. Quiet Frank Thompson, sandy hair looking greasy, his tan eyes seemed to question. And to the rear Billy Templeton squinted up at Butler, elbows propped on his knees where they poked through the holes in his gray pants with the stripe down the seam. Phil Vail, green eyes worried, ran fingers through his cinnamon hair, then shrugged as he looked away. Francis Parsons and Matthew Johnson watched him nervously from the other side, as if he were Moses on the mount.

"*Où avancer?* Where we going, Cap'n?" Kershaw asked.

Butler pointed. "North. Across the basin. Paw always talked about the Shining Mountains when I was a kid. That's where he hunted beaver. Fought the Blackfeet. Said he was nothing but an illiterate fur hunter when he first got there, but he learned to read around the fire in winter camps. Met William Drummond Stewart. A Scottish lord, can you believe? Changed the course of his life. Lived with the Indians. Learned their ways."

"Cap'n, suh?" Phil Vail asked. "With permission, suh. Y'all reckon home is that way? Or shouldn't we be skeedaddling back toward Phillips County, Arkansas?"

Butler saw the conflict in the man's eyes, the fragmented hope. "We tried Arkansas, Private. Our homes are lost. Our families dead and buried." He smiled wistfully. "Any hope for Arkansas was lost when Tom Hindman was forced to give it all up. And like the beast, Arkansas rose and devoured its own tail until it was no more."

"Heard the general fled to Mexico," Kershaw said softly, his voice barely audible over the wind.

Butler squinted up at the sun, letting Apple crop grass. "Yes, he's in Mexico. Him, Joe Shelby, and so many others. And, that being the case, gentlemen, what does that tell us about Arkansas?"

"Don't rightly know, Cap'n," Pettigrew answered. "But it don't set right well, does it?"

"Not at all, Corporal. If there's nothing for the likes of Tom Hindman, there's certainly not a thing for us."

"So, it's the Shining Mountains, then?" Private Vail stood, head cocked as if waiting.

"Paw always said he wanted to see them again. The fight at Shiloh took that away from him. Maybe we'll go see them for him. Maybe that's where we'll all find a home."

"Yes, suh," Kershaw said, and Butler thought he heard the snap of a salute. "But, if'n the Cap'n might consider? I'd suggest a slower pace. We don't want t' kill these hosses you bought. Or the men, neither."

"Good advice, Sergeant."

664

Butler put his heels to Apple, and the tired buckskin started down the long hill. Behind him, Shandy followed on her lead rope. Forming ranks, the men marched along behind, their feet swinging through the grass and wildflowers.

84

May 20, 1867

"It's a total loss," George Nichols said as he leaned on his polished ebony cane and looked at the charred wreckage of Aggie's parlor house. He wore a black sack coat with matching vest, a paisley-patterned shirt beneath the white silk scarf at his neck, and striped trousers cut longer at the heels. His hooded dark eyes were fixed on the blackened timbers, ash, and ruin. Melted glass, the crumpled stoves, fire-grayed tins, and broken porcelain lay in heaps. The burned hulk of the piano was particularly poignant. The two billiard tables in the new addition had been turned into slate and charcoal.

Sarah took a deep breath. The smell of fire and wet ash filled her nostrils, although the last of the embers had died out days ago. She had put off seeing this. It had taken nearly a week before she could even think after the blow to the head Parmelee had dealt her. Then had come Bret's funeral, an event held up at Nevadaville. They'd stood in a misty mountain rain as his earthly remains were lowered into the ground.

Solicitations had come from all quarters as rock and soil were shoveled in to resonate hollowly on the pine casket. She had forced herself to remain until the man she loved lay beneath six feet of mountain dirt.

I buried my heart and life down there with him.

After that she'd endured the lonely, quiet nights in her silent and dark house. There, Bret's ghost had stalked the floors, anguished and forlorn, as she had alternately wept, screamed her anger, and beat her fists.

Maybe she'd gone crazy. First she had thought to drag the bed outside. She'd been raped on the thing. Thought to douse it with coal oil and set it afire. Had actually started, pulling the mattress off the frame and into the front room.

Somehow she hadn't been able to drag it over the bloodstain Bret had left on the floor. Bret's bed. The one he'd made his own. Burning it was like burning him. So she'd put it all back.

It had taken her days before she'd forced herself to scrub Aggie's clotted blood from the table. The ropes they'd cut from her wrists had still been around the table legs.

Sarah had finally retrieved them. Burned them. As they'd been consumed in the stove, Sarah had screamed her hatred and anger.

Yes, she'd been a madwoman. She'd pulled Dewley's old Colt from under the bed and checked the loads. More than once she'd cocked it, placed the muzzle to the side of her head, and laid her finger on the trigger.

Each time, she'd looked toward the mirror, wanting to stare into her eyes as she blew her brains across the room.

But Parmelee had smashed it. As he'd smashed so many things. Unable to watch herself die, to see that last explosion of her skull and being, she'd lowered the pistol each time.

Who am I? What am I?

She hated that little cabin. But within its walls, she'd been loved and cherished. Bret's warm eyes stared out from every corner of the room. Either she was weeping over lost and reverent moments, or her skin was crawling as she relived those last hours of death and violation.

Opposites. They were tearing her apart.

"You had everything invested here, didn't you?" Nichols asked as he gazed at the wreckage.

"Not quite everything, George. But almost."

He pointed with his cane. "Parmelee didn't just want to burn the place, he wanted to kill everyone inside it. He poured coal oil over the back steps, lit it, and went around front where he smashed one lamp in the entry. He threw a lit lantern through the front window to set the parlor afire."

"Why?"

"My guess? He wanted people burning alive to focus the whole town's attention here while he dealt with you, Bret, and Aggie. Thank God construction here is as shoddy as it is. Mick was able to break a hole in the wall and they all got out. Still, if Pat hadn't been there when Aggie arrived, Parmelee's plan would have worked. Pat was the one who sent a rider up to check on you. When he knocked at the door, Parmelee pulled a pistol and shot at him. Fortunately he missed, but before we could get up the hill, he was gone."

"I guess I owe Pat my life."

"There are worse men to owe it to. But that said, how much was outstanding on Aggie's loan?"

"I'll write off what she owed me. But she's still a little more than two thousand in the hole to Pat." Sarah shifted, her gut curdling at the sight

668

and smell. But for a miracle of the wind, the whole block might have burned — and after that, the rest of Central City, built as it was of a mismatch of closely packed timber and frame buildings.

"Then I assume I needn't ask if you need assistance, Mrs. Anderson?"

She glanced at him, reading those dangerous and dark eyes. "George, I would never take assistance from you. Even if it meant starving in the street."

"Hard words, Sarah."

She answered him with a bitter laugh. "Oh, stop it. You know exactly what kind of man you are. In a nickel melodrama you'd be the villain seeking to ravish the innocent virgin, but in real life, you're just waiting to shoot the hero dead when he arrives at the last moment to save the girl. With you, it's about taking it all no matter what the cost."

"You sound oddly rational when you say that."

Sarah shrugged. "I'm smart enough to do business with you, George. But only when the terms are spelled out. I'd never, in any way, seek to interfere in your dealings."

He chuckled to himself. "By God, you are a remarkable woman."

"Am I? All I can feel is grief and emptiness. Nothing's left. I poured all of myself into Bret. All of my dreams into our future. I thought life had beaten all the love and trust out of me. But as soon as I found real happiness, that filthy beast . . ." She swallowed hard, fists knotted as the rage pulsed through her.

"Want some revenge?"

"Nothing would make me happier than to spit in his face the moment before I put a bullet through his brain." She paused, considered her words, then said, "And afterward, I'll cut his cock and balls off and stomp them in the mud."

George shot her a sidelong glance. "Even harder words . . . from a lady."

"I'm no lady, George. That's for women who don't hate life. Who don't hate themselves." She gave him a hard glare.

"I've learned that Parmelee owns a parlor house in Denver. A couple of weeks back, all of his girls vanished. His professor disappeared with the house take. Word is that Parmelee owes Francis Heatley money. Heatley holds the title. Pat has known Heatley for years. With a word, Heatley might call the loan."

Sarah considered. "George, I'm going to cover Aggie's debt to Pat. That's the least I can do." She gestured toward the ruins. "This is all my fault. Well, mine and Bret's."

"I could loan you the money."

"I told you. I'll conduct a fair transaction with you, but that's all. And I don't have anything to sell."

His hard black eyes fixed on hers. "Of course you do. Five hundred dollars a night. Four nights. That's two thousand dollars, *Mrs.* Anderson. Just about what Parmelee owes Francis Heatley. And I can think of no more salacious revenge."

She actually laughed. "Are you out of your mind, George? I just buried *my husband.*"

"One thousand a night."

She stared at him, almost uncomprehending. "Men in this camp work for two to three dollars a day. Even the best engineers only get ten. Even as a joke that's —"

"One thousand dollars. Two nights."

Her heart skipped. "Dear God, you're serious."

"I am."

"For Pete's sake, George, why?"

His smile thinned under those deadly eyes. "Did you know that in all the time I knew him, Bret never looked twice at another woman? One night I asked him if he were made of wood. He told me, 'Nothing compares with what's waiting for me at home.' I've always wondered what it would be like to share your bed. We call you the goddess, you know."

Sarah blinked, shaking her head. "You'd bed me, knowing all the time that I despised you? That while you were on me, I'd be dreaming of Bret?"

"I've never offered a woman a thousand dollars a night. I'm not sure anyone has."

She struggled to understand. *A thousand dollars a night?*

What would Bret say?

"Don't be a fool, Sarah. Two thousand dollars is one hell of a salve for any woman's conscience."

And it wasn't like she was guarding anything men hadn't used before.

As if Nichols could see her struggling, he said, "Call it a fair business transaction. Straight service for fee. Do that, and I'll hand you Parmelee."

Parmelee? Hers? That easily?

"I'm like cracked glass, George. Even if I decided to do this, there's no telling but I might break down into a sobbing wreck right in the middle."

Twitches of amusement formed at the corners of his mouth.

"You won't. You will give me full measure because, first and foremost, you're a business-woman."

85

"Not a word, Doc. It's like he dropped off the face of the earth. Not even so much as a rumor. And you know your brother. If he's around, people do talk." Those were Big Ed's last words as Doc walked out of the Cricket Club after stitching up two of the burlesque girls who'd gotten into a fight. Their weapons of choice had been broken bottles.

He stepped out onto Blake Street, finding the day warm as the morning sun rose high in the Colorado sky. The trash-strewn street with its bottles, flattened cans, and bits of paper had that acrid tang of ground-in horse manure, urine, and dust. Mixed in were the smells of burning coal and the rich aroma of baking bread. His stomach growled, adding to his hunger.

"Butler, where the hell are you?"

Deep down, the worry just kept building. He'd expected Butler to come back. But in the following days there had been no word. As his anxiety built, Doc played to his strengths; what was the point of knowing people who knew everything if they couldn't locate a lost lunatic? But no one in Big Ed's, Francis Heatley's, Ed Jumps's, or Patrick

O'Connell's circles had heard anything. These were the people who made it their business to know everyone else's business, and they had their networks alerted to report any sighting or rumor about Butler.

Doc had even gone to the extreme of offering a hundred-dollar reward. The culmination of that so far apparently futile venture was that every lunatic in the city had been rounded up by various posses of drunks and delivered to Doc's doorstep in hopes that it might be the wayward Butler. It had been a hell of an incentive for creativity. For a hundred dollars a man could stay "roostered" on hooch for a couple of weeks.

"Me and my damn mouth," he whispered to himself as he stepped around a battered freight wagon and its team of drooping oxen. From an alley came the clatter of tin cans. Moments later, a pack of half-starved dogs shot out, startling a passing rider's horse into a bucking fit. Hot on their heels a man appeared in pursuit, waving a stick and cursing as the canines vanished into the thoroughfare.

Ah, Denver!

What the hell had possessed him that day? Was he just as crazy as Butler? Throat tickling, he stifled a cough, and shook his head as he batted at the flies that buzzed up from a slimy green puddle of something in the street.

He'd gotten his fill of flies in Camp Douglas and hated the damn things. Denver City's manure-filled streets, lines of rickety outhouses, piles of half-rotted garbage, and tossed tins bred millions of the buzzing beasts — not to mention the alleys where drunks and vagabonds shit, pissed, and vomited their guts out. Nor was there any shortage of animal carcasses decomposing in the sun and crawling with maggots. Denver swarmed with flies like hell swelled with sin.

At his surgery, Doc fought a constant war with the beasts. Even in benighted Camp Douglas, they'd finally figured out that flies carried contagion.

At the corner, a man perched on a freight wagon and called out, "I got the last canned peaches in Denver! Two dollars a can! Ain't no more to be had! Get 'em now! Twenty cans left! Won't be no more."

A small crowd stood around, most with hands in pockets, some fingering their last coins and wondering if it was worth the cost. Back in the United States a can of peaches might have sold for ten cents.

Being summer, the grass was up, which meant the Sioux, Cheyenne, and Arapaho had shut down the Platte River Trail in the north, the Smoky Hill Trail across Kansas, and the Kiowa and southern Cheyenne had closed the Arkansas River route in the south. Word, however, was that some fool general named Custer was chasing back and forth across the Plains in an effort to defeat the heathen once and for all.

Good luck on that.

Doc, as he always did, experienced that little surge of hope as he opened the door to his surgery and stepped in. A quick scan of the room showed no Butler. Instead a thick-shouldered Irishman sat across the desk from Aggie. He wore a fine broadcloth sack suit over a shaw-collared vest. An expensive dark-brown felt homburg rested at his elbow on the desk.

As the man rose to his feet, Doc figured him as

being in his early forties, maybe five foot six, and white was infiltrating the fiery red hair at his temples. Whiskey or frostbite had left its trace in the veins in his pug nose, but the green eyes that fixed on Doc were as shrewd and cutting as a ten-dollar Bowie.

"Ah, let me guess," the Irishman said, offering his hand. "Ye must be Dr. Hancock. I'm Patrick O'Reilly and most pleased to meet ye. Jist come t' check on Aggie, here. An' 'tis a wonder. Yer a miracle worker, Dr. Hancock. Me Aggie, she's near to the perfect rose I've always known."

"Philip Hancock, sir. At your service." He glanced at Aggie and winked to set her at ease. He'd often wondered at the relationship between these two. In the weeks since Aggie had been boarding with him, his interest had grown as had his discomfort.

She'd been the madam in one of the most prominent parlor houses in Central City. He'd also heard that it had been burned the day of her assault. That she was essentially wiped out and destitute, yet here sat O'Reilly, looking after her welfare? He cringed at the history they must have, at the intimacies they'd shared.

Over the weeks, he'd rather taken to Aggie's company. And, though it seemed sacrilege to admit, her cooking was a thousand times better than Butler's. Even given the scanty rations that dwindled with each day that the trails remained closed.

She delighted him with her little jokes, the wry sense of humor, and quick wit. More than once, she'd assisted him with emergencies in the surgery when Dr. Elsner wasn't available. Aggie didn't have a squeamish bone in her body when it came to blood, effluvia, pain, or excrement.

And now her rich and powerful patron was back, smiling at her across the desk.

Doc wanted to laugh with futility.

"Doc?" She pointed to a covered tin resting on the side of the desk. "I brought hot biscuits, butter, and side pork. I figured you'd have a hunger on." She paused, brow lifting. "How was the stitching?"

"Mostly cosmetic and restricted to the forearms and hands. If the girls hadn't been staggering drunk, the damage might have been considerable." He gestured to O'Reilly. "Have a biscuit?"

"Thank'ee laddie, but I've eaten at the hotel. Do help yourself, sir. I jist stopped in t' see to Aggie."

She glanced at Doc, a curious mixture of excitement and sorrow behind her green eyes. "Pat tells me that Sarah has paid my debts." A faint smile came to her lips. The pink weblike tracery of scars on her forehead and cheeks bent and flexed with the power of it. "She's coming to Denver. Has title to a new house." Her eyes hardened. "Parmelee's."

"Now, isn't that a turn of fate?" Doc asked as he bit his biscuit. Damn fool that he was, of course she'd go back to a house. "I helped to bankrupt the son of a bitch, and I didn't even know him."

"And how moight that be, sir?"

"I helped Parmelee's battered girls escape beyond reach. His professor cleared out the next morning, figuring he'd be held to blame. Last I heard, Francis Heatley had a lien on it. It's a nice house. One of the best in Denver. Brick construction. Two stories. Phillipa spared no expense when she built it. And the location couldn't be better."

676

"Sarah wants me to come and help her," Aggie said, hesitation in her voice for the first time. "It's such a relief, Doc. First the attack, then my house is burned, my people scattered. Because of you, I may be scarred, but I'm not a monster. Then I learn my debts are cleared, and I have a place to go."

You could stay with me, a voice in his head said, startling him. Did he want that? A madam? A purveyor of prostitution?

"Which brings me t' me purpose." O'Reilly placed his hand on the desk. "What do I owe ye, Doctor, for all ye done for Aggie, here?"

"Nothing, sir." Doc took another bite of biscuit, the panic settling like a rat down in the pit of his stomach.

"Nothing?" O'Reilly and Aggie asked in unison.

Doc smiled at her, a melancholy sorrow building. She'd told him that she'd been born Bridget O'Fallon in New York. Her parents were famine Irish. Crowded ten to a room on the east side of the city, the family had scraped by. Her father had scrounged menial day labor. Brought home moldy bread for the family and watered alcohol for himself.

As a young girl, Aggie had had a choice to make. She could scrub floors for twenty-five cents a day, which she'd have to surrender to her father. She could marry one of the local boys, move into his tenement, and bear his children in squalor. The third option had presented itself on the street one day; a man in a flashy suit promised her a passage to Chicago, employment at two dollars a day, room and board included in what he called, "a house of entertainment."

On arrival, she'd discovered that her virginity

was worth an extra five dollars to her first client. Being no one's fool, she had bargained it up to ten, and never looked back.

He remembered the night she'd told him. They'd been seated across from each other at his table, sharing a cup of tea by lamplight. "Philip, in my world, a poor woman with no education sells her body one way or another. The only man who will marry her stinks of old sweat, stale tobacco, and cheap whiskey each night when he crawls into her bed. She prays he won't beat her too hard or often, and that he keeps a little food on the table while she pops out his kids one after another.

"She can get work for a tenth the wages a man can make in a factory, or maybe cleaning in a business or household, but she'll live ten-to-a-room in hungry filth. Either way she's sold her body whether it be to bear a man's children or for the labor it produces. But if she sells her cunny the work isn't as hard, the hours shorter.

"Sure, she'll face a brief and fast life. Odds are, one way or another, she'll be dead by the time she's forty. However she ends, it won't be pretty. If it isn't disease, beat to death by a johnny, or suicide, she'll finally starve to death in the streets when the drunks won't even pay a penny for her. The brave ones conjure up the cost of a bottle of laudanum and drink it down to end it all."

"But you did well?"

"I paid attention. Learned to read and write. Taught myself to talk to a man about more than his johnson. Listened when smart folks talked. And I gambled everything when I walked out the door in Chicago and spent every penny I had on a ticket to Colorado."

Where she had put her body up as collateral, and this man, O'Reilly, had bankrolled her.

And why the hell is that bothering you?

"You're smiling, Doc." Aggie's voice brought him back to the present.

"Aggie, truth be told, I amuse myself sometimes. Any idea when your partner will arrive?"

"End o' the week," O'Reilly told him. "About your bill, sir? We owe you."

Doc waved it away. "Mr. O'Reilly, Aggie has cooked, straightened, assisted me in the surgery, and scrubbed up the gore afterward. She's kept the ledger. For the first time, I know my accounts! She has reassured me that my wayward brother is all right. Dear Lord, she's cleaned my house spotless." He gestured down. "My clothes are immaculate. And my trousers pressed. My shoes are blacked and polished. I . . . I can't take a penny."

"You housed me, Doc. Bought food," she said. "Gave me your brother's room."

"Well . . . it felt better. Like he wasn't gone. If I'd been in that house alone, it would have all come crashing down like . . . like . . ."

What the hell, he couldn't find the words. He shot an imploring glance at Aggie. Bridget. Whoever.

"If you'll excuse me," O'Reilly said, rising and collecting his hat. "I think the two of ye need t' work some things oot."

At the door O'Reilly looked back, a smug smile on his face. " 'Twas a pleasure t' meet ye, Dr. Hancock. Take care of the lassie, will ye?"

And then he was gone.

Doc took a deep breath, the biscuit forgotten in his hand.

Aggie was looking up at him, a question in her

679

knowing green eyes. "Ah, I see. Doc, you're not developing a case for me, are you?"

"What? No. I . . ." He gestured helplessly with the biscuit.

"Over supper the other night you told me about Ann Marie. She wasn't the first girl to break your heart, was she?"

"No."

Aggie's smile rearranged her scars. "Companionship? Someone to talk to? Especially when you're feeling guilt over Butler? A wounded woman, one for whom you feel both sympathy and responsibility? Those can lure a man into making a fool's decision."

"What fool's decision?"

"You're a smart man, Doc. Especially when it comes down to anything but yourself." She reached out, taking his hand. "You think a woman like me don't know the signs? Haven't had men get that moon-eyed look you've started to give me?"

"What moon-eyed look?"

"The one you're giving me right now, you fool. I could bat my eyes, tell you that with Sarah coming to town I was hanging on the edge of perdition. I could change my posture, just so." She shifted slightly so that her muslin dress accented her breasts and narrow waist. "It would take me no more than five minutes, admitting how much I was going to miss you, and what a wonderful man you are. I could work you like putty around a windowsill. All I'd have to do is take this hand, lead you back to that examining room, bolt the door, and I'd have you wrapped up like a fly in a spiderweb."

Doc blinked. "Aggie, I really don't think you

could . . ."

She stood, stepped around the desk to slip her arms around him. When she leaned her head on his chest he could smell her hair, feel her body pressed against his, conforming. Her breasts, hips, and thighs felt so firm. His heart began to pound, his penis rising.

Feeling it, she chuckled and stepped away. Retreating to the desk, she seated herself and arched a knowing but scarred eyebrow. "Eat your biscuits, Doc. I don't want them getting cold. Ain't that much baking powder left in Denver City with the trails closed."

With a smug smile, she propped her elbows, laced her fingers together, and cradled her chin as she studied him with those thoughtful green eyes.

"How did you do that to me? I'm a physician, for Pete's sake."

"You're a lonely and desperate man grasping at straws, Philip Hancock. A bloody fucking martyr ready to be led to the stake and set afire. Now, I been in that room back there hearing you talk about bodies, medicine, and relief. How long has it been since you bedded a woman? Be honest with me?"

"Maybe ten years."

"A lamb to the slaughter."

"Why are you telling me this?"

This time, there was radiance to her smile. "Because, Doc, these last weeks with you, they've been some of the finest in my entire life. I've never just lived with a man. I damn sure never expected to admire and trust one, let alone want to protect him. And as easy as it would be to trap you, all it would take would be the right words, the right look, and you could reel me in like a hooked fish."

Doc felt his heart lurch, his muscles beginning to tremble. He whispered, "I'm sorry. I just wanted to make sure . . ."

"You can't even finish a sentence, can you?"

"It would be easy to fall in love with you."

"And what then? You want to keep me as a mistress? Maybe marry me?"

"I haven't thought that far."

"No. You haven't. Right now you're in the hot rush, Doc. Like you just took a swig of laudanum. So we fall into each other's arms, ride the high. We laugh. We wear out the bed springs. What happens after the rush fades? When you finally come to your senses and realize you're married to a cut-up whore? You going to buy me nice dull brown frock dresses and take me to the theater? Escort me to supper invitations at the Moffat house? Maybe even Governor Evans's? Or up at Walter Cheesman's fine mansion?"

"Don't say it so bitterly."

"I'm being frank. You always see the hope, the goodness in people. That's one of the things I love about you. But high society? They're a mean, backstabbing lot by nature. And they'll torture you if you take a whore as a wife."

"I'm lost here, Aggie. What do you want to do?"

She stood again, walking around the desk to place her hands on his chest. Looking up into his eyes, she said, "First off, for you, and only you, call me Bridget. Second, I won't marry you. I won't be your mistress, either. But I will . . ." She frowned. "Oh, hell."

"What?"

"My God, Bridget, you fool," she said to herself, "you're smarter than this!"

"Smarter than *what?*" Doc cried.

She looked up at him, indecision in her normally self-possessed eyes. "I got where I am by being smart. Every instinct tells me this is a mistake, and it ain't gonna end well."

"Ag . . . Bridget, what are we talking about?"

"I don't want to hurt you, Doc. And I sure as hell don't want you to hurt me, either!" She took a breath. "Can we just . . . I mean, I don't want to be your mistress, but maybe . . ."

"I don't understand."

"I don't, either." She vented a lusty laugh. "I could really love you, you fool. I like being with you, watching you. I like looking into your eyes, and talking about all the things we talk about. I don't want to lose that."

"Listen, Bridget" — Doc set the biscuit down — "why do we have to lose anything? We can just continue on as we are. You do the books, learn to be my medical assistant. You've shown a natural aptitude in the surgery. I will pay you a wage. Not for your body, but for your skills and talents."

"You just make it worse for me, don't you?"

"How's that?"

"Because I want you in a way I've never wanted a man." She laughed at herself. "So, who's the bigger fool? You, or me?"

Doc took her hand, coming to a decision. "If you're willing, come. We're locking the surgery and going home. We're going to lock the door and draw the blinds. You and I are going to spend the day together, in bed, and out of it. And some way we're going to figure a way through this."

Her smile displaced the scars as she pulled his head down. "I'm going to do something I've never done with any man."

"What's that?"

"This." She placed her lips on his, kissing him with depth and feeling.

86

June 20, 1867

Sarah stared up at the tall, two-story redbrick building. Unlike its fellows, which were cramped wall to wall, the house stood on two lots, leaving it freestanding. Some of the window frames needed paint. From what she could see, the roof looked good. Bay windows stuck out on either side of the porch-covered entry. The door had a glass window and a big brass knocker.

Behind her, traffic passed to and fro on the street.

"One hell of a house," O'Reilly said beside her. " 'Twas a bit of a mess inside, but I've had word from Heatley that he had it cleaned. Still, there's no tellin' what we'll find when we go in."

Sarah glanced sidelong at him. "Well, Pat. Let's see."

He handed her a key, doffing his homburg and bowing. "Yer pleasure, Mrs. Anderson."

Sarah glanced back at the brougham that had brought them; her trunks were strapped on the back. To the driver, she said, "If you would place the luggage inside the door, I would appreciate it."

"Ma'am," the driver replied, touching his hat brim.

Sarah climbed the dressed-stone steps, O'Reilly a half step behind. She inserted the key and opened the door. To her surprise the air smelled of soap and wax. The foyer sported hangers and benches. Doors opened on either side into two spacious parlors, each lit by the bay windows.

"Spruce floors," O'Reilly called positively as he stepped into the eastern parlor.

Sarah followed, her heart lifting at the engraved and fitted woodwork, the marble fireplace. "Not the sort of construction I'd have anticipated in a mining camp."

" 'Tis said Phillipa hired wagon wrights for the trim work."

She fingered a couple of scars in the wood. "Parmelee didn't care for it well, did he?"

"He's not a mon to take care of things, lassie. Apparently he caught word that George and I were after 'im. There's not been hide nor hair of him seen." O'Reilly glanced around. "We'll have men to stand guard for the toime being in case he comes back."

She laid her fingers on the shoulder bag she carried, feeling the Colt's hard outline. "It is inevitable, you know."

"Eventually" — O'Reilly turned serious eyes on hers — "ye'll have to broker yer own arrangements with Heatley, Ed Chase, and the rest. A word of advice. I'd not mention George t' Big Ed. There's bad blood there. Smart as ye are, 'twon't be a challenge."

She passed the stairway in the rear and walked into the bar, finding four tables and — a rarity — matching chairs. A large mirror hung behind the

686

bar. Some stock had been left, but she supposed that Heatley would have taken most of the quality drink.

The kitchen was in the rear, the stove satisfactory to begin with, but when the trails opened, she would have to order a larger one. Looking out back, she found a trash-filled small yard open to the alley and a four-hole privy. Room to expand the kitchen?

Opposite the bar was a paneled room with lamp sconces. Dining room? It sat right off the kitchen with a door leading to the other parlor.

Walking into the west parlor, she found it covered with velveteen wallpaper. Scars on the floor showed where a piano had been moved out.

"It's better than I imagined, Sarah," O'Reilly said, turning as he took in the room.

"Let's see what's upstairs." She led the way, hiking up her dress as she climbed the steps. The two front bedrooms with bay windows were slightly larger. She immediately chose the one on the east. No doubt it had been that bastard Parmelee's, but the wallpaper was a brighter light blue. Aggie could have the one across the hall.

The girls' rooms lined the hall, six of them, perhaps eight by ten, with small windows. In the rear was a washroom with a pitcher stand, sink, and drain. The hall was carpeted; dark pine wainscoting rose halfway to the ceiling.

"What do you think?" O'Reilly stuck his thumbs into his waistband.

"I think once it's furnished, I can make it pay. Come on. I'll buy you a drink in the bar."

She led the way, almost enjoying the sound of O'Reilly's heavy boots clumping on the stairs behind her.

He pulled up a chair as she slipped behind the bar, found two glasses without spots, and studied the selection. Overlooked in the back was a bottle with a real label. She pulled the cork, sniffed, and decided it might actually be Kentucky whiskey.

Pouring, she set the bottle on the table, and seated herself opposite Pat. "Well, here it is." She waved around. "My life's dream come true. As a girl I prayed I'd be in charge of a beautiful two-story brick house with expensive furnishings in the city. That I would orchestrate fine parties and gala events. I would be in charge of servants, dress in splendid clothes." She paused, smiled. "And then I damned myself: I promised God I'd do anything to get it."

She shook her head, lifting the whiskey and sipping. It *was* real Kentucky whiskey.

O'Reilly took a hesitant drink, ran it over his tongue, and took a bigger one. "Why'd ye do it, Sarah?"

"Do it? Dream of a big fancy house and —"

"George Nichols. Four days ye spent up t' yer cabin with him. Four days. And when ye come oot, lassie, ye set fire and burned it all to the ground."

"It was just business, Pat." She stared absently at the brown liquor, letting the aftertaste linger on her tongue.

"If you needed money, ye could have come t' me."

"I had to bury Bret. Bury him deep and forever. And not just in the ground. I couldn't stand the pain, the empty aching hole. I had to punish myself. Abuse myself. And then wall it off. Brick over it with something else."

She shot him a hard look. "During the war

bushwhackers came to our farm in Arkansas, Pat. They killed Maw. They took me, staked me to the ground, and one after another, they raped me for two days. My brother got me out, and a couple of days later I killed the man who took me. I listened to him squeal, looked into his eyes as I cut pieces of him off with a Bowie knife. He's still one of my nightmares."

She tossed off the rest of her whiskey and poured another. "I couldn't stand the way my brother looked at me. And then he brought a friend, and I got a glimpse of what life would be like. Everyone knowing I'd been . . . So I left, floated. Did what I could and tried to hide my shame. Then I met Bret.

"Hell, Pat, he just kind of worked his way into my soul, loved me, held me. We saved each other. Lived in each other. For that one brief, shining time, he and I loved like you couldn't believe." Wistfully she added, "It was a mythical, magic sort of love. The kind the bards would write and sing of."

"Doesn't mean —"

She waved him off and poured another glass for O'Reilly. Setting the bottle down, she snapped her fingers. "Like that, Bret's dead! I'm beaten and raped, Aggie's mutilated, and her house is gone."

"It didna mean ye had t' turn to Nichols."

"I had to teach myself, one more time, who men are, Pat. What kind of creatures they are. Had to build that wall between Bret and everything we shared. It had to be impregnable. Right down to the cabin. I had to burn it to snuff out every last trace of happiness."

She wiped a tear from her cheek, and sniffed. "And I did. I put Bret in the ground in a way that

689

he couldn't come creeping out to stare at me with those loving brown eyes. Couldn't allow myself to imagine his fingers caressing my cheek."

"And Nichols did that fer ye?"

She chuckled without humor. "Who? George? You bet he did. I didn't just have to kill Bret, I had to kill me. George is as cold and unforgiving as a steel drill, and I had to prove to myself I was worth a thousand-dollar fuck."

She fingered her glass, frowning. "But after that first go? How did I maintain the value once the fruit had been bitten into and tasted? Was I smart enough? Talented enough? Could I keep the honey sweet?" She paused. "I used every bit of ingenuity I could imagine. By the end of the fourth day, you couldn't have hung a flag from George's pole, let alone played taps over it."

"George says . . ." Pat seemed to think better of it and looked away.

She cocked her head, wondering at the smile that fit so easily on her lips. "Does he say I was worth it?"

"Aye, lassie, he does." O'Reilly took a breath. "But t' burn yer cabin?"

"It was tearing me apart. A secure womb of tender love and happiness one second, a prison filled with grief, death, and degradation the next. It had to go. Like cutting the last rope."

"So, ye're fixed on yer future?" He lifted the glass in his fingers, eyes thoughtful. "But for a handful of us, yer still Mrs. Anderson. Ye don't have to do this. You can be a silent partner. Let Aggie run the house. I know you're grieving, lass, but yer life's not over. There are those of us who care fer ye."

"Get to the point, Pat."

690

"If ye'd take a while. Grieve fer Bret. There are those of us who'd like to see if we could bring a smile back t' yer face. Perhaps prove that not all men are like Parmelee and Nichols." He gave her a level gaze. "I'd like that chance meself."

"Marry the grieving widow?"

"After ye'd had a chance to foind yerself."

She reached across the table and took his hand. "You're a good friend, Pat O'Reilly. A hard man, but a kind one. I would only bring you to ruin. If you want me in your bed, you can have me. But it will cost you a thousand dollars."

"Sarah . . ."

"I had my one love. A love of a lifetime, and one the likes of which you and I could never approach. And if we did, God would strike you down as a way to punish me."

"God? Punish ye?"

She held his gaze. "It was preordained from the moment the war started. I had to watch my home destroyed, be broken of all my dreams and hopes. Become a sullied pariah. God used Parmelee to drive me from Fort Smith all the way to Colorado. God put Bret in my bed so I could learn all the ways a woman can use her body with a man. Aggie showed me how to run a house. I showed her how to make it pay. And then, finally, God sent Parmelee back to give me that last violent slap and humiliation."

"Lass? To blame God? He's not —"

"Oh, come on, Pat. As I look back over my life, I can see that God has been driving me toward this house as surely as if He had a whip in one hand and reins in the other. I'm going to call this the Angel's Lair because this is God's will. And I'm exactly as He made me."

87

June 22, 1867

Sarah met Aggie at the door, pulling it open, enjoying the slanting afternoon sunlight as it shone in Aggie's red-blond hair. She'd been alternately aching for and dreading this moment. How did a woman apologize?

"Aggie?" she asked, seeing her friend's familiar face through the veil she wore. Pat O'Reilly had told her the surgeon had performed miracles, but that Aggie would never be the same.

"Hello, Sarah. Dear God, it's good to see you."

Aggie stepped in and wrapped her arms around Sarah, hugging her tightly. "God, I've missed you."

"I'm so sorry, Aggie. So very, very sorry. It's my fault. Bret's and mine. You shouldn't have come that day."

"He'da kilt you both, you fool!"

"I wish he had. You'd still have your house . . . your face. That mother-humping bastard killed Bret as it was, and part of me died with him."

Aggie pushed back, staring up through the veil. "You sound hard, Sarah. Pat won't tell me nothing. What happened while I was down here?"

"Come on in. Drink? I've got good stuff."

"Well, hell yes."

"Welcome to the Angel's Lair."

"So, this was Parmelee's?"

"It was indeed. Seems while he was up in Central ruining our lives, his girls tucked and run. Then his professor took the cash box and fled. Left Parmelee without funds to cover a note owed to Francis Heatley. Pat pulled strings, I paid the note, and now it's ours."

"Ours?"

"Such as it is." Sarah gestured to the empty parlor as she led the way to the bar. "On the few occasions it's been working, I've been to the telegraph, wiring back East. With the Sioux and Cheyenne out raising hell on the trails, Denver might as well be an island. Might take a while to get furnishings like I want, but they're on order."

"What about Parmelee, Sarah? He could come back any time."

"Both George Nichols and Pat have their people in Denver on the lookout. If he does make it back, he'll want to gloat before he does anything. Make sure I see his face. Take up raping me where he left off."

She reached around, slipping the small .36-caliber, five-shot Colt pocket pistol from the holster in her bustle. "This place has a cellar. I've been practicing down there every night. I can put five shots into the size of a playing card from eight paces." She paused. "And I do it every night. I get faster and faster."

Aggie took a deep breath. "What if he gets you by surprise? He done it before."

"Maybe he'll kill me, maybe I'll kill him. Everything's different, Aggie. I'm different. I've stopped fighting it." She gestured to a chair in the

bar, pouring two drinks from the Kentucky whiskey.

Aggie sat, her gaze taking in the room.

Sarah said, "Let me see your face, Aggie."

Aggie took a deep breath, lifted the veil, and
raised her head to the light. The thin lines were
pink, little scabs here and there where stitches
had been. Which didn't make any sense. But all in
all . . . "My God, Aggie, he saved your face."

"And he's still working on the scars," she said
proudly as she lifted her glass. "To life!"

"To the Angel's Lair. And us." Sarah took a
drink.

"Us?" Aggie asked, looking around again.

"I can't run this by myself. Half of it is yours.
That's the least I owe you."

Aggie's voice dropped. "Sarah . . . I know you
paid off what I owed Pat. And I'll make it right
with you. Somehow. Some way."

"We are right," Sarah insisted. "Look at this
house. We can make money here that we couldn't
make in Central, even sitting on top of the mines."

"How?"

"High dollar." Sarah studied her friend. "Think
a step up from what you planned in Central. Then
think another step. Like the best of Chicago, or
even New York, or San Francisco."

"Hard to get the girls. That kind of quality? That
takes money." Aggie leaned back, a frown twisting
her scars. "And Sarah, it's short-term. High
overhead. Limited clientele. Not many men
around who can afford talented cunt, new and
strange, or a trick."

"A trick?"

"Make-believe. And it better be good. Like
dressing a girl up like Helen of Troy. Fixing the

694

room to look like Ancient Greece. Making the johnny part of a theater." She was thoughtful. "If the money's right, you could lure the right girls. But the local talent? They're trained to get johnny in the saddle, get a squeeze on his cock, pull his trigger, then get him out the door and another one in."

"That's why I need you, Aggie."

"Damn, Sarah! You're talking like you're in the business. You did something, didn't you? With Pat? Is that why he's so closemouthed about you?"

"George Nichols," Sarah said softly. "He calls me the goddess. A thousand dollars a night. That's some kind of record, ain't it?"

Aggie shook her head. Green eyes on Sarah. "It won't last. You're novelty. Men will come just to see you. But there's maybe ten men in the territory who would pay that much for a fuck, no matter how good."

"Maybe I want to be exclusive."

"Maybe you're going to end up humping for what the traffic will bear when the cash runs out and the bills are due."

"So, how do we keep that from happening?"

"You really want to do this? Take up whoring?"

"You taught me that there's a difference between a madam and a whore."

"Best you can do? You drop the advertised price of your personal slick down to two-fifty a throw, but you take a hundred from very special clients. That's still ten times the price of any other tail in town. And you've got the right to say no if you don't like the johnny."

"And if some filthy miner comes stumbling in with a chunk of gold in his hand and pus running out his prick?" Sarah asked softly.

Aggie arched a scarred eyebrow. "We wine him, dine him, and dope his drink so he thinks he had the ride of his life when he wakes up the next morning."

"You still think it's short-term?"

"Sarah, I paid attention in Chicago. A lot of houses specialized, but it's still a business. If one of them figured an angle, some trick, wasn't long before a couple of the other houses copied it. You start making money, you can damn bet that Big Ed, Heatley, and the others will want a piece of the market. They got more money than you do, more power than you do, and they're just as smart."

"Damn, you're depressing." Sarah took a deep breath.

"You gotta understand your place. You're a woman trying to win a hand in a world where men hold all the cards and can shuffle them any way they please. You got one ace. One. They got the whole deck. You build something they want, they'll take it."

"How?"

"Pass a law, arrest your girls, send in thugs to break the place up, run articles in the paper that your girls are diseased, threaten your customers, order the merchants not to sell to you, raise your taxes, declare your title to the property invalid, file a lawsuit, bribe a judge. They got a thousand ways."

Sarah felt her heart sink.

Aggie sipped her whiskey. "My advice? Build your Angel's Lair for the short-term. Then, when it looks flush, sell it to Big Ed, or Heatley, or whoever."

"Aggie, you sound like your heart's not in it.

And maybe you don't understand what I'm asking. I don't expect you to be competing with the girls to gin up income. I've got a head for figures and, for the moment, an exotic reputation. You have a feel for how to make the business work."

"Things have changed, Sarah."

"I'm sure as hell not blind to what Parmelee did to you."

"That . . . and there's Doc."

The way she said it caused Sarah to arch an eyebrow. "You giving it out for free? Or just in trade for medical services? Pat hinted that this doctor wasn't charging."

"It's not that." Aggie looked down at her hands. "Doc's . . . just . . . different. God Almighty, Sarah, I'm in love with the man. It's just impossible. That's all. He's a real physician, trained back East. He survived a prison camp during the war. He's lost everything. Even his crazy brother. But he still cares. It's like living with a damned saint." Then she burst into giggles. "Some saint, he can't keep his cock out of the honey pot!"

"Must be the whiskey getting to you." Sarah paused. "Why's it impossible?"

" 'Cause of what I am." Aggie ran nervous fingers down the whiskey glass. "Never felt this way before, Sarah. It's hard to keep my balance, to remember that, like this house, it's a short-term proposition. I wake up every morning afraid he's going to realize that he's got a whore in his bed when he should have a respectable wife."

Sarah sat back and rubbed her face. "Live it while you've got it, Aggie. The ones who will love you don't last very long."

"You're going to need a physician when you

open. Doc Hancock sees to girls all over the . . . What?"

"Sorry, the name startled me. He has a first name?"

"Philip. With one l. Like you, he came from Arkansas."

Sarah took another swallow of whiskey to brace herself. A funny feeling, like insect wings, fluttered around her heart. "You said he had a crazy brother?"

"Butler. He lost his mind at the battle of Chickamauga. What Doc calls the fatigue. But I only met him for a moment the night they took me to Doc's surgery."

Sarah leaned her head back, taking a deep breath. Below Aggie's hearing, Sarah whispered, "God, won't this be one miserable family reunion?"

88

"Where we goin', Cap'n?" Kershaw asked as Butler turned off the Overland Trail and headed north toward the gap between the distant Ferris and Green Mountains.

Ahead of them lay a basin, grass-filled, with sagebrush and intermittent greasewood flats. Patterns of old sand dunes, now covered with sparse grass and rabbit brush, marched off toward the east. The white dots of antelope could be seen in the distance.

On the western horizon low lines of sandstone-capped ridges disrupted the constant wind. Puffs of cloud seemed to dash toward him from the west, and an impossible blue infinity colored the sky.

"At that last station, they said the trail to the Shining Mountains lies ahead." Butler pointed between Apple's ears as the buckskin walked, head down. "Through that gap between the mountains lies the old Oregon Trail and the Sweetwater River. He said we couldn't miss the ruts or the telegraph line. That we follow that to the Sweetwater Station, and from there take a trail north, down the Sweetwater Rim."

"And then what, Cap'n?" Pettigrew asked, his voice almost a whine. Butler wondered how the man had ever made corporal, given the way he complained. Pettigrew was marching, dispirited, his rifle over his shoulder, blanket roll around his torso.

"The Wind River," Butler told him, his voice awed. "Paw said he did his best trapping at the head of the Wind River. Prime beaver, that's what he called it."

"We ever gonna eat anything but rabbit, suh?" Phil Vail asked. "And even then, some of us is startin' t' worry 'bout ammunition. Y'all ain't such a magnificent shot with that Yankee rifle."

"We'll get a deer or antelope as soon as we get away from the trail."

"Cap'n," Kershaw asked, "y'all still ain't tolt us why we a-headin' into them far mountains."

"Got to get away," Butler said softly, almost under his breath. "I dreamed last night while we were bivouacked. I was back at Shiloh. It was the morning of the attack. I was riding behind Tom Hindman when we charged the Federal camps. Caught 'em by surprise. But I remember the oddest thing. A young private. Not more'n seventeen. Parrot shell exploded just as it hit him."

Butler closed his eyes, seeing it in his mind. "That boy just vanished into blue smoke and red haze. I remember thinking to myself, that can't be real."

"Suh?" Kershaw asked.

"Was any of it real, Sergeant? Or did I dream it? All of it? Am I still at home? In my bed on the farm?"

The wind lifted his hat brim and laid it flat against the crown. It pulled at his clothing, ruf-

700

fling it. Gusts hissed in the brush and grass. But for the creak of the saddle, the occasional farting horse, it was the only sound.

He asked, "Am I about to wake, only to discover that everything's just fine? That Paw's at the legislature, and Billy's dodging chores?"

Butler closed his eyes, but Kershaw didn't answer. For long moments, he swayed with the horse's steps, willing himself back to that place. He pictured himself in his bed, the cotton-ticked blanket up to his chin. Each sawed-plank board overhead was familiar right down to the dark knots and pattern of the grain. He could hear Maw and Sarah clinking ceramic bowls in the kitchen. The hollow sound of boots on the floor.

Doc had insisted he was crazy. Maybe that was the explanation. Only a crazy man could have imagined the war. Could there be any other reason for millions of men lining up and shooting each other down by the tens of thousands?

You just ain't right in the head. It didn't happen.

Yes, he'd be home. In his bed. Maw would have breakfast ready. Sarah would be making biscuits. He'd just wake up.

Except that when he opened his eyes, the sun-swept ridges, the turquoise sage, and lonely wind remained. He was still out in western Dakota territory. Which meant he'd left Doc in Denver. Maw was dead, and the farm taken. Billy and Sarah were vanished. Paw was rotted to bones at Shiloh.

That terrible war had been real. That innocent seventeen-year-old private was blown away by that exploding shell.

"Maybe I just haven't run far enough," Butler told himself, unwilling to look back. What if he did, and the men weren't marching along behind?

What if they really were dead back at Chicka-mauga?

"I couldn't stand that," he muttered under his breath where he hoped Kershaw couldn't hear. "It would kill me."

89

July 1, 1867

The steamboat was called the *G. A. Thompson* and she was berthed, bow to the current, at the Fort Benton levee. Five other boats — also recent arrivals — were nosed in behind her. This was the season of high water on the Missouri River as the surge of spring runoff peaked. Fort Benton was the head of navigation. Upstream the river entered a gorge filled with rapids and rocky drops.

In the darkness the boats had a fairylike appearance; their fine, two-story woodwork, railings, and windows glowed yellow in the July night. The light flickered and danced on the midnight-black water as the Missouri sucked and curled around the hulls.

Outside of the boats, there wasn't much to Fort Benton: Two stores; a couple of hotels, the haphazard collection of tent warehouses; thrown-up, plank-sided shacks called shebangs; tents and lean-tos; dugouts; and even tipis. Camps had been set up by freighters awaiting the offloading of goods as the river boats steamed and chugged their way to the levee. Word in the camps was that five thousand tons of supplies would be unloaded by the arriving boats. These were mostly the staples: whiskey, flour, coal oil, powder, lead, tools, tin goods, nail kegs, canned food, canvas, rope, bolts of cloth, boots, shoes, and overalls. Most of Montana Territory's heavy mining equipment — stamp mills, winches, boilers, and the like — arrived by wagon from the south.

Billy studied the boats as he waited in the night, batted at a swarm of mosquitoes, and chewed a sweet stem pulled from a clump of prairie grass. From one of the temporary tent saloons behind him came the sound of a violin playing "My Old Kentucky Home." It was accompanied by whistles and hoots.

For most of the year, Fort Benton was a trading post with a population of fewer than fifty people. But for the summer months it swelled into a thriving metropolis. Then, as the boats were loaded with downriver goods and the wagons and newly arrived passengers lined out on the trails to Helena, Virginia City, and Canada, it shrank to its former insignificance.

Like everyone else, Billy was here because of the boats. And specifically, a man who had come to meet them.

He studied the *G. A. Thompson* through narrowed eyes. He'd seen steamboats a couple of times down on the Arkansas River, but only from a distance. To inspect one right up close like this was a marvel. By damn, they really were big. Like a downtown city building. Way up there, atop the second story, perched a high pilothouse. Shooting up beyond it were the two tall stacks, both with faint threads of smoke snaking out against the stars. And these were small boats with shallow draft capable of navigating the upper Missouri. He couldn't imagine the behemoths that plied the

Mississippi waters.

Billy chewed his grass stalk and waited.

A plank had been run from the deck to the shore, and in the lamplight's glow, a black crewman stood watch. From time to time he'd strike a match and smoke a cigar. Occasionally he would pace, otherwise he'd sit on a barrel head, apparently cogitating on the night.

Over the soft slap of water on the hull and shore Billy heard steps coming down the deck from astern.

The guard turned his head and stood as Danny walked up to him and said, "Go get some shut-eye. Macky's got the watch. I'll keep an eye until he arrives."

"Who you?" the black deckhand asked.

"Danny Goodman. Figured Macky would have said something about me. Been playing poker with him these last two days. Go on. He's taking a shit off the stern. Said he'd be here as soon as he can button up his breeches."

"All yourn, then," the deckhand told him as he snuffed out his cigar. He nodded and walked down to the amidships doors, where he vanished inside the boat.

Billy hurried down the plank to the deck where Danny waited. By damn! He was really on a boat! He took the thong off his pistol, and asked, "How does it look?"

"I knocked on General Meagher's door. He's sick. Got the runs. But said he'd meet us on the stern. I put two of the lights out so it's pretty dark."

"What did you tell him?"

"Said there was a messenger from Governor Smith what needed to see him. That there was trouble with Major Lewis."

"And who's he?"

Danny dropped his voice to a whisper. "Lewis? He's an army major sent here by General Sherman. It's all a mess. This fella Meagher? He's just the territorial secretary, but he called up a militia to fight Indians. He don't have the authority, but he did it anyway. He's here to pick up a load of guns due upriver on another boat any day now."

"If the guns is on another boat, why's he on this one?"

"All the passengers got off, right? So the boats is empty. Ain't but two shabby hotels in the town, and all these people come in. Where would you rather sleep? Out there on the ground? Or here in a fancy stateroom with a roof and a feather bed? Captains turn the boats into hotels, make extra money that way."

"Damn, I'd stay here. Hell, I'm on a real steamboat! And I can't even look inside?"

"Let's just do the job, Billy. Lay low a couple of days, and we can come back and do it! Rent staterooms. See the engines and the wheelhouse and everything."

"By God, I love this job!"

As they passed the last of the cabins he asked, "What do you think Meagher did to rile George?"

"Could be anything. Montana's politics is a worse mess than Arkansas's if you can believe it."

"Maybe I can't."

"Meagher pardoned a man a couple of weeks back that George wanted hung. And Meagher knew it. Feller named James Daniels had tied a knot in one of George's ropes. Kilt one of George's friends and queered a business deal. Cost him title to a bunch of claims at a place called Silver

Bow Creek, over the other side of the mountain from Helena."

"It don't do to rile George," Billy agreed.

"You there?" a voice heavy with Irish accent asked from the darkness by the stern rail. "You're the man looking for me?"

"General Meagher?" With his left hand, Billy eased the Bowie from its scabbard. "Major Lewis wanted me to give you a message, sir. 'Specially with as illegal as the militia is."

Billy offered his hand to the dark-bearded figure.

As Meagher grasped his hand, Billy pulled him close, running the Bowie up under the man's breastbone and through the heart. Meagher stiffened, a croaking in his throat. He rose up onto his tiptoes, as if he were trying to lift himself off the blade.

"Message is, don't never buck George Nichols, you Yankee piece of shit." Danny had stepped close. Together they eased Meagher off the stern and into the water.

"Hold his hand," Danny ordered as he bent down and tied a length of rope to the dead man's wrist.

"What are we doing?" Billy pulled a meadowlark feather from his pocket and stuck it in a crack between the deck planks.

"You wanna just let him float? They's gonna find the body, Billy. See that he was stabbed."

"So?"

"Ain't it better that he just disappear? Make it more of a mystery? You hold the rope, and we'll pull him to shore, toss him over a horse, and haul him out into the middle of nowhere to bury."

"Thought we was gonna come back and see the boats."

"After he's buried, Billy. And they got good whiskey on these boats. And card games. I been practicing. I can win as often as I lose these days."

As Danny left for the shore, Billy floated Meagher's body over toward the levee bank. At Danny's call, he tossed him the rope, then walked casually down the deck, looking at the fancy woodwork, hearing the hollow thump of his boots.

It was but a moment's work to drag the general's limp body from the dark water, and together he and Billy slung it over the roan's saddle and tied it in place. Billy caught a stirrup and vaulted onto Locomotive's back.

As they started into the darkness, Danny turned on his saddle, cupped his hands around his mouth, and shouted, "Man overboard!"

But Billy never looked back. He'd never heard of General Meagher. Wouldn't have cared if he had. But at least he'd set foot on a steamboat. Maybe, if he was sleeping on one of them steamboats, in a real bed, with a whiskey load on, Maw wouldn't rise nightmarelike from her grave.

Maybe there'd be peace.

"Danny?"

"Yep."

"When we get back to Helena, I'm gonna wire George. Tell him I'm gonna stay in Montana for a while."

"Think he'll let you?"

"Don't care. I'm gonna do it."

90

Sometimes it didn't matter how hard a man tried; he had to stand by and watch. Doc should have been hardened. He'd seen death often enough. Lived with it like a companion.

The worst part this time was the parents, both bending over the examination table. The mother, a narrow-faced woman dressed in dusty gray gingham, sobbed into a handkerchief. Her back was bowed as though bearing a great load, and her hair was coming loose from the old-style net she wore.

The father stood with slumped shoulders, head down in defeat. He kept kneading his worn felt hat with thick, dirt-encrusted fingers. The look on his face was what Doc called shock stupid. Hollow from disbelief and the inability to comprehend. Even simple words seemed beyond him.

The boy on the table had just turned six. He would never turn seven. Wouldn't even see the sunset, given the sound of his labored breathing. Blood had run from his nose, mouth, and ears. His head was oddly distorted, flattened, the skull having been crushed. A dark bruise ran across the snapped jaw, cheeks, and bloody ear. The parents' story was that the boy, Arnie, had fallen from the wagon. Landed just so on Market Street, and the combination of pulling oxen and the momentum of the wagon had rolled both right-side wheels over the boy's head.

Doc had given the child just enough chloroform to deaden his senses. Now he waited, staring sadly down at the unnaturally flattened head, at the wispy blond hair, the half-lidded blue eyes, and the manure-stained, hand-stitched canvas clothing the boy wore. Occasionally the boy's little hands would twitch, or a leg would spasm as the abused brain sent out some signal.

"Please, God," the woman kept repeating through her sobs.

Then the boy's lungs sucked. After a soft rattle in the throat, he stilled.

"I am so sorry," Doc told them. "He's gone."

"Are you sure?" the woman pleaded, peering anxiously at him through reddened eyes. "Cain't ye do sump'thin?"

"Ma'am, I . . ."

She turned on her husband, crying, "You kilt him! You big stupid Swede! I told you not to let him stand on the seat! You . . . You *worthless* . . ."

"He be all right," the man whispered, eyes unfocused. "Ja, sure. You'll see. Arnie, he's a tough sprout for sure."

"It's no one's fault," Doc said in his soothing voice. "People are run over by wagons all the time. Kicked by horses. Maybe it's just the slip of a knife. A gun goes off by accident. The world is a dangerous place."

The woman was still staring daggers at her husband. He had worked his hat into a cylinder of tight felt.

Doc took a deep breath, reached down and lifted the boy's body. "Do you want him delivered to anyone in particular? Perhaps the undertaker? Or will you be taking Arnie with you?"

The man blinked, instinctively extending his arms as Doc offered the boy's deadweight. Urine was spreading in the boy's crotch now that the muscles had let loose.

"Ja, I take him," the man said woodenly.

The woman watched, mute, eyes disbelieving.

"Again," Doc told them. "I am so sorry."

Bridget looked up with somber eyes as Doc led the bereaved parents out into the office and opened the door to the street. Closing it behind them, he sighed.

"Didn't charge them?" Bridget asked, her thoughtful look rearranging her scars.

"Figured they had enough hardship for the day. I can make up twenty-five cents' worth of chloroform from someone whose world didn't just collapse." He paused. "Dear Lord, I hope she gets over this enough to stop blaming her husband. If not, their misery is just starting."

"God takes people when their time comes, Philip."

He walked over to the stove and poured a cup of stale coffee. "Does He? I've looked for His hand on the battlefield, in prison camp, among the displaced from the war, and among the poor line girls. I've looked for it among the just and righteous . . . and among the fallen and discarded. And then you see a little boy like that, just dead from a slip and fall?"

Doc sucked at his lukewarm coffee. "That notion that God knows when every sparrow falls? Something's wrong with the entire premise. If

711

He's in charge of everything? Running the whole shebang? I've seen no proof of divine will, no rhyme nor reason in the way things work out. Life's nothing more than a random madness of events and endings. God's either a piss-poor steward, or He's a capricious and callous bastard."

"Don't blaspheme, Philip. It's dangerous." She fingered the scars on her face. "In the end there's always punishment for our sins and transgressions."

"Tell me what possible sin that little boy had time to commit? Or that little newborn girl I went to treat last night? Dead of the bloody flux. If she had time to commit sin — weak as she's been since I delivered her — she's wickeder than black-hearted Charlie Harrison was on his worst day? Old Charlie just shot down innocents, beat his wife to death, and garroted honest folks in the alley behind his bar. But he's still alive and kicking."

He shook his head. "No, my dear, I've been in misery's front-row seat, and I don't see God's hand in any of it. Just random living and dying. Sure, the hard cases tend to die quicker than the rich and prominent, but they associate with a rougher and more dangerous company in the process."

"When you get in these black moods, I wish I could cheer you."

"You do, my dear. More than I could ever tell you. If it weren't for you, I'd crucify myself. Go mad with guilt for driving Butler away. God, I worry about him."

She stood. "Come. It's time to lock up. I need you to hurry home and change into your good clothes. I'll meet you at the Angel's Lair."

"This must be some dress you've got stashed away."

She stepped up, straightening his lapels, a sly smile on her scarred face. "I don't know how Sarah managed to find it, let alone in my size. The dressmaker has just finished with the alterations. I want you stunned and astounded, though I'm sure Sarah will steal the evening."

"And I finally get to meet your mysterious partner? Discover if the goddess of rumor is really just a mortal woman?"

Bridget studied him thoughtfully. "You really don't approve, do you?"

"Bridget, I understand that you're just a partner. I realize that the house will cater to a higher standard of client. It's just . . . Well . . ."

"A whorehouse is a whorehouse?" She arched a scar-lined eyebrow.

"No. Um . . . Hell, I don't know. I want you home safe with me. Remember what I just said about the company people keep? I don't like the odds."

She remained thoughtful. "Do you ever dwell on it, Philip? Perhaps in the middle of the night, during the hour of the wolf? Does it bother you that I was with so many men?"

"A little, I suppose. I always wish I could have been there on that New York street."

"Ah yes. What a weight we put on a man's shoulders. The old, desperate 'if only' of the male savior. If I'd never chosen the houses, I would never have ended up in your bed, my darling. Now, go on with you. I'll see you at half past six." She turned in the door, flashing her red-blond hair as she donned her veil. "Oh, and don't forget to lock up."

"Yes, ma'am."

She blew him a kiss and was gone.

Doc chugged the last of his coffee and banked the stove, not that it had anything but a few coals left aglow.

"And had I been there to find her on the streets of New York, she wouldn't have been *this* woman."

He made a face. Yes, damn it! The thought of all those men who had crawled between her legs bothered him. He hated and resented each and every one of them. Not just that they'd discharged their penises inside the woman he loved, but that they'd known the magic of her body.

He'd had no idea that sexual intercourse could be an art, or that two people could conjure such sensations and pleasures. He just couldn't stop imagining her using those same skills as she serviced other men.

From the beginning, however, she had told him: *"When I was with a johnny, he was a nameless, faceless job. He might have paid for the use of my body, but I never gave so much as a sliver of my heart. You're the only man I ever loved, ever told I loved. Damn, Doc, till you I'd never even kissed a man! My cunt may have been used, but my heart was chaste, untouched, and virgin."*

"So what would you change, Doc?" he asked himself as he strode home in the late afternoon. Flies buzzed where someone had a shot a dog and left it in the street.

He averted his gaze to the distant mountains. Clouds were building in the peaks to the west, their bottoms black and inky with rain as they sailed out from Lookout Mountain.

By Bridget's own admission the seventeen-year-old girl he would have rescued on the New York streets had been ignorant, unlettered, her accent untenable, her etiquette unmannered, and mind empty. Everything that Bridget had become — the intelligent, smart, brave, and resourceful woman he loved — was the culmination of her years in the houses.

"Dear God," he whispered to himself as he climbed the steps to his house. "I'm still a fool."

He never darkened the door of his house without the hope that Butler would be waiting — that silly grin on his bearded face, his blue eyes slightly unfocused as his listened to the phantoms in his head.

The house greeted him with emptiness.

After he had dressed in his new black broadcloth sack suit, Doc ran a comb through his sandy locks and checked himself in the mirror. Still struggling over the dilemma Bridget presented, he walked slowly to Blake Street and arrived at Phillipa's old house more than fifteen minutes early.

He stared up at the brick structure, thinking of his history with the building. Of the role he'd played in bringing Bridget's attacker down. He'd spirited Parmelee's girls away at the same time the blackguard had left to rape and mutilate the woman Doc would come to love. That act, in turn, had brought her here to this very same building. Couldn't that be said to be God's hand?

He blinked. Suddenly shaken down to his core. Was he twice the fool?

Even if it was God's hand, he surely wasn't being punished for blasphemy. He'd ended up with Bridget. Or at least the part of Bridget's life that this damn pile of brick and her mysterious partner didn't lay claim to.

Doc smiled wryly, amused by his silly preoccupation. He climbed the steps and lifted the old familiar knocker before letting it clank.

A young woman in her early twenties opened the door and met him with a smile. She wore a light green poplin dress with silk trim and a curved corset that left no doubt about the swelling endowment beneath her silk-trimmed bodice. Raven-black hair was piled high and hung around her ears in ringlets. A smile lay behind her green eyes and dimples formed in her cheeks as she greeted him. "How may I help you?"

"Dr. Philip Hancock, ma'am. I'm afraid I'm early. I'm a guest of —"

"Oh, yes! Aggie's Doc. Do come in! I'm Agatha." She led the way through the parlor and into the handsomely furnished bar. Compared to the last time Doc had seen it, the wood was waxed and polished. "Might I get you something? Perhaps a Madeira?"

Doc had heard about the trials and tribulations of not only minimally furnishing the house, but obtaining symbolically exotic drink. Scarcity was everywhere with the trails closed. Nevertheless, one of Pat O'Reilly's agents had happened upon five cases of Madeira, which — being in greatest supply — would be the most promoted drink of the evening.

"Madeira would be fine, and I'll do my best to steer the others away from the sour mash." Somehow Sarah had also cadged the last two bottles of Tennessee whiskey in the territory. Those drinks were to be judiciously dispensed.

Agatha continued to smile as she stepped behind the bar and poured Doc a full glass. "Your help extending the sour mash will be most appreciated."

"You are the actress, if I recall."

"That's right." She leaned forward, glancing slyly to the side. "With the show I's paid to act, but had to give it out for free. Here I'll be paid for the lay *and* the acting. We're gonna be putting on performances. Not like the stage, but costumed readings and such. What's different from the troupe is that Sarah an' Aggie ain't gonna be slipping a'tween my covers at night with a hard prick and all sloppy drunk and stinking."

"One doesn't think that of actresses, I mean that they'd be taken advantage of that way. I know Aggie will treat you fairly."

She glanced speculatively at him. "You gonna be attending to our female needs?"

"I've been asked to see you all once a month, but you're welcome to send for me at any time."

The rustle of fine fabric announced the arrival of another woman, older, perhaps closing on thirty. She wore a lace-trimmed yellow silk taffeta with a tightly corseted waist. Cut low over the bosom, it exposed considerable cleavage. The Basque sleeves were short, accenting pale white forearms. She had done her hair up in ringlets that hung to either side of her head. Her smile was practiced and didn't extend to the familiar wariness in her blue eyes.

"This is Aggie's Dr. Hancock," Agatha said. "Doc, this is Theresa. She's been with Aggie for a while."

The wariness faded slightly as Theresa offered her hand, a genuine delight in her eyes. "I'm most pleased to meet you, Doctor. And not a little curious. Especially after the trouble with Parmelee. You've done what I never thought could be done, saved Aggie's face, and swept her off her feet."

717

"As she has swept me. My pleasure, Theresa. Bri . . . Um, Aggie speaks highly of you. I know you're the only one of her old employees she has honored with an invitation to the Angel's Lair."

"Bri . . . ?" Theresa glanced at Agatha. "Oh my. Did you mean 'bride'?"

Flustered, Doc winced, hands up. "No, I'm sorry I —"

Theresa's eyes widened. "She *told you* her real name?" She lifted fingers to her lips. "Dear God, she's really in love with you."

"Aggie" — he forced himself not to stumble — "and I seem to be rather fond of each —"

"What's her real name?" Agatha interrupted.

Doc gave her an apologetic smile and said nothing.

"I don't even know that," Theresa mused, thoughtful eyes on Doc. "You be damned careful with her. You hold her heart in your hands, Doc. Don't. Fucking. Drop it."

He smiled at the irony. "As she, it seems, also holds mine. Which of us, I wonder, has the steadiest grip?"

"Reckon we'll see," Agatha noted, turning as Bridget entered the room wearing a turquoise silk dress. Black embroidery, topped by bands of dark blue velvet ribbon, decorated the hem. Additional black embroidery trimmed the bodice bottom; her corset emphasized her narrow waist before curving up to her full bust. Black velvet stripes ran down the sleeves to dainty black-lace cuffs. The velvet collar contrasted with her pale and freckled chest and shoulders. She wore her red-blond hair long in the back and contained by a beaded net that merged with her light veil.

"What do you think, Philip?" she asked, drop-

718

ping into a curtsy.

He stood paralyzed. Turquoise was definitely her color, setting off the tones of her skin, eyes, and hair. "If I hadn't been in love before, you'd have me prostrate." He swallowed hard. "You have to be the most beautiful creature on earth."

Walking up to him, hoopskirt swaying, she lifted her veil and kissed him tenderly on the lips before backing away and saying, "You're a dear one yourself, Doctor."

At the knock, Agatha excused herself and went to greet the next arrival.

"So that's your new girl?" Doc asked.

"One of them. Three more are on the way. One from New York, one from Washington City, and another from Philadelphia. All enticed with the promise of riches and a novel working environment. They've money enough to ride the rails to End-of-the-Tracks, and from there, stage service on into Denver."

Theresa shrugged. "Assuming the railroad don't make it to Cheyenne first. Heard General Dodge has laid out a city. They're already selling lots. And if the railroad don't come to Denver? Why, hell, we may all be moving north with our fancy house."

The new arrival proved to be Pat O'Reilly dressed in a neat brown suit. "A hale and hearty welcome to ye all!" he cried, marching through the parlor with Agatha on his arm. " 'Tis a joy and an honor t' be here fer the lovely opening of Angel's Lair."

"Hello, Pat," Aggie greeted, giving the man a peck on the cheek. "This is as much your celebration as ours. We're so delighted that you took the time from your duties to come."

"Aye," he replied jovially. "I've got me engineers and superintendents whipped into shape. We're stockpilin' the gold. Casting what we have in two-hundred-pound ingots and ready to run the tailings through the new smelter. I tell ye, lass, 'tis going to be the making of Colorado, 'tis."

He offered a hand. "Doc, good t' see ye. Hear ye're still taking roight foine care of Aggie, here."

"As she's taking care of me."

"A word, if ye will?" Pat took him by the arm, stepped to the side, and lowered his voice. "From what I hear, Aggie's become a real help t' ye in the surgery. That she's as much nurse as office help t' ye. That she's learning the medical trade."

"She is." What the hell was the man's point?

O'Reilly studied him thoughtfully. "Ye could do a lot worse, Doctor. And fer what it's worth, I think yer a roight foine man." He took Doc's hand, shaking it firmly.

"Mr. O'Reilly, I thank you for your high opinion of me, and when it comes to Aggie —"

"Gorgeous, ain't she?" O'Reilly inclined his head in Aggie's direction. "I've nivver seen th' woman this happy. She glows in yor presence, Doctor."

"She does, indeed. Did you have a point, Mr. O'Reilly?"

"Aye, don't muck it up, man. Marry her while ye've a chance. Otherwise yer a damn fool."

Turning on his heel, O'Reilly raised his voice and called, "Now, lassies, whar be the drink? Ah yes. Thank ye." He lifted the glass Theresa handed him. "The Angel's Lair. Health and prosperity."

At the same time, two violins and a cello began to play in the far parlor. Doc recognized the selections as Brahms. Or thought he did. It could have been his poor ear, or being so long away from the concerts he'd attended in Boston, or the quality of the musicians. Denver, though filled with musicians, wasn't exactly known as a musical mecca.

Big Ed Chase made a grand entrance, having to duck his head as he entered the bar. He greeted O'Reilly. Introduced himself to Aggie, who had lowered her veil, then shook hands with Doc. The man's cold blue eyes took in the surroundings, as he said, "So tell me, Doctor, what's your interest in Angel's Lair?" He hesitated. "Beyond the lovely Miss Aggie, that is."

"Just their medical care."

Big Ed glanced sidelong at him. "A suspicious mind might think you were most adept at maneuvering Parmelee out, and the goddess in. Were that the case, I'd say well done. Saves action on the part of me and my associates to deal with the scoundrel. Beyond that, I don't care, Doc. Town's better served with a high-end house. But just between the two of us, if, shall we say, concerns come up. Who do I deal with? You, Aggie, or this Sarah Anderson?"

"Seriously, Mr. Chase, I have no stake in this. And while Aggie is a partner, most of the day-to-day decisions are made by Mrs. Anderson."

"The Goddess?"

"So they say."

"Is she as beautiful as they claim?"

"Honestly, I've never met the woman."

Big Ed's cold gaze fixed on his. "I've heard that George Nichols shelled out a thousand a night for the privilege of bedding her. Makes me wonder what sort of a woman could command such a price. Our Mr. Nichols — bag of shit that he may be — is nevertheless no one's fool."

At the foot of the stairs, Agatha called in a theatrical voice, "Gentlemen! If you will raise your glasses in toast, I present to you the most beautiful woman in Denver, Sarah Anderson!"

Doc and Big Ed turned.

She descended the stairs with an almost magical grace, her hips swaying, each step languid. Her dress created the most incredible image, one of shimmering gold and black. The silk conformed to her waist, but instead of the fashionable oval hoops, Sarah Anderson's dress slimmed around her hips and narrowed at the thighs before expanding to a ruffled wealth at the hem. The fabric accented her flat abdomen and outlined each forward movement of her legs, while the train flowed down the stairs behind her. Rising from the waist, the fitted bodice was cut and trimmed in black braid and cut low over each swelling breast. The sleeves were hemmed eccentrically, ending in black lace cuffs. The effect was provocative, lean, and reeked of exotic female sexual allure.

"Dear God in heaven!" O'Reilly sounded awestruck. "Sarah? Is that you?"

She turned her head regally, her blond hair in a ringlet style Doc recalled was *à l'impératrice.* He wondered if Sarah had copied it from the same worn copy of *Godey's* that he'd seen Bridget reading.

Sarah's face was classic, the nose delicate, straight, and thin in the patrician manner, her brow high, cheeks exquisitely modeled over a full mouth and perfectly proportioned jaw. Every feature was magically sculpted atop her swanlike neck. She smiled, lips parting to expose straight white teeth behind rouged lips. One by one she met the men's eyes, inclining her head slightly.

When she fixed on Big Ed, Doc heard him take a breath, as if he'd been holding it.

Then she was looking at him, and despite the powder and rouge, her mascara-darkened eyes seemed to burn right through to his soul. Something in his gut squirmed uncomfortably, as if she had singled him out for some special scrutiny. Her smile went from practiced, to reflect wry amusement, and then perhaps . . . disappointment? As if she'd expected something from him. But what?

O'Reilly broke the spell when he stepped forward, taking her hand. Only then did Doc realize how tall she was, and how perfectly proportioned.

"There," Big Ed whispered under his breath, "is indeed a goddess."

"I have *got* to make that woman's acquaintance," Francis Heatley said from behind Doc's elbow. Doc wondered when he'd arrived.

"Take your turn, old pard. But after me," Big Ed told him before stepping forward.

"She does make an entry, doesn't she?" Aggie said as she moved up and took Doc's elbow.

"Where did she learn that skill? One of the better houses in San Francisco? Europe?"

Aggie laughed as the men swarmed Sarah. "Hardly. She was just a gambler's wife until Parmelee killed her husband. Since that day she's reached down inside herself and pulled all of this out. As if she's inventing the goddess as she goes along. I mean, damn! She's got the brains and the beauty, as well as a natural sense for what men want. Hard to see that coming out of backwoods Arkansas, but there you have it."

In the parlor the musicians had tackled Bach.

Doc watched Sarah shaking Big Ed's hand, her face lighting as she traded smiles and glances. "Hope she's as good as you think she is, Bridget. Big Ed is one of the most dangerous men I've ever met. Not the sort to trifle with. By day he has a seat on the city council and acts the politician, but at night most of his 'enforcement' is done by hired men who aren't chosen for their manners."

"Shh! Don't call me Bridget. Not here. And damn it, Doc, yes. I hope she is as smart as she thinks she is. She's gambling everything with this house. We've got a plan, and if by some miracle we can make it work, we'll be rich."

"And if not?"

"Worst case? You and I stand over Sarah's grave to ensure that John Walley actually buries her in the coffin we buy for her. Word is that he buries a lot of corpses out there on the hill, but doesn't waste a coffin if he can help it."

Doc felt a shiver as he watched the beautiful young woman. What was she? Twenty-five at most? But as Denver's lords of the demimonde swarmed around her, she seemed every bit as confident and poised as they were.

"Come on." Doc took Aggie's arm. "I'm starved. Take me to the dining room. I know you couldn't get salmon, oysters, and caviar with the trails closed. So you and I are going to listen to music, eat roasted buffalo tongue and stuffed prairie chicken, while I look into your eyes."

Aggie laughed, and let him lead her through the arch beneath the stairs and into the dining room. The food was exquisite and spiced with New Mexican red peppers and wild sage. The cook, Mam, had also managed a surprise: pickled elk's heart. As with the dresses and furnishings, Doc wondered where they'd found the cook.

"Mam? She used to cook for a planter in Mississippi," Aggie told him when he asked. "Just before the end of the war she poisoned the old man as payback for selling off her daughters and all the years he used her for sexual services. Then she ran off to join the contraband and ended up here."

Later, when Aggie was called away for some consultation, Doc retreated to the parlor — a glass of Madeira in hand — to listen to the musicians. He had no idea what the piece of music was, but found it soothing, especially after the trials of the day.

Where, he wondered, was little Arnie? Had his parents taken him out to Jack O'Neill's ranch — as the local boneyard was called? Or had they just driven him out onto the short grass and dug a hole?

"Are you enjoying yourself, Doctor?" Her voice was a pleasing contralto, and yes, he could hear Arkansas twang beneath the cultured tones she had adopted.

He stood as Sarah Anderson appeared and stopped before him.

"Yes, ma'am," he told her. "I hadn't realized how much I've missed music. You and Aggie have built a delightful establishment."

She was watching him through those hard blue eyes, as if, again, she expected something from him that he didn't understand. "Would you accompany me upstairs for a moment? I think there is something you and I should discuss."

"Of course." He let her lead the way, felt curious at the number of male eyes that watched him

as he followed her golden and provocative posterior up the stairs.

As she turned toward her room, she said, "Aggie has told me a great deal about you. About the
war, the prison camp, about Butler. She said you
went back to Arkansas, that the farm had been
seized by squatters. She didn't say, but have you
heard from your other brother, Billy?"

Doc shot her a nervous glance. What *was* it
about her? Those eyes, he almost felt as if he
should know them. Then it hit him. They reminded him of Paw's eyes.

She closed the door behind him, indicated a
chair, then seated herself on the edge of her much
too plush-looking bed.

"Billy? Not a word." He shook his head as he
sat. "Nor from my sister. They're just gone.
Vanished. I've placed ads in the Fayetteville paper.
Little Rock, too. But nothing. I don't even know if
they are alive."

Again she was looking at him with those haunting eyes, so he asked, "What about your family?"

"My paw was killed at Shiloh. Billy and I buried
Maw behind the house . . . and you still have no
idea, do you, Philip? That just stuns me. Have I
really changed that much? What was I? A gangly
girl of twelve when Paw used Sally Spears to
humiliate you? Has life beaten and battered us so
much that we're unrecognizable?"

She stared away then, her eyes hurt and distant.

Doc swallowed hard, his heart beginning to
hammer. *Oh, dear God!*

"Sarah?" But looking close, peering beneath the
powder and rouge, he could see Maw's cheeks
and nose.

As it all came crashing down, he stood, met her

726

as she rose and wrapped her arms around him. The tears caught him by surprise.

She, however, seemed immune, whispering, "It's all right, Philip. There will be time to tell it all." She paused. "But not tonight. I have a client."

"Who?" Doc rasped, trying to find his voice. "Pat?"

"Big Ed Chase."

"His wife's name is Margaret."

"That's his concern. Did you know he hates George Nichols? Big Ed has offered me eleven hundred dollars for the pleasure of my company." She pushed him away, staring into his eyes as if to see his soul. "So we'll talk tomorrow, or the day after."

She used a cloth from the stand beside the bed to wipe his tears. "Now, promise me something. Go down, enjoy the evening, but don't tell Aggie who I am until tonight when you're both home, and holding each other in bed."

"Big Ed and George Nichols? Sarah, you're playing with fire. They'll kill you if you get in the way."

"They can't kill what's already dead, Brother. Now go. I have a job to prepare for."

God had *done this. Played him after all — like a trout on a line.*

91

According to the soldiers at Camp Brown on the Popo Agie River, they called it the Valley of the Warm Winds. To the west rose the jagged and pointed Wind River mountain range, its peaks still spotted with snowfields even this late in the season. The foothills beneath the steep and timbered slopes were the most unusual Butler had ever seen, the terraces being composed of piles of boulders and gravel, all mixed and tossed together in a way that made no sense.

The rocks appeared as insane as he was, which brought a cackle of laughter to his lips and askance glances from the men who marched to either side.

On his right the Wind River ran clear and cold, its waters splashing over the rocky bottom where the shapes of fast trout darted. Ospreys nested in the cottonwoods, and antelope watched from the far buttes, making their chirping calls.

Across the river, the land was as different as could be; flat-topped, sandstone-capped buttes rose in banded shades of gray, buff, and reddish brown. The northern horizon was blocked by the Owl Creeks — irregular mountains whose slopes looked tough and scarred behind the fortlike ramparts of foothills. Off to the northwest, they merged with the Absaroka Range, where its peaks seemed to chew at the sky.

The smell of the sage carried on the wind, the air fresh and crisp as it rattled the cottonwood leaves.

"Cap'n?" Kershaw asked cautiously. "What are we doing clear out heah? Ain't even a road. We's off 'n de map."

"Least we ain't eatin' rabbit no more," Pettigrew mumbled from where he walked alongside Butler's horse.

Phil Vail called from up front, "Glad the cap'n shot that prairie goat. Men can't march 'thout rations."

The rest of the men were giving him sidelong glances. He could feel their unease. Doc would have told him it was the expression of his own mind. That his delusions were tossing his own growing disquiet back at him.

Maybe that's what it meant to be crazy.

"Bet they ain't never heard no cannonade out heah," Jimmy Peterson observed as he looked at the rock-studded terraces they passed.

"Y'all ask me," Templeton groused, "it's a damn desert."

"Fayetteville had water." Pettigrew wiped his dirty and torn sleeve over his powder-grimed face and gave the country a worried look.

"You men just wait," Butler told them. "Paw said the upper Wind River and the Jackson's Hole country is, as he put it, 'some spectacular.' Said water boiled out of the ground, as if bubbling up from hell."

"We been in hell already, Cap'n." Kershaw

sounded short. "Think that's what they called Chickamauga. Remember that place where we was all shot down? All the stink of sulfur and blood and death? Hell busted out on earth, and you could have stopped us from charging into it. Could have ordered us all back."

Butler's body spasmed as if his muscles had received a shock. His heart began to thud inside his chest.

"Stop it! Right now!" He swallowed hard, throat oddly tight. "Never mention that day. Not ever! You all hear me?"

He blinked, Apple nervous as the trembling in his hands ran down through the reins. He had proven a good mount — not very energetic, but calm and capable.

"Cain't never run full tilt through no forest at night th'out running into de trees, Cap'n. An' dat's just a fact."

"Your meaning is unclear, Sergeant."

"Maybe time's come foah you t' recognize you's runnin,' and Chickamauga be dem trees."

The horse sidestepped uneasily as tremors ran through Butler's body. He couldn't breathe, as if his lungs were suddenly starved for air.

"Calm, men. Calm," he ordered, willing himself to breathe; he knotted the muscles in his arms to keep his hands from shaking. Spots had formed in his vision, a darkness creeping in from the sides. He blinked, gasping for air, and felt the world settle back into place.

Panting from the sudden fear, he said, "Sergeant Kershaw, you will *never* mention that place again. If you do, I will charge you with insubordination."

"Truth be what it be, Cap'n."

"Stop it! Go away! *Get out!*"

Hearing Doc's words in his own mouth, Butler couldn't help but hunch down in the saddle, almost flinching as he awaited his sergeant's response. The only sound was the wind in the sagebrush and cottonwoods and the happy sounds of the river running over stone.

"Sergeant?" Butler snapped.

"Reckon he gone, suh," Johnny Baker said warily.

Butler fixed his swimming vision, seeing the men, their faces ashen, their torn clothing hanging in tatters. Fear, like cold splinters, shone in their eyes.

"He be back." Pettigrew shifted uneasily. "That damn Cajun'd do anything t' keep me from making sergeant."

"Forced march, men. Forward!" Butler spurred the horse, leading the way at a trot. When he looked behind, the men were following the packhorse at the double-quick.

"Kershaw, what were you thinking, mouthing off like that?"

Butler's vision of the trail where it skirted a patch of willows shimmered and silvered as tears welled in his eyes.

92

August 20, 1867

Butler poked at the crackling fire with a stick. The men sat in a circle, quiet. Somber. He'd been forced to stop early that day, having pushed the horses too far, too fast. The animals were simply exhausted.

Pettigrew, the complainer, had called it to Butler's attention when he announced, "Cap'n, keep it up, and you're gonna kill that hoss. Then where all will y' be?"

They'd passed beyond the low, piled rock and gravel foothills with their sprinkling of giant boulders — and skirted the base of blood-red sandstone cliffs where the Wind River looped close to the mountains. The range to the north, the Absarokas, were closing in now, jutting ever higher into the crystalline blue of the sky. Soaring gray cliffs, spotted with high snow patches, contrasted with the vault of the heavens.

The river remained a dividing line between worlds. To Butler's left grew timbered patches with pines, groves of quaking aspen, and thick stands of willow that gave way to white-barked pine then fir-and-spruce-covered slopes.

On the right, across the river, lay a fantastic and

colorful landscape — a layer cake of red, white, yellow, brown, and tan formations cut by drainages and eroded into spires, hollows, and patterns mindful of pictures he'd seen of mighty cathedrals.

The fire popped, sparks twirling up toward the night sky. Butler leaned his head back and filled his lungs with the cool, forest-scented air that blew down the valley from the northwest.

"Reckon ya'll got to admit" — Billy Templeton had mimicked Butler's posture — "them's more stars than a feller ever sees back t' Arkansas."

"The scientists would tell you the air is thinner here," Butler told him.

"How could air git thin? It's jist air, ain't it?" Johnny Baker asked.

"Something about being higher here than in Arkansas." Butler smiled faintly as a meteor shot a sliver of light across the blackness.

Coyotes yipped and carried on to the south. Wolves howled in a lonely tremolo to the north, as if in answer.

"Is the water thinner, too?" Phil Vail asked. "Seemed every bit as thick and fast when we forded the river this morning."

"I don't know if the water is thinner," Butler answered. "Maybe everything is. Maybe if we just keep climbing, we'll become less and less substantial until we're mere shadows of ourselves. And if we could climb high enough, we'd just vanish into nothingness."

As soon as he'd said it, he wished he hadn't. Sometimes he could see through the men as it was, only to have them firm up again. Or they'd be in one place one instant, and somewhere different the next.

He glanced around anxiously, nodding to each

of them, assuring himself that they were still present. He hadn't heard from Kershaw since dressing down the sergeant. Not since the near paralysis of fear that had left him weak and whimpering.

Tell me the men didn't see that.

An officer's first responsibility was to his men.

Corporal Pettigrew paced nervously where he guarded the packs, and said, "We're down to seven rounds for the Spencer, Cap'n. A couple of pounds of flour, and a half tin of lard. Reckon come breakfast mess, the last of that antelope is gonna be gone, too."

"Sounds like supply and commissary is gettin' thin along with the air." Frank Thompson was jabbing a stick into the ground. "But . . . guess it ain't the fust time we all been on short rations."

As Butler looked around, the men had turned somber, eyes either on the distance or the ground at their feet.

He couldn't stand it. "Have any of you seen Sergeant Kershaw?"

No one so much as met his eyes.

"I just can't take insubordination. An officer *must* have obedience."

"Kershaw's right," Pettigrew told him, "you caint miss all them trees. They's there whether y'all wants t' see them or not."

"That day is done, gentlemen." Again he felt the throb of fear growing around his heart.

Don't go there, Butler. If you do, it will destroy you.

"How about a song?" Butler asked, and began singing. " 'Hurrah! Hurrah! For Southern rights, hurrah! Hurrah for the Bonnie Blue Flag that bears a single star. Hurrah for our Confederacy . . .' "

His voice faded. None had joined in.

"Would you rather we sang 'Lorena'?" Seeing only sad expressions, he asked, "What about 'The Rose of Alabama'?"

Billy Templeton stared into space. Jimmy Peterson slowly touched his fingertips together and pulled them apart, only to do it all over again. Pettigrew was shaking his head, gaze vacant. None would so much as look him in the eye.

"We had to leave," Butler said, hating the emptiness inside. "Doc wanted us out of his life."

One by one, he looked at them, saying, "We can do this! It's not the first time we've faced long odds. You should have been with Tom Hindman and me in Arkansas. We had *nothing*. The state was lost! But we brought it back. Yes, it was hard. Yes, we made difficult choices. But damn it, men, we built an army."

"And lost it at Prairie Grove," Pettigrew reminded. "And all them partisan rangers? Wasn't they the ones who tore the state apart? Drove the people away from their homes? How'd that work out, Cap'n? Arkansans killin' each other instead of Yankee invaders? If Tom Hindman was so all-fired smart, why'd they th'ow him outta Arkansas? What's he doing in Mexico? Why'nt he win the damn war?"

Butler shivered, leveling a shaking finger at Pettigrew. "Stop it! I don't want to hear any more. Not a word. We did what we had to. Don't you see? Killing those men . . . those boys? They were deserters. Right down to those children the Texans shot down. That wasn't *my* fault. No sirree. They abandoned their oath and their state."

He swallowed hard, looking down at his shaking hands. "Not my fault," he whispered. Damn it! Why couldn't he stop the spasms in his hands?

"Didn't have to let us charge up that hill," someone muttered.

Butler snapped his head up. "Who said that? Speak up."

The men seemed frozen, flickering ghostlike at the edge of the firelight. None of them would meet his eyes.

The trembling in his hands was worse, as if the muscles in his arms had lost all control.

"It wasn't my fault," Butler whispered. "It wasn't me."

93

September 1, 1867

Maybe shooting the calf elk would change things. At least, Butler hoped so as he stood over the brown carcass. He pulled a hind leg up and propped it against his back to expose the light tan underbelly. Working carefully, he sliced through hair and skin to open the belly, slitting from the brisket, past the penis, to the pelvic bone. The warm smell of blood, fat, and the hot sweet scent of elk internals rose to bathe Butler's face. In the cold morning air, steam from the guts rose in delicate tendrils.

Please, let this change things.

He wasn't sure he could stand the growing strain, the long periods of quiet as the men avoided him. It was horrible the way he'd catch them casting accusatory looks in his direction when they thought he wasn't looking.

It was all because Kershaw had left.

Damn him anyway.

Then, that morning, this bull calf had burst from behind a patch of willows, water dribbling from its mouth where it had been drinking. Two cow elk had exploded from the other side of the thicket and fled headlong for the timber a couple hundred yards up the slope.

Confused, the calf had stared openly at Butler and his horses. In that moment of hesitation, Butler had pulled up the Spencer, eared the hammer back, and shot the calf in the chest as it whirled and ran after the two bounding cows. The way the beast had run full-out up the sage-studded slope toward the timber left Butler wondering if he'd missed. Impossible as that seemed.

Apple hadn't appreciated the carbine's sharp report and made life interesting as Butler tried to control his crow-hopping mount, keep his seat, and maintain his grip on both the carbine and the packhorse's lead rope.

As the horse had settled, the distant calf had slowed, staggered, and finally fallen just shy of the timber. It had been a remarkable run for a lung shot.

Butler and the men picked up the first frothy crimson spots halfway to the animal, and the blood trail had increased until they reached the calf, lying on its side, eyes wide and dark.

"You see," Butler told them. "We're back on full rations. Tonight we'll feast on backstrap. No Confederate commissary ever fessed up the like of that, now did they?"

He pointed his bloody knife at Pettigrew. "Corporal, you've been bitching like an old one-legged hen in a muddy barnyard." He waved around at the rest of them. "You all have. Which is what soldiers do. I understand. But lookee here. An officer's first responsibility is to his men. And tonight, we're feasting like we were in Richmond at Jeff Davis's table. Not even Tom Hindman could have provided the like."

Butler bent to cut out the anus and core the pelvis before reaching into the gut cavity. He jerked everything loose, and pulled the intestines and bladder out into the sagebrush.

Two ravens had appeared, both cawing to each other as they bounced from branch to branch in the closest fir trees and watched with beady black eyes.

"Reckon we owe y'all an apology, Cap'n," Phil Vail admitted, dropping to his haunches to stare out across the valley at the high cliffs off to the north.

"I should have been more appreciative to the needs of my men," Butler admitted.

He stopped where he'd been cutting out the diaphragm and stepped over to Pettigrew, looking him in the eyes. "But you, Corporal, during Sergeant Kershaw's absence, are second in command." He pointed a finger. "I expect more from you."

Pettigrew, however, stared back stoically, as if not hearing.

"Oh, for Pete's sake!" Butler stomped over to Vail. "Don't you see? I've never shirked my responsibilities to any of you. I realize you've had your doubts, not only in battle, but on this march. Nevertheless, I know what I'm doing. It should —"

"Ain't seen any beaver," someone said.

Butler whirled, wondering which of the men had blurted it out, but Templeton and Peterson were watching the ravens hopping about in the branches and waiting for their chance at the gut pile.

"Who said that? Step forward, and be a man."

When none of the men moved, Butler told them, "Paw trapped beavers on the upper Wind. We'll

739

no doubt find them as we get higher. I've brought you this far, haven't I?"

He shook from a sudden surge of anger, snapping, "Goddamn it! What do you expect from me? I'm doing the best I can."

He muttered under his breath as he pulled the ruined lungs from the chest cavity. The shot had been good, but the .50-caliber bullet had only destroyed the left lung, stopping halfway through.

"At what point in the animal's death did the bullet fail to perform?" Butler asked himself.

Nevertheless, he glanced at the men. "Don't think we want to tackle a grizzly with a Spencer, though. Paw says they're tough as sun-cured rawhide, big, and meaner than the devil himself."

He sliced open the throat, cutting out the trachea and severing it just below the jawbone. This he tossed to the ravens who fluttered down and began squabbling over it.

Butler walked back to the packhorse and retrieved his ax. With sure strokes, he split the rib cage and propped it wide with a stick to cool. The men had watched with unusual attention, respectful for the first time since Kershaw had left. And, since that fateful day, Butler finally felt more sure of himself.

Maybe an elk would do that.

Butler glanced at Shandy, wishing he had a good pack saddle and panniards instead of the tarp he'd tied on with a diamond hitch.

"What ch'all gonna do next, Cap'n?" Vail asked. "I ain't never packed nothing bigger'n a deer or hog."

"We're going to cut the carcass into halves," Butler told him. "Front and back. It's a trick Paw taught me. Then we cut each half down the

740

middle through the backbone, but we don't cut the hide. That holds the whole load together when you lay it upside down and inside out on the horse with a quarter hanging off either side."

He pointed. "Front half goes on Apple, the lighter, back half, on Shandy. I'll lead the horses to where we're going to camp tonight, and we'll spend the next couple of days cutting up the meat and smoking it dry over a fire."

He heard whistles and stamping feet as the men approved.

Right up until the time came to load.

Loose, limp halves of elk were almost impossible to lift. And this was only a calf? Then, as he strained, his legs trembling, blinded by the hairy burden, the horses shied away every time he staggered close to them.

Finally he collapsed onto the fragrant sagebrush, panting and gasping. On one side the horses watched him with wary eyes, the men from the other.

Butler blinked, muttered under his breath, and the horses shifted their wary prick-eared attention to the trees.

The ravens leaped into the air, each with a dangling and bloody treat hanging from its beak. They flapped away, wings slashing the air.

The horses shifted nervously, the air having gone remarkably quiet beneath the breeze blowing down the valley.

He first saw the Indians on the slope below. They had formed a line in the sagebrush. With hand signals, they were ordering several large dogs to circle to the side. Indians for sure, their dress and long black hair could be no other. They had bows in hand, arrows nocked but not drawn.

Butler called, "Atten-shun! Corporal Pettigrew, have your men form a line."

"Form a line," Pettigrew bellowed. "Look sharp now!"

Butler wished he had a bugler and drummer, but would make do as the men formed up, looking downhill. Indians! A thread of fear pulled tight in his gut.

"Cap'n, suh?" Kershaw whispered behind his ear. "Reckon y'all otta look to the rear. They done flanked us, suh."

Kershaw! He's back!

Butler whirled around, seeing no less than ten warriors emerge from the trees no more than forty yards away. And in that moment, he steadied, almost smiling his relief. Kershaw was back. He could face this new threat.

"Been missing you, Sergeant."

"Reckon y'all needed some he'p."

The Indians wore their hair piled high and roached up before it fell down their backs in black waves. Two held large-caliber flintlock muskets, the others carried finely crafted bows with nocked arrows. They had hard, dark faces, their features hawkish, noses thin and cheeks wide and angular. They watched him with wary and unforgiving dark eyes, wide mouths pinched into angry lines. Some had feathers in their hair, others woven strips of fine and glossy fur.

They moved with a fluid grace as they surrounded Butler and his command. And it hit him, their hunting shirts — more like coats actually — were finely tanned and tailored, clean, and trimmed in wolf, coyote, and bear hide. Tall moccasins rose almost to the knee and colorful breechcloths hung at the loins.

"Hold your fire!" Butler commanded his men. "Sergeant Kershaw, order the men to fix bayonets."

"Fix bayonets," Kershaw bellowed from behind Butler's ear.

"Fix bayonets," Corporal Pettigrew repeated.

One of the Indians, more lightly complected, his hair wavy and brown, stepped forward, hands raised. Staring warily around, he finally focused light brown eyes on Butler, asking, "What's yer name, pilgrim?"

Butler snapped to attention, saluting. "Captain Butler Hancock, Company A, Second and Fifteenth Arkansas Volunteers. You have the advantage of me, sir. I cannot see your rank or martial affiliation."

The Indian cocked his head slightly, looking perplexed. "That ain't palaver this coon's ever heard. Ain't even heard it amongst the missionaries, and they talk plumb odd of an occasion."

Butler blinked, hearing Paw at the supper table when he fell into the vernacular of the mountains. "Y'all are common folk, then?"

"We're what ye'd be calling Sheep Eaters. Can ye ken that, pilgrim?"

"Sheep Eaters." Butler laughed and slapped his thighs. "Reckon this coon can. My pap larn'ed me when I was a young 'un. He spoke highly of the Sheep Eaters. Said they were brave and men of honor. Said he lived with the Dukurika Sheep Eaters for a couple of years. Said they were some of the best days of his life."

"Who you talk to?" The Indian gestured around at the sagebrush.

"I am an officer. I am responsible for these men."

Again the Shoshoni looked confused. He spoke rapidly to the others in his own tongue. One, an older man — streaks of white lining his temples and deep lines in his face — kept studying Butler intently. A thick necklace of animal bones, claws, and beads hung down his chest. He asked something of the young warrior.

The young man shrugged, then stated, "We don't see no men but you, coon."

"My men are soldiers, Second Arkansas. They're standing right there." Butler pointed. "I see them plain and clear as I see you."

Again the Dukurika conversed.

"You see them, but others do not?"

"Some call me crazy," Butler told him with a smile. "But tell me this? Who's got the right of it? Me? Who can see them? Or you that can't?"

Butler reached out with his left hand, grabbing his right to keep it from shaking.

The old man watched him as he did. Meanwhile the speaker translated.

Then the older man stepped around the elk's gut pile and stopped a pace away, staring into Butler's eyes. The effect was eerie, as if those stone-black eyes were looking down into Butler's trembling soul.

"Who're you?" Butler asked.

"He is Puhagan," the speaker told him. "What you would call medicine man. He has asked to see you."

"To see me? How did he know I was coming?"

"We been watchin' fer days, Man Who Speaks to No One." The young man gestured with his hands. "We watched you. The ravens watched. The elk and wind have watched. We all talked

744

about you. You fed the ravens, reckon now you c'n feed us."

Butler was still looking into the old man's eyes. It was as if he were falling into a deep and dark hole. A place where dreams and the real world mixed and flowed together.

Puhagan said something.

The speaker translated, "Puhagan says that you are to come with us, Butler Hancock. He says he knows what you are. A party of the Injuns you call Crow is a half day's ride over east. He would rather that they don't carry your carcass off ter their land."

"He knows who I am?"

The speaker shrugged his young shoulders. "A *puhagan* palavers with the spirits, maybe like you do, Butler Hancock."

"Where'd you learn to talk English?"

"From the traders, coon. My mother lived in a mountaineer's lodge fer nigh on ten years afore he went under. She brung me home, remarried."

"Hold!" Butler called as Billy Templeton tried to shift out of line. "At ease. Form the men, Sergeant. Prepare to move out."

The *puhagan* had watched him, eyes gleaming and thoughtful.

At the old man's orders, the elk was easily lifted onto the horses and tied down with lengths of braided leather rope the Sheep Eaters provided. As quickly and expertly as the warriors tied on the load, they might have done it a thousand times. The heart, liver, kidney, and tongue vanished into sacks and bags.

The men who'd cut off retreat downhill were approaching now, the dogs called to heel. They were big beasts, splotched with color, panting from mouths where most of the teeth were filed flat. They watched Butler and the elk with alert and interested eyes.

Then, at an order, the dogs literally leaped on the gut pile, devouring the lungs, paunch, and long strings of intestines.

"How are you called?" Butler asked the speaker.

He rattled off something in Shoshoni. "Means Cracked Bone Thrower, after the man who done taken the last bone from the feast, cracks it open and sucks out the marrow. Then, when there is nothing left, he throws it out beyond the camp circle. My white name is Dick Hamilton. After my grandfather Richard. That ol' coon trapped beaver and traded all through these parts."

Puhagan asked something, and as he did Cracked Bone Thrower translated, "We do not want to walk on your spirit men. Can you show us how to avoid them?"

"Tell your elder that the men appreciate his concern, but they'll do fine on their own. They're used to staying out of the way."

When this was translated, the *puhagan* gave Butler the most unsettling stare, as if the man were passing judgment on Butler's suddenly nervous soul.

"Cap'n?" Kershaw whispered behind Butler's ear. "I reckon we be in a heap of trouble."

"Why is that, Sergeant?"

" 'Cause my mam done tol' me about the evil eye, and I reckon that old man's done fixed it on you."

"What does that mean?"

"Means you and him's gonna have to do battle afore this is over, Cap'n."

94

September 2, 1867

In Billy's eyes, Helena was high, wide, and hand-some. The placer claims were pretty well played out, but talk was that a wealth of gold and silver lode deposits lay waiting for the miners' pick and drill. That several of the new-fangled smelters were going to be built, and the moment they were, all of those stubborn lode deposits were going to place Helena at "the top of the heap."

He and Danny had rented rooms in a two-story firetrap on Boulder Street just off Montana Avenue. Danny had actually managed to show a profit on his gambling, having established a table in the back of Follet's saloon just off the Last Chance Gulch road.

"Play at it long enough," Danny had told him, "and I could even make you a poker player."

"I'll stick to guns and knives," Billy had replied with a smile.

If Billy had had any good news it was that he'd cured the nightmares for the last couple of days. They had been getting bad, leaving Billy shivering with night sweats after Maw's or Sarah's ghosts had haunted him in the middle of the night.

Then two nights ago, shivering and shaken, Billy

had dressed, and in the wee morning hours, found Lizzie's crib — a rickety plank shebang housing her bed, an oil lamp, and table. Lizzie — homely as a plain board fence — had laid back on the bed, pulled up her skirts, and given Billy a gap-toothed grin as he blew out the light.

In the darkness, he'd been able to close his eyes, imagine Sarah, and pay her back for the suffering and humiliation. As she'd bucked and contorted beneath him, he'd pumped his loins. When he came back to his senses, she lay limp and unfeeling beneath him.

Billy had felt around until he found the lamp, lifted off the chimney and unscrewed the lamp and wick from the bowl. He had poured coal oil over Lizzie's body and bedding. Then, at the door, he'd struck a match and tossed it. He'd watched blue-based flames start in the bedding as he'd closed the door behind him.

All that remained the next morning had been a pile of charred ash, burned planks, and a half-cooked corpse in the wreckage of what once had been a bed.

Word on the street was that it had been a terrible accident. Lizzie was known to drown herself in drink and opiates. Speculation was that she'd knocked the lamp over in a drunken stupor.

Billy appreciated the people of Helena. They didn't bother themselves to think beyond the obvious.

He considered that as he and Danny walked through the cool evening, boots leaving tracks in the dusty street where boardwalks hadn't been built. Billy looked up at the nighthawks where they flipped and flittered against the darkening sky.

"Long way from Elkhorn Tavern, ain't we?"

Danny cast a sidelong glance at him. "Where the hell did that come from? You been having them nightmares again?"

Billy shrugged. "Not so bad these last couple of weeks." He barked a laugh, then lowered his voice. "Can you believe? They done offered up a ten-thousand-dollar reward for old Meagher's killer and ain't nobody found his body."

"Why'd you suppose that is?" Danny answered with a sly grin.

"Aw, I reckon sometime a hundred years from now, somebody's gonna be building something out there in the uplands and dig up bones. They'll be a story in the Fort Benton paper. Folks'll find his buttons, the belt buckle, and the like. Reckon they'll know it's a white man, but that's about all there'll be to it."

"It ain't gonna last, you know."

"What ain't gonna last?" Billy glanced Danny's way as they passed a saloon. Inside mediocre musicians were playing "Union Forever," but the singers — most of them drunk and off key — were belting out the Confederate verses, singing, " 'Down with the eagle and up with the star! Won't you rally 'round the flag, Won't you rally 'round the flag, Dixie forever, hurrah, boys, hurrah!' "

That was another of the things he liked about Montana. Most of the men were Democrats — a bunch of them unrepentant Rebels — and though the black damn Republicans ran the government — what there was of it — they were in the minority.

"You being dream-free, the money, the job, what we got. It *ain't* gonna last."

"What are you talking about? We're the best they is, Danny."

He shot Billy a measuring glance. "We been lucky. That's all. What if that old nigger deckhand had forgot something and stepped out just as you was sticking Meagher? What if someone had been looking out a slit in the door when I knocked on the old man's stateroom that night? Somewhere, just like in cards, there's gonna be an ace turn up at the wrong moment."

"Such as?"

Danny lowered his voice. "Might be some bull-whacker sleeping in the alley under a tarp who just happens to wake up and see you step out of some whore's shebang. Sees you moments before the thing goes up in flames. Maybe pulls her dead body out of the blaze."

"You saying what I think you are, Danny Good-man?"

"Billy? We made us a pile of money. Hell, more'n I ever figgered to see. We could just up and quit. Go home. You ever thought of that?"

Billy kicked at a rock as they walked, happy with the cool breeze blowing down the canyon from the west. "I can't go home. Ain't nothing left there."

"What about the farm?"

"Too many ghosts. If Sarah ain't dead, she's running it now. Or maybe Butler if he ever come home from the war. I ain't never setting foot in Arkansas again."

"What are you going to do?"

"Keep one step ahead of the devil for as long as I can. Ain't no happy ending to this, Daniel."

"Don't have to be that way, Billy. You got enough to buy yourself a nice place. A tavern, a sporting house. A store if you wanted to be respectable. Me, I think I could enjoy bossing a gambling house. Run a couple of tables, have games like a spin-the-wheel, maybe one of them fancy roulette tables."

"House always wins?"

Danny smiled. "That's where the real money is. You got enough you could go someplace like Oregon, maybe Texas, or just stay here if you wanted. You could buy a place up in the hills, run some cattle, and market-hunt to keep busy."

"What are you really saying, Danny?"

"I'm saying I want you to think about it. Not for tomorrow, not for next week, but sometime soon." He raised a finger, eyes sincere. " 'Cause sometime soon, Billy, that ace is gonna come up, and they're gonna hang you."

"What the hell difference does it make? I ain't got nothing to live for anyway."

Danny spread his hands wide. "Then, for God's sake, find something, you damned fool! There's got to be something else in this old world that puts that joy in your heart besides sticking a knife in some johnny's guts, or popping your cork in a whore while you're choking her."

"Ain't found it yet." He considered the implications as they resumed their way. "You ever going back to Arkansas? You still got family. They might even have moved back to Benton County."

"Maybe. Someday. After it's all rebuilt. I'm kinda like you, I guess. When I look back at Arkansas, all I see is ruin and death and war. Never figgered I'd live this long. But since I have, and I got a stake in my sock, I'm thinking I might like to try life without the bloodshed and fret."

They reached the front door of Follet's. Billy

reached out, stopping his friend. "I don't know how long I got till the Devil snaps me up. But till then, I need you, Danny. Ain't a better front man in the country than you. Hell, you're the only reason I'm still alive."

Danny grinned at him. "You know why, don't you? It's 'cause I figured out how to talk to a man, string him on, and he ain't got a clue about what's running in my mind. He thinks I'm his best friend, right up to the moment the Meadowlark slips in the back door. Reckon it's like a sixth sense, knowing when the time to act is 'thout the other guy catching wise."

"And don't think I don't appreciate it. That's why I can't quit. Not yet. But maybe in another six months or so. Maybe we'll both just ride away."

"Hell, just for you being willing to think about it, I'll buy you a whole bottle of Follett's best." Danny slapped him on the shoulder, and led the way into the log-and-tent saloon.

When Billy blinked awake the next morning, he was lying on the sawdust-covered floor. His mouth was dry as Montana dust, his head pounding, and his stomach flipping and tickling with the urge to puke. Sunlight could be seen through the cracks and gaps in the walls. Men talked softly, and glasses clinked from the bar. Billy's eyes might have been full of gravel as he blinked to clear his sight.

He still clutched a whiskey bottle in which a swallow or two remained. Tilting it to his lips, he sucked it down, reveling in the taste and wetness on his tongue.

Sitting up, he brushed sawdust from his clothes, groaned, and staggered to his feet. Damn, he was still drunk given the swimming and wobbling.

Nevertheless he staggered out the back to the two-hole outhouse. Made it halfway through a piss before he caught the odor coming up through the hole. At just a whiff, he bent double and threw up. Then came the dry heaves; with each convulsion of his guts, he thought his head was going to explode.

Exhausted and weary, he staggered back to his room, drank the entire pitcher of wash water, and collapsed on his bed.

Dusk was darkening the sky when his bladder insisted he rise and stumble over to the chamber pot.

It wasn't until the morning after that that he discovered that Danny was gone. Not only was his room empty and his bedroll and war bag gone, but so was his horse from the livery.

"He left this fer ye," the hostler told him, handing him a folded piece of paper sealed with a drop of candle wax.

Billy broke the seal. Read the short note. He crumpled the paper in his fist. A curious weakness in his knees caused him to lean against one of the support posts. Like he'd gone hollow inside.

Printed in Danny's poor block script was written: *Cant Do this no Mor yor frend Dany.*

95

"These mountains are old, coon," Cracked Bone Thrower told Butler as they sat on the edge of the high mountain camp. The Sheep Eater village literally perched at the top of the world, on a long, knifelike ridge between two rocky peaks. Hardly the place anyone sane would think to put even a temporary camp. The aerie was so high, Butler was surprised that when he reached overhead his fingers didn't rake the clouds.

Groves of white-bark pine lay to either side, the occasional nutcracker flying past on black-and-white wings.

But, God in heaven, did it ever have a view! The majesty before him — ragged peak after ragged peak fading into the distance — seemed to swell his heart. His men, dressed in their rags, were seated in a line behind him, quiet and awed, as if they'd become acolytes desperate for knowledge.

Cracked Bone Thrower, his half-white face passive, gestured toward the panorama of distant snow-capped crags. "In the beginning, Tam Apo, our father, lifted hisself from Tam Segobia, our mother, to create the arch of the sky. That was the beginning of everything. And it was plumb mixed up as the spirit beings and the first creatures come up from the Underworld, and the springs began to flow. From them came the spirits of the Underworld. Beings like the *nynymbi,* the little people. The rock ogres we call *dzoavits,* and the Giant Cannibals. All walked the earth. Some still do."

"Sounds like demons t' me," Billy Thompson muttered.

"Amen to that, friend," Johnny Baker agreed softly.

Cracked Bone Thrower laced his fingers around his knees and leaned back, the mountain breeze tossing his long brown-black hair as he continued, saying, "The Water Ghost Woman, her name is Pa'waip, rose from the watery depths, beautiful and deadly. Her sheath is forever desperate for a man's pizzle. With a smile and flashing dark eyes, she draws a man close. Such is her beauty that when she lies down and spreads her legs, a man cannot help himself. It is said that at the moment his seed squirts into her, she rolls him into the water and drowns him. Then she devours his souls and leaves his empty corpse to float away."

"Reckon they's Natchez whores rougher'n that," Pettigrew noted.

Butler shot a warning glare over his shoulder to silence the corporal.

Cracked Bone Thrower inclined his head toward the women working on the slope below. They bent over mountain-sheep hides, hacking and scraping to flesh them. "As cunning as Pa'waip is when it comes to seducing and killing men, so are the Water Babies skilled at trapping women. We call them the *pa'unha,* and they look like abandoned infants left beside the waters of a creek. When a woman picks one up and places the *pa'unha* to her breast, it grabs her by the nipple. It never lets go, and bite by bite eats the rest of her."

Pettigrew snickered rudely. "Puts a whole new twist on 'breast feeding,' don't it?"

"Corporal, you will be silent!" Butler snapped.

Cracked Bone Thrower ignored him, as he often did when Butler talked to his men. "In the middle world, Wolf and Coyote and Rabbit and Pack Rat fought the monsters and created life and death. In the sky world Eagle, Falcon, Hawk, Hummingbird, and Chickadee learned to fly and to work the Powers of the sun, clouds, wind, lightning, and rain.

"The first humans were born after Coyote snuck his pizzle into a spirit woman. That old coon had to knock the teeth out of her cunt with a rock before he could have her. Afterward she gave birth to the first people. Kept these newborn people in a basket, but they eventually got out and ran around fucking and having babies. And some became the *Newe*. Our people."

This time Butler turned far enough to glare at the men, ensuring their silence.

Cracked Bone Thrower pointed to the peaks across the valley. "White coons call those mountains Absaroka. Dukurika call them the Wind River's Mountains because they are the birthplace of the water. Water is everything to my people."

Butler stared at the distant peaks, feeling the slight chill to the air. Behind them, just down from the ridge and sheltered from the west wind, the Dukurika had set up their hide-and-brush lodges in little hollows cut into the slope. It might be hell to climb to, but from here he could see clear across the Wind River Basin to the distant Green

Mountains. Had to be a hundred and fifty miles or so.

Butler had counted sixty-seven men, women, and children, and sixteen of the big dogs. Just below the alpine camp lay a snowfield, its surface covered with bighorn sheep carcasses — and the reason the high-altitude camp was occupied.

The day after they'd brought Butler here, the band had managed to herd a flock of bighorn sheep into a V-shaped drive line on the other side of the ridge. He'd watched from a distance as the people and dogs had slowly eased the animals into the trap's confines. At the *puhagan*'s cry, they had rushed the milling sheep, funneling them between the narrowing drive lines and into a log pen. Even as the sheep piled together a large net had been thrown over them. As soon as it settled, the panicked sheep had crouched down as though paralyzed.

Butler had turned away as men and women with clubs waded in, whacking and smacking. It may not have been pretty, but it was over within a minute. Then the real work began as the carcasses were dragged out one by one, gutted and quartered, and carried down to the snow patch to cool.

"Winter food," Cracked Bone Thrower had told Butler and the men. Though Butler had offered to pitch in and carry his share, Cracked Bone Thrower had told him, "You stay away, Man Who Talks to No One. Puhagan is still uncertain about your Power, or even if it is good or bad. People don't want you close yet."

And maybe it was for the best. To Butler's chagrin, even when he went about collecting firewood for the camp, all but the littlest of children worked harder than he could. He'd stop,

757

gasping for breath, while the little tykes would race up and down the slopes, hopping from rock to rock like Shakespearean sprites.

Though the people treated him with reserve, not wanting to get too close, he'd gotten a good look at them. Unlike the Cherokee, or the Cheyenne he'd met on the trail, these were a tall, muscular, sun-darkened people. They worked almost naked while mucking around in the blood and gore of the kill pen and gut piles, and then scrubbed themselves clean with snow before dressing again for the evening. He had never known Indians as clean and well dressed. Or nearly as attractive.

He was constantly disciplining the men, minding them to keep their tongues civil, especially when it came to comments about the half-naked young women with their glistening black hair and supple, bare-breasted bodies.

When the Dukurika thought Butler wasn't looking, they laughed, joked, sang curiously unintelligible songs, and played, often slinging guts at each other, or pulling other tricks. The children were obviously loved and indulged as they crawled over the adults, got their heads patted, and were constantly attended to.

The men were all muscle and sinew, and possessed of a self-assured virility. The women, too, were lithe and muscular, with an almost irresistible allure, as if their athletic bodies exuded some elemental sensuality. The pregnant women were the most remarkable to Butler, working right alongside everyone else, apparently oblivious to a condition that would have required their enforced isolation back in American society. Here they carried on as if their swollen abdomens and protruding navels were no more out of the ordinary than the clouds in the sky.

Was this what Rousseau had been thinking of all those years ago when he wrote his *Discourse on the Origin of Inequality*?

That afternoon the Sheep Eaters started down the mountain. Packing camp hadn't taken more than fifteen minutes. The brush-and-branch lodges were simply abandoned, along with the grinding stones, heavy butchering tools, and even the big net, which was stuffed into the dry shelter of a rock overhang.

"It will be waiting for us next year," Cracked Bone Thrower told him with a shrug. "We know these hills and camps. Why carry heavy tools when you know there's another one just like it waiting where you left it last season? And shelters are easy to make. It doesn't take more than an afternoon."

Butler had offered his horses, both of which were packed with meat. So, too, were the big pack dogs, each loaded with the weight of a sheep. Every man, woman, and child carried his share.

"We're headed for a camp down in the canyon," Cracked Bone Thrower told him. "From there it is a couple of days' travel to a special place. One where Puhagan wants to take you. It is an old place, one where *puha* rises from the ground through cracks in the stone. A place where Water Babies and *nynymbi* and *dzoavits* emerge from the Underworld."

"And what does that have to do with me?"

"He will see if you are good or evil, Butler Hancock. There, he and the spirits will look into your souls."

Butler had to turn his concentration to a tricky descent where the trail pitched almost straight down. Here he had to skip to stay ahead of the horses, hooves locked as they slid. The pack dogs, he'd noted, had simply jumped from boulder to boulder. No wonder these people didn't have horses.

When the trail went back to simple switchbacks, he asked, "What do you mean, souls? I've only got one."

Cracked Bone Thrower raised a skeptical eyebrow. "You plumb sure about that, coon? You see ghosts, yes? You say you see them with your eyes, but my eyes don't see nobody. Maybe you got another soul in yer body? Puhagan, he wonders if 'n you got the usual three souls, or maybe a fourth."

"Three souls? A fourth? That's . . ." But he couldn't quite allow himself to say it was crazy.

"Sounds like satanic nonsense to me," Pettigrew grumbled where he walked off to the side.

Cracked Bone Thrower might have been loaded with feathers, instead of the eighty-some pounds of meat slung on his back, given the way he hopped onto a log that had fallen across the trail. He said, "Among the *Newe* we know a person has three souls. Your *suap* is the soul that fills your lungs and breath. The *mugwa* is the soul what lives in your bones and blood. Finally your *nuvashieip* is the seeing soul that slips in and out of your body. You see through its eyes when you dream, when you see faraway places. Puhagan wonders if perhaps you somehow have *two* different *nuvashieip* locked inside you."

"And how is he going to find this out?" Butler asked skeptically, glancing sidelong to where his men marched beside him; somehow they maintained their footing on the steep mountainside.

Pettigrew was grinning, shaking his head dismissively. Billy Templeton, however, looked worried. The others, marching along, kept shooting Cracked Bone Thrower wary sidelong glances.

Kershaw, however, had been missing since he'd announced the arrival of the Sheep Eaters. That realization sent a tingle of warning through Butler's gut. The sergeant hadn't been acting right. Not since Butler's stern rebuke for bringing up Chickamauga on the trail.

But this notion that he had another soul stuck inside him?

Silly heathen superstition!

"And what will the *puhagan* do if he thinks my souls are evil?" Butler asked.

"He will kill you. And then, as each of your diseased souls emerges from your body, he will destroy them. If your *mugwa* is good, he will leave your body for the wolves and coyotes. If it is evil, he will roll a big boulder onto your bones to trap them there forever."

Butler ground his teeth, seeing hard promise in Cracked Bone Thrower's black eyes. Little sparks of fear began to flicker around his heart.

96

September 8, 1867

"I now pronounce you man and wife," the preacher said, one hand on the pages of his open Bible. "You may kiss the bride."

Sarah watched Doc lift the light blue veil from Aggie's scar-lined face. No, not Aggie. Bridget. Bridget O'Fallon Hancock. It had come as a shock to Sarah when the preacher called her friend Bridget, but of course Aggie would have wanted to be married under her given name.

Doc leaned forward, placing his lips on Bridget's, kissing her with a sensitive passion Sarah had only known with Bret. The two of them seemed to melt together, as if the small church were illusory and the two lovers the only reality in the firmament.

The preacher cleared his throat, slightly embarrassed, and murmured, "Reckon y'all got the rest of yer lives fer that."

Doc and Bridget broke apart, grinned, and turned, both shooting radiant smiles at Sarah.

Doc took Bridget's arm and marched her up to Sarah. "May I present my wife, Mrs. Hancock?"

"My pleasure," Sarah told Bridget, folding her into a hug. "I couldn't wish you a better man.

And look! We're truly sisters!"

Bridget hugged her fiercely. "This is the happiest day of my life."

"Come," Sarah said as they parted. "I've taken the liberty of ordering food to be delivered to Doc's . . . uh, *your* house. I thought we might have a quiet supper before I retire and leave you to contemplate your happiness. It *should* be a family celebration."

Doc was giving her a thoughtful look as he held Bridget's arm and walked from the crude little church. Why Doc had chosen it was beyond her, given his constant preoccupation with God, justice, suffering, and the inherent flaws in the universe.

A carriage waited to take them the three blocks to Doc's. An indulgence Sarah had insisted on.

"Don't be a silly duck," she'd told him. "I insist. You shall be treated as royalty."

She'd been ready to pull the cord on the cannon and shoot the moon when it came to the wedding, only to have Doc and Aggie demur.

"We want it small," Doc had insisted. "Just the three of us and the preacher. We don't want anyone counting the days. And we sure don't want announcements in the *Rocky Mountain News.* God alone knows what that skunk Byers or his team of scribblers will publish. It's enough that Aggie will be my wife, due and legal, and that she and I will wear our rings."

At Doc's she led the way up the stairs and into the small living room. Mam had done herself spectacularly, having laid the table with a roasted goose, a baked potato, and a loaf of fresh-baked bread with chokecherry jam. All of which, given the shortages and deplorable lack of fresh vegetables in the city, was a culinary miracle.

"Oh, my God," Bridget cried, placing hands to her face. "This is a feast for kings!"

"Well," Sarah admitted, "at least for a king and queen. I shall act as your squire and handmaiden." She stepped around the table as Doc held Bridget's chair, then she held his as he was seated.

Sarah poured Madeira from the last bottle surviving from the Angel's Lair opening, and offered the toast. "To Mr. and Mrs. Philip Hancock. Huzzah! Huzzah! And may love and prosperity fill all the days of your lives."

"Here! Here!" Doc and Bridget cried in unison.

Sarah served — a feeling of contentment warm in her breast. "I do wish Maw, Butler, and Billy could be here to see this."

"Life didn't quite give us the paths we hoped to walk, did it?" Doc asked, taking a bite of roast goose. "Oh my, that is wonderful. Mam just makes miracles, doesn't she?"

"The way she tells it," Bridget added, "slaves had to find ways to make do with almost nothing, so they figured out recipes that made food their masters wouldn't eat into delicacies."

"In the end, it's always about making the best out of hard times, isn't it?"

"You referring to my condition, Doc?" Bridget said hesitantly, her fork halfway to her mouth.

"Good God, no!" Doc replied in shock. "I was thinking of prison camp, and how men with nothing, not even hope, managed to hang on." He took a deep breath, reaching across the table for Bridget's hand. "*We* are having a child. Together. As a husband and his wife do. I love you, Bridget. More today than I have ever loved you. Events forced us to move with greater rapidity than perhaps I would have liked, but as I told you, I've been thinking of marriage for some time now. I could not be happier."

Sarah watched them staring into each other's eyes, at the way they smiled with such intimacy. Damn, she missed Bret. Too often she caught herself dreaming of his smile and laugh. At times she practically ached for his company, especially that wry amusement with which he viewed the world. For those months that she and Bret had been together, she'd had a fit mate for body and soul. In the aftermath of his murder, she'd been lonelier than even during those terrible days after she fled from Billy.

"What's wrong, Sarah?" Bridget asked, sensitive as usual to her moods. "That's the missing-Bret look."

Sarah smiled, spread her hands wide. "Guilty. If the two of you have half, just half, of what we had, you'll be daisies for the rest of your lives."

"We'll make do," Doc said, thoughtfully watching her. "With a child coming, Bridget and I have been talking. It's no longer just the two of us. The child will change things."

"Doc and I will want to relocate," Bridget said. "Sometime. After the child is born. We're thinking maybe California. Someplace where Doc can establish a surgery where no one knows who we are. What we've been."

Sarah gave Bridget a wink. "Were I in your shoes, I'd do the same." She cut a thick slice from the breast. "My goals are compatible. I think we should sell the Angel's Lair by next summer, Aggie. The new girls are working out. The playacting is popular, and we've added an element the johnnies have never known they were missing. If we were to push it to two years, I think the newness would be worn off, or someone is going to copy our action."

"And then what are you going to do?" Doc asked.

"Property." She glanced between the two of them. "I've been buying up lots in Cheyenne. Railroad should be there in a month or so. And believe me, the railroad is going to change this country like nothing else. You'd be surprised what a girl can learn when Big Ed, George Nichols, or Pat O'Reilly is whispering in her ear."

"You worry me sometimes, sister," Doc told her. "Your playmates are scary."

She smiled wistfully. "Philip, my world started to crumble the day Butler and Paw rode off to war. Silly girl that I was, I thought all I had to do was marry the right man. Which, of course, Paw would see to. I only needed to look pretty and offer myself as a brood mare to produce my husband's children. It wouldn't have been on the basis of love as you and Bridget are doing, but a service in return for a place in my husband's house, and the status I derived from his."

"And how is that different from what you have now? You're still depending upon men. A lot of them as they pass through."

"Aggie and I *own* the house," she told him with a deadly smile. "And we're using it as a stepping-stone. But true power, brother, lies in money and property. I may be a fancy whore for the moment, but only until I can grow the value of the Angel's Lair into enough capital to acquire the right property. And when I sell that, I'll acquire even more property, until I can buy and sell the men who've bought and sold me."

766

Philip looked at her through somber eyes. "That sounds hard and cold, little sister. You used to have a romantic side, almost dreamy eyed as you talked about the future."

"That Sarah is long dead, Philip. Maybe it happened when men were bleeding and dying on our living room floor. Or the wagonloads of half-frozen, half-rotted corpses I hauled for the Yankees. Might have been Maw and me starving when the armies took our food. Anything that was left was gang-raped out of me by Dewley and his men. When I finally found I could love with all my heart, Parmelee shot it dead in my front door. Every lesson I've learned has taught me that the world is heartless, ruthless, and fit only for the strong and smart."

"And Parmelee's still out there," Bridget noted.

"And Parmelee's still out there," Sarah repeated softly.

Doc's eyes mirrored a wounded soul, as if he shared every bit of her suffering and anger. Bridget, lips pursed, glanced anxiously at her husband.

"We have all lost so much," he said softly. "Suffered so much. I just wish . . . Well, never mind."

Sarah shook her head, raised her hands. "But let us forget about me. Today is about you. Both of you. And it is about family, and the realization that even though there are only three of us left, you and Aggie are building the future with that wonderful new life within her womb."

Sarah lifted her glass again. "To both of you, and to a better and brighter future!"

"To the future," they chimed, a rosy glow in Bridget's cheeks. She looked so happy, so flushed with joy, that for a moment at least, Sarah could almost believe in hope again.

97

September 22, 1867

The fire popped and crackled, shooting sparks up into the chilly night sky. Butler sat naked but for a sheephide blanket wrapped around his shoulders. His breath was visible with each exhalation and shone in the firelight as though golden.

He, Cracked Bone Thrower, and Puhagan had traveled here — a three-day journey back down the Wind River and then west into the foothills, following the channel of a rushing, clear-watered creek that Cracked Bone Thrower had told him was called Water Belonging to Pandzoavitz — where on the northern bank, above a small clear-water lake, the *puhagan* had ordered a camp made just up from the shore and below a boulder-studded field that rose to a steep and rocky valley slope.

"You must be clean inside and out, Man Who Talks to No One. There will be no food. No water. Just the praying."

Puhagan had erected a small, domed shelter with Cracked Bone Thrower's help. For a solid day now, Butler had been walking down to the lake, bathing, and climbing the slope to the little sweat lodge where the *puhagan* had brushed

Butler's naked body with a branch of sagebrush, then scooped smoke from the fire with an eagle-wing fan and wafted it over Butler's flesh. All the while the old man kept singing in the soft and sibilant Dukurika tongue.

After each of these cleansings, Butler was urged into the cramped sweat lodge. Cracked Bone Thrower would lift stones from the fire with mule deer horns, and lay them inside the small lodge.

After the *puhagan* had entered, he would close the flap, sealing them in darkness. Then, from a bladder, he would douse the white-glowing stones. Steam would explode in an angry sizzle. Within moments, Butler would be gasping for breath, his skin prickling, and sweat would run from his hide as if he were being baked alive.

Having endured all that, he threw his head back and blinked up at the night, seeing a billion stars like frost across the sky. The Milky Way ran in a forked streak from horizon to horizon, only to be blocked by the black shadows of the narrowing mountain valley to either side.

The men were crowded around, just out of the fire's light. More than seeing them, Butler could feel their presence. Pettigrew — usually the complainer — was unusually sullen. And while Kershaw remained missing, Butler could sense the Cajun's fear.

That sent a shiver down his back. He'd never known Kershaw to be afraid of anything.

At Puhagan's barked command, Cracked Bone Thrower said, "Put your blanket down. Then lay on your back, looking up at the sky."

Butler nodded, arranging the sheep-hide blanket on the scrubby grass and lying down. The chill immediately ate into his chest, stomach, and

770

thighs. He could feel his testicles knotting, his skin going to gooseflesh. Nevertheless, he endured, looking up at the night sky in all its crystal brilliance.

Still singing, Puhagan leaned over him and began thumping on Butler's body. First he tapped on his arms, then his shoulders, his chest, and belly. Next he thumped on Butler's right leg starting at the thigh and moving down to the foot. Finally he did the left.

Sitting back on his haunches, the old man raised his hands to the night sky, and sang with greater emphasis. When he finished, he reached into a pouch and removed a stone tube maybe five inches long, an inch in diameter, with a hole drilled through it.

The man bent down, placed the tube to Butler's shivering skin, and sucked vigorously at the upper arms. Then above Butler's right and left breasts. Just up from his navel. In the hollow above his pubis bone, and on both thighs.

"What was that?" Butler asked, as Puhagan straightened.

Cracked Bone Thrower told him, "He has found poisoned places in your body. He has sucked them out."

Even as Cracked Bone Thrower said this, the *puhagan* bent to the side, spitting what looked like a stream of bloody spit into the flames. As the expectorate hit the fire, it burst into a malignant yellow smoke that rose in a pillar.

"Dear God," Butler whispered.

Puhagan turned, staring thoughtfully at Butler who was now shivering from the chill. He said something in Shoshoni, his voice firm.

"Eat what the *puhagan* gives you," Cracked

771

Bone Thrower told him. "It is *toyatawura*. The Power plant. It will free your souls and allow you to see into the places of Power. Only when *toyatawura* has separated you from yourself, can you travel to the dark water world beneath the earth."

Butler took the bits of woody root the old man gave him, and chewed. It was all he could do to keep from making a face at the bitter taste. Even harder to finally swallow the stuff. It seemed to stick in his throat, sort of like trying to choke down a cocklebur.

"Go," Cracked Bone Thrower told him. "Take your blanket and follow the trails to the boulders. The spirits will watch you. Judge you. If you are lucky one will call to you. When you hear the voice calling from the stone, lie down before the spirit. There you will sleep. The *puhagan* will watch and see which spirits are called to you. Then they will tell him what to do with you."

"Just get up and walk up through the boulders?" Butler asked as he got to his feet, still trying to get the chewed root to go down.

Did they really think a piece of woody root would separate him from his body? And what silliness was this anyway? Venturing to the water world? Spirits? It was the year of our Lord eighteen hundred and sixty-seven, for God's sake! Not the Middle Ages when idiot superstition ruled the world.

Cracked Bone Thrower pointed up the slope, his expression stern.

Toyatawura? What kind of word was that?

In the darkness, hobbling on his bare feet, Butler made his way up into the scattered boulders, some as large as a freight wagon. He tripped over low

772

sagebrush, stubbed his toes on stones, and felt his way.

His stomach pitched suddenly, an eerie tingle running through his arms and legs, down into his hands and feet. His penis began to warm, as though immersed in hot water. The air rushing into his lungs with each breath seemed to vibrate. Around him the night turned liquid in his vision, as though he looked at it from underwater.

Here, a voice called, eerie and soft on the night. Where?

This way.

He found a level spot, as though it had been dug out before a flat-sided boulder. The great stone was as tall as he. On this boulder-studded slope, one rock was as good as the next. This one felt curiously warm. He took a deep breath, wrapping the sheephide blanket around his shoulders. Cracked Bone Thrower had given it to him. Superbly tanned with the hair on, embroidered, and decorated with porcupine quills, it was remarkably warm.

Butler blinked. The sensation that rolled through him was as if the world were washing back and forth amid waves, surging, ebbing, and flowing.

Looking back toward camp, he could see a solitary figure who stood before the fire. He was glowing as if lit from within.

The puhagan. *Watching. Yes, that's who it is.*

"I am supposed to sleep," Butler whispered to himself, feeling odd prickles run through his muscles and bones. As if *that* was going to happen. He was being judged, after all. And if he failed, the *puhagan* would kill him.

Who could sleep feeling the way he did, all prickly and hot, knowing his life was forfeit if he

773

failed the medicine man's test?

"Does it even matter anymore?" Butler asked himself.

Power brought you here. It wants you to do this.

"To do what?"

Learn.

His eyes felt leaden. Tucking the blanket around his shoulders, he hunched forward and sat in the boulder's lee. Whatever the *toyatawura* was, it had fogged his head, heightened his senses. His insides continued to prickle and tingle. Every sound came clearly to his ears. The very act of breathing preoccupied him with wonder; his heart — the pump of life — kept swelling and constricting within his chest.

Why had he never noticed what a miracle it was just to be alive?

Images came slowly at first, just hints, flickers of sights and sounds long gone. Then his memory opened like a rush; the visions spun through his head: scenes from his childhood on the farm. Paw at the supper table, leaned back, his big hands slapping his thighs as he told a tall story about the mountains. These mountains.

He stared into Tom Hindman's preoccupied face that first day in the hotel lobby, the man clutching Butler's letter of introduction in his hand.

Images shifted, and suddenly he was back at Shiloh, watching men shot apart and murdered by Federal fire. Death. So much death. In the blackness of a cold Arkansas night, he watched hogs eating partially cooked human bodies in the burned remains of haystacks.

Saw the men and boys shot down for being deserters.

And then, moment by moment, he relived

Chickamauga . . . and terror, and fear, and guilt . . .

He threw his head back and screamed.

98

September 23, 1867

Butler remembered the coming of daylight, how it shot spectacular colors across the morning sky and set high, threadlike clouds afire with orange, gold, blazing yellow, and violet. The mountains around him emerged from the gloom and seemed to throb with color: purple, green, and gray running together and smearing like melted rainbows.

He was floating, his essence borne aloft by the spirit plant's wings. His soul hovered in the air above his body. With each puff of breeze, he bobbed like a stem of grass, bending, rising, but unable to blow away.

Toyatawura. This was magic, powerful, ancient, and pure.

And then he began to dream . . .

Looking down, he could see his body where it crouched before the stony boulder's face. When he truly looked at the rock, it was to find a small creature staring back at him from a carving in the stone — a being with a curiously inverted triangular face in an oblong and squat body. It wore a sort of wavering headdress. Pencil-thin arms emerged from the shoulders and bent, as if thrust up and out in surprise. The hands each sported three long flowing fingers. Sticklike legs curled down into long three-toed feet from which sinuous lines of magic flowed down into the ground.

"You called me last night."

"You called me," the being replied, its voice reedy inside Butler's head. *"You are lost and need a guide."*

Even as the little creature spoke, he turned, calling, *"If you would find yourself, follow me."*

"Follow you? Into the rock?"

"It is the way."

"Who are you?"

"I am nynymbi. *Come."* It gestured, and Butler followed, squeezing down through the crack in the rock, as if it were the most natural thing in the world.

The way was narrow, dark, and gritty as Butler eased his way through the thin passage.

"Where are we going?"

"To find out how many souls you have." Nynymbi stopped when the way opened into a small hollow. He reached his three-fingered hands into a pool of water close to Butler's bare feet. When he withdrew them they were covered with slime.

The *nynymbi* said, *"You will pass the rock ogre first. He has skin of stone and hands covered with sticky pitch. He will try and grab you. If he succeeds, he will carry you off and eat you. When we come to him, pull your hair forward over your face so that the rock ogre cannot see your eyes, nose, or mouth. That way he cannot recognize you as human. Meanwhile, I will smear trout slime on your skin, so that when he touches you, his fingers won't stick. When he smells them, he will think you are a fish."*

Butler struggled not to make a face as the *nynymbi* slathered smelly fish slime on his skin. Then, according to instructions, he pulled his hair over his face as best he could.

And a good thing. They had no more than rounded a bend in the fissure, than what looked like three boulders piled atop each other rose on stony feet. Slender arms reached out with sticky-looking three-fingered hands. The ogre made a sound like stone grating on stone as its fingers traced over Butler's skin. Then it smelled them, sighed, and settled back into what looked no more offensive than a pile of rocks.

The *nynymbi* slipped sideways down a small tunnel and stepped out on the shores of an underground lake.

Butler stared around, hearing the drip of water echoing in the underground cavern. The lake's surface looked smooth, black, and heavy where it rimmed the stony shore.

The *nynymbi* stopped and looked up at Butler through hollow circles of eyes. *"This is as far as I can take you."*

"Where do I go from here?"

"I will take you to her," another voice told him from below.

Startled, Butler leaped away, realizing he'd almost stepped on a mossy-backed turtle that had looked like just another cobble on the stone-strewn shore.

"Who are you?" Butler asked warily.

"One of her servants. I can take you to her." The turtle paused. *"If you have the courage."*

Butler shot the *nynymbi* a worried glance, then reluctantly followed as the turtle clambered up and over the rocks, its shell scraping, claws scratching across the stone.

In the end, Butler couldn't help himself. "Can you tell me where we're going?"

"To find out about the dead clinging to your dream soul. That's what you came here for, isn't it? To determine why you cannot rid yourself of the dead?"

The turtle continued to scuttle awkwardly over the rocks, its shell knocking hollowly. The still black water lay unmoving to the right.

The lake ended where the cavern roof dropped down to a small grotto. The turtle scrambled its way into the mossy opening, beyond which lay a low chamber whose shape reminded Butler of a long bottle laid on its side.

She stood in water up to her waist; her large dark eyes fixed on his as he slowed and stared in disbelief. What looked like a huge wolf lay curled on the moss to her left. The beast fixed its deadly yellow eyes on Butler, then yawned, rose, and strode past him and out of the chamber with languid strides.

The turtle slipped off the moss and vanished into the dark water, its passing not causing so much as a ripple.

Butler turned his attention back to the woman. His heart skipped at the sight of her. Had he ever seen such rich, thick black hair? It hung about her like a raven-dark mantle, gleaming in the darkness as though it were a robe. Her wondrous dark eyes were possessed of an inner light; the face in which they resided a perfect and exotic blend of high cheekbones, lush lips, and a straight and regal nose. With slender fingers she clutched a rattle in her right hand, a bow and arrows in her left.

As she stepped toward him the water didn't so much as stir, as though she flowed magically forward. The seductive sway of her hips hearkened of unadulterated sexuality.

Butler might have been frozen, his heart hammering, as she gave a graceful flip of her head, and the glossy wave of her hair curled back behind her. Her naked body seemed to pulse with each beat of Butler's heart. He couldn't help but stare at her full breasts topped by hard brown nipples, at her narrow waist, and the dark shadow of her navel. Between her muscular thighs, her midnight pubic hair beckoned, looking thick, warm, and soft.

He tried not to stare. Knew it was rude. He just couldn't help it. Nor did she appear the least alarmed by his gaze, but seemed to undulate toward him in a most sensuous manner. Her smile widened, the endless depth in her eyes welcoming, warming.

She stopped before him, eyes locked on his, lips parted. The odor of mint perfumed her breath.

Senses swimming, Butler squirmed from the ache in his hardened penis and the tension in his testicles. His breath came in short gasps, his skin electric, heart hammering. Every nerve in his body seemed to be singing. To gaze into her wide eyes was to fall into their bottomless depths.

She melted against him, arms wrapping around his back. Ecstasy shimmered through every inch of him that touched her. Which was nothing compared to the liquid thrill that ran into his pelvis and up his spine as she slid onto his throbbing erection.

She pulled him down onto the moss, her hips rocking in time to his deep strokes. Excitement mirrored delight as her eyes flashed and her mouth opened. Her arms tightened, pressing him against the cushion of her breasts. Like a vise her legs had locked around his hips and thighs.

Butler gasped as the tingle built in his loins.

The very instant he filled his lungs to cry out, she rolled him into the water.

Butler inhaled, sucking liquid. His body remained locked with hers, paralyzed by the sensation as his genitals throbbed and tingled. His sudden terror did nothing to stop the waves of pulsing delight bursting through his body.

Butler thrashed, trying to break free. Her arms were like iron bands. Even as he fought, they tightened and forced air out of his starving lungs.

He coughed, half crazy at the water in his nose and mouth. Wild with panic, he sucked it into his lungs. He jerked, struck, and bucked against the woman's unforgiving restraint. His penis continued to spasm inside her, as if she were draining him.

The frantic panic of suffocation crested. Subsided. His vision drowned in blackness. Faded. He could no longer feel the water in his nose, throat, and lungs. The pounding of his heart slowed. Even the honeyed sensations of ejaculation faded into the distance.

His last memories were of stygian eternity. Weightless. The woman's body locked around his. The feeling of her long hair drifting against and tickling his skin.

Sinking faded into nothing . . .

Awareness came slowly. Naked, he sat on a rock. He might have been sitting there for a long time. Perhaps even forever.

At his feet, still water met the rocky shore, dark, black, and eternal.

He was in a cavern. Somewhere deep underground.

"Are you back?"

He turned at the voice. The woman sat beside him. Her luxurious black hair draped around and conformed to her remarkable body. Through gaps he could see the pale swell of her breasts, caught a glimpse of her thick pubic hair. Her luminous dark eyes were fixed on the water before them.

"Back?" he wondered.

"From death." Her dark eyes seemed to enlarge in her face. "A man and a woman can make the most exhilarating things happen when they are locked together. It was a surprise to discover you'd never been with a woman before."

"You drowned me."

"I had to kill you to separate you from your souls."

"Who *are* you?"

She turned those large midnight eyes on his. "The *Newe* call me Water Ghost Woman. *Pa'waip* in their tongue." She gestured toward the cavern roof. "They are calling for you up there."

"Who?"

"The parts of yourself that you left behind. They know that you are dead and are frightened. They fear what you might discover about yourself."

"I don't understand."

"Of course you don't. That's why you came here. To find yourself."

"Puhagan brought me here."

"He, too, knows that you are dead. He wonders, Did one of the monsters, perhaps the rock ogre, kill you? Did a Water Ghost drag your dream soul into the darkness and devour it?"

"But I'm alive."

"Are you?" She laughed, flashing strong white teeth. "Why did you flee to this place? Travel all this way just to let me kill you?"

"Paw always talked about the mountains."

"Ah yes. The father. The man behind it all. The reason you clung to the dead . . . why you won't let them go. Your greatest fear has always been that you might not live up to his expectations."

She reached out, running long sensuous fingers along his shoulder and arm. Her slightest touch stoked that sexual tingle in his loins. "Your soul wasn't made for war and horror. You knew that, didn't you? But once you'd been thrown into the battle, you tortured yourself to become someone you could not be. And when you failed, it was easier to exploit the dead than to live within the shadow of a father's disappointment."

"How do you know all this?"

"You ate *toyatawura.* You shot your souls into me with each hot jet of semen. You are mine, wounded man."

"What will you do with me?"

She studied him, her infinite gaze picking out each of his souls, warming it before she went to the next. Her hair swayed with each movement of her head. "You interest me. It was your choice to live with the dead. You called them, bound them into your service."

"They *need* me to take them home!"

"No man is as blind as when he turns his eyes upon himself. Why do you lie to yourself?"

"I . . . I . . ." To admit anything else would be too painful.

She spoke the words he could not: "They *take care* of you. Shield you from the world. Keep the pain at bay."

Butler gasped, tucking his arms around his stomach and blinking back tears. The essence inside him twisted, spun, as if to fly away. He felt sick.

"If you were a vain man" — her voice softened — "or arrogant, I would devour you. But you came here as a supplicant, showing both courage and humility. Instead of death" — her smile was chilling and cold — "I give you what you seek."

"What I seek?"

"A chance to escape the contradiction that consumes you. To understand the root of your fear, and face the truth. Only then will you find illumination and happiness."

"You don't make sense. Understand what?"

"Your confusion." She paused, head back to expose her slim throat. "That the living are dead, and dead are living. The knowledge may destroy you. Come spring, I will give you the Silver Eagle. By saving the Silver Eagle, you condemn him. But understanding never comes without a price. Life, hope, love, and salvation all hang in the balance."

At that, she reached out and touched her fingertips to his forehead. A sense of peace washed through him.

Then a black haze drifted softly down around his body . . .

Butler blinked, shivered, and tried to swallow. His mouth was filled with a bitter taste. His head ached as if his skull were split. He lay on his side in dusty dirt, a soft sheephide blanket over his shoulders.

Groaning, he sat up and realized that his head was covered, a sort of blindfold over his eyes, a binding across his mouth.

Frantically, he clawed the coverings of cloth from his head, sucking in deep breaths. He blinked to clear his hazy vision and discovered he wasn't wearing so much as a stitch. Worse, some red paint had been smeared in patterns over his chest and stomach. Lines of blue clay ran down his thighs. What looked like a coating of white clay was flaking off his penis.

The sound of voices came to him. Men singing in Dukurika Shoshoni. Two of them. He shifted, made himself sit up. Mountains rose around him, a crystalline blue lake just down from where he lay. Overhead the sky was light blue, sunlight just cresting a ridge. The smell of sagebrush, juniper, and water rode down from above on the chilly breeze.

He was sitting before a big gray boulder, and as he started to stand, he froze. There — engraved on the rock — was the *nynymbi*. The short and squat figure seemed to stare out at him from the depths of the stone.

"Holy jumping Jesus," Butler whispered.

Images came rolling up from his memory. It had to have been a dream — and a fevered one at that. Or it had been a version of madness that would have even horrified Philip.

He sucked in gulps of cold air, his body shivering. *Nynymbi,* rock ogres, Water Ghost Woman, these were stories. Stories he'd heard from Cracked Bone Thrower. But why would he have fixed upon them and dreamed so fervently . . . ?

The spirit plant. What was it called? *Toyatawura.*

He'd heard of the phantasms conjured in opium dens. It had to be similar, a drug-induced haze of imagination.

He stood, bracing himself on the rock and avoiding the *nynymbi's* gaze. Looking down the slope he could see the two men. Recognized the rounded shape of the sweat lodge.

Puhagan sat cross-legged, head back, his painted face turned to the sky, arms resting palms up on his knees. Cracked Bone Thrower was thumping a small drum, his eyes closed. He sat across the fire from the medicine man.

I don't take care of the men? They take care of me?

He stumbled slightly, Water Ghost Woman's eternally dark eyes watching from the depths of his soul. He'd *never* had a dream that vivid, erotic, or terrifying.

His stomach felt like an empty hole. His bladder ached with the need to empty itself.

"Hey?" he croaked through a rusty and swollen throat. "What the hell happened? Where are my clothes?"

Cracked Bone Thrower opened his eyes, the drumming stopped. "You were dead."

"Pa'waip killed me." He made a face. "But that was only a dream. My dream. You couldn't know."

"Your body was dead, Man Who Talks to No One. You stopped breathing. Your heart no longer beat. We have been making medicine to appease your *mugwa* and *suap* so that they would not come back and plague our people."

"Pa'waip?" Puhagan asked. His eyes opened but remained fixed on the sky. He said something that Cracked Bone Thrower translated as, "She is not known for mercy. The *puhagan* asks why she let you live?"

"She said I was a good man."

When that was translated, Puhagan asked something else.

786

Cracked Bone Thrower seemed to hesitate, then asked, "Did she tell you anything? Give you a gift?"

"Something about a silver eagle. If I save it, I condemn it." Butler couldn't stop shivering. His flesh felt like ice. "Puhagan, she's not merciful. I wonder if it wouldn't have been better if she'd just devoured my souls."

"Why is that?" Cracked Bone Thrower asked.

"Because she left me with the truth, and now I have to live with it."

99

November 26, 1867

That day in Fort Benton, Billy sat at a back table in the restaurant at Baker's Chouteau Hotel. He had his foot up on a second chair. His cup of coffee rested by his right hand, and a cigar perched on a tin ashtray before him. Even at midmorning the establishment was busy. Billy could hear the hollow thump of boots through the plank floor overhead. The place was loud with the clink of dishes and utensils and the animated talk and laughter shared by the patrons.

In the wake of Danny's betrayal, he'd come back to Fort Benton, certain he'd take a berth on one of the boats. That he'd ride on a steamboat. Go to St. Louis. See what a real city was like. Try once and for all to rid himself of Maw's and Sarah's ghosts. Maybe drive the demons from his head.

But the last of the boats had gone, racing winter and low water.

He'd tried drink, but that didn't seem to make a difference. Strangling a whore? Sometimes it worked, other times she just fixed herself in his dreams with the other ghouls, and stared hollowly out from his memory with dead eyes.

He picked up his cigar and drew, enjoying the

euphoria that tobacco sent pulsing through his veins. One thing for sure, if you could afford it, Fort Benton had everything. Fine cigars, good drink, real beds with mattresses, tinned oysters and pickled fish, fine clothing, and anything a fella needed to freshen his trail outfit.

Word was that no less than thirty-eight steamboats had unloaded their cargo at the levee that summer. One boat had carried more than a million dollars in gold back to St. Louis. If there were a center to Montana, Billy was smack in the middle of it. But it was a curious sort of center: a smattering of frame buildings in the midst of a haphazard mixture of tents and dugouts that looked sort of half circus and part prairie-dog town. So copious had been the cargo unloaded at the levee — and the transport so insufficient — that bullwhackers were still arriving, loading their wagons, and pulling out next day for the mining camps. Even at this late date and after the first hard blizzard.

He washed down the taste of the cigar with another swig of coffee. Real coffee. At I. G. Baker's store he'd even traded in his old worn Sharps for a brand new Model 1863 sporting rifle. It shot flatter than his old gun, and he was still learning how to adjust the sights at distance.

He nodded as the boy came around with the coffeepot and watched as his cup was filled. At the nearest table, one of the bullwhackers laughed at a joke. The four of them looked the worse for the morning, having bucked the tiger in the all-night saloons. They would load their wagons today, and be off at first light tomorrow for Helena.

Billy smiled warily and puffed his cigar to keep

it burning. He was a man of leisure. That's what having money was all about.

"So what are you going to do?" he asked under his breath as he stared into the coffee. Damn it all, he'd never been this lonely. He'd expected Danny to come back. To have at least sent word. But no post was forwarded from Helena. Nor was there a message in Helena's *Herald* paper — though Billy had seen one from George Nichols dated a couple of weeks back.

He needed only telegraph if he wanted a job.

But did he?

Would it be the same without Danny?

He lifted his cigar and took another puff. Chairs scraped as a group of rough-looking men — woodcutters from their clothes — took the last empty table. They draped their thick buffalo coats on the chair backs, frozen snow melting from the hair and dripping on the floor.

It would be risky without Danny going in advance to do the scouting. More people would see him. No one would be watching his back.

"Damn you, Danny," Billy whispered under his breath. He was the Meadowlark. Powerful men feared him, knew from his reputation that were he hired to kill them, their lives were forfeit. And here he was, wounded, a half-man because Danny had left him. And worse, Danny had fled knowing that after his desertion, if Billy ever caught up with him, that his onetime friend wouldn't suffer the slightest remorse over shooting him dead.

It's because of what you've become, the voice inside his head told him.

"And what is that?" he asked himself softly, his eyes on the rising streamers of smoke coming off the cigar ash.

You're a monster!

For proof he need not look any further than the fragments of nightmares brewing behind his eyes. Maw — clotted dirt clinging to her grave dress — her bent finger pointing at him, red-hot anger in the empty sockets of her eyes. Or Sarah's ghost reaching down for his hard cock, her facial features mixing with those of dead whores he'd buried, sunk, or burned.

Odd, wasn't it? How the men he'd killed never came back to haunt him, but the women he'd wronged remained so fresh? Sometimes Sarah's blue eyes transformed into Margarita's doe-dark ones the moment she grabbed him. Her mouth would shape itself into Lizzie's gap-toothed grin.

What kind *of a monster are you?*

The voice was probing, deep, and reverberating, as though it shook his very soul.

"The kind who belongs to the devil himself," Billy whispered under his breath as his empty gaze fixed on the tabletop. For what seemed an eternity he stared at the grease-stained wood marked by old coffee rings.

He felt something through his boot, shocking him back to the world. Billy looked up, startled, to see the man who'd kicked the chair.

He was tall, dressed in a thick wool winter coat, a dusting of snow melting into droplets on his shoulders. The slouch hat sat crooked on his blond head, and cold blue eyes were taking Billy's measure. The mouth behind the dark-blond beard had an amused pinch to it, as if derisive.

"Sorry to wake you, friend," the blond man told him. "But you've got the only free chair in the house. Either I talk you into moving your foot and sharing your table, or I have to sit on the floor."

"Sorry," Billy said, removing his foot. "Lost in my head."

The big blond seated himself, a plate of bacon and beans in his hand. "Lost ain't the word for it. You was plumb vanished in the wilderness on beyond Jordan. First I thought you were drunk, then I wondered if maybe you was just deaf."

Billy took the man's measure in turn as the newcomer shrugged out of his thick wool coat; a Remington revolver had been tucked in a cross draw at his belt. He was a little over thirty, with a hard look. Deeply seated anger lay behind those slightly crazy blue eyes. Something about him bespoke a military bearing. Not that that was so unusual given the war or the disenchanted men from both sides that had flocked into Montana. What was unusual was that he hadn't shed it as so many had. As if that strict bearing were somehow important to who he was.

Billy said, "Don't be prodding, mister. It's my table, and it's a mite early in the day to be raising a ruckus."

The blond studied him as he forked a load of beans into his mouth and chewed. Swallowing he said, "Hard case, are you?"

"Did you come here to eat breakfast or get shot?"

A slight quiver of the blond man's lips, a cooling of his expression, seemed to stretch time. Then he smiled, a faint chuckle barely audible in his voice. "Fair enough. I just needed a place to eat. Guess I shouldn't hold it against a man who was just looking for a place to think, should I?"

"Reckon not. And I should have been paying

better attention. What brings you to Fort Benton? I haven't seen you around."

"Got in a couple of days ago." He looked around. "Heard there was great doings up to Fort Benton. That this was the richest town in Montana Territory, and there was money to be made. Thought it would be like Denver or the Colorado strikes. Had it in my head to take over a fancy house, one suited to a better-heeled clientele. And what do I find? Blow-down tents, underground hovels, bullwhackers, two-bit monte dealers, and cold bitter enough to freeze a Massachusetts man's arse off. And that, friend, is God-Almighty cold."

"There's money right enough," Billy told him. "But it's in freight and supply. You might make a fancy house pay, but only in summer when the boats are in. This time of year? I doubt you could count six hundred people in the whole of Chouteau County."

The blond shrugged and shoveled another mouthful. "Where's the best place? Helena?"

"Maybe. They're just opening the lodes. Might take a couple of years to see the likes of the Colorado strikes or the Comstock. And even then it'd be a mighty different class of people."

"Seems to me all these Rebels can have this damn frozen waste. And good riddance." His eyes narrowed. "But then, from your accent, you're a damn Rebel yourself."

"Nope. Not really. Had kin that fought for the South. I didn't figure it was my war. I was ready to live and let live." He smiled thinly. "But sometimes some son of a bitch just comes along and sticks a finger in your eye."

"They conscript you?"

Billy shook his head. "Bushwhackers. Killed Maw, took my sister. Mean bunch. Took me to nigh on the end of the war to run down and kill every last one of the whoresons. By then wasn't a hell of a lot left of Arkansas but ruins."

"I was in Arkansas there at the end. You're right. Not much left." He stared thoughtfully at nothing, as if reminiscing. "It was always the chase. They leave traces when they run. Letters home, some mention to friends. I sure miss it."

Billy narrowed his eyes. "That what you're doing now? Hunting someone?"

The blond laughed bitterly. "Don't I wish. They say my means are too harsh." He gestured with the fork to make his point. "You want to get anywhere hunting men? You've got to go for their throats. Especially the dangerous ones. Like pulling up weeds, you gotta yank out the whole rotten plant. Rip out its jugular, break its neck, and jerk up the roots. Then you burn the very ground it grew on and teach a lesson by destroying everyone close to the traitorous son of a bitch. Friends, wives, whores."

His eyes seemed to flicker, lips quivering. "And somehow . . ." He cocked his head. "It's just bad luck. Who would have thought a homeless cunt . . . ?"

He seemed to have lost his train of thought.

"You going to stay around Fort Benton?"

The blond man shrugged. "Might try Helena. Maybe follow one of the freight companies down to Virginia City." He seemed to forget the question, then looked up, gaze brittle and cold. "You see, I learned. A smart man lets them relax. Think the danger is past. Then, when they least expect it, that's when you catch them in their doorway.

794

That's when you *really* make them pay."

Billy studied him warily. "Thought you were looking to run a fancy house?"

"Man can have two skills, can't he?" The blond smiled coldly. "Running special whores and killing, can't call either one exclusive, can you?"

"Nope. Reckon not." Billy picked up his cigar. Maybe it was time to drift back over the divide to Helena. Send a telegraph to Nichols. Maybe a winter job was what he needed.

"Call me Billy Nichols. Who are you?"

"Win Parmelee."

Billy frowned. Where in hell had he heard that name before? Colorado? Something about a parlor house? Lord knows, a man heard a lot of names out here.

"Tell me," Parmelee asked casually. "You ever hear of a man who calls himself the Meadowlark?"

Billy stiffened, his heart skipping. "Nope. Where'd you hear that?"

"Drunk gambler I met. Barely made it onto the last boat headed downriver. Said he was lucky to get away with his life. Funny how things work out, isn't it? All them odd coincidences in life."

Danny? Had to be.

"How's that?"

Parmelee shrugged. "You ever hear anything about this Meadowlark, I'd pay to get a line on him. That's all."

"Why?"

"Might have some work for him."

Billy took a draw on his cigar, only to find the ash gone cold.

100

February 18, 1868

Had you asked Butler, he would have told you it was a rotten night for a celebratory feast, especially given the blizzard that raged outside. Nevertheless, a celebration it was. Every now and then a severe gust of wind rocked the hide lodge, and drafts of cold — bearing a dusting of snowflakes — would trickle down from the smoke hole. As they fell into the warm interior, the flakes vanished.

And a snug lodge it was, crafted from scraped and tanned elk hides and wrapped around a conical framework of lodge poles. Tied to the inside of the poles, a thin calfhide liner rose two thirds of the way up the walls and acted to create an insulating layer of air.

The inside was just large enough for him to sit in the guest's place beside the door. To his left sat a pretty young woman dressed in a beautifully beaded and quill-worked dress that sported chevron patterns of elk teeth. Her woman's name was Wobindotadegi, or Mountain Flicker in English. Tonight they celebrated her passage from girl to woman.

Cracked Bone Thrower sat in his traditional spot

in the rear as lord and master of the lodge.

Beside Cracked Bone Thrower, and across from Mountain Flicker, the man's wife, Ainka Wei, or Red Rain, perched uncomfortably given her swollen and very pregnant belly. She was also Mountain Flicker's older sister, and the resemblance was plain to see.

Finally, opposite Butler, Cracked Bone Thrower and Red Rain's two little boys, five-year-old Cricket and two-year-old Water Snake, wiggled and fidgeted more than they actually sat.

In the center of the lodge — and in front of the anchor rope — the hearth crackled and burned cheerily. Resting on hearthstones sat a soapstone cooking pot, its contents bubbling and filling the air with scents of wild onions, sego lily, and biscuit root taken from the family's dried stores. All were swimming in melted buffalo back fat.

The centerpiece of the meal was baked elk heart seasoned with dried biscuit root leaves. Strips of the succulent meat steamed on the wooden plate in Butler's lap. He glanced at Mountain Flicker and grinned as he chewed off another bite.

He had grown fond of the girl over the months since his return from the journey to the Underworld. She had been fascinated by him and his invisible men, and she'd taken to teaching him Shoshoni as he'd instructed her in English. Together they'd tackled chores, played tricks on each other, and teased. But now, for reasons Butler could barely understand, things had changed.

She matched his grin, eyes sparkling. They were celebrating the conclusion of her first woman's flux. In the white culture Butler had come from, even hinting at a woman's monthly discharge was forbidden. Here, among the Dukurika, the event was cause for feasting. During her ten-day isolation from the community, Mountain Flicker had been instructed on a woman's duties by Red Rain and Flowering Sage. At the end of Mountain Flicker's passage into womanhood Red Rain had painted her face, and the part down the center of her scalp, in crimson, which marked her as an adult.

Butler thought Mountain Flicker was an enchanting girl. Her partly white ancestry — going back to her grandfather, a trapper named Travis Hartman — had given her a perfectly proportioned face, wide cheeks, and straight nose. Tonight she wore her long black hair loose, and it hung down over her shoulders to pile on the buffalo robes behind her.

Butler made the hand sign for "Are you doing well?"

"Ha'a," she called back. "It's good to get out of the women's lodge."

He wasn't sure what to make of their relationship. He'd never really been close to a girl before. And Lord knew, they'd had a lot of fun together. More like they'd been best friends. And she'd never flinched on those days when Pettigrew, Baker, Peterson and the rest of his men were being pesky.

Red Rain and Cracked Bone Thrower had watched, but said nothing. For Butler, however, his attraction brought unease. Mountain Flicker was sixteen, but her supple young body was fully female with muscular legs, rounded hips and flat belly, broad shoulders and full breasts. She moved with a fluid grace, and he loved to watch her dance, her body undulating as her feet flew. When she did, her hair would catch the sun and shine, swishing behind her like a liquid wave that washed down almost to her knees.

Sometimes he couldn't help but think of Water Ghost Woman, and the desire that Mountain Flicker aroused, unbidden, within him.

But then the Dukurika were anything but chaste. To Butler's initial dismay, carnal relations between a man and wife were considered a natural behavior as unremarkable as eating and sleeping. The first time he had heard Red Rain and Cracked Bone Thrower connubially joined under the robes had shocked him. Red Rain made sounds of delight deep in her throat that ended in little yips of pleasure when she reached her paroxysm. Or a whole string of them if Cracked Bone Thrower was on his game. One thing was sure: pelvic congestion wasn't on Red Rain's list of concerns.

No sooner had Butler come to terms with his own physical reaction to the goings-on, than he'd been abashed to find himself dreaming of Mountain Flicker in that way.

To his further dismay, it had become a major topic of conversation among his men.

Mountain Flicker had come to Cracked Bone Thrower's lodge with the intention of marrying him. Among the Dukurika, Butler had learned, it was actually expected that when a man took a second wife, it should be his wife's sister.

And now Mountain Flicker was officially a woman.

Which meant that, inevitably, Butler would have to listen to his friend and this sparkling young woman he so adored make those sounds. Do what he more and more longed to do himself.

The blizzard made a howling out beyond the

799

lodge, another twist of snowflakes pushing their way past the smoke hole to vanish in the heat.

"I am very happy for you," Butler told her, allowing his soul to ache a bit as he stared into her eyes. And he *would* be happy. Cracked Bone Thrower *had* become his friend. Red Rain and Mountain Flicker had made him part of their little family group. Accorded him every respect after hearing of his Underworld adventures with Water Ghost Woman. No matter how he had come to obsess over Mountain Flicker, he would force himself to be joyful when she and Cracked Bone Thrower married.

Might even be tonight.

"And how will y'all deal with that?" Kershaw's thick drawl asked behind Butler's ear.

"I will do my duty, Sergeant," he said crisply. Damn it, it was a measure of his disquiet that Kershaw had come. The Cajun only spoke when Butler's turmoil was roiling.

"Reckon, Cap'n, yer gone on the girl."

"I will acquit myself as a gentleman, Sergeant. I am delighted for my friends, delighted for Mountain Flicker." And before Kershaw could goad him again, he ordered, "That will be all, Sergeant."

Cracked Bone Thrower, Mountain Flicker, and Red Rain were watching him with knowing eyes.

"What was the dead man saying?" Cracked Bone Thrower asked. "The sergeant only comes when you are unhappy or worried."

Butler smiled wearily. "You know him too well. I was just telling him that I am happy for Mountain Flicker, and how her life will be changing."

He could sense the sudden tension. Even among the little boys. They were all looking at him expectantly.

"Yes" — Cracked Bone Thrower thoughtfully set aside his plate of meat — "Flicker is now a woman. It is time that she took a man. Her father is not around to speak for her. So she has come to me. She would have you for as long as you would keep her."

Butler stopped short, as if he had imagined the words coming out of Cracked Bone Thrower's mouth. "I thought she was to marry you."

"I will gladly take her for my second wife if you don't want her, Butler. We are *naatea,* family. You have come among us, shown us honor and respect. Red Rain and I have watched you with Flicker. We have seen your attraction, how you look at her with fond longing. And she has told us she would be your wife."

Butler, his heart still pounding, turned to her. "You would be my wife?"

"The word is *gwee.* Say it." Flicker seemed unusually nervous.

"Gway."

"Close enough," she told him. "I will call you *nadainape.*"

He knew that word, it was what Red Rain called Cracked Bone Thrower and what Puhagan's wife Flowering Sage called him. The Dukurika used it suspiciously like Americans used "husband."

"And if I have to leave? Would you want to come with me? Go with me back to America?"

"I don't know," she both said and signed with her hands.

Cracked Bone Thrower shook his head. "She would not like the white world. I myself tried it when I was younger. You know that among the Dukurika, a man is expected to marry his wife's sister. If your *puha* says you must leave, she will become my second wife."

"Just like that?" Butler asked, amazed.

Mountain Flicker shot him a shy smile. "We are not white men, Butler. We are *newe* Dukurika. If you become part of our *naatea,* call me *gwee,* you will take responsibility for Red Rain, as well. If anything should happen to Dick Hamilton" — she smiled as she teased Cracked Bone Thrower with his white name — "you will call my sister *gwee,* wife, and care for her as well as share her bed."

"What're y'all gonna do now, Cap'n?" Kershaw asked dryly behind Butler's ear.

"Do you really want this?" he asked Mountain Flicker.

Her smile widened. "You are a puzzle. Filled with *puha,* you see the dead. You faced *Pa'waip* and she gifted you. These things scare me, but you are a kind man who works hard. You help with the hunting and packing, and make me laugh. You have known pain and terrible things, but they have not made you bitter. I think you would make a good father for my children."

"Father?" Butler asked himself softly, somewhat stunned.

He looked into her thoughtful dark eyes, his heart pounding. She wasn't fooling. None of them were. He was being asked to join their family. He wasn't a lunatic in their eyes. Not some piece of broken human being to be kicked, shunned, pitied, or humiliated. They wanted him because of who he was. Because he was crazy!

He reached out, drew her to him, and hugged her. Kissing the top of her red-lined head. "I would be delighted to call you *gwee.* I will cherish it every time you call me *nadainape.*"

To Cracked Bone Thrower, he said, "You, I will call *babi,* my older brother. And Red Rain, you are *gwee* to me."

That night after the lodge had been made ready, and the last trips had been made outside for relief and to check the dogs and horses, Flicker knelt in the dying light of the fire and slipped her beautiful dress off.

Butler had already undressed and crawled under the robes. His hands were trembling; his heart beat in anticipation and terror as she slipped in beside him. He'd never felt a woman's body against his, and for a moment, she just lay there, as if savoring the feeling herself.

Then she leaned her lips to his ear and whispered, *"Nadainape."*

"I have never done this before," he whispered.

"Me, either," she whispered back.

She took his trembling hand, placed it between her breasts so that he could feel her pounding heart. Then, sighing, she led him in an exploration of her body.

They didn't sleep much that night. Butler was too delighted with the soft sounds of pleasure that Mountain Flicker made deep down in her throat.

101

February 28, 1868

The wind couldn't have cut more keenly if it were a knife. Backed by small flakes of blowing snow, it sliced through Billy's coat, finding every small crack and gap. Locomotive, powerful beast that he was, nevertheless showed signs of fatigue. The packhorse following behind kept stumbling, jerking on the lead rope every time he did.

Billy knotted the muscles in his leg, arm, and side on the left. Then he'd tense his right in a futile effort to keep warm. By constant exercise he built heat, but it sapped his energy, and his stomach felt like a chafing and empty hole. Every muscle had gone stiff, as if it were made of wood.

He kept Locomotive moving on the rocky road, the horse's hooves clacking on the worn river cobblestones, the cleat-tipped winter shoes slipping on ice. On his right, just past the line of winter-stark cottonwoods, the Missouri River's course was marked by a broken, piled, and snow-covered swath of ice. The wind-torn bottom country almost looked smoky, an illusion created by the gray cottonwoods and their interlaced branches. Snow streaked the upland bluffs to the east where it had filled in drainages and cuts; the sides of the slopes drifted in rounded and sculpted mounds behind bare, windblown patches of sage.

The trail turned toward the river, and squinting against the bitter wind, Billy could see the ferry at Eldorado Bar. It was drawn up on the far side, choked with ice; the little shack just opposite it looked snug with a streamer of smoke curling out of the stovepipe to be wicked away by the wind.

Picking his way along the bank, floundering through drifted drainages, he kept staring longingly at the river. Back at the Great Falls, they'd no doubt found the body. One more in a long list. A man Billy hadn't known. Just a name on a telegram. A poor bastard that somehow stood in George Nichols's way. Already frozen, the corpse would have been hauled off to a shed to await the spring thaw and burial. They would be speculating about the meadowlark feather in the corpse's pocket. That storekeeper's wife would have told them about the young man in the slouch hat that rode the big black horse.

She might have even gotten a good enough look at Billy to draw a likeness of him. Though none of them would know his name.

He stopped Locomotive, feeling the big black tremble as he looked out over the broad Missouri. Here the ice was smooth, not cracked and piled, as if the river ran slower.

He fought a bout of shivering.

"God*damn* it!"

He couldn't stay out — not given the bruise-dark band of clouds rolling down from the northwest. He could sense the building fury. This was going to be one hell of a blizzard. The kind that killed men and froze animals stiff. And just over there, beyond that far shore, the road led to

Helena, a stable for the horses, and a warm hotel room for him. Maybe with a hot bath. And afterward, a woman to keep his bed occupied.

If he could cross that ice.

He should dismount, but as cold as his legs were, would he be able to mount again? He blinked his eyes, then had to place a mittened hand to them where the tears froze his lashes together.

"God *fucking* damn," he whispered. "Locomotive, reckon we're gonna die one way or another, and what the hell, Devil's gonna get me in the end anyway." He glanced around. "Sure as shit, we can't stay here."

He tapped spurs lightly to the black's side, and — dumb trusting brute that he was — the big black horse slowly minced his way out onto the frozen river. Once on the ice, Billy turned the packhorse free. The buckskin would either follow or not.

"Easy there, hoss," Billy whispered to Locomotive's frost-whitened ears. "One step at a time."

He heard a hollow crack.

Damn it!

"Whoa, now." He almost fell as he climbed off, easing his foot down on the snow-streaked ice. Shivering, taking the reins, he half stepped forward. Locomotive had his eyes rolled back and worked the bit.

"Gotta go slow, old friend," Billy soothed, leading the way. To keep on line he picked a toppled cottonwood on the far bank, and kept sliding his steps forward. If the ice broke, if Locomotive fell through, Billy could hurl himself headlong. Maybe he'd have a chance.

Sure. A chance to freeze to death as the blizzard

raged down on him and buried him in a whiteout of howling snow.

Off to the right he could see an open patch. Black water running fast before vanishing down into the darkness and cold depths.

What would it be like, falling through? Feeling the cold shock of icy water through his clothes, the grip of the current. To grab at the lip of the ice, fighting, struggling, terrified as the cold ate his strength? That moment of desperate realization, knowing that nothing could save him. Right up to the moment his fingers let go and he was dragged down into the blackness. Thrashing, bumping up against the ice, feeling it slide past. The air in his lungs would begin to burn, bitter with cold, and he'd finally blow it out and suck frigid water into his chest.

There, he would die. Down in the black depths. Floating along, arms and limbs akimbo, hair playing in the current. And no one would ever find him.

Forgotten by everyone but the Devil.

Damnit all, how thick is the fucking ice?

He'd never been so scared in all his life. If only he'd waited. Shot that fancy-dressed son of a bitch *after* the weather cleared.

He shook, jaw muscles in such a spasm that his teeth clacked like castanets.

He'd worked wide around the black hole.

Heard the ice crack beneath him again.

Froze.

His heart skipping.

But nothing happened.

Step by step, he shivered his way, expecting at any instant to hear that final crack. Each step was made with the expectation that the ice had to give way.

What the fuck had possessed him to try this? Better to have just kept riding until he froze in the saddle and fell off into a drift.

But he'd made it halfway. Maybe more.

"Slow, you stupid idiot," he whispered, the wind tearing his breath away.

Again the ice cracked, seemed to shift. Locomotive pulled up, muscles tense, head up, on the verge of panic.

"Easy there, old friend. Whoa, now. Easy. That's it. Just stand for a bit. Get your bearings. That's my good old horse."

And once again the stupid beast believed him.

"One step at a time," he told the horse, worrying that he couldn't feel his feet anymore, and that his knees were so stiff he could barely bend them.

Damn, had he ever been this cold?

And then they were across, scrambling, slipping, as they climbed the icy bank and onto the snow-packed rocky shore.

He couldn't bend his legs, couldn't find the strength to climb into the saddle. He might have crossed the river, but he was still going to freeze.

Until he fixed on the fallen cottonwood.

"Come here, boy. That's it."

Took him three tries to clamber up onto the log, then to launch himself halfway into the saddle and swing over.

Two hours later, his body like senseless clay, he topped the rise from the Prickly Pear Valley and into Last Chance Gulch. His brain numb, he passed the shacks and cribs on the outskirts, then into town. He passed J. H. Ming's books, Cannon's Steam Bakery, Binzel & Hamper's, and the Occidental Billiard Hall.

At the livery he staggered off the horse, pounded on the door, and mumbled something incoherently at the hostler before stumbling to the small heat stove in the man's office. In bliss, he shucked off his frozen and snow-packed coat. Practically hugging the stove, he had to wait nearly a half hour before he could talk rationally to the proprietor.

"You just made it," the man told him. "Cain't hardly see across the street the way it's coming down."

Billy sucked at the cup of hot coffee the man had given him. "I couldn't think. Hands were too numb to move."

He sipped again, belly happy. "I was starting to feel warm. Ain't that something? To look down and see all that ice on my legs . . . and feel like it was July?"

"Yep. And next you go to sleep. Not a bad way to go, I guess." The old man pointed a knobby finger at him. "Son, yer jist damn lucky you made it." He paused. "Thinking of sleeping here, are ye?"

"No. I'm good enough to find my way to a hotel and a meal."

Billy wrapped himself in his coat, pulled his hat down, and stepped out into the storm. He knew the way from his previous visits, but in the blinding waves of snow, he still had trouble finding the hotel.

To his relief he got the last room, left his coat and war bag, and wearily made his way to the restaurant for the obligatory meal of elk, beans, and biscuits. He couldn't have cared less as long as it was piping hot!

It was a measure of his fatigue that he was halfway through the meal before he noticed the blond man across the room. The gent was staring at him through eyes as cold and blue as the blizzard blowing outside. That same man he'd sat across the table from in Fort Benton.

Win Parmelee. The fellow looking for the Meadowlark.

102

Sarah — dressed in a robe — allowed George Nichols to take her arm and escort her down the stairs to the Angel's Lair dining room. He was dressed in the finery he'd been wearing when he arrived the night before: a tailored black sack suit, starched white shirt, with a silk scarf at the neck. His long wool coat was hanging in the foyer along with his silk hat.

"That really was exquisite, I'm all abuzz," he told her as he held the chair for her. After she seated herself, he pulled his chair next to hers and sat, elbows propped on the table as he clasped both of her hands. The look in his dark and dangerous eyes was almost worshipful.

Mam burst out the door, a silver coffee service on a tray with two cups.

"Morning, Mam!" Nichols greeted.

"Mr. Nichols, suh," she told him with a slight nod of acknowledgment. "Y'all ready fo' breakfast?"

"At your convenience," Sarah told her with a smile, knowing full well it would be delivered within minutes.

After Mam left, Nichols took a deep breath,

then, as if embarking on a perilous path, said, "I would like to think that if there was a limit to what the human body could sense and experience, I had already discovered it in your bed. But each time . . ." He shook his head. "Dear God, Sarah, my entire body tingles just thinking about it."

She gave him a satisfied smile. "It was rather pleasant. I imagine I shall have to nap half the day just to recover. Last night was . . . well, let us call it special."

Something powerful lay behind his black eyes, an intensity to the set of his face. "I find myself drawn to Denver with ever greater urgency. No sooner do I return to my work in Central City than I find my mind obsessed with you. It's enough to drive me mad."

"We make a study of obsession at Angel's Lair. Did you enjoy the play last night? I thought Agatha gave a wonderful performance of Helen being seduced by Paris. That was the beginning of the Trojan War, you know? I think it fed your appetites more than a little."

"I thought you were crazy when you mentioned this theater nonsense." He paused. "I never liked theater."

"Until it consisted of torn clothes, and overcoming the resistance of reluctant women? Agatha was marvelous, don't you think?"

"And that actor? David? Is he one of yours, too?"

"He was one of Langrishe's theater troupe. We hired him for the week. Generally it takes that long to train them how to act at the same time they're, um, doing the deed. Some men just can't keep their rods stiff, remember their lines, and still give a credible performance. It takes a special sort."

"I don't think I could." Nichols sighed. "Sarah, let's get back to the subject."

"And that is?" She freed her hand to pour coffee for both of them.

"You and me."

"What about us?" she asked as Mam pushed the kitchen door open, two steaming plates in her hands. These she set first before George, and then Sarah. With a slight bow, she left.

Nichols had picked up his fork, glanced to be sure that they were alone, and said, "I want you."

"You had me all night, George."

"I mean I want you all the time."

Sarah laughed, giving him her conspiratorial half wink. "Then I'm still worth the price."

"I want you to be my wife."

The way he said it, she knew he wasn't joking. A coldness slipped down her spine.

"I've thought about it all night. I am in love with you. The knowledge that you entertain other men . . . that callous and beastly Chase, Pat O'Reilly, others . . . it almost makes me insane."

"That's my business, George. And it is strictly business. I am an entertainer, but in addition to spinning a story, or playing a part, I use my body and a man's to explore delight. I think there's an entire science to be made from the study of sexual union. Given what I've learned so far, any man who spends the night with me never views his sex, or a woman, in the same way."

"But I want more than the short hours we get here. Come with me. Move back to Central City. Marry me."

Dear God, how do I handle this?

813

She patted his hand and began eating. Between bites, she said, "George, you don't want me. You, Pat, you both honor me with proposals, but I'll never love again. You don't even know the kind of woman I am. How I came to be here."

"I don't *care*."

She studied him as she chewed the venison in gravy. "As a girl I dreamed of a family and society. Funny, isn't it? On the day Paw left for war, I had no idea that my hopes had just died. It didn't set in when men were bleeding to death on our floors, or even when the armies took our food. Nevertheless, I clung to that misguided hope right up until Dewley and his raiders killed Maw and packed me off."

She saw his face go slack, saying, "See. You don't know me at all. That revolver hanging behind my bed? I took that from Dewley. You should have heard him scream when I cut him apart. Even after that I still had to be betrayed, humiliated, and hounded to the lowest rung on life's ladder."

"But you came back," he told her forcefully.

"Bret brought me back. Taught me to love, to trust, and I gave him everything that I ever was or would be."

She paused, seeing the turmoil in his black eyes.

"Parmelee shot Bret down in front of me. I still can't remember what was going through my mind while Parmelee had me tied to the bed. I have a vague memory of the pain and violation, but mostly all I recall is a weird, savage scream howling in my head. Didn't matter that I opened my mouth and filled my lungs. I just . . . couldn't . . . get it out."

She shook her head, taking another bite. "It's still there, George. Way down deep. Can't hardly hear it at all these days, but it's there."

"You know I've had people looking for him." George smiled. "One of my sources who works for the Helena *Herald* sent word he was in Montana earlier this year but couldn't confirm it." His eyes sharpened. "Now, if I was to kill him for you, would that be proof enough of my devotion?"

She arched an eyebrow. "One day he'll show up here full of anger and revenge. After I've shot him dead, you could show your devotion by disposing of the body."

George laughed from deep down in his belly. "By God, Sarah, you are a woman after my own heart. Marry me!"

"Not a chance, George. I might have you bedazzled for the moment, but your true love is power. You mean to make yourself the richest man in the Rockies no matter who you have to kill, bully, or intimidate."

"Would it be so bad to stand at my side when I become that man? You could have anything you wanted. Wealth, property, or —"

"I mean to have them on my own." She gave him a conspiratorial wink.

"Marry me, and you'll have them sooner."

"George, I'm a momentary obsession, just like so many of your mines and properties have been. But once acquired, they've vanished into your vast holdings. Forgotten, but for the money they make." She shook her head. "I will not marry you."

Nichols pushed back, his black eyes seething like heated cauldrons. "Don't spurn me, woman."

"Never, George." *Careful now!* She met his stare with her own. "But if we were to marry? Given what I want and what you ultimately want? One or both of us would be dead within a year."

"What if I can't take no for an answer?"

"You'll have to."

"No one has ever told me no before."

"You could abduct me. Carry me off and rape me. You wouldn't be the first. But the magic would be gone." She hesitated, heart racing as she fought for the right words to mollify the black anger in his eyes. "Too many people would be looking for me. Would you kill the magic?"

"I don't know."

"Sometimes, George, the only way you can win a woman is by accepting who she is, and letting her go."

"That's your final word?"

"It is."

His face like dark granite, he pushed his chair back and stood. Wheeling, his heels beat on the spruce floor as he stalked from the room.

Sarah dropped her head into her hands. *Dear God, I've played hell.*

103

April 1, 1868

"Philip?" Her voice woke him from a sound sleep.

Doc blinked awake, fragmenting dream images splintered and fell away. Images of James huddled on a bunk in the Camp Douglas barracks, of a young man's pain-glazed eyes as they laid his bullet-shattered body on the table in that farmhouse at Shiloh, of maggots crawling through damp muck on the prison camp hospital floor.

He stared up at the darkness, taking a second to remember where he was: home. His bedroom in Denver. A faint beam of moonlight angling down from above the curtain rod and across the foot of his bed.

"What is it?"

Bridget took a deep breath. "I'm bleeding. Don't know when it started, but the bed's a mess."

Doc sat up, puffed in the cold air, and reached for the matches. Striking a Lucifer, he lit the lamp and adjusted the wick. "Let's take a look."

Bridget had thrown back the covers, and as Doc turned, his soul froze. Her cotton nightgown was soaked at the crotch, the blood bright red.

"Dear Lord God," Philip cried.

Bridget's eyes had gone wide, her mouth dropping open. She seemed frozen, propped up on her elbows as she stared over her protruding belly at the spreading gore. Her hair lay in tangles around her shoulders.

Doc ripped off his nightshirt, then pulled Bridget's hem up above her waist. She'd been bleeding for a while, lines of blood having caked on the inside of her thighs. As she spread her legs for him, Doc used his nightshirt to wipe away the blood. A thin stream of bright red continued to seep past her labia.

"Is there any pain?" Doc asked, using his fingers to press around the swell of her distended abdomen.

"No," Bridget told him in a weak voice. "I just felt funny. It was the wetness that woke me up. I don't hurt at all."

Doc's heart began to race. Fear made him want to knot his hands.

"What is it, Philip?" Bridget asked him, her eyes searching his face. "You're scared."

"No pain. Sudden onset bleeding late in pregnancy. I think it's *placenta previa.*"

"Is it bad?"

Doc hesitated, the platitude rising to his lips. But he couldn't lie. Not to Bridget. "It's bad."

"Can you fix it?"

Doc rubbed his hands to stop the sudden shaking. "I saw this once as a student in Boston. The placenta is in the wrong place. Over the cervix. It's torn loose, which is why you're bleeding."

She closed her eyes, face ghost-pale, her cheeks hollow in the light. "Am I going to die? Is the baby?"

"Not if I can help it."

Doc wadded his nightshirt and used it to absorb

818

the blood. "Just stay there and don't move." He tugged on his pants and shirt, found his boots. Looking at his watch, he saw it was a little after three. Where in hell would he find a carriage at this time of night?

Frantic, he bent over Bridget, scooped her into his arms. Surely he could carry her as far as the surgery. Even as he lifted her, he could feel Bridget's blood, warm, wet, dribbling her life and their child's life away like sand through an hourglass.

Three blocks.

All he had to do was make it three blocks.

104

April 6, 1868

Spring was coming to Virginia City, laid out as it was along the westward-trending Alder Gulch. To the north and south the logged-out slopes were green with grass, the black stumps of long-gone trees speckling the rocky ground. Outcrops, roads, tipples, and prospect holes gave the mountains a hivelike look. Overhead a spring-blue sky was dotted with clouds that drifted serenely up from the southwest.

Virginia City's element-gray, plank-board buildings contrasted with the painted establishments, many of them weather-faded. Whitewash was expensive and hard to come by, having to be shipped in from the east to Salt Lake and then north, or by ox train from San Francisco. Most structures were allowed to just warp and fade with the seasons.

Two days ago, Billy had made use of just that weather-dry character to set fire to a miner's cabin down on the Ruby. After Billy had cut the man's throat, a sprinkling of kerosene from one of his lamps and a match had sent the shack up like a torch. Before the ashes had cooled, one of George Nichols's agents was filing on the man's claim.

Being no miner, Billy couldn't make sense of it — most of the valley looking like nothing but granite and quartz outcroppings.

But that wasn't his business.

His war bag packed, hat clamped firmly on his head, he felt jittery. His dreams had been haunted with Maw's body rising from the grave, as if she were stalking him. The line girl he'd slept with last night didn't know how lucky she was. He'd kept from choking her as he bucked up and down on her body. Maybe it was her half-lucid brown eyes, vacant from the opium she'd chugged down from a patent-medicine bottle. Maybe it was the slack way she'd held her jaw, as if it were already dislocated. Whatever the reason, he'd popped his cork, rolled off her, and found himself somewhat relieved that she was still breathing when he'd awakened that morning.

The snow high up on the mountains was mostly melted. Grass was up. Time had come to make his way back toward Colorado. Truth be told, he was tired of being alone. Not that he and George had ever had much in common, but he wondered if maybe he shouldn't see the man one last time and close the books on the Meadowlark's activities.

"And do what?" he asked himself as he strode down to the Pork and Bean, a moderately acceptable eatery featuring hot-cooked meals. Stepping in the door, he made his customary scan of the clientele.

He stopped short. At a back table, Win Parmelee sat over an empty plate, a cup of steaming coffee resting by his right hand. His cold blue eyes were fixed on Billy, and narrowing. The man's lips quivered, then he looked away.

Win Parmelee. Seemed that wherever Billy went, he stumbled over the man as if he were a stone in the road.

Billy found a table across from Parmelee and tried to ignore him. It wasn't like Montana Territory was that all-fired big despite the distances. Benton, Helena, Virginia City, Dillon, Bannock, Bozeman, and a handful of failing placer camps were about the only real towns. If a man did business in Montana, he'd be in one of those few places.

Or was it that Parmelee suspected who Billy really was? The thought of that sparked an almost insatiable curiosity. He fought down the impulse to walk over and ask the man flat out.

A girl of about ten came with a coffeepot and cup, asking if he wanted breakfast. At his nod she filled his cup and flounced off for the kitchen.

The rest of the clientele were the normal miners in their filthy boots, saloonkeepers in decidedly natty dress, freighters and mule skinners, and even a fellow in a sack suit who might have been a banker.

Through breakfast, Billy remained acutely aware of Parmelee. Watched him pick up his travel satchel, and step warily out the door.

Definitely a hunter.

"Just like me," Billy whispered under his breath as he chased boiled beans across his plate with a piece ripped from a loaf of bread. But, did he really suspect?

Leaving a fifty-cent piece for his two-bit breakfast, he picked up his war bag with his left hand, leaving his right to dangle by the Remington's butt. At the door, he glanced both ways, then stepped out on the street.

Despite having a woman in his bed, Maw had come last night. There would be trouble today. She'd warned him from the grave. The Cherokee used to tell him about how important it was to listen to the dead.

"Whatever happened to you, John Gritts?"

A one-legged Indian? John had sided with Stand Watie's Confederates. John Ross's Union faction had won in the end. If Billy knew anything about Cherokee they would continue killing each other for years after the whites had finally made peace. It sure didn't take no fortune-teller to figure that out.

But, damn it, he'd like to see John again. Sit with him on a porch, smoke a pipe, talk about old times. A sudden longing — almost a physical pain — brought tears to Billy's eyes. By Hob, he wished he was home. Wished he could hear Maw's voice, smell Paw's pipe. See Sarah, still innocent and pure, prancing in from the springhouse with her water pails.

Foolish damn nonsense.

Billy wiped away a sudden tear, glanced around the rutted and rocky street, seeing no sign of Parmelee.

Odd to think of John Gritts. To think of home. Maybe it was a sign. Maybe time had come to go back to Tahlequah, look up the Gritts family and find John. Hell, he had plenty of money. It wouldn't take much to set John up with a small cabin, keep him in food and company. He owed the man that much.

Or was that just the devil playing him, baiting a hook to see if he'd take it?

At the livery where he'd stabled Locomotive and the packhorse, he took one last look around, and stepped inside.

"You looking for me?" a voice asked from the shadows.

Billy turned slowly, hand resting on his pistol.

Parmelee was watching him from the shadows, a rifle held low at his waist.

"Nope. Just come to head out, is all."

"Where to?"

"Colorado. California. Salt Lake. Maybe that ain't your business."

"I'd hate to see you show up on my back trail. Might give me the wrong idea."

"Seems to me a man with those kind of worries has enemies." Billy kept his hands wide. "All my enemies are dead, which means you're not one. I got no quarrel with you, Parmelee."

The man stiffened. "How'd you know my name?"

"You told it to me across the table up at Fort Benton over breakfast."

Parmelee seemed to deflate. "Yep. Reckon I did." He snorted derisively. "Man can be a damn fool sometimes."

Maybe he didn't suspect. Still . . .

Billy lowered his hands slightly. "I'm fixing to leave Virginia City. You got a problem with that?"

"I do." Parmelee raised the rifle slightly. "How about you wait a couple of hours and let me get a head start? That way I know for a fact you ain't gonna ambush me."

"How do I know you won't be laying in ambush for me?"

"Thought you said you didn't have any enemies."

"A couple of hours? Sure. I'm a maudlin sort. Reckon I'll go see what's in the stores, maybe smoke me a cigar in the sun. But this is the only time I'll play the tune for you."

With that, Billy backed out, holding his war bag wide so that Parmelee could see his revolver.

Billy frowned, wondering what had Parmelee up in a snit. Nevertheless, as he walked back toward the street, he was instantly aware of the two men who leaned against a blacksmith's wall. Something about their posture, the Henry rifles propped beside them, and the way they were dressed wasn't right.

Billy gave them a slight nod as he passed, feeling their hard eyes, the threat in their expressions.

An hour later, figuring Parmelee had had enough time, and wouldn't dawdle on the trail, Billy saddled Locomotive and tied his packs onto the packhorse.

He headed out on the Bozeman Road, climbing up over the divide to the Madison Valley. Locomotive was making good time, seeming to relish being on the road again. Last night's rain had softened the tracks, and so far, only one rider was ahead of him.

This, he assumed to be Parmelee, having not stood around to watch the man leave. The blond man was making good time, apparently well mounted given his horse's stride.

As the shadows lengthened, Billy followed the trail down toward the Madison River. Where the trace dipped through a draw, Billy was surprised to see tracks coming in from either side. Four of them. He could see where Parmelee's horse had pulled up, sidestepped, and then stood for a moment before heading out at a walk, followed by the others.

Billy chewed his lip, glanced uneasily around,

and backtracked two of the newcomers to the place where they'd been in wait. Boot tracks, piles of manure where the horses had been tied, told him they'd been there a while.

Reining Locomotive around, Billy resumed his way toward the Madison. He'd heard that, being a day's ride, most folks camped down by the river where they could water their animals before or after the pull from Virginia City.

As he neared the trees, Billy slipped the Sharps from its scabbard and laid it across Locomotive's saddle bows.

He saw them as soon as he rode under the first of the cottonwoods; the branches had barely sprouted green with the first leaves, the ground covered with fallen blossoms.

The rope was already over a limb, Parmelee's hands tied behind his back.

Two of the men turned toward him, riding out, their Henry rifles at the ready. Nothing in their expressions had changed since Billy had seen them leaned against the shop.

"Hold up!" one called, leveling his rifle.

"Why, I do declare," Billy cried. "Reckon you all are riding for that vigilance committee we hear so much about. Who you got there? Some road agent? Who'd he kill?"

"I said, hold up!" the man repeated.

"Aw, you're not gonna shoot me," Billy told him. "I ain't a robber or a outlaw. You all only hangs bad men. And if that's Win Parmelee you got yonder, he's one of the worst. What the hell did he do?"

"Murder and rape," the man barked.

"Son of a bitch," Billy drawled. "Hell, mister, I'll help y'all pull on the rope."

Daring the devil, he rode right up to the men, his heart pounding, knowing he was beaming his excitement. By God, he was tired of sneaking. He could feel the thrill, missing for so long. The same as when he'd walked into the middle of Dewley's camp.

Then he was in the middle of them, grinning, staring at Parmelee, seeing the man's fright — the half-crazy look of a galoot facing his final extinction. Under the rope, the pulse was beating in Parmelee's neck; he kept swallowing as if his throat had gone dry.

"Who are you?" one of the men asked, his old Colt Army leveled on Billy.

"Billy Hancock. You sure you want to hang him? Might be money for handing him over."

"All it takes is his head," another said. "We pack it in a nail keg filled with salt and ship it."

"Damn, do declare?" Billy shook his head. "Well, come on, boys, let's see the son of a bitch swing!"

Parmelee whispered, "I'll see you all in hell!"

"Maybe so, you piece of shit," one of the men replied, stepping off his horse and walking over where the loose end of rope lay. He was in the process of wrapping it around the tree to knot when Billy eared the hammer back on the Sharps and shot the nearest man through the chest. At the big gun's concussion, the horses shied. By the time he had Locomotive under control, Billy had the Remington leveled and shot the mounted man to his left.

Wheeling the big black horse, he spurred it toward the third rider, one of the Henry riflemen, and shot the man through the face as he fought his bucking horse.

Wheeling around, Billy instinctively ducked the shot as the man on the ground thumbed the hammer back on the Starr revolver he'd pulled from his belt and triggered it.

Billy took a breath, aimed, and shot him through the forehead as the vigilante leveled his pistol for another shot. The man dropped as if he were poleaxed.

But for the scattering horses, one tripping over its reins, the evening had gone quiet.

"By damn!" Billy cried. "Now that's just daisy, ain't it? Haven't felt this fucking good for ages!"

He slipped the Remington into its holster, pulled a cartridge from the box on his belt, and after inserting it into the rifle's chamber, he plucked a cap from its tin and pressed it onto the nipple.

Only then did he ride over to where Parmelee sat on his horse. The animal had backed away, pulling the rope up over the branch.

Billy caught up the animal's reins, turning Locomotive so that he could reach out with the Bowie and sever Parmelee's bonds.

The man wasted no time peeling the rope from around his neck and throwing it aside. For a moment he just sat, hunched in the saddle, breathing heavily.

"Reckon you got a right to be shook up some," Billy remarked as he considered the men he'd killed. One was going to need another bullet or he'd linger.

"I've got no idea why you did that, Mr. Hancock, but I'm damned sure glad you did."

"Reckon I been curious about you since Fort Benton."

"Why?"

"That a fact? That you murdered and raped?"

828

Parmelee was recovering his wits, the cold glare was back. "The man was a deserter. The women were both his whores. By definition, you can't rape a whore."

Billy walked Locomotive over and pulled the Remington. Calling, "Whoa, now," he steadied the horse and shot the lingerer through the head.

Rather than reload his empties, he pulled the loading lever down, pressed out the cylinder pin, and reached into his pocket for a second cylinder with five loaded chambers. Fitting it into the frame, he pressed the pin back in and clipped the loading lever home.

"We'd best take them Henry rifles," Billy said. "Especially for the trail on the other side of Bozeman. A smart man wouldn't risk his hair crossing the Powder River country. I figure it's chancy enough if we head down through the Big Horn Basin. Them Henrys might come in handy."

"You always thinking?" Parmelee asked as he stepped down from his horse and started rummaging through the vigilantes' clothing.

"Yep. Like it might not do to have those horses get back to where people could recognize them any too quick. I'll be back just as soon as I get them."

As Billy rode after the horses, he felt jubilant, as if his chest were going to explode with sheer unadulterated joy. In his mind he kept replaying the shooting, seeing it over and over again.

By damn, he did good work when the devil was in him!

105

April 10, 1868

They called the windswept cemetery hill just east of town Jack O'Neill's Ranch in honor of the well-liked bartender who'd been buried there. John Walley — self-declared undertaker — had claimed possession of the graveyard. Walley had started out as a cabinetmaker. A talent that easily had been turned to the manufacture of coffins — a commodity in perpetual short supply on the Colorado frontier, but in particular demand in violence-prone Denver.

Sarah stood in the blustery cold, bracing herself as the wind tried to billow her dress into a sail and blow her off to Kansas. Low blue-black clouds scudded toward the southeast; misty drops, little more than drizzle, beaded on her wool coat, turning the black fabric light gray. Here and there droplets had streaked.

She kept her back to the wind, as did Philip. He stood, head down, hat off, heedless of the fine misty rain that was already darkening his blond locks and sticking them to his skull. His gaze was fixed on the two freshly dug graves. One large, the other small.

God, Sarah's heart ached for him. He looked as

if he were a husk. Nothing more than skin wrapped around a frame of bone and absently clothed. Emptiness lay behind his eyes — a blue vacancy that had retreated beyond distance and time. The old Cherokee stories about soul loss that she'd heard as a girl came back to haunt her.

Philip had thrown every bit of himself into his marriage. He'd worshiped Aggie, blossomed with the growing promise of a child. Having invested that much of himself, the loss of lover, wife, partner, and child had crushed him the way a stone did a berry.

Had Aggie's and his unborn son's deaths forever ripped the soul from his body?

"And so we lay our beloved sister, wife, and mother, Bridget Hancock, to rest," the preacher droned on. "At her side, taken too early, we inter the physical remains of her son, James Butler Hancock. Yet, in doing so, we are reminded that the dead are resurrected in eternal glory. Ashes to ashes, dust to dust."

As the preacher went on to recite the Lord's prayer, Sarah stepped up to Philip and took his hand. Followed his gaze down into the ragged holes Walley's men had hacked through the plains' sod and down into the buff-colored dirt. Both coffins were covered with a smattering of wildflowers that Agatha had purchased for a penny from a street urchin. At least they hadn't had to use paper flowers as was the winter custom.

After saying the obligatory amen at the end of the prayer, Sarah squeezed Philip's hand. "She was my dear friend. Odd, isn't it? For all the family's prominence in Arkansas, we children had so few friends."

"How am I going to live?" Philip's voice sounded distant.

Sarah glanced at Walley, standing in the rear, and nodded her head. The two gravediggers started forward with their shovels. They drove their blades into the dirt piles, and tossed the first shovelfuls back into the holes. The soil thumped hollowly on Aggie's casket. Little James Butler's barely made a sound.

Aggie's casket. Not Bridget's. It was how Sarah would remember her. That part of her friend's identity was hers, while Philip could claim all of her that was Bridget.

"Dear brother" — she took a deep breath — "how many times have you told me that a physician is one of the most impotent of men? That so many maladies defy your skills?"

He glanced at the small grave immediately to the right. "My little boy was dead in the womb. I can take that. But not Bridget." He closed his eyes, tears trickling down to mix with the light rain in his beard. "I don't want to live. Not without her."

She pulled him to her shoulder, pressing his wet head against her, feeling the sobs rack his body.

"Wasn't your fault. You did everything you could."

"I couldn't *stop the bleeding*!" He swallowed hard. "And the worst part was, she *knew* she was dying, and she kept saying 'Don't blame yourself, Philip. Promise me.' But I couldn't . . . couldn't . . ."

"Are you God, brother?"

"My wife and my son are dead" — he shivered against her — "I'm not even dirt."

832

106

As Butler rode up the mountain pass he realized he'd never been better. The whole of his life had changed, and for the first time ever, he felt truly happy.

He'd just spent the winter in a four-pole Sheep Eater tipi in the high mountains. The winter's diet had consisted of pit-roasted mountain sheep, elk, sage grouse, fish, and stews made of netted waxwings. Along with root breads, he'd devoured cakes made of crushed crickets and buffalo pemmican. His body had never been stronger, his wind deeper, or his thoughts more clear. He was possessed of a new energy.

The men watched him with worried eyes, sometimes they even faded, seemed to slip away for hours, even a day or two.

Nights around the fire with Mountain Flicker at his side, Cracked Bone Thrower and Red Rain across the fire, not to mention the boys, had been among the finest in his life as he'd found a home in Puhagan's small family band.

Cracked Bone Thrower had taught him to make and walk on snowshoes, and he'd learned how to snare elk with a braided rawhide lasso and a bowed fir tree. *Snare* elk? Who would have ever thought?

Better yet, on those days when Pettigrew and the men pressed in on him, no one in the Dukurika camp looked at him askance. Not even when he spent hours talking to Jimmy Peterson about St. Francis County, or listening to Johnny Baker chatter on about his two sisters back in Arkadelphia. The Sheep Eaters just shrugged and considered it his special Power — along with those granted him by Water Ghost Woman.

Though no one had any idea who or what the silver eagle might be.

The winter had given him time for introspection. He could recall his boyhood in the Arkansas mountains with joy. Remember hiking and hunting in the forested uplands around the White River; reading by the nightly fire during winter's chill; and the joy of dressing out a hog with anticipation of Maw's culinary magic as she cooked the loin. It all lingered like honeyed joy in his memory.

His days in the academy in Pennsylvania had been filled with thrill and terror as he pitted his brain and intellect against that of other students, sometimes retiring in triumph, other times in ignominious defeat. Challenging. Fun. And forever filled with the stress of constant study and testing.

And then had come the war.

As his horse climbed the trail behind Cracked Bone Thrower and his pack of dogs, Butler struggled to make sense of the things he'd witnessed, participated in, and somehow survived.

Glancing off to the side, he could see the men marching along in their tattered uniforms, rifles pitched across their shoulders.

Phantoms. The creation of his broken mind.

Doc had told him over and over that they were a figment of his madness, but Water Ghost Woman finally had convinced him. Some part of his white man's brain had wanted to blame the narcotic Power of the *toyatawura.* But, damn it, he'd seen Water Ghost Woman, felt her body against his. Died down there in the watery Underworld. And what the hell? He *was* crazy. If he could see dead Confederate soldiers marching along in ranks, of course he could see terrifying mystical Indian spirit beings.

That day back at the lake when he'd related the story to Cracked Bone Thrower, who'd told Puhagan, they'd sure as hell believed. Though it amazed them that a *taipo,* a white man, had survived one of their most dangerous spirit journeys.

Apple's hooves cracked hollowly on the rocky trail as Puhagan — up in the lead — pulled up. He was surrounded by six pack dogs, all panting under their loads. Behind the elder followed Cracked Bone Thrower and Red Rain — with her infant daughter in her cradleboard on her back.

Butler was proud of that little baby girl. He'd been called to help deliver her. Cracked Bone Thrower and Red Rain's two young sons, Cricket and Water Snake, each with their own packs, immediately threw themselves down to rest. Among the Sheep Eaters everyone carried part of the load.

Mountain Flicker turned back toward Butler. As she smiled, her teeth gleamed in her triangular face with its broad cheekbones.

Butler grinned back. My, how life had changed. Checking on the men, he saw that they had

835

already dropped onto the rocks and taken seats in the sagebrush. Over his shoulder the view was spectacular. He could see clear across the basin, rimmed as it was on the west-southwest by the Wind River Mountains, and on the south by the Sweetwater Rim. To the east and below he could make out the green line of cottonwoods that marked the Wind River's course. It was said that it ran through the Owl Creeks in a narrow-walled canyon.

The trail followed a small canyon cut into the limestone slopes. Ancient, it was said by the Du-kurika to have been used since the beginning of time. Clear back to when the first humans escaped from First Woman's basket. Butler could believe it. The ground was scored by the passing of numerous old travois poles, and winter-bleached piles of horse apples could be seen here and there.

Earlier Puhagan had told him, "We wouldn't take the Red Canyon Pass if the snows were not so deep in the high peaks. Too many enemies use this trail. But this early in the season we should be able to get through and down to the safety of Anikahonobita Ogwaide."

"Red something." Butler had struggled with the words. He was learning, but Shoshoni was a difficult language.

"Red Canyon's Creek," Cracked Bone Thrower had told him. "That is where the injured *taipo* is. The one they have asked the *puhagan* to heal. The one that perhaps you, too, can help heal."

Maybe it was Water Ghost Woman's gift. Maybe it was the time he'd spent with Philip, but he did have a gift. In addition to delivering Red Rain's baby, he'd helped Puhagan set broken bones, stitch wounds, and treat fevers. To his, and the

836

men's, amazement, his patients had all gotten better.

And then, three days ago, a runner had arrived from Ducha Goobai's camp by Red Canyon's Creek informing Puhagan that a white man had been badly mauled by a spring grizzly. Ducha Goobai, Dirty Face, was a longtime friend of Puhagan's. Would the Spirit healer bring the Man Who Talks to No One — the one who had been given healing Power by Water Ghost Woman — and come immediately?

Butler wondered how Dukurika from all over the mountains seemed to know about him. As far as he'd seen, throughout the winter, most everyone had spent their time in the lodges.

The climb continued up through the shallow valley, and over the divide. As they passed through the summit, a panorama unfolded to the north bounded by the tall Absaroka Mountains on the west — the crags dominated by the peak called Iszupa Wean, the Coyote's Penis. The lower peaks and cliffs were gleaming and snow covered. In the east, the Big Horn Mountains — capped in pristine white — towered over the basin. And in the far north, Cracked Bone Thrower pointed out a mountain. "The whites call those the Pryor Mountains. Named for one of Lewis and Clark's men. That's Crow country. Mostly they are horse people, we avoid them by staying in the high mountains."

Before them the trail descended in a long slope toward a magnificent line of bloodred sandstone buttes and upthrust ridges. As the sun sank toward the northwest, Puhagan followed the trail — marked as it was with elk and bison tracks. While snow still filled the narrow drainages that incised the slope, green grass, sagebrush buttercup, shooting star, and the first shoots of balsam were coming up.

Flicker had slowed to walk beside Butler's horse. Maybe he should have walked like the rest of them, but he'd dedicated himself to leading the packhorse, loaded as it was with the folded covers of three small elkhide lodges and baskets full of provisions. Among the Sheep Eaters it was considered rude to just show up without bringing some contribution to the stew pot.

And besides, he didn't trust leaving the horses with the other Wind River Dukurika. It would have been shirking his responsibility to the animals. Even the biggest antihorse skeptic had admitted that the animals had been most helpful packing meat for the camp, but Sheep Eaters were dog people. And with good reason. When they retreated to the high peaks for summer, most of the trails were impassible to horses. Dogs, however, could scamper up and down rocks and over fallen timber, and leap from boulder to boulder with the same agility as people.

"How far is Red Canyon's Creek?" Butler asked Mountain Flicker, at the same time keeping an eye on the two boys. Off and on Butler had taken turns walking, and letting them ride on the saddle. From the looks of their stumbling fatigue, it was almost time again.

Flicker pointed. "There. Just around that red cliff. It is a place of springs. We will be there by dusk."

"Does Dirty Face have a bigger band than Puhagan?"

"All Dukurika camps are small at this time of year," she told him, mixing Shoshoni with English words and hand signs. "Mostly just families, no more than ten or twenty people. As the snow goes away we will move up into the mountains. In summer these lowlands are too dangerous. There is too much war and raiding with Sioux, Cheyenne, Arapaho, Crow, and Blackfeet passing through."

Butler glanced over at the men, calling, "See. There's trouble everywhere that men are men. War and raiding. Even here in paradise."

"Maybe we're all mad," Corporal Pettigrew called back.

"Maybe we are," Butler agreed.

Mountain Flicker glanced at the emptiness where Butler directed his remarks, and a knowing smile followed.

The shadows were long by the time Puhagan led them down a drainage and into a small valley marked by red cliffs on the west and steeply sloped beds of sandstone that gave way to soaring limestone on the east.

Two young runners came trotting up the trail, long hair bobbing behind them, dogs leading the way. It created a small melee as dogs and people sorted themselves out amid wagging tails, growls, and called greetings.

After that it was another mile or so before the youths led the way into a gap in the upthrust sandstone. Behind it lay a sheltered cove beneath high stony slopes. Here water bubbled up out of the ground in a small stream. Above it, amid juniper and pines, a winter camp of brush structures had been built against a sandstone incline.

Mountain Flicker pointed out the people. "That's Dirty Face. And he's the elder here. That tall young man is his oldest son, Chokecherry Eater. The two older women are Dirty Face's wives, both sisters. The one with the limp is Ripe Currant, the younger one is Moon Cloud. That pregnant woman is Chokecherry Eater's wife, White Hand."

Introductions continued as Butler dismounted and helped Cracked Bone Thrower unpack Shandy's load. He led the animals to water and then to a grassy flat where he staked them on pickets.

By the time he made it back to camp, a good fire was burning. Puhagan's and Cracked Bone Thrower's small tipis had been pitched, and Mountain Flicker was halfway through the task of weaving branches she'd stripped from juniper into a conical structure for Butler and herself. As soon as she finished with the frame, she'd wrap their lodge cover around it.

"Go and see the hurt *taipo*," she told him as her nimble fingers wove the prickly juniper. "This will be finished by the time you get back. Then we will eat."

"Yes, ma'am," Butler told her with a salute. She always smiled when he saluted her, knowing it was a gesture of respect.

"That big earth lodge," she told him, pointing to a domed structure back in the trees.

Butler made his way to the low entrance, calling, "Puhagan?"

"We are here, Butler," Cracked Bone Thrower replied.

Butler ducked into the low, warm interior, finding it lit by a stone-slab-lined fire pit just inside the door. The odor of stale sweat and sepsis made him grimace; flashes of memory took him back to Camp Douglas, and filth, despair, and death.

The *taipo* lay in the back. In the dim light Puhagan was peeling back a blanket to expose long gashes that ran diagonally across the big man's chest. The right hand was missing, the forearm a lacerated mess — skin and muscle stripped from the bone — and dripping infection. The left hand was chewed and missing the ring finger and pinky. Dark scabs could be seen across the man's scalp where teeth or claws had ripped through the long white hair.

"It was a spring grizzly," Cracked Bone Thrower told Butler. "She had just come out of her cave with two cubs. The Silver Eagle" — he indicated the wincing white man — "came upon them by accident. She would have killed him and eaten him, but he managed to jump off the trail and fell down a steep slope. At the bottom a juniper tree stopped his fall, but even then, his leg is broken."

The Silver Eagle.

Water Ghost Woman's gift.

It all made sense.

Cracked Bone Thrower was giving him a "see, I told you so" look. *Puha* was at play here. He felt the Power of it settle on his shoulders like a heavy cloak.

Butler fixed on the man's thin face, on his high forehead, the matted beard, and hawkish nose. Behind the parted lips he could see the chipped tooth, the gap worn in the teeth from years of clenching a pipe stem.

As if he were hearing it again, Water Ghost Woman's words echoed in the cramped structure. *"By saving the Silver Eagle, you condemn him."*

"I have the *puha* to heal," he whispered, heart pounding.

"What was that?" Cracked Bone Thrower asked, the men looking up at Butler.

841

"He has to be cleansed," Butler told them. "The claw marks and bites are infected; I've seen it before, after the battles. You've told me of the Smoking Waters, where hot water bubbles from the earth. The Bah'gewana. We need to take him there if there's to be any chance of saving him."

Cracked Bone Thrower had translated and Puhagan straightened, asking in Shoshoni, "You know this?"

Butler nodded. "Can we go there tomorrow? Pack him on the horse?"

"Ha'a," Puhagan told him. "But we need to set that broken leg first."

Butler dropped on his knees, laying a hand on the fevered man's forehead. Delirious blue eyes wavered in their sockets as he stared up at Butler. The man's lips parted, his tongue working as if he were trying to speak.

"It's going to be all right, *puha* has brought me to you. Water Ghost Woman said I could save you."

"Butler?" the man finally managed to whisper.

"It's me, Paw."

107

The play that night at Angel's Lair was *Caesar
and Cleopatra.* The back of the parlor sported five
chairs in which the clients sat, cigars and their
liquor of choice at hand. On the raised stage, two
male actors played Julius Caesar and Mark
Antony. The background looked like a dressed-
stone wall, and the only props were two velvet-
upholstered chaise longues.

Resources in isolated Denver being what they
were, Caesar's and Antony's helmets might have
looked more like buckets, and the breastplates
they wore like stove parts; nor did the red kilts
resemble the pictures of Romans that Sarah had
seen in the magazines. The sandals had been borrowed from an acting troupe, as had the swords.

Across the foyer, the two violins and a cello
added a musical background while the actors
spouted their lines in the glow of the floor lamps.

The one playing Caesar — a tall black-haired
Ohioan — declared in his nasal twang, "I tell you,
Mark Antony, I shall burn Egypt! Raze it to the
ground! I am Caesar! I come, I see, I conquer!"

"But Caesar," Antony objected, "this is the land
of Pharaohs, birthplace of Moses. To simply lay it

waste is a hideous bit of business."

At this juncture, Theresa, dressed in a simple shift, entered the room, bowing down in such a manner as to tease the audience with her rounded buttocks.

"Hail, Caesar!" she cried. "I am Memnis, servant to Cleopatra, Queen of the Nile. She has sent me with a gift for the noble Caesar!"

Mark Antony stepped forward, laying a hand on Caesar's arm. "Before you unleash havoc on the Egyptians, Caesar, at least see what the queen sends."

"I only do this for you, Antony," Caesar quipped, gesturing.

Into the room came Mick, bare-chested, wearing a pair of baggy yellow pants. A roll of carpet was carried crosswise in his arms. This he laid on the raised platform at Caesar's feet, bowed, left.

"She sends me a rug?" Caesar complained. "I could find the like at the local bazaar!"

Sarah, from the back of the room, glanced at the rapt expressions on the johnnies' faces. The ash on their cigars gave them away. Short ash, they were bored. Long ash, the cigars were forgotten in anticipation. Now all eyes were fixed on the roll of carpet, shaped as it was in a most female form.

Sarah slipped silently out and closed the door behind her as she entered the dining room. In the process, every male patron in the room strained to catch a peek. Callie and Ginnie, dressed to look like Egyptians, kohl dark around their eyes, were already waiting for the finale. Arms crossed to emphasize their busts, they'd been teasing the men at their suppers.

Sarah gave them a nod, looked at the men, and

said, "Don't be left out, gentlemen. There will be another show tomorrow night. Make your reservations with Mick, and you'll get a thrill you won't soon forget."

"The only thrill I'd never forget is taking a roll with the Goddess!" one called jovially.

"I will anxiously await your increase in prosperity, Joshua," Sarah shot back with a wink, and stepped into the bar. Another ten men were drinking at the tables, poker games forgotten, heads cocked in the attempt to overhear the "play."

The bartender, washing glasses, gave her the "all's well" nod, and went back to his duties. At that moment the musicians hit their cue — a dynamic crescendo as Agatha was unrolled from the carpet.

From here on, as Cleopatra, she would slowly seduce Caesar, thereby saving her kingdom. Meanwhile, Callie and Ginnie would attempt to distract Mark Antony, who, despite both women's attentions, would look longingly and jealously at Cleopatra as she enticed Caesar onto the chaise.

Sarah glanced at the clock. The girls had another twenty minutes before the play was over and the johnnies would be desperate to get them upstairs.

Mick descended the stairs, dressed again in his usual fine silk vest, pressed trousers, and starched white shirt.

As he resumed his station below the stairs, Sarah stepped close and asked, "How are we doing?"

"Five hundred up from last night, ma'am. Frankie, Sally, and Ceylon should be finishing their johnnies." He indicated the men at the bar, every one of them imagining what was happening in the show. "Reckon by the time the show's over,

845

there'll be demand enough that we'll have a full house."

Keeping seven girls busy on show nights — in spite of the outrageous prices Sarah charged — was never an issue. Yet. Word was that after seeing one of the shows, Big Ed and some of his partners were working on two houses that would offer competition. As Aggie would have told her, "It's short-term."

The presence of the new houses would add to the struggle of finding male actors. It wasn't the money, or male willingness, but duration — finding the ones who could keep wood in their peckers long enough to end the play.

A smart woman would seize the moment. She could almost imagine Aggie's green eyes, her ironic smile. Practically hear her Irish-inflected voice saying, "Quote Big Ed a price. Worst he could do is say no, second worst is a low counter-offer, but then, he might just buy you out on the spot."

But what should she ask? What was Angel's Lair worth? With Aggie's death, she owned it all free and clear. She not only had investments in lots in both Denver and Cheyenne that had started to pay off, but through the lawyer Bela Hughes she had also invested in the Denver Board of Trade — a committee of influential men desperate to bring either the Union Pacific, Kansas Pacific, or a third line of their own creation, the Denver Pacific, to the growing city.

The musicians hit another crescendo, the signal that Cleopatra had allowed the last of her garments to fall away.

Whistles and applause could be heard, the music softening sensually. Agatha was peeling away

Caesar's armor.

During the show, clientele were directed around to the back, entering through the kitchen so as not to distract from the action.

Sarah wasn't surprised, therefore, to see George Nichols emerge from the kitchen. He carried his cane, was dressed in a magnificent sack coat with matching vest, his black wool trousers pressed and immaculate over glossy black leather shoes.

She needed only a glance at his face, however, to tell that this was trouble. George was drunk, his eyes glassy, the normally dark face ruddy. A wicked smile crossed his lips as he laid eyes on her. He wobbled on his beeline toward her.

From a pocket, he pulled a packed roll of coins, tossing it to Mick. His greeting to Sarah was "Upstairs. Now."

She glanced sidelong as Mick poured out the golden coins. Sarah guessed it at a little over two hundred dollars.

"You know my price," she told him.

His dangerous black eyes hardened, and he seemed to sway. "It'll do. I want you now."

She gave Mick the desist sign, nodding at George. "Let's go discuss this, shall we?"

Yes, better this way.

He'd make a scene otherwise, and the last thing she wanted was a row with one of the most dangerous and powerful men in the territory. And, who knew, drunk as he was he might just step into her room and pass out if she could stall him long enough.

She reached the top of the stairs, led the way to her door, and closed it behind Nichols.

He was having trouble shedding his coat. Wavering on his feet.

"George, you're drunk. You couldn't put wood in your pecker if you tried." She poured him a generous whiskey, handing him the glass. His black eyes burned, as if enraged. He chugged it down and ran his sleeve over his lips.

"I want you, bitch." He gestured with the empty glass. "Tonight. Now. Every night. I want to fuck you like no man's ever fucked you. Like I fucked you that first time. Remember that? Four days and nights!"

"Why don't you sit down and let me —"

He tossed the glass over his shoulder. It clattered off the wall, hit the floor, but didn't break. Stepping forward, he laid his hands on her shoulders, staring hotly and balefully into her eyes. She saw a black maelstrom there, a swirling of anger, lust, and frustration.

"George . . ."

His head shot forward, kissing her, shifting his hands to the back of her head, holding her in place. She stiffened, tasting whiskey as his tongue probed her mouth.

His body was like a tense spring, his erection hard against his trousers. Then he pushed her, toppling her back onto her bed. Before she could right herself, he was on her, clawing at her dress, ripping the low-cut neckline. Buttons popped on her bodice, and he tore the fabric away, dropping his mouth to her exposed breast. She whimpered as he took her nipple in his teeth.

"George! All right! All right! Let me get out of this dress."

He was panting, something feral in his eyes as he released her, his lips parted in a desperate grin.

She tried to wriggle out from under him, but he clapped a hand to her neck. Shifting, he pawed frantically at the ruin of her dress.

She was able to reach behind her head, pull herself higher on the bed, get her back against the ornate brass-rail headboard.

"You are *mine!*" he told her, blinking, his breath thick with alcohol. "No woman ever told me no. As if a whore like you was too good for George Nichols. Sarah, I *own* you. I *made* you. You don't want to marry me? Huh? That it? Well, you don't have to. But you'll be my bitch, or I'll bury you."

"You're drunk, George." The fear had burned loose, the feeling of helplessness, the old terrors leaping up from the past. Flashes of Dewley's eyes, of the smell of sour breath being blown in her face as men grunted and rutted.

"You tell me yes, Sarah," he insisted, his hand tightening on her throat like a clamp.

She tried to break free, only to have him crush her windpipe. Panic lent her strength, but when she clawed at him, he smashed a vicious right to the side of her head. Pain and lights burst through her brain.

Half stunned, she slumped, letting her arms fall away. She managed a weak nod, body going limp.

Nichols grinned, exposing tobacco-stained teeth. With both hands, he tugged on her dress, ripping it down.

When he lifted himself and frantically began to unbutton his trousers, she shifted her grip on the headboard. Her fingers encountered cold metal, the smooth feel of wood.

He pulled up her skirt, his breath gone to ragged panting. As he threw himself onto her, she tightened her grip on the wood and metal, bracing herself.

His eyes had gone distant, expression hollow

with anticipation. As he sought to insert himself, she drew her arm back.

She could hear the music downstairs as Caesar, unable to resist, mounted Cleopatra.

The voice seemed to come from a distance.

Do it!

Nichols barely had time to react, confusion flickering in his drunken eyes.

With all her might, Sarah slammed Dewley's heavy .44 Colt against the side of Nichols's head. He twitched and collapsed on top of her.

She lay there, exhausted, panting in the wake of the rushing fear, and rubbed her throat. When she'd hung the holster there, behind the headboard, she'd known this day was coming. Had thought it would be Parmelee. The feel of the revolver's cool wooden grips reassured her.

She felt Nichols convulse and managed to roll him off onto the floor before he doubled and vomited onto her throw rug.

108

April 29, 1868

The knocking kept repeating before it finally brought Doc awake. Logy, he blinked his eyes open and realized the insistent pounding came from his door.

He staggered to his feet, half stumbling in sleep, and made his way to the front door. Opening it, he squinted into a lantern's light, recognizing Mick, Sarah's professor from the Angel's Lair.

"What's wrong?" *God, tell me it's not Sarah!*

"Got a man in the wagon, Doc. Sarah asked that you look him over at your surgery. See if he's all right."

"What time is it?"

"A little after two, sir."

"Let me get dressed."

Doc blinked, half staggering back to his bedroom where he fumbled for his clothes. Damn it, he shouldn't have had that last glass of whiskey. Problem was, whiskey helped. It deadened the sucking emptiness and softened the features of Bridget's face, forever hanging, as it did, in his hopes. Just beyond his vision, as if he could reach out and touch her.

While one glass might get him to sleep, it wasn't

enough to keep him from popping awake a couple of hours later. That was when the emptiness and pain were the worst. That's when he'd slip his hand onto her side of the bed only to find cold sheets.

Two glasses would conjure a stupor that would carry him far enough through the night that he would wake headachy, mouth dry, his tongue like a stick. But lately that hadn't been enough, either, so he'd gone to three glasses a night.

"Physician, heal thyself."

He finished dressing, grabbed his hat and coat on the way out of the house, and locked his door behind him. A man didn't leave his house unlocked. Not in Denver with its hordes of destitute and broken men — the ones who'd flowed west after the war to make their fortunes. All but a lucky few had discovered that if they'd been failures in the East, they'd be failures in the Rockies. But without family and friends to cadge from. Here they found only starvation, pneumonia, exposure, and exploitation by the gangs.

Doc climbed onto Mick's wagon seat and bent over the back. A man lay there, wrapped in a blanket. From habit, Doc checked his pulse and breathing as Mick started them for the surgery.

"Who is he?"

"George Nichols."

"Jesus! What happened?"

"He come to the house tonight with a load on. Sarah took him upstairs to avoid a scene. Nichols got violent. Sarah pistol-whipped him with that big Colt she keeps. She wants you to take a look at him."

"Is she all right?"

"A little shaken, Doc. Going to have a bruise on

852

her throat, but she told me to tell you, don't bother to come check her."

"She worries me."

"If there's any worrying to be done, it's about Nichols, here. His brougham and driver are still waiting out front. We took Nichols out the back. The driver isn't a concern yet, he's waited till nigh on midday before, but if Nichols doesn't eventually come out? There, uh, could be complications."

Doc rubbed his face and tried to order his mind as they pulled up at the surgery.

It took the two of them to carry Nichols back to the table. Most of the time, the man muttered and tried to stumble along.

Doc lit his lamps and winced at the smell of vomit and stale drink. He slapped Nichols on the face, peering into the man's eyes when he blinked. "Wake up!"

Nichols made a face, squinted against the light, mumbling, "Where am I?"

"You're at Doc Hancock's. What do you remember?"

Nichols's gaze wandered in confusion. "You said . . ." He blinked. "Where am I?"

"Concussion," Doc told Mick. He cleaned the cut on the side of Nichols's head. "That and he's so drunk he can't stand. Hard to tell which is worse."

"So he's going to live?"

"I'd say so."

"Think he'll remember what happened?"

Doc shrugged. "Hard to say."

"Where am I?" Nichols asked.

"So, what do we do?" Mick asked.

"I'd say take him back, have his driver load him in the brougham, and haul him back to wherever he's supposed to be."

Mick studied Doc warily. "If he remembers that Sarah whacked him in the head . . . Well, he ain't the forgiving kind, Doc."

"With that goose egg on his noggin, he's going to know it wasn't just an ordinary fling with Sarah."

"Either way," Mick told him, "Nichols is going to be trouble. He's asked her to marry him more than once. She thinks she can handle him, but Doc, I been around. He's a powerful man, and folks who stand in his way have a funny way of up and dying. Word is he's got a killer working for him. Calls him the Meadowlark. No one's ever seen him. But Nichols don't need no help. If he is of a mind, he can break Angel's Lair. Ruin it one of ten different ways."

"I've heard." Doc stared down at Nichols. He'd closed his eyes, snoring softly.

It would be so easy. He could soak a rag in chloroform and hold it over the man's nose until he stopped breathing. No one would ever know. Tomorrow morning, Mick could have the body carried out to the brougham, claiming, "He just died in his sleep."

If there were questions, Doc, as the house physician, could certify that the man's heart had stopped. While he was known to serve the demimonde, he had enough influential clients that his reputation would be untarnished.

"Is this what I've come to?" he asked himself, feeling suddenly weak, as if his very soul had come unmanned.

"What's that, Doc?"

"Nothing. Let's get him back to Angel's Lair."

But one thing was certain, Sarah was dancing

with a serpent, and if she wasn't damn careful, it was going to get her killed.

109

April 30, 1868

The water was as hot as Butler could stand as he waded in naked and kept his father from sinking. The Smoking Waters were indeed hot springs, big ones that gushed up from the ground at the base of a series of low red hills and upthrust ridges. To him it looked as if the sloping mountains to the south had been broken, bent, and cracked. Where it emerged from the narrow canyon carved through the mountain, the Wind River ran clear, cool, and deep, passing within an arrowshot of the great springs.

"Got to get the sepsis out," Butler told his father as he brushed at the dead and necrotic tissue with a brush made from a frayed willow stem.

Tears ran from his father's face, suffering sounds came half choked from the man's convulsing throat.

"Please, stop!" Paw whimpered, struggling weakly against Butler's grip. "God . . . *that hurts!*"

Butler glanced at the shore. His men sat in a line just off to the side of where Puhagan, Cracked Bone Thrower, Red Rain, and Mountain Flicker waited. Dirty Face and several of his young men squatted to their right, concern in their eyes.

"I have to cleanse you, Father," Butler told him. "I have to wash away the corruption. The slashes on your chest should have been sewed up, but they've healed too much now, so we'll let them go. The same with the lacerations on your scalp."

"Just let me die?" Paw wheezed, still trying to break free. Impossible given his right arm was shredded and useless, a chokecherry-stave splint immobilized his broken leg, and that he was drained by fever.

When Butler was finally finished, his father floated in the water, gasping and exhausted. Butler turned to Puhagan and nodded. The medicine man waded out, not even making a face as the hot water swirled around him.

Butler got a grip under Paw's right armpit, and together he and Puhagan dragged the man up onto the stone-hard mineral of the shore. Mountain Flicker supported Paw's broken leg.

Butler waded back into the water only long enough to splash himself all over to wash off the sweat that beaded and trickled down his hot skin. After the heat it was a delight to just stand, naked, letting the breeze blow over his red and dripping body.

Mountain Flicker stepped close and used her hands to slick the water from his hide, asking, "Will Silver Eagle be well now?"

"I have more to do." Butler glanced uncomfortably at his father where he lay gasping and limp on the blanket. "The arm's ruined."

"Puhagan says the same," she told him.

"It's gonna be plumb ticklish," Kershaw whispered from behind Butler's ear. "Reckon I wouldn't give yer paw a coon's chance, Cap'n."

"I have to try, Sergeant. He's my father."

"Butler?" Paw asked after Butler had pulled on his clothes and bent down. For the first time, his father really seemed lucid. His lips were working, sweat beading on his forehead.

"The arm has to come off," Butler told him. "It's dead, Paw."

"No." Paw licked his lips, his chest rising and falling.

"What are you doing here? What happened at Shiloh?"

Paw glanced at him, worked his mouth, and looked away. "Shiloh? Can't . . . bear it. Death all around. The sounds . . . screaming, shrieking bullets . . . they sing . . . sing of death . . ."

Butler nodded, a pain in his heart. "I need you to chew on something for me."

"What?"

"It's called *toyatawura.*"

Paw blinked, throat working as he swallowed. "You a *puhagan,* son?"

"No. Water Ghost Woman just said —"

"Jesus, Butler, what happened to you?"

"I had to bring the men home. The ones who were killed at Chickamauga. Philip threw me out. Said I was crazy. So the men and I marched here; because you always talked about it when I was a boy. And Water Ghost Woman said she had a gift, the Silver Eagle."

"That's what they call me now." Paw glanced at him, his thoughts seeming to scatter. "Ain't never been nothing but a failure. Tell Maw . . ."

When no more was forthcoming, Butler said, "She's dead and buried behind the farmhouse. Everyone's gone but me and Philip. And now you."

He took the *toyatawura* and slipped it into his

858

father's mouth, ordering, "Chew that, Paw. Chew it hard."

For whatever reason, his father's jaws began to work as he ground the bitter plant between his remaining teeth.

"What next?" Puhagan asked as he settled beside Butler.

"We have to cut this arm off. Can you smell that? It's rotten, what's left of it."

Puhagan glanced at him. "You can do this? Pa'waip showed you?"

"No. But Philip did."

Butler glanced at the men where they crowded around, faces hard and skeptical. Butler waved them away. "Sergeant, set up a perimeter. We don't want to be caught by surprise if enemy vedettes are in the area."

"Yes, sir."

To Mountain Flicker he said, "I'll need that thread and the iron needle I asked you to bring. I'm going to have to sew arteries closed."

She nodded and went to retrieve her pouch.

Paw's eyes had gone glassy and vacant. Butler wondered what he was seeing in his vision.

"You know," Corporal Pettigrew told him from where he stood with arms crossed, "you're gonna kill him."

Then, with the men slowly shaking their heads, Butler reached for the knife he'd spent the last two days sharpening.

110

May 3, 1868

The light blue taffeta day dress Sarah wore had a high collar to hide the bruises at her throat: they'd turned that hideous yellow-green and were still sore to the touch. She had added a hat, which though a couple of years out of style, matched the dress's color. She'd had Agatha cinch her curved corset a bit too tight, but then this wasn't just an ordinary meeting.

She was through with having choices made for her, of suddenly and traumatically finding the course of her life irrevocably changed. One way or another, her days of being a victim were over.

She'd come to that conclusion the night George Nichols had tried to force her. She'd let her rage get the best of her. Some unfettered insanity had goaded her to write a note on a scrap of foolscap stating: *I will never marry you. Do not come back!*

When no one was looking, she'd unbuttoned his fly, used a bit of string to tie it around his limp penis, and buttoned him back up before he'd been carried to his brougham. The rest of that day she'd waited with her five-shot pocket revolver. George hadn't come.

But he would. And the tension was killing her.

She made her way across Lawrence Street to the office on the northeast corner of Fifteenth.

Opening the door to the law offices of Hughes & Welbor, she found Doc already waiting. She stopped short, really seeing him in the light of day. His features were sallow, the flesh of his face sunken, his eyes bloodshot and set back in their sockets. His hair hadn't been washed in days, and his clothes were rumpled, food stains on his coat.

I haven't been seeing to him as I should.

Fact was, she'd been avoiding him since the funeral. Some part of her was made uncomfortable by the hideous depth of his grief. Another part of her justified her abandonment of him with the self-serving platitude that just being around him was a reminder of Aggie — and only served to pick the scab from a poorly healing wound.

"Philip," she greeted him warmly, stepping forward. "Thank you for coming."

He glanced to where the legal secretary sat behind a desk, pointedly pretending to ignore them. "Want to tell me why you called me here?"

"I need you. I'm a woman, Philip. A condition which the laws of men insist make me both incompetent, unreliable, and impotent. You, however, were born a man, and therefore wise, temperate, and in remarkable control of your faculties. Should I succeed in my endeavor today, you shall become the senior partner whose lawful signature will guarantee the legal validity of any silly actions my flighty female mind might have led me into."

"What *are* you talking about?"

"Business, Philip." She placed a hand behind his shoulder, directing him to the desk. "I think Hancock and Hancock shall do nicely."

861

Now the secretary looked up, a nice young man, moderately well dressed, a trimmed beard on his cheeks. "May I help you?"

"Dr. Philip Hancock and Mrs. Sarah Anderson to see Bela, please. We have a two o'clock appointment."

"Yes, ma'am," he told her, rising. "If you'd follow me, I believe the other parties have already arrived."

Sarah gave Doc a suspicious smile, and lowered her voice. "Whatever on earth could they have been discussing prior to our arrival?"

Doc shrugged his bony shoulders, looking even more mystified. She noted how her brother's coat hung on his rack of a body. What was the man doing, starving himself to death?

Perhaps he was. She remembered how little she herself had been interested in food after Bret's death.

Well, brother, if today works out, I promise I'll take better care of you.

They were led upstairs, down the hall, where the clerk opened a door and stepped back.

Sarah strode into a corner conference room dominated by a long and well-worn table. Serviceable chairs, most of them matching, lined the sides, and a double-hung window provided a view down both Lawrence and Fifteenth Streets. Beyond the clutter of buildings, she could see past the uplands where the distant mountains, still snowy, seemed to huddle beneath a bank of clouds.

The men in the room stood: Big Ed Chase, his tall body dressed in a fine charcoal-gray suit, his partner Francis Heatley, and Pat O'Reilly. Bela Hughes, Denver's most prominent lawyer, stood

862

at the head of the table, his back to the window.

Hughes was already in his fifties, with a thick white mustache, his gray hair combed over his receding forehead. He now studied Sarah through baggy brown eyes, his full body filling his suit.

"Gentlemen," Sarah greeted them, "good of you to meet me. Mr. Hughes, I don't think you've met my brother, Philip."

"How do you do?" Hughes shook Philip's hand.

"How do you do?" Philip responded.

"Can I get you anything?" Hughes asked.

"Coffee, if it wouldn't be a bother," Sarah said, and was pleased when Big Ed held her chair while she was seated.

Hughes nodded to the clerk who closed the door behind him.

Philip, still looking uncertain, seated himself beside her.

"Looks like rain's coming," Heatley said as he glanced out the window. "Heard the Smoky Hill Trail's already been raided."

"At least our noble red brothers haven't figured out how to raid a train!" Hughes remarked. "Thank God for the iron horse. Those bastards in charge of the Union Pacific might be a bunch of lying skunks when it comes to getting a spur line to Denver, but at least we can get supplies to Cheyenne these days."

"Kansas Pacific will get here eventually. Then the damn Indians can have Kansas." Big Ed leaned back, his hard blue eyes thoughtful as they studied Sarah.

The clerk entered, handing Sarah a cup of coffee, black and steaming. "Thank you," she told him.

After the clerk left, Hughes leaned back in his

chair. "Now, Mrs. Anderson, shall we get down to business?"

She glanced back and forth among them. "Pat, thank you for coming today."

"Aye, lass." O'Reilly gave her a smile. "Ye've got me curiosity up."

Sarah reached into her purse, removing the quit-claim deed that O'Reilly had signed over to her. "Pat, I really only need you to verify your signature on the deed to the Angel's Lair. To vouch that I own it outright."

He glanced at the paper, nodding. " 'Tis indeed the deed."

Sarah, folded it, returning it to her purse. "Mr. Chase, I've —"

"God, Sarah," he said with a smile, "call me Ed. I get enough pomposity at the council meetings."

"All right, Ed. You and Francis are in the process of starting two houses with . . ." She frowned. "Shall we call it carnal theater?"

"As good a name as any," Heatley replied with a shrug. "If you're thinking of stopping us, Sarah, I don't think you've got a legal leg to stand on."

"Indeed?"

"Well, why else would you call us to Bela's?"

She gave Heatley an amused smirk. "Oh, Francis, you are a dear sometimes. I've no interest in stopping you. Quite the contrary, I've heard of the troubles you're having finding talent and putting the houses together. If I'm right, you're still months out from an opening."

Heatley and Chase glanced knowingly at each other.

Sarah set her ledger on the table. This she slid across to Big Ed. "Those are the figures for Angel's Lair. If you need confirmation, we can

864

stroll down the street and have a little chat with Luther Kountze. I stopped by the bank on the way here. He'll be in all afternoon."

"Sarah?" Philip asked, "What are you . . ."

She silenced him with a gesture.

Chase and Heatley were bent over the ledger. O'Reilly leaned back, having withdrawn a flask from his coat to take a sip. He grinned at her, gave her a wink — cunning co-conspirator that he was.

Hughes sat thoughtfully, fingers laced over his chest, a frown on his face. He'd obviously been an attorney long enough to know that whatever the hand, the cards would be shown soon enough.

Big Ed was the first to look up. "If these figures are true, you're not exactly dissuading us from horning our way in on the action, Sarah."

"Then you agree that what we've put together at Angel's Lair is a valuable business?"

"Which is why we're going ahead with our own," Ed told her. "If you want us to stop, not even begging will help. And if we don't do it, someone else will."

She cradled her coffee, sitting back, giving them a demure smile. "Why saturate the market? Angel's Lair has an established clientele, a reputation that has spread far beyond Denver. We're doing four shows a week now. If my projections are correct — despite the outrageous prices I'm charging — by the end of the year we can fill every seat, every night of the week. We'd have waiting lines if we could get the railroad here."

Heatley slapped a hand to the table. "We agree."

Now Sarah leaned forward. "So why should we fight over johnnies to fill the seats? Come on, Ed, you worked out the formula yourself when it comes to the gambling hells. You run honest games, and your tables are full because you offer the chuckleheads a square deal. Your theaters are packed because you provide superb productions and top actors. Why ruin a good thing like Angel's Lair with cheap imitations?"

Heatley shrugged. "We'll figure out how to do it ourselves, Sarah."

"Sure. But why not have it all ready-made?" She shot Ed a smile. "Like I said, I'm not here to stop you. We've established that I own Angel's Lair, lock, stock, barrel, and band. You can see that it's making me a tidy profit. That could be *your* profit."

She paused. "Gentlemen, I brought my brother today in case I need a family member to cosign any of the paperwork. There are things I'd like to do in Denver." She glanced at Bela Hughes. "Investments I'd like to make in the Board of Trade. So, Ed, I'm offering you Angel's Lair."

She slipped another piece of paper across the table to Big Ed. "That's my price and the conditions of the sale."

On cue, Pat O'Reilly leaned forward, saying, "Lass, I thought ye were supposed to offer Nichols first —"

"He didn't meet my price."

"But he never offers full price at first. He likes to whittle ye down," O'Reilly countered.

Big Ed had glanced up, his glacial eyes narrowing.

Sarah gave a slight shrug, not wanting to overplay the rivalry between Big Ed and Nichols. That hook was now set.

Heatley was still studying the figures in the ledger, then glancing at her conditions. "Agatha, Theresa, and Mick stay with the business?"

866

"Agatha is the brains behind the shows. Don't meddle. Theresa has a knack for keeping the girls happy. Mick's been keeping track of inventory, and you'd be a fool to lose Mam. Her cooking is twenty percent of our income."

Big Ed asked, "And what are you going to do? Start another house? You're the Goddess, after all. You're part of the allure."

She glanced at Pat. "How are we doing on the Cheyenne lots?"

"Ye've doubled yer money, lass. And that's after me percentage. As for the other project, between us, we're currently holding forty-six percent of the investment. All we need is another five percent and we have control."

Sarah nodded, saying, "Ed, I've created and run the best house in the Rockies. I'd rather retire offstage, conduct affairs where I'm *not* the center of attention. There's my offer. Take or leave it."

Because George Nichols is out there, and he'll be coming for me one of these days.

Sarah sat back; the chair was uncomfortable as hell, but she'd endured worse.

And she'd wait.

If it took all afternoon.

111

May 15, 1868

Butler sat in the sun, his back to an aspen tree. With his knife he whittled on a chokecherry stem. He had stripped the bark, already steeple-notched one end, and was working on the other. When it was finished, he'd stretch sinew netting across the inside of the square he was making; it would be a light, portable drying rack. Propped on supports, it could be placed high enough over a pit of glowing coals that roots, fruits, meats, and leaves could be desiccated for storage. They'd also receive a slight coating of smoke. This, Mountain Flicker assured him, would keep them from molding, even in damp weather.

A smart and cunning people, these Mountain Shoshoni.

"Makes a heap more sense than Rebel commissary ever did," Johnny Baker noted where he sat on Butler's saddle.

"Thinking of all them roots and berries we been eating, I sure do miss salt pork," Phil Vail added where he crouched in the crushed grass.

"I don't know about you all," Butler told them, "but I've never felt better. I know you're missing your wives and families, and if —"

"We ain't the ones living wild and free," Pettigrew announced as he slung his rifle over his shoulder and stared out over the vista.

"Then what are you doing?" Butler asked. "You're marching everywhere I do. Seeing the same country. Would you rather be back in the army? Camped in the rain and mud, making sloosh out of moldy cornmeal and rancid bacon? And not enough of that to keep your belly from being ganted?"

"Butler!" his father's voice snapped.

He laid his whittling aside and crossed over to where his father lay on the travois. His broken thigh had mended to the point that he could hobble around camp on his crutch as long as someone helped balance him. People didn't think about how awkward a one-armed man on a crutch was, especially on rough ground. And Paw's leg, despite being mostly knit, pained him to walk on.

Butler crossed by the smoldering fire and glanced out at the slope below. The women, children, and some of the dogs were scattered across the landscape. Each place a bobbing white sego lily or onion grew, a woman would stop, plant her digging stick, and with a pop, lever it out of the ground. The child following behind her with a sack would pluck up the bulb and stem, clean the dirt away, and drop it into his or her sack.

This was broken country where Owl Creek ran out of the mountains; it consisted of tilted layers of sandstone, with rocky outcrops on either side of the valley. The sage-grayed, juniper-spotted slopes slowly gave way to conifer forest as the mountains rose behind the broken hills. To the south, the horizon was dominated by the peak known as Coyote's Penis.

Looking back down the valley, Butler could see the distant Big Horn Mountains, looking blue in the misty haze. Fresh snow capped their heights. Here in the lower basin it had rained for a solid week, and now the moisture-laden air almost reminded Butler of Arkansas. "Almost" being the key word.

Most of the Dukurika men and dogs had left before dawn, following Owl Creek farther up into its mountains, their intent being to hunt the elk calving grounds in higher meadows.

Butler would have gone had he not been needed to care for his father.

"What do you need, Paw?" Butler dropped to a crouch beside him. The man's hawkish eyes were filled with that old irritation Butler had known so well as a child. Years of cringing under their glare now faded as Butler realized it was an improvement over the glassy and wavering emptiness that had possessed Paw's stare for the past week. The fever had finally broken, and the watery pink pus that drained around the stump of his right arm had slowed.

Since Butler had cut his arm off, Paw had mostly raved in delirium. Then he'd been so weak he could barely move. For days it had been all the man could do just to draw breath.

Puhagan had looked on as Butler and Mountain Flicker had tended Paw, and shaken his head. They'd made teas from red willow and aspen bark, adding rose hips and sage leaves. Mountain Flicker had made diapers woven of juniper bark and stuffed with powdered, sun-dried buffalo dung that proved to be a remarkable absorbent.

"Just like with a *teaippe*," she told him. The word meaning "baby."

870

Now Butler smiled down at his father. "I've been telling the men how ironic life is, how the way we care for —"

"I wish you'd stop that!" Paw snapped.

"Stop what?"

"Talking to nothing like some lunatic. It sends shivers down my spine. It's not bad enough that I'm in this fix? I have to watch you acting like the village idiot? What the *hell* is wrong with you?"

"Doc, um, Philip, calls it the fatigue."

Paw made a face, glancing away. "Your high-and-sanctimonious brother. Gone off to Boston. Well, it was good riddance. Hope he used my money to set himself up."

"I told you about Philip, what happened to him. And about Maw, and the squatters. About the graves behind the house. Do you remember?"

Paw kept his head turned away, nodding. "I was a little woozy. Think you said you thought the two graves were Maw and Sarah, but no idea about Billy?"

"He was in the hills last time I was able to visit. That was back in . . ." He frowned, trying to remember.

"Back in sixty-three, Cap'n," Parsons told him from the side.

"Thank you, Private. Yes, back in sixty-three. Winter. Before Prairie Grove."

"There you go!" Paw griped. "Looking off and talking to the air. Man Who Talks to No One. You're a lunatic! My crazy son of a bitch of a son! I won't have it! From here on out you're —"

Butler changed the subject. "Your fever's broken. The delirium has passed. You can finally understand the question. Why didn't you contact us after you ran from Shiloh?"

871

Paw's lips bent into that old smile that always presaged a lie.

"Don't even think it," Butler ordered. "Shiloh. Remember? You were with a Mississippi regiment. I know you marched into the fight. Talked to some of the boys when we got back to Corinth. They said sometime around mid-afternoon, you disappeared."

Paw's expression fell. The crafty look was back, but when Butler narrowed an eye and pointed with an accusatory finger, it faded.

"Tell the truth, Paw. You owe me that."

"Disappeared?" Paw stared off toward the distant Big Horns. "Hell no. Ran. Hid in the brush in a creek bottom, and come nightfall I did a craw-dad outta there."

He swallowed hard, voice dropping. "You had to have been there. Like nothing I'd ever seen. Not even in Mexico. It was the boys being shot down all around me. Falling, bleeding, scared and dying. The smoke and stink and sound of it. God, the sounds. The minié balls whizzing, singing by my head. I couldn't take it. That voice in me screamed, *'Run!'* and by thunder, I did."

"Because you were scared?"

"Scared like I ain't never been." Paw looked at him, arrogance twitching his lips. "If you ever got close to that fight, you'd know."

Butler lifted his hands. "I don't understand. You're not a coward. You shot men in duels! You had half the men in Benton County scared of you."

"What are you? A Papist priest?"

"Just tell me!"

Paw started to rile, then snorted in self-derision. "What the hell. All right. Here's the way of it: first

872

one I shot was Pat Phillips. He was so drunk he couldn't find his pecker, let alone the sights on a pistol." Paw shook his head. "Second one, Brandy Hayes, I bullied into it, knowing he couldn't hit a barn from three paces. Eli Johnson? He was shaking so hard, he wet himself just before I blew his brains out. After that, I never had to fight another duel."

Butler sighed and rubbed his forehead. "Thousands of men ran that day. You weren't the only one. But what about Maw and Sarah and Billy? What about me? Why didn't you send word you were alive? If you'd gone home —"

"Maybe all this wouldn't have happened? Maybe you wouldn't be a goddamned raving lunatic? Maybe Maw and Sarah'd be alive? Or maybe they'd have shot me for desertion, and it all would have worked out the same. Except that you'd have had to live with the reputation that your father was a coward and a deserter."

"Why here?" Butler asked, gesturing around.

"Won't make no sense to you."

"Try me. I read Kierkegaard at the academy."

Paw actually smiled, then said, "Here in the mountains was the only place that I wasn't a lie. For a while, at least."

"You saved Tom Hindman that night he was going to be beaten, maybe killed."

"Ha!" Paw almost spat. "I'd lost every cent I had at the poker table. Hindman was just another gamble. I knew the ruffians who beset him. Dangerous chuckleheads as long as they had the advantage. When I whacked 'em from behind, it put the scare in 'em and they run. See, Hindman thought he owed me his life. Good temperance man that he was, he still bought me drinks all

873

night long."

Paw raised a finger on his mangled left hand. "That's the thing, Butler. You can always game a 'man of honor.' Just like those canny politicians gamed all those thousands they sent into battle. I recognized that on the first day at Shiloh. I shouted 'Death before dishonor!' and my boys all cried huzzah and marched headlong into massed Yankee fire."

He shook his head. "Not me. This child ain't no man's patsy for a cause."

"Why even enlist, then?"

Paw shot him a look like he was an idiot. "I didn't think the fools would keep fighting, killing, and tearing up the country. Anyone with sense would have said, 'We ain't dying like flies in a tannery. Stop this nonsense.' And it would have been over."

Paw grinned. "Hell, boy, I didn't figure it would last six months. When it was over I'd be known to have been a Union man, but I'd go back to Arkansas having served as a Southern officer. Down in the legislature, I could have played both sides. Maybe even been governor."

Butler glanced at the men; they were watching with somber, sometimes tortured eyes. "It was always about you, wasn't it? Why'd you even marry Maw in the first place?"

He sniffed, as if derisive. "She was a beauty. Tall, hair like corn silk, with a face that would have shamed immortal Helen. Hell, I was just back in America for a season before heading back to the mountains. But here was a woman the likes of which I couldn't turn down. Insisted we be married a'fore she'd let me take her to the blankets."

"And Grandfather was a lunger," Butler added, remembering the story. "He'd just sold his farm. Gold that would be Maw's. Which meant yours. Gold that built the farm."

Paw shrugged, the action making a mockery of his stumped arm. "You think I ever got my fingers on a coin of that? Your maw was no fool. Then, something changed in her when Philip was born. She wanted more than just the adventure. Demanded roots. I'll say this for your maw, she kept me on a string."

He frowned, searching Butler's eyes, "Why the hell do you think I ran off to Mexico? Robbed that damn church and melted all the gold into bars?"

"You *robbed* a church?"

"Papists, son. Not fully Christian. And wasn't nobody around, them Spanish bastards having all scampered off like rats ahead of the *yanqui* army."

Butler sighed and glanced sidelong at the men. Did they see his shame? "Did any of us mean anything to you?"

Paw blinked, worked his lips. "You made me feel like a real gentleman. And I appreciated it more than I could tell you. All I had to do was go home, and there was the house, the fields, and your mother and you. All looking prosperous. I could bring anyone I wanted, and for a day I was a lord in his manor. Complete with a beautiful wife, a library, and two boys who weren't going to be mere farmers.

"I tell you, men were impressed. Even the plantation scions, because unlike Phillips County, this was the backwoods, a plantation and empire in the making."

"Don't heah nuthin' 'bout nuthin' but yor paw,"

Kershaw whispered behind Butler's ear.

"Makes me wonder why Maw stuck with him," Butler said for Kershaw's ears alone.

"Probably warn't no other way," Pettigrew told him. "Hell, for all you know, he'd a shot her for throwing him out."

"Would you?" Butler asked his father.

"Would I what?" Paw asked, confused.

"Have shot Maw if she'd divorced you?"

That seemed to set him back. "Divorced? No. She just figured a man was a man, having been raised by the likes of her own father. Her only interest was in you kids . . . and making the farm a success. She always gambled that I'd be shot by some jealous husband or lover. A divorced woman gets nothing. A widow gets it all."

"Why'd you break Philip's heart, Paw?"

"That Sally Spears he was in love with? I knew her for what she was. She'd set her sights on Philip as her way out of Elkhorn Tavern. The boy didn't have a chance once she'd grabbed him by the pizzle. I only knew of one way to keep him from marrying her."

"What would it have hurt?"

"He'd have never become a physician."

"You made him hate you."

Paw chuckled weakly. "I needed *successful* sons more than I needed their love." He sighed, "And here, in the middle of no place, you show up, a broken lunatic worthy of the asylum."

"What *you* needed? That was the only thing?"

"It's a hard lesson, boy. But if you'd learned it you'd be teaching in some academy or university instead of ending up exiled from civilized society and mumbling to the air." He closed his eyes, adding, "Just as well I ended up here. You're a disgrace."

Butler said nothing, his insides crumbling.

Paw shot him a sidelong glance. "My only regret? Running into that silvertip sow and her cubs on the trail." He used his ruined left hand to indicate his amputated arm. "I *ain't* living like this, Butler. Ain't gonna be no hobbling, one-armed, three-fingered cripple. Wish you'd a let me die."

112

Maybe it was the weather that brought it on. In the afternoon — on the day Sarah had sold the Angel's Lair — dark clouds rolled in off the mountains and intiated weeks of off-and-on rain. Denver's streets, normally foul with trash and fly-filled manure, reminded Doc of the Camp Douglas yard — a liquefied quagmire of filth.

Additionally, there had been no business because of the black wreath he refused to remove from the surgery door. And then, that morning, he discovered that in the night someone had made off with it. Even now it was probably in some drunk's possession down on Wazee Street, or hung around some corpse's neck where he lay propped on a tin-can pile behind a Blake Street saloon.

Sitting at his desk chair — where Bridget once had held court — he stared through the wavy glass panes in his window to the drizzle outside. Word was that the constant storms had nearly shut the mountains down. Stories of avalanches and stranded travelers filtered down from the gold camps. The Platte and Cherry Creek were up, and people feared another flood like back in '64.

Doc stared down into his cold coffee, and found

his reflection like a midnight mirror image. All he could see was the outline of his head. No facial features. Just black emptiness where eyes, nose, and mouth should be. Never had he seen such a true reflection of himself. An outline surrounding a stygian void.

Bridget laughed, somewhere, far away, at the edge of his consciousness. Her smile hung wistfully in the distance . . . an evaporating memory. Her presence seemed like an echo coming from the very room, fading by the instant. When the last of her finally seeped away into infinity, what would be left? So little of her remained here.

At home at night, he took out her dresses, one by one, and laid them on the bed. Lifting them, he would bunch the fabric, place them to his nose, and sniff, desperate to inhale her odor. But more and more, the only scent he could recognize was stale cloth.

Her things remained as she'd left them, though Sarah had insisted on putting the kitchen in order and cleaning it. So, too, had she insisted on throwing open the curtains. Curtains that hadn't been touched since Bridget closed them before bed that last night.

Why are you sitting here?

The faceless reflection in his coffee cup had no answers.

You don't have to be so pathetic.

It was a choice. One he could change. He didn't have to do this, live like this. If living was indeed what he was doing.

"God, I'm tired," he whispered to himself.

Then stop it. Stop it all.

Chuckling hollowly at himself, he set the coffee cup to the side and reached into the drawer.

Bridget had kept a store of hard candy for the children, handing out the sweets as the child was leaving.

Doc took a peppermint. Setting it on the desk, he began carving with his penknife, hollowing out the center. The only sound in the room came from faint scraping. Fine white powder floated down to coat his black trousers like dust.

He glanced at the gray beyond the window, realizing that dusk was closing in. Rain pelted the glass and rattled on the tin roof. It would be a cold and miserable walk back to his empty house. And, to be honest, he was tired. As tired as he'd ever been.

And as hopeless.

Doc forced himself to stand and walked back to his pharmacy kit. He found the vial with its garish label. Using the small measuring spoon, he scooped out more than enough of the powder and dropped it into the white ceramic mixing cup. With care he made a paste and used the spoon to press it into the hole he'd carved in the peppermint. As a final measure, he sealed it with a plug of damp flour.

Then, knowing his pharmacy would surely wind up in another's hands, he carefully washed the mixing cup, and returned everything to its proper place.

Taking the candy, he returned to the front room and resettled himself at his desk. The room was gloomy now, cold, the fading light of day feeble beyond the rain-streaked window.

Doc stared at his deadly candy, resting so innocently on the battered wooden surface of the desk.

"Don't torture yourself because of me, Philip." He

heard Bridget's voice in his memory. *"Dying is part of life."*

She had kept repeating that over and over as her life seeped away. Whispered how much she'd loved him. Pleaded that he not mourn.

"Dying is part of life." He nodded, thinking back to his training, to the lectures he'd first listened to about losing patients. And then working with Benjamin Morton in Memphis, how the old man had given Philip that gleeful wink when they'd pulled off the impossible and saved a life.

And Ben Morton — a picture of health — had died in his sleep.

Then had come the Fourth Tennessee, and boys wasting away right and left from dysentery, cholera, typhus, pneumonia. And nothing he could do about it. Clear up to Shiloh.

Dear God, Shiloh!

How many of his nightmares were filled with the terrified eyes, the pain-glazed disbelief sculpted into the faces of those dying boys. It was as if Doc could feel the blood caked on his fatigued hands, the exhaustion and horror in his soul as they died on the table. He'd never forget the limp and sodden weight of their amputated feet, legs, hands, and arms.

The Federals had marched him across the battlefield to Pittsburg Landing. He'd seen with his own eyes. Impossible things: the bloated bodies rotting in the sun; the broken guns and dead horses; the splintered trees; and blasted soil.

One Shiloh should have been enough. How did a reasonable man get his brain around twenty of them, from Manassas to Shiloh, and on to Gettysburg, Chickamauga, Cold Harbor, and Franklin?

And then James was staring up at him, his eyes

fever-bright in the barracks at Camp Douglas. *"Don't grieve for me, Doc. You've suffered enough."*

"Saint Hancock?" He rubbed his weary face, the deadly candy but a shadow on his desk. "You were like a brother to me, James. Unlike Butler, I didn't betray your trust."

Butler.

He closed his eyes, wondering where he was, if he even were alive. What happened to a lunatic in the wilderness? Had he been killed by the rampaging Sioux and Cheyenne, frozen in a blizzard while out in the open? Murdered, shot down by someone too frightened to share the world with a crazy man? Beaten to death because he couldn't stop babbling?

If so, he should have found his final rest behind the farmhouse next to Fly, Maw, and that unknown bushwhacker who'd stood up for Sarah.

God, how much would have been different if he'd just told Ann Marie no when she'd suggested enlisting. As a physician in Memphis, could he have convinced Maw and Sarah to come join him for safety's sake? They'd had no place to go as northwest Arkansas descended into madness, murder, and butchery.

"If I could have saved them, I would have lost Butler," he told himself. He wouldn't have been at Camp Douglas to keep the ragamuffin from freezing to death in the snow that day.

And God alone knew what had happened to Billy.

"I wouldn't have known you, Bridget. Wouldn't have loved you until I'd given you all of me that there was to give," he told her ghost where it lurked in the darkest of the shadows. As he closed

882

his eyes, the extent of his loss came hammering home.

A man can only bear so much.

But tonight, it would be over. God could chide him for being a coward, or slap him down as a fool.

"Let the Christians be right," he whispered. "Let me see Bridget again."

He turned the candy in his fingers, feeling the round essence of it. He'd want to wash it down with the last of his cold coffee, ensure it was deep in his gut when the cyanide began to —

Someone tried the doorknob, found it locked. A frantic hammering was accompanied by a woman's shout. *"Hello! Help me!"*

Doc set the candy aside, stood, and walked to the door.

"Dear God!" the panicked voice cried. *"Somebody, be here!"*

Doc slid the bolt and pulled the door open.

The frantic woman was soaked to the bone, her hair hanging in straggles that leaked water. She wore a sodden wool coat, and behind her a man, bareheaded, shivering, his face a mask of torture, held a child in his arms, his posture that of a supplicant.

"You're a doctor?" The woman almost pleaded.

"Philip Hancock. Yes, ma'am. What's wrong?"

"She's *shot!* It was an accident. Her brother . . . with the shotgun. He was shooting a rabbit. It ran in front of Bessie!"

Doc waved them in, hurrying to the desk, fumbling for the matches. Cranking the chimney up, he lit the lamp and adjusted the wick.

"Bring her." He led the way to the surgery, painfully aware that it was in disarray, hardly the pin-neat facility he'd kept when Bridget . . .

No, don't go there.

He swept the clutter off the table and said, "Place her there." Then he went about lighting the other lamps.

Turning to the girl, he figured her for about eight or nine. Her dress was homespun and worn, mud and blood splotched her coat. "Help me here."

With the mother's help he got the dripping coat off the girl, and unbuttoned her bodice. Slipping her arms out of the sleeves, he got a good look at her chest; rain-wet bloody punctures in the girl's left side were leaking red.

"How long ago?"

"Maybe an hour or two. We unhitched the horses, rode straight here. A man on the street pointed your way."

The little girl's eyes were open, half lidded. She whispered, words inaudible, as if her voice were gone.

"Help her!" the mother pleaded.

Doc turned to his surgical kit, thankful once again that Butler and his men had stolen the best.

"This may take a while. Nor should you watch. Please. Go back to the office. There's coffee and water. Wood and kindling next to the stove. If you need food, I'd suggest sending one of you down to the Planter's House. They can fix a meal in a tin to go."

They stared at him as he turned back to the little girl, his probe in one hand. Ether bottle in the other. "Go on! I'm going to do the very best for Bessie that I possibly can. This isn't my first gunshot."

After they'd closed the door, he looked down

into the little girl's half-vacant eyes. "Sweetheart, we're going to do everything we can."

And he did.

Three hours later, his feet and back aching, Doc walked out into the office. The way the man and woman were seated on the bench, it was as if they were propping each other up. Expressions of agony were replaced with desperate expectation.

Doc reached out. The man extended his hand, and Doc dropped four buckshot pellets onto his palm. "If she makes it, you'll want to give her those as a remembrance."

"*If* she makes it?" The mother stared up with bloodshot and swollen eyes. She'd have been a pretty woman had her thin face not been hardened by sun, worry, and deprivation.

Doc took a seat opposite them. "Bessie's sleeping. The bleeding is stopped. One lung was collapsed. I've got it reinflated and her chest drained and sealed. She's breathing normally again, and the strain on her heart has been relieved. From here on out, it's up to Bessie, and if she can tolerate the infection."

The man nodded, the woman staring vacantly, as if unsure what to believe.

"I'm going to keep her here," Doc told them. "I've slept in the chair before. Do you have a place to stay?"

"My sister's husband is a baker here in town. We can stay there," the man said. "Theodor, Bessie's brother, will see to the farm."

"Go get some rest," Doc told them. "Come back in the morning."

He saw them to the door. Watched them disappear into the rain-black night.

Sighing, he realized he was starved for the first

time in days. Again, he longed for Bridget, for the hot meal he knew she would have had waiting for him. He could see the concern in her green eyes as she watched him eat, the smile she'd give him, filled with pride for the work he'd done on little Bessie.

And he *had* done good work on the little girl. If the infection didn't take her, she'd live. He'd done it. Given her a chance where none had existed.

Glancing at the desk, he stopped, cold fingers sending a shudder through him. The candy lay there beside his half-empty coffee cup.

What if Bessie's father or mother had picked it up? Popped it into their mouths?

"Philip, you are an imbecile!"

Picking up the candy with careful fingers, he unlocked the bottom drawer, opened the cash box, and tossed it back into the tin box's interior.

113

Billy fingered the stubby copper cartridge as he relaxed against his saddle. He'd laid it over a log, and with the stirrup shoved back, used the fender as a backrest. Firelight flickered, and sections of branches cracked and popped as they burned. Overhead the trees gleamed yellow in the pale light of a quarter moon. The stars seemed unnaturally bright as they cast patterns beyond the treetops.

"I don't think these are such a good idea," Billy said as he held the .44 cartridge between his fingers and studied the rimfire.

"Why's that?" Parmelee asked from across the fire. The man was in his underwear, hemming the ragged cuffs of his pants. He glanced up from his needlework. The man's sun-ruddy face had surrendered to a reddish-blond beard that made him look older, almost sagacious.

"Well, imagine that all we had were these Henry rifles. We got a total of fifty-six cartridges for the two of them. That's all them galoots was carrying. So we get in the middle of the Big Horn Basin, like we was, and run smack inta a big party of Sioux. We fort up and swap shots with 'em for a

887

couple of days, and shoot these little cartridges up. Now where in the name of hell are we gonna find more? I tell you, we'd have to ride plumb to Denver or Salt Lake or back to Virginia City."

"You don't *have* fifty-six rounds for that Sharps of yours."

"Parmelee, I got a hundred caps, a bullet mold, and a half pound of powder. I can find lead in most any place: Fort Caspar; one of the telegraph stations; a stage stop on the Overland Trail; Fort Bridger; Virginia Dale; even Sweetwater Station or Camp Brown."

"Same problem with the Spencer rifle," Parmelee said, looking thoughtful. "Carried one during the war. Even then sometimes supply didn't have cartridges where you needed 'em. Heard that Sherman carried whole wagons full so's he'd have enough for that march through Georgia."

"Notice you don't carry one now."

Parmelee stared from under his hat brim. "I got a Henry with fifty-six cartridges."

"Twenty-eight. Half of them's mine."

"You got a Sharps. You can find powder and lead anywhere."

Billy grinned and tossed him the cartridge. "There, I give you that one. Makes twenty-nine you got now."

"We come out of these hills, End-of-the-Tracks is just yonder in the flats. You ever been to End-of-the-Tracks? It's a whole town they set out for the railroad workers. Saloons, stores, whores, gambling, hot-cooked food. Then, when the rails move on so far, they pick it up. Even the boardwalks. Haul it another twenty or so miles down the line and set it all back up again."

"So why are you figuring we need to go there?"

Parmelee gave him a flat look across the fire. "Money. Or you got something hid out I don't know about?"

Billy nodded thoughtfully. Parmelee had been a right fine traveling companion. He didn't ask prying questions. Didn't offer much about himself. His only explanation for the hanging party was that the Virginia City vigilantes had heard he'd raped two women in Colorado. Then he'd dryly admitted he'd never been made a Freemason. It being well-known that the vigilance committee was run out of the local blue lodge.

Riding cross-country as they had, Billy had shot most of the meals, using his flour and salt sparingly for biscuits. But that was mostly gone now. Even then, he'd never hinted that he had money hidden away in the lining of his buffalo coat. The heavy coat now rode folded atop the packsaddle, looking like anything but a bank.

"How do you figure to get money?" Billy asked as he tossed another pine branch onto the fire.

"My considered opinion of you, Billy Hancock, is that you're a man who don't mind busting a few heads if it will advance your cause in the world. In this case, getting us enough of a stake to see us back to Denver."

"And how's this supposed to work?"

Parmelee studied him across the fire. "At End-of-the-Tracks the gambling hells are big tents. The games run all night. Latrines are dug out back. The play works for one night. I go in and keep watch, playing occasionally at the tables. You wait in the darkness out by the jakes. When I spot a winner, he'll have to piss eventually. I follow him out, which is your sign to step up behind him. As he's draining his johnson, you sap him.

Meanwhile, I'm back inside where I can be seen. You tug his sorry hide into the dark, bind and gag him, and relieve him of the cash. A couple of hours before dawn, we're off down the rails where we don't leave tracks. When we find some rocky ridge, we cut away across country."

"The railroad just lets folks get away with this? Ride in, break heads, rob, and ride out?"

Parmelee grinned through his beard. "I used to be a provost. I know how they think. They'll figure first that it was someone in End-of-the-Tracks. One of the locals who knows the layout. Most likely a johnny who lost at the tables, owes someone, and needs money fast to pay off. That two strangers rode in from Montana, gave it to four or five guys in the neck, and rode out for Denver in the same night? Sure, possible, but that's pretty far-fetched."

"What's in Denver?" Billy resettled himself, glancing over his shoulder to where Locomotive cropped the short high-country grasses.

"Payback for a whore."

"This is the one you said stole your house?"

"Her and her backers." Parmelee finished his stitching and inspected it in the firelight. "I've listened to you talking in your sleep, Billy Hancock. I *know* you don't have no special love for whores."

Billy ground his teeth, studying Parmelee through slitted eyes, but the older man didn't seem to want to make anything of it.

Parmelee stood, pulling on his trousers, threading his belt through the loops. "Can't say there'd be much money in it, but if you wanted to follow along, maybe lend a hand, I'd be obliged." He shot a look at Billy. "You ever heard of the Meadowlark?"

Billy had wondered when it was going to come up again. Said, "Well, of course, you fool. We been listening to 'em since before Bozeman."

His heart was skipping.

"Not the bird. The killer."

"The one you asked about clear back in Fort Benton?"

"George Nichols. You ever heard of him?"

"Mining speculator. Rich. I hear a lot of people don't like him, but I don't hear why?"

Parmelee reseated himself. "That deserter I shot? The one the vigilantes was talking about? That was his whore I took. He was a gambler. Thick as thieves with George Nichols. Now, here's the interesting part: no sooner was Bret Anderson buried, than I hear that George is bedding his whore. Supposedly he gives her four thousand for the fuck, and she uses it to pay a note I owe on my parlor house in Denver. Then, somehow, she ends up running *my* parlor house."

"Why are you telling me all this?" Billy realized he was nervously chewing his lips and made himself stop. "What's it got to do with this Meadowlark?"

"He's George Nichols's hired killer. The notion of a killing for hire gave me an idea. You ever seen three hundred dollars before, Billy Hancock?"

"That's a lot of money."

"I got that much in the Colorado National Bank in Denver." Parmelee watched him through pensive eyes. "I haven't made up my mind yet, but if you're as good as I think you might be . . ."

"At what?"

"We'll see at End-of-the-Tracks. If you're good,

I might pay you that whole three hundred dollars to do some killing."

"The whore?"

"No, she's mine. Very *personally* mine. I'm thinking about you dry-gulching George Nichols. His people won't have a single notion of who you are or why you'd kill him. The Meadowlark would have no idea who to hunt down for making his boss into dust."

"All that for three hundred dollars?"

"That's a year's wages, my friend."

Billy broke out in laughter. By damn, the Devil was playing him good. One thing Billy had never been short of was a sense of humor.

114

June 1, 1868

These were halcyon days for the Dukurika. Yet again Butler found himself amazed by the genius of the Sheep Eaters and their resource-filled world. What looked like rough and mountainous country was a virtual breadbasket. From strategically placed camps, hunters had a wealth of different animals to pursue. Within a day's walk downhill were long-established antelope drive lines and traps. In the foothills, cunning hunters set braided rawhide snares for mule deer along narrow paths between choke points on steep and rocky trails. Up high, mountain sheep could be stalked in the open meadows, and marmots on rocky slopes. Rabbits and grouse were common fare, brought down by throwing sticks. Nets were placed at exits, and pack-rat nests set afire to drive them out. By careful herding, bison were driven into dead-end canyons, and high-country hunters returned with pika and ptarmigan. If it ran, slithered, crawled, swam, or flew, it was fair game for the stew pots. Even coyote — which other Shoshoni considered taboo — was cut up and thrown into the Sheep Eater larder.

In addition the sego lily, bitterroot, shooting

star, biscuit root, bladderwort, wild onions, cactus blossoms and tunas, elk cabbage, juniper berries, yucca blossoms, pine nuts, balsam, pond lily and cattail roots, wild licorice, breadroot, tobacco root, mint, and many other plants added variety. To Butler's delight, not only were the soups and breads delicious, but a tea made from blazing star seeds reminded him of lemonade.

Not all of the harvest was consumed. Even now, portions were placed to one side to dry before being processed for winter storage. Plant material in particular was desiccated and compacted into rawhide parfleches. Wild hemp and milkweed were stripped for fibers, as was juniper bark and yucca leaves, the fibers processed into cordage. If the Sheep Eaters depended on any piece of hunting gear, it was nets — they used them for everything. Small nets were for catching crickets, fish, pack rats, and rabbits. Medium sized for netting grouse, coyotes, and beavers. The large ones for deer and mountain sheep. Second in priority were the braided ropes for snares that ranged from elk-sturdy at the top, to cord capable of suspending a flopping rabbit.

While nets and snares provided most of the catch, a man's most prized possession was a sinew-backed horn bow. Each one painstakingly crafted from the heavy boss of a fully mature mountain ram. Such bows might take a year to manufacture, and Butler had seen one drive an obsidian-tipped arrow past its fletching into a bison's chest. Despite never having been stronger, it was all he could do to pull Cracked Bone Thrower's, let alone hold and aim with it.

That day Mountain Flicker led the way as they walked down an elk trail that skirted the bottom of a thick patch of subalpine fir and lodgepole pine where they had been working.

They had spent nearly an hour collecting pitch from old cuts in the fir trees. The balls of hardened sap would be moistened and mixed with crushed larkspur and gumweed. Then the concoction was boiled into an insect repellent that, when mixed with fat, could be rubbed on to keep off ticks and mosquitoes.

Like most things in the Sheep Eater world, this patch of trees was cultivated. As they left each tree, Butler had been instructed to slice additional gouges into the bark so that whoever came back later would find a new and plentiful source of the sap.

Sheep Eaters didn't just live in the world, they changed it, guided it, and shaped it to produce for their needs. One of the first things he'd helped Cracked Bone Thrower and Puhagan do after his journey to the Spirit World was set fire to a large meadow over on the Wind River.

"Too much sagebrush," Cracked Bone Thrower had told him. "We burn it now. When we come back next fall, this will all be filled with goosefoot to harvest. That slope up there. It used to be full of rice grass. If the sagebrush continues to grow, there will be none. But if we burn it now, in two years, it will be full of rice grass again."

Life among the Dukurika was all about long-term planning.

Butler let his gaze travel across the narrow mountain valley with its rock outcrops, grassy meadows, and mixed patches of timber. When he thought about it, it was a lot like managing a farm to keep it productive.

Farther up the valley and above, elk grazed a

lush meadow, their pale tan catching the bright sunlight. He could still see the skeletons of burned trees dotting the slope. Flicker had told him that it had been purposely set afire four years ago in hopes it would become elk pasture.

How odd; he would have thought this entire country a wilderness, untouched by human hand. Instead, most every inch of it was being manipulated with the same careful forethought that a Mississippi planter gave to his plantation. Jean-Jacques Rousseau and his happy forest savage was no more true than the Eastern notion of the ignorant and unwashed Indian. The Dukurika were as clever and calculating as Yankee bankers when it came to future investments. How many of the illiterate trappers and traders who journeyed among them understood that?

"What are you thinking, *nadainape*?" she asked over her shoulder.

"I have never been happier." He glanced back, realizing he hadn't seen the men as much today. Reassured, he found them following, Phil Vail out front.

He'd barely noticed it in the beginning — just an awareness that they'd been gone. But when he checked, they were always where he expected them to be. None of them ever seemed concerned. Therefore, neither was he.

Maybe they'd had their own interests in the timber? Maybe this was just a phase of his madness?

He turned his attention back to his wife. She'd braided her hair for the day, and it swayed provocatively in time with her stride. She wore a doeskin dress that hung down from her shoulders in a fringed yoke, conforming to her hips before dropping to a knee-length hem. As she preceded him on the narrow trail, he enjoyed the sway each step imparted to her lovely hips. Thought of how it felt when he placed his reverent hands on their full swell, of the magic they contained: the enchanting essence of womanhood. The ultimate cradle of new life.

Just the thought excited him.

And she was his. Her smile, her teasing, the sparkle in her eyes. He could watch her by the hour, marveling as her quick fingers worked hides or did quillwork. He loved the way she gripped the mano as she ran it back and forth, grinding seeds and dried roots into flour for baking. Everything about her was fresh, young, and powered by an essential vitality.

"There should be new people by the time we get back," she told him. "My father's *naatea* is supposed to be coming along with Antelope Fire's people."

The Dukurika did that in summer. The families and small bands all congregated at predetermined locations to socialize, trade, and catch up on old friendships.

"So I finally meet your mother and father? What if Hard Hand and Fall don't like me?"

She shrugged. "Why would they not like you? You are a good hunter, a responsible man. You do your share. You are not stingy."

"I'm a crazy *taipo*."

Again she shrugged. "Unlike most *taipo* you are not lazy and arrogant. You don't see others as being less than you. You are a blooded warrior. A war chief. You have made a *Puha* journey, survived *yokoh* with Pa'waip." She grinned. "You are even kind to dogs!"

"All those things don't make me likable, Flicker."

She shot a look over her shoulder. "Butler, you worry about the silliest things."

He grinned, reslinging the sack of pungent sap on his shoulder. Dear God, he loved this woman.

The encampment filled the head of the valley and consisted of small family groups and their extended kin and close friends. Most had settled on the same small plot their families had occupied for generations, though this particular valley hadn't been the gathering location for several years. Here, as well, the Sheep Eaters had given it time to grow new plants, attract game animals, and for the areas they'd burned to recover.

Butler remembered how Puhagan's wife, Flowering Sage, had cried out with delight as she turned over a sandstone grinding slab, its concave surface having been left facedown after her last visit to protect it from the elements. Old lodge poles — carefully propped back in the trees — had been recovered from where they'd been stashed, and within a day, Puhagan's small band had reestablished themselves.

For Butler, going native had its limitations. Especially when it came to his father. Somehow he just couldn't invite the man into his lodge. Couldn't stomach the idea of his *father* being aware of what he and Mountain Flicker were doing under the robes at night. Therefore, they'd built him a shelter several paces away under the aspens.

For his part, Paw Hancock continued to recover. He could manage on his own now, pulling himself up and hobbling along on his crutch, though he said the leg still pained him.

Upon their return to camp, Butler, first thing, looked in on his father. Paw had settled himself on a bench Butler had made of poles laid across two small boulders. It seated Paw high enough that he could get his good leg under him to get up. Paw's parfleche bag was on the ground beside him. It contained all of his remaining possessions: a knife, a Starr revolver with its flask, balls, and caps. His strike-a-light, and other possibles.

"Had a good hunt?" Paw asked, the breeze teasing long strands of white hair across his fresh, pink scars. He didn't bother to look up as Mountain Flicker walked past and checked the stew steaming by the fire. From a brass bucket she added water and moved it closer over the flames.

Butler slung the sack of pitch down before walking over to the bladder water sack and drinking. "Red Rain and the kids went after larkspur. The way Flicker tells it, they'll dig a hole, line it with a hide, and use hot rocks to boil the sap and larkspur. All them mosquitoes and deerflies will be a thing of the past."

"Stuff works," Paw growled, still refusing to look up. "Used it in the past."

Butler gave his father a questioning glance. "So, with all the world to escape to, you came here. You said it was the only place you weren't a lie."

Paw fixed his eyes on the creek where it ran through the willows a hundred yards to the north. With his remaining hand he batted at a fly. "Come out here with the Rocky Mountain Fur Company. Bridger and his boys. Seems some woman back in the settlements had led me astray, and her male kinfolk wanted to place the blame on me. Mountains was a heap safer."

He gestured around. "Lot of us ended up as

899

free trappers. Took up the life with the Snakes, Crow, and Flathead."

"Like Richard Hamilton and his kind?"

"Hamilton? You heard of him? He never thought much of me. 'Course it looks like I ended up more of a mess than that bastard Travis Hartman he used to travel with." Paw indicated his stump.

For a moment, Paw's smile was filled with irony. "Fool that I was, I thought if I came back to the mountains, I'd be a big man. Last time I was little more than a kid. This time I could be a booshway, a boss. Respected like William Drummond Stewart was. Spent the first year after Shiloh out here with the Crow."

He made a face. "One of them bastards finally remembered who I was. Rather than lose my scalp, I hurried on over to the Fort Hall country, but the Shoshones over there was going to war with the whites. Then, after that shit, Patrick Conner, killed all them women and children at Bear Creek, I thought the country around Fort Bridger might be a bit more healthy. Somehow I ended up with Bazil's band of Shoshoni. They're mostly half-breeds. Horse Shoshoni, buffalo hunters. Wintered with them, helped with the trading down at the fort. With whites moving into the Green River country, I followed Chief Norkok here to the basin and wintered with Dirty Face in Red Canyon."

He shook his head. "One instant I was on the trail hunting sheep, the next I'm face-to-face with that sow."

"So, did you find what you were looking for?"

Paw shook his head. "All I found is ruination."

"People coming," Mountain Flicker noted, standing and shading her eyes. "It's my father,

900

Hard Hand! And look. Beside him is Antelope Fire."

Butler stood, suddenly feeling panicked.

"Easy, Cap'n," Kershaw said. "Reckon we're behind you. *C'est bon?*"

"My wife's father," Butler said, as if in explanation.

Hard Hand was a medium-sized man, dressed in a finely tailored hunting shirt that hung open to expose his muscular chest. Long black hair had been combed up in a high wave in the front and pinned to fall down behind his left shoulder. Travel-stained moccasins shod his feet. A thick sinew-backed horn bow hung from his left hand.

Hard Hand smiled, ran forward, and wrapped his youngest daughter in his arms, a smile breaking his wide lips, his angular-planed face alight with joy.

The second man, Antelope Fire, was older, his pomped hair mostly gray. A heavy-barreled, half-stock Plains rifle hung from his hand. The man's face reminded Butler of a storm: tortured, lined, and threatening with its leathery and wrinkled skin. A deep scar ran from the corner of the man's nose just under the cheekbone and back to the ear. His eyes, like black stones, fixed on Butler — the impact almost physical.

The moment he turned them on Paw, it was as if psychic lightning had struck. For an instant, the air literally tingled between the two, and then a slow, deadly smile curled Antelope Fire's hard lips.

"Butler!" Mountain Flicker took his hand, distracting him from the interplay between his father and Antelope Fire. She led him forward, face beaming. "Here is my *apo.* His name is

901

Getande'mo. Hard Hand." To her father she said in Dukurika, *"Apo,* this man is my husband. His white name is Butler Hancock, but he is known among us as Man-Who-Talks-to-No-One. We are *naatea."*

Hard Hand's face had gone from beaming love to implacable stone, betraying no expression. The man's dark eyes, however, seemed to burn into Butler's, as though demanding to know the worth of his soul. Or souls, as the Dukurika figured it.

Butler offered his hand. "I have heard a great deal about you, sir. I am honored."

Hard Hand glanced down at the hand, then back into Butler's eyes. In Shoshoni he asked, "Is he a good man?"

Mountain Flicker replied, "He is a very good man, Father. Everything a man should be, more so since he's a *taipo.* One who has *puha* and does not abuse it."

"Why are you keeping the one who calls himself Silver Eagle? Why is he in Puhagan's camp?"

Butler was having trouble following the rapid Shoshoni as Mountain Flicker responded, "Silver Eagle is Butler's father."

"Dog shit!" Antelope Fire said through gritted teeth. "That's what he is!"

Butler stepped back at the violence in the man's voice, seeing Mountain Flicker's surprise and disbelief. For a stunned moment, she could only gape, then weakly asked, "You *know* him?"

Antelope Fire hissed through his teeth, a distasteful gesture among his people. He kept his angry gaze locked on Paw's, who stared back uneasily, his blue eyes wavering, face a mask of guilt.

His muscles trembling, Antelope Fire asked in

broken English, "Why you return?"

Paw chuckled dryly to himself. "Thought you were dead."

"Dead." Antelope Fire seemed to swell with hate. "You walking shit, bastard fucker."

"Wait!" Butler cried, stepping forward, arms raised. "What is this?" He stepped in front of Antelope Fire, crossing his arms. Meeting the man's fiery stare, he asked, "What did Paw do to you? *Gwee,* help me with the words I don't understand."

Antelope Fire struggled, as if to keep from spitting. "That man came as a youth. Wild, full of himself. And where he went, he left suffering. He was a *taipo,* and rich. With his smile and his trade, he lured my sister into his lodge. She worked for him, and he decorated her with beads and bells, and when the winter was over, he went to trade at Fort William. He went with Ainka Pakan, Red Arrow and his two wives. And at the fort he drank whiskey and went insane. He *gambled* my sister off to a *taipo* whiskey trader. He sold her to men for money. Within a moon, she had cut her own throat because she couldn't stand it.

"Back at camp, the Two Footed Shit found Red Arrow's youngest wife alone, and though she fought, he took her there in the dirt.

"Red Arrow came back then, caught the Two Footed Shit raping his wife. When Red Arrow cried out, the *taipo* stuck a knife in his friend's belly. The Two Footed Shit looked around. Couldn't find Metsa, Mountain Lamb, Red Arrow's first wife. She'd seen. Ran and hid.

"The stinking *taipo* couldn't let Red Arrow's young wife live. She would tell. And he didn't know that Mountain Lamb had seen him kill her husband. So he cut the young wife's throat and carried both of the bodies to the river the *taipo* call Platte. He just let them float away.

"Mountain Lamb was headed home, alone, on foot, horrified. That's when the Crow found her. Took her to their village.

"The Two Footed Shit knew she must have seen, so he started back to the Wind River, thinking he would find her on the way and kill her. But he didn't. He came back to our band and my sister's lodge. But he was always out hunting alone, searching to see if Mountain Lamb was coming. And for more than a year, she did not."

Antelope Fire almost trembled, his hands knotted. "When she did come, late the next summer, the Two Footed Shit had decided that she was dead. Mountain Lamb was no one's fool. She came to my lodge at night, told me what had happened. She had had time to think during her stay with the Crow. She knew that if she just showed up, it would be a fight in the camp, that other people might be hurt. So we waited. Then one night after a father dance, when several *naatea* had gathered, she appeared at the fire as a surprise.

"The Two Footed Shit could do nothing but call her a liar, and when he came at her, I was there with a knife." He pointed to his cheek. "He gave me this before others intervened. We tied him up, but before morning, he had vanished, taking four of the horses. We were never able to catch him."

Butler turned to his father. "Is this true?"

"I couldn't understand that singsongy clucking he was making."

"About Red Arrow, and his wives . . . did you kill them?"

"That's all a bald-faced lie. All of it." Paw's face had stiffened into his arrogant and appalled expression. "If I could, I'd face him down over a pistol!"

Dear God, he'd seen it so many times. Butler sagged, his heart like lead in his chest. With an aching sorrow that leached the starch from his bones, he turned to Antelope Fire. "I am so sorry. I never knew. None of us did."

"What?" Paw cried, struggling to rise. "You taking *his* side?"

Butler stalked up to his father, who balanced on his crutch. "You *raped* a man's wife! *Gutted him!* Hid the bodies, and denied it!"

"You had to be there! I don't know what happened! I'd been through most of a jug!" He gestured feebly with his mutilated hand, eyes half rabid with worry. "They was just Indians, boy!"

"Just Indians? Like *my wife*? My friends? My *naatea*? Just Papists? Just Mexicans? Just a whore? Is there *nothing* in your life that you can be proud of? Is it all ruination and lies?" He pointed at his father's lodge. "Get out of my sight, Paw."

Paw blinked as if confused. Glanced sidelong to where the others were watching, Mountain Flicker whispering a translation in Dukurika.

"You don't know shit, boy." Then Paw turned. Awkwardly he propped himself. Reached down for his parfleche, and clinging to it and his crutch, stumped awkwardly to his lodge.

Butler glanced around, seeing his men. In a ring at the edge of camp, they watched him through stunned eyes. Then he lowered his head, tears of shame and sorrow mixing as they trickled down his cheeks.

He sank to his knees, bereft. He didn't hear

Hard Hand or Antelope Fire leave. Didn't know how long he knelt there, but Mountain Flicker placed a hand on his shoulder, saying "I hurt with you."

"What should I do with him? He can't stay here. Not among the *newe*. It will be all over camp that my father is a rapist and murderer, and we're keeping him here."

"Puhagan will be back tonight. We can ask him."

Butler pursed his lips. "When I was little, I worshiped my father. Thought he was the most powerful and grand man alive. He made me read, encouraged me to be a scholar. And it was all built on lies."

"We cannot help who our parents are. They have different souls, *nadainape*."

"Is there anything else he can do to disgrace me?"

The bang of a pistol shot made him jump.

Scrambling to Paw's lodge, he pulled back the cover. The smoking revolver lay on the hides. Paw sagged against the poles, eyes oddly bulged and bloodshot, crimson leaking from his mouth, nose, and ears.

115

Butler looked back at the packhorse that followed along on its lead. The travois poles extended in an X above the horse's withers. The blanket-wrapped body was riding perfectly where it had been lashed to the travois frame.

Beneath the blanket, Paw's head had been tightly wrapped; his eyes, nose, mouth, and ears covered with rawhide bindings. At Flicker's instructions, that had been done to keep his breath soul and dream soul trapped inside his corpse along with the *mugwa,* or body soul. The precautions were necessary. Not just because Paw had been a violent suicide, but that he'd been a rapist, murderer, and liar.

It wasn't that suicide was prohibited among the Dukurika, just that there were acceptable methods: most generally walking away into a snowstorm; refusing food in the middle of a famine; leaping into raging rivers; or flinging oneself from a high point.

Blowing one's brains out with a gun in the midst of a social gathering wasn't among them.

It had been Butler's decision to drag the corpse not only out of Owl Creek Valley but clear out of

Shoshoni territory before he finally disposed of the body.

Had he not done so, a half-terrified Mountain Flicker had promised that every lodge in the valley would have been packed and gone by morning. And not only that, but the local bands wouldn't have returned to the vicinity, fearing Paw's malignant and evil spirits.

Why inflict such intense and long-term misery upon the people?

Glancing back again, Butler called, "Even in death you're a perpetual goddamned *pestilence,* aren't you?"

He looked up at the tan sandstone ridges to the south. The flat stone beds were dotted with juniper and pines. And beyond them lay the Owl Creek divide, its timbered skyline rounded and rumpled.

He'd take the trail south across Mud Creek, past Rattlesnake Springs, through the Red Canyon and over the pass to the Wind River Basin. From there he'd top the Sweetwater Rim, hit the Oregon Trail, and follow the telegraph to Muddy Gap. Then he would cross to the Laramie Basin, and somewhere in that vastness, be far enough away from Shoshoni country that Paw's malignant ghost, if it ever escaped, could harass the occasional passing Arapaho or Sioux. Because he sure wouldn't worry any white man.

"Got to bury you, Paw. All tied up like you are, we want your ghost deep underground where it can't get out and bother decent people."

"Y'all expect him to answer?" Corporal Pettigrew asked as he marched at the head of the men. They followed in the wake of the travois, tramping along on either side of the two drag marks.

"Absolutely not, Corporal." Butler smiled to himself. "With most of a company of dead men already at my beck and call, what do I need another one for?"

"Don't make fun of us, suh," Jimmy Peterson called back.

"Just feeling sorry for myself, Private. Thinking that Water Ghost Woman played me for a fool. Told me I could heal, and gave me the one man on earth I should have let die."

Butler shook his head, swaying in time to the horse's pace. "If I hadn't interfered, but let Paw die back in Red Canyon, we'd still be with Mountain Flicker, laughing and eating fine. The Dukurika wouldn't be staring nervously over their shoulders. Hard Hand wouldn't be thinking his daughter married a monster's son, and Puhagan wouldn't be wondering what he's going to have to do to cleanse me of soul pollution before I can return."

"Soul pollution, suh?" Frank Thompson asked.

"Reckon that means the cap'n's gonna have to do another *puha* journey to the Underworld, with all them sweats and fasting," Phil Vail told them.

Kershaw spoke up for the first time. "Not only that, Cap'n, but this time of year? Yor paw's gonna be turning a mite ripe. Reckon he's already drawing flies, *comprendre?*"

"We could drop him anywhere," Pettigrew groused. "How are the Dukurika gonna know any different?"

"We will *not.*" Butler shot a hard glance at the recalcitrant corporal. "Paw might have been a liar, but I'm not. I gave my word. We will see this through in the honorable tradition of Company A, Second Arkansas."

"Be just as like to run into a passel of angry Sioux out here all alone."

Butler thinned his eyes. "And what chance does a party of Sioux have against a company of the Second Arkansas Infantry? As upset as I am right now? We could take half the Sioux nation."

"What about Philip, Cap'n?" Kershaw asked.

"What about him?"

"Reckon he ought ter know 'bout his father, *le père, oui?*"

Butler winced. Philip had hated Paw, but he was still the man's son. And there were only the two of them left.

You can write him a letter from one of the stage stations on the Overland Trail.

But after lecturing the men on honor, was that really the thing to do?

116

June 6, 1868

The thrill of the hunt pulsed with each beat of Billy's heart. End-of-the-Tracks was all that Parmelee had promised. And sure, it was small-time compared to the stakes he was used to. But that old joy of watching the approach of prey — in this case a half-staggering man appearing from the tent door — of seeing Win Parmelee reach up and touch the brim of his hat to signal the go-ahead, and then following behind the unknowing victim just plain made Billy's bones quiver.

Adding to the thrill was the sense of danger, of knowing that a mistake would mean discovery, flight through the darkness, and the chance of being caught.

Billy, moving silently on his feet, stepped behind the latest target. The man was big, heavy through the shoulders. Most track builders were, from pick-and-shovel men, to graders, to the ones who carried the ties or unloaded the rails. Let alone the ones who swung the jackhammers all day pounding in spikes.

Win Parmelee's weighted-leather sap wasn't the tool for this kind of hunting. Instead, Billy carried a pick handle. More wallop and less room for error.

The man he now crept after was whistling softly, wobbling as he made his way to the line of outhouses. Billy set himself, swung.

Some sense warned the mark at the last instant; he ducked. The thick end of the pick handle glanced off the side of the man's head. Definitely not enough of a blow to flatten him, but enough to topple him. As he hit the ground, he let loose with a loud bellow, followed by, *"Son of a bloody bitch!"*

Billy made a quick calculation of his chances, figured it was time to blow, and with all his might, slung the pick handle at the galoot. He didn't look back as he made fast tracks for where he'd left Locomotive.

Shouts rose behind him, with calls of "Thief!" and "Some dirty beat's just tried to bushwhack me!" "Where'd he go?" "That way! Christ, my head hurts!"

Billy rounded a corner just as a man with a lantern emerged from a shebang shanty. Billy plowed straight into the chucklehead. Face-to-face as they collided. He had an image of a green-eyed man with a mashed nose, thick beard, and breath like rotted onions.

Then Billy was on his feet, half blinded by the lantern. Blinking at the afterimages, he damn near made a wrong turn. Caught himself at the last instant, and plunged between the two wagons that hid his horse. He paused only long enough to tighten Locomotive's cinch, then he was in the saddle, letting the big black horse find his own way in the dark.

"By God." Billy chuckled to himself. "That was some doings!"

Hard to admit, but he hadn't had that much fun for a coon's age. Reaching down, he felt the thick stash of cash he'd wadded into his shirt for safekeeping. Good enough for a road stake, and Parmelee wouldn't be asking any stupid damn questions about Billy Hancock's money.

"All right, Win, you old fog, that ought to just about do us, don't you think?"

Riding with Win was almost like old times, but different. Billy had always been able to trust Danny. Win was different, unnerving in ways. The man took pains to hide it, but couldn't quite corral his belief that he was Billy's better. Behind it all, Parmelee was driven, possessed of a plumb cruel streak. He just plain hated this whore he called the Goddess, and he downright loathed George Nichols.

But most irksome of all, Billy knew he was being played. That behind Win's smiles and assurances of friendship, the son of a bitch was figuring to set Billy up for George's murder. That somehow he'd be left holding the bag.

"Yep," Billy told the night. "But we'll see who's playing who, Win."

117

June 15, 1868

Doc stopped beside one of the freshly planted trees that lined Grant Street. Denver had its own committee dedicated to the planting of trees; they'd popped up along all the major streets. He stared up at the two-story brick behemoth of a house.

The design, with two round towers, one on either side, had reportedly come from New York. The big corner lot on Grant Street and Colfax Avenue originally had been purchased by a young man whose father owned a prosperous foundry in Cleveland. The young man — expecting to open a Denver branch of the family business — had begun construction on the great house, only to relocate to Cheyenne upon notice that the railroad would be routed to the north.

Sarah had been able to pick it up for a song, and even now workmen were still finishing the interior. What Sarah would do with the fifteen-room monstrosity — let alone how she'd maintain it — was anyone's guess.

Some of the windows were still boarded over, awaiting the arrival of beveled-glass panes that would eventually overlook the street. The yard was dirt, though to Doc's eye, it had plenty of promise for a fine garden.

Doc shifted his grip on his medical bag and nodded to Pat O'Reilly's driver where he waited out front on the phaeton's seat. So, Pat was here. Doc always felt uncomfortable in the man's presence, knowing that he'd been one of Aggie's regulars. And how did one act casually with a man known to have paid handsomely to bed one's sister on multiple occasions?

Ah, the tangled webs we spin!

Skipping up the stairs, Doc knocked at the pine-plank door, having heard that an engraved-oak specimen was somewhere between St. Louis and Cheyenne.

Sarah opened the door, smiling as she ushered him in. In the foyer he divested himself of his hat and coat, glancing around. The stairs in the back still lacked a handrail. Sawdust seemed to be everywhere.

"Philip, welcome. It's good to see you." Sarah stepped close and kissed him on the cheek. "Come. Pat's already here."

She led Doc through what would be the parlor and to a dining room off the kitchen. A south-facing bay window provided plenty of light. The back wall would be a built-in hutch, to be filled with plates, cups, and porcelain. The drawers were for flatware, napkins, and the like. Everything remained unfinished — including the utilitarian table and mismatched chairs where Pat waited.

The Irishman stood, taking Doc's hand, and crying, "Ah, Doctor, a good day t' ye. And I hope yer doing roight foine."

"Pat, good to see you."

"Can I get you a drink, Philip?" Sarah asked, of-

915

fering a bottle. "Sherry. Just the thing for an early afternoon."

"A small glass," he told her, setting the bag on the table.

Pat gave it an askance inspection. "Expecting trouble, are ye, Doc?"

"Showing off." He unbuckled the strap. "I'd forgotten I'd ordered them, it's taken so long." He lifted his prize.

"That doesn't look so frightening," O'Reilly decided as he took the small glass rod. "What is it?"

"The new Allbut-patent medical thermometer. Just six inches! I'd used thermometers at medical school. Big things, over a foot long. But look how small and compact. Imagine, a thermometer that small!"

Sarah set his glass of sherry before him. "But Philip, whatever is it good for?"

"*Accurately* diagnosing and measuring a patient's fever, dear sister. And look at this." He lifted out his true delight.

"Now, that scares the bejeezus outta me." Pat made a face.

"It's called the binaural stethoscope."

Sarah pulled up a chair, staring at the thing. "What on earth would you ever use it for?"

"Auscultation," Doc told her. "Isn't that apparent? It's such an improvement over the old monaural tubes." At her blank look he said, "I can listen for irregularities in heartbeat, hear the lungs as they breathe. It will make the detection and treatment of pneumonia so much faster."

Pat nodded. "Now that, Doc, is worth something. I lost nigh on thirty men to pneumonia last winter alone."

For long minutes, they listened to each other's hearts, Sarah and Pat absolutely enchanted. All three of them were within a degree of 98 degrees Fahrenheit.

"And you think it will change medicine?" Pat marveled. "It's not jist amusement?"

"It will," Doc promised.

Sarah tossed back her sherry and refilled her glass. "The reason I asked you here, Philip, is to discuss a different kind of payoff. How are we doing, Pat?"

He gave her a saucy wink. "Closing the deal, lassie."

"What deal is this?" Doc asked.

Sarah's smile was triumphant. "You remember the company we set up after I sold the Angel's Lair? I need your signature on some Hancock and Hancock documents. We're selling our interests in a mining venture. Just speculation."

"A mine? Sarah, what do you or I know about mining?"

"Aboot as much as I know aboot med'cine," Pat told him. "But laddie, moines are my particular charm. 'Tis called the Piute Lode, about seventy-five moiles east of Virginia City, Nevada. According to the stories, the prospects are unusually promising."

Sarah sipped her sherry, a crafty smile on her full lips.

"And are they?" Doc asked.

"If you b'lieve the stories, laddie." Pat's smile had turned predatory.

Doc knew he was being played. "I take it you don't?"

"Reckon not," Pat agreed. "But, more t' the point, George Nichols does."

Oh, dear God.

Sarah told him, "For the last month, our partnership has bought up every claim there is on the Piute Lode and filed on as much of the mountain as we can. Rumor is that William Ralston and Pat's old pal, Johnny MacKay, are battling to obtain it. Those men are bitter rivals who'll do anything to get one up on the other. If George can get a controlling interest in the Piute Lode, he'll play Ralston against MacKay for the highest bidder."

"So, we're beating George to the punch? And who are Ralston and Mackay? I don't understand."

Sarah said softly, "William Ralston is head of the biggest bank in California. MacKay and three of his friends are mining investors who are competing with Ralston in the development of several mines in the Comstock." She inclined her glass toward O'Reilly. "Pat met MacKay when he was running a placer operation in California before coming to Colorado."

"We're old friends," Pat said easily. "And I staked him a while back when a decision he made wasn't the right one."

Sarah added, "George got word of the Piute Lode, that both MacKay's group and Ralston's were trying to move on it. It is his intention to scoop them all. He has placed *all* of his assets as collateral against a loan to buy the eighty-five percent of the Piute Lode that Pat and I own. If his agents can close the deal, he intends to dangle it between MacKay and Ralston."

Doc lifted his hands in confusion. "Why don't *we* sell the Piute Load to the highest bidder ourselves? Especially after what George Nichols tried to do to you, sis."

Pat sighed, looked across the table at Sarah, and shook his head in futility.

Sarah laid a long-fingered hand on Doc's. "Philip, the Piute Lode isn't quite worthless, but almost. And while George has come into possession of a series of letters a geologist has supposedly written to MacKay about the Piute Lode, I can assure you that neither William MacKay, nor Ralston, have the slightest interest in the Piute."

"But George Nichols is going to pay . . . ?"

"That's right, laddie." Pat savored his sherry. "I nivver loiked the mon in the first place. 'Twill leave me with a warm spot in me heart to break the boy-buggering sot."

Doc took a deep breath, the impact hitting home. "Jesus, Sarah. He's going to know you did this to him."

She gave him a hard-eyed stare. "No he won't. If he traces the Piute Mining Company to its source, he'll find an empty office in a building in St. Louis. Piute Mining Company's papers of incorporation are on file with a law firm in Sacramento. If he manages to discover the company's bank account, and should he somehow gain access to it, he will discover that it sold its assets to Hancock and Hancock, and that the account has been closed."

"Dear God." He glanced at Pat. "And you're party to this?"

Pat winked at him again. "Aye, and fer a noice profit, laddie. Yer sister won't marry me any more than she'll marry George, but unloike him, I niver take personally what moight make me a tidy sum."

Doc blew out a worried breath. "God help us if George ever figures it out."

Sarah arched a stately eyebrow. "If he does, it will be because one of three people told him. And they're sitting right here at this table." She placed papers on the table before him along with pen and ink. She tapped them with a slim forefinger. "Just sign on the bottom, Philip. Pat and I will take care of the rest."

He did, wondering all the while if it was a death warrant.

118

Billy sat at the table in the dim rear of Central City's Colorado Nugget saloon and leaned his chair back on two legs; his left foot he propped on the chair across from him.

Down in Black Hawk work was progressing on Hill's new smelter — the supposed key to unlocking a wealth in gold from the recalcitrant ore. New buildings were going up everywhere. Talk was that a railroad would be built up Clear Creek from Golden — even if the rails and the locomotive, in pieces, had to be hauled in from Cheyenne.

He sipped rye with his left hand, the fingers of his right resting on the Remington's polished grips.

The revolver had been a good one, though it didn't look the same as when he'd taken it from the sallow-faced man that day at Dewley's camp. The bluing had worn off, and though he'd taken the best care of it he could, the metal had pitted in places. The grips, once dark walnut, now balanced between weather bleaching and the darkening oils from his palm. The action, however, remained tight, and he kept it clean and oiled.

The bartender, Mooney, had five clients. He

921

kept them up by the front. As if they understood Billy's need for solitude, the men spoke softly, rarely glancing his way.

Would George come? Billy had sent a message to the man's boardinghouse mistress asking that George meet him at two at the Nugget. If his pocket watch was correct, it was now five after.

The hinges squeaked as the back door was opened, and the smell of rot, urine, and feces blew in.

Billy tightened his grip on the Remington.

George — clad in his long duster, the hat pulled low — emerged from the narrow hall, his hands held wide, as if in surrender.

Billy used his foot to push the chair out, and resettled himself, using the table to hide the fact that he'd slipped the Remington free of its holster. "Hello, George."

"You got a reason for showing up just at this particular time?" George's voice sounded like a wire pulled too tight.

"Thought I'd drop in. Pay a social call. You remember social calls? Say hello to an old friend?"

"Not funny. Tell me why you're here, Billy. Is it about the Piute?"

"What the hell would I care about any old Indian?" Billy cocked his head, trying to read George's posture, the weary slump of his shoulders. Below the hat brim, the man's shadowed face looked strained.

George glared balefully. "Is it about that trouble at End-of-the-Tracks?"

"End-of-the-Tracks?" How the hell would George know about that?

"What were you doing? Rolling track layers, for God's sake!"

"What makes you think it was me?"

George reached into his duster and pulled out some folded papers. These he slid across the table.

With his left hand, Billy picked them up, unfolded them, and stared. The best likeness was a drawing of his face, almost good enough to be a tintype. Below, it proclaimed:

Murderer and Thief
$500 Reward.
Wanted for the brutal murder and robbery of Angus McFarley and Sam Howell

The fine print went on to note that the reward was offered by the Union Pacific and would be payable upon delivery of the miscreant.

"Seems a remarkable likeness of you, don't you think?" George asked. "My agents tell me that McFarley was one of their route surveyors, and when you hit him with that pick handle, you hit too hard. Same with Howell, though it took him four days to die."

George pointed at the drawing. "Seems that you almost ran over a man getting away. Turns out he was an artist back East before his wife left him and he ran off to build a railroad."

George gestured. "Those other two are just circulars. One from Helena, the other from Virginia City. Both of them looking for whoever strangled and burned a couple of whores. I thought it looked like your work."

Neither of them had a picture to go with them, just a request for information leading to an arrest and conviction.

George asked, "Want to tell me why you, of all people, were killing railroad men for a couple of dollars like some chucklehead?"

Billy flipped the papers away and took a sip of his rye. "Mostly to keep Win Parmelee from getting suspicious about who I was?"

George seemed to freeze, his eyes like daggers. "Parmelee? You were riding with Parmelee? My people thought they had him in Virginia City. Somehow the son of a bitch killed several of my associates and got away. And *you* end up traveling with him?"

Billy shrugged, fighting a smile. The stranglers had been George's men? What kind of strange was that? "I knew I'd heard of him. Seems to me, it was right here, in this place. Mooney mentioned him to you. But here's the thing, I never knew what your interest in him was until Win told me about the Goddess, and how he killed her man. He says she stole his whorehouse."

George was stewing, chewing his lip. "So, where's Parmelee now?"

"Headed to Denver to kill this Sarah Anderson. Reason I'm here? I thought I'd see what you wanted me to do about him. 'Specially after he kilt the whore."

With tentative fingers George reached up to absently probe the side of his face where a small scar was whitening on his cheek. "That son of a bitch. When's he planning on doing this?"

"He had some things to do over in Cheyenne. Don't reckon he'll be in Denver till tonight at the earliest. Figure he'll take a day to scout out the whorehouse, lay his plans."

"The scheming cunt's sold the place to Big Ed and his partners. She's bought herself a house at the edge of town. Figured I'd pay her a visit before I headed west. 'Vengeance is mine, sayeth the

Lord'? In a hen's ass!"

George narrowed an eye. "That walking-shit friend of yours is forcing me to move my schedule up. Parmelee might be a cock-beater of the first order, but *she* threw it in my face! Ain't nobody gonna get away with that. Not in light of what those California peckers just did to me."

"What California peckers?" Billy asked.

George studied him from under his hat. "You know the names William Ralston, John MacKay, James Fair, or maybe James Flood?"

"Heard of 'em in Helena, for sure. Mining bosses. Fighting with each other, ain't they? Out in the Sierras? What they call the Comstock."

"You think Meagher was your biggest kill? Why, Mr. Meadowlark, after you get done filling out my list in California, you're going to be the most wanted killer in all the world."

"What did they do to you?"

"Took me for a fucking fortune over the Piute Lode. Don't know if it was Ralston or MacKay, but someone sold me a pig in a poke."

"How bad?" Billy wondered, thinking of George's fortune.

"Bad!" He pointed a hard finger. "But that ain't your concern."

"So, after I kill Parmelee, we're going to California?"

George stood. "Right now we're riding to Denver. Seems I've got to get the Goddess before Parmelee, or that sick buckey is going to ruin her before I get my chance."

925

119

Butler stepped down and loosened Apple's cinch. Taking Shandy's lead and Apple's reins, he tied the animals off on the hitching post ring. Patting Apple on the neck, he added, "You be good now, old friend, and feel free to add to the piles."

A ring of old manure was visible around the hitching post where it had been beaten into the street by countless hooves. Business at Doc's must have been good.

Butler glanced up and down Fifteenth Street. Denver really was turning into a city. New three- and four-story buildings were going up; teams of bricklayers on scaffolding labored in the midday sun. Despite being gone for just shy of a year, he found the changes dramatic.

"Reckon this heah might be the equal of Memphis in a year or two," Phil Vail said admiringly where he stood to the side. The rest of the men were crowded around the boardwalk in front of Doc's.

"Don't seem yor brother missed you none," Corporal Pettigrew muttered, his hands on his hips. He was looking up at the newly painted wood. Things must have improved. Paint had been scarcer than hen's teeth, and twice as expensive. Now half the frame buildings on the street sported color.

Butler's chest began to tickle with that odd mix of excitement and fear. He couldn't help but remember the anger and pain in Doc's voice as he'd thrown Butler and the men out of this very building.

"Jus' get it over with, Cap'n, *ça va*?" Kershaw insisted. "Otherwise you stand out heah all day, *mais oui*?"

Butler glanced at the men for reassurance and reached for the doorknob. It rang a bell hanging from a hook. Otherwise the office and waiting room looked about the same. Maybe the bench was more polished, and the clutter of papers on the desk not as neat.

"Be there in a moment!" Doc's familiar voice called from the surgery.

Butler stepped over to the surgery door, butterflies in his stomach as he peeked in.

Doc was bent over a little boy whose shirt was off, his suspenders down. Back to Butler, Doc leaned over the lad, listening to his chest through some device with tubes that were inserted in Doc's ears. A worried-looking woman stood beside him, holding what was obviously the little boy's shirt.

"You say he only gets this when he's helping stack the hay?" Doc straightened and removed the tubes from his ear.

"Yes, sir." The woman's voice was filled with twang. "It gits so bad with the coughing, little Jake here th'ow's up. Then, to a night, he cain't hardly breathe a'tall."

"It's the hay fever, Mrs. Smith. Sometimes they

927

grow out of it. My advice, and I know it's hard, is to keep him away from the haying. If he absolutely has to, you give him half a teaspoon of codeine just before bed. But no more. And only when he needs it."

Butler backed away, smiling. Doc was like himself — if a little thinner-looking.

"Looks like he need t' clean a little more." Frank Thompson bent to inspect the coffee stains on the side of the pot where it rested on the stove. Butler shooed him out of the way, carefully tested the pot with a quick tap of the finger, and found it still warm. Taking a tin cup from the rack, he filled it and took a taste.

"God, I've missed coffee," he remarked.

"Reckon them Dukurika could larn a thing er two 'bout a good drink," Jimmy Peterson added.

"I really miss that phlox tea Mountain Flicker makes," Butler told him. "Coffee's good, but I really wish I was back there."

"Missin' the missus?" Pettigrew fixed hard eyes on Butler. "Reckon y'all know how we feel."

"Not all of you had wives," Butler pointed out, "but Corporal, I never discounted what you all gave up when you enlisted."

"So, what's next, suh?" Billy Templeton asked. "You dead set on going back to the mountains?"

"We told Mountain Flicker we'd be back." At movement, Butler turned, nodding and touching his battered hat brim as Mrs. Smith herded her little boy out, stepping wide of Butler in the process and avoiding his eyes.

"That's a nice little tinkle bell Philip put up," Vail noted as the woman left.

"It is, Private." Butler studied the thing. "But I guess without us to keep watch, it's the next best thing. Sort of like a picket you don't have to feed or relieve from duty."

"Dear God!"

Butler turned at Doc's cry. "Hello, Philip."

Doc stood in the door to the surgery as if frozen, his face expressing wonder and disbelief. His right hand clutched a couple of greenbacks. Then he rushed forward, wrapping arms around Butler, hugging the breath out of him.

"God, I've missed you! Worried about you! Don't you *ever* leave me like that again!"

Butler smiled, tears, unbidden, trickling down his cheeks as he hugged his brother to him. "I'm sorry, Philip. So sorry."

120

Doc pushed his brother back, searched his face, took in his travel-filthy clothing. Butler looked like he'd been in the wilderness, pants threadbare and grease-blackened. He smelled of campfire smoke, stale sweat, and dust. Instead of boots, heavy trail moccasins of a style Doc had never seen clad his feet. A holey excuse of a felt hat — worse than the scarecrows at Camp Douglas used to wear — topped his head.

But beneath the wild tangle of unwashed hair and beard, Butler looked tan, lean, and healthy as a wildcat. His eyes were clear, without that anxious wavering and insecurity.

"Are you all right? Where in God's name have you been? I've been worried sick."

"I went to the mountains."

"Where? Idaho Springs? Central City? One of the camps?"

"The Shining Mountains. Up on the Wind River. Where Paw always talked about." The old fear rose behind Butler's gray eyes, hard-edged and painful. "I found Paw."

"What do you mean you found Paw?" Philip knew that look. Butler wasn't happy with what he

930

had to say. "Don't tell me he's in your head, too. Like Kershaw and the rest of your phantoms. You are still seeing them, aren't you? That's who you were talking to when I came out."

Butler glanced to the side in irritation, then waved it away. "I know he's never liked you, at ease, Corporal."

Turning back to Doc, Butler said, "Paw ran at Shiloh. Deserted. He never told me where all he went. Mostly I suspect he drifted from tribe to tribe, wearing out his welcome. He ended up with a Sheep Eater band. Before they could drive him out for being a lazy shit, a bear got him. Mangled him pretty bad."

"Wait" Doc put a hand out, pleading. Realized it was still full of Mrs. Smith's money, and took long enough to unlock the drawer and stick it in the cash box. Then he seated himself on the corner of his desk, watching Butler's delighted expression as he sipped Doc's mediocre coffee.

"You mean he's *alive.*"

Butler shook his head. "Was alive. The bear mauling was bad, Philip. Shredded Paw's right arm. With the help of the men, I performed the amputation. Paw was barely . . ." He glanced to the side. "Yes, Private, he'd have died if you hadn't remembered that double knot to tie off the brachial artery."

"Stop it!" Doc cried, his heart pounding. Then added, "I'm sorry. Please. Just tell . . . *ask* the men not to interrupt."

Butler shot a smug, slightly superior look to the side, saying, "See? What did I tell you?"

Then to Doc. "Paw lived. We took him with our *naatea,* our family group, up into the headwaters of Owl Creek. He was recovering, learning to

931

walk . . ."

"What?"

Butler looked down at his dirt-encrusted hands. "Someday I will tell you the whole story. But the things Paw confessed to? Let us just say he shamed me before my men and wife and family."

"Wife?" Doc swallowed hard. "You're *married?*"

To whom? What woman would have a delusional lunatic?

"Her name in Dukurika is Wobindotadegi. Mountain Flicker. And I see that look you're giving me. I'm not a madman among the Shoshoni; they believe I see the Spirit World, that I am a sort of *puhagan.* Especially after I went to the Underworld and lay with Water Ghost Woman."

Doc barely caught himself in time. *God knows what kind of insanity he has imagined. Don't drive him away!*

Butler might have read his mind, a weary smile coming to his lips. "You won't understand, Philip. It's all right. The men and I are not here to be a burden. I only came to tell you about Paw. In the end, disgraced by all his lies and sins, he shot himself in the head rather than face it. I had to get him out of Shoshoni territory, bury him where his souls, if they got loose, couldn't plague the *newe.* I dug a hole and put his putrid body in it. Filled it full of rocks to keep him in, and covered the grave. I put the sod over it, and no one will ever know where he's laid."

"You really believe all of this? I mean . . ."

Butler chuckled, as if in amusement according to some internal whim. He gestured for Doc to wait, stepped to the door, and rang the bell as he stepped outside. Butler reentered with an Indian suitcase, what they called a parfleche.

This Butler laid on the desk, saying, "That's all of Paw's possessions. Everything but the revolver. It's a nice Starr and I'm keeping it."

Doc unlaced the ties and opened it. Inside was a small framed photo of Paw in his major's uniform. No doubt taken just before Shiloh. His gold watch and chain, the one he wore so proudly at the legislature. A small sack of gold coins and a sheaf of Confederate and Federal money. His wedding band, a deck of cards, dice, a folding knife and Bowie, a strike-a-light and box of matches. The pin he insisted he'd taken from a Mexican general's chest.

Paw's things, all right. "Jesus. You really found him."

"Divine justice." Butler's smile faded. "It was fitting that I was the one to find him. When I told him about Maw, Sarah, and Billy. About the farm. It might have been water off a duck's back, for all he cared."

Doc glanced up. "Sarah."

Butler shrugged. "Paw had no news. He never so much as wrote to —"

"Sarah is here. In Denver."

Butler blinked, as if processing this new revelation. "Is she all right?"

Doc took a breath. "Brace yourself. She's . . . changed."

Butler's gaze slid to the side — the way it did when he glanced at his men. "Imagine that," he said dryly. "As if any of us were left untouched."

"Untouched by what?"

"The ways of *puha.* The cockeyed strings of fate, Doc. Of course she's changed. We all are."

"Up until recently she ran one of the most prestigious parlor houses in the city. She's . . .

933

well, a madam is a nice way to say it."

"And Billy?"

"No news."

"I'll want to see her before I go."

"Go?" Doc asked, spreading his arms. "Go where? That night that Aggie came, I was just upset. I didn't mean those things. I have cursed myself over and over for my stupid tongue. The endless nights I've lain awake . . . I beg you to forgive me."

Butler reached out, laying a hand on his shoulder. "Long forgotten. I needed to go. Had to go. I found my place. I have a wife, a family. I only came back to tell you about Paw. Do it face-to-face. The men and I figured we owed you that."

"And then you're going back?"

Butler nodded, firmness in his eyes. "I don't belong in your world any more than you'd be happy in mine."

"But you'll stay long enough to see Sarah?"

A tease of a smile bent Butler's lips. "Of course. But Philip, give me your word. You won't conspire with her to keep me. You won't lock me up or drug me, or do something I wouldn't approve of."

Doc looked into his brother's clear blue eyes. He might be a delusional lunatic, but he'd never looked as sure of himself.

"My word, Butler."

"You keep Paw's stuff. I need to clean up, maybe find presentable clothes. I left a shirt and pants at your house. Then we'll go see Sarah. I'd like to know how she got here, what happened to Maw in those last days."

"It's a hard story to hear, Butler."

"Aren't they all?" he asked softly, his gaze distant.

121

June 29, 1868

Sarah closed her door, and the messenger boy went skipping down her front steps. She picked her way around the workmen who were gathering their tools in the foyer, and retreated to her dining room. The last of the banging and sawing signaled the end of the workday.

She used her hand duster to whisk the sawdust from her chair. Pulling up her skirt, she settled herself at an angle so her bustle cleared the chair back. Then, with a thumb, she broke the seal on the envelope Doc had just sent her.

She scanned the few lines, then reread them just for the enjoyment. Butler was back in town! Apparently still mad, but tanned and healthy. Would she mind if he and Philip paid a call at seven?

She smiled at that, remembering the last time she'd seen her brother — a dashing lieutenant on a warhorse, riding at the head of a detachment of cavalry. God, had it been so long?

And what would he think of his sister the whore? Ex-whore?

Could one ever really be an *ex*-whore?

Butler had been the epitome of a Southern officer. Would there be censure in his eyes — that aloof distance spun of moral superiority? God, it would wound her if there was. She'd always admired Butler and his well-read knowledge. Looked up to him beyond all of her other brothers.

Damn, she wished she could have ten minutes alone with Philip before they arrived. A chance to ask, "What does he think of me?"

"Sarah, what the hell does it matter?" she asked herself. "After everything you've been through, you're worried about the look in your crazy brother's eyes?" She laughed at herself.

No matter, she would be gracious, proud. If she had learned nothing else, it was how to put up a façade and hide the real Sarah.

"Mrs. Anderson?" the last of the workmen called. "We're leaving. Good night, ma'am."

"Thank you!" She shifted, glancing around the room as the front door closed authoritatively. She'd have to clean up a little. At least sweep up the sawdust in the dining room and wipe down the chairs so fine powder didn't stick to their clothes.

In the kitchen she poured water onto a rag from the keg she had delivered every other day, and attacked the worst of the mess. Nothing much could be done about the rest of the house. She'd give the tour, of course, but construction was construction, and Butler would just have to understand.

She thought back to the Butler she'd known in Arkansas. His distant gaze as he'd worked cutting tobacco and doing chores; all the while his thoughts had been focused on Romans and Greeks and ancient kings. That dreamy smile that would animate his lips as he told her of history and literature.

How changed he had been the last time she saw him; his once sensitive eyes had betrayed a wounded soul. She could still see the waver in his eyes, how his hands had twitched when the subject turned to war and battle.

"People born to be saints shouldn't be trying to stuff themselves into a soldier's uniform, brother. The cut and angles are all wrong."

She climbed the stairs, being careful of the lack of railing — although the dowels had been delivered and piled in the hallway just beyond her door.

She opened the door to her bedroom wide. She kept it closed during the day to keep out the dust, and because the workmen needn't be speculating on her big, plush bed.

She stepped toward her wardrobe, thinking that the light gray poplin would . . .

The floor creaked behind her.

She whirled and froze.

"Well, well," he said, stepping out from behind the bedroom door. "You've become quite the lady, haven't you?"

Parmelee shook his head, grinning. He wore sawdust-stained trousers stuffed into rider's boots. His shirt was in need of a wash, and his beard looked like it had been trimmed with a knife. His oily blond hair curled where it had been sweat-soaked by a tight hat. The grin on his lips, however, was predatory; his blue eyes deadly with threat.

"How did you get in here?" She struggled to sound in control. God, she hated being afraid.

"Passed myself off as a workman. They didn't look twice at the fella carrying them turned pieces up the stairs. Gonna be a fancy hand railing. But you ain't gonna see it finished."

She backed toward the bed, heart hammering against her chest. "You know they'll kill you."

"Gotta catch me first. I hear you turned into quite the whore. The Goddess? How's that for ripe? Washerwoman to Goddess. Talk about a fairy tale. I like to think I gave you your start. That having a real man inside showed you what you were missing. 'Specially after that milksop of a deserter."

"Bret was five times the man you'll ever be," she told him, stepping back to the headboard, slipping her right arm behind her.

"Go on," he told her. "Try for it."

A hand of ice might have taken her by the heart. "Try for what?"

"That big pistol you hung behind the headboard." He waggled a finger at her. "I put it somewhere safe."

With his left hand he pulled out a wad of stout cord, his right slipped a Bowie from its sheath. "I'm gonna have to tie you again. Don't want you fighting or screaming. You understand, don't you?"

He paused. "Hope it's still tight after you been riding so many cocks. I'd be damn disappointed if it ain't."

Sarah took a deep breath. "I don't suppose there's any other way? Like I could just promise to lay back, give you the best I could, and you'd be on your way?"

He barely cracked a smile. "Sometimes a thing's got to be done just so. It's putting you in your place . . . causing pain and fear. Knowing you're hating my cock hammering away, but praying it'll last 'cause when I ride you that last bit, you're gonna die. That's what makes it so good."

"You're a sick pile of shit, did you know that?"

"So I've been told. Now, you can turn around and let me tie you easy, or we can start with a beating." He flicked the knife back and forth, as if teasing. Then he started forward. She could see his nostrils flaring with each breath.

Sarah's chest felt as if it would explode, her limbs charged and trembling.

Now or never.

122

June 29, 1868

"This damn thing looks like a castle," Billy noted as they rode past the big house on Grant Street. The sun sat at an angle, dipping toward the distant Rockies. It shot bars of light through the smattering of clouds that seemed to glow above the city's smoky air.

"Guess she poured all the money she got from the Angel's Lair into this monstrosity," George said through a growl as he reined his horse up, hard eyes on the big brick house with its two towers.

"Son of a bitch," Billy muttered under his breath as they rode around to the rear. "That horse tied behind the outhouse? That's Parmelee's buckskin. From the piles of horse shit behind him, I'd say we're a couple of hours late and a dollar short, George."

"Well, shit. Let's go see what's left of Sarah. That sick bastard has a thing for playing with knives while he's fucking them."

Billy rode up behind the house, tied his horse off on a heavy sawbuck, and walked up to the back door. Locked. Down beside the stairs a workman had left a crowbar.

Ten seconds later the door was open — if a little splintered.

"Follow me," George told him, leading the way. "If that bastard hasn't left me something to humiliate, and hurt, and pay back, you can kill him twice. Slowly."

Billy shucked his Remington and kept a couple of steps behind. One thing he could say for Sarah Anderson, she was building one hell of a house. What was a lone woman going to do with a rambling hulk like this? Turn it into an orphanage?

George led the way through the kitchen and into a dining room. Billy spotted the liquor bottles on the back wall's unfinished hutch and grinned. If he had to wait on George, there'd be liquid entertainment. Quality if he could judge from the labels.

They'd just made it into the parlor when a muffled bang from upstairs brought them both to a halt. Pistol shot?

"Son of a bitch!" Parmelee's shout carried from above.

Another bang.

A door slammed open, boots pounding on stairs as someone hurried down.

Parmelee came reeling in from the foyer, a hand to his cheek, face like a strained mask. Blood, like a crimson blossom, spread on his shirt just below his right collarbone.

He stopped short, gaping at George, and then Billy. "What in tarnal hell?"

"Win Parmelee," George drawled slowly. "Run out of a woman's bedroom."

"Who the hell are you?" Parmelee dabbed at the blood leaking out of his cheek and grimaced. "She

941

shot me in the fucking face! Bloody fucker, that hurts!"

Billy covered Parmelee with his Remington as he heard footsteps on the stairs. The woman was coming, which meant things might get a little interesting if she had more than a two-shot derringer.

George sounded pleasant. "How'd you get away from my men outside Virginia City, Parmelee? Heard that they had you to rights, but somehow you killed them all."

"Billy did that." Parmelee sounded dull, his voice starting to slur as if in great pain.

"Indeed," George whispered. "Sometime in the future that will make for an interesting conversation."

"She shot me in the face!" Parmelee moaned. "It's like a hot poker shoved into my head!"

"It's about the pain and fear," a woman's cultured voice said from the foyer. "Or so I've been told." Then she added, "Hello, George. Is Parmelee one of yours? Or is this just happenstance?"

Billy began to shake. Sarah's voice!

From the dreams.

But different.

His mouth went dry, blood rushing. Clutching the Remington, he began to tremble.

Visions flashed behind his eyes, Sarah rising naked and abused. Towering over him, her eyes like blue burning fire. She was reaching down for him, death and horror in her eyes.

He stumbled back into the dining room, ducked behind the partition. Back to the wall his knees went weak, and he slid down to the floor.

Images of the nightmares kept playing behind his eyes; he began to weep.

123

June 29, 1868

Sarah stepped into the main room, her .36-caliber Colt pocket revolver ready, hammer cocked. Parmelee's face was a mask of pain, blood streaming between his fingers. The wet blossom on his shirt had begun to soak down in a V.

George Nichols, wearing a short black sack coat and starched white shirt, stood with one booted foot forward. Neither his fine black linen vest with its wide lapels, nor the jaunty, flat-topped felt hat with narrow brim, offset the .41-caliber Sharps single-shot pistol he held. They just emphasized the black rage seething behind his eyes.

"I'm glad to see you've still got your clothes on, Sarah," George greeted her. "Ripping them off gives me something to look forward to."

Sarah thought she heard a mewling sound from the dining room, as if someone were whimpering.

"I'm delighted to see you, too, George." Who did she cover with her revolver? Parmelee, or George? She had three shots left. George had one.

And who, in God's name, was sobbing behind the wall in her dining room? As if it stroked some distant memory . . .

The spell broke when Parmelee's eyes rolled

back in his head. His knees buckled. She felt it through the floor when he hit with a bony thump.

Sarah shifted her aim to George. "So, here we stand. Each of us armed, and —"

"No one gets away with what you did to me. I came to close accounts, to pay you back for —"

"Heard you're broke," she told him dryly. The sham was over. She could see it in his eyes. Nothing left to lose. "Is what they're saying about the Piute Lode true? That you bet everything on a hill of worthless rock?"

His face blanched, a snakelike emptiness behind his eyes as he raised the pistol, shaking it at her as if the jerking pistol could emphasize his words. "How did you hear? What do you know about . . ."

She was looking into George's eyes when his gun went off. Saw the surprise there as the report cracked in the room.

She felt the impact in her left thigh, like a painless slap. George's mouth was open, eyes wide.

"You son of a bitch!" She took her time, raised the Colt. Over the sights she saw his shock mixed with glassy terror. He pitched sideways as she shot. Even without the smoke and flame, she couldn't have seen if she hit him. As he whirled away, he threw his pistol at her.

She tried to duck, the heavy Sharps glancing off her thrown-up left arm, giving her a hard knock on the head as it went by.

She eared the hammer back, snapped another shot as Nichols fled through her dining room. He hurled a chair to the side to clear his way. Then he was gone, boots hammering through her kitchen and on out the back.

She stood in sudden silence, blue smoke rising, the smell of sulfur and blood in the room.

The whimpering cry from the dining room came again. She glanced down at Parmelee, bleeding on her floor. The man's eyes were open, as vacant as glass marbles. His beard now matted with blood. It frothed in his mouth and bubbled in his nostrils.

The whimpering came again.

She cocked her revolver, took a step, and almost toppled. Her left leg didn't seem to work. She locked her knee, hobbled to the wide arch that separated the parlor and dining room.

Leaning against it, she glanced down. Saw the man who huddled into a ball. He wore a fringed buckskin jacket. The wool pants were travel-stained and tucked into high cavalry boots. Dirty blond locks straggled out over his shoulders, his head hidden by a weathered felt hat.

"Who are you?" she demanded.

"Don't hurt me, Sarah," he whispered. "I don't want to kill you no more. Don't . . ." He sucked in a terrified breath. *Don't fucking touch me!"*

She blinked, aware of the growing ache and weakness in her left leg. "Billy?"

She let herself sag. Crouched beside him. "Billy?"

"No!" he cried. "Tell Maw to leave me alone! I'm sorry! I'm so sorry!"

She reached for him, only to feel a shock run through him as she grasped his arm.

He looked up, terrified. In that instant, he screamed, *"You demon bitch!"*

He knocked her backward, his hands going for her throat. She fought, clawed, as he bowled her onto her back. "Billy, for God's sake, it's me! Sarah!"

He was leaning over her, hair hanging down, tears streaking from his eyes to patter on her face.

A wild insanity twisted his expression, teeth bared. His eyes were possessed of a weird blue light.

She felt her throat crushing under his grip.

Driven by an animal terror, she pulled her hand back and drove the revolver hard into the side of his head. The force of the blow knocked the hat off his head.

As he collapsed sideways, she managed to scramble out from under him. Scuttled away. Her left leg like numb meat.

Across from him, she lifted herself up onto one of the chairs and, over the cocked pistol, watched him pant as he lay there.

"Sarah?" he whispered hoarsely.

"What in the name of hell are you doing, Billy?" she rasped. It hurt when she coughed, and she fingered her throat. Why did men always go for her throat?

He looked up, half dazed, raised a hand to the side of his head. "You're . . . alive?"

"Not by much," she told him wearily. "What the *fuck* is wrong with you?"

"You're . . . not a demon?"

"Do I look like a goddamned *demon*?" She shook her head, glancing back at Parmelee, now apparently dead on her floor. "What the hell are you doing with Parmelee and George Nichols? How did you get here? Just tell me what's going on!"

"You're . . . the Goddess?" he rasped. "Thought you were dead. Haunting me. The nightmares . . . the endless goddamned nightmares . . ." He started to cry again. "I'm sorry. I'm so sorry."

She swallowed painfully. "I'd never haunt you." She paused. "Billy, I'm the one that's sorry. Back at the trapper's cabin, I was lost. More than a little crazy. A thousand times I've wished I could have gone back, told you it was all right."

"My fault," he told her through streaming tears. "All my fault."

"Wasn't anybody's fault. Just the damn war. The madness. Men turned to animals. That's all."

"I got 'em all," he whispered. "Dewley's bunch. Ran every last one of 'em down and killed him. But you still kept coming to haunt my dreams. All naked and raped. Reaching out for . . . for . . ."

"Jesus!" She sucked a breath, suddenly starved for air. "Damn it, listen to me! I'm alive because you *saved* me. Now, get up. I'm shot! Parmelee's dead on the floor. I think I shot Nichols, but he's running. Philip and Butler are due here any minute. Philip's a doctor. Here in Denver."

She pulled her skirt up, blood was leaking out of a hole about four inches below the point of her hip. It should have hurt worse than it did.

Billy's expression seemed to clear, and he wiped the tears from his face. "George? How did you know he's broke?"

She thinned her lips, balanced the revolver in her hand. If Billy went crazy and started to strangle her again? Could she shoot him?

Hell yes!

"I broke him. I'm tired of men raping me. Abusing me. Parmelee, George, it don't matter, little brother."

"George . . . raped you," Billy said absently, as if his mind were a thousand miles away.

"Tried to." She indicated the revolver. "Reckon when it comes to men, I'm getting right practiced at beating 'em off."

Odd how the mere presence of her brother made her language slip back to the Arkansas hills.

948

"He can't let this go," Billy said, picking up the big Remington that lay on the floor beside him. He climbed wearily to his feet. "Is there some reason why I'm always proved to be the fool?"

"Where are you going?"

"To get George," he told her.

"Billy, wait. Philip and Butler are coming. We need to talk. There are so many questions."

He gave her an eerie, half-possessed stare as he paused at the kitchen door. "It's my responsibility, sis. Has been since Paw left. I gotta finish it."

Then he was gone.

"Billy!" She rose to start after him, only to have her leg give out. Grabbing at the table, she barely kept from falling. For a moment the room spun. When it cleared she heard the back door slam.

For the time being, all she could do was prop herself up, cling to her revolver, and pant.

124

June 29, 1868

God — or the Devil — has played me for a fool!
A bitterness like he'd never known leached his insides like lye on raw meat.

Billy trotted Locomotive to the livery where George liked to stable his mount. The blood-bay mare was there; and tossing the hostler two bits, Billy ensured that Locomotive would be fed and watered and ready to go.

Stepping out onto Wazee Street, he took stock as the sun began to fade behind the distant Rockies. God might have played him like a fool, but no one was a better hunter.

There had been no blood on George's saddle, which meant Sarah had either missed him, or barely nicked him.

Sarah!

Alive.

Not a demon.

"Well, God, or whoever you are, you son of a bitch, you ain't playing me no more."

All those years he'd been trying to kill something that wasn't dead. Bitterness churned as self-loathing took over.

"Time to square the accounts," he told himself.

Where would George go? Not to one of Big Ed's establishments. No, it would be one of the other taverns.

Why a tavern?

Billy licked his lips as he started for Blake Street. George would want to lick his wounds, salve his defeat with a couple of drinks. It wouldn't be a cheap hole, but somewhere with style. He'd want to figure his next move. On top of being broke over the Piute Lode deal, he'd be smarting. Sarah had beaten him again after whatever setback she'd handed Nichols earlier. Was that why he'd been fingering that new scar? He'd tried to rape Sarah, and she'd beaten him off with a pistol?

He grinned. A man had to love a sister with that kind of grit.

But George? He'd be seething.

Billy started with the Tremont House, then the Broadwell House, followed by the American. One by one he went through Denver's finer establishments.

"Did you hear?" one worthy asked at the International. "George Nichols and a friend went after Sarah Anderson at her house. One man's dead, and she's shot!"

Billy stopped at the edge of earshot, listening.

"Word is that Marshal Cook's looking for Nichols," the worthy's friend replied. "Bet he don't try an' force no woman with a pistol in her hand. Heard she's got bruises on her throat." The second man shook his head, spitting on the floor.

On her throat? I did that.

Billy ground his teeth, feeling sick to his stomach. Damnation and hell! One minute he was on the verge of rage — the next his eyes were burning with tears. He staggered out into the night, leaning against the saloon wall, one hand to his heart.

When he remembered Sarah, it was as a girl. How she smiled, the way she teased. The time she'd set him up, tripped him so he fell headlong into the river.

Damn and hell, they'd been great friends as kids: her chiding, his practical jokes. The time he'd put pine pitch in her comb. Sarah's shrieks as Maw had washed her hair with turpentine. How Sarah had finally gotten him back, dropping a mouse in his pants pocket, the one with a hole in it. How he'd gone berserk with the little beast scampering around his cock and balls and then down his leg.

When did we lose that?

The pain built.

In the end, the sense of desolation was too much to bear; he threw his head back and laughed, and laughed. Soul screaming at the trick fate had played on him.

It took a couple of hours, but he found George. He was drinking upstairs at the Criterion — the infamous tavern and gaming hall started by dangerous Charlie Harrison and now run by Ed Jumps. The upstairs was separated from the riffraff, reserved for the more respectable clientele.

"Hello, George," Billy said, walking up behind his friend.

George whirled, hand reaching for the pocket where he used to keep his single-shot Sharps. Then his slow smile spread. "Billy, where the hell you been? What happened to you? One minute you're behind me, the next you've vanished! Goddamn it! You were supposed to back me up!"

"How much is Sarah Anderson's life worth to

you? Assuming I kill her tonight?"

"Five thousand."

"Oh, I forgot. You're broke. Sarah took you on the Piute Mine deal. Maybe I better do it for free?" Billy smiled, gesturing for the bartender down the way. "Best you've got," he called. "George is buying!"

"Like hell," George whispered, his eyes like black pits. "You *crawled* on me back there!"

"Odd turn of events," Billy told him as he took the amber liquor and drank it down. "That *is* good stuff. What's it cost?" He gestured the bartender for another.

"Four dollars a glass," the bartender told him, filling it and retreating.

"And it's such a small glass," Billy noted as he tossed off the second.

George was red-faced, the corners of his lips trembling. "You and Parmelee. Start at the beginning where you killed my men."

Billy shrugged. "Not much to tell. I'd been running into Parmelee up and down Montana. Couldn't remember where I'd heard of him. So, outside of Virginia City, a bunch of stranglers had him. Rope around his neck and all. Devil just gigged me, so I saved him."

Billy gestured for another whiskey.

"See, George, this is all like one of them puppet shows. You know, the ones that dangle odd-looking little fellas on strings? I haven't decided if it's God or the Devil that's been playing us."

"Do you know how goddamned crazy you sound?"

"Reckon you ain't up on the half of it." Billy lifted the whiskey glass. "All them whores I been strangling and burning? It's 'cause my sister's ghost kept coming in my nightmares. What she'd do to me? If I told you, it would make your skin crawl. Let's just say I'd wake screaming. And sometimes it was Maw rising out of the grave all full of hate."

"You *are* one insane son of a bitch!"

Billy raised his voice. "Just your hired killer." Felt the devil break loose in his chest. "The Meadowlark! At your service."

The bar had gone quiet. The bartender, a couple of paces down, stopped short, gaping, eyes wide.

George had stiffened like an oaken rod. "I *don't* know what you're talking about."

"Want me to deal with Sarah Anderson? Kill her for running you out of her house? You were going to rape her before cutting her throat, weren't you, George?"

Billy gestured grandly with his glass. "I mean, you can't let her get the best of you. So now, after all them men you hired me to kill, you'll *pay* me five thousand dollars to shoot Sarah Anderson in the face. Not because you want to get your fingers on a mine, like them other times, but because she drove you out of her house when you went to rape her."

"Shut your *lying* mouth!" George started to walk away.

"You take another step, George, and I'll shoot you down."

George stopped, his breath coming in fast gasps. "Billy, you're drunk. Talking crazy. You been in the opium again?"

"That odd turn of events I was talking about? Sarah Anderson is *my sister,* you pile of walking shit. She was Sarah Hancock before the war. Me, I let her down once. She and Maw both. I let her down again today. But it stops here. Turn around, you belly-crawling worm."

George turned, the only sound in the room coming from the raucous celebrants in the room below. George's face was a conflicting mix of anger, disbelief, and soul-blanching fear.

Billy said, "Time to give the Devil his due," and shot George Nichols through the heart.

George was gasping, his legs pumping weakly in the sawdust. Billy stopped long enough to pull a meadowlark feather from his pocket and stuck it in the bullet hole. Then he glared around the stunned room and started down the stairs.

He was most of the way to the door before a man came pounding down after him, pointing, and crying, "He just kilt George Nichols! Grab him!"

Billy pulled his pistol, waving it around, shouting, "Get your drunk carcasses away from me!"

When one burly bullwhacker grabbed at him, Billy calmly shot the man in the face. Then he was out into the night, charging up Blake Street, feet pounding on the rutted thoroughfare.

They came pouring out of the Criterion in his wake. Several pistols banged in the darkness. Billy flinched as a ball buried itself in his shoulder. Then came a staccato of gunfire like a string of Chinese firecrackers.

The louder bark of a rifle accompanied a numbing impact in his hip. Something else slapped low into his back.

Turning, he thumbed the hammer back on the Remington; his return fire scattered them into the darkness. A deep ache burned through his right hip, that leg going weak.

Blinking, he stiff-legged into the sanctuary of an

955

alley, found a board for a crutch, and hobbled forward. The pain was atrocious. Warm blood drained down the inside of his thigh. He stopped only long enough to throw up, then staggered on.

He had just stepped out on Fifteenth Street. In one sense, he only had made it for a couple of blocks. On the other, he was as far from salvation as he'd ever been.

That's when a voice called, "There he is, men. I want him surrounded and unable to flee."

125

June 30, 1868

Doc poured coal oil into one of the lamps, then screwed the lid back onto the tin. After setting the tin back in its place, he threaded the hot lamp back together, lit the wick, and replaced the chimney. With three lamps burning, the surgery was as well illuminated as it could be for this time of night.

He crossed to where Sarah lay on the cot. He'd just used his thermometer, finding her temperature a little high at 98.8. She usually ran about 98.5.

"How's the leg?" he asked.

"A slight ache," she told him, looking up at him with dreamy eyes. "Removing the bullet hurt worse than being shot."

"It wasn't the bullet that worried me. It was the fabric it carried in with it. One of these days we're going to understand why foreign objects cause wounds to infect. But cleaning out a wound and irrigating it with boiled water seems to help."

"I like morphine," she told him. "It's like floating in warm water."

"Don't like it too much. You'll end up like so many of the girls down on the line. If it's such an easy way out, why do they always end up dead?"

She shook her head. "I'm past that trap, Doc. What am I? Twenty-three? I feel like an old lady." She paused. "Butler's a kind man, isn't he?"

"Him and all of his soldiers." Doc reached for his coffee.

"He's so . . . odd. Talking to the air, but he seems to think like a normal person. Outside of losing the thread of the conversation on occasion." She shook her head. "I keep thinking he's fooling with me, playing games."

"It gets worse when he's worried, like at your house tonight. Sometimes, when everything is going well, you can almost forget that he's a lunatic."

She frowned. "Do you really think that letting him go back to the Indians is a good idea?"

Doc sipped his coffee. "He seems happy, sis. He lights up when he talks about this wife and family of his. But as to letting him go back? I think now that Billy's here, maybe it ought to be a family decision."

"Perhaps." A flicker of dreamy smile crossed her lips, and she asked, "Do you believe what he says about Paw?"

"I'm not the one to ask. I always saw through Paw's clapjaw and bluff. Maybe because I was the oldest."

She stared distantly at one of the lamps. "I fell for it. He was going to take me to Little Rock, find me a husband who would make me a lady. I'd be a happy brood mare, dressed in finery. The perfect accoutrement to augment a prominent gentleman's social position. Envy of Arkansas high society."

"And?"

Her lips twitched. "I suspect Paw would have

pawned me off to whomever offered him the greatest gain. If I could go back I'd slap that little bitch silly, stand her on her own two feet, and start her practicing with a revolver at the age of eight."

"That sounds hard."

"It's a hard world, brother." She made a face. "Discovering that? Well . . . believe me, the epiphany is not only humiliating but rather painful." Her drugged gaze wavered. "Thank God for bustles. The lords of fashion never could have devised a better place for a hideout gun."

"Those were good shots on Parmelee. I'll see if I can't get over and clean up the blood before you get home. Dave Cook's deputies should have carted the body off to Walley's by now."

She stared into the past. "I gave him a hell of a lot more chance than he ever gave Bret, or me, or Aggie."

After a long silence, Doc asked, "I know you spend time with Pat O'Reilly on occasion. Think you'll ever marry again?"

"What I had with Bret was a miracle. God doesn't grant two such in a lifetime. Pat's a . . . what? Business partner? Friend? Sometime lover? I don't know. But I'll never marry again." She glanced at him. "You?"

He shook his head. "We understand each other."

The door to the street opened, the bell ringing.

Doc had no more than started for the surgery door when Butler called, "Philip? Assistance, please!"

Doc burst into the dimly lit front office to find Butler staggering under a young man's weight. The newcomer wore a fringed buckskin jacket; one arm was hung around Butler's shoulder. He

959

was staggering, dragging a leg, and even in the dim light, the dark stain down his trousers had to be blood.

Doc got a hold, and together he and Butler dragged the bleeding man into the surgery. They heaved him up onto the table, where Doc stripped off the coat. He was checking the young man's eyes as Butler held up the coat, saying, "Four bloody holes in the back. Turn him over."

With Butler's help, he rolled the body.

"Dear God," Doc whispered as he cut away the bloody shirt and took in the entry wounds. Butler pulled the trousers down; the wound in the buttocks looked the worst. "It's Shiloh all over."

"God, Billy," Sarah whispered. "What did you do?"

"Billy?" Doc wondered, bending down to inspect the young man's bearded face. Yes, he could see the family resemblance. How had the boy he had once known grown into this face, lined with pain, and groggy as it was.

Faces. Memories of them — young like Billy's — came flooding back from the past. The feel of blood caking on his fingers. Of impotence as desperate eyes looked up at his, praying for a miracle.

I couldn't save them.

As he reached for his surgical kit, his vision began to silver with tears.

126

"*C'est bon.* Reckon she be one beautiful woman," Kershaw noted.

"She is indeed," Butler replied.

"Too bad," Pettigrew muttered where he leaned against the surgery wall. Beside him morning light streamed in through the dirty-paned window.

"Woman like her" — Phil Vail bent over Sarah's sleeping form — "why, she could have had any man."

Pettigrew smirked. "Hell, given her profession, she's probably *had* 'em all a time or two."

Butler stiffened, pointing a hard finger at Pettigrew. "I thought you all heard my orders. You're to keep a civil tongue. Or I'll bust you right down to private."

He must have spoken too loud. When he looked back, Sarah's eyes were open, looking steely blue in the morning light.

"It's unsettling when you do that," she told him. "Doc says it's one part of your brain dealing with another part. That you've given different bits of your mind an imaginary character. That it's your way of arguing with yourself."

"Doc is a very bright doctor. Maybe that's

exactly what I'm doing." He gave her a welcoming grin.

"Then why don't you stop, Butler?" She sat up, almost yipped with pain, and eased back down. "Son of a bitch!"

"You didn't used to talk this way."

"And you didn't carry on conversations with the empty air." She paused. "Sorry my language bothers you."

"Why don't *you* just stop, Sarah?"

She arched an eyebrow. "Throwing my own medicine back at me? Maybe I'm no longer a lady, big brother." At his smile she pulled her long hair back and looked at the far bed. "How's Billy?"

"Philip dosed him rather heavily with morphine. He removed the bullets and irrigated the wounds. Billy's got a broken shoulder blade, a bruised kidney, two bullet-broken ribs, but the worst is the wound to his buttock. A rifle ball. It tore up the muscles pretty bad. How Billy could even stand, let alone walk, is beyond me."

Sarah said, "It's a miracle you found him last night."

"That was Phil Vail's work. He's always been our best scout."

Off to the side, Vail gave a two-fingered salute.

She stared at Butler as if uncertain if he were making fun. Then she shook her head — as though banishing an irritating fly — and asked, "Where's Philip?"

"Out on the waiting bench, trying to sleep. I told him the men and I would stand watch."

"The men and you," she said absently.

"Coffee?" he asked.

"I'd worship you. And food if we have any."

"I'll bring you a cup and then walk over to the

Broadwell Hotel. They let Doc charge for meals to go."

It took Butler longer than he thought, it being almost a half hour before he was back with a basket. It was going to be a hot day, one of those brassy-skied, bake-you-dry ones.

He slipped in the door, careful to open it slowly so the bell didn't wake Doc. The man looked uncomfortable with his head on the railing, his feet hanging off the far edge.

"Poor Doc," Johnny Baker noted as he followed Butler in. "He tries so hard."

Butler led the way into the surgery to find Sarah white-faced, her position on the couch changed. On the floor, the thunder mug was full.

"You should have waited for me," he told her. "I could have helped."

Her look was scathing. "Somehow, after working with Doc at the Angel's Lair, helping him examine the girls, and watching him dig a bullet out of my leg, it wasn't as embarrassing with him helping last night. He's a doctor. You . . . and your men? That's another matter."

"But you let so many strange men who . . ." He froze, quivered. Set the basket down and tried to stop the twitching in his hands as he went to check Billy's fevered breathing.

"Sometimes, Cap'n," Kershaw told him, "you jus' ain't smart."

"Sergeant, I don't need you to remind me of my shortcomings."

"It's all right, Butler." Sarah's voice was forgiving. "I've done what I've done. Philip told me to expect occasional, well, uncomfortable moments when talking to you. Now, why don't you stop torturing yourself and bring me that basket? And

963

while you do, you can tell me about this Indian princess of yours."

"She's not a princess." Avoiding her eyes, he set the basket on the examining table and began removing biscuits. "She's just a woman. I call her *gwee,* which means 'wife.' We have our own lodge and what you'd call a family. I really, really miss her. If it hadn't been for Paw, I'd have never come back."

Sarah took the plate he handed her. "What about us? Your family here? And Billy's back. We still haven't heard his story."

Butler glanced shyly at the men. "I only came back to tell Philip about Paw. I guess it was just luck that you and Billy showed. It was worth it to know how Maw got in that grave, and to see that you're alive. But I have to get back. There's winter to prepare for, and I have to make sure that everyone knows I properly disposed of Paw's evil."

"Are they that much better for you than we are?" She took a fork and stabbed at a sausage.

"They don't judge." Butler tried again to still his hands. "My wife loves me for who I am. She doesn't care if I'm crazy. And when I talk to the men, her eyes don't get that worried look. We laugh, and share, and hold each other. We work side by side, and it's . . . well . . ."

"Go on."

He wiped at a sudden pesky tear, his chest full as if to burst. "I *love* her! I really *miss* her, and I can't wait to get back."

Sarah was studying him with thoughtful eyes. "But Butler, Philip and I, we love you, too."

"Then I am doubly blessed. But Sarah, don't fight me on this. I'm going back. I have to."

The bell out front rang, a voice calling, "Sorry

964

to wake you, Doc. Can I have a word?"

"Marshal." Doc sounded groggy.

Butler walked to the surgery door, seeing Dave Cook, the city marshal.

"Don't look like the marshal got much sleep last night," Phil Vail noted.

"Neither did we," Pettigrew retorted.

Butler waved them down, noting the bland look on Cook's face. The man had a high forehead, straight nose, and a knobby chin — all emphasized by his full mustache. He wore a long linen coat over a colorful checkerboard-patterned vest, and baggy trousers. A polished leather gun belt hung at the man's hips.

"Doc?" Cook asked. "You got a man here? Young galoot, blond, maybe twenty? Might have a couple of gunshot wounds?"

Cook held out a paper flyer, that Doc took, asking, "That man look familiar?"

Doc rubbed a hand over his face as he studied the picture. "My brother Billy." Then his expression fell. "What's this wanted business? A reward? For murder?"

"It gets worse," Cook told him. "You ever hear of the Meadowlark?"

"The hired killer?" Doc asked. "Thought he was more myth than real?"

Cook took the flyer back. "If that's your brother, he was bragging to half the Criterion saloon that he was the Meadowlark. That he worked for George Nichols . . . doing his hired killing."

Doc looked sick, his face lining with worry. "My sister says Billy went after Nichols after the shooting at Sarah's yesterday."

"Well, he found him. Shot him down in the Criterion in front of about twenty witnesses.

Paused long enough to put a meadowlark feather in the bullet hole. Nichols was unarmed. Which, given what went on at Mrs. Anderson's, might have been justified. I'm not sure it even would have gone to trial. But on the way out, your brother shot and killed a bystander who tried to stop him. Fella by the name of Swede Halverson. Well liked by his friends."

Cook paused. "And then there's the warrant from End-of-the-Tracks."

Butler's heart was thumping, a hollow desperation beginning to ache. "Our Billy?"

Cook shot him a look. "So, you're back? Must be a Hancock family reunion."

Doc rose unsteadily to his feet. "Butler found Billy on the street last night. He's in the surgery. He was pretty shot up. Especially the hip. Femoral artery stopped the rifle ball without rupturing, if you can believe it."

"Doc." Cook lowered his voice. "I need to see him for myself."

"Of course, Dave." Doc led the way, Butler retreating and the men scattering to clear a path.

Cook removed his hat, nodded respectfully at Sarah where she sat frozen, a buttered biscuit halfway to her mouth, having no doubt heard the whole conversation.

"This is your brother? Billy Hancock?" Cook asked, matching the face with the drawing as he leaned over the comatose Billy.

"It is." Doc sounded half dazed.

Cook lifted the blanket, inspecting Billy's wounds. Then he asked, "Son, can you hear me?"

Doc replied, "Dave, he's drugged. It will be hours before —"

"Sssss awright, Doc," Billy whispered hoarsely,

blinking his eyes open. "I'm tougher than I look."

Sarah called, "Billy, you don't have to —"

"Sis," he rasped, "can't cheat the Devil forever. I been dreaming. Maw's rising from the grave, telling me it's time. She's coming to get me. Gonna drag me to hell where I b'long."

"Son, did you kill those men at End-of-the-Tracks?" Cook asked.

"Yep. And I left a string of dead whores behind me. Started with little gal named Margarita down to New Mexico. Thought she was Sarah's ghost . . . reaching . . . reaching down . . . And I'd try to kill her."

"I don't understand," Cook said.

"Isss th' demons." Billy licked dry lips, eyes vacant. "Ol' Hob had his joke on this child, didn't he?"

"And the Meadowlark murders?" Dave Cook leaned forward.

"Make you a deal, Marshal. When Philip fixes me up to where you can get me to a jail? You hand me a pistol with one shot. You do that . . . and I'll tell you the whole thing in front of a court recorder. Full confession."

"Billy!" Sarah snapped, struggling to stand. Face strained with pain, she wobbled forward on her wounded leg. "Don't you say a word! Not until you talk to Bela Hughes."

"Who?" Billy asked dryly, then waved it away with a feeble flip of the wrist. "Don't matter, sis. I been tempting the Devil to come get me. Took the lazy old shit way too long as it is. Just give me that one shot, Marshal, and the rest is all yours."

Butler waved the men down as they broke into a cacophony of questions and protests.

"Dear God," Philip whispered under his breath.

"Is this true?"

Billy smiled wearily, eyes closed. "Best hunting there ever was."

Dave Cook straightened. "Doc, you're a good man, and I hate to do this, but your brother is under arrest. How soon can he be moved?"

"Maybe a week depending on how bad the infection is," Doc said dully. "Especially in that pelvic wound."

Given the confusion in Doc's expression, Butler ached for him. He winced at the horror in Sarah's face as she stared disbelievingly at her brother. Billy and Sarah, they were the close ones.

"You give me your word, Doc?" Cook asked. "You won't let him out of here? Won't put your brother in a wagon some night and sneak him outta town?"

"You have my word, Marshal." Doc closed his eyes, looking as stricken as if he were denouncing Jesus in the garden.

"And mine as an officer and gentleman," Butler told him. "The men will follow my orders regarding my brother's disposition." He glanced at his men, all crowded and cowed in the back of the surgery. "Isn't that right?"

At their assent he added, "There, Marshal. See?"

The corners of Cook's mouth tightened, but he nodded and looked at Sarah.

She pursed her lips, eyes thinned in misery, and nodded.

127

July 2, 1868

Butler stood with his hands on his hips as he studied Sarah's parlor floor. He couldn't help but admire his work. The floorboards still had a slight discoloration in the grain — but only if a person knew what to look for. Had Parmelee's blood not sat for so long, he might have even managed to scrub that out.

The men had provided encouragement as he'd worked with the bristle brush, and they'd pointed out places he needed to concentrate on.

The sound of hammers and sawing reassured him. The workmen were back at it. A sign that Sarah's life was returning to normal for her. Or as normal as it would ever be again.

Life just seemed to kick her around.

He tossed the brush up and caught it, then stooped to pick up the rags he'd used to dry the floor. Walking into the dining room, he disposed of them in a bucket and went to pour a cup of coffee before seating himself at the table across from Sarah. Sunshine beamed in through the bay windows.

"Unless you know what to look for," he told her, "you'll never know it was there."

"I really appreciate it," she told him. "I feel guilty."

"You were shot in the leg. You can't be bending down and breaking that wound open. You worry us enough when you climb up and down the stairs."

"I wanted to sleep in my own bed. With my big revolver at hand." She drew a breath that thinned her nostrils. "Didn't entirely work. It's one thing to know that Parmelee and Nichols are dead, and another for the feeling of threat to go away." She glanced off to the side. "Assuming it ever really does."

Butler shrugged. "I lived in terror from the moment I was placed in command of Company A. I should never have agreed to lead the men up that hill." He shook his head. "Funny, isn't it? I can remember the charge, the Yankee guns and smoke and noise. And then it's a haze of dreamlike images. I remember pain. And then waking up among a group of prisoners and feeling such relief that so many of the men were still with me."

He glanced at where they lounged at the peripheries of the room. Several nodded in reply.

She rubbed her eyes, looking exhausted. "I think we're all crazy in one way or another. You hallucinate dead men to soothe your guilt. Philip's a suffering saint trying to save the world when he can't even save himself. I turned to prostitution as a way to punish myself for something that wasn't my fault. And Billy? My God, he's a . . ."

She knotted a fist, knuckles going white. "I should have stayed with him back at the trapper's cabin. But, damn it, Butler, I couldn't face it. Day after miserable day. Couldn't stand the way he'd look at me. It was the horror and pity in his eyes.

And then he brought Danny to see, to share . . ."

Butler stared into his coffee. "Maybe we're all bad seeds. Maybe that's why Maw stuck it out. She was trying so hard to turn us into good people, all the while wondering about the sins of the father, and wondering if they'd come home to roost."

"It would break her heart to know about Billy." Sarah stared dry-eyed into the distance. "And he knows it. That's why he goes on about his nightmares, about Maw rising from the grave. And God knows what part I play in them. He said I was naked and raped, and I reached for him. Damn, he won't even look at me when he talks about them. It must be so horrible . . ."

"It's partly my fault."

"Yours? How?"

"I should have talked Tom Hindman out of issuing Order Number 17 that created the partisan rangers. Of all the mistakes, that was the worst." Butler gestured in futility. "In the end we just turned the people loose on each other. There would have been no Dewley. No Darrow. So what if the Federals had taken the entire state back in sixty-two? Yankees were going to win in the end anyway; and you, Maw, and Billy would still be at the farm. The mills wouldn't have been burned, northwest Arkansas wouldn't have been turned into a wasteland. I could have stayed a staff officer, and maybe someone competent would have kept Company A from disaster."

Around him, the men were giving him a hollow-eyed look. Butler realized his heart was pounding. He swallowed hard and took a swig of coffee.

Sarah drummed her fingers on the table. "What would I change if I could go back? I'd shoot Dew-

971

ley off his horse the day he rode into the yard. Fight him off from the house, even if it meant they burned it down around Maw and me. But it would have saved me the rape and all that followed. Saved Billy the guilt. Kept him from having to find me like that. I think that's what really drove him crazy."

"You're the strong one, Sarah." He reached out and took her hand. "After I'm gone, Philip is going to need your strength. The men and I have discussed it. They are going to hang Billy. He's evil, and he knows it. But Doc is only going to see his little brother going to the gallows, and it's going to crucify his soul."

She met Butler's eyes and nodded. "Hell, it's going to be hard enough on me. I'm the cause of it, even though it wasn't my doing. Damn it! It was all I could do to save myself, let alone him."

"This is Billy we're talking about," Butler said softly. "He was bound to be a hellion. Maw knew. So did John Gritts. Paw might have had a hint, but he wouldn't have cared. Billy always hung on the edge. If the war hadn't come. If Gritts had stayed around, and Maw had been there for a guide, maybe they could have taken the sharp edges off Billy's nature. One thing I can tell you, he wasn't ever going to stay and be a farmer."

"You were going to be a scholar. Now what? You're going to be a wild Indian?"

He smiled at that. "Not wild. Just free. For as long as it lasts."

She pursed her lips. "I wish you wouldn't go. I've heard talk. The man Billy killed leaving the Criterion? Swede? He has friends. They're burying him tomorrow. There's talk of forming a vengeance committee."

"Dave Cook won't let them." Butler glanced at the men, reading their expressions. Pettigrew tilted his head, as if indicating it was time to head north. "I know, Corporal. We've been away too long already."

To Sarah he said, "A couple of days. Just long enough to get to know you again, and maybe talk to Doc about Billy. Then we're heading north."

He thought her eyes had changed. More of a steely blue now. Harder. After his last visit to the farm he'd left hoping that Sarah would one day be the dreamy-eyed girl he'd known before the war. Before blood and dying men. Before the famine and hard times. Instead, after fate had played its hand, she'd become this beautiful, tough, and calculating woman. God help the man who tried to cross her.

She said, "I can promise you one thing: I don't know how, but one way or another, I'm not letting Billy hang."

128

July 3, 1868

The pain was down to a dull ache, except when Billy moved. Then it blasted through him like lightning, causing his eyes to water and his guts to squirm. A part of him cussed and fretted about being laid up like this. All that time, all those fights, and he'd never so much as been scratched. Now Philip told him he'd never walk without crutches. His physician brother might fret about the wound in Billy's ass, but the one that played hell was the two smashed ribs that had stopped one of the pistol balls. If he so much as drew a breath too fast, his chest stitched itself in agony.

And God help him if he sneezed or coughed.

Billy glanced sidelong at where Philip sat at the small desk. In the glow of a coal oil lamp he was reading a medical journal. Not much more than a pamphlet that Doc subscribed to from Boston.

"What time is it?" Billy asked.

Doc pulled his pocket watch. "A little after eight."

"Got to take a leak."

"Well, do it." Doc looked over from his journal. "That's why you're on the table with the hole in it."

Billy made a face, letting go and listening to his urine dribbling into the thunder mug under the table.

"Hell of a circumstance," he muttered under his breath.

"Believe me, you really don't want to try and stand up and urinate like a man."

Doc set his medical pamphlet aside, stepped over, and removed the chamber pot. Eyes thoughtful, he inspected the pot's contents. "Good, the bleeding in your bruised kidney has slowed. You're healing."

"Wish t' hell that bastard had used a bigger gun."

"If it hadn't been a .32, it would have killed you, little brother."

"That's the point I was trying to make."

Billy waited while Doc went out back to the jakes and emptied the pot. When he came back in and replaced it, he studied Billy with pained eyes. Damn, did he have to look that way? Half crazy with worry?

"What?"

"I can understand you going after Dewley's rapists. I'd have done the same." Doc pulled his chair over and sat where he could look Billy in the eyes. "But the first time you took money to kill someone? You *had* to know that was a step over the line."

Billy smiled faintly, thinking back to Charlie Deveroux. "That was Texas. It was war and war's paybacks. The man I killed was the enemy, a skunk who'd used his position to kill others and take their property. Wasn't much of a moral line to step over."

Billy slowly shifted his good arm. "See, the thing

975

is, I could have looked all I wanted to, and I never would have seen no line, Doc. It's like what shade of pink is the difference between white and red? And one day it just plumb hits you that you're something you never quite thought you'd be. And you know what? You're already damned by then, so what the hell?"

"When did these dreams about Maw and Sarah start?"

"After I found Maw's body. She come that night and damned me. Told me I done let her down." He ground his teeth. "Hell, seems I was always letting her down one way or another. I just never could be the boy she wanted me to be. But that day I found her dying in the house? I knew there wasn't no forgiving me for nothing after that."

"I think you wrong her. The woman who raised me wouldn't condemn you for not being there to be killed when the bushwhackers rode in. She'd have wanted you to rescue Sarah. To live."

Billy used his good hand to make a fist and prop his chin so he could see Doc better. "Maybe. But things changed when you left. She and Paw went at each other. Not tooth and nail like bobcats in a bag, but cold and hard and silent. Paw moved his bed into the spare room. That's when she really come down on me. 'Don't you become a wastrel like your paw, boy!' she told me one time when I didn't get the chicken coop cleaned out."

He grinned. "Tarnal hell, what's chicken shit compared to a two-day hunt with John Gritts?"

Doc sighed. "Butler told me that she knew about Paw and Sally Spears. You heard that story?"

"Somehow I missed that one. Reckon it would explain some things, though."

Philip hesitated. "Tell me about these dreams

you have. I understand Maw rising from the grave. But what about the one with Sarah? You said she was naked and raped."

Billy chewed his lips and frowned. Did he dare tell?

What the hell, you're already dead and dying.

"You promise me what I tell you is atwixt you and me, and no other? And never, on your holy honor, do you mention a word of this to Sarah?"

"I give you my word." Doc laid a hand on his heart.

Billy exhaled slowly so as not to hurt his ribs. "I'm laying on my back, buck-assed naked, and Sarah rises up looking like she did at Dewley's camp. She's stripped bare. All covered with bites and bruises, and from her privates . . . well, you can tell she's been used hard. Her hair's mussed and blowing like in a wind. She walks over, looks down at me with hell-burning eyes, and reaches down. I can't stop her when she lays hold of my johnson. And then she lowers herself and . . ."

Billy swallowed. "Well, hell, Doc. There ain't no way fittin' to talk about it. I just wake up shamed and hating myself. Sometimes I go through weeks of it. Dreams of Maw, dreams of Sarah. Sometimes the whores I killed change faces with Sarah. You see, I got the Devil inside, and he tortures me something fierce."

Doc sat silently, a frown lining his forehead.

Billy made a face. "Devil's been in me since the day I walked into Dewley's camp and shot those bastards down."

"How do you know that?"

" 'Cause I could *feel* him in my chest, Doc. I didn't have no fear, didn't have a hesitation. He was there, making sure I done it right. I don't remember giving him my soul in return for getting Sarah out, but he must have known I'da said yes if he'd a bothered to ask."

Doc rubbed his face, as if exhausted. "I don't know that I can stall Marshal Cook, but I have some influential friends. Men who, for a price, can probably get you out of Denver. It will —"

"Thought you give your word to that marshal."

"You're my brother, Billy."

"Fuck that! Did you hear a word I said? I'm tired of hurting all the time. I've lived with hell bottled in me for too long now." He blinked back tears. "There ain't no happy ending out there. Ain't no redemption. I want the hurting to stop. *I just want it over!*"

"Billy, there are places that might be able —"

The bell in the front rang.

"Hold that thought. We'll pick it up when I get back."

Billy watched his brother rise and hurry through the door.

Goddamn you, Philip. Last thing I need is some damn hero figuring he's a-gonna be a fucking saint.

Billy couldn't hear the words out front, spoken as low as they were. He heard what sounded like a bench being shifted. Some soft thumps. Most likely someone injured being laid out.

He closed his eyes, trying to keep from breathing hard and hurting. All of life had funneled down to a desperate hope that in return for that damn confession, Dave Cook would give him that one shot. It wasn't such an impossible thing to ask for. Why the hell stretch it out?

He heard Doc coming back, his boots scuffing on the floor.

Billy opened his eyes, staring into someone's

belly: a check-patterned linen vest with brass buttons partially covered with a polished gun belt, the holster empty.

Billy winced as he turned his head, looking up at a stranger. Revolver in hand, the man stared down with hard brown eyes. A mustache flared over wide lips. Homburg-style hat set forward on his head. Then more came flooding in. Maybe ten altogether. Most had bandanas over their faces, some wore bags over their heads with cutouts for eyes.

"Who'er you?" Billy asked.

"Friends of Swede Halverson's." The man's smile carried no humor. "You know why we're here?"

Billy swallowed hard. "Yep. And if you can't get this job done right and fast I'm calling you all a bunch of bleeding cunts."

Someone shoved a wad of cloth into his mouth. Quick hands tied his ankles together. His scream died in the gag as they jerked his arms behind him and bound them.

He would have smiled as the hard hands grabbed onto him, but pain blasted hot and white through his chest and shoulder.

As they carried him to the front, he was relieved to see Philip, hands and feet tied to the bench, a gag in his mouth. His brother's panicked eyes met his, and Billy found the courage to shoot him a wink in return.

And then they were out into the night.

Billy was thrown into the back of a wagon; his muffled scream elicited no response. Damn, that hurt! It brought tears to his eyes.

Then the wagon started forward.

Fuck you, Devil! He kept repeating it over and

over in his head. Like a prayer. The way he'd heard that the Catholic monks did in their monasteries.

He heard the horses and wagon cross onto a hollow bridge, and the driver called "whoa" as he pulled to a stop. Was it no more than a couple of minutes that had passed?

Billy lost his senses — blinded by pain as they tossed him from the wagon and onto the bridge. Claws might have been tearing his wounds in all directions.

He was gasping, pulling at the gag in his mouth, sucking all the air he could through his nostrils.

Fear had finally come to claim him, his bowels loose, heart hammering.

The rope was cool as they placed it around his neck, and he flinched as they jerked the knot tight.

He was lifted. Heard a weird wail coming from his throat. Then they tossed him out, body flopping.

For a moment, he fell. Weightless.

He heard the pop as lightning flashed, blinding and eternal . . .

129

July 4, 1868

Sarah used the toe of her shoe to close the damp-ers on the cookstove in her kitchen, and winced as it pulled at the wound in her thigh. With a hot pad she shifted the fry pan to the side and dished out fried eggs mixed with bacon, thin-sliced potatoes, and bits of fresh red pepper and onion.

She tried not to limp as she carried the plates into the dining room. Butler sat, elbows propped on her table. A cup of coffee steamed in his hands as he stared out the window. Her dirt yard was il-luminated by the slanted light of dawn, the distant horizon green.

"I do appreciate you staying here last night," she told him as she eased into her chair. "The few times I woke up in the night, all I had to do was remind myself that you were in the next room. I think that's the best night's sleep I've had in years."

"And this is the best breakfast I've had in years," he told her. "Well, maybe right up there with the buffalo tongue stew that Mountain Flicker makes when the sego lilies are fresh." His expression warmed. "I know she'd hate it here, but I wish she was with me."

"You really do love her, don't you?"

"Were I Sir Walter Scott I would write epic poetry about her."

"I'm lucky enough when I can write a check without errors." She had just picked up her fork when the banging came at the door.

"Oh, sit," she told Butler. "If I don't use this leg, it's going to stiffen. Besides, it's probably just one of the workmen arrived early."

Still, as she hitched her way to the front door she reached back, reassured that the pocket revolver in her bustle was easily at hand. All it took was a jerk on the bow and the holster pocket opened to expose the pistol grip.

At the door, she undid the bolt and opened it, stepping back.

To her surprise, Dave Cook stood there, hat in hand, his coat open to expose his badge. "Mrs. Anderson," he greeted. A tightness lay behind his eyes, his expression pinched.

"Marshal? Can I help you?"

"Is your brother here?"

"We're just having breakfast. If you'd care to join . . ." She saw his expression harden. "What's happened?"

"If you wouldn't mind, Doc's down at his surgery. He's a bit banged up, but he's going to be fine. It's about Billy, ma'am. I'm afraid some of the boys formed a vigilance committee last night. His body was found this morning hanging from the Lawrence Street Bridge."

The world seemed to sway. She could imagine the scene, had seen it before. Vigilantes liked using the Lawrence Street Bridge. The drop was far enough to break the neck, the railing sturdy enough to take the weight. In the morning the corpse would be seen by many, hanging limp, the head to the side, eyes bugged, tongue stuck out like a swollen plumb.

Not Billy!

She turned, feeling sick. "Butler! Hurry! We have to go."

"What about breakfast?" he called.

"Leave it. Something's happened to Billy!" She turned just long enough to grab her bonnet, and thrust Butler's reprehensible hat into his hands as she hobbled her way out and down the stairs to Cook's spring wagon.

"Tell me what happened?" she demanded as she climbed painfully into the seat and arranged her bustle. Butler had clambered into the back and was carrying on a disjointed conversation with his men.

"Butler, stop it!" she told him. "Now quiet the men and listen."

Dave Cook slapped the reins, saying, "According to Doc, they walked into his office last night just after dark. Someone shoved a shotgun under his chin, and others gagged him and tied him up. Then they went in and carried Billy out."

"Did he recognize any of them?" Sarah asked, a cold anger building.

"No. Doc said they were hooded when they came in."

"And Billy?"

"It was quick and clean. I had him taken down first thing. He's at John Walley's. Soon as I saw to him, I hotfooted to Doc's. Got him untied and had Doc Elsner check him out. He's hopping mad and blaming himself."

Cook stuck a finger under Sarah's nose. "Wasn't a damn thing he could'a done. Not unless he'd'a got his fool head blown off fighting with that shotgun."

"God . . . not Billy," Sarah whispered. "When does it ever end?"

"Right here and now," Cook told her. "Sarah, you think about this long and hard! You know damn well that I've got contacts all over the territory through the Detectives Association. So I know what Parmelee did to you and your husband. Parmelee's dead. I know Nichols was up to no good at your place. Your brother's gone and killed him. But Billy sure as hell had no business shooting Swede. And he told me he killed them track layers. Now he's paid."

She glared into his hard eyes.

"You following me, Sarah?" he demanded. "I know he was kin, but the balance is paid. You gonna give me your word that you'll let a sleeping dog lie? Or do I gear up for a string of vendetta killings that tears this city apart?"

Sarah ground her teeth.

"Where does it end?" Dave Cook asked softly as they pulled up in front of Doc's. A small crowd had gathered, all talking among themselves.

"All right," she lied, her heart like a stone in her chest. "It ends here."

Dave seemed to smell her rat. His eyes narrowed. Then he asked, "What about you, crazy man? You give me your word as, what was it you said? An officer and a gentleman?"

"If Sarah does," Butler said softly. He paused, his voice changing as it did when he talked to the men. "It's because of Paw, Corporal. Everything goes back to Paw."

Sarah eased her wounded leg down from the seat, ignoring the onlookers, and limped, seething, into Doc's office.

He sat in his chair behind the desk, cheek propped on a hand. She could see the raw red where his bonds had chafed the skin on his wrists.

"Philip? Are you all right?"

"I'll never be all right." He looked at her, a desolate emptiness behind his pale eyes. "He winked at me as they were carrying him out. The way they were holding him, it had to hurt like thunder, but he winked at me. Told me it was all right."

She stepped forward. "In a pig's eye. They *lynched* our brother!" She glanced back to see Butler closing the door behind him. Through the window she could see Dave Cook driving away. "I'll need to have a talk with Big Ed and have his —"

"Let it go, Sarah," Doc whispered.

"Philip?"

"These stranglers? What they did? It was a kindness."

"Are you as crazy as Butler?"

He shook his head. "I'm as sane as I've ever been." A flicker of a smile died. "After the things he told me? I'd make a terrible priest. I'd wave my hand and say, 'Go forth, my child, and throw your sinning soul off the nearest cliff.' "

She struggled for words, trying to understand.

"Billy was *hurting,* Sarah." Philip seemed to choke back tears. "Deep down in his soul. In a place where there was no healing. He wanted it over."

"How do you know?"

"Because he told me. Because I have been there. So many times." He raised a hand, stalling her protest. "Sarah, the difference is that I wasn't

985

haunted by the men and women I'd murdered. I might have been miserable when I wanted to die, but I wasn't condemned by my own self-loathing."

"Holy sweet Jesus," she murmured, dropping limply onto the bench. "What did I do to him when I left him?"

"Nothing," Doc told her. "If you've got to go back to the beginning, it was when I caught Paw with Sally. Hell, maybe it goes clear back to him marrying Maw."

"Or back to the mountains," Butler said. His gaze flicked to the side. "You heard him, Sergeant, he started destroying people early on."

Sarah clamped her hands against her ears, leaning forward, feeling sick. Moments later she felt Doc settle beside her, his arm going around her shoulder.

"Someone needs to see to arrangements for Billy," Butler said, walking over to the desk. "He's going to need a coffin. This time of year, warm as it is, we don't want to tarry. Since it's the Fourth of July, John Walley won't be staying at his office for long. He's going to need to find gravediggers. I'll see if we can't have the service tomorrow."

Sarah was barely aware of Butler pulling Doc's drawer open, removing the cash box. Her soul felt as if it were bruised, raw, and floating. There were things she needed to tell Billy. Confessions of the heart she would never be able to make now.

Butler rifled through the cash box, rattling coins, and stuffed his pocket full. Then he closed the tin box, replaced it, and shut the drawer.

"I'll be back," he promised, before shooting a glance at the men. Then he was gone, the bell ringing as he closed the door.

Doc pulled his arm tighter around Sarah's

shoulders as they sat in silence. Not since Bret had held her had any human offered her comfort.

God, I'm lonely.

And sad.

And tired.

She was wondering when it would ever end. Which was when Doc jerked upright, every muscle going tense. "The box!"

Sarah shifted. "What box?"

But Doc was on his feet, flying to the desk, clawing at the drawer. He ripped out the cash box, opened it, and stared in horror.

"Doc? What's wrong?" she demanded.

"He's got the candy!"

His face blanched with panic, Doc flung himself at the door. Wrenching it open, he raced out into the morning, crying, "No! Dear God, No!"

130

Butler tried to ignore the men as they trooped along at the edge of his vision. The saloons were going full blast. With the exception of the merchants trying to capitalize on folks come to town for the holiday, most businesses were closed. Horses, buggies, and carriages didn't exactly clog the streets, but traffic was brisk.

The sound of Federal martial music filled the air. He could tell it bothered the men, but secession and the war had forever changed the way the Fourth was celebrated. And Denver had been a Union town, having spawned the Colorado Volunteers.

Butler could feel Kershaw hanging just behind him and out of sight as he made his way down the boardwalk, tipping his hat on occasion to the ladies, and trying to sort out the conflicting emotions in his breast.

Ruffians had murdered his brother in the night. Tied a rope around his neck and tossed him off a bridge. God knew he'd seen plenty of that during the war. Even been party to it when it came to deserters and spies.

It wasn't as if young Billy hadn't deserved it. If

Butler stood back from his roiling emotions, thought about Swede Halverson, about the men Billy had murdered for money, and God forbid, about the prostitutes he'd strangled in fits of madness, it was high time he paid the ultimate price.

"But he's my brother!"

Images swam through his memory. Billy as an infant, cradled in Maw's arms. The two-footed bundle of trouble he'd been when he was two. The time he'd stolen Butler's jackknife and laid his hand open "knife fighting" with imaginary raiding Choctaws. He'd been what? Eight? As Billy had grown older, he'd pitched in with the farmwork, taken on his share of the chores. When he worked, he worked hard. By the time he'd been ten, he could best Butler when it came to putting up tobacco or corn. And John Gritts had been taking him out hunting since he was little. No one could track, stalk, or fill a larder with game the way Billy could.

"That child!" Maw's voice came unbidden from the past. "I swear, he'll put me in my grave! If he ain't the spittin' image of his paw, I don't know doodle when I see it."

And strangers took him, and hung him.

"My fault," Butler whispered, stepping around a family that had stopped to stare into a store window. "Mine and Tom Hindman's. We made Arkansas into the kind of battleground it was. We were the ones who unleashed the whirlwind. Once Maw was dead and Sarah raped, what did Billy have left but raiding and ambushing?"

"Don't you go puttin' all de blame on yorseff, Cap'n." Kershaw's deep voice rumbled. "*Avec certitude,* yor brother make his own decisions."

"Can't live no other man's life for 'im," Corporal Pettigrew agreed from behind. "Ain't yer fault, Cap'n."

"What would have been different if I'd been there?"

"Reckon nothin'," Vail called from the side. "Somebody would'a conscripted your sorry hide, Cap'n. They'd'a made you fight, one way or t'other."

He turned onto Larimer Street and made his way to 1412 where Walley did his undertaking business. He hammered on the door. Then hammered again.

"Coming!" The cry was barely audible over the noise in the crowded street. Two open-air bands were playing. One down by Cherry Creek, the other up on Sixteenth. Nor was Larimer Street short on saloons, each with its door open to allow piano and horn music to spill out in hopes of luring additional patrons.

John J. Walley unlocked his door, staring out at Butler. "Yes?"

"I'm Butler Hancock. Come to see about Billy. Dave Cook's deputies brought his body in this morning." He took a breath, trying to still his grief. "I'm one of his brothers."

"Ah yes, come in." Walley closed the door behind him. "I haven't prepared the body yet. What did the family have in mind?"

"Just a quiet burial tomorrow morning." Butler tried to keep his hands from twitching like butterflies. "I hear that Doc buried his wife out at the boneyard. Maybe next to her?"

Walley lifted an eyebrow. "You familiar with the hill out there? It's three hundred and twenty acres. The top of the hill is . . . well, for our better citizenry. One section is Jewish, another Catholic. Dr. Hancock's wife, given his reputation in the community, is on the edge of that higher ground. It's rather more expensive than the area off to the southeast." He shrugged slightly. "Your brother Billy, having been involved in a shooting, claiming to be this Meadowlark —"

"How much for him to lie next to Mrs. Hancock?"

"Fifty dollars for the plot, a fir coffin, the excavation, and refilling the grave. Another twenty for embalming if you want it. Ten more if you want me to make the deceased presentable for a viewing."

"Can I see him?"

"Mr. Hancock, I haven't had time to —"

"Would I be seeing anything I haven't seen on the battlefield? No? Then let me see my brother, please."

Walley led the way through the front office and into the back. Butler felt his skin crawl at the sight of a woman laid out on her back, a series of tubes actually inserted into her veins and attached to a hand pump atop a brass tank.

He'd never seen embalming before. Wasn't sure he wanted to know any more about it.

Billy lay on a stained pine table just inside the big sliding rear door. At the sight, Butler stopped short. His brother's eyes were open and bulged, his tongue jammed out, the jaw dislocated, broken, and lopsided. Billy's neck — oddly elongated, the skin chafed — looked unnatural, and for reasons Butler couldn't quite understand, reminded him of a plucked turkey neck.

"I can make him look like he's just asleep," Walley said softly.

Butler drew a short breath. "No need, sir. Closed coffin. No embalming." Butler reached in his pocket, pulling out coins. In the dim light he sorted through them, finding two twenty-dollar gold pieces and a ten. "There's fifty for the lot and the rest."

He dropped what remained in his pocket — all except the piece of hard candy he'd found in Doc's cash box. That he cradled in his hand, thinking it inappropriate to pop it into his mouth when his brother lay there, cold, covered with a sheet, after having been viciously executed by hooded and masked stranglers.

"I'll leave you alone, sir." Walley retreated on silent feet.

"Well, Billy," Butler said softly, "they sure played hell this time, didn't they?" He reached out, pulled the sheet back so he could hold Billy's cold hand. "It's too late to ask now, but I hope you'll forgive me for my part in all this."

He sniffed, feeling an unfamiliar hole emptying in his heart. So this was what it was like to grieve?

"I'm going to tell Doc and Sarah not to come. I don't think it would do any good for them to see you like this. Instead, I'll say good-bye for all of us."

He sniffed. "I wish . . . I wish we would have had the chance to talk. Like in the old days. Remember all those insane and impossible stories you told? How they made me laugh? I just wish we'd had the chance to do that again. One last time."

He closed his eyes, whispering, "I will miss that."

He patted Billy's hand, and turned to go.

Butler had passed the woman on the table with

her tubes and pumps when he remembered the candy cupped in his hand.

131

Doc ran as he had never run in his life. Arms pumping, feet flying. His leather-soled shoes slipped on the boardwalk. People stared at him in surprise as he careened through them, many diving out of the way at the last moment. He crashed into others, only to stumble before charging on.

"Move!" he screamed at the top of his lungs. "Out of the way! Emergency!"

As he ran, lungs burning, he cursed himself for the despicable idiot that he was. What vile failing of character had caused him to concoct that deadly candy in the first place?

Let alone leave it in the cash drawer!

Butler, please! Tell me you kept it for later!

He brutally plowed through a gaggle of children, knocking one or two sprawling, hearing bursts of crying behind him, mixed with shouts.

Let them curse him! Hate him for being a brute.

Wasn't a candle to how he hated himself.

Let me make it in time!

Just the fact that he hadn't stumbled onto a crowd gathered about Butler's dead body was cause for hope. His brother must have put it in a pocket for later.

God, don't let him eat it! Please!

Tears were running down his cheeks, adding to the dismay in people's faces as he gasped and panted his way, arms out.

"Move!"

"Out of the way!"

He slipped as he rounded the corner onto Larimer Street, fell, tore his hand and knee on the boardwalk. Bowling to his feet, he knocked a woman onto her butt. She was screaming, a man pounded along behind Doc, shouting threats.

Beat me senseless later.

And God, yes, the man could have him. Cane him to within an inch of his life, or beyond, for all Doc cared.

At Walley's, he grasped the doorknob, wrenched it open, and hurtled inside. Walley gaped, sitting at his desk, a cash box open before him.

"Butler! Where is he!"

Walley had just opened his mouth, pointing to the rear as Doc vaulted a chair and straight-armed the door.

Please, God! Please.

"Butler!" he bellowed. "For God's sake, don't eat that candy!"

And then he was in the back, sliding to a stop.

Staring.

Eyes wide, arms out.

"Dear God," he whispered through sucking pants, sinking to his knees.

132

September 28, 1868

Butler wondered if he'd ever been this tired and out of breath. His ribs and belly ached, each heaving breath feeling for all the world like it was tearing his lungs out of his chest.

He paused, struggling for air in the high altitude. Spots flashed before his eyes as he dragged a sleeve over his sweaty forehead. Blinking to clear his vision, he looked out across the high, gray peaks, lines of them, growing ever more distant until they faded into the horizon. Snow already whitened the northern slopes, the southern exposures having been melted by the slanting fall sun.

A cool wind tugged at him from out of the west as he thought, *This is how God sees the world. To do so is to be blessed.*

Mountain after mountain, peak after ragged peak, the long, timber-clad slopes slanting off to the blue-gray sage-blanketed basins. And in the bottoms, the dark green meandering line of the Wind River, marked as it was by cottonwoods and willows. This was the view commanded by eagles, and now it was his.

"You coming?" Cracked Bone Thrower asked,

grinning, his white teeth shining in his brown face. "Or are you just another lazy *taipo*? Come to buy favor and lay with one of our women because you have the wealth to do it?"

"Never," Butler puffed, resettling the freshly gutted sheep carcass on his shoulders. He could feel the animal's blood draining onto his bare shoulders; the sweet pungency filled his nostrils. He'd smelled enough blood tainted by unjust death on the battlefields. This, in contrast, was the blood of life. This death would feed his *naatea* through the long winter months. And in return the people offered their thanks to souls of the sheep who had died that they might live.

Butler's shoulders were already streaked and smeared with caked sheep blood. After the last of the carcasses had been carried down to where the women were butchering, he would scoop up handfuls of snow from the big drift. Half stunned by the cold shock, and with Flicker's help, he would sponge the blood and gore from his naked body.

"Little children have better wind than you do!" Cracked Bone Thrower called over his shoulder.

"I've been down in the flatlands," Butler protested. "Doing *taipo* things! They are all lazy. You've told me that so often, you should believe it yourself. Once I train my lungs, the men and I can outwork you all."

He shot a sidelong glance at the men where they had seated themselves on rocks and in places in the sun. That was the thing about being crazy. His men never changed, never looked any more ragged in their holey and tattered uniforms. They didn't look bedraggled in the rain, never cared for their rifles or gear. They didn't shiver in the cold.

And, like today, they never did any work.

Sometimes he wondered about the rules of his madness. The men were never in his lodge. Never watching or making comments when he and Mountain Flicker were locked together under the robes.

Sometimes — when he was particularly happy — they vanished for long periods of time.

Because, as Water Ghost Woman taught me, I no longer need them. Then, later, they just appeared as if nothing had happened.

That had been the case ever since his return from Denver. As if, having cast off the last links to the white world, he had found a growing peace of mind. His madness didn't matter when he was surrounded by people who didn't care if he kept the dead around when he needed a shield.

In addition, his hallucinations seemed to recede in intensity following a session in the sweat lodge, or in the days after he had gone with Puhagan in search of a spirit vision.

For the moment, however, he needn't think about that. It took all of his concentration to pick his way down the trail to the snow patch. His muscles were trembling, knees shaking. But in the end, he waded out into the mushy snow and dropped the ram's gutted carcass. With bloody hands he scooped snow into the gut cavity to cool the carcass and straightened.

Mountain Flicker worked at Red Rain's side just down the slope. He shot her a happy smile. She grinned back, pausing to push back a strand of long black hair. Her finger left a bloody streak on her smooth cheek.

Butler scooped up a handful of snow for himself, packing it in his mouth and crunching it for the water it contained. Then he walked down to crouch beside Mountain Flicker. She had half skinned an ewe, and was competently running her knife around the connective tissue as she pulled with a firm brown hand.

"How are you?" he asked.

"Happy," she told him, a twinkle in her dark eyes. "We will have plenty of meat for the winter. And that rack you made allowed me to dry more than enough of the roots, leaves, and flowers. We had a good harvest of white-bark pine seeds. Best of all are the cactus tunas. A lot of them this year. You'll like them. Very sweet. Like *taipo* candy."

Butler grinned at that. He liked candy. Which made him think back to Doc crashing into the undertaker's, throwing his arms out and falling to his knees, face tear streaked, as he cried, *"Don't eat that damn piece of candy!"*

"You laugh?" she asked.

"And my brother calls me crazy."

"Tonight I shall make you crazy." She winked at him and wiggled her hips suggestively.

"And why is that?"

"It has been a half moon since my woman's blood. I have the tenderness and the craving." She wiggled her hips again. "This is the best time for your seed to make *dudua'nee.* A child. I've been waiting."

"So have I," he told her, standing. "But for the moment I had better climb back up to the trap and haul down another sheep for you to skin. If you're going to grow a child, you'll need the meat. And Cracked Bone Thrower already accuses me of being a lazy *taipo.*"

Butler chuckled to himself, turned, and started up the steep slope to the kill pen.

Glancing toward where the men of Company A

lingered, he said, "Reckon you all won't mind that if it's a boy, I'll call him Billy? No? Good, 'cause being crazy, I can do any damn thing I like."

In the west a line of clouds were bunched on the tops of the Tetons, and he thought he smelled rain on the wind. Somewhere down in the timber, an elk bugled, its sweet high strains carrying on the fall air. The scent of lodge-pole, fir, and spruce mingled with the last of the fall flowers. Around him, the mountains seemed to pulse with life.

Once, he would have been a gentleman scholar as his father had wished. Then a war had come and gone, and here he stood, defiant of the odds, a wild man awash in liberty.

He shook his head, lungs straining in the thin air. "And those fool secessionists thought they were fighting to be free? Tom, we had no idea, did we?"

133

October 1, 1868

Sarah lit the lamps and checked the clock. Doc should have been here by now. She walked to the window, peered past the curtains, and checked the dark street below. A misty drizzle was falling, the effect haloed in the streetlamps. The cobblestones reflected lights from the houses lining the street.

Three stories high, of frame construction, her house perched on the hill overlooking the city. On a clear day she could see across the span of San Francisco Bay to the distant uplands beyond. She'd painted her mansion a bright yellow, the windows and trim done in white. Protruding bay windows allowed her the opportunity to enjoy the splendid view, and she enjoyed reading in the light of the afternoon sun, a cup of tea near at hand.

Commensurate with her wealth, she had furnished it with the finest of Oriental carpets, brass lights, and furniture crafted from exotic tropical woods. The entire first floor, she'd given to Philip. One room he had dedicated to his study, another to his growing medical library. And its street access made it easier for him to respond to late-night emergencies at the hospital.

He should have been here by now. And yes, here he came. In the light of the gas lamps, Philip's tall and lanky frame couldn't be mistaken as he climbed the sidewalk. On the cobble-paved street, a horse-drawn barouche clattered past, a couple holding hands in the backseat.

Sarah breathed out her relief. When Doc was late, it always worried her. While they lived in one of the better neighborhoods, Philip had insisted on having his surgery down by the wharves.

"There's no one close," he had told her. "Besides, I can see to the houses down there."

"What about a more well-to-do clientele, Philip? You're a *real* physician. A mountain and a mile beyond most of the charlatans practicing in San Francisco."

"Sarah, I do my share of surgeries at the hospital, but I've found my calling and place." He had smiled wistfully. "Once I thought as you do. I wanted to be rich and respected. A man of such prominence I could look down my nose at Paw. I've paid the price for my arrogance and pride. My only goal now is to alleviate suffering."

The irony was that, as her brother, he had that standing — though he had yet to recognize it. Every time he escorted her to the opera. Or the theater. Or a musical production. San Francisco's greatest would stare speculatively at the man upon whose arm Sarah's hand rested, and say, "There go Dr. Hancock and his lovely sister, Sarah."

And she was lovely, dressed in the latest of high fashion from London, Paris, and Italy. As the richest woman in the city, she made it a point to be among the best dressed. Of course the men came flocking, only to find her politely intimidating, and forever disinterested in their favors.

Another ultimate irony. She was surrounded and desired by the kind of men Paw would have salivated to have her marry. Men for whom she had no interest or desire.

If there was one thing Sarah knew, it was men. In all of their guises, strengths, and weaknesses.

She had loved, and been loved, by a real man. Once. Which was good enough for any lifetime.

She arched an eyebrow, stepped back from the window, and hurried to the kitchen. There, she pulled the roasted salmon from the warming shelf above the stove. A puff of steam rose, carrying scents of curry, saffron, and cilantro as she lifted the lid on the roasting pan.

She was just pouring the wine when Philip entered, hanging his hat on the rack and shrugging out of his black wool coat.

"Interesting day?" she asked.

"Quite," Doc told her, slapping the newspaper onto the table by the foyer. "Sorry I'm late. Had a last-minute patient. Man with a crushed foot."

"Supper is ready. Wash up. Water's on the stove."

"Where is Molly?"

"I let all of the servants go home early."

She arranged her crimson satin dress with its bustle-holstered revolver, and seated herself. She lifted the roaster's lid and began spooning out sweet potatoes. Another of the wonders they'd found in San Francisco: foods available nowhere else. Things like fresh fruits and vegetables brought in by ship from South America. Remarkable fish, oysters, and clams. Epicurean delights and spices from the Orient. After the deprivations in Arkansas and Denver, it was culinary magic.

Doc dried his hands and seated himself. "I was thinking of Butler all day." He gestured to the

1003

paper. "Do you remember General Tom Hindman?"

"Butler's commander?"

Doc nodded. "After the war he escaped to Mexico with a lot of the other Confederates. It didn't work out, and he went back to Arkansas. Was making a political comeback. A couple of nights ago he was sitting in his parlor easy chair. Someone shot him through the window. He died a couple of hours later." He paused. "I wonder what Butler would think?"

She studied him in the lamplight, seeing the lines in his face — as if they were scars from his wounded but poorly healed soul. Lost love, dead friends, shot-mangled bodies, the hell of prison camp and disease, and then his struggle through the ruins of their world. It had left her brother a fragile and cracked human being.

"Butler would cry for him, Philip. You know that. Some souls are too good for this world."

"If they'd just left him alone. Let him be a professor of history. Maybe we'd still have him." Guilt tightened his expression. "Poor deluded soul, what do his wild Indians give him that we couldn't?" He knotted a fist. "Damn that war for what it did to him." A pause. "For what it did to all of us."

In the following silence, she thought back to Pea Ridge, to the boys dying on the farmhouse floor. To starvation and Dewley, Billy, and her flight to Fort Smith. She smiled at the memory of Bret's eyes, and of the desperate flight to Colorado. And everything that culminated in Billy's body hanging from a bridge.

"If I could go back" — she balanced her fork — "I would throw the secessionists like Hindman,

Jeff Davis, and the rest right into hell. And just as soon as they'd dropped into the flames, I'd shovel John Brown, Abe Lincoln, Grant, and the rest of the Black Republicans straight in after them. Let them scream and burn together."

Doc's gaze went distant. "So much could have been so different if the Federals had just let the Southern states go. James would be alive. So much suffering . . ." He shook his head. "Water under the bridge."

"Slavery is gone."

"And the murder of a half million men, and the maiming of millions more, the destruction, the looting, and burning of half the country was the *only* way we could find to end it?" He gestured with his butter knife. "That's the *best* we could do? As a species we're condemned to self-immolation."

She arched an eyebrow. "Maybe my next investment should be in matches?"

"Mark my words." Doc cut a bite of salmon. "Tom Hindman won't be the last. If I know my brethren, the smoldering hatred in Southern hearts is going to burn for generations. They've been humiliated. They're going to make the freed blacks suffer for it in the end, no matter what kind of promises the Yankees make."

She shook her head. "God, Doc, just once, can't you be wrong?"

He stared absently at the lace-covered table. "I think we're all crazy. We believe in impossibilities. Not even so much as a touch of sanity. Fools for the impossible. Invest in those matches . . . and I'd stock enough coal oil to go 'round as well."

"What would you change if you could go back?" she asked.

His smile flickered and died under his mustache. "Me, I could have stopped it all. He told me. Just before it started."

"Who did?"

"A crazy man in a New Orleans brothel. If I'd known so much hung in the balance, I would never have cut off that lunatic's leg."

ABOUT THE AUTHOR

William Gear is an international, *New York Times,* and *USA Today* bestselling author who holds a master's degree in archaeology. *This Scorched Earth* is his magnum opus, a riveting family saga that combines his passion for the subject with his expertise in research, historical record, and archaeology.